THE MARY STEWART OMNIBUS

Book Two
LORD IN WAITING

Scotland in the 15th century was a divided and troubled nation, presided over by the weak and foolish James the Third. Before long, John, Lord of Douglas, a born leader and a man of conscience and vision, was to find himself wishing that James' wise and strong-minded sister, Princess Mary, had succeeded in her brother's place.

A wish compounded by the feeble king's habit of ignoring the advice of high-born nobles and succumbing instead to the malign influence of the astrologer and alchemist, William Sheves, Archdeacon of St Andrews, one of the cleverest and most unscrupulous individuals in Scotland's history.

Also by Nigel Tranter
(in chronological order)

The Mary Stewart Omnibus

Price of a Princess

Lord in Waiting

Nigel Tranter

CORONET BOOKS
Hodder and Stoughton

First published as two separate volumes

Price of a Princess © 1994 by Nigel Tranter.
First published in Great Britain in 1994 by Hodder and Stoughton
First published as a Coronet paperback in 1995

Lord in Waiting © 1994 by Nigel Tranter.
First published in Great Britain in 1994 by Hodder and Stoughton
First published as a Coronet paperback in 1995

This edition 1998
A Coronet paperback

ISBN 0 340 71755 6

Printed and bound in Great Britain by
Clays Ltd, St Ives plc

Hodder and Stoughton
A division of Hodder Headline PLC
338 Euston Road
London NW1 3BH

Price of a Princess

Book One

Principal Characters in order of appearance

James the Third: Youthful King of Scots
Princess Mary: Elder sister of above
Gilbert, Lord Kennedy: Great noble, brother of former Bishop Kennedy
James, Lord Hamilton: Great noble, Head of the house of Cadzow
Sir Alexander Boyd of Duncow: Keeper of Edinburgh Castle
Thomas, Lord Boyd of Kilmarnock: Elder brother of above
Thomas, Master of Boyd: Son and heir of above. Later Earl of Arran
James, Lord Livingstone: Great Chamberlain
Lady Annabella Boyd: Sister of above
Patrick Graham, Bishop of St Andrews: Primate of Scottish Church
Princess Margaret: Younger sister of the King
Alexander, Duke of Albany: Younger brother of the King
John, Earl of Mar: Youngest brother of the King
Andrew Stewart, Lord Avondale: Chancellor of Scotland
Patrick Fullarton: Son of the Coroner of Arran
Andrew Durisdeer, Bishop of Glasgow: Envoy
William Tulloch, Bishop of Orkney: Envoy and interpreter
Rob Carnegie: Shipmaster
Christian the First: King of Denmark, Norway and Sweden
Martin Vanns: Grand Almoner
Princess Margaret of Denmark: Daughter of Christian and Dorothea
Magnus, Archbishop of Nidaros: Metropolitan of the North
William Boyd, Abbot of Kilwinning: Another brother of Lord Boyd
Archibald Douglas, Earl of Angus: Chief of the Red Douglases
Elizabeth Boyd, Countess of Angus: Daughter of Lord Boyd
Nils Larsen: Danish merchant
Wilhelm Schoenbach: Senator of the Hanseatic League
Lord Haliburton of Dirleton: Privy Councillor

1

The hunt was well past Duntarvie, and now heading almost due southwards towards Niddry Seton, downhill through undulating country of scattered woodland, the stag a notable runner but carrying a splendid head of antlers, well worth this long pursuit, the deerhounds still unable to run it down or corner it. Some of the more experienced horsemen might indeed have been able to use knowledge of the land to head it off, in this western part of Lothian, but could scarcely do so ahead of the King – who was, not unnaturally, less experienced, being of only fourteen years. Nor was His young Grace the best of riders as yet, being a studious and less than vigorous youngster, unlike his late and impetuous father, James the Second of that name. Even his sister had had to rein in on occasion at his side, for Mary Stewart was a more vehement character and, at seventeen, a fine horsewoman.

They had already come more than five round-about miles from Linlithgow, and it looked as though there would be more miles ahead of them before they killed, if ever they did, with the stag showing no signs of flagging.

The Lord Kennedy, at the other side of the young monarch, pointed and panted out, "The burn, Y'Grace. Niddry Burn. Water. That . . . our best hope . . . I judge. Quarry making for . . . water, belike." A man of later middle years, now inclining to corpulence, *he* was not having to rein his, his breathlessness very evident.

"A burn? A river. Will we have to cross a river?" James demanded, a little anxiously. "Is it . . . deep?"

"The Niddry is nothing that our mounts cannot take, Jamie," the princess reassured as they pounded on. "It is the boggy edges that we will have to watch for. Where the deer can cross lightly, but our beasts' hooves will sink in."

"Right, Highness," Kennedy agreed. "A pity that Seton . . . did not come . . . this day. He knows this country best . . ."

They were approaching thicker woodland from a lengthy

1

downwards slope; and already the stag and pursuing hounds were disappearing into the trees. Mary was having to restrain herself and her mount from forging ahead, as were others behind – although she perhaps was the only one there who could have outridden her brother without seeming guilty of *lèse-majesté*.

Actually it was the girl, the only female present, who perceived the situation first, or at least was first to utter it. "Look – men!" she exclaimed. "There, within the trees. Many men. Mounted."

Kennedy stared, his sight scarcely as keen as that of the young woman.

"Who are they?" James asked, ever ready to be alarmed.

"They will be the Lord Seton's people," his sister suggested. "We are near Niddry Seton here. I have been here before. But for these woods we could see his castle, I think."

"Should we not halt? There are many. In case . . ."

"The Setons are your good friends, Sire," Kennedy said. But he did seek to slow down his pace a little, although that was not easy with them all thundering downhill, many of the other huntsmen close behind. Any sudden reining in, and the foremost could be ridden down.

Then Lord Hamilton's voice sounded from their backs – he was usually to be found as near to the Princess Mary as he could decently get. "It is Boyd! I see the Boyd banner. And Somerville. See – there is the white on blue of Somerville."

All who might have been apprehensive relaxed at that, as they saw horsemen emerging from the trees under colourful heraldic flags. Lord Boyd of Kilmarnock was a trusted supporter of the crown, and his younger brother, Sir Alexander, more prominent in national affairs, was indeed Keeper of Edinburgh Castle, the second most important citadel of the land. But it was strange to be intercepting the royal hunt thus. They must be bearing some vital news to account for it.

Their fine stag looked like escaping, in these circumstances.

There were about a score of horsemen coming slowly to meet them. Everywhere now the more numerous huntsmen, by unspoken consent, were drawing in their mounts, recognising these ahead as friends.

Lord Kennedy, whose brother, the late renowned bishop who had more or less ruled the realm for both the young King and his father, gave no impression of annoyance at this interruption of their sport. "It seems . . . we must leave . . . this chase meantime, Sire," he advised. "These . . . would not be here . . . thus . . . without cause." The Lord Boyd's son and heir, Thomas, Master of Boyd, was after all contracted to marry Lord Kennedy's daughter.

The two groups drew together, and not a few hands were raised in greeting, for all knew each other well enough. There was cap-raising towards the monarch and his sister.

"We regret the spoiling of Your Grace's sport, Sire," one of the newcomers announced, with a flourished bow from the saddle, not the Lord Boyd but his brother, Sir Alexander, a fine-looking man of early middle age, richly dressed. "But the matter is important."

"It is no matter," the youth said. "I think the stag was winning away." He was no great one for hunting, this James Stewart. And indeed this day's hunt had been something of a surprise altogether, at least to his sister, proposed suddenly by Kennedy as a relief from the admittedly boring business of the annual Exchequer Audit, which had been going on for three days at the palace of Linlithgow, and at which, by established custom, the monarch had to be present. She had been glad enough to take part in it, for she loved the chase, even though she did not always relish the kill itself. But her brother had not been enthusiastic.

"We were on our way to Linlithgow, Sire, when we heard of this hunt," the Lord Boyd said. He was a heavier man than his brother, massively built and square-featured. "We understood you to be at the Exchequer Audit there. But perceived the hunt coming down this way."

It occurred to Mary Stewart to wonder, then. How had these lords, from Edinburgh, heard of this hunt, which had been decided upon only this morning? And had assumed that the King would be with it? She did not voice her questions, however.

"Your Grace's presence is urgently required at Edinburgh." That was the Lord Somerville, a younger man, of somewhat haughty bearing.

"Why that?" somebody asked, from the ranks of the hunters behind.

Lord Boyd frowned. Then glancing over at all the interested faces of the listening horsemen, waved. "It is a privy matter. Of some . . . secrecy."

"Shall we return to Linlithgow, then, and consider the matter?" the Lord Hamilton said. "His Grace agreeing."

3

"No, my lord. And Your Grace. There is some urgency in this. Better for His Grace to come with us to Edinburgh now."

"But . . . the others? The Chancellor, Lord Avondale – he is at Linlithgow. Livingstone, and other lords of the Council. They must be informed."

"No time for that," Sir Alexander Boyd said crisply. "A messenger has arrived from Edward of England. From Carlisle. His mission requiring the royal reply and signature."

"The Chancellor, then, must hear of it. We are but five or six miles from Linlithgow . . ."

"No!" That was definite. "We must go at once." This was not the normal mode of speech where the monarch was concerned.

Kennedy, strangely, said nothing.

Mary wondered the more. There was much here that she did not understand. She scanned the faces of the newcomers. Of the score or so, most were men-at-arms, a mere escort. As well as the two Boyds and Somerville there were two others whom she knew slightly, Andrew Hepburn, Master of Hailes, and Andrew Ker, heir to Ker of Cessford, both daredevil young men, Borderers. But there was one whom she did not recognise – and she certainly would have done so had she seen him before, for he was the most handsome young man she had ever set eyes upon, well built, tall, bearing himself proudly and seemingly almost amused by the present situation, certainly in no awe of the company he had joined.

She was reverting to a consideration as to how this party could have known of today's hunt, when she realised that the good-looking stranger was eyeing her with frankest interest, all but assessingly. She was used to admiration, of course, not only as a princess but as a very lovely young woman, tall also, slender and lissome but amply rounded, dark-haired and fine-featured, her grey eyes large and expressive. Those eyes met the young man's, and they locked for a moment or two before she turned back to her brother.

James was indeed addressing her. "Must I go with them, Mary?" he asked. Ever since their mother, Queen Mary of Guelders, had died three years before, the young King had looked to his elder sister for guidance, help and comfort, a somewhat bewildered youngster requiring much support and fondness, no very adequate monarch for a nation as turbulent as

4

Scotland, and following a headstrong father. It was to be feared that he would never be a forceful monarch.

"Wait!" she said, and turned to Lord Kennedy who, since the good bishop's death a year before, had more or less assumed the duties of the monarch's principal adviser. "Such haste? Could the English messenger not have been brought here, to His Grace? Rather than the King having to go to *him*?"

Kennedy looked uncomfortable. "I know not, Highness. Perhaps he was wearied with long riding." That sounded feeble indeed.

Alexander Boyd reined his horse closer, to speak low-voiced. "This is important, Sire and Highness. The messenger must return to Carlisle, whenever he is sufficiently rested. King Edward is urgent. He leaves for the south. Prithee, come!" And he actually reached out for the reins of the boy's mount.

"No!" Mary declared. "Jamic, I say that we should rather return to Linlithgow. First. Here is something strange." She turned, tossing her long hair back from her brow, a habit of hers. "You, my Lord Kennedy – say you not so?"

That man hesitated, glancing left and right.

From behind, Hamilton spoke. "I agree with Her Highness. Back to Linlithgow."

Alexander Boyd acted rather than argued. He grabbed James's reins and tugged. "Come, Sire!"

Mary, kneeing her beast's flanks, cried, "No! No, I say. Stop him!" It was Kennedy whom she so urged.

That lord, the King's cousin and her own, at one remove, made an indeterminate gesture, part shake of the head, part shrug. Then he seemed to decide, and urged his mount over nearer to the King's again, which was being pulled round. His hand went out.

Swiftly Sir Alexander twisted in his saddle and lashed out with his fist, striking the older man on the shoulder, and all but unseating him with the vehemence of the blow. At the same time he spurred his horse into vigorous motion, back towards the woodland, and perforce dragged the boy's beast with him.

Immediately all was changed as to tempo, urgency, atmosphere. There arose exclamations and shouting, much clamour and jerking of horses' reins and heads, much concern; but also a deal of uncertainty. For all the men there knew each other, had their links and friendships – and the reverse to be sure. For her part, Mary Stewart spurred after her brother without delay. Lord Kennedy, breathing stertorously, biting his lip, remained where he was.

James, reins wrenched from his not very firm hands, was clinging to his saddle-bow for support, and looking back over his shoulder. "Mary!" he cried, "Mary – do not leave me!"

"I will not!" she shouted after him, and heeled her mount the harder.

There was a notable confusion of riders on that grassy slope, decision and indecision equally evident. Amidst the cries and beat of hooves, Mary heard the thudding crash of a horse falling behind her, and glancing back saw the two Andrews, Hepburn and Ker, reining back from the sprawling, kicking mount of the Lord Hamilton, who himself was now asprawl on the grass, clearly having been ridden down by the pair as he came after her and James. She almost drew up, to go to his assistance, then perceived that her brother's need was the greater, and pounded on.

Another horseman was coming fast from behind and drawing level. She saw that it was Fleming, another important lord.

"Better back, Highness," this one jerked. "No ploy . . . for a woman!"

She ignored him.

Then she realised that a second rider was close at her other side, the handsome young man whom she had noted earlier. And he was laughing, the only one there to be showing amusement. He reached over to pat her arm, their mounts almost touching.

"I salute you, lady!" he exclaimed. "Spirit! Fear nothing. All will be well."

"James!" she panted. "The King."

"He will be well enough, also. Here's to your spirit! I like it."

Mary, just then, could do without compliments, and rode the harder.

The Lord Fleming dropped back – but not the girl's good-looking admirer.

They were almost up with Sir Alexander and the young monarch now, and she called out reassuringly to her brother. Boyd looked round, frowning.

"All is well, uncle," the young man shouted. "Hamilton took a fall! Others . . . less eager! Save this princess. All in order."

Which was a strange way of describing the situation.

6

Level with James, Mary cried, "Fear nothing, Jamie. They will not harm you, the King."

Tense, anxious, the boy shook his head.

As they entered the woodland she looked back, expecting pursuit. But there was none. The hunt-followers were clustered round Kennedy, Fleming and Hamilton and other lords. All seemed to be more or less stationary, Hamilton mounting his horse again. Indecision triumphed, apparently. Or connivance!

The Boyds and Somerville were by no means glancing back apprehensively.

Presently, deeper within the trees, Lord Boyd's party pulled up, to consider the position – and it was at Mary Stewart rather than at the abducted young sovereign-lord that they stared, obviously put out and at something of a loss by her presence.

"Highness," Lord Boyd said, "I regret that you have been . . . troubled. By this. That was not intended. This way is best for His Grace. But you . . . ! This is no concern for a woman." He changed that. "For a young lady such as Your Highness."

"What *is* this concern, my lord?" That came out strongly, if a little breathlessly, with another toss back of her dark hair.

"It is for . . . for the realm's weal, Highness. And His Grace's own. That, I do promise you. And you, Sire. It, it had to be this way. Lest there be . . . difficulties." Boyd was clearly having his own difficulties, with this delivery.

The Lord Somerville was less troubled. "Better that you get back to Linlithgow, lady," he said curtly.

"I stay with His Grace," Mary told them simply.

"But, Highness . . . !" Boyd wagged his head. "Best indeed that you return . . ."

"No!" That was James Stewart, in agitation.

"This is man's work, Highness. In the kingdom's cause. For betterment therein," Sir Alexander Boyd put in. "His Grace will be very well with us."

"Perhaps, sir. Although I doubt it, by this present! But His Grace has suffered much, the deaths of his royal father, and his mother, none so long past. He must not suffer the loss of his sister also! If he goes with you, I go also."

There was muttering and growling amongst her hearers, but another voice spoke up, that of the next youngest person present after the monarch and Mary, the so handsome stranger.

"This lady is brave as she is fair, uncle. And could aid us all,

7

with the King. A useful friend!" And he flourished a bow at the girl. "Let her bide, I say."

Alexander Boyd shrugged, and nodded towards his brother. "Come, then. We have wasted sufficient time." He still retained the reins of the King's horse.

Lord Boyd looked doubtfully at Somerville; but it was clear that his younger brother was the strong character and the real leader here. He gestured onwards.

In the woodland track there was room only for riders to go two abreast; so Mary, unspeaking, drew in immediately behind Sir Alexander and her brother. She found her personable admirer at her side.

"I am Tom Boyd," he said. "And find Your Highness to my taste!"

"And I find nothing of this to *my* taste, sir!" she told him, and looked firmly away.

He laughed. "My taste in women seldom errs, I think! You will come round to it!"

She did not have to answer that, for along the track before them appeared three of the hunt-servants and two of the deerhounds, evidently coming back to discover what had happened to the hunt. At sight of this party with the young King these drew up and pulled aside, in astonishment and uncertainty.

The Boyds and their friends ignored them entirely, as they trotted on.

The track led them, presently, down to softer ground and then to a shallow ford of sorts over the Niddry Burn, up beyond which was the major road between Edinburgh, Linlithgow and Stirling.

They had some ten miles to go to Edinburgh, and it was not long before they could actually see their destination away eastwards ahead of them, for its great fortress-castle, atop its lofty rock, stood out as a landmark from afar. Mary's self-appointed escort pointed to it.

"You will know yonder citadel, lady?" he asked. "*I* find it less than comfortable."

The girl did not answer.

He went on, cheerfully. "We must seek to make it more suitable lodging for a princess. And, to be sure, for our liege-lord!" There was something like mockery in that last.

She did rise to that. "Lodging, sir? I thought that we went but to sign papers and speak with an English courier?"

8

He laughed. "That was as useful a pretext as any. A little longer stay will be called for, I think!"

"What do you mean?"

"Why – only that the realm's business may take some of its sovereign's time. And if Your Highness prefers to bide with him – for which praises be, I say! – then you may require some comforts in Edinburgh Castle, lady. And some comforting, perhaps!"

She stared at him, as they trotted along. "Do I take you aright, sir? Is this then some shameful . . . device? Some unlawful and treasonable seizure and constraint of the King? For the advantage of . . . these!"

Still he seemed to find amusement in even that dire challenge. "Not how my father and uncle would name it, I swear! Say, rather, for the advantage of all the kingdom and the King's folk. Even for His young Grace's self. Better keeping than he has been in, from those old men, the Kennedys."

"You mean that you and yours are going to hold James? To rule the realm, or seek to, through him, as your prisoner!"

"Never prisoner, no. Guardians, perhaps. His advisers, counsellors. Needful guardians. Since Bishop Kennedy died, the rule of this land has been but slack, has it not? Or so my father and uncle declare. Allowing much of ill to arise. So now there is to be . . . improvement. Should we not rejoice?"

Her lovely features set, Mary Stewart digested that as best she could.

He reached over to pat her sleeve. "If you do not like it, Highness, it is perhaps not too late for *you* to turn back. Go back to Linlithgow. I will escort you most of the way, if need be." But that also was announced with a laugh which held mockery.

She tossed back her hair. "I stay with the King," she said.

"And I am glad of that! Heigho – I have found Edinburgh dull indeed after my Kilmarnock and Ayr. You will improve it, I have no doubt!"

She shook her head wordlessly, seeking to order the tumult of her thoughts. Responsible as her nature, training and circumstances had made her, for a girl of seventeen this situation was upsetting to say the least. And the young man's familiarity of tone and manner were insufferable. Yet, presently, she turned to him.

"You say that it is your father and uncle who lead in this . . . felony and folly! And you come from Kilmarnock? A Boyd?"

9

"I told you – Tom Boyd. I am Thomas, Master of Boyd, yes. At your service, to be sure."

"I see. So – you are deep in this plot also?"

"Not so. A mere onlooker, Highness, unconcerned with affairs of state. I prefer affairs of the heart!" He waved a flourish. "I came from Dean Castle, our house in the west, only a week past. And now, this! So unexpected a satisfaction!"

"Unexpected, sir? I think not. Much about this day's doings I deem strange indeed. Planned in advance, well planned. I have noted much. No sudden whim of you and yours. This hunt, see you. It was only decided upon this morning – or so it seemed. To enliven the dull work of the Exchequer, for James. Yet your father said that he knew of it. And some of the lords in the hunt itself have acted very strangely. The Lord Kennedy himself. And Fleming. Hamilton alone sought to prevent this, this outrage. I think that the others knew that it was planned. Or some of them."

He glanced at her more carefully, at this, assessingly. "Perhaps these recognised it as for the best?" he suggested. "After all, they know my father and uncle. He, my uncle, is married to Janet Kennedy. And I, would you credit it, am supposed to be be marrying Kennedy's youngest daughter one day! Plain of face and person as she is!"

"Whom do I condole with, sir? You – or her! But . . . could my Lord Kennedy so betray his trust? His brother, the bishop, would turn in his grave, I think! To yield up the King so – he, his protector and supporter, since the bishop died . . ."

"There are more sorts of betrayal than one, lady. Before ever Bishop Kennedy died, his brother had a band with my uncle. And Fleming. And the Earl of Crawford. Each to support the other in all matters and interests – all save, to be sure, such as might be against the interests of the crown. And this present, I am assured, is in His Grace's best interests! Much so. Where, then, is the betrayal?"

"Words, sir! Words do not alter deeds. I have heard of these bands, between lords. And mislike the sound of them. Fleming also, you say? He, too, held back, there. But Kennedy – his is the greater betrayal. He is keeper of the King's royal castle of Stirling. James's home. And mine. Brought us to Linlithgow, for this audit. Arranged this hunt – and then hands over his charge to Sir Alexander Boyd . . ."

10

"Who is also keeper of the other royal castle, of Edinburgh! A fair exchange! What is so ill in that?"

"Do not play with me, sir! But – tell me this, pray. You who know so much. Why did Sir Alexander strike Lord Kennedy back yonder? When he reached out to James."

The master shrugged, but grinned too. "You should ask him that yourself, Highness. Myself, I was surprised. But I jalouse that it was a kindly blow, well meant! A precautionary gesture, shall we say? Lest aught went wrong. Hamilton was questioning. So – none could accuse Kennedy of . . . perfidy. But ask Sir Alexander."

"I do not think that I would place more faith in *his* answers than I do in yours, Master of Boyd!"

"For one so fair, you are hard, hard, Highness. But we shall convince you of our goodwill, never fear. I, in especial!"

Her head-tossing was eloquent.

The road being broader here, as they neared the city, Mary took the opportunity to spur forward level with her brother, at the other side from Sir Alexander. The boy turned to her anxiously.

"Is it . . . is it well, Mary? Why this? I do not understand. Lord Kennedy? Lord Hamilton? Where are they? They have not come . . ."

"I have explained to His Grace, Highness, that we act only for his weal, and that of his realm. As I have heard my nephew telling yourself. Heed us."

She eyed him, above her brother's troubled head, heedfully indeed. For this man deserved heed, in more regards than one. He was able, strong, dangerous, yet attractive, if scarcely as brilliantly handsome as his nephew. Moreover, not so long ago he had been her mother's lover – or one of them. When King James the Second had died, at the bursting of that cannon at the siege of Roxburgh, aged only twenty-nine, he had left a very beautiful young widow of the same age, Mary of Guelders, of strong character and talents and equally strong desires, with no lack of personable would-be partners. Her elder daughter had not failed to be aware of it, and to recognise the problems and dangers involved, in royal circumstances. This had, perhaps, helped to make Mary Stewart the more mature for her age.

"I cannot think, sir, that you go about your well-doing in the most leal and kindly fashion for His Grace!"

"It was necessary." That was brief and discouraging of further discussion. They rode on in silence – save for the Master of Boyd, who continued to discourse in lively and amiable style.

In due course they reached the West Port of the walled city, and passing through, trotted down the narrow streets to the Grassmarket, under the towering crags of the castle rock. Then up the steep climb of the West Bow into the Lawnmarket, with its tall gabled tenements and the booths of its traders and craftsmen, to the tourney-ground which led up to the lofty citadel itself, walls, towers and gatehouse frowning across the deep water-filled ditch and over the town and farflung prospects of land, hills and sea. It was extraordinary how alike it was to the castle of Stirling, the royal family's principal seat and home.

There was little homely however, once across the drawbridge and within the ramparts, about this fortress, grimmer than Stirling's and scarcely welcoming. James and his sister had been here before, of course, but had never lodged in it, the Abbey of Holyroodhouse, a mile to the east, providing preferred accommodation for royal visits.

"We do not go to the abbey?" Mary asked, as they clattered up the cobblestone ascent to the upper courtyard.

"His Grace will be safer here," Sir Alexander said.

"Safer? In his own realm of Scotland? His Grace has been safe enough, until this day!"

"The abbey would not be . . . suitable, lady."

"I do not like it here," James declared.

"We must take good care of Your Grace and Highness." That was the nephew. "The city folk could be lacking in respect."

The girl turned in her saddle to eye him witheringly.

Strangely, when they drew rein outside the governor's quarters, it was the Lord Boyd who took over from his brother. He had ridden ahead all the way, without word with the royal pair. Now, dismounted, he gestured them within.

"You will find the lodging well enough here, Sire. We had not looked for a lady, but it will serve, to be sure. I shall have a woman sent for, to see to your needs. All will be well."

"Well for whom, my lord?" Mary spoke for her brother. "We were very well at Linlithgow and Stirling. What is your purpose in bringing His Grace here? Sir Alexander says that it is for weal. No more than that. Are we not to be told more?"

"The realm requires better rule, Highness. Since the Bishop

12

of St Andrews died it has drifted, the ship of state lacking a firm hand on the helm.It is intended to improve on that."

"*Your* hand, my lord?"

"With others, yes. Many others."

"But in the King's name?"

"To be sure."

"And the Privy Council? And parliament? Do these not . . . signify?"

"They will . . . approve. In due course. These matters have to be devised in stages, lady. All will be done lawfully, I assure you."

"Will be? But has not been done so this day, I think!"

Boyd glanced at his brother and son. He seemed now to be in charge, but less sure of himself than had been Sir Alexander. "We shall put all in order. Have no fears, Sire." He avoided the girl's eye. "We shall do all to Your Grace's best advantage. Now . . ."

His son came to his rescue. "I will show Their Highnesses to their quarters," the master said, bowing. And taking two royal arms, he ushered them within from that doorstep.

Mary shook her arm free, even if the bewildered young monarch did not.

They were conducted along a vaulted passage to a door which opened on to two intercommunicating chambers, windows facing north across the Nor' Loch and the rolling grassy, cattle-dotted slopes which sank down to the shores of the Scotwater or Firth of Forth. The rooms were sparsely furnished, one with a table, chairs, benches, chests and wall-closets; the other a bedroom – but with only one bed, although a large one. The master waved to it all.

"You will do very well here, no? We will make all more comfortable, I promise you. Refreshment will be sent. And attendants. It will be *my* pleasure and honour to attend you, to be sure." It was at Mary that he looked, smiling.

The young woman managed that flick back of her hair, so telling. "When His Grace, or I, summon you, sir!" she said coolly. "Jamie, give the Master of Boyd permission to retire.

"Yes," the boy said. "Yes. Go away, sir."

The man spread eloquent hands, then changed the gesture into a flourishing bow, as he bent low – but never losing his grin.

"At your royal service!" he declared. "Always." And backed out.

Brother and sister, alone at last, eyed each other, his face crumpling, hers set, tight-lipped. Then she stepped over to clasp and hug him.

"Jamie, lad – I am sorry. Sorry! For this that they do. It is shameful. But they will not hurt you. Never think it. You are the King. They need you, to advance their plans. Whatever these are. So they will do you no harm. Be strong. They must cherish you, gain your help, or they lack the authority to act as they intend. I will be with you, always, aiding you. Fear not."

He shook his head. "I do not understand. When do we go home? To Stirling?"

"I do not know. They may bring them here. Or Lord Kennedy may keep them safe there. We shall see. But . . . keep courage, Jamie. You are their sovereign-lord. Crowned King of Scots. They have sworn allegiance to you. They cannot do without your goodwill. Remember that, always. Now . . ."

A knock sounded at the door, and Thomas Boyd ushered in two servitors with trays of viands – cold meats, oatcakes, honey, a flagon of wine. He drew up chairs to the table, three chairs. It looked as though he was intending to eat with them.

"That will be sufficient, sir. His Grace and I prefer to rest now. And eat alone," Mary told him.

"As you will." Waving the servitors aside, he poured out goblets of wine for them, before taking genial leave.

There was a key in that door, on the outside, and the girl took it out and, transferring it to inside, turned the lock. They had had enough of company for one day.

Sitting down, food untouched, suddenly she was overwhelmed, and sinking forward, head on arms, she sobbed, quietly. It had all been a dire and testing experience, and she had held up, played the princess and the elder sister as best she could, for Jamie's sake. But although no weakling and with her own understandings of due and suitable behaviour, she was of no hard or over-proud nature, no arrogance in her. And she was still only a young woman of seventeen years, King's daughter or none.

"Mary – are you, are you unwell? What is it? Mary, do not cry!"

She looked up, pulling herself together, to muster a watery smile at the boy's worried face. If Mary was in some ways older than her years, James was the reverse, an unsure and hesitant youngster, clever in book-learning and amenable, but always requiring guidance and backing.

"It is nothing, Jamie. I am but tired from long riding. And talk with these lords. You also, to be sure. Food and drink is what we require. And rest. Come – eat you. We will feel the better. We have had a long day of it."

"Yes. I hope that we will go home tomorrow. If we were to ask that man, the one that you call the master – will he take us, do you think? He is much better than the others. Kinder."

"Over-kindly, by half!" she declared. "But, no – I do not think that they will let us go very soon. They have taken too much of trouble to get us here. Or you – for *me* they do not want. But I will not leave you . . ."

"That one, the master, likes you well."

"It is but his manner. A man who makes much of women – and expects much! Do not heed him greatly, Jamie."

They ate, once they had started, more heartily than they had thought to do, young bodies demanding sustenance, for it was dusk now, of a July evening, and they had not eaten since breakfast.

A knock sounded at the door presently, and when Mary signed to ignore it, Thomas Boyd's voice sounded.

"Candles, Highness. Lit. You have locked this door?"

"Yes. Leave them there."

"A pity. I would wish you a good night. Both."

"Well, you have done so, sir."

"And nothing such for *me*, in return?"

"Others, who have had a better day, I think, can give you that!"

"Cruel!" That, however, came with a laugh. "Sleep well, then." They heard his footsteps fade.

"There is but the one bed!" James said, questioningly.

"Then we must make the best of it, must we not? It is large. And we can do without the candles!"

"I . . . I have never slept in a bed . . . with a girl."

"Nor I with a boy! But we shall not die of it!"

"How, how shall we do it?"

"Just as you bed always. There is plenty of room for both of us. Without coming closer than you wish! Go you first, and undress. Call me when you are bedded."

15

Doubtfully the monarch did as he was told, and entered the bedroom. His sister went to the window, to gaze out over the darkening prospect.

She sought to gather and discipline her tumult of thoughts, impressions, questions, fears. These Boyds were clearly hard and dangerous men. And she and Jamie were completely in their power, whatever sort of a face *she* had put on it – no happy situation, however much she sought to reassure her brother. But she had been right in insisting on coming with them. He needed her, as never before. She owed him all her aid and care and support. For, strangely, was he not her own liege-lord and sovereign, as well as her brother, James, by the Grace of God, King of Scots! Of the oldest line of monarchs, possibly, in all Christendom. But she was worried, also, about her two younger brothers and sister, at Stirling. Was Kennedy to be trusted to look after them now . . . ?

A somewhat uncertain call came from the next room.

James was lying close to one edge of the huge bed, with the covers up to his chin, his clothes in a heap on the floor. Going over, she stooped to pick them up and arrange them in some order on a settle. She sat on the end of this, to draw off her long riding-boots – for of course, she was clad as for the hunt, unsuitable as these clothes were here and now.

Then she undressed. She was well aware that the boy, almost a youth, was watching her, for it was not so dark yet in that room that she could remain in any degree unseen – and at fourteen he was old enough to be interested, however shy about his own unclad appearance. He would have seen his *young* sister unclothed, no doubt, but Margaret was only seven, a child yet. Mary was no prude, no prim maid, and not unaware that she was well made, entirely womanly; and while she was not going to flaunt it, nor was she going to hide it foolishly.

Naked, she climbed into the great bed – and saw that the boy was seeking to draw still further away. "I will not bite you, Jamie!" she told him. "Have you said your night's prayers? No – then do so. And you will feel better." She reached over, to pat his arm.

He was silent for a while. Then presently he said, "Mary, you are kind. Thank you. For coming with me."

"Now – go to sleep, Jamie. Goodnight. All will seem better in the morning."

It was surprising how short a time it was before his deep breathing told her that he slept, whatever his anxieties. For herself, she lay long awake, pondering. If only their mother had been still alive, she would have been able to deal with all this, known what to do. This might not have happened then, of course, especially with that Alexander Boyd there. She was strong, able . . .

Mary was, at long last, about to drop off, when with a muttering, James turned over, and a hand came groping out towards her. Rousing herself, she leaned across and drew him to her, and he came, wordless. She clasped him close, hushing him – not that he spoke.

So they lay, silent. And strangely, now she slept almost as quickly as did he.

2

Up and dressed before James was awake, Mary went to unlock
that door, after making use of the garderobe and sanitary chute,
a new determination about her. Outside sat a serving-woman,
half asleep, with jugs of steaming water, basin and towels.
She said that she would be back with the breakfast when her
ladyship was ready. Thanking her, Mary took the water to the
bedroom and washed thoroughly, having partly to undress again.
James wakened and watched, but this time with little sign of
embarrassment. Nevertheless, when she had finished, and told
him to rise and wash also, with breakfast coming, he would not
get out of bed until she had left the room.

The outer door was still unlocked, and when a knock sounded
she opened, and found four persons standing there, the woman,
the two male servitors of the evening before, and Thomas, Master
of Boyd again.

"Ha, Highness, a very good morning to you!" he greeted
cheerfully. "I hope that you slept well? Here is the best this
castle will rise to, to break our fast. We will do better in future, I
promise you; but here is porridge, cream, eggs, cold venison and
bread. Also ale, if you so desire." And he took a tray from one of
the men and led the way in. Thereupon, he proceeded to set out
all on the table – and Mary noted that it was three places that
he set again. This was a determined young man, clearly. That
made two of them, then.

But this morning she did not curtly banish him. For one of
the decisions she had made last night, before she slept, was
that, in this difficult situation, it would be wise to make use
of almost the only asset they seemed to possess, apart from
the royal status, and that was the so evident eagerness of this
so handsome character to be friendly. Too friendly, no doubt,
and she must keep him in his place, if possible. But that place
might well be useful, helpful. So although she did not exactly
smile upon him, when thanking the servants she did not dismiss

him with them. Instead she called to James to come, that breakfast awaited him.

Owl-eyed, the boy came through, to be bowed to deeply and greeted warmly. He was not yet fully clad, and tousle-headed and barefooted – as indeed was his sister, her long riding-boots unsuitable wear for breakfast. She felt, to be sure, distinctly at a disadvantage, sartorially, her hunting-jacket discarded meantime and the sleeveless bodice she had worn beneath looking rather ridiculous above the heavy, long and full skirt, and revealing as to figure into the bargain. Whereas, despite the hour, the young man was dressed brilliantly, in the height of fashion. This was no help.

"You are very . . . attentive, sir," she said. "I wonder why? The others a deal less so!"

"It is my pleasure, Highness. And my leal duty." That to James. "I would wish all to be to your satisfaction, as far as is possible. While you are here."

"Yes. And for how long *are* we here? Against our wills."

"That, I fear, I do not know. And, no doubt, you will come to see that it is for the best. And be less displeasured."

"I doubt it, sir."

"I, at least, will seek to pleasure you! And Your Grace. To my best ability. And I am practised at it, see you!" That was added with a wave of a hand. "Now, shall we eat? While this porridge is still warm."

The King, for one, required no second invitation. He sat down to porridge and cream without delay.

Mary, although of a good appetite, was less eager. "If we are here for some time, sir, we require clothing, gear, attendants . . . other than yourself! These are at Stirling. Why must we be at this Edinburgh Castle? Why do you and your father, and the others, not go there instead of us being held here? Surely your purposes could be served equally well from Stirling?"

"The decision is not mine, Highness. But the rule of the kingdom has been from Stirling, since Bishop Kennedy died, and has not been . . . of the best. Good. Strong. It needs improvement. And those who failed to lead fittingly, hold Stirling. So, the new rule will be from Edinburgh. And better, surer."

"And *your* part in it?"

"Myself, I am but a looker-on. My father's son, my uncle's nephew. But anxious for your welfare. Sire, more porridge?"

"So – His Grace and myself are, in fact, your prisoners here! Is not that the truth of it?"

"Not so. Never think it. All will be done for your comfort . . ."

"Such as a second bed provided, perhaps?"

He raised eyebrows. "You prefer that? I swear His Grace does not! How fortunate and happy a bedfellow! I could wish . . . !" He sighed. "Ah, well – another bed, if so demanded. Possibly other apartments, an extra chamber. We had planned only for His Grace. We shall send to Stirling for your clothing and attendants. But meanwhile, I will have my sister, Annabella, come from Kilmarnock to be Your Highness's lady-in-waiting. She is a mite younger than yourself, I think – but sixteen years. But not uncomely or lacking in manners. And she could bring women's clothing with her."

"I see. And meantime we remain in this fortress, like cooped fowl!"

"Scarcely that, to be sure. With suitable guard, His Grace can ride abroad – for the King of Scots must not go unprotected, must he?" A chuckle. "Venison? And you, Sire? As for yourself, Highness, I will escort you where and when you will. Hunting. Hawking. There is the royal forest of the Holy Rood, around that great hill here, Arthur's Seat. The Braid and Pentland Hills also, I am told, are good for the chase. And lochs for wildfowling. We could go visit my sister at Tantallon, down the coast – she is Countess of Angus. No need to play the cooped fowl – you the fairest bird to fly this land!" And he bowed across the table.

"I find your empty compliments wearisome, sir. Boyd deeds do not match your words!" She rose. "I have had a sufficiency now, of provender as well as of talk! His Grace, I think, also. James, will you again give the Master of Boyd leave to retire?"

Mouth still full, the monarch nodded.

"Heigho – dismissed! But I shall be back, presently, to see if you would desire to go riding. It is a fine day. Too good to sit indoors."

"Yes," James answered for her. "I would like that. Could we climb that big hill yonder?"

"Arthur's Seat? I doubt whether we could get horses up to the top, Sire. I have never been there. But – a royal command, and we can try!" He turned to salute the girl. "In an hour, shall we say?" He took his leave, all smiles.

20

"He is very good," the boy asserted. "I like him, Mary."

She reserved her own opinion as to that. But she certainly did not wish to be immured in these two rooms all day. And at least she had clothing for riding.

In due course, then, their so diligent squire came to usher them out to the upper courtyard, where about a dozen men, mounted and wearing the colours of Boyd, awaited them, with their horses. There was no sign of Lord Boyd or Sir Alexander. The master made a great show of hoisting Mary up to her saddle, with considerable clutching, and taking the opportunity to murmur that it was a pity about the guard, but it was unthinkable that the monarch should go about without due and proper escort. She replied that she understood perfectly – and the first smile she had bestowed on him was a mocking one. She added that she was quite capable of mounting her horse unaided.

They rode down to the gatehouse and out across the tourney-ground beyond and into the Lawnmarket. The walled city of Edinburgh was highly unusual in its siting and layout, being in the nature of a mile-long ellipse, narrow, and flanking a central spine of rock which ran down from the castle-fortress to the Abbey of Holy Rood and the open woodlands which surrounded the extraordinary towering peak of Arthur's Seat and its cliff-girt outliers. From this central spine, which comprised the Lawnmarket, the High Street and the Canongate, alleys and lanes and wynds branched off, inevitably all downhill, left and right, like herring bones, with tall tenement housing rising everywhere, and all but meeting each other overhead, darkening the alleys, with booths and workshops and ale-houses in the arcaded basements, the town-houses of great ones, lairds and prosperous citizens on the first and second floors, and the teeming warrens of the lesser folk soaring six and seven storeys above; so that, although the city, within its sheltering walls, did not cover a great deal of area, it housed a notably large population in its restricted space.

Interested enough in what they saw, they rode down High Street, past the Mercat Cross, the High Kirk of St Giles and the Tolbooth to the Netherbow Port. Beyond this was the Canongate, strangely, a separate burgh belonging to the abbey, although there was no break in the housing. Down this they came to the Abbey Sanctuary, a girth or place of refuge for offenders against certain laws, debtors and those awaiting trial. Then they were at the great abbey and monastic establishment itself, founded by James's ancestor, David the First.

"I do not see why, if we must remain in this Edinburgh, we cannot lodge here, in the abbatial quarters," Mary said. "I have been here before. My father always bided here when in Edinburgh. The place is spacious, comfortable, much better than up in that castle. Better for all. The Lord Abbot would welcome us."

"It is the matter of security, see you," Tom Boyd told her. "These great monkish buildings, spread as they are, in gardens and orchards, cannot be guarded as can the castle. You must see that."

"Guarded against whom? The citizens of this Edinburgh are not going to attack you. Or us."

"Others could seek to do so."

"So! I think that you mean the lords from whose care you . . . stole us! Or some of them? You fear that they may seek to win His Grace back? The Lords Kennedy, Fleming, Hamilton, Crawford and the rest?"

"Not Kennedy or Fleming, I think."

"Why? They were our guardians. Still are, for our brothers and sister."

"We have our bands with them."

"Ah, yes – your bands. These bands are so strong? They bind and tie all hands? Stronger, it seems, than your oaths of allegiance to your sovereign-lord!"

"No-o-o. They are strong, yes. They bind lords to mutual support, not to injure each other's causes. Saving, to be sure, treasonable offences against the crown."

"And doing what you did yesterday is not treason against the crown? Forcibly abducting the King!"

"Not so. What was done was for the King's good. And the realm's."

"I think that you play with words, sir. You stole His Grace from those the Privy Council chose to guard and guide him, the monarch. For *your* ends, not his. And the Lords Kennedy and Fleming also, with others, did not seriously oppose you. Because of their bands with you. Hamilton tried – but perhaps you had no band with the Hamiltons? So – you fear reprisals. As well you may! And so we must be kept secure. Prisoners in yonder castle!"

"Save us, if you are hard to convince, Highness! While Scotland was being well governed, by your royal mother and Bishop Kennedy, there was no need for this. But now, the lords at Stirling are weak, feeble. The realm drifts. The Lord of the Isles and the Earl of Ross actually swear allegiance to the English, so long as they are left to hold all the Highland west and the Hebrides. And the Earl of Dunbar *bides* at the English court, and threatens invasion of the borderland. With a child King, the realm needs a strong hand, and has not had it, this sorry year."

"And could that not have been arranged decently, in order, by the Council and parliament? Not this unlawful grasping?"

"The other was talked of, yes. But no agreement was reached . . ."

"Even with your banded friends?"

"Not so that it was sure. Firm. As it had to be."

"So you have been tying men's hands, with your bands! For long. In preparation. All a plot! To move when all was ready. Now you hold the King, but fear reprisals. I think that you are a little unsure of your hands, you Boyds!"

"Not me, lady. I am but my father's son. Not consulted. But I say that you are hard on us. This was only a necessary device, a means to effect the required change. All will be put in order, you will see. A parliament will indeed be held. A new Council sworn . . ."

"When?"

"A parliament requires forty days of notice to be lawful. And the King's signature and seal. So that it will be six weeks yet before all is settled . . ."

"Six weeks! In yonder prison!"

"Is this prison-keeping?" He waved at all the parkland, woodland and steep whin-clad slopes. "Am I not doing my best for you?"

She relented a little. "As gaoler, you are more . . . friendly than your kin, perhaps! But we are prisoners, none the less."

James had been showing little interest in this conversation, gazing around him as they rode, especially up at the abruptly climbing hillsides beyond a small lochan from which wildfowl rose as they drew near.

"Can we not get up there?" he asked. "I would like that."

"We might try, Sire. But the last part, I think, will be too steep for horses. And rocky. And for ladies, belike!"

"I can climb hills as well as any," Mary declared – although

23

admittedly she was not clad for this, with her long riding-skirt and boots. But then neither was the young man, in his fine clothing. "Why not do that another day, Jamie, when we are better clad for it? Today remain a-horse."

"I agree," Tom Boyd said. "But I am told that we can ride quite high, round the far side of the hill. Up beyond this loch. They say that there is another loch up there, set high. And still another, large, far below, providing much sport for hawks."

Disappointed, James acquiesced. His was not an assertive nature. If the guard, behind, heard any of this, they would be relieved, no doubt.

Leaving the low ground, they trotted on by a climbing track up the eastern flanks of what was really a small range, with all the Lothian plain of Forth spreading before them now, to the green Fawside and Garleton Hills, the leviathan-like Traprain Law, the isolated conical peak of North Berwick Law and the mighty stack of the Craig of Bass soaring out of the waves beyond, then the limitless plain of the sea, a glorious prospect indeed, which had the monarch exclaiming, for he enjoyed beautiful things and showed a burgeoning talent for drawing and painting.

His sister, whilst appreciative of scenery, was more concerned with the situation into which they had been plunged.

"Who leads, in all this?" she asked. "Your father or your uncle? Sir Alexander appeared to be the leader, yesterday, the younger as he is. Yet, at the end, the Lord Boyd took over command, it seemed."

"My uncle is the man of action, my father has the wits! Uncle Sandy is the soldier, the knight-at-arms, the tourney-master. He has been called an ornament of chivalry! Your royal mother, I think, found him so?" He glanced sidelong at her. "Which gives me hope!"

When he got no response to that from Mary, he went on. "My father plans and judges and sees ahead. They make an effective pair."

"And you?"

"Why, I seek to learn from both. But have my own notions." He laughed, but eyed her keenly. "What, may I ask, is *your* position, Highness? I heard that you were contracted to marry an Englishman, their King indeed, Edward. King meantime, at least! Although with these Wars of the Roses, as they are called, who knows."

24

She tossed her head. "That is by with. It was but talk. Talk between my mother and Margaret of Anjou, Henry's Queen. A match for this Edward. I was not consulted. Now, with my mother dead, all that is forgotten."

"How blessed a relief! We must do better for you than that! To wed an Englishman! Even their King."

"*We*, sir?"

"The Council. The parliament. The realm. Scotland's fairest and most proud daughter, marry English! Never!"

"I hope to wed whom *I* will, sir – not who others may choose."

"Well said. My own attitude, entirely. My father formerly contracted me to that pale young Kennedy female. But I have persuaded him otherwise . . ."

"There is a heron!" James cried, pointing to a long narrow lochan they were now approaching, high in a sort of hanging valley. "And a flock of teal. Mallard amongst them. And – yes, it is a goose, only one. Is it a greylag? Or a pinkfoot?" The boy was good on birds.

His companions could not inform him.

"The hawking here will be excellent," the master said. "I will send to Kilmarnock for my falcons."

"We have many at Stirling. Will you bring them to us, sir?"

"I will see if it is possible, Sire. But – I have plenty. Fine birds. We will have good sport."

Soon they were out of that loch-cradling valley and able to look down far below, where there was a quite major sheet of water ringed with reed-beds, with beyond it more low hills beginning to lift up towards the lofty serried ramparts of the Pentlands.

"That will be Duddingston Loch, the largest here," they were told. "You see – you will do well, very well, at Edinburgh."

James at least was beginning to think likewise.

Back at the castle they found a second bed being installed in their chamber, a smaller one, necessarily further restricting the space in the bedroom. Refreshments were produced for them but no large meal was served, word being given that they would feed presently in the great hall – with His Grace's agreement. Tom Boyd seemed less than elated over this, obviously preferring a private threesome. Mary declared that if that was to be the way of it, then she must have clothing other than her riding-gear. To go dressed so would look ridiculous. Could the master not find some women's garb for her, about this castle? It need not be handsome or even especially well fitting. But she was not going in that scanty bodice, heavy skirt and long boots!

Approving of this request, the man went off to see what could be found. Unfortunately the female members of his family had been left at Kilmarnock during this venture; and his father was a widower. There *were* a few women in the citadel, however, in addition to servants. He would see what he could do.

When he came back almost an hour later, he brought a buxom, bold-eyed lady with him, both bearing armfuls of clothing and shoes. This was Isabel Cunninghame, he introduced, a friend. She was perhaps a little larger than Her Highness, but they might be able to make something here fit reasonably well. A tuck here and there? Shoes might be more of a problem. They should go through all, and try them. He led the way into the bedroom, the newcomer skirling a laugh.

Mary gestured for all the gear to be put on the new bed, then turning, pointed to the door. "Thank you. But we shall essay this the better for your absence, Master of Boyd!" She called, "Jamie, summon the master to you."

By royal command, however vague and non-spontaneous, the man had to leave them, protesting, to more mirth from the newcomer.

In fact, the dressing situation was less difficult than it might have been, with quite a choice of garments and sizes, and only minor adjustments required, presumably not all the offerings pertaining to this Isabel Cunninghame. A leather belt helped to reduce the waist-fitting, and the bust excess was not great, for Mary was quite well developed there, and a silken shawl served to hide any maladjustments. The footwear was less simple to fit, but by using ribbons to tie soft leather slippers in place, a fair comfort was achieved. So, arrayed in an olive green velvet skirt, a more ample bodice under an open quilted doublet of brocaded purple and gold satin, and that shawl, Mary sallied out to face male inspection – and found herself, in fact, concerned that the effect should be favourable.

The man clapped his hands at the sight of her. "Bravo!" he cried. "Here is wonder, delight! The vision fair! You gladden the eyes, Highness. And . . . more than the eyes!"

James could not have been less interested, at least in his sister's appearance. "The master was telling me that Boyd means fair, comely, Mary. The Erse, *boidheach*. And he *is* fair, comely, is he not? They come of the old Celtic people, before ever the Stewarts came to Scotland. Or the Bruces. Is that not notable?"

"The master is fair of talk, at least! Over-fair, I think!" But she did not frown as she said it. She turned to thank the Cunninghame woman for her help. Whereupon the master took that woman's arm and ushered her to the door.

"Come, Isa," he said. "I will be back for Your Grace and Highness shortly, to conduct you to the hall. When all is in readiness."

Mary noted that, as they passed out, the lady's hand went up to stroke Tom Boyd's head and neck affectionately.

When in due course they were escorted to the great hall of the castle, scene of many a parliament, it was to discover that quite a banquet had been prepared and a large company assembled to partake of it. A trumpeter sounded a flourish, and all stood as the monarch entered. In place of the Lyon King of Arms — who of course was at Stirling — Lord Boyd himself came to lead the royal pair up past the long table and bowing guests to the dais-platform at the far end, which they mounted, and where a group of notables awaited them. One was a short, corpulent, red-faced man wearing a handsome cloak and a chain of office, and bearing a cushion on which lay a golden key. This was the provost of the city, who thrust out the cushion to James, bowing as low as his build would allow, all but upsetting cushion and key in the process.

The boy, who had never been given the key of a city before, glanced at Mary for guidance. She nodded, and murmured, "Take it. Then put it back." Her brother lifted it up, admired it, declared that it was very heavy, and returned it to the cushion.

"Sire, come and sit here," Lord Boyd directed.

There was a throne-like chair at the centre of the dais-table, somewhat large for this King of Scots. To him there were brought the magnates who had stood waiting, the Lords Somerville, he who had taken part in the abduction, Hailes, and Livingstone, with the Master of Hailes and Ker Younger of Cessford. All now made respectful obeisance towards the sovereign.

The Boyd brothers seated themselves on either side of James, with Mary between Sir Alexander and the master. Much attention was paid to the boy.

A quite ambitious meal was served, entertainment proceeding

27

throughout down beside the long table, in the form of fiddling, dancing and a gypsy with a dancing bear. Sir Alexander addressed little of his attention to Mary, but she heard him enlarging on the military arts to James, and promising to organise a tourney for his edification shortly. It was evident that efforts were now being made to gain the sympathies and goodwill of the youngster, as well as holding his person.

The master made up for his uncle in attentiveness to the young woman, so much so that, removing a hand that was stroking her wrist, she asked him why he had not brought his friend Isabel Cunninghame up here to sit beside him; she could be seen placed well down the lengthy main table. Laughing, he told her that Isa was well enough where she was, and not over-particular as to the company she kept. Ask Uncle Sandy!

Mary did not pursue the matter, but sought to maintain her cool distance-keeping, difficult as this was in physical terms.

James ate heartily, enjoyed the bear's antics particularly, and listened to his two mentors, clearly appreciating all this new-found care and solicitude.

With the eating over and the entertainers beginning to repeat themselves, Lord Boyd, turning in his chair, signed to the waiting trumpeter, who thereupon blew another flourish. From the end of the dais-table the Lord Livingstone rose, and came along with a paper, ink-horn, quill and metal seal. He was Lord Chamberlain, and had been at Linlithgow for the Exchequer Audit. Now he was here; so he must have been in league with the Boyds, although not taking part in the abduction. He presented the paper to James, opened the ink-horn, dipped in the pen, and handed this to the young monarch. Boyd explained that this was the official summons, to the kingdom, for a parliament, to be held in forty days' time, requiring the signature and seal of the King. Would His Grace sign there at the bottom?

The boy looked quickly along at his sister. It was obvious to her that this was the real reason behind this evening's activities, James's co-operation now essential. If he refused, what would they do? Was there any point in refusal? Would not a parliament, in fact, be advantageous? Once the realm's parliament met, they could hardly keep the sovereign-lord a prisoner any longer. This entire situation should be bettered, regularised. Anyway, they might force James to sign, one way or another. Half shrugging, she nodded, wordless. The boy somewhat laboriously appended his signature, the quill rather spluttering ink.

Livingstone took the document, declaring that he would have wax prepared and the seal appended, and bowed himself off. Boyd rose and indicated that James should do so also. All then had to rise, when the monarch stood. Clearly the evening's importance was over. Amidst more trumpeting and bowing, the entire dais-table group escorted the monarch to the door – whereafter, however, the Master of Boyd was left to take the royal pair back to their quarters, their importance abruptly dispensed with. James, however, was well pleased with it all, almost excited.

Tom Boyd, of course, would have come in, to continue the evening's entertainment in his preferred style, but Mary was quite firm in directing otherwise. He did, then, kiss her hand, and was proceeding on up her arm, when she twitched it away.

"Go back, sir, to yonder hall," she advised. "You have gained your ends sufficiently for one night, I think! And you will find more . . . accommodating company back there, no?"

He sighed, shaking his head at her, but went.

Having to shorten her brother's encomiums on the evening's satisfactions, especially his approval of the bear-dancing and the promise of a tournament, Mary got him off bedwards. She hoped that she had done rightly in guiding him to sign that summons to parliament. But . . . these ones would have achieved it anyway, somehow, she had little doubt. A parliament, although obviously necessary for these Boyds' plans, was also best for James himself and the nation. Had she shaken her head, then, and James refused to sign, they might have separated her from him, as a hostile influence – which would have been a grievous development.

When, presently, she in turn entered the bedchamber, it was to find James, as before, lying in the large bed. It was later and darker than the previous night, and she was able to discard her borrowed clothing in more privacy. She went over to give the boy his goodnight kiss. He clung to her for a little, in her nakedness. She was making back for the smaller bed when he spoke.

"Will you not come back, Mary? To this bed. There is much room. It was good, last night. Was it not? Together."

She hesitated. Had she not been talking about suitability, earlier? Was this suitable? Yet . . . if James wanted it, was there any harm in it? He was going through a very upsetting experience, for a boy. If it helped him to feel her, his elder sister, close, a reassurance, was it wrong? And herself – she could do with a little togetherness perhaps. These last two days had been . . . testing. She went round to the other side of the great bed, and got in.

James reached out to her, but taking his hand, she did not encourage him to come closer. He said, "Will the master take us climbing that hill tomorrow, Mary?"

"He might . . ."

"If I said that it was my royal command, would he do it?"

"That is hardly a subject for a royal command, Jamie!"

"If *you* asked him, he would. He likes you."

"We shall see. I am not eager to ask favours of that one! He is over-eager for favours from *me*! These Boyds are ambitious men, Jamie. They act of a set purpose. They need you, the King. As when they had you sign that parliament summons. I think that was right to do. But you will have to beware of them, not trust them too greatly. The master is very friendly, but you must watch him also."

He yawned. "A tournament would be splendid. I hope that they have one. Would they let me take part? Not just watch? What could I do?"

"Tournaments are for grown men, Jamie. Jousting on horse-back, with lances. Swordplay. Duels. Archery contests. I do not see that you could take part in any of these. The last, perhaps. You could practise with a bow. I could show you. I have done a little archery. Not that I am good at it. I do not think that you have ever tried it?"

There was no answer. The King of Scots slept.

The next day was wet, and scarcely suitable for climbing hills, to Jamie's much disappointment. But the indefatigable Tom Boyd, who appeared to conceive it his pleasure, if not his duty, to be responsible for keeping the royal pair entertained, took them on a tour of the fortress itself. They started with the extraordinary topmost structure of all, a tiny chapel perched on the naked summit of the vast rock, severe, plain within and without, its whitewashed interior containing little more than a simple stone altar, a holy water stoup, a lectern and a kneeling-stool. This was Queen Margaret's Chapel, he explained. Why so small, so modest, when built by a Queen, he did not know, for the good King David's mother had erected the great Dunfermline Abbey, where the Bruce was buried, and other major shrines; but this place was considered to be very holy, for some reason, nevertheless. He was not very strong on matters religious, himself, but no doubt there was some reason . . .

Mary, although no know-all, took the opportunity to demonstrate that they were not all ignoramuses in the royal family of Stewart, and was quite pleased to be able to suggest that if indeed the Boyds were of the old Celtic race, as their name indicated, then the master ought to know what this chapel represented. She had never seen it before, but had heard of it. Queen Margaret Atheling, of the English royal house, believed that Almighty God must have sent her to Scotland for some especial purpose – after all, she was on her way to Hungary, her mother's home country, when their ship was driven ashore in a storm, and Malcolm Canmore, King of Scots, had captured her and, captivated in turn by her beauty, had wed her. She believed that God's purpose must be her conversion of the old Celtic or Columban Church, which had been Scotland's Kirk for five hundred years, since Columba's time, to her own Roman Catholicism. And, almost single-handed, this young woman in her twenties had achieved this, and turned the Scots to Rome. Whether this was indeed God's will was doubtful, for the old Church had suited the Scots people, independent folk who took but ill to domination in spiritual matters from the Pope, cardinals, archbishops, bishops and legates and nuncios, preferring their own monastic abbots, and small shrines to the grand abbeys and cathedrals of Rome. However, in middle life, when disaster took her husband and eldest son from her, and her favourite youngest son David was a captive hostage in England, with another son deserted back to the Celtic faith, Margaret came to doubt the rightness and wisdom of what she had done. She became all but an anchorite, shutting herself away, castigating herself, all but starving; and when sickness overtook her, holed herself up in this castle, and built this tiny, simple chapel, in the ancient tradition, for her dying worship. So this, not the great abbeys of the land, was her final statement of faith, possibly remorse, a monument to a woman's flexibility of mind.

James was not very interested in all this, but Boyd was, not so much probably from the religious or even historic aspect but in that the young woman knew of it and had elected to tell him. He said that he would not forget it and, patting her shoulder, added that it was a blessing that women could change their minds!

From the chapel they went down to the Governor's House where, it seemed, the Boyd family were installed. While they did not examine it all, although by no means palatial it was obviously a deal more comfortable and well appointed than were the quarters presently allotted to James and his sister – a point on which Mary did not fail to comment.

Boyd had his own answer to that, waving an eloquent hand. "If *I* had my way, Highness, you would be *sharing* these lodgings with me, I do assure you!" And she could take what she would out of that. Her tossed hair was as eloquent as his arm-waving.

Their next stop was at the fortress prisons, a row of dark, underground cells cut in the solid rock, provided with staples and iron chains, all fortunately empty at this juncture. Glad to get out of that horrible place, Mary could not resist a comment.

"At least you did not instal us *there*, prisoners as we are!"

Even she had to acknowledge his quick thinking and spirit when he answered, "Never. That is folly. But, even there, it would have been my pleasure to join you!"

Passing their own quarters, across the square from the palace building with its great hall, galleries and armoury, he took them down to see David's Tower, easternmost of the eight towers of the citadel, built by Margaret's youngest son, David the First of proud memory. And here he showed them the renowned cannon, Mollance Meg – which greatly intrigued James, if not Mary. She had something of a horror of such things, for it was, of course, the explosion of a cannon which had killed their father, who had been all too interested in artillery. Young James knew of this great piece by repute, the mightiest in Scotland, and recited for Boyd's benefit its story, how it had been constructed by a Galloway blacksmith on the orders of Maclellan of Bombie, and made powerful enough to smash through even the walls of Threave Castle, the seat of the Earl of Douglas who had slain Maclellan's father. This it had achieved, its huge ball, the weight of a Galloway cow allegedly, said to have taken off the hand of the Fair Maid of Galloway as she sat at meat with the earl. The castle had fallen, and its lord with it – and since he was the enemy of the King, that James had bestowed on its maker the farm of Mollance, formerly Douglas's, in gratitude. The smith's wife's name was Meg, and so the great piece had become known as Mollance, or Mons, Meg, and was brought to Edinburgh and installed here, the monarch's pride. Tom Boyd almost certainly knew all this, but he listened attentively to the boy. Made of staves and hoops of iron and mounted on a low trolley, it was impressive only by its size, weight and story; yet Mary's companions obviously found it fascinating – which led her to consider, not for the first time, the difference of what might impress males as distinct from females.

The rain had now ceased, and nothing would do but that, in the afternoon, they must climb Arthur's Seat, wet grass or none, Mary's protests about unsuitable footwear being dismissed by her brother as feeble. So, with the strongest of the borrowed female shoes which would approximately fit, they set out, horsed and with the required escort again, down through the town to the hillfoot, the enthusiasm one-sided indeed.

The master had been told that if they turned up from the parkland of the royal hunting forest, between a knoll called the Haggis Knowe and St Anthony's Chapel, just before they reached the first of the lochs, St Margaret's, they would find a rising valley which would take them almost two-thirds of the way up, still mounted, before they had to leave the horses and clamber. The floor of this quite wide valley had to be carefully skirted on the right, for it was waterlogged, indeed it was known as the Hunters' Bog; so the riders had to pick their way, James urgent, Boyd consistently cheerful, Mary patient and the escort glum.

Up on the final shoulder of hill before the ultimate steep and rocky peak, they dismounted, for a windy conclave. None was really dressed for climbing, the master probably the best so, even James having only riding-boots; and clearly none of the escort was properly shod for this – nor eager to make the attempt. However, the guard was there only to ensure that the monarch was not the target for any recapture attempt, and the climbers would be in sight throughout, so it was decided that the men could safely be left with the horses, and their three betters go on alone. The top of Arthur's Seat was hardly likely to be the scene of any reprisal raid.

So they set off, the King leading and determined to show his prowess, Mary kilting up her skirt and shaking off the master's helping hands.

It was indeed a steep and rough ascent, with much of bare stone and moss, slippery after the rain; and the wind, from the south-west, in their faces, did not help. Soon all were panting, and even James glad to pause with increasing frequency, the young man urging the girl not to overdo it, to go slowly, and when she breathlessly declared that she was perfectly able to master this hill unaided, pointing out appreciatively that her heaving bosom gave the delightful lie to her assertions.

Grasping tussocks and outcropping stone, and seeking to use the sides of her ill-fitting shoes rather than the toes to aid her, Mary pulled herself up. With perhaps three hundred feet to surmount, and so steep in parts that they had to pick a circuitous route rather than going straight up, it was a demanding business, with false crests to contend with. She would have copied her brother, who was largely going on all fours, but perceived this as undignified for a woman, princess or other, particularly with a man all too anxious to give her physical support. She was no weakling, but found it a trial.

At the summit, at length, it was probably worth it, however, so tremendous was the prospect on every hand and, yes, the sense of achievement, James capering about in triumph and exclaiming, and the master taking the opportunity to clutch the girl, to steady her against the wind's buffetings, in necessarily all-embracing fashion. There were these varieties of reward.

Going down again was as difficult as coming up had been, if less exhausting, slipping now the danger, and Mary not ungrateful for a hand on occasion – especially when, all but involuntarily, it was *her* hand which once shot out to prevent Tom Boyd from falling. That made her feel better, strangely enough. James was on his bottom as frequently as on his feet, but shouting his mirth.

Mud-stained, breathless and wind-blown, they reached the horses again, to their escorts' ill-concealed smirks.

That evening, when the master ushered in their meal, he brought news. It had been decided that he should go to Kilmarnock on the morrow, to the Boyds' Dean Castle there, to bring back Annabella Boyd, a supply of women's clothing for Mary, and to exchange some of their fighting men for a new batch – these being mainly the sons and brothers of tenant farmers and field-workers, cattle-herds and the like, who could not be away from their other duties for too long at any one time. It was suggested that Mary Stewart went with him, to select the clothing and other plenishings which she might wish, and for the chance to get out of their cramping quarters for a while.

She hesitated. The opportunity to go riding free appealed, even though she recognised that she would have to be constantly on her guard over Tom Boyd's advances throughout – but was she not that anyway? And she was reasonably confident that she could cope with him. But James . . . ?

The boy at once asked whether he could go also, to be told that unfortunately that was not possible in the circumstances. The royal protests were immediately forthcoming, when the master revealed that this had been foreseen by their captors, by declaring that Sir Alexander was desirous of discussing the tournament details with His Grace; and also, if he would wish it, give him some instruction in the martial arts, swordplay, lance-aiming at targets on horseback, archery and the like. This, of course, much altered James's attitude and priorities. When could they begin, he demanded?

Mary, for her part, asked how far it was to Kilmarnock – since distances she could see might complicate the issue as far as she was concerned, if an overnight halt was required. She was told, quite casually, that it was some sixty-five miles, but no really difficult riding – to which she replied that she had ridden further than that in a day ere this; and her mare was of excellent quality.

The man eyed her carefully, and shrugged.

3

The following morning they were up betimes, with James suddenly anxious and having to be reassured by his sister that she would be back in but three days and all would be well. He was to pay careful heed to Sir Alexander over the arms exercises, for these could have their dangers; but to remember always that he was the King, and not to be persuaded to anything that he judged unsuitable. This matter of suitability was becoming something of a preoccupation for that young woman.

The boy was a little tense at the parting, for he had never hitherto been left alone for more than an hour or two lacking the support of members of his family; and Mary asked herself whether she was in a way failing him, doing the right thing. But it was too late to change her mind now, and the boy was probably the better of learning to stand on his own feet on occasion; she must not seem to cosset him too protectively.

They rode off with a party of some two score men-at-arms, some of these of the Arthur's Seat escort, a cheerful company glad to be going home, the master in dashing mood. Fortunately it was a fine sunny morning.

They left the city by the Grassmarket and West Port, and took the road south-westwards as though making for the northern skirts of the Pentland Hills. Tom said that there were two or three routes they could follow, but the easiest as regards terrain for fair riding, although not the shortest, he reckoned was by the drove-road to Lanark by the upper Water of Leith, the Pentland hillfoots, the Crosswood and Medwyn Waters, to Carnwath and so to Lanark. From there, over the moors to the Avon Water and Darvel, it was but another score of miles to Kilmarnock. Put thus, it sounded no major journey.

The men-at-arms were on the whole well mounted, for the Ayrshire land of the Boyds was notable for raising cattle and horses; but Mary was afraid that they might hold them back nevertheless, her own and the master's animals being of course especially well bred. It was not so much their speed that she was concerned with, but the ability to cover the long journey in one day. An overnight stop could present opportunities for her companion to press his unacceptable attentions – although the possibility of putting up at some religious house or hospice did occur to her, where presumably women would be kept apart from men anyway. Or would they be? She had never been in such situation before. Were there any religious houses between Lanark and Kilmarnock? And if so, would such be prepared to entertain some forty men-at-arms? She could hardly put these queries to Tom Boyd however.

Not that there was much opportunity for converse at the pace they rode, her companion certainly not limiting his pace for whatever reason. No doubt he too was glad to escape the restrictions of the last three days. He led with a spanking canter for the first few miles, before settling down to a fast but steady trot, which ate up the distance satisfactorily. It was a good feeling, of a summer's day, the larks trilling and the curlews wheepling from the heather.

This road, made for cattle-droving, although flanking the hills all the way, nowhere rose very high, the moorlands on the whole providing fairly firm going, and the valleys, being those of cascading hill-streams, not boggy. So they made excellent time, with a minimum of talk.

When, after three hours of it, they reached Carnwath, to water and rest their mounts, Tom remarked that she was a good horsewoman to add to her other attractions. She pointed out that, with the father she had, she had to be – the late James being of an impatient and impetuous nature, to put it mildly.

They reached the River Clyde soon thereafter, and followed this most of the way to Lanark, where they fed after a fashion, at three ale-houses, for forty men-of-arms called for the facilities of more than one, and Tom Boyd was apparently not the kind of man to stint his supporters. Then on, still in the Clyde valley, to the inflowing River Nethan, up which they turned. They were here mounting to a central watershed of south-west Scotland, where many rivers were born, new country for Mary. They had to pick their way over dividing ridges and escarpments, none high, from one valley to the next, to maintain their true direction, from Nethan to Candor to Avon, the most difficult part of their journey, but picturesque. Thereafter reaching Strathaven, they followed that river for a dozen miles up to the highest point of their journey, where Wallace and Bruce had fought some of their fiercest battles against the invading English, in the Loudoun Hill area; indeed Boyd pointing out the site of Wallace's camp, and asserting that he had Wallace blood in him.

Over this pass they were into the valley of the Irvine Water, a major stream, which would bring them almost all the way down to Kilmarnock, by Darvel, Newmilns and Galston, the final dozen miles. It was only early evening, so there would be no question of having to halt for the night, to Mary's distinct relief. Although what conditions would be like at Dean Castle remained to be seen.

Saddle-sore and stiff, but not too weary, they came at length, with the dusk, in sight of the town of Kilmarnock, its smokes blue haze to the evening. But they did not enter it, swinging off northwards to reach the Kilmarnock Burn in about a mile, where in open meadowland the tall, massive, square keep of a castle rose out of a high-walled courtyard enclosure, extensive, with its own parapet and gatehouse. At first glance it did not appear to be a very strong defensive site, however powerful-looking and impressive was the fortalice itself; but closer approach showed that meadowland to be largely waterlogged, and the Kilmarnock Burn used to provide a wide moat around the castle. An easily defendable causeway crossed this to give access. A dean or hollow might be no typical position for a stronghold, but Dean Castle was obviously not lacking in strength.

"Our poor house is perhaps no abode for a royal princess," the master observed, as they rode up to the gatehouse. "But we shall do our best to cherish you therein."

"I shall be surprised, sir, if it is not more comfortable than the quarters you allotted us at Edinburgh!"

"Not *I*, Highness. That was my elders' doing. And they had not looked to entertain a lady."

They had been dropping off men-at-arms for the last two or three miles, and it was only a small group which now passed under the gatehouse archway and into the large cobbled courtyard lined with lean-to outbuildings. Their approach evidently had not gone unobserved, despite the dusk, Boyd colours presumably sufficiently evident, for the drawbridge had been lowered and the portcullis was up, and a girl stood watching, waiting, up on a small stone platform projecting from a first-floor doorway. At some distance out from this a flight of steps rose, and from its top a removable wooden gangway crossed to the doorstep platform. The Boyds clearly could be concerned with their privacy.

"My sister Annabella," Tom said. "A saucy piece – but with her parts." Leaping down from the saddle, he went to aid Mary from hers.

Waving a hand, but with a smile, at his upstretched arms, she deliberately turned to the other side, flung a leg over the saddle as modestly as she might, and slipped to the ground unaided, there to brace her somewhat travel-aching shoulders. Let the Lady Annabella perceive, from the start, some hint of attitudes.

At least the man could not be prevented from taking her arm to escort her up those steps. "Anna," he called, "here is a guest indeed – Her Highness the Princess Mary, sister to His Grace the King."

The girl awaiting them was not handsome like her brother, but not unattractive, round-faced, sparkling-eyed, with a wide, smiling mouth and dimpled cheeks, less tall and slender than Mary but well built. Her examination of the other, crossing the gangway, was humorous rather than impressed.

"You fly high, Tom!" she greeted, and made an incipient curtsy.

Standing behind, in the iron-grille-guarded doorway, were now to be seen two small boys, aged eight and six. The master had not mentioned that he had brothers, only that their mother had died three years before.

"These are Sandy and Archie, scoundrels both!"

Mary offered them all a tentative smile. None of the offences committed by the older Boyds could be laid at *their* door, at least.

"You have come far this day?" the Lady Annabella asked, standing aside to let the visitor enter.

"All the way. From Edinburgh. So – food and drink, lass. We have scarce eaten since."

"So far?" the girl exclaimed. "Then you are a notable horse-woman, Highness. I do not know whether *I* could do the like."

"You will have to," her brother told her. "For you are coming back with us!"

"I am . . . ?"

"Yes. That is why we are here. If the princess will have you! You are to become a lady-in-waiting, Anna. So be on your best behaviour – less than excellent as that may be!" He kissed the girl however, and slapped his young brothers' shoulders. "In, in!" he commanded. "Do not stand there staring."

Mary spoke. "You have a forthright brother, Lady Annabella. *I* was not long in discovering that. Forthright and . . . pressing!"

"Like most dogs, his bark is worse than his bite, I think!"

"Enough! Food, I say."

"I would prefer that I might wash first," Mary said.

"As you will." Annabella hesitated. "Not knowing of your coming, Highness, I have no chamber prepared. So – you had best come to mine, meantime. Sandy, go down to the kitchen and have Jeannie send up hot water to my bedchamber for the princess. Sufficient."

"And for me," the master added. "I think our mother's room for Her Highness, Anna."

The younger girl led the way upstairs two flights, pointing out one of three doors on the first landing in passing, which she said would be the chamber for Mary. That young woman noticed that the man entered one of the others alongside. On the floor above, she was ushered into a room, less than tidy with scattered clothing, but well enough furnished, particularly with a fine, large canopied bed, cupboards and chests, and its own seated garderobe in the thickness of the walling.

"I will make use of that, if I may," Mary said, pointing to the last, and did not wait for permission. Such a facility had not been available since Lanark.

The other laughed. "Even princesses can be so incommoded, then!" she commented. "Hot water will be up shortly. I will seek to see to all, for your comfort."

When Mary emerged, she found the other girl gone, but a pail and ewer of steaming water awaiting her, with towelling. She was thankful to disrobe partially and wash, having something of a preoccupation with cleanliness, something her brothers and sister found strange.

When Annabella came back and Mary was drying herself, she eyed her up and down frankly. "You are well made, Highness," she observed.

"You think so? You Boyds seem to be . . . concerned with such matters!"

"Oh, I did not mean to offend, Princess. I . . . admire!" She moved over to a doored cupboard, which she threw open. "Some of my clothing may fit none so ill, if you would wish to change, after long riding. Take whatever you require. I will go down and prepare the bed in the chamber which was my mother's."

Mary looked up, and over. "I think . . . if you do not mind it . . . I would prefer it here. With yourself. Here is a large bed. Room for both. And pleasant female company! If you do not find it to your displeasure? I will not disturb you."

The other blinked, but then smiled. "Surely. I used to share a bed with my sister, before she married. If you so wish it, Highness."

"I thank you." Mary moved over to scan the clothing in the wardrobe. "I fear that I cause you much trouble, Lady Annabella. I am sorry. But all this was no notion of mine, to come here. Your brother urged it on me."

"I can see why." That was simply said.

"Can you? The master is . . . urgent."

Annabella gurgled a laugh. "Yes, he is. And apt to get his way. But *you* will be a match for him, I think!" She paused, and threw up a hand to her mouth. "Oh, I did not mean, by match, a, a match of that sort . . . !" Her voice tailed away.

"I understand. Think naught of it. Now, this dark grey gown would fit me adequately, I judge – if I may borrow it?"

"To be sure. Anything. I fear that I am not provided as would be a princess . . ."

As they descended the stairs to the castle's hall for their meal, and passed the first-floor doorways, Annabella grinned and pointed to two of these. "I think that I know why you chose to sleep in *my* room!" she said.

"As to company of a night, I choose my own, yes."

Below they found Tom waiting with what patience he could muster, with the serving-woman Jeannie spreading a very adequate repast of soup, cold venison again, sweetmeats and cream, with wine. He eyed Mary's change of clothing critically, observed that her good looks transformed even the dull grey, but that the skirt was on the short side – on *her*, the better for that!

Annabella winked openly and sighed loudly.

The travellers did full justice to the provision, Annabella, having already eaten, contenting herself with the wine. The small boys had disappeared. When it was over, Mary announced that it had been a long day and her couch called. Gallant, the man rose to pull back her chair and aid her up.

"I will escort you to your chamber," he informed. There was a giggle from behind.

At the first-floor landing, he went to open the door next to his own, but Mary proceeded on to the next flight of stairs.

"A good night to you, Master of Boyd," she called back over her shoulder. "I have elected to share your sister's bed, of her kindness. I have been deprived of women's company and chatter, you understand. Sleep well."

She heard his exclamation, and glanced briefly back. The man was staring after her, expression eloquent of various emotions. But at his sister's tinkled laughter, humour of a rueful sort triumphed.

"Women!" he cried. "I vow you will make ill bedfellows . . . and keep each other awake!"

They proceeded to climb the stairs.

Undressing, they made a delectable pair – so much so that Annabella remarked cheerfully on what Tom, or any other man, was missing. Mary decided that she liked this girl.

In bed, and certainly not shrinking away from each other, she was further confirmed in her estimate, as they talked together easily, companionably. The younger girl admitted that she had known something of the design of her father and uncle to seek to obtain the keeping of the young King, and her doubts as to the propriety of it all; but she had learned no details. Mary recounted the tale of the hunt and forcible abduction, and the fact that clearly the thing had been arranged with the co-operation of Kennedy and the other lords, save it seemed Hamilton, and their shameful inaction at the deed; to which the other commented that their mutual-aid bands, tying their hands, had been well prepared. To Mary's charge that these had made unworthy guardians of the monarch, Annabella suggested that perhaps the Boyds might prove better ones, despite this doubtful start.

They left it at that, and soon thereafter Mary slept.

In the morning, the master, after pointed enquiries at breakfast as to whether they had passed a disturbed night, did his sister snore, and suchlike witticisms, announced that he had to go round the Boyd lands to collect a new batch of men, or at least pick them and order them to assemble here, well mounted, next morning early, for their journey back eastwards. So the young women would have to entertain themselves. They could decide what clothing and gear they wanted to take back with them, and Anna, who was good at falconry, could select three of his favourite hawks, for sport at Edinburgh. Very much the master, the master went off about man's work.

Mary spent a pleasant leisurely day with the other girl and the two small boys, being shown over the castle and its surrounding gardens, orchard and pleasance, admiring the hawks and hounds, and going over much clothing left by previous Boyd women, from which Mary was not too proud, in the circumstances, to accept some for her use. She found a distinct affinity developing between herself and Anna, and they quickly were on first-name terms, save in servitors' company; after all, they had much in common. Both had lost their mothers at about the same age, and had had to try to act as such to young brothers and sisters; both were horsewomen, fond of hunting, hawking and outdoor activities; both girls of spirit. For a lady-in-waiting, Mary decided that she was fortunate with this one.

Tom got back for the evening meal, evidently satisfied with his mustering activities, and reporting that the hay harvest was almost all in and the oats well advanced with full heads. Keeping up the high standard of horseflesh was his one problem, his father having taken the best for his own trip eastwards; and not all their tenants, farmers and herdsmen breeding the highest quality. Some of his recruits' beasts would almost certainly not be able to cover the distance to Edinburgh in one day, so he had decided to take only the best-mounted with them on the morrow, leaving the others to come on at a slower pace.

They spent the evening agreeably enough, the vaulted hall lit by candles and a small birch-log fire, with music and singing, Anna playing the harpsichord and Mary not refusing to pluck the strings of a lute, accompanying herself in songs Scots and Flemish, learned from her mother. Tom proved to have a fine tenor voice and a quick ear for picking up melodies, refrains and choruses, demonstrating loving and amatory passages with gestures and embraces, suitable or otherwise, mainly directed at their guest, and difficult to reject when playing on instruments. Later, he gave a display of Scots dancing, very agile, and inevitably sought Mary as partner, to Anna's music. This, to be sure, involved much hugging and clasping and birling. The young woman, while seeking to keep this within bouncing bounds, could not but acknowledge his untiring persistence.

When it came to bedtime, and with an early start in prospect, of course the man could not fail to suggest that Mary would be better bedded in the other room than with his unrestful sister – with predictable answer. Probably he felt that it was incumbent on him to try, at least.

The girls discussed men and their ways and foolishness at some length before sleeping.

They were a deal less talkative in the early morning of a dull, grey day, saying goodbye to the two small boys, left in the care of Jeannie, a motherly soul of whom they were obviously fond. The troop of mounted men was waiting for them beyond the causeway, cheerful enough, apparently looking on this interlude as something of a holiday. Selecting about a dozen of the best horsed to accompany them, the master told the rest to follow on at their own speed, and rode ahead.

They followed the same route as they had used to come, and although there were spots of rain soon after they started, it came to nothing, and by Lanark there were even glimpses of sunshine. Anna rode well, and they were not delayed by pack-horses, for Tom had distributed the bundles of clothing and gear being taken amongst the men-at-arms. Each of their betters carried a hooded and jessed hawk at wrist, the birds remarkably little trouble.

They took slightly longer on the return journey than on the outward, this not on account of Anna but on the quality of the escort's horses; but even so they reached Edinburgh before the city's gates were shut for the night – not that the master would have worried about demanding the watch at the West Port to open up for them.

James welcomed them effusively – not, it seemed, because he had greatly missed his sister but in order to recount at length his adventures and prowess in various branches of the martial arts, particularly archery and quarter-stavery, the pleasures of tilting at hoops and pegs, with lances, and the saddle-posturing necessary to avoid the impact of enemy assaults. He had not so much to say about swordplay, the great two-handed weapons being rather heavy for his young wrists, and the short stabbing variety suitable only for men-at-arms. He found the shields heavy also, but Sir Alexander had promised to have a lighter one made for him, painted with the red Rampant Lion on gold. He was loud in his praise of the said Sir Alexander, who had said that he would organise a tournament in the royal honour in a week or two.

In all this the monarch more or less ignored Anna as irrelevant, and was even a little superior in his attitude to his sister, such matters being of course beyond womenkind.

Getting the boy to bed thereafter was a delayed process, especially as no provision having been made apparently for quarters for Anna, and suitable lodgings in the fortress limited to say the least. It was evident that she had to share the royal rooms, meantime at least, Mary nowise objecting. So the obvious procedure was to put James in the smaller bed and the two girls share the larger – at which the monarch was not enthusiastic. However, the pleasures of watching the two young women undressing made up for that, with Anna nowise bashful.

The girls continued to get martial talk across the bedchamber, with scant response, until tired, they slept.

Next day, the master took them all to try out the hawks at Duddingston Loch, the large one on the south side of Arthur's Seat, a third of a mile long and half that across, and surrounded by reed-beds. It was a great place for wildfowl, varieties of duck, the occasional goose, herons, swans and sometimes oyster-catchers and other waders from the nearby Scotwater of Forth. So there was always plenty to fly hawks at; the problem was retrieval, both of the prey and of the hawks themselves. If the alarmed fowl flew off inland, as it were, it was not so difficult, for the horsemen could ride after them to collect; but if they took refuge in the high reed-beds then it was otherwise, and retrieval all but impossible, for the reeds grew out of mud and surface water capable of bearing neither horse nor man. This was why Tom had brought only his best-trained hawks, those which could be relied upon to return to the hawker after a strike, not to go down and seek to devour their prey. Falconers, the trainers of hawks, had to be expert at their task; and the sportsmen also, for they had to be selective about which wildfowl to loose their hawks at.

James knew all this, of course, but the master reminded him of it as they rode out to Duddingston. The secret was to keep the hawks hooded until a high-flying duck or goose soared off away from the loch, or a group of such, ignoring the low-fliers which would be apt to settle again on the water or in the further reeds. Heron and swans were less of a problem, for these were not so apt to come down again in the reeds but tended to flap away in a wide circle, to come back to the disturbance-point to see if it was clear. They were slower fliers also, and so more readily caught up with by the hawks; but of course they were much larger, stronger, and less easy for the hawks to kill.

The party was seven-strong, for they had brought along three of the Kilmarnock men to act as tranters, or retrievers. With only the three hawks, the two young women agreed to take turn about with one of them.

James was all excitement as they reached the loch, at its west end, near the monastic property of Priestfield, a grange belonging to the Abbey of the Holy Rood. Since that abbacy was a royal appointment, the King did not have to seek permission to hawk and hunt here. Before ever the horsemen got close to the reed-beds, the duck began to fly up with a great quacking, in ones and twos and groups. These all went off low, some even skittering along the surface of the water, eastwards, to the King's disgust.

"Wait you," the master advised. "These are but the easily scared ones. See – we will ride a little into the reeds. Not far, or our beasts will get bogged down."

The boy urged his horse on impatiently, and before he had gone a dozen yards a heron rose, a great grey bird with long legs trailing behind, to flap off seemingly lazily after the ducks' swift wing-beating, rising to only some twenty feet or so.

"Right! Fly!" Tom cried.

The boy, in his excitement, fumbled with his hawk's hood, and got its jesse, the leg strap, already loosed, caught in his fingers; and in those few seconds' delay, a pair of mallard burst out nearby and soared up, quacking. The hawk, freed, saw these as its prey, and launching upwards beat wings to gain height rather than going directly after the ducks. These were heading southwards, not down-loch.

"Stupid bird!" the monarch exclaimed. "Look – it has gone after the wrong game! And it is too slow! They will get away. It will lose them. And the heron get away too . . . !"

"Give it time. It needs height. Till then, it rises. Then it will fly swiftly enough. It will not lose sight of them." The man turned to Mary, who was taking first turn. "The heron!" he jerked. Then he turned to one of the men, and pointed wordlessly after the pair of mallard. That individual spurred off.

Mary had been ready, jesses loosed, and had the hood off her bird with a flick, almost throwing the hawk after the larger bird, now at least one hundred yards away. Again this hawk began to mount at a fairly steep angle, whilst the heron increased its distance.

"Never fear," the master cried. "Better to let the heron gain some distance. We do not want it brought down in the water. Without dogs to retrieve it . . ."

"I have been hawking since I was a child!" she returned. "Save your breath! Aye, and your eyes!" She pointed over to the right, where another heron, no doubt the first's mate, had risen out of the reeds to beat off southwards.

Cursing, the man unhooded his own hawk and flung it after. There was mocking laughter from Anna.

So, within mere moments, all three hawks were in the air, and climbing.

The term hawk-eyed was proven to be no misnomer. Those birds, although firstly concerned with gaining height, never lost sight of their chosen quarry, despite James's fears and impatience. Once sufficiently high, and well above their hoped-for victims, they could plane down at a slant at fearsome speed, and drop on their prey from above for the kill.

The two other retrievers were already riding off after the birds, one due southwards over the parkland, the other along the reedy shores of the loch. The four remaining backed their horses a little way on to firmer ground, and waited.

"Your pardon, Highness, for seeming to instruct you," the master said, waving a hand. "I had not realised that you were so knowledgeable about hawking."

"My mother was enamoured of the sport, and taught me," she replied. "She taught me about men also, sir. And was experienced with them likewise!"

"So there you have it, Tom!" his sister chuckled. "Beware!"

Unabashed, he inclined his handsome head. "I may always hope that Her Grace's daughter might be as kind as was Queen Mary of Guelders!" he replied. "I must seek my uncle's guidance!"

Which might be said to even the score.

James, uninterested in this exchange, let out a whoop. "See – your heron, Mary!"

At the far end of the loch, Mary's hawk had got above the first heron, and dropped like a stone upon it, to strike at the base of the long outstretched neck in an explosion of feathers. The larger bird, three times the size of its attacker, plunged downwards in an ungainly sprawl of wings and legs, whether killed or not they could not tell at that range. Unfortunately, it fell into the water, although not far from the shore.

"A pity! If that hawk had but waited just a little, it would have been over the land," Tom declared. "I do not see your tranter getting through those reeds to collect it." He turned to observe the progress of his own hawk.

"*I* can swim," the King announced. "I will get it."

"Jamie, what nonsense!" his sister exclaimed. "It is not worth that. If the man cannot get it, leave it . . ."

"There goes mine!" the master cried. "Into those trees. Down. The tranter will get that one, to be sure."

"Look!" Anna called. "Here is *your* hawk, Sire. Returning." She pointed. Quite high, a hawk came to hover above them, and then circled down to them, coming to flutter wings above the man, not the boy.

"Good bird! It knows *me*, not you." Tom held out his gauntleted arm, for the creature to land on. "See – duck's feathers caught in its talons. It will have killed."

The bird settled on the man's gauntlet and folded its wings. He handed it over to James, who took it and hooded it, stroking its back feathers approvingly.

"Your hawk is better trained than mine," Mary observed. "See – it has come down and landed on the heron. What now?"

Tom frowned. "It is because the heron has fallen in water, I wager. The hawk will be unsure. Perhaps it will come, presently . . ."

They could see that tranter on his horse, stationary amongst the reeds perhaps seventy yards from the birds. They all commenced to ride round the loch thitherwards.

"I will get them both!" James asserted. "I will swim."

"Not so, Your Grace. That would never do."

"I will . . ."

"I forbid it, Jamie," Mary declared. "A King cannot do such a thing!"

"If any has to do it, I will," Tom said. "But the hawk may come back. The heron can lie."

When they reached the man, the hawk still rode on the heron's back. The latter had ceased to flap.

"Can you swim, man?" the master asked.

"No, lord, I canna. And it's ower soft for the horse. Thae reeds . . ."

Cursing, Tom whistled through his teeth and held up his gloved arm. But the hawk remained where it was.

"Devil-damned bird!" its owner muttered. Dismounting, he began to strip off his doublet.

"No need to go to such lengths, surely?" Mary protested. "It will come in time, no?"

"It may not. And it is a valuable bird – too much to risk losing. It is a haggard – a wild-caught adult, and could go wild again. A female peregrine . . ." The man was kicking off his riding-boots now.

"I say that he is but eager to display to you his matchless man's body!" Anna suggested.

"Why can *he* do it, if I may not?" James asked plaintively – but none attended to the royal demand, being frankly intrigued by the master's progressing disrobing.

Tom's own hawk was now circling above the party, possibly itself somewhat confused by its flier's behaviour, unusual in that sport. Anna whistled to it expertly and held up her leather-protected arm, and the bird dropped down to settle on it obediently; it would know her as well as it did him. Just then its tranter rode up, with a dead heron. But this passed barely noticed by the onlookers, as the Master of Boyd stepped out of his breeches and stood naked on the grass, a notably well-formed figure, wide of shoulder, narrow of waist and hips, with quite an abundance of hair on chest and at groin. He made no attempt to hide his masculinity, but nor did he flaunt it, before striding down to the first of the reeds.

"A pity to spoil all that revelation with mud, is it not?" his unreserved sister observed. Mary remained silent.

Plunging into the high reeds, Tom's feet and ankles quickly began to sink in and emerge with each step, black before the greenery hid him, and his progress was indicated only by the waving of the rushes and the noise of his squelching. Then, and rather thankfully, they heard a major splashing – for that mud could have been deep enough to endanger the man – which indicated open water reached, although, because of the height of the reeds, they could not see the splasher.

"Are you duly impressed, Highness?" Anna asked.

"Folly, I think. But sportive folly. There he is, out."

With a strong over-arm stroke the man came into view, with only a dozen or so yards to the birds.

"He swims well," Mary said. "But how will he deal with the hawk, while swimming?"

"The good Lord knows! But if any could, Tom can."

"You admire your brother more than you seem to, I think, Anna!"

The man reached his objective. They saw him swim round the birds, prospecting the situation. Then he turned on his back, using his feet to propel and steady him. The girls saw him stretch out and up one bare arm for the peregrine to jump on to – and both winced as they recognised what those sharp talons could do gripping naked flesh. The hawk obediently transferred itself to the arm, kept high. Then he grasped the long legs of the heron with the other hand, and paddling round in a semicircle, still on his back, commenced to kick his way to the shore.

"He has them both!" James cried. "The heron is dead. Good! Is that not splendid?"

The young women did not deny it.

Tom splashed his way into the reeds with his burdens, the tranters hurriedly dismounting to go down to the edge to relieve him. Presently the waving greenery parted to reveal him, hawk held high, heron dragged behind, black well above the knees, and much elsewhere, with clinging mud, but grinning triumphantly. Something not unlike a cheer came from the watchers, Mary included.

A tranter took the heron but the master took the offending hawk to his sister, then turned back to the loch's edge to splash himself with water to wash off the mud. He paid particular attention to his hairy groin. Mary transferred *her* attention to Anna, asking whether she intended to fly the errant bird any further.

Tom answered for her. Yes, they would go round to the other side of the loch, once he had his clothes on, and try a sally or two from there. Perhaps, if that peregrine misbehaved itself again, one of the ladies would choose to act the swimmer? Anna could swim, he knew. And, pulling on his breeches, he looked enquiringly at the other girl.

Mary told him that, although she *could* swim, she was less concerned to demonstrate her prowess than he seemed to be. Then, glancing round, she changed her tune.

"You are hurt!" she exclaimed. And flinging her leg over

saddle, she slipped to the ground and went to him. Black mud was now being replaced by red blood from a gash in his arm. Those talons had indeed sunk in.

"It is nothing," he asserted, wiping away the blood with the other sleeve of his silken shirt. "A scratch, only."

"Nonsense! It is deep. There is dirt in it. Come." And taking his hand, she drew him down to the water's edge again. Perhaps that peregrine had served him none so ill, after all.

Although protesting vocally, the man by no means held back; this was the first time that she had voluntarily taken his hand. Telling him to stoop, she bathed the gash with water thoroughly, examining it for any remaining mud. Then, ordering him to hold the sleeve-silk padded firmly over it, she left him to walk back along the lochside a little way. "Come," she commanded.

"Why? What is this?"

"Meadowsweet," she called back. "Much grows in this marshy place. I saw some nearby. There it is. Beside those yellow flags."

Mystified, he followed on.

She stopped at a clump of golden iris. Beside this was another clump of growth, long-stalked weeds with small white-flowered heads. Plucking a handful of these flowers, she raised them to her mouth and chewed at them. Then, putting the resultant paste on to her fingers, she turned to take his arm, remove the pad of silk, and spread the paste on the gash.

"There. That will staunch the bleeding and aid healing," she said. "Hold the cloth on it again. Firmly." She led the way back to the horses without further remark.

"Well, well! So you are physician as well as all else," he commented. "Who would have thought it?"

"Not that. But my mother taught me of this of plants. As she did other things. In Guelders they are wise about the like. Meadowsweet grows there also. Other plants she showed me, with their merits. Coltsfoot, tormentil, buckthorn berries, even nettles . . ."

She helped him to put on his doublet carefully, so that the sleeve held the padding in place. Mary was then for turning back for the city, but James's complaints were loud. Tom backed the boy, saying that he was very well and quite able to continue with their sport, especially so well looked after as he now was.

They rode on east-abouts round the foot of the loch.

51

In the event, there was precious little more sport for them on the north side. There were fewer reeds here, no herons, a couple of swans which merely paddled out into mid-loch – and swans were not hawkers' sport save when they flew. Some duck they did put up, but most of these only squattered across the water to the other side. One pair of teal did rise high, however, and swinging round in a circle, beat up as though climbing the steep hillside behind, obviously making for the high-set Dunsappie Loch up there. James had his hawk after them promptly – to the scowls of his tranter, who was faced with the daunting task of following up that difficult slope, and the Lord knew how much further beyond, to try to retrieve any kill; and all for a small teal.

With no more suitable game starting up, and the hawk returning presently, whether successful or not they could not tell, the party left the poor man to it. Enough for one day. The master did not admit that his arm was stiffening. Two heron and one mallard drake represented the day's bag.

That evening, Thomas Boyd joined them again for the meal. Clearly he considered it his duty and privilege to see to their provision and to eat with them. By the way he held his arm it was evident that it was sore, but he made light of it.

James was very vocal over the day's activities, much impressed with the man's swimming act, and saying that he had never tried to swim on his back. Would the master teach him? There was a loch below the castle rock, he had seen – the Nor' Loch. They could go there next day.

Mary told the monarch not to be impatient. It would be some days before the master's arm was fit for more swimming or lessons. Tom declared that he would be happy to oblige, but thought that the Nor' Loch was scarcely the place to do it, being the destination of much of the city's refuse and excrement. In a day or two he would take them to Restalrig Loch, near to Leith, where one of his uncle's lairdly friends, Logan of Restalrig, said that there was excellent fowling and no reed-beds. They could both hawk and swim there. Although, for swimming, the seashore would be better, did they not think, less muddy?

Mary had her doubts on this subject.

4

Two wet days intervened, to the King's disgust, and indoor
entertainment had to be devised for him – the young women
being more able to interest themselves, at this juncture largely
with needles and thread, adapting the Dean Castle clothing to fit
Mary better. They were summoned, however, to watch James's
efforts at mastering the arts of quarter-staff, throwing-spear,
hand-ball, skittles and the like. The master's damaged right arm
was a disadvantage in this, so his uncle had to be brought in on
occasion, when he could spare the time. Just what Sir Alexander
was busy at elsewhere was not clear, but frequently he was away
from the castle. James assumed that he was off arranging details
of the promised tournament. It was noticeable that Lord Boyd
himself seldom presented himself to them, almost all contacts
being with his brother. It had always seemed, indeed, as though
the younger was the real leader in it all. Mary said as much,
one time, to Thomas, and got a careful reply, whether accurate
or not, to give her the impression that there might be some
hostility between the two brothers, possibly the elder resenting
the prominence and driving force of the younger. Yet this entire
policy, if that it could be called, on the bands between lords and
the taking into custody of the young monarch, was evidently of
the Lord Boyd's devising, Anna asserted.

Having Anna always with them improved matters for Mary
greatly, not only in companionship, aid with James and other
helpful services, but as regards her brother's ever-pressing attentions. Tom just could not make himself quite so suggestive and
demanding with her about; and, the girls quickly becoming good
friends, Anna recognised Mary's need of her in this respect as in
others, and took her side against over-active masculine advances,
making something of a joke of it all, which helped the older girl.
The master was as much in their company as ever, but as far as
Mary was concerned, conditions improved considerably.

After the rainy days, they went hawking at Restalrig Loch and had better sport than at Duddingston, thanks partly to the lack of reed-beds; also the fact that Logan of Restalrig, a swarthy man of middle years, joined them with his own hawks and dogs, these last able to retrieve fowl which fell in the water. The shores of the loch were somewhat muddy however, moreover directly under the windows of its castle on a rocky knoll, which rather inhibited the idea of swimming, to Mary's relief.

Another day, they went hunting deer in the Pentland Hills, a few miles to the south of the city, and although they failed to make a kill, lacking trained huntsmen, they had two exhilarating chases over steep hillsides, screes and high moorland, to lose their quarry both times in wet peat-bogs in which horses and men could not follow.

James declared that he preferred life at Edinburgh to that at Stirling, where he had had to spend overmuch of his time being tutored in dull subjects such as Latin, French and handwriting.

Then, one day in late August, Sir Alexander announced that the looked-for tournament would be held in two days' time. Great was the excitement, hawking and hunting paling into insignificance for James. It could not be on any large scale, in the circumstances, he was warned, no great assemblage of lords and knights being advisable from the Boyds' point of view; moreover the tourney-ground before the castle entrance was of only modest dimensions. But for the boy it was all a great event, his first – for his father had been too busy with real warfare for tournaments, and his mother scarcely that way inclined. And it was being organised in his name and honour. He would be allowed to take part in one or two events himself; and his sister was to be the traditional Queen of Beauty, and to bestow the awards and prizes.

There were fervent prayers for good weather.

The great day dawned, dull but not raining, and for once the King was up betimes, even though activities were not due to start until noon. He had to inspect the lists, the stand erected for the Queen and principal onlookers, the pavilions for refreshment and gear-changing and the like; and impatience prevailed thereafter until proceedings were to start. Eager as he was to be involved, the boy was informed that it was unsuitable for the monarch to be seen awaiting the arrival of others; he would have to make a staged appearance once all were assembled. He would then be escorted out with due ceremony.

So the King of Scots had to wait, fretting, while shouts arose, trumpets blew, cheering echoed from beyond the gatehouse.

At length the Lord Boyd arrived, to make one of his few appearances, and conducted the royal party out, under the gatehouse arch and across the drawbridge, to a fanfare of trumpets. The open space beyond was thronged with people and horses, flags and banners flying, half the city seeming to be present, children yelling, dogs barking, a lively scene.

The provost, magistrates and deacons of guilds came forward to greet their young liege-lord, with much bowing. Instead of the key of the city he was presented this time with an illuminated scroll – which he did not so much as glance at, being intent on greater things than paper. Then he and his sister, with Anna, were led to the stepped platform, with seats, from which they could view the contests. Around this were clustered the nobility and gentry, with only one or two of their ladies, and there was more bowing and curtsying. The Lords Somerville, Hailes and Livingstone were there, their sons and lairds and a number of knights and lesser magnates. Also the Abbots of the Holy Rood and Melrose and the Prior of Soutra, to add Holy Church's dignity to the occasion. Mary guessed that this was all as much an exercise in gaining public acceptance for the Boyds in national affairs as an entertainment for the young monarch.

They were escorted up the steps to the platform, amidst cheers from the crowd, to seats behind a table spread with chaplets, bouquets and posies of flowers, with ribbons and tokens, as prizes; also flagons of wines, with sweetmeats. The red and gold Lion Rampant standard was erected to fly above them – but with two other banners only a little less large on either side, the blue with red fesse-chequey of Boyd.

Despite all the respect and attention, James was still agitated. He did not want to sit up here, being a spectator; he wanted to take active part. Tom assured him that all would be as he wished. The churchmen had to have their say first.

The three clerics mounted the steps, and the Abbot of the Holy Rood held up his hand for silence. Apart from dogs and children he got it approximately. He then intoned a prayer for God's blessing on their sovereign-lord and his realm, on his royal sister, and on all who worked for their weal. Also upon this day's activities and knightly prowess. Whereafter the other abbot gave a comprehensive benediction for all present, James fidgeting the while. This was not what tournaments were for, he asserted.

There followed a great marshalling of horses, and the Lord Boyd came to conduct the King down to the head of this cavalcade, leaving the women on the platform. The boy was then mounted, and flanked by the two Boyd brothers, he led a procession round the tourney-ground behind four trumpeters blowing lustily, to the huzzahs of the populace. Back at the royal platform again, all except James bowed to Mary, the Queen. This ended the preliminaries, and Tom, as Master of Ceremonies today, announced the first contest, which would be a display of knightly skills between the Lords Somerville and Livingstone.

This took a little while to develop, since the said two nobles had to retire to a pavilion to change into armour, covered by heraldic surcoats, their horses also suitably and colourfully caparisoned. As tourney-jousting went, this was to be a mere demonstration, for these lords, one the Chamberlain of the realm, were much too important to risk the physical injury quite frequently resulting from such bouts. But presently coming out to place themselves at opposite ends of the ground, lances held high, at a single blast of a trumpet they lowered these, and shields held before them, spurred their mounts into a trot, then a canter, to bear down on each other in impressive style, armour gleaming, to the cries of the onlookers.

James, agog, demanded whether they would kill each other, adding that he did not much like the Lord Somerville anyway. Mary assured him that this was unlikely, this being a gesture rather than a serious trial of strength. She was proved accurate in this as the two charging duellists came together, each jerking his beast's head a little aside so that they would pass close by rather than collide, and at the same time raising their heraldic-patterned shields high to act as targets for the lances. Even so the impact was forceful and resounding, so much so that Livingstone's lance shattered, and Somerville's shield was jerked from his arm and fell to the ground. The contestants pounded on past each other until they could rein in their mounts, and then turned to bow, first to each other and then towards the royal platform.

It was now Mary's duty to declare the verdict, advised by the Master of Ceremonies.

"I would think Livingstone wins, since Somerville's shield fell and he became as it were disarmed," Tom suggested.

"No – it was a draw," the girl decided. "If they had continued the contest, Livingstone would have been at the mercy of the other, having no lance. I declare a drawn contest."

"A draw, a palpable draw!" the master shouted, to a mixture of cheers and boos from the onlookers.

The two contestants came, to dismount and climb the steps, to receive posies from the Queen, who made tactful praise of their efforts.

After more trumpeting, the master announced that there would now be a very special event, a three-a-side jousting between Sir Alexander Boyd of Duncow, one of the flowers of chivalry, Boyd of Bonshaw and himself, against the Master of Hailes, Hepburn of Waughton and Hepburn of Whitsome. This would be won by whichever team first unhorsed one of the others, by whatever means.

There was a stir at this unusual announcement, five young men against one of middle years. Mary found herself a little concerned over Tom taking part, when his right arm was still not entirely healed, some infection having swollen the wound. But he asserted that it would not incommode him, it being almost back to normal. James and Anna wished him well.

Adam, Master of Hailes, who led the opposing team, was one of those who had taken part in the abduction at Niddry. Once armoured, he led his Hepburn colleagues to the far end of the enclosure. Sir Alexander Boyd placed his kinsmen on either side of him, and gave them their instructions. At a sign that all was ready, the trumpet sounded and the six horsemen, lowering lances, charged.

This time there was no attempt to avoid headlong clash, and the two teams, riding neck-and-neck, cannoned into each other in mid-ground with a resounding crash. There was seeming immediate chaos, men all but unseated, lances askew, two shields falling, both Hepburns', Boyd of Bonshaw's horse staggering back on its haunches and seeming almost to topple but recovering itself. The impetus was maintained, however, in some fashion, and although raggedly, each trio did emerge, to proceed on a little way before being able to rein round and face each other again, now not very far apart. It was to be seen that Bonshaw had lost his lance altogether, whilst Tom's had a third of it snapped off.

Sir Alexander wasted no time, but with barely a pause for recovery or instructions, led his two back against the other group, spurring fiercely. The Hepburns, two lacking shields but all having lances intact, recognised the danger of being ridden down if they were not in forward movement themselves, and heeled their mounts to meet the next onslaught.

This time the collision was less dire, insufficient speed having been attained. The horses were now wary also, not having enjoyed the previous impact, and took their own avoiding action. As a result, the clash was scarcely headlong, partly slantwise indeed, but this had a major effect nevertheless; for it meant that the long, unwieldy lances, aimed for direct contact, tended to miss their marks – this to the Boyds' advantage. Whereas these three still had their shields, and these could be used almost as battering-rams. Both Tom and his uncle tossed away their lances, and reining round as best they could, rising in their stirrups, leaned over to smash their shields against their opponents, with all their force and weight, all but unhorsing themselves in the process. But the tactic succeeded, for the Hepburns now found their useless lances only a handicap, in the road, and without shields to counter the attack, took the smashing weight of it on their armour-plated torsos. The Masters of Hailes and Whitsome toppled over out of their saddles, and fell with a crash to the ground.

Boyd of Bonshaw was less fortunate than his fellows. Having no lance, he had drawn his sword. He sought to slash this at his chosen opponent, but achieved only a glancing blow because of his mount's swerve. And Hepburn of Waughton, a big, powerful young man, managed to find some use for *his* lance, swinging it round in a driving arc, not point-on, to smash it against Bonshaw's back with force enough to unseat him. He in turn fell heavily.

The three survivors sought to control their quivering mounts, and reined up.

Mary raised her hand, beckoning to the trumpeter to sound an end to the contest, lest there be any more mayhem. It was obvious that the Boyds had won, two against one, however unorthodox their methods. The two victors came trotting over towards the platform, while men ran out to deal with riderless horses and assist the vanquished to their feet, often necessary in heavy armour. The two Hepburns rose, to stand shakily, but Bonshaw lay still.

When Sir Alexander and his nephew dismounted and climbed the steps to the table, Mary was gazing past them, and pointing.

"Your friend," she exclaimed. "He lies there."

The others looked back. "He will be but stunned," the knight said. "Often a fall in armour can do that. A mouthful of wine will revive him."

"I hope that is all that it is. I have to congratulate you two on your win, sirs. However oddly achieved! But . . . perhaps you Boyds usually contrive your achievements oddly?" That was said significantly. "Here, then, are your so Boydly earned chaplets!"

They took their floral tributes, bowing.

James was chattering eagerly. "That was good, good! Is the other man dead?" he asked, all but hopefully.

"I think not, Sire. He was only knocked out of the saddle. That would not kill him. Bonshaw will be well enough presently . . ."

"When do *I* take part?" the boy demanded. "You told me that this was to be *my* tournament. I want to do something."

"Your Grace's turn now," Sir Alexander assured. "We will have the tilting at targets. You will show your skill, Sire, never fear."

Mary and Anna were dividing their attentions between concern for the master's arm and watching to see the person of Bonshaw being carried to one of the pavilions. Blood trickling down Tom's wrist they had not failed to perceive, and although the man declared that he was very well, they were insisting on him discarding his steel gauntlet and rolling up his sleeve. The swollen talon wound had burst open, no doubt with the impact which had broken his lance, and it was looking decidedly unpleasant.

"No more tourneying for you this day!" Mary declared. "Go and have this seen to by the physicians . . ."

"It is nothing . . ."

"It is not nothing. Forby, it stinks! So perchance the bloodletting will help it. But I have no meadowsweet here! It requires a salve. See to it. And have word sent to me, as to how is your friend Bonshaw."

"Yes, Princess. Your word is my command! Always!"

She eyed him levelly. "Indeed? *You* remember that. As will I!"

Sir Alexander went to divest himself of his armour and to direct the arrangements for the next contest – nothing so dramatic as the last but a trial of skills nevertheless. Gallows-like posts were erected in the middle of the ground, and from the cross-trees of these hung ropes, two to each post, these ending in circlets woven of reeds and flowers, of about six inches diameter, which hung and swayed in the breeze.

These were the targets and hoped-for trophies. There were five such posts.

The first batch of contestants were lined up, mounted, ten of them, the King placed on the extreme right. He was given a shorter, lighter lance than the others, with no armour worn. He almost dropped it, in his excitement. Those with him included young Ker of Cessford and the Master of Somerville.

At the first blast of the trumpet, all lowered their lances, to point; at the second, the line spurred forward, if somewhat raggedly – to Tom's criticism.

This was meant to simulate an onset in battle, and the targets the enemy line. So the riders were placed close together, to form a fairly solid front – and this, of course, was a handicap in their lance-aiming, with jostling and the necessity for careful horse-management to avoid contact, bumping. This was why James had been placed at the outer end, so that he might be less concerned with collision.

The less than lateral line beat down on the targets. The object was to spear one of the circular wreaths on the lance-point, no easy endeavour with the things swinging, the horses' up-and-down cantering, and neighbours so close as to be distracting – as in war. In fact, at that first drive, only two of the ten gained their trophies, and James was not one of them.

However, this was not unexpected, and while the two winners trotted off to present their wreaths to the Queen and be given chaplets in exchange, the other eight were lined up at the other side of the arena and given a second chance. And this time the King, and three others, did achieve success – and great was the royal delight, as he went to receive a small posy from his sister.

Another ten, of lesser rank, then were marshalled – and these, in fact, did rather better, keeping a straighter line, four winning their trophies in the first run, two in the second. From the platform, James was able to point out to the girls errors made.

Thereafter it was time for a change in the programme, with archery the sport. Butts were erected, with curtains of sheepskins hung behind, to prevent stray arrows going on to injure onlookers beyond. The monarch was anxious to demonstrate his skill in this also, and did fairly well – although, as it happened, not so well as did his sister who, after enquiring whether it was permitted for the Queen of the Tournament to try her hand in one of the events, showed that she was indeed expert with the bow and arrow; she it was, in fact, who had given James his first lessons in the art. As the Master of Ceremonies, Tom Boyd thereafter presented her with a bunch of flowers, which he made a dramatic display of pinning on to her bosom, to cheering.

Quarter-staff duels followed, using six-foot-long poles, well greased, which were wielded in various strokes, sliding the grip up and down the shafts, to deliver and counter stylised blows and defences, with much swiping, whacking and dunting, but all done according to the rules, and requiring a quick eye and swift reactions to anticipate and thwart smites and to glimpse opportunities for return blows. James found this sport to his taste; but the difficulty here was in finding anyone suitable to exchange strokes with the monarch – who of course must not receive possible injury, but who, on the other hand, must not be given too obviously easy a win. In the end Thomas himself was appointed as acceptable opponent, his injured arm serving as sufficient handicap, shake her head over this as Mary would. Dozens of competitors took part, in pairs, but owing to the need for each couple to be carefully watched, for blows which did strike home, bungled strokes, quick recoveries and the like, to count for points, only three bouts went on at one time. So the entire contest took a considerable time, especially as the procedure was that the winners of each bout should then fight each other until one final champion was left. This, of course, again presented the difficulty of matching the King against all and sundry; so it was carefully decided that his bout with Tom should be declared a draw and neither should go on to the finals – to some protest on the boy's part.

There followed wrestling matches, in which few of the nobly born participated but which provided opportunity for much wagering. Then there was a wall-scaling competition – which again took time, since it demanded much preparation, timber palisades having to be carried out into the centre of the lists and fixed firmly in place. The object was for armoured contestants to lumber out, swords in hands, to seek to clamber over these ten-foot-high barriers, as though they were assaulting a castle's outer defences; no easy task, although productive of much hilarity on the part of the spectators. If one lost his sword in the process, fell heavily on the other side, or simply failed to get over at all, points were deducted.

James, who was small for his age, and had no armour which

would fit, could not take part, although in his eagerness to attempt it, he was allowed, at the end, to make a solo run, wearing a helmet and carrying a light sword. He did manage to get over his wall, but left helmet and sword behind.

The final episode was a massed double-charge, of practically all the horsed men present, from the two ends of the lists, banners flying, shields high, but with no intention of actual impact. This was less of a mere gesture than it might sound, for four score horsemen approaching each other at a fast canter, in a comparatively confined space, and seeking to pass through each other's lines without clash, was no simple exercise. And in fact three men, one the Lord Livingstone, the Chamberlain, were unhorsed in the process, and sundry banners fell to the ground. But it made a stirring finale to the day; although not to the evening, for a banquet was laid on in the castle for all the participants, and an ample if less ambitious feast spread in the tourney-ground itself, for all who cared to partake.

That night, as the master conducted the trio to their quarters, clearly in some pain from his arm but making light of it, Mary bade him goodnight, with her comment.

"A notable day indeed, Master Thomas. You Boyds do not lack cunning, I recognise! All this will much enhance your name and fame, I am sure. And have my royal brother thinking the better of you – which was your intention, no? For your further purposes hereafter!"

"Ah, me! Would that the Queen of Beauty was as caring as she is beautiful!" he returned.

She touched the damaged arm lightly. "*This* I am prepared to care for. Today has not furthered that, at least. It was folly to go jousting with it."

"If it arouses even such kindness in you, it was worth it, Princess. This enheartens me."

"It is your arm I am concerned with, sir – not your heart! Goodnight."

Anna dipped a curtsy. "Master of Ceremonies, Master of Boyd – but other masteries you lack, Tom. Perchance you will learn!" She blew him a mocking kiss.

It was September, and Mary had rather hoped that James had forgotten about demonstrating his swimming abilities, and the season for swimming for pleasure all but over, when, one sunny day, the master announced that the boy, having requested a visit to a seashore to spear flounders, flatfish, such as they did in the Ayrshire estuaries, he had accordingly made enquiries. He had discovered that there was a place at the mouth of the Figgate Burn, midway between Leith and Musselburgh, a mere four miles away. Would the ladies care to accompany them there? The sport might amuse them.

This put Mary into something of a quandary again. She enjoyed most sports, and had heard about this of spearing fish – they actually managed to spear salmon, from horseback, in the shallows of the Solway Firth, although this for flounders was done wading, she understood. She would like to try it, but if it entailed paddling about in the sea, it might well bring on Jamie's swimming ambitions. Not that she was against swimming – she enjoyed that also; but she foresaw complications with Thomas Boyd.

She decided that she was being feeble in this – and that young woman was ever against feebleness in herself as in others. Also, Anna wanted to go.

They set off down to the abbey again, and round the northern skirts of Arthur's Seat, to head eastwards by a well-defined road. The master explained that this was called the Fishwives Causeway, and was the route for two kinds of traffic, he had been told: the said fishwives of the fishing town of Musselburgh, who brought their menfolk's catches in creels on their backs, actually supported by straps slung from their brows – they might see some on their way, for there was a great demand for the fish in Edinburgh; and the other was the night-soil of the city, which was carted daily down to the market-gardens and fields of the Musselburgh area, for manure – a less than delightful conception but apparently productive. There was a tradition that this causeway had once been a Roman road, although that was doubtful; admittedly the Romans were known to have had a station at Inveresk, near Musselburgh.

Sure enough, soon after they reached a quite large stream, apparently the Figgate Burn, the banks of which their road followed, they passed a group of women, all clad in dark blue heavy cloth, and carrying on their backs large basket-work creels, obviously very weighty, these held in place by leather straps, dark with sweat, which were braced round their foreheads, a device which looked uncomfortable indeed but which the women, young

63

and old, seemed not to mind, for they were all singing as they trudged city-wards, a cheerful band.

Tom was not making for Musselburgh, however, and where the road swung away southwards from the stream, in an area of rough pasture and gorse bushes where cattle grazed, obviously common land, they continued on down the burnside. Presently they came in sight of the sea.

The master had been told to seek out a couple of cottages of salmon-netters, in the Figgate Whins area, where they could borrow the necessary short stabbing-spears for their fishing. They had no difficulty in finding the houses; they had poles outside for drying the nets – and anyway, there were no others in sight. Two men were sitting outside, mending nets.

Of these the master asked if they might borrow spears, and for any advice on how best to go about the sport. When the fishermen heard that it was the King who sought their help, they promptly downed their tools and offered to come and instruct. This was well received, and dismounting, they left the horses with one of the men, while the other went to a shed and produced five spears, and led them down to the little estuary where the Figgate Burn entered the firth.

This was a pleasant place of rippling shallows, with the stream now fully fifty yards across, flanked on each side by long stretches of golden sand backed by small dunes.

The fisherman took off his boots, and explained, with much bobbing of head towards the young monarch. This fishing was done barefooted, by wading in the shallows. The flounders or dabs lay just below the surface of the sand, and the wader could feel with his toes and the soles of his feet the fish as they darted away. This movement set up a flurry of sand in the water, and the art was to stab down the spear swiftly into this, in the hope of spitting the fish. It had to be quickly done – and care taken not to spear the wader's toes in the process, easily done. The spears each had a little spur projecting near the sharp tip, and this, once in, held the fish secure. He would show them. There were usually lots of flounders here; they seemed to like the fresh water mixing with the salt.

Rolling up his ragged breeches, the man waded in towards mid-stream, and had not gone a dozen splashing paces before he suddenly plunged in his spear. They heard a smothered curse as the weapon came up empty; but only a few yards further and he stabbed again, and this time, when raised, he had a flapping flatfish impaled. Detaching it, he smashed its head against the shaft, to kill it, and proceeded on.

James was immediately agog, already kicking off his riding-boots and removing his hose. Grabbing a spear, he plunged in.

"Watch your toes, Jamie," his sister warned.

Thomas Boyd was not long in following him.

The girls eyed each other, and nodded in unison. Stooping, they too discarded their boots, and then raised their heavy riding-skirts to belt them to hang above the knees. Then they too laughingly waded in.

The fisherman had another dab now, and came with his catch to the King.

Before he reached him, the boy yelled out, "I felt one! I felt one! It wriggled. Where is it? I cannot see it."

"Och, they're just below the sand, laddie. You dinna right see them, just the bit birl o' the sand in the watter. You hae to be quick."

Tom let out a cry, and stabbed. But without result.

It was Anna who made the first kill — or not exactly kill, for when she drew her spear out it had a quite large flounder transfixed almost at the tail, and flapping wildly. She shouted for help, not knowing what to do with it, and Mary nearby was going to assist her when she too felt a wriggling beneath her toes, saw a little moving cloud of sand, and plunged in her spear. She felt the movement at its point, and lifting it out found that she also had a dab, smaller than Anna's, sand-coloured on back, with red spots, and white beneath, flapping. Unhooking it, she banged its head against the spear and it went limp.

Anna was still ineffectual in dealing with her vigorous catch, finding the fish slippery to grasp as well as over-active, she with the use of only one hand. Mary was even more handicapped, with her own fish to hold, but using the butt-end of her spear, she brought it down on the other girl's fish. Three times she had to do this before the creature was still, Anna giggling uncontrollably.

They both waded ashore, to deposit their booty.

Neither of their companions had in fact achieved a catch as yet, James complaining loudly that there were no fish where he was, and Tom shouting that the devilish brutes seemed to zigzag away so that he missed them. The fisherman however had another two.

The triumphant young women, wringing out their skirt hems which had got splashed, decided on another attempt. This time it took them longer, but eventually Mary skewered one, better than the last. Although Anna did get one, it was not properly impaled by the spur, and fell off before she could grab it. Despite much splashing about by the pair, they could not retrieve the fish, getting not a little wet in the process. They came to the conclusion that they had proved themselves sufficiently for one day.

Much humiliated, their male companions came ashore empty-handed, although the fisherman now had five. James asserted that the girls had clearly struck the lucky patches where the fish lay; and Tom took the opportunity to declare that it was all women's wiles, the ability to allure and ensnare flounders as well as men.

The fisherman presented them with his catch, which meant that they had eight fish which they could have for their evening meal. And then came what Mary had rather feared. James declared that the water had not felt cold. He liked to swim. There was lots of sandy beach. He wanted to go swimming – no doubt anxious to indicate that he was good at this, if not at flounder-spearing. Tom Boyd was not slow in supporting this royal edict.

The girls exchanged glances. Mary could by no means forbid it. "Swim if you wish," she said. "But not, I think, near these cottages." She looked at the master. "Your arm . . . ?" she wondered.

"The salt water will do it good," he asserted. He pointed. "Along there, where there are higher sand dunes."

Leaving the fisherman with the spears, and a coin in thanks, they walked along the shore in the Musselburgh direction.

At least there was ample privacy, a couple of miles of empty sandy beach backed by the lowish dunes, small waves rolling in and no rocks in sight. James was all but undressing as they went.

Quarter of a mile on, Tom suggested that this would do. The inevitable followed. "You will join us, no doubt?" he challenged the young women.

Anna gurgled.

Mary inclined her head. "I enjoy a swim, yes. As to joining you, scarcely that! You, Anna? We will go in further along there."

"M'mm. Not too far, I hope!" the man protested, James already half unclad.

66

A smile. "Shall we say we shall be within sight, sir! Come, Anna."

The girls went about another two hundred yards. "This will serve, I think," the elder said. "We will be . . . generous, no?"

"If I know my brother, he will come swimming along!"

"No doubt. But we shall be in the water by then."

They moved into the dunes to undress. When presently, naked, they ran down to the tide's-edge, they made a lovely sight undoubtedly. They could see the other two already splashing in the water.

Mary was quite a strong swimmer, and struck out vigorously, the younger girl less venturesome. When, tiring a little, she turned on her back to rest, legs in a gentle paddle, it was, as she anticipated, to see the man coming towards her, using a powerful over-arm stroke, whatever the effect on one of his arms. She smiled to herself.

"You swim . . . as well as . . . you appear!" he panted, as he came up.

"Ah, but then appearances can mislead, no? Especially under water. As you discovered with the flounders!"

"You do not . . . resemble a . . . flounder, even so!"

She turned over on to her front. "Should you not be looking to your liege-lord's safety, sir? In case he gets into difficulties." And she pointed.

"He seems to swim very well. He says that you taught him."

She had begun to swim shorewards, and found that he was accompanying her. So she changed direction, back towards where her brother was ducking and surface-diving. Perforce the man had to do the same.

"Your arm?" she enquired. "Does it not hurt?"

"A little," he admitted, possibly hoping for female attention.

"Then you were foolish to swim at all. And more so to have come thus far along."

"It was worth it," he averred.

Near the boy, Mary turned on her back again, and began to kick large fountains of white water with her feet. Under this screening, she waved to the man.

"I require no escorting back!" she called mockingly, and left them.

But the Master of Boyd was not readily discouraged. The girls were only just out of the water when he and James came running along the firm sand towards them – which set Mary and Anna running, in turn, for the cover of the dunes.

"Come running. To dry off," they heard, and ignored, that shouted invitation.

"I wonder . . . that they do not come . . . to help us to dress!" Anna panted, as they donned clothing over distinctly wet bodies.

"Was he always like this?"

"Tom is six years older than I am. But ever since I have known enough to watch him, he has been very strong on women. The castleton girls all had to beware of him – such as did not encourage him! My other brothers do not seem as though they will be like Tom."

"Boyds! Give them time . . . !"

Clad, they all returned to the horses. The King of Scots rode back with a string of eight flounders slung round his neck.

5

The forty days were up, and the parliament assembled. Right up to the last the Boyds and their allies were cautious. Usually parliaments met in the great halls of Stirling or Edinburgh Castles, but the Boyds saw possible danger in allowing all who were entitled to attend into the fortress here, and had arranged for the session to be held in the Tolbooth of Edinburgh. All the lords, barons, prelates, officers of state, commissioners of the counties and representatives of the royal burghs could take part, if so they desired. How many would do so on this occasion remained to be seen. And how many might be hostile to the Boyds, and what they had done? The carefully contracted bands would deal with not a few of the nobility, of course; but there were inevitably large question marks as to majorities. The Boyd hope was that most hostile or condemnatory ones would absent themselves, rather than come intending battle, in words or even deeds. So the atmosphere in Edinburgh that ninth day of October 1466 was tense.

The Master of Boyd however showed no sign of this when he came to escort Mary and Anna down to the Tolbooth, a tall, five-storey building set in the middle of the High Street near to St Giles High Kirk, through the crowded streets; the King, on this occasion, would be led thither in royal style, later, by the Lord Lyon King of Arms and his heralds.

The Tolbooth, despite its height and twin stair-towers, was scarcely the most illustrious venue for a national parliament, but was heedfully chosen as a difficult place to bring any large number of armed men against, in its narrowing of the street and with the booths of merchants abutting; the city crowds would bar the way and give any required warning. But the courtroom on the first floor was comparatively small for any such large gathering, more apt for the city council. But there was a gallery, and it was to this that the master took the two young women. Already it was full, with bailies, councillors and dignitaries not of parliamentary status, but seats had been reserved for the trio at the front. These two were the only women present.

The courtroom below was also filling up, and Tom was carefully identifying those present, although giving no sign of anxiety. Mary was aware of a general air of wary vigilance however.

They had not long to wait, with the space below becoming crowded and ushers leading lords, prelates and lesser magnates to their due places – which in fact were only rows of wooden benches, plain and less than imposing. A flourish of trumpets outside heralded the incoming of the official party. The crown, sceptre and sword of state could not be carried in, for these were still at Stirling Castle; but a substitute regalia had been improvised, the Earl of Crawford bearing aloft a great two-handed sword, the Earl of Argyll a marshal's baton on a cushion – these two both having been summoned back from England where they had been on an embassage – the Lord Somerville carrying another cushion on which lay a pair of golden spurs, and the Lord Livingstone, the High Chamberlain, bearing a scroll of unknown significance but looking impressive. These four came to stand in front of a table and throne, brought from the castle, erected on the judges' dais.

Another trumpet blast brought in the new Bishop of St Andrews, the Primate, Patrick Graham, and his colleagues of Glasgow and Aberdeen – notable as the only bishops present out of thirteen, to represent the support of Holy Church.

There was no sign of the Lord Boyd, although Sir Alexander sat in a comparatively humble position, as keeper of the royal castle of Edinburgh.

Then the final great fanfare. The Lord Lyon strode in at the head of his heralds, all gorgeous in their tabards, insignia and batons. And behind them, alone, came James, looking embarrassed and nervous, far from resplendent in his very ordinary clothing. He squeezed past the row of dignitaries to the throne, and sat down, biting his lip. Quickly his eyes rose to search the gallery for sister and friends.

"Poor Jamie," Mary murmured. "He will prefer swimming, even flounders, to this!"

"I hope that His Grace remembers his words!" the master said.

"He has words to speak?"

"Oh, yes. Important words."

"Then he will have been well schooled, I vow!" The boy had had a long private session with Sir Alexander that morning.

Lyon thumped his staff. "James, by God's grace King of Scots, ordains this parliament of his realm to be duly constituted and in session. I call upon the Primate of Holy Church to open the proceedings with prayer. God save the King!"

"God save the King!" all echoed.

Patrick Graham, Bishop Kennedy's successor in St Andrews bishopric, then asserted that they met on this very important occasion to make decision for the weal of the King's realm, and prayed that Almighty God would guide them in wisdom and prosper their conclusions. Amen.

The four lords bearing the emblems laid down these on a table near the throne, and bowing, proceeded backwards to their due seats. The Bishop of Glasgow, who was apparently to act Chancellor, or chairman, on this occasion, went to sit at this table, while a couple of monkish clerks scurried in, all bows, to take their places, with papers, at the other end of it.

All sat.

There was a pause. James glanced about him, anxiously, fairly obviously wondering whether *he* ought to be doing something. Mary felt for him.

Nobody else seemed to know quite what to do, either. Anna murmured, "Where is our father?"

"Wait, you," her brother advised.

The door by which the official party had entered was suddenly thrown open again, with something of a clatter, and in strode the Lord Boyd, alone. He was magnificently dressed, head held high. Straight to the throne he paced, ignoring the acting Chancellor at the table and Lyon with the assistants behind, and, in front of the King, sank to his knees and bending forward low, clasped arms about the boy's ankles.

"Sire," he said loudly, "I beseech you to tell me, to tell all here, whether Your Grace has conceived any indignation or offence against your humble servant and loyal subject, or against any of my companions, for our riding here to Edinburgh with you after the Exchequer Audit at Linlithgow? Answer, if you will, whether you bear any royal rancour or concern in this matter." This to the gasps of the company.

James moistened his lips. "I . . . *we* are not . . . we do not

71

so conceive, my lord. No. Not so. It, it was done by our royal command and desire. I say it, yes. Er . . . rise, my lord."

Boyd got to his feet, bowed deeply again, and went to stand behind the throne, nudging the Lord Lyon slightly aside.

"Save us – is that our father!" Anna exclaimed. "Abasing himself like that!".

"Wait, you," her brother counselled again.

Boyd tapped the boy's shoulder. "My lord Bishop?" James said then, hurriedly.

The acting Chancellor inclined his head. "As Your Grace commands." He consulted papers on the table put before him by the clerks. "This parliament of the realm, duly called by royal authority, is now in session. It has much of great import to decide and homologate. But first, His Grace has certain edicts of his royal will of which to inform you." He rose, and went to present one of the papers to the King.

James took it almost gingerly, looked up at the gallery, round at the Lord Boyd, and cleared his throat.

"I, James, King of Scots, do hereby make, make declaration," he read carefully, if with scant conviction. "For the necessary weal and gov . . . governance of my realm, I do hereby . . ." He seemed to lose his place and repeated, ". . . for the governance . . . I do hereby . . . declare, appoint and, and nominate, to be my royal governor and regent of my kingdom until I become of full age, the Lord Thomas Boyd of Kilmarnock. From this present. I . . ." His hands trembling obviously, the boy dropped the paper. Alarmedly he looked round at Boyd, who frowned, and gestured to a herald to pick it up as the monarch himself was stooping to do so. There were seconds of uncomfortable silence while the boy found his place again.

"From this present, I appoint the Lord Thomas to have governance of my royal person. Also to have the governance of my royal brothers, Alexander, Duke of Albany and John, Earl of Mar," he went on, at something of a gabble. "Likewise to take into his care my royal castles, each and all, the keepers thereof to, to deliver them into his hands forthwith . . . I . . ." He peered more closely at the paper, as though the writing thereon eluded him. "I do hereby pro . . . promul . . . promulgate, aye promulgate, as my royal will, that he, the Lord Thomas, shall have the execution of all my, my authority and justice, in my name, until I reach the age of twenty-one years. This, my, my sovereign will." With a sigh of relief, James rose and went to hand that paper back to the bishop – an unscheduled move, which had not a few there hastily rising from their seats, since none should sit while the monarch stood. As James got back to his chair, Lord Boyd waved them all down.

"God save the King's Grace," he called.

There was a complete hush in that courtroom as the significance of the boy's reading sank in. Thomas, Lord Boyd, was no great magnate, not even an earl; and here he was suddenly, it seemed, complete ruler of Scotland. What had been declared on that paper, pronounced by the monarch before parliament as his edict and will, gave Boyd the control not only of the King's person but of everything pertaining to the rule and direction of the kingdom. He was now the Regent, with the monarch's powers delegated. That thought took a deal of digesting.

Mary turned to gaze at the master. "So – there was the aim of it all," she said, accused. "The regency! The Boyds to be rulers of the land. All to be subservient to Boyd!"

Even that young man looked a little uncomfortable. "For the good of all the kingdom," he asserted. "Since Bishop Kennedy died, and your mother, all has been weakness. No firm direction. This will make improvement . . ."

The Lord Boyd was speaking. "My lord Bishop, to business," he said crisply. There was no doubt now who was in charge.

Andrew Durrisdeer, Bishop of Glasgow, rapped on his table. "This parliament has to consider the due carrying out of the King's wishes for the best governance of the realm. Further, the Lord Boyd requires that these important decisions be recorded amongst the acts of the parliament, and provisions registered under the Great Seal of the kingdom, that there be no question as to the legitimacy and authority thereof." He did not ask for parliamentary approval of this, it was to be noted. Then, "Certain lords to be appointed, to have full power to act in the name of this parliament, until another is called to consider and approve the reforms instituted in the interim. Such parliament to be summoned early in the next year, 1467."

The Campbell Earl of Argyll was on his feet immediately. "I agree such provision," he said. "I nominate my lord Earl of Crawford to such council."

"And I second," the Bishop of St Andrews added.

"And I nominate my lord Earl of Argyll," the Lord Livingstone said.

"And I second," Crawford agreed.

"I nominate the lord Bishop of St Andrews, Primate." That was the Lord Somerville.

"And I second," Lord Hailes confirmed.

Like the rapid hammer-blows of a smith at his anvil, the names rang out, all the supporters of the Boyds, those with whom they had exchanged bands, their kinsmen and friends. The thing was done in almost less time than it takes to tell.

"Now, the matter of the royal castles," the acting Chancellor went on. "Some are known to be in the hands of those disloyal to the crown. Notably Dunbar, Lochmaben and Stirling. These are held respectively by Kennedy of Kirkmichael, Kennedy of Blairquhan and Gilbert, Lord Kennedy. These named to be requested to yield them up forthwith, and to the Lords Montgomery, Maxwell and Cathcart, as keepers."

"Considering that you were affianced to the Lady Janet Kennedy, you Boyds are hard on that house!" Mary observed.

"*Was* affianced – but no longer." That was brief.

"Fortunate Janet!" Anna commented.

No comment on these appointments came, however, from the assembly's members – who, no doubt, were busy making their calculations as on which side their bread was buttered.

"Parliament is now required to consider the important matter of the eventual marriage of the King's Grace," Glasgow's bishop went on, consulting his papers. "It was intended that, for the good of the realm, and peace with the realm of England, the King's sister, the Princess Mary, should wed Edward of York – this arranged by the late Bishop Kennedy." He glanced up at the gallery. "But now that Edward is King of England, he has wed a woman of the House of Lancaster." He did not add deplorably, but implied it. "Now it is proposed that our young sovereign-lord James be found a suitable partner, possibly one of the English royal family, York or Lancaster. Also the marriage of his brothers, the Duke of Albany and the Earl of Mar, be considered, whether to ladies of England, France, Flanders or elsewhere. Therefore this parliament is requested to appoint the Earls of Crawford and Argyll and the Bishops of Glasgow and Aberdeen to consider this matter, and report to the next parliament. Is it agreed?"

No disagreement was voiced – save by implication, and quietly, from the gallery.

"What is your Boyd motto?" Mary wondered.

Thomas raised his eyebrows. "Motto? Why? *Confido*, it is."

"I think that it should be changed to *I Waste no Time!*"

He shook his head. "In this matter I do not agree with my father. I see the King's marriage as best with Norway, or Denmark. For young Albany and Mar, who knows? But . . ."

"Norway . . . ?"

"Aye. It would solve much . . ."

But the bishop was speaking again. "For the future Queen, a suitable dowry must be offered. It is suggested that one-third of the crown's rents, with the use of the palace of Linlithgow, as was His Grace's late mother's portion, should be offered. Is it agreed?"

No contrary voice was raised, but the Primate spoke. "I would add the provision which the good King Robert the Bruce imposed, that as to dowry moneys, none should be permitted to be exported to England, whomsoever the lady. Lest it provoke . . . interference."

A dozen voices seconded that.

"As to this of moneys and exporting," the acting Chancellor went on, "it is important for the royal treasury, and the better care of the kingdom, that there should be greater export to foreign lands of the realm's goods and merchandise. This not only to fill all the empty coffers, and aid the public weal, but to pay for goods imported from other lands, in especial arms, wines, silks and other cloths, and other items which we ourselves cannot produce. This important matter has been but insufficiently considered of these last years. We must export more wool from the Lammermuir Hills, for which the Flemings cry out for their cloth mills. Also hides and salt-fish. In these Scotland is rich. Other goods also. A council to see to this. Who will so act . . . ?"

He was interrupted by an authoritative voice from behind the throne. "My brother, Sir Alexander Boyd of Duncow, will attend to that."

There was a moment or two of silence. This was the first mention of Sir Alexander's name so far – and for a far from resounding office, however necessary; dealing with mere trade, moneys, merchandise, would be considered below the dignity of most lords there. Anna looked past Mary to her brother.

"Uncle Alex, the Mirror of Chivalry?" she wondered. "*He* did not so choose, I think!"

The master said nothing.

Almost hurriedly, the bishop went on. "So be it. Sir Alexander Boyd to see to it. Lead a council, and report. Now – the matter of officers of state. justiciars, sheriffs of counties, customars and the like. This will, to be sure, take some time. Is it the wish of His Grace and of this parliament that the filling of these offices be dealt with now? Or at a further sitting on the morrow? For other necessary business will require a further session assuredly."

"I move adjournment. Sufficient for one day," the Lord Boyd announced – and only just seemed to remember to add, "if His Grace agrees?"

His Grace, bored by now, nodded hearty concurrence, and was on his feet before even Lyon signed for his trumpeters to sound.

All rose, although probably all did not realise yet that a new chapter had commenced in Scotland's eventful story.

Mary Stewart had some inkling of it, at least. "So now we know who rules the land! Thomas, Lord Boyd. Whoever *reigns*. But – what of his brother? Aye, and what of his son?"

"We shall see," the master said carefully. "At least there have been no interruptions from without." He sounded almost grim for that so confident character.

"You feared such?"

"Aye. Come, you . . ."

6

At first, in the days that followed, for the royal pair at least, it might almost have seemed as though that parliament had never taken place, so little difference was there in their conditions and daily programme. The only noticeable change was that they saw practically nothing of Sir Alexander Boyd, to James's disappointment – and they could not conceive that he was already away on his new duties as trade commissioner. Yet he was the Keeper of this royal castle of Edinburgh – or had been.

James had to attend two more sittings of the parliament, to his boredom; but the girls elected not to go, finding it scarcely enthralling.

The master, strangely, appeared to think as did they; of course he had no part to play therein, and was no born spectator. He preferred female company, it seemed, and presumably his father did not need him – as certainly was proved by the word coming from others, that Lord Boyd had now had himself appointed not only as Regent but as Chief Justiciar of the Realm and Lord High Chamberlain, this latter office giving him access to the monarch at all times. At any rate, the master continued to escort the young women assiduously; Mary was glad that in James's absence, Anna ever remained close. They went riding and hunting, especially in the Pentland Hills of which Mary had become fond, with the season now getting past for seashore activities. Tom was much his usual too-attentive self, never failing to seek to exploit every opportunity for amatory gestures, physical contacts and gallantry, yet there was something of preoccupation about him not previously noticeable. Anna saw it also, and did not fail to remark on it. She opined that it behoved them to watch out.

Then, only a week after the final sitting of the parliament, it was announced that all were to pack up and go to Stirling. It was an order, no royal agreement being sought. The Regent was now in full command. Not that Mary objected. Stirling Castle had been her home, scene of her childhood, where her belongings and clothes still were, set amidst a country she knew and loved. James was less pleased. He had come to like Edinburgh – and there was no sea at Stirling; but he was not consulted.

On 25th October they set out on the thirty-five-mile ride, a large and now fairly resplendent company, well escorted by armed men, with a lengthy baggage-train coming along more slowly behind. Sir Alexander Boyd presumably remained at Edinburgh. They passed Niddry Seton and Linlithgow, halfway, without comment.

It was almost dark when they reached Stirling and, tired and hungry, rode up through the narrow, steep-climbing streets of the town to that other fortress-citadel on its great rock-top, so like Edinburgh's but more commodious and less grim, the ancient seat of Scotland's monarchy, which dominated the waist of the land.

At the drawbridge and gatehouse an extraordinary scene was enacted, in the nature of play-acting but significant enough. Gilbert, Lord Kennedy stood there awaiting them, alone, a ceremonial rope tying together his wrists, but loosely. In his hands he held a bunch of great iron keys, not like the golden one the provost of Edinburgh had presented to the King. Bowing low, these however he did not offer to James, but came to Lord Boyd's horse and held them up to him. This was the first meeting of these two since the interrupted hunt. He said nothing.

Boyd eyed him, expressionless, but took the keys. Then he turned to the Lord Hailes, who rode behind him, and silently pointed, first at Kennedy, then into the castle before them. The Hepburn chief nodded, and urging his mount forward, stooped low in the saddle to reach down for the rope which tied together Kennedy's wrists – but not so very low, for that man raised arms to facilitate the process. Then, thus linked, the two nobles moved off together, one mounted, one afoot, over the bridge and under the gatehouse arch, gaoler and captive. Most obviously it had all been arranged beforehand.

"Your band with the Kennedys included this?" Mary asked the master, not troubling to lower her voice.

He shrugged, wordless, but his father looked round, frowning, before leading the way into the fortress, after the other two.

Dismounted, stiff and saddle-sore, at least it was good to be able to go, with James and Anna, to their own rooms in the palace block, infinitely more handsome apartments than at Edinburgh, and found their royal servants there to attend them.

Mary had a large bedchamber and anteroom, and James similar adjoining on the same floor. When Anna asked where she was to go, Mary declared that, unless she wished otherwise, she should continue to share accommodation with her; the great canopied bed was large enough for two, and there was ample cupboard and wardrobe furnishing for both. They had proved good boudoir companions hitherto, had they not? The other girl was more than agreeable, delighted; her brother might be less appreciative, they both recognised with small smiles.

The reunion with the other royal children provided an affecting occasion. Margaret was ten, a shy, gentle child, with little to say for herself; Alexander, Duke of Albany and Earl of March, a year older, was very different, a hot-tempered, opinionated boy, who rather dominated his younger brother John, Earl of Mar, aged only seven, but who had his virtues, being ingenious, quick-witted, clever – more so than was James, undoubtedly. They were all very fond of their elder sister, who had acted mother to them for three years; they had obviously grievously missed her these last months. They were now less excited over James's return, and at first a little suspicious and resentful over Anna – but soon they accepted her, and indeed found her good company.

As it happened, Mary, in her first weeks back at Stirling, had something of a remission from the attentions of Tom Boyd. Presumably lacking Sir Alexander's presence – for whatever reason, the brothers now appeared to be at loggerheads – Lord Boyd required his son to act for him where his brother would have done so before; and the master was sent off on various missions and errands for the new ruler of Scotland. With her young brothers and sister to look after again, and something of her old life to resume, Mary was kept a deal more busy than she had been at Edinburgh; but despite this, she had to acknowledge to herself, on occasion, that she missed the young man's company and challenge.

More than once, Mary asked Anna about the curious situation anent Sir Alexander Boyd. Although even that forthright and uninhibited young woman was reluctant to appear openly critical of her father, it did seem as though the elder brother had used the younger, who had so much more polish, style and good looks, with a gallant reputation, as against his own rather chill and colourless, not to say dull-seeming, self, to further his schemes and designs.

Possibly the elder was the more clever of the two, in fact; but the other had the more useful image and was the man of action. Now that Lord Boyd had got what he wanted, however, it seemed that Sir Alexander was to be dispensed with. There may have been jealousy involved. Mary was the less enamoured of the man who now ruled them all.

Her lack of approval was to be notably enhanced that Yuletide. One day, just before Christmas, James came back to their quarters from one of his now frequent sessions with the Regent and the Chancellor, now reappointed, Lord Avondale, to sign and seal documents, charters, edicts and the like, full of talk about this Lord Avondale, who was in fact a sort of cousin of his own, an illegitimate son of a former Duke of Albany, and who had been away in England and France acting as a special envoy. He had come home, and presumably thrown in his support with the Boyds, since he had been reappointed Chancellor of the realm. James quite liked him; but would have preferred the Master of Boyd to have been Chancellor, since apparently he had to see so much of him. It was a pity that he was away so much these days. He was good, interesting, very kind. He hoped that once he was married he would not be so often gone. It had been good at Edinburgh, much better . . .

"It will be long before you are married, Jamie," his sister told him, smiling. "That talk of marriage at the parliament was only policy, at this present. Much will have to be decided as to which realm will offer the best terms, which princess will make the best match for the King of Scots. Ambassadors will be sent out . . ."

"Not *my* marriage, Mary – the master's. And yours."

"What . . . !"

"The master is going to marry *you*. Did you not know?"

His sister stared at him. "Marry? No!" she gasped.

"The Lord Boyd says it, so it must be so. Will you not like that?"

"No! No!" She turned abruptly, and went over to a window, to stare out, back rigid.

Anna moved over to her, and took the other girl's arm, silent.

Almost fiercely, Mary turned on her. "Did *you* know of this? All along? Has this been planned from the beginning? I will not! I will *not* wed him, I tell you! Never!"

Anna shook her head. "I am sorry. I knew naught of it. Tom has never spoken of it. Nor our father. But . . ."

"They cannot *make* me do it. I will not be sold, traded, like some new mare! This is too much – you Boyds go too far! Jamie, you must stop this."

"But why, Mary? He is kind . . ."

"He is a Boyd. Until three months ago I had scarcely heard his name! I am Mary Stewart, not some chattel to be married off at will."

"But you like him, do you not? And he likes you, I think."

"You know nothing about it. Marriage!" Mary turned, to glare at them both, so unlike her. Then she strode over to the bedchamber, entered, and slammed the door behind her.

The master arrived back at Stirling in time for the usual Christmas festivities, and was not long in presenting himself at the royal quarters, still travel-stained as he was from long riding. Had he seen his sister before he saw Mary, presumably he would have been warned of impending trouble; but Anna was with the other girl in their anteroom when he appeared, and in no position to sound the alarm.

"Ha – as beautiful as ever!" he exclaimed, and came to reach for Mary's hand to raise it to his lips, all urgent satisfaction.

She snatched it from him, and turned her back on him.

"Save us – here's no way to offer Yuletide greetings to the weary traveller from across the sea, no less!" he protested. "I've come from Arran itself. Have you not missed me?"

Mary did not reply, but moved further away.

"I have ridden from Dumbarton since disembarking, all but killing my horse, the sooner to see you, to salute you, to warm myself in your fair company! And now, this! What is to do?"

Anna spoke. "She knows. Her Highness has been told. This of . . . marriage."

That silenced him – but only for moments. "So-o-o! Our sire has spoken! I had hoped . . ." He shrugged. "Princess, I am grieved that you should have learned of this, this decision, thus. Not from myself, of my love and devotion. My seeking of your hand in suitable fashion, in humble duty and esteem . . ."

She whirled round on him. "Humble! You! Spare us more, sirrah! Let us be honest, at the least. *I* shall be honest with you, I assure you. I will not wed you!"

He eyed her distressedly, an emotion seldom seen on those handsome features. "Mary! Highness! Do not take it so. I am sorry that it has come this way. My true caring and admiration. It is not as it should have been. However you heard of this projected match, the proposal should have been mine . . ."

"The proposal perhaps, Master of Boyd. The *decision* is mine. No, I say! And again, no!"

"But . . ."

"Master Thomas!" James, having heard the man's voice from his adjoining room, came hastening. "You are back. How good! We have missed you. Where have you been . . . ?"

It is to be feared that Tom Boyd quite failed in his loyal duty and respect towards his sovereign-lord, indeed ignored him completely.

"Mary, hear me," he pleaded. "Give me opportunity to express my feelings for you. You must have known of them, surely? I have not sought to hide my regard and fondness – aye, my love. These months you have been my joy, my need, my hope. I have not declared myself in words. But my strong desire and need of you must have been apparent to you. I have been waiting. Waiting until I had something to offer you, other than just myself, my heart. Now I *have* something. I could not ask the King's sister to be but Mistress of Boyd, to descend to that. But now I have Arran, the whole great island. Other lands also. And the promise that it shall all be erected into an earldom. Now you will be Countess of Arran . . . !"

"Think you that I care for Arran or any other stolen lands, sir? Or being your countess. I am of the blood royal, and will not be married off to any – at your demand, or your father's . . ."

"Mary," James said, "do not be so sore against the master. He has been good to us. Kind . . ."

"Be quiet, Jamie! You know not what you say. Know nothing of marriage and a woman's needs and concerns."

The boy bridled. "I am the King!" he said.

"And a foolish one! Spare me your guidance."

"His Grace is kind, Princess. Can you not be a little kind also? At least hear me out. For you are not a hard woman."

"In this you will find me sufficiently hard! What have you to say that you have not already said?"

"This. You, His Grace's elder sister, one of the two princesses of Scotland, will fall to be wed. To someone. Possibly a prince or even a King of some land. Or a great noble, here. It is always so – you know that. Call it your fate, if you will. The choice is scarce likely to be yours. You know that also. So what would you? Myself, a man who loves you, is devoted to you? Or some stranger whom you know not, who may care nothing for *you*, only wish to marry into the Scots royal house?"

"As do you!"

"As does my father, *for* me. Myself, I want *you*, Mary – not Her Highness! And, and I think that you have found me none so grievous a companion, these months? At least, you know me, and my caring. Where you would not know another. And I am to be made a great lord – for none rank higher, in Scotland, than its earls, save only the dukes of the royal house. See you, you could do worse, Mary, in your marrying!"

"If I sought to marry – which I do not. And when – and if – I do, I will seek some say in whom I wed."

"You will find none more devoted than am I . . ."

Anna coughed and made a brief but complicated gesture, part shake of the head, part nod towards the door.

The man drew a deep breath, then shrugged. He bowed, and turned. "Have I Your Grace's permission to retire?"

"I will come with you," James said.

At the door, the master turned. "Think on it, Highness," he urged, all but pleaded, and went out.

Mary stared after him, biting her lip.

Anna discreetly left her alone.

In the days that followed, with traditional Christmas festivities prevailing, much feasting and entertainment, the question of marriage, if question it was, remained undiscussed. Tom Boyd sought to make all as it had been before, as far as the royal pair were concerned, or to seem so, a good companion. He organised amusements and sporting activities, although the weather was not of the best for such, spending most of his time in their company, whether desired or not – James at least encouraging him in this. But there *was* a difference. The man was less bold, less demonstrative in his attentions, less of touchings and sought intimacies, however heedful of the young woman's needs and desires. For her part, Mary, well aware of this, while by no means encouraging him, did not maintain too hard an attitude, too hostile a front, for all their sakes. It was not in her nature to do so, to be sure, and she recognised realities when she saw them. Also that he was trying to be placatory.

Twelfth Night came and went, the end to Yuletide. And as though to emphasise that festivity was now over, the very next day it was not the master who came to the royal quarters but Lord Boyd himself. He dismissed his daughter with a flick of the hand, and looked meaningfully at the King, who took the hint and retired to his own room.

"Princess," he said, without preamble, "I understand that you are informed that it is decided that you shall marry my son, Thomas. This for the benefit of all. He will be created Earl of Arran as from the day before the wedding, which will be on the last day of this present month. Certain details have to be arranged first, and of these I come to inform you – "

"I think, my lord, that you can spare yourself in this," the girl interrupted. "I have no wish to marry, the Master of Boyd or other."

Undoubtedly the Regent had been warned that this interview might not be all plain sailing, for he showed no surprise nor indeed any change of expression on his fairly consistently expressionless face.

"This is not a matter of wishes or preferences, Highness," he observed, flatly. "It is policy, state policy. Taken by the Council, for the good of the realm. His Grace's sisters should be wed, for many reasons, but first and foremost for the sake of the succession. Only two young boys represent the succession, both children; and boys do not always reach manhood. So, with His Grace not yet himself of marriageable age, although he must be affianced soon, it's important that the succession be strengthened, assured. So . . ."

"So you, sir, would seek to have a grandson, a Boyd, to sit on the Scottish throne! The Kilmarnock lairds aspire to become royal!"

That did make the man blink. "Not so. That is not my intention. It is but a precaution. Ever necessary in the royal house, Princess. His sister, wed, will strengthen His Grace's hand, and His Grace's regency. You must see that . . ."

"But not necessarily to *your* son, my lord!"

"My son regards you highly. He will make you a good husband."

"A good husband, perhaps – but not for me!"

"For you, yes, Princess."

"No!"

84

"You cannot disobey a royal command, lady."

"*Command . . . ?*"

"Yes. The King has signed a decree to that effect. And to create the earldom."

She stared at him. "James . . . has done . . . that!"

"His Grace has, yes. At the Council's request."

Wordless now, the girl turned away.

The Regent, point made, went on, addressing her back. "There will be great benefits for you, Highness. You will be Countess of Arran. All that great island yours. Large lands in Fife, Lothian, Ayrshire and Galloway, also. Thomas will be one of the richest earls in the land."

"Think you that I care for that!"

"Would you liefer have wed an unknown foreign prince, lady? As part of a treaty?"

She did not answer.

"Kings' daughters seldom can choose whom they will wed," he told her. "I would say that you are more fortunate than most. Consider you that, I charge you." With the sketchiest of bows, he left her to her consideration.

7

Mary Stewart was not a fool, nor afraid to recognise and accept unavoidable facts. She had strength of character and will; but she knew how to bend to necessity. That is not to say that she thereafter surrendered meekly or became patiently accepting, reconciled to her fate. But, perceiving that she was not going to alter that fate, short of a miracle, she sought to adapt her behaviour so as to make the best of it, for herself and for others. Whilst making it clear, especially to Tom Boyd, that she was still no willing bride, she did not refuse all preparation for the marriage, nor make life miserable for her brothers, sister and Anna.

As for the bridegroom-to-be, he trod warily indeed for that man, still attentive but never assertive, not exactly apologetic but ever seeking to reassure, to allay fears, to indicate that his caring was real and included concern for the young woman's feelings. This was obviously difficult for a man of his temperament and lead-taking nature; and at times Mary was actually almost sorry for him, well aware of his efforts and strains.

It was towards James that she was most distant, finding it hard to forgive that he had been persuaded to sign the marriage documents, and charters of Arran and other lands, for Tom. She told herself that the boy did not fully understand, of course, that he had grown fond of the master, provider of so much that he enjoyed, probably thinking indeed that he was doing his sister a favour. But it rankled.

It was to be a most brilliant wedding, inevitably, Lord Boyd seeing it as the crowning evidence and symbol of his achievement and success, the flourished confirmation of the Boyd rise to supreme power. No expense was to be spared, no detail of the splendour of a royal occasion overlooked. These weeks of January were all too short for the scale of the arrangements, the provision of magnificent clothing, the preparations for feasting and the sending out of invitations to the illustrious – the haste was to have it all over before the fasting season of Lent. So the first weeks passed quickly.

Anna, not to mention the royal children, grew much excited.

There was a distraction however, before the due day. An envoy arrived at Stirling, from Norway. King Christian thereof sent, not felicitations and congratulations on the royal match, but urgent complaint. It was, as ever, concerned with those bones of contention, the isles of Orkney and Shetland. These clusters of islands, although lying off the north coast of Scotland, belonged to the Norse kingdom, and had done since Viking times, this despite the fact that they constituted a Scottish earldom and bishopric. Usually, the trouble was about the latter, for, because the Scottish Church had no Metropolitan or archbishop, the Archbishop of Trondheim, who called himself Metropolitan of the North, claimed spiritual jurisdiction over the See of Orkney. This was disputed by the Archbishop of York, who made similar claims – much to Scotland's resentment, the Scots prelates accepting the claims of neither, an ongoing clerical war. However, the present incumbent, William Tulloch, was a careful and diplomatic prelate, who got on well with the Norsemen. Unfortunately, William St Clair, Earl of Orkney, was of a very different character, a harsh and violent man, and the two seldom were in agreement. Now, according to this Norse envoy, the earl had actually laid hands on the bishop and locked him up in one of his castles, a prisoner – to the great offence of the Archbishop of Trondheim and King Christian; and, incidentally, when he heard of it, to the Scots Primate, the Bishop of St Andrews.

There was much concern at Stirling, not so much perhaps on account of Bishop Tulloch's fate as at the danger of trouble with Norway – for Scotland had only what amounted to a lease of the Northern Isles, and was considerably in arrears with the rental, one of the many problems of an all but empty treasury, finances neglected since Bishop Kennedy died. The last thing they wanted, at this stage, was King Christian's ill-will, and demands for indemnity – and payment of arrears.

Lord Boyd, faced with his first major challenge, in a sphere in which he had no least experience, sent for the Primate, from St Andrews. Bishop Graham, hastening to Stirling, not much more than a couple of weeks before he was due there to celebrate the royal wedding, was much upset, both at the outrage perpetrated upon one of his bishops, and on the Norse reaction, fearing that the Archbishop of Trondheim might do what had been threatened more than once before, petition the Pope to have the Orkney diocese removed from the Scottish Church to the Norse one, a dire development, especially over this question of Metropolitan status. Something must be done, and at once.

Lord Boyd's dilemma was acute, his courses of action limited indeed. The Earl of Orkney had to be dealt with, and vigorously, obviously; but that was not so easy, up there in his island fastnesses; and he was a formidable individual, apart from his hot temper – he had indeed been Chancellor of Scotland once. No sort of military persuasion was to be considered, even possible; so diplomacy it had to be. But who was to apply it, and what? The fire-eating earl had no regard for churchmen, obviously, to imprison a bishop; so there was no point in sending up the Primate or any of his fellow-prelates. Who, then? Boyd himself, although Regent, was only a Lord of Parliament, no earl, and undoubtedly the St Clair would refuse to heed any less than of his own rank. As it so happened, the Boyds' friends and allies and supporters included only the two earls, Crawford and Argyll, the Lindsay and Campbell chiefs, and these were both away on the embassage to seek a suitable bride for King James. The two others were keeping their distance, to see how this Boyd regime developed. Certainly none would or could go on this awkward mission to Orkney and Shetland.

It was the Primate himself who came up with a possible solution. He said that he would have proposed Sir Alexander Boyd for the task, as the sort of man old St Clair might listen to, soldier and known as the Mirror of Chivalry; but he recognised that a mere knight would probably not carry sufficient weight, even if supported by some of the lords. So – postpone the wedding, but have the Master of Boyd created Earl of Arran forthwith, and send him. He was a personable and effective young man, and about to be wed to the King's sister.

For want of a better suggestion, or indeed any other, Boyd agreed, and the master given his instructions. The wedding to be held over meantime, but not the earldom. The King would sign the necessary documents right away, and the new Earl of Arran, with, say, the Primate himself and Lord Somerville, would sail from Inverkeithing for Orkney, just as soon as a ship could be got ready. No argument was permitted.

Tom Boyd came to Mary with mixed feelings, obviously uncertain as to her reactions, whatever his own.

"Behold, Highness, an errant bridegroom indeed!" he began, with an attempt to mix apology with both concern and banter. "Matters of state are to give you remission, for a little while, of being wed to your unworthy suitor! I am to go to Orkney, to beard the earl thereof in his den, and seek to free the good bishop. This is not of my choosing, I do assure you. Indeed, it may be the end of me! The Earl William is said to be a fierce character, and I may end up sharing the same cell with the bishop!"

"I think not," she said. "The St Clair may be a hard man, but he would not do that. He was Chancellor of this realm once. He is bitter, yes, but may have reason to be." That was levelly said.

He looked at her curiously. "You sound as though you know more of him than do I?"

"Perhaps I do. Perhaps I have reason to do so. Since he represents, in some measure, a stain on my father's honour." She was looking away from him, but speaking firmly. She had heard something of what was to do this day in Stirling, from James.

"Your father? The King? The late King?"

"The same. This Earl William of Orkney had a sister who wed the Earl of Douglas, the seventh of that great line, James the Gross. And my father, with his own hand, stabbed the son of that sister, the eighth Earl of Douglas, with his own dagger, at a banquet here in this Stirling Castle. To bring down the great power of the House of Douglas, which he feared was threatening the royal power. That was some fifteen years ago – but it is not something that I can forget. I do not think that ever before had a King of Scots done the like. My father was . . . impetuous. He lived to regret it, I know. As must all of his family."

He reached out to touch her – but thought better of it. "I knew of the death of Douglas, yes, But not that he was nephew to this Earl of Orkney."

"He was. And because Orkney supported the Douglases, he lost much. He resigned the chancellorship. Also the position he held of Admiral of Scotland. Much else. So St Clair is a bitter man."

"I see. This will scarcely help my mission, then!"

"What is that mission? What do you go to say to him? What have you to offer St Clair? Since you cannot threaten him with men, with violence, in those far isles. You would require a great fleet of galleys – which you have not got. Whereas he has. The other islesmen who have, the Lord of the Isles and his like, will nowise help you in this. Nor my lord of Argyll, I think. What have you got that the St Clair may want, as a price?"

"Lands. The offer of lands here in the south. And the threat of seeking to use the King of Norway's power against him."

"Think you that the Norse would not have done that ere this, if they were prepared to do it, rather than appeal to the King of Scots?"

"M'mm. You seem concerned, Mary? And knowledgeable about it all?"

"Not greatly so, no. But I heard my mother and Bishop Kennedy discussing a similar situation, when the earl gave up the chancellorship and the rest. They feared his power, allied to what was left of that of Douglas. I was young then, but I was interested. For the bishop took me to see the splendid chapel which St Clair had built at Roslin, near to Edinburgh, where the line hailed from. I said that a lord who built so fine a church could not be so ill a man."

"Roslin? I have not heard of this. A chapel?"

"One of the finest in the land. Renowned elsewhere – if not in your Kilmarnock!"

He grinned. "You think that I may survive, then? And our wedding be only delayed!"

"I can bear the delay, sir. However long!"

"I was afraid of that! Whereas *I* can not."

"May I at least hope that the marriage will now not be held until after Lent is past? If it must be, even then!"

"Oh, I think not, no. Easter is not until mid-April. So Lent does not start for six weeks yet. Lord help me if I am away for *half* of that time. It is but three days' sail to Orkney, they say – if the ship does not sink in the winter's gales! Two or three days at Kirkwall or Stromness or wherever the earl bides in those God-forsaken isles, and then home. I should be back in two weeks."

"I think that it will take you longer. Unless you have some strong lure to tempt him. More than any mere gift of lands. He has a sufficiency of lands already, I would say."

"Since you appear to know more about it all than do I – or my sire, I think – have you any suggestion as to what could well please the man?"

"It is scarcely for me to say. But . . . I would think that to assuage his hurt pride over what was done to him over the Douglas cause – for the St Clairs are notably proud – that would be best. He can hardly have back the chancellorship, nor want it now. But it would cost little to rename him Admiral, would it not? There is no Admiral of Scotland at present, I think? And he has the ships. And that might serve to help keep the turbulent Lord of the Isles in his Hebridean place, no? It could do the realm no harm . . ."

The master wagged his head at her. "Save us, here is a wonder! So young, so fair – and such wits! Such knowledge of affairs. A King's daughter, indeed. That might serve . . ."

"Also, there is this of the Roslin chapel. It is not only a chapel, of course, but attached to a collegiate church, if I remember rightly, with a provost and priests. If the Primate was to elevate Earl William in some way, or at least elevate his foundation of this collegiate church, as its patron, might this not please him? He is no young man, and will be apt to be considering his latter end, on occasion – as older men can do, they tell me. A raising of his status with the Church, after this of imprisoning a bishop, might well appeal to him – and help to release the poor prelate. To ensure for him some credit on the Day of Judgment!"

Tom Boyd was lost for words. "I think . . . I think that you should come with me to Orkney!" he got out. "You would make the best envoy!"

"A woman? Women are meet only to be men's playthings, and married off to whom men will!"

"Do not say that . . ."

"Is it not true?"

"No. And a plaything *you* could never be." He wisely changed the subject. "You will come tomorrow, to see me invested as Earl of Arran? Since it is only because of you, that I wed you, that so I am to be."

"If you will . . ."

In the morning, it was a somewhat abbreviated ceremony held in the great hall of Stirling Castle, with Thomas due to leave almost immediately thereafter for Inverkeithing, on the Fife coast, where a ship had been found for them, strangely enough by the Abbot of Dunfermline, whose abbey and lands, the richest in the land, did a great trade with the Low Countries, in timber, salt-fish,

91

hides, and beeswax for candles. The Primate feared that it might smell somewhat of the hides, but it ought to be sturdy enough to get them to Orkney, and its shipmaster experienced and skilful. There was only a comparatively small company present in the castle to see the investiture, momentous as it was, the first creation of an earldom for many a day. All indeed could be accommodated on the hall's dais-platform.

The proceedings, however shortened from the traditional, had to be celebrated in two parts, for it was unthinkable that any man could be created earl who was not already a knight; so knighthood had to be conferred first. The Lord Lyon King of Arms dispensed with a trumpeter on this occasion, and thumped his staff on the floor to have all to stand – although all were standing already – for the entry of the monarch. James, on cue, came in. All bowed, and he was handed a sword by Lyon, who declared that by His Grace's royal command, Thomas, Master of Boyd, was to be admitted to the order of knighthood, in token of his services to the crown. The said Master of Boyd to kneel.

Thomas got down on his knees and James rather gingerly raised the sword.

"I, James, by God's grace King of Scots, do, do hereby . . ." He hesitated over getting the wording right. ". . . hereby dub thee, Thomas, knight." He brought down the flat of the blade rather more heavily than necessary on one Boyd shoulder, then transferred it to the other, with some risk to the recipient's head in the process. "I charge that you, you fulfil your knightly vows. Yes, and remain a good knight until your life's end." That came out in something of a gabble. "Arise, Sir Thomas." Thankfully he handed back the sword to Lyon.

There were murmurs from the company as the new knight stood, looking, for him, almost embarrassed. Considering the greater honour to follow, nobody felt that congratulations were convenient at this stage.

The Primate thought that a prayer might be suitable here, to mark the interval, and besought the Almighty to bless and cherish Sir Thomas Boyd, about to be raised to the rank of earl, by His Grace, on the eve of a most important mission on the King's behalf; and thereafter to prosper the said mission with divine aid, and bring all to a worthy conclusion, including the release and restoration of William Tulloch, Bishop of Orkney, presently in durance vile.

That over, Lyon thumped again, and declared that, with His Grace's royal permission, the sponsors for the bestowal of the earldom should stand forward.

The Lord Boyd, as Regent, and the Lord Avondale, as Chancellor, moved over to the King, the latter bearing a golden banner over his arm. Drawing this aside, he revealed beneath it a golden belt. This, most obviously weighty, he handed to the Regent.

Lyon bowed to James.

"I . . . we, James, King of Scots, having approved that . . . the elevation of the . . . *Sir* Thomas Boyd, to the rank and dignity, aye and the honourable estate of earl of my kingdom, do hereby . . ," Looking very uncertain here, he paused.

"His Grace names, appoints and raises the lands of the Isle of Arran." That was the Lyon, helpfully.

"Aye. I name, appoint and raise the lands of the Isle of Arran to the, the status of an earldom. And I hereby . . ."

Lyon coughed warningly, and the boy stopped.

"My lord Regent, and my lord High Chancellor, sponsors, will present the earl's belt to His Grace."

Lord Boyd stepped forward and held out that golden, gleaming trophy to the King – who, obviously unprepared for the weight of it, all but dropped it.

Actually this procedure lacked some authenticity. It was the custom for two earls to sponsor the newcomers to their ranks, but today no two earls were available. There were no great numbers of earldoms anyway, and some were vested in the crown itself, some in the hands of minors. And only Crawford and Argyll were openly supporting Boyd.

James took a deep breath. "I hereby call on the master . . . Sir Thomas . . . Boyd to, to kneel again."

Tom duly got down, and managed an encouraging smile to his liege-lord.

The boy raised the massive chain with difficulty, and as the other ducked his head, managed to get it over without actually striking Tom's face with it, to deposit it on one shoulder, the rest to be draped down to the waist at the other side. Earls' belts were not to be worn round the middle, but hung thus from one shoulder, intended for the better carriage of a heavy sword.

"I hereby create you an earl of Scotland and invest you with the earldom of Arran, Sir Thomas," James got out with a rush. "Arise, my lord Earl."

There were exclamations all round as the new earl stood, adjusted the massive belt slightly, and bowing, reached for the King's hand, to take it between both of his own, in the traditional gesture of fealty, before backing away.

The thing was done.

Congratulations were now in order. Presently Tom came to Mary, where she stood with her brothers, sister and Anna. He searched her face almost anxiously.

"Your lordship!" she said. "Should I be overwhelmed by your increase in stature? Dazzled by more than this golden chain?"

"You, you do not resent it, Mary?"

"Why should I? Some of it will represent one more seal on my marriage contract! I can hardly escape you now, can I, my lord?"

He shook his head.

Anna kissed him, with a smile and a mock curtsy.

James came up. "What must I call you now?" he demanded. "Are you to be always my lord Earl?"

"Surely not, Sire. I was Master Thomas until this day. To Your Grace I will be proud to be Master Thomas always."

"Good! That is well. Mary, did I do it properly?"

"Very well, Jamie. I was afraid that you might stun his lordship with this chain!"

"It is heavy, yes. Do you wear it all the time, Master Thomas?"

"Lord, no! I hope not. I, I have enough on my shoulders!" And he glanced at Mary.

"My heart bleeds for you!" she told him, but lightly.

"Will you come to bid us farewell, Mary? And wish me success. Aye, and safety."

"To be sure."

"Glad to see the back of me, for a space?"

"As backs go, my lord, yours is well enough."

With that he had to be content.

Later, down at the gatehouse and drawbridge, the Primate, Lord Somerville and the new earl, with a small party of monkish clerks, servants and an escort, took their leave, to the advice and well-wishing of all. Tom bade farewell to the King first, and to Mary last.

"Well . . . ?" he questioned. "What is your word for me?"

"Safe journeying. A successful mission – remembering pride. Not *your* pride, but the St Clair's. I think that it will all turn on that."

"And . . . ?"

"Would you expect me to say haste ye back?"

"Not expect – but wish it, Mary."

"Very well. Haste ye back, Thomas, Earl of Arran."

He gripped her hand, kissed its back, then turned it over and kissed the palm, before swinging on his heel and striding off to his horse, only remembering, with a foot in the stirrup, to turn and bow towards the monarch. He did not wait for the Primate and the others, but urged his beast away.

Mary looked after him less calm than she seemed. As the others rode off, she raised that hand, to wave.

8

The weeks that followed were strange, in that all urgency seemed to have gone out of living, for Mary Stewart at least. The wedding preparations continued, but with less immediacy. She saw little or nothing of Lord Boyd or his colleagues, although James was frequently summoned to give royal assent to edicts and to sign papers. So the royal group had considerable time on their hands. Unfortunately, as so often in Scotland, the snow came as January passed into February, and this restricted excursions from the castle, under escort as these still had to be. There was a renowned sport, however, unique to Stirling Castle, known as hurly-hackit, in which the participants went tobogganing down a steep slope at the northern tip of the castle rock to a little green terrace meadow called Ballengeich, halfway down, where the two milk-cows for the fortress's inmates were pastured. This pastime was pursued sitting on the skulls of oxen, using the horns as handles to grip on the bumpy ride over the grass and outcropping stone, no gentle proceeding. But in snow, north-facing as it was, this slope became a deal more smooth than normal, and with rough sleds instead of the ox-skulls it made an exciting descent – one where steering was very necessary if minor disaster was to be avoided, for there were many large boulders, outcrops and miniature cliffs dotting the slope to be dodged – and fast-moving sleds are not the easiest vehicles to steer. So the royal sledgers, and Anna, had to be prepared for rough riding and upsets, but were by no means off-put by that, not in spirit however much they were apt to be in person. Young Margaret *was* the least enthusiastic, and never went on a sledge alone. The favourite sport was to have races, two sleds with three on each. Anna came to enjoy it, although scarcely as much as did Mary who, she declared, was determined to try to kill herself in order to avoid having to marry Tom.

During this waiting period Mary sought better to prepare herself to accept the inevitable as best she might. She told herself that countless women had had to do this down the ages, in every period and in every land, especially royal and noble women, married off for dynastic and policy reasons. Many undoubtedly had found their fate none so grievous. And she was possibly more fortunate than most, in that Thomas Boyd was a much more attractive man than many she might have been saddled with, young, good-looking and most evidently not only desirous but fond of her. She might have been landed with a harsh, sour, older man, who would have made her life a misery. This one might do that also, of course, once they were wed – although she rather thought not. And he could be good company, she admitted; indeed in this interval, she had moments when she actually missed him – at the sledging for instance, and of a long evening by the fireside. Sometimes she even worried about his present safety. More often she wondered what he would be like in bed. She had no actual experience in this, to be sure; princesses were apt to have their virginity emphasised, for obvious reasons. But her mother, a lusty woman, had told her not a little, and not all of warnings and the need for care, but of pleasures and indeed delights also. Often Mary Stewart lay awake of a night beside the sleeping Anna, wondering what it would be like with brother exchanged for sister.

There was, of course, no means by which the people at Stirling could learn how the Orkney mission fared. With varying degrees of anxiety, all waited.

Then, on a snowy Eve of St Finnan, a single horseman arrived at the castle on an all but foundered mount, having ridden from Inverkeithing, the port of Dunfermline – the Earl of Arran himself, having far outridden the Primate, Somerville and their escort in his haste to get back. And it was very clear that it was not so much the urgency of the news he brought as his desire to see Mary Stewart at the earliest possible moment – to his father's disapproval. It so happened that the young people were at their sledging at Ballengeich when he arrived, and he came hastening over to them, all still clad for hard winter's riding as he was. Mary, rising from her sled alone, at the bottom of the slope, all breathless and rosy-cheeked, was astonished to see the man come plunging, sliding, slipping down to her, frequently on his bottom, long riding-boots no help to him, an extraordinary sight.

Her companions above were waving and shouting.

He could hardly avoid cannoning into her – not that he tried. Even as she stared, he was upon her, and she was caught up in

97

his arms bodily, in headlong, stumbling career, to stagger on a few yards together and then collapse into the snow in a heap, the man on top.

"You . . . great . . . witling! Fool!" she gasped. If she had been breathless before, she was more so now.

"Fool . . . as to . . . you!" His own breath was scarce now. "In especial . . . as thus!"

"Had I . . . foreseen *this* . . . I would not . . . have prayed . . . for your return!" Even as she was, panting, she amended that. "Your *safe* return."

"You did that? Prayed? God be praised!" Almost reluctantly lifting himself off her, he rose, to aid her to her feet.

"I prayed for . . . the Primate and . . . Bishop Tulloch also!" she pointed out.

He still held her by the arms, all but devouring her with his eyes. "It has seemed an age, endless . . ."

"Yet you are back sooner than we looked for you."

"Once we had gained our ends, I would have no lingering, I promise you! Bishops or none."

"You did succeed then?"

"Aye, he was none so ill. St Clair. I remembered your advice. His pride! Played on that. He is Admiral again, now. And the Primate made him Commendator of Roslin, which seemed to please him. Although not Bishop Tulloch! But we did get that one freed. He was scarce as grateful as we thought he should be. He is now off to Denmark, to see King Christian. But . . . enough of all that. This is not what I came hastening to tell you!"

"No? Yet it is good news. You earn your earldom!"

"Would that you said that with a kinder smile! I tell you . . ."

What he would have told her had to be postponed, for the other sled, with James and Anna aboard, came hurtling down to join them, amidst cries of greeting and a flood of questions. There could be no doubt about the man's welcome from these two, at any rate. He released Mary, whom he had been clutching the while, sketched some sort of a bow to the monarch, and returned his sister's kisses. Anna at least sought no account of his mission, although James was interested to hear how near to shipwreck they had been and whether the famous tidal whirls between Caithness and Orkney were as fierce as they were said to be.

Presently they all climbed back up the hill, to where young Alexander, John and Margaret awaited them, snowball fighting meantime. Tom admitted that he had never thought of sledging here – but then he had never lived in Stirling Castle previously. He would have to try it, later.

Back at the palace block, it was not long before the ex-envoy found his way to the royal quarters, changed as to clothing, presumably leaving the Primate and Somerville to report in detail to his father and the other lords, while he recounted his adventures to the younger folk. Actually, he did not make a great deal of it, over their meal, but he did describe the "rousts", as they were called, the whirlpools amongst the isles where the Atlantic tides met those of the Norse Sea, hazards for shipping indeed, not unlike the notorious Corrievreckan of the Hebrides. He told them of the mighty cliffs of Hoy,. the swirling winds which prevailed, the multitude of the islands, treeless but not infertile, the rich fisheries, the friendly enough folk, more Norse than Scots with strange names, the small but sturdy cattle and horses, some of the latter barely larger than a dog.

James declared that he would like to go there, one day. Would Master Thomas take him? He had never been on an island, a real one. He was told that it might be possible, although Orkney and Shetland were the Norse King's territory and they might have to get especial permission. But meantime there was Arran to visit, and much to see there.

The mention of that island produced its own effect, on Mary at least, and while she did not ask the question foremost in her mind, and probably in Anna's also, James had no such inhibitions.

"Will we go there, after the wedding?" he demanded. "When is the wedding to be?"

Tom answered that carefully, for him. "It should be soon. As soon as possible, with Lent ahead. Weddings are not held in Lent. So, at Her Highness's convenience, the sooner the better."

"*My* convenience! You are most thoughtful, sir!"

"I rather conceived the time of the month to be important, Princess!"

Anna's glance darted from one to the other.

"You *would* think of that!"

"Would you have me not to care, Mary?"

She did not answer.

"Would a week hence serve?"

"As well as any. Since . . ." She left the rest unsaid.

"Everything is all but prepared. This delay . . ." He looked at her almost appealingly. "It will be none so ill, Mary."

She changed the subject. "Tell us more of Orkney and Shetland. And the St Clairs. This earl's father, Henry St Clair, played guardian to our grandfather, James the First, when his uncle Albany sought to slay him as he had slain his brother Rothesay, to gain the throne for himself, a vile man. So we Stewarts have our links with the Earls of Orkney. That one suffered much for us."

"He took our grandfather to safety on the Bass Rock, in the middle of the sea," James added. "Near to North Berwick. Until they could go to France. We saw the Bass from Edinburgh, from the top of Arthur's Seat. I would like to go there, one day."

"One day, Sire . . ."

Later, when Tom left them for his own chamber, a tired man after his long day and journeying, he contrived a private word with Mary.

"See you, my dear, do not dread this of our marriage, I beseech you! It will not be so ill, I swear it. For you. For me, I can scarce wait! But I recognise your . . . fears. Apprehensions. I am willing to be . . . patient. To consider you."

"You Boyds are always considering, my lord!"

"No — not that! I mean it, lass. I know that this is no desire of yours, however much it has become mine. But *you* consider. Together, we shall make it . . . serve."

"Serve? Who serves who, my lord Earl?" Then she relented a little. "But I thank you for your intended reassurances for an unwilling bride. I am, shall we say, partly reconciled to my fate! Almost. And I perceive that I might have had a worse one! Let that suffice, for this night."

He half nodded, half shrugged, and reached for her hand to kiss it as he had done before, back and front, and left her.

The Chapel Royal of Stirling Castle was modest in size however splendid as to style and decoration, and was packed on this occasion. No expense had been spared, no detail and embellishment overlooked. The guests were illustrious as they were numerous, even though there were not a few notable absentees, for this being a royal wedding, not merely a Boyd one, some who were not in fact in favour of the Boyd faction were present, as a mark of respect for the crown, all clad in their finest. The church was lit by candles innumerable, hung with banners and standards, and rich with the scent of incense. Instrumentalists and a choir of singing-boys made sweet music.

There were four small preliminary processions. First came the Lord Lyon King of Arms and his four heralds and trumpeters, leading in Alexander, Duke of Albany, John, Earl of Mar and the Princess Margaret, to seats at the front. Then came the clergy, led by the Dean of the Chapel Royal and the Primate, with four bishops, four mitred abbots and sundry priors, who moved into the chancel. Then a single blast of trumpet ushered in the bridegroom and his father, and two young Boyd brothers, Tom magnificent in blue and white velvet of their heraldic colours with the red and white fesse-chequey as a silken sash over his right shoulder and his golden earl's belt over the left; his father notably plainly dressed by comparison. There was no sign of Sir Alexander. The younger Boyds went to seats beside the royal children, while their father and brother went to stand centrally before the chancel steps.

There was a distinct pause, which produced some shuffling of feet, murmuring and even a few sniggers, before Lyon signed to the two trumpeters who, waiting, promptly produced a tremendous flourish of a fanfare – which shook the rafters and actually brought down some bat-droppings and dust on distinguished heads. But even when this ended there was some delay, to the frowns of Lord Boyd and some anxious looks from the bridegroom, before the vestry door opened to admit King James, more handsomely garbed than he had ever been, a golden circlet round his brow, and on his arm, his sister.

Mary, however unenthusiastic a bride, had never looked more lovely. She was dressed all in white damask with the raised patterns in gold, having little other decoration, but superbly cut and fashioned by the best dressmaker Stirling could boast. The coif, which sat lightly on her long, dark hair, was simple but beaded with pearls from the River Tay, a gift from her father to her mother. She held her head high, features unsmiling but nowise sour. James looked the more nervous and excited of the pair. Behind them came Anna, glancing all around cheerfully.

All stood – and must remain standing while the King did.

To the choir's chanting, James led his sister to Tom's side, that man turning to her eagerly and receiving an inclination of her head and a direct look which was almost questioning. Anna stood a pace behind.

So they waited, while the Dean, from before the high altar, opened the proceedings with prayer to the Almighty, that He might bless what was being done this day. An anthem followed.

Then the Primate came forward to stand before the five principals. He declared that they were here together in this place, in the sight of God, to enact a great matter, no less than the union of two of God's children to be made into one, one in the sight of God. This was a notable and enduring mystery, the entry into the estate of holy matrimony. Man might pronounce it, all unworthily, but only the Almighty Father of us all could make it real. It therefore was not to be entered upon lightly or with lack of due understanding. Was that recognised by the present applicants for the sacrament of marriage?

Tom shot a swift sideways glance at Mary, cleared his throat, and made an approximately affirmative noise. The girl said nothing, but meeting the prelate's eye, raised her brows slightly.

Bishop Graham presumably accepted that as sufficiently positive, for he went on.

"Marriage, as well as for the union of two persons to be one hereafter for all time, is also for the procreation of children. Offspring to be raised for the service of God, and nurtured in the fear of the Lord, if the union is blessed with children. This must be understood by those who seek their Maker's blessing upon their union. Is it so understood?"

Again the man's swift look at the woman. This time she returned his glance levelly. Neither spoke.

The bishop no doubt was aware of something of the situation between these two, since he had been Tom's close companion on the Orkney visit. At any rate, he appeared to be content with their reception of his statements. He in fact seemed to speed matters now, as though having made his point, he was concerned to spare the couple anything more than the essentials. Almost businesslike, he asked who gave this woman to wed this man?

James said that he did.

The vow-repeating, after the Primate, followed, Tom's strong, Mary's merely a slight movement of her lips. Then, for the ceremonial of the ring, with the bridegroom having no other supporter than his father, Lord Boyd handed over the symbol to his son, and stepped back beside Anna. James did the same.

Fitting that ring on the girl's finger, so almost defiantly thrust out, had even Tom Boyd's hand trembling a little. But he got it in place, and squeezed *her* hand thereafter, searching her face.

Another hand raised, the prelate declared that these two, Thomas and Mary, were undoubted man and wife, in the sight of God and of all men. He signed to them to kneel, and with a hand laid on both heads, blessed them in the name of Father, Son and Holy Spirit.

The kneeling pair could scarcely believe that that was all, that the deed was done.

The Primate turned to the altar, and on that cue the choir broke out into a joyful chorus of hallelujahs and hosannas, which went on and on, while high above them all the chapel's bells rang out. Long the resounding praise and thanksgiving went on, and even Mary was not exempt from some emotion as they rose and stood. For his part, Tom seemed as though he was going to take her in his arms and kiss her rapturously, but with an effort contented himself with kissing that beringed hand.

"Your hand . . . in marriage!" he got out.

Anna did not hesitate as her brother had done, but flung her arms round the bride, in a mixture of tears and laughter. James, as yet not at the kissing stage, pecked at his sister's cheek and backed away to safety. The Lord Boyd looked grimly satisfied but made no gestures.

A nuptial hymn from the choir, and a general benediction from the Dean, completed the proceedings.

Led by the monarch, the Earl and Countess of Arran paced down the aisle to the west door, his arm in hers, to the congratulations and plaudits of all.

The banquet which followed was on a scale seldom seen in Scotland previously, in richness as in variety, with ongoing entertainment of performers, dancers, acrobats and musicians, as well as set scenes of masques and play-acting, all this ordered by the Regent although not devised by him – he was scarcely that way inclined; but by another brother, William Boyd, Abbot of Kilwinning, who was having his abbey erected into a regality, with all the financial and other advantages accruing, a man of talents in more than religion. He sat at Mary's left at the dais-table, an entertainment in himself, even though she had some difficulty in concentrating on his witticisms and anecdotes this evening, an unlikely brother for Lord Boyd. Tom, at her other side, was not as attentive as he might have been either; the thoughts of both tended to be elsewhere.

Indeed, throughout what to him seemed a never-ending trial of patience, that young man's glance was more often towards his new wife than on either the entertainers or on his rich food and drink. And, considering his normally confident, not to say ebullient, nature, a sort of apprehension could not be concealed, indeed more apprehension than was apparent in his partner – although perhaps she was merely becoming better at hiding her feelings. He kept glancing sideways at her, rather than any gazing or consistent eyeing; he did not actually address her much, but frequently his hand went out to touch her arm or squeeze her wrist. Mary did not return these gestures, but nor did she move hand away; and once or twice she met his glance and nodded slightly.

James, at the other side of Tom, with the Regent on his left, at least fully enjoyed and appreciated the proceedings more adequately. This, in time, oddly enough, in part contributed to the bridegroom's impatience and concern – for with the King present, none might rise and leave the hall before he did, without his express permission; and he seemed in no least hurry to do this. Normally a newly-wed couple could, and did, leave a nuptial feast considerably before the end, to frequently outspoken advice and comments from the guests; but this was not possible here.

At length, with James applauding vigorously and demanding a replay of an acrobatic display by four almost naked performers, two of each sex, presumably considered by the abbot as suitable wedding-night entertainment, Mary took pity on her new husband, recognising that putting off further was not going to aid *her* in any way. She did what only she there could do. Briefly touching Tom's elbow, she rose and went behind him to her brother's back and stooping, murmured in his ear.

The boy looked up, surprised, but listening, shrugged and stood. All had to rise, the music stopped, the acrobats paused in an uncomfortable stance, and silence descended save for the growling of deerhounds under the tables, squabbling over bones.

"My sister . . . the princess . . . Her Highness the Countess of Arran . . . she has my royal permission to leave my presence. And, aye, Master Thomas, Earl of Arran," he announced somewhat uncertainly, and sat down.

Cheers and laughter sounded from the crowded tables down the length of the hall. Thomas rose, bowed to the monarch, and taking Mary's arm, led her down from the dais-platform and on down that length of the hall, nodding right and left to the sallies and guidance offered, crude as much of it was. Mary played the princess, possibly her last opportunity to do so that night.

Out into the February dark and wind, they hurried across the palace yard's flagstones to the opposite wing, a long handsome range of building, at the north end of which were the royal apartments. But it was not to these that the couple now headed. The man's quarters were at the other end.

Mary, in fact, had never been in Tom's rooms, and now entered them with mixed .feelings. She found them spacious and comfortable enough, lamps lit in both chambers and fires burning brightly in each. She was surprised to find Anna waiting in the outer one. She had not seen her leave the hall. It was a kind gesture.

"Highness." The girl dipped a curtsy. "At your service, as always!"

"Thank you, Anna." She looked from sister to brother. Whose unexpected notion was this?

"All is prepared. Warming-pans in the bed. The morn's clothing laid out. Bed-robes to hand. Also towels. Warmed water. Cloths." That seemed to Mary to be rather spelling it out.

Evidently Thomas thought so also. "We shall manage," he said shortly.

"No doubt. *You* will not find it all so . . . strange!" Anna answered. "But we do not all have your experience, brother!" Smiling, she turned to Mary. "If you need me, Highness, there is also a bell on the floor by the bed. I shall be in the chamber along the passage. His Grace will have to do without near company tonight."

"You. are kind, Anna . . ." It occurred to Mary that perhaps Anna was not herself wholly without experience in such matters.

Raising a hand, the other girl departed.

Tom drew a deep breath, looked at his companion, but found no words.

"You have been very patient, husband," she said. "Now – it is my turn!"

"Patient? I hope . . . I trust that patience is not what you will

105

find necessary. It need not be so ill, see you. Others have not found it so, Mary. Or, leastways . . ."

"And you will have, shall we say, instructed not a few?" When he did not answer, she shrugged. "Well, Thomas, I see naught to be gained by delay. Now, shall we seek our couch? So well prepared for us!"

He eyed her questioningly, as though he had scarcely expected *her* to take the lead in this matter. He gestured towards the open bedroom door. "Do you wish . . . to go first? To, to make ready? To . . ." he left the rest unsaid.

"Do *you* so wish?"

"No-o-o."

"Then come, my lord of Arran. And of myself! Since I have, I think, much more to, to undergo this night, let us not make much of this. After all, you have seen me unclothed, in the sea, have you not. And I you, running along that fishwives' beach!" And she preceded him into the other chamber.

It was less brightly lit than the first, but the fire was even better, indeed the birch-log flames producing much of the lighting. A massive urn-like sitting-bath stood before the fire, with a lidded pail, from which steam curled, beside it. The bedclothes were turned back, with bed-robes lying there, the other conveniences listed evident. There was even a flagon of wine and beakers on a chest nearby.

"Your sister is very thoughtful. And . . . knowledgeable. For one of her years," Mary commented, going over to the fire. "How think you – the firelight? It is more kindly, perhaps, than these candles." Not waiting for his assent, she went and snuffed out the four candles with her fingers.

He stood watching, silent.

She removed the lid from the pail and dipped in her fingers, to clean them of the soot. "It is sufficiently hot," she reported. "After all this day's events and excitements, I vow a bath will not come amiss. How say you?" She was removing her coif now.

"If you . . . yes."

"Help me then, with this gown. At the back   "

Still remarkably silent for that man, he stepped over, and making something of a fumble at it, undid the buttons at the rear of that splendid damask dress.

She moved aside and let the gown drop to the floor, and so stood in her knee-length linen shift. This she raised, to take off

106

garters and to roll down and remove her silken hose. Stooping to gather up these, with her gown, she went over with them to one of the chamber's chests, laid them thereon, and then slipped off the light shift from her shoulders and let it fall away, to stand quite naked.

"Pour the water, Thomas," she directed – although her voice thickened just a little as she said it.

Tom Boyd did not move. He was staring, quite frankly staring. And he had something to stare at indeed, for she had, by any standards, a quite superb body, beautifully proportioned, from her long, graceful neck and sculptured shoulders down to full, rounded but not heavy breasts, well apart, tipped with generous pink aureolas and nipples. Below, her stomach was by no means flat but firmly rounded above a dark triangle which notably served to emphasise the white of long and shapely thighs to slender calves and ankles. No man could do other than stare. She made no foolish attempt to hide any of herself.

"Water, my lord," she repeated.

He mumbled something, and went over to the pail and bath, while she waited.

When he had done it, and turned back to her, he found words. "You are beyond all beautiful! A joy to behold. Perfection itself!"

"Scarcely that, I think. Although it is not for me to point out my failings!" She moved across to the bath, and he took her hand to help her step into it, and steady her therein.

The nearness of all that warm loveliness seemed almost to affect his breathing, the more so perhaps in that her own was not unaffected by the situation, as the slight stirring of her bosom testified.

"I . . . I . . . it is not too hot? The water . . . ?"

"No. It is very well. One of those cloths, if you please."

He hurried to pick up what proved to be a towel, and at her pointing this out, changed it.

"May I . . . could I . . . it would give me great pleasure to bathe you. Wash you down." That came out in a rush. "If you would permit it? I have never . . . so done."

Mary stooped to dip and squeeze the cloth in the water – and the change in posture in itself added further enchantment and stimulation for the man, front and rear.

"I do not see why not," she decided. "If you so wish." She handed him the wet cloth.

He took it, swallowing audibly, seemed doubtful as to where to begin, and bent to wet it further, although it scarcely needed that. Whilst down, he evidently decided to start thereabouts, as the least taxing probably upon them both. Sinking to his knees, he began to wash her feet, her ankles, her calves.

She looked down on his bent head. "Is this normal usage? A wedding-night custom?"

"I do not know. All I know is that I, I rejoice in it." He moved his busy hand higher.

"You are very thorough, at least, sir!"

"You do not mind it?"

"I think not, no."

"Do you sit down. There is not a great deal of water."

"And you are spilling some, splashing it over. To make it less. No, I will remain standing."

At her groin and middle he was careful indeed, clearly anxious not to offend; but round the back he allowed himself more scope, more freedom, almost lovingly massaging those firm rounded buttocks with the cleavage between. Then, making something of a show of re-dipping the cloth, he rose to his feet, to tackle those challenging breasts, which became the more so when she raised her arms high that he might wash below them.

"As well that all be done . . . properly," she murmured. "If that is the apt word!"

He found no answer, other than active but far from rough hands – for he now seemed to be requiring both – that cloth tending to figure less prominently than did his fingers. Her bosom had never been so meticulously bathed before. When he appeared to be about to repeat the process, she took the cloth from him.

"My face I can deal with myself," she observed. "The towel now, if you will." And she stepped out on to the floor.

Emboldened now by what he had achieved, Tom did not hand over the towel to her but started on the drying treatment himself, patting and dabbing and gently rubbing in a comprehensive coverage, until she declared that there was surely no least drop of wetness left on her, and she was going to bed. Would he put a couple of logs on the fire . . . ?

Mary all but ran over to the wide bed and got in under the blankets and between the sheets, to cover herself, somewhat belatedly, perhaps.

Tom busied himself with the fire.

Watching him, the girl said, "I will let you bathe yourself!"

He shook his head, decidedly. "I think not. I will not trouble with it. Tonight. I bathed before the church, the wedding. I, I have better things to do!" He was divesting himself hurriedly, as he spoke.

It did not take him long. He had indeed some small difficulty in removing his fine velvet breeches, for masculine reasons – but for the same reasons wrenched them off vehemently. And for his part there was no tidy picking up of discarded clothing and putting it on a chest. Observing this last, Mary transferred her gaze to the flame-flickering on the painted ceiling rafters.

He came to the other side of the bed and jumped in. At once his hands reached out for her – but not to grope nor to draw her to him, only to hold her.

"You are . . . well enough?" he asked, seeking to keep the urgency out of his voice.

"Well enough? I am washed. And naked. And, and wed to you! Is that not sufficiently well for you?"

"I mean . . . see, Mary, I know that this is not of your choosing. That therefore it could be . . . difficult for you. Something of a trial, perhaps. Yet . . ."

"Yet it is my duty now. And your right. Is it not?"

"I would have you to think, to *feel*, otherwise." His hands began to slide lightly over her soft warm skin. "There should be pleasure in this, lass. For you, surely, as well as for myself. Will you not . . . seek it so?"

"If you say so, I will try."

His hand continued to caress. At her breasts she did not stir, but when it moved down and down below her midriff to her groin, she drew quick breath, and stiffened.

His own breathing was growing the more evident by the moment, stronger, deeper, as he sought to hold himself in. He was moving over to her now, gripping her. She remained rigid, as that exploring hand went probing.

"My dear, my dear!" he almost groaned. "I . . . I . . ."

Mary could not fail to recognise his need, his urgency, that he was undergoing his own testing struggle, however different in character from hers. She forced herself to aid him a little, even as he was presumably trying to aid her.

Then he was on to her, above, his hand superseded, and basic masculinity took charge. She almost bit *his* lip instead of her own as he forced his way. She knew sudden hurt, yes, but more hurt of mind, of her inner self's privacy, integrity, than of her violated physical person, and twisted beneath him, this way and that, in her extremity.

He was panting, gasping, blurting out incoherent words, but so active upon her, his weight so heavy, his sheer dominance over her so overpowering, that she lost all sense of anything but his mastery and ascendancy over her, his undeniable demand, under which she could do nothing but accept. And as it went on, the acceptance grew the less hurtful to her pride, as to her body. A sort of yielding grew in her, a feeling of self-immolation, and yes, wonder in some measure.

Then, suddenly, his gasping changed to a strange cry of mixed triumph, fulfilment, relief, and yet somehow regret also, as the pent-up pride of his manhood burst its bounds, his struggle over. And in that strange, violent, aggressive moment she nevertheless felt all woman as she had never felt before, receiving if scarcely receptive, as, in his final throes, he more or less collapsed upon her, chest heaving now to match her own.

As he lay upon her but still within her, spent, where she was anything but, she gazed up at the firelit ceiling and wondered. She was surprised to feel no offence, no real resentment, however much her physical discomfort. She did not speak.

At length the man did. "I am sorry! Sorry, Mary. That, that I had to . . . could not . . . contain myself. Gave you no time. Overbore you so, so hardly. I sought to wait, but . . . I am sorry, lass."

She rather wondered what he meant by giving her time. Time for what? She had been as prepared for his assault as she would ever be. What would further waiting have availed? She did not answer him other than by patting his sweating back a little.

He lay some moments longer, while his breathing became more normal. Then he rolled away, to lie at her side, on his back, although one hand still held a breast.

Mary stirred a little, moistening her almost bruised lips.

Presently he asked, thickly. "You are . . . well enough?"

"Well . . . *enough*! Yes."

"I am sorry . . ." His voice tailed away. He sounded sleepy now.

Still she stared up at the ceiling, herself far from sleepy and relaxed, going over and over what had happened to her, her mind

110

darting this way and that. This, then, was what was meant by losing one's virginity, her innocence. She had, of course, heard women's talk of this, and not usually with any signs of great concern. She had not failed, to be sure, to wonder what it would be like. Was it so grievous once the mind was schooled to accept it? All women, or most, had to go through with it. Many, no doubt, almost rejoiced to suffer it – that is, if they loved the man, or themselves felt the desire for him. Or of what it could lead to.

Presently the clutch at her breast relaxed, and Tom's breathing deepened in sleep.

Long she lay, wide awake, pondering, wondering. This then was marriage, this sleeping man her husband. She had taken vows before God, however unwillingly. Did a lifetime of this stretch ahead of her? Was that a cause for dread? Her own mother had not felt that way, assuredly. From all accounts she had had many lovers once her husband died – or, if not lovers, at least bedfellows. Including this man's uncle. That was no road to follow, surely; but there could be *something* to be learned from it all? This, of possible pleasure in the act . . . ?

How long Mary lay thinking thus there was no knowing, before there was a stirring at her side and that hand came reaching out once more.

"Mary," she heard. "You, you sleep?"

"No."

"You are very lovely. Desirable. And patient, too. I am grateful. I failed you then. But – not again. I shall not fail you again, my dear."

She shrugged, under the hand which had begun to caress her bosom again. "I did not esteem you . . . failing!" she said. "You seemed sufficiently . . . active!"

"Aye, too much so! I had waited for you, desired you, ached for you, overlong, you see. So that I was at, at bursting-point! But that is over now. Now we shall do better."

As he moved close again, hands only a little less eager than heretofore, she realised that what he meant by not failing her again was not that he would not use her again, and right away. The not-failing was to be otherwise. What? How? Her ordeal for this night was not over, then! If ordeal it was . . . ?

Tom Boyd changed his tactics indeed. He threw back the bedclothes, so that they both lay bare, all her lovely nakedness fairly apparent, even though the firelight was much less bright now, although the room was comfortably warm. Then he began to kiss her, not just on the lips now but comprehensively, all over her person, lingeringly, lovingly, in no haste. She did not seek to stop him, since this was presumably him not failing her again, even when he told her to turn over, so that he could start on her back. Besides, she had to admit that it was not an unpleasing sensation.

Then commenced as comprehensive a fondling of her, high and low. This continued for some considerable time – not that it seemed overlong for the still somewhat apprehensive girl. But clearly he knew what he was doing – had not Anna said that he was an experienced lover? So perhaps this was meant to be an aid to her, as well as to himself, and certainly she sensed his masculinity nowise reduced. For herself, something of a strange and not unpleasant lassitude seemed to be coming over her – no doubt lack of sleep, after a long and tiring day, beginning to tell? Not that she felt actually sleepy herself . . .

He talked quite a lot while this was going on, quiet, murmurous talk, hardly soothing but certainly reassuring, whispering endearments, declaring love, admiration, fascination. She realised that she was finding no real fault with it all.

Then, with this continuing, he found his way on top of her again. But now there was no hasty aggression, only a sort of playing and testing – so much so that she began to feel that it would be better if he got it over with, since it obviously had to come. She was scarcely impatient, but . . .

And then, with his assertion becoming stronger, more commanding, abruptly, almost without warning, she knew a great surge of feeling, emotion, urgency, desire, need, a demand indeed such as never before experienced or even imagined could be hers. Aware of it, then, the man responded strongly, as a man should, and like flood-gates opening, her own woman's tide overwhelmed her. She cried out, clutching his shoulders convulsively.

They moved as one, as Tom Boyd cried out also, for the second time that night.

Thereafter, he muttered no apologies, nor did Mary Stewart put her wonder into words, although she stroked his shoulders which she had clutched, till he slid over.

"Man . . . and wife!" he got out, before he was part asleep again.

She nodded, all but questioningly, at that. Soon she also slept, not caring about those down-turned bedclothes.

9

It was Anna who wakened them, belatedly, next morning, having dismissed the servitors who brought the hot water and breakfast viands. She knocked, entered, and eyed the pair on the very rumpled bed interestedly, assessingly.

"The sun is up. Perhaps you should be also?" she said. "Unless the night was too ill for your rising? Yet I heard no call for my services."

Mary yawned and stretched, frankly. "I think that we have survived it," she gave back. "But – ask Thomas."

The man opened one eye. "Why the haste? Begone, Anna." He turned his back on his sister – and then his hand went out to touch and caress Mary's white shoulder. "Begone!"

The young woman beside him, becoming aware now of the signs, rose quickly and jumped out of bed, reaching for the fallen bed-robe to cover her nakedness. Smiling, she pointed to the bath.

"Some warm in last night's water will serve," she suggested. "For only I used it!"

"Ha! So that was the way of it!"

"Begone!" repeated her brother from the bed.

"Not so, my over-weary lord of Arran! So weak and worn! I am Her Highness's lady-in-waiting, and have Her Highness's care to consider, if you have not." She was carrying forward the steaming pail. "Perhaps you should not have wed a princess?"

Mary was quite glad of the other girl's attentions this morning, for she had not failed to note the gleam in the man's eye. "Thank you, Anna," she acknowledged "And, now that we are good-sisters, I think that we can forget the Highness, save in company."

"As you will, Mary." Anna busied herself with laying out the daytime clothing and carefully folding the wedding gown, while the other, discarding the bed-robe after all, washed herself all over, as carefully, but turning her back on the others. Anna came over with a towel.

From the bed Tom watched the two girls interestedly and a little ruefully, so obviously did they work together – and *his* interests would be apt to suffer.

When, the drying over, Anna was assisting with the dressing process, he made further protest.

"Off with you, girl! *I* do not require, nor relish, a lady-in-waiting."

"Wheesht, you!" his sister returned. "Your princess's hair has yet to be seen to." And she brought brush, comb and mirror.

"You can comb your own hair, Mary, can you not?" And then, with a jerked exclamation, he climbed out of bed. "Anna – go!"

Mary smiled. "Wives have their rights, as well as husbands," she observed.

At sight of her brother's state of aggressive nudity, Anna emitted a squeal of feigned shock, and made for the door, but scarcely in a hurry. She looked back, indeed, with a typical gurgle.

"Breakfast is here. You both need it, I swear!'

At the bath, Tom reached out to take Mary in his arms and to kiss her eagerly. "Lass, I thank you! I thank you, indeed. For last night. For your, your patience, your help, your forbearance. You were very kind."

"Was it indeed all those, Thomas? I but sought to . . . play my part, however unlearned."

"You did well. But – you did learn a little, no?"

"I think it, yes. I recognise that I received some . . . tutoring!" Very much aware of the male pressure against her middle, she disengaged herself. "Now, I will go and aid Anna with the meal."

"Save us, what is the haste? The least that you can do, surely, is to wash *me*, as I washed you last night."

Glancing down, she pushed him away. "I think not, my lord. Lest there be . . . problems. Enough tutoring for the moment!" And she fled.

Thereafter, breakfast, distinctly delayed, was interrupted by the arrival of the monarch. James came not so much to see how the newly-weds had survived the night as to enquire when they were going to Arran. It was usual for a bridal couple to seek to betake themselves off on their own for a few days, and they had

115

decided that, despite the time of the year, a visit to the new earldom would be suitable and useful. But James had declared that he wanted to come with them – and besides this being in the nature of a royal command, it would have been difficult to deny, since Arran, up till now, had been a crown property, part of the royal earldom of Menteith and Knapdale, which the Regent had persuaded the boy to alienate

Tom told him that there would be some matters to see to first, but that they would be going in a day or two. The first of March was St Marnock's Day. Would not that be an apt time to go, since he came from Kilmarnock? The King had no views on that, and his only other comment was that they were very late with their breakfast.

Mary was very much aware of the glances which came her way that day from the castle's inhabitants; however, she did not have to mingle greatly with the company there, and the Regent kept his distance. These two would never be friends. The younger royal children, less affected even than James by the wedding and its consequences, were clamouring for their favoured sport of hurly-hackit, of which they had been deprived these last few days inevitably, and which they were not allowed to engage in unattended, for safety's sake. Their elder brother supported them in this, so quite a proportion of the day following the so important event was spent hurtling down and climbing up, both breath-taking, the steep slope above the Ballengeich terrace of the fortress. The snow had gone, so the sleds were exchanged for the traditional ox-skulls with their curving horns, which actually made more manageable and manoeuvrable vehicles, if less comfortable to sit on. The snows had left the soil, such as there was, slippery, muddy, and many were the tumbles, upsets and rollings-down, an odd sport for royalty, with dignity at a minimum, clothing derangement normal – and female legs apt to be much in evidence, however muddied.

The new earl was good at it, but was glad enough when he could decently claim that he had many arrangements to make for their Arran expedition, and brought the entertainment to a close.

That night, Mary received further tutoring, and learned not a little, physically and mentally. Perhaps the latter was in fact the more important now, in that, once her mind and inner self were prepared to accept the physical side of it all, the satisfactions began to come of their own accord. Tom's care in the matter was evident and she appreciated it – although he clearly nowise lacked his own satisfaction, and at certain stages was less than gentle.

It did not make for undisturbed night's sleeping, however. Anna's kindly enquiries were variously received.

An improvement in the weather enabled the royal party to get out on horseback. One of the drawbacks of living in a rock-top fortress, however finely housed and comfortably furnished, was the sense of constriction, of being closely cooped up behind stone walls, trying for active folk and young people especially – hence the popularity of hurly-hackit. Being able to ride abroad, weather being kind, was a great relief. And Stirling's vicinity was even better than Edinburgh's, since the town was much smaller and open countryside more swiftly available. And there was great choice all around. To the south lay the great Tor Wood, next to Ettrick in the borderland the largest forested area of the Lowlands. East of that were the meanderings of the Forth, before it changed from river to firth, where the great victory of Bruce at Bannockburn had been won; here careful riding was required, because of the pools, bogs, ditches and marshland, but which made exciting territory to explore, if the tracks were held to, hunting country, with deer abounding and even wild boar quite frequently to be seen. Northwards, once across the ancient Stirling Bridge and mile-long causeway beyond, where William Wallace had gained *his* victory, all the foothills of the Ochil range were available, although the upper ground here was still snow-bound, the peaks dazzling in the sunlight. But it was westwards that there was most scope for them, for, over twenty miles stretched the vast flood-plain of the Forth known as the Great or Flanders Moss, a strange land unto itself – although land perhaps was not the most apt description – of some one hundred square miles, waterlogged miles, through which the river wound its way, spreading here and there into ponds and pools and even lochs, but more often mere swampland and brush, with islands of firmer ground, some quite large, all again swarming with deer, boar and wildfowl. James, hunting-mad, looked upon it all as next to heaven, and deplored that it was not now the hunting season. He knew it fairly well, of course, and was so eager to show Master Thomas his favoured areas that he almost would have put off the Arran trip until he had demonstrated all.

But, King or not, the Arran arrangements stood, and on the first day of March, a dull but not cold morning, the party of

117

four set out, with the necessary small escort. They would head for Kilmarnock again, for the first night, although the shorter sea crossing would be considerably further north; but Tom had his reasons.

The going was somewhat poorer than on the previous occasion, the melted snows having left the ground muddy and soft, with no real frosts as yet to firm it. But they were all good horsemen, and it was of course different territory to cover from the last time – indeed none of them had ridden from Stirling to Ayrshire. The most direct route would be south-westwards through the Gargunnock Hills and Campsie Fells to Glasgow, and thence on in the same direction. But with snow still lying fairly deep on the hills, it was decided that they would in fact be quicker to go by the more round-about way, by the Tor Wood to the Carron valley at Denny and then round the foot of the Kilsyth Hills, by Kirkintilloch, and so to Glasgow, some thirty miles. There would still be almost another thirty miles to Kilmarnock, but used to long riding as they had to be, Tom did not have to make a challenge of it. The escort, on somewhat less mettlesome steeds, probably did least well – but these Boyd retainers, carefully chosen, were not going to be outdone by women if they could help it.

They reached Glasgow, after an early start, by midday, and making use of the royal prerogative, called at the bishop's palace, beside the mighty cathedral-church of St Mungo, for sustenance. Bishop Durrisdeer was not in residence but the provost found them excellent provender, and would have provided more if they had not had to press on, to cover as much ground as possible before darkness reduced their pace. Tom remarked that the churchmen always knew how to look after themselves – as witness his uncle of Kilwinning.

They again had some high ground either to surmount or avoid, inevitably, this being Scotland, but this time there were no really major heights, so they took the direct road, having to climb after Rutherglen by the Mearns heights and the Earn Water, over to the Fenwick Water, Hamilton country this, and down eventually, with the dusk, to the low ground of the River Irvine, where they could just discern the white cone of Loudoun Hill away to the left. Weary, mud- and spume-spattered, they rode up to the Dean Castle gatehouse in the half-dark – and with the drawbridge up and portcullis down for the night, had some difficulty in gaining entrance to courtyard and keep.

That night, despite tiredness and saddle-ache, Thomas Boyd was somewhat more aggressive than heretofore. Perhaps it was being in his own house that did it. At least Mary considered this, and whilst not actually chiding him, suggested that no doubt in this chamber he had had so many other young women that he felt spurred on to make comparisons and to demonstrate his virility?

Perhaps that was *her* weariness of body speaking?

They rested for a day at Dean, for the Lord Boyd had given his son instructions to see to various neglected matters here. Moreover, the horses required and deserved remission. Mary and Anna had a women's day to themselves, for James elected to accompany Tom, king and new earl making a large impression on the vicinity.

The following morning, after a more leisurely night, they were off again, still south by west, ten miles to Ayr town. This was not the usual port of embarkation for Arran, too far south, but it was where the Boyds, quite mercantile nobles – indeed only ennobled for one generation before – kept their three merchant-vessels, for trading with Ireland, Cumbria, Man and even Wales, when the English were not at war with Scotland, and would not act pirate. These were larger craft than normally plied over to Arran, Bute and Cumbraes, from Irvine, Ardrossan, Largs and the like, but with the dozen of escort, the party had sixteen horses to transport and these were necessary.

The port of Ayr was quite large and thriving, and the monarch for one was much excited by it all, his first real experience of shipping and seafaring. Arran, although its white mountains looked large, indeed all but dominating the wide Firth of Clyde, might have been as far voyaging as to Orkney itself for young James Stewart.

Only one of the Boyd ships was in port, and busy loading tanned hides and salt from the local salt-pans. Its skipper was somewhat put out by the demand to halt this and put the travellers across the twenty miles of sea to the port of Lamlash in Arran. But the authority behind the requirement was undeniable and the grumbles muted, however much of a nuisance those horses represented for the crew.

It took a while to effect, but presently, sails hoisted, they

119

sailed out of the harbour and river mouth, to head north-westwards. This was not too difficult, for the wind was consistently south-westerly and only minimum tacking was required. No great seas running, as sometimes there could be in this firth, nobody was seasick.

Mary was interested in all that she saw; but also in what their reception was going to be like at Arran. She had not realised that the island was so mountainous, and wondered what sort of an earldom this would make, more apt for goats and deer than for themselves by the looks of it. Also how the islanders would react. It had been part of the royal lands, yes, the present Earl of Menteith, a distant cousin, forfeited and in England – or the place could not have come to Thomas. But she, at least, had never heard of any member of the royal family visiting Arran or even mentioning it. Presumably there would be a land steward. How would such see them? Tom expressed no least worry about that.

The crossing was uneventful if scarcely pleasurable, even though a fitful sun did appear and made their destination look the more dramatic with its great shadow-slashed snow peaks, wooded valleys and green but narrow coastal plain. It was a larger island, obviously, than Mary had realised, almost a score of miles long and perhaps half that in width, hilly throughout but the major mountains in the northern half, rising to mighty summits. The lower, southern end, which they approached from this angle, was cliff-girt, with rocks and skerries and little bays, more typical of the Hebrides. Tom named various landmarks, although he admitted that he had only been on the island once.

They were heading for Lamlash and its great bay, one-third of the way up the eastern side. This was the best landfall, for the bay was sheltered by a notable lesser island, providing a safe anchorage whatever the wind direction.

Well before they reached this haven, Tom pointed out, on the very southernmost clifftop, Kildonan Castle, a small, stark hold. There it was that King Robert the Bruce, their royal ancestor, one hundred and fifty years before, had awaited the fiery signal from the Ayrshire coast to bring him across by night to commence his seven-year desperate struggle to free his occupied kingdom from the English invaders, after his earlier defeat and almost exile. Yes, they would visit it one day. There would be much to see on this great isle.

Beating up the coast, the shipmaster having to deal with down-draughts from the hills so close, they came to Lamlash Bay; and Mary for one was surprised to discover that what had seemed to be just one more pointed hill, close to the shore, was in fact a mountainous offshore island, with the inner bay tucked in behind. This was Holy Isle, they were told, so called because there was a renowned and ancient monastery thereon, founded by Ranald of the Isles on the site of the hermitage of the famous St Molas, come from Columba's Iona. This they would visit also, in due course.

This Lamlash Bay itself was notable, having sheltered many a fleet in its time, but especially interesting as where that other Orkney overlord, King Haakon of Norway, had reassembled and rallied his host of galleys after his defeat by Alexander the Third in 1263 at the famous Battle of Largs. James was enthusiastic over this. Had other predecessors and ancestors of his been here, besides the Bruce and Alexander?

They landed at a sizeable jetty, backed by a long, straggling shoreside community, more than just a village, obviously occupied mainly by fisherfolk, with boats drawn up on the curving sandy beach and drying nets much in evidence. This was not the chiefest place on Arran, it seemed; Brodick, where there was a larger township, another port on a more exposed bay, and the main castle of the island, being three miles to the north. They would ride there forthwith, where they ought to find the steward of the lordship.

Bidding the shipmen farewell, and mounting, the party rode northwards, starting to climb almost at once. Obviously there would be much climbing on Arran. Their road turned away from the coast, which here swung out to a headland, the northern horn of the bay, and quickly rose between small hills, these notable in being dotted with many standing-stones, cairns and stone circles of their ancient Pictish ancestors, who evidently had found the island to their taste. Mary, interested in the Picts, or Albannach as she preferred to name them, said that she understood why St Molas had come here. They must come back and examine these Tom said that he understood that there were plenty of others the like, elsewhere.

That was true, for they saw others as they began the descent to what was obviously a major valley coming dow the western heights to enter another bay, this shallower ar open. Clearly there was a township where the glen opened to the sea; and up on the high ground beyond was a red stone castle, their immediate destination.

Clattering through the strung-out village, and raising surprised stares from the folk – clearly the islanders were unused to horsed parties, with ladies and men-at-arms – they mounted the steep slope beyond and came to Brodick Castle on its spur of hillside. There was no sign of watchful wariness here, the gates open and drawbridge down, and looking as though it was usually thus. They rode into the courtyard, Tom hallooing loudly.

Servants appeared, and then a young man of about Tom's own age came to the keep's door, most evidently astonished. He was carelessly clad but clearly no servitor.

"Ha, friend – is the steward here?" Tom called. "I am Thomas, Earl of Arran." He said that a little self-consciously, the first time that he had had to announce the fact. "And here is His Grace, the King. And the Princess Mary, my countess."

The other's eyes widened and his jaw dropped a little. "Eh . . . ? You . . . is it . . . ?" He recovered himself, as he took in the fine clothing, the splendid horse-harness and the two pennants bearing the royal and Boyd arms carried by men of the escort. "Yes. Yes, my lord. And, and Your Grace!" He contrived a bow of sorts. "I greet you. I, I will get my father. He is within." He turned to leave them there, then recollected suitable and respectful civilities. He waved to the staring servants. "Aid them down. His Grace. The ladies. The earl . . . and see to the horses . . ." Then he departed.

They dismounted, not waiting for help, Anna declaring that that young man deserved their pity – but was none so ill-looking.

Presently a stocky man of greying head and stern expression appeared, with the other behind him, to eye the visitors carefully before making brief obeisance.

"Is this true? That it is the King's Grace? And the new Earl of this Arran?" he demanded.

"Think you any would claim it if not true, man?" Tom asked im. "Are you steward here?"

"Yes, my lord. I am John Fullarton of Kilmichael, Coroner of an. I act steward also, and have done these many years."

ood. Then you will be able greatly to aid and guide us. But llartons are an Ayrshire house, surely? Of Dundonald?"

"A forebear of mine wed a daughter, a bastard daughter, of an Earl of Menteith, and was appointed Hereditary Coroner of Arran and also steward here." He looked the other up and down. "I have heard of your appointment, my lord." That sounded questioning, as though the man was wondering whether his position now was in doubt.

Tom nodded. "I shall need a steward, sir – if scarcely a coroner!" he said. "So, if it serves us both . . ." He left the rest unsaid. "Now, there are quarters for us, in this hold? Suitable for His Grace and his royal sister?"

"Quarters, yes. I can have them made ready, my lord. And Sire. Unused for long. But . . ."

"I understand. We shall not be over-particular, meantime, Fullarton. Will my men find quarters here? Or will they return to Brodick?"

The other counted the escort. "I say that they would do better downby," he decided. "And, my lord, Brodick is the name of this castle, see you. Invercloy is the name of the village and haven."

"Ah, I stand corrected, Master Coroner! You can feed us all here?"

"To be sure. We can find a sufficiency. Then my son here will take your people down to Invercloy and find them lodging. Come you, within, Sire, and my lord and ladies . . ."

Brodick Castle proved to be very like Dean, only somewhat smaller, very similar as all these fortalices were, as distinct from the great fortress-castles like Stirling, Edinburgh and Dumbarton. A vaulted basement contained the kitchen, dairy and storage cellars, a turnpike stair led up to the great hall and withdrawing-room on the first floor, and there were three storeys of bedchambers above, the last attics within a parapet and wall-walk. John Fullarton, they found, had a cheerful, bustling wife, who presumably had been listening somewhere in the background to the exchange at the door, for she seemed to know the position and seemed quite prepared to cope, bobbing curtsies, smiling and waving hands about. Mary and Anna declared that they would help if required, but she shushed them away. She had lassies to aid her, she assured, down in the castleton. She would have a meal prepared for them forthwith, even though much of it would be cold, with water heated for washing, and while they made use of these she would have their bedchamber readied. How many would they require? Themselves, they used only two, their son Patrick's and their own. There were six others above . . .

She was told that three would serve. And they would be happy to eat in the kitchen meantime.

No, no, the lady asserted. She was obviously much more forthcoming than was her husband, possibly something of a blether, but seemingly her wits and hands could be as busy as her tongue. The Fullartons themselves used the withdrawing-room to live in, she informed, so the hall was free for the visitors. She would have a fire lit there right away.

The newcomers decided that they were fortunate, after having arrived thus without warning. The young man Patrick took them upstairs to select their rooms while the meal was being put together. They found the castle only fairly basically furnished, but when girls appeared with armfuls of blankets and sheets, and men with baskets of logs for the fires, they perceived that they were going to be comfortable enough.

They sat down to a substantial meal of hot soup, cold venison, bread, oatcakes and honey, with home-brewed ale to wash it down, Patrick and his mother waiting on them assiduously, the former paying particular attention to Anna – who indeed more or less asked for it, by her glances and reactions. James, mouth full, announced that he liked Arran, Brodick and the Fullartons.

The hall, large and bare and draughty as it had seemed when first they arrived, looked much better with a great log-fire blazing and candles lit, and the travellers stretched themselves pleasantly in front of it, while Patrick took the escort down to Invercloy, where the River Cloy, in its glen, reached salt water, and the community was strung along the shore, as at Lamlash. Indeed, by the look of it, all the communities, of this side of the island at least, would be so placed, for there was seemingly little breadth of land between the mountainsides and the sea.

When Patrick came back, it was to announce that his mother would be bringing them hot drinks of her honey wine before bed, a speciality of hers. He was clearly a friendly young man, and Anna kept him talking. He was able to tell them something of what there was to be seen and considered on Arran, and they realised that he would make an excellent guide, such as they were undoubtedly going to require.

The honey wine proved to be potent stuff, despite its sweetness, and sent them off to their couches more heavy-eyed than they had already been. Fires in each bedroom welcomed them.

Sleepy or not, Tom Boyd was not going to waste a bedding, especially as their couch was somewhat smaller than that at Stirling, which made for closer proximity. Mary, without actually reaching any heights of excitement, was no way aggrieved, and sank to sleep thereafter almost as quickly as he did.

Tom had a consultation with the Fullartons, father and son, next morning, as to the state of the island, its extent, its revenues and how it was administered, Mary sitting in on this and asking her own questions, since this great property was in the nature of a dowry for herself. In time, James burst in, demanding when they were going to go see and do something? He wanted to climb those mountains, especially the pointed one.

Tom agreed that this would be something that they might do; but there was a lot of snow up there meantime, and it might be better to wait awhile. A survey of the island first would be best, he suggested, and since it had a seaboard of no less than eighty miles, they were told, that was going to take some time. John Fullarton proposed that, to get some notion of the place as a whole, they should take a ride westwards over the spine of the island, from the crest of which they would see much, and then down to the western coast, which was very different from this eastern side, more exposed to the winds but not the seas, because of the shelter of the long Kintyre peninsula; and it had much more low ground. Patrick would show them.

This programme was acclaimed. The question was, whether to take their escort with them? They scarcely required them here, indeed would be better without them; but they might get into mischief, idling down in the clachan. Fullarton reckoned that his islesmen and fisherfolk could well look after themselves.

So the five young people set off, in very much a holiday mood. They rode down to the village in the forenoon sunlight, to tell the Boyd men-at-arms that they were not required, but to behave themselves, and then turned westwards. They found that although the community was called Invercloy, it was actually at the junction of three glens, that of Cloy being the southernmost and largest. Glen Rosa, which probed up behind the castle, was the north one, but it was the central one, Glen Shurig, which they took, heading due westwards and starting to climb almost

125

at once, its burn cascading, its well-defined track the main access between the two sides of the island, and apparently called the String. Mary declared that this was obviously a Lowlander's corruption of their Gaelic ancestors' word *streap* or *streapadair*, which meant ladder or climb, to a pass. She knew of other similar names in the Highlands, usually called struie. Tom was impressed by his wife's erudition and interest in the past.

They saw plenty of signs of that distant past on their climb up Glen Shurig, Pictish burial-cairns, standing-stones and, right at the summit, a grass-grown fort with three layers of ramparts and ditches. Not that they spent much time on examining this, so stupendous was the view which here burst upon them. In every direction the prospect was breathtaking. Before them, the land sank into a widening valley, which itself opened on to a much wider coastal plain than on the eastern side, with the blue, firth-like Kilbrannan Sound beyond, six or seven miles wide, bounded by Kintyre, the longest peninsula in Scotland, almost seventy miles of it. This last was hilly, and so not to be seen over from here, save for a gap of lower ground to the south, across which they could glimpse the vast plain of the ocean, the Atlantic – and, according to Patrick, on a very clear day, the shadow which was Ireland itself. Stretching southwards from this summit was a great jumble of hills and valleys, leading the eye to the sea again, the mouth of the Firth of Clyde, with the Ayr and Galloway coasts and the isolated stack in the midst which James asserted was like the Bass Rock in Forth, and was told was the Craig of Ailsa. Northwards were the mighty ranked snow-peaks, starkly challenging in their proud aloofness.

All explanations, pointings and questionings, they proceeded down to what they were told was the Machrie Water, leading to Machrie Bay.

Pictish relics became even more numerous, circles, inscribed monoliths, cairns, tombs. When Patrick learned that Mary was especially interested in these, he told them that there were so many on this western side as to defy description. At Tormore, for instance, above Machrie Bay, there were actually eight stone circles, some with as many as a dozen monoliths still standing, all connected, of course, with sun-worship. He pointed to a prominent headland to the south-west, which he named Drumadoon, on the summit of which there was an enormous Pictish fort covering no fewer than twelve acres. And carvings and inscriptions everywhere. Tom admitted that he had never realised that the Picts, or Albannach, had been so numerous, so active, so concerned with setting up monuments, not just uncultured barbarians. Mary told him that he should be prouder of his Boyd Celtic heritage.

Down on the low ground, quite fertile here, with cultivated rigs and grazing cattle, they crossed from the Machrie to another river, the Black Water of Clauchan, on the bank of which they were shown another feature, a burial-ground made out of a stone circle, notable for a different kind of inscribed stone, with Christian symbols. This was the grave of St Molas, of the Holy Isle, who came from Columba's Iona to convert Arran's Picts, and lived allegedly to the age of one hundred and two. This monumental stone had been brought from Iona itself, as suitable token.

They rode on south-westwards for another couple of miles, to Drumadoon Point, and there ate the provender Patrick's mother had made for them, within the tiered ramparts of the huge fort above the foaming tides of the Kilbrannan Sound – this, they were informed, called after another of Columba's missionaries, St Brendan. Indeed, the folk of these parts called themselves Brandanes, after Brendan and this long arm of the sea.

Anna remarked that Arran seemed to be a very holy place, with so much sun-worship and saint-worship. Were they all as saintly today? And Patrick was a saint's name too, was it not? Even though a far-away Irish one!

The young man rose to that, pointing out that St Patrick was a good Scot, or at least a native of Strathclyde, born near Dumbarton in what were now called the Kilpatrick Hills, before ever he went to convert the heathen Irish. So Columba, coming over from Ireland a century or two later, was but repaying a debt. Did her ladyship object to saints? There were very muscular ones, he judged!

James, who found all this talk of Picts and saints something of a bore, wanted to know what the hunting was like on Arran, whether they went in for hawking, and whether Patrick had ever tried spearing fish, flounders? Thomas, for his part, was more concerned with having details of lands, properties and wealth-production pointed out to him. This western side seemed to be much more fertile, with not a few farms, holdings and grazings. Were their rents and dues properly assessed and collected? Patrick assured that this was so, his father looking after that, and making account to the crown commissioners – and now no doubt to his new lordship. This side of the island did produce more grain, beef and mutton; but the east had much better fishing, and of course trade with the mainland. There were a number of small lairdships on both sides, vassals of the earldom, his father's own Kilmichael one, Machrie here, Kilpatrick, Dougrie, Shiskine and others. All of their holders, no doubt, would come to pay respects to the new earl – and to His Grace of course – when they heard that they were here. There was, however, one property which would not send a representative – that of Lochranza, in the far north of the island. This was a strange situation.

Demands for the reason brought forth a significant story – with the young man glancing sidelong at the monarch and his sister. It seemed that His Grace's royal father, for some reason, had, some fifteen years before, granted Lochranza Castle and its estate to Alexander Lord Montgomerie, alienating it from the rest of the island lordship. He had no sure notion why, although there were tales. But all the rest of Arran's hundred thousand-odd acres remained with the crown, save these four hundred. And he pointed northwards, beyond the high peaks.

Mary at least guessed what had lain behind this, the same old sorry story. Fifteen years ago, 1452, was the same year of the bringing down of the Douglases. Lord Montgomerie had no doubt assisted at the grim murder of the Earl of Douglas at Stirling, by the King, her father, and fell to be rewarded or quietened, paid off. Thus was Scotland governed, on occasion. She did not say so, however.

Tom, for his part, was concerned. He would have to see his uncle about this – for it happened that Lord Montgomerie had married Tom's aunt. He had not known about this Lochranza. He could possibly exchange some other lands on the mainland for it. He could not have a ridiculous bite out of his earldom like that.

Their midday break over, Patrick led them southwards above the shoreline and into the hillier country again. This was little less rich in relics, and he pointed out a cashel at Kilpatrick Point, one of the early Christian monastic settlements of the converted Picts, long deserted but clear enough. And so onwards, down towards the southern tip of the island. Mary asked whether they were going to be able to visit that Kildonan Castle they had glimpsed from the ship, where the Bruce had waited for the signal to return to the mainland to start his long campaign; but was told that this would be too far for them to ride this day, if they were to get back to Brodick before dark. They would turn northwards soon now, to go up the Sliddery Water, and this would lead them through the central hills eventually to Lamlash Bay. Even so, that was a ten-mile traverse. Kildonan would have to wait.

There was somewhat less to see on this north-eastwards route, apparently known as the Ross Road, through a positive welter of hills, with the waterfalls of the Sliddery most of the way testifying to the steepness of the ascent. But even here there were Pictish remains. Arran, Mary declared, instead of being named after *aran*, the Gaelic for a kidney – which admittedly was almost exactly its shape – should have been called Eilean Albannach.

Much more aware of the size and character of Tom's earldom, they came down to Lamlash Bay again, with the dusk. Mary, commenting that it was a strange name, learned that it was really only another corruption, of Eilean Molas, the saint's isle. James tried that on his tongue, and wondered why there should have been two languages in Scotland. Explanations and examples kept them going all the way to Brodick.

They could well have reserved that discussion on place-names, Picts and Albannach, Scots and saints, until a later occasion, for there followed two days of continuous rain and winds gusty but warm, with outdoor pursuits contra-indicated, and the filling-in of time something of a problem, especially where James was concerned. Tom had much debate with John Fullarton over the island's profitability and where improvements could be made, having the local lairds over to meet him, and the like. Meg Fullarton did her best to make the accommodation more comfortable, as well as over-feeding them. Patrick was good company and consistently informative – as well as good at contriving to disappear with Anna on occasion. And Mary sought to curb her brother's impatience, and to instruct him, in so far as she was able, in his realm's long story. She had also to attempt a certain amount of impatience-curbing where Thomas was concerned, this of a different sort, especially in the evenings, when her husband saw little point in sitting by the hall fire when they might be more effectively employed elsewhere.

It was on the second evening, however, with the rain stopped at last and the skies clearing that, venturing outside for a breath of fresh air, they could hear a sort of distant roaring sound which none had noticed before. Patrick told them that this would be the Glenrosa Water in spate, that all the rivers would now be in flood, but the Rosa more especially so, since it drained the high mountains to the north, where the snows would have been melting fast. This of course had James agog. Would the snow indeed be gone? Could they go climbing? Patrick was a little doubtful, but if they went up to the summit of a nearby hillock they would be able to see the great peaks. By royal command, they marched over the wet terrain to ascertain – and sure enough, only small patches of snow were left on the high tops ahead. That was it, then, James declared; they would go climbing on the morrow. Patrick warned that the ground would be very wet and slippery, but such feeble attitudes were brushed aside by their sovereign-lord. They would go.

In the morning, the question of suitable clothing and footwear for the girls inevitably came up, and James was for declaring their attendance as unnecessary anyway. But Mary, and to a lesser extent Anna, was not to be thus discarded. Heavy riding-habits and long, high boots were out of the question for climbing, and their house-shoes quite inadequate. It was Meg Fullarton who provided an answer, even though she seemed to think that high-born ladies should not contemplate such activities. Nevertheless, as a girl she herself had gone climbing on rocky hills on occasion, and had found the common rawhide brogans apt enough for the exercise. Some of the castleton lassies would have such footwear, to be sure; and since they were tied on with lacing, they could be made to fit well enough. She herself could lend them rough and shortish homespun skirts, which would serve – if the ladies were prepared to wear them? So the two girls went down to the castleton cottages and had no difficulty in borrowing brogans which, by their lacing design, could fit almost any woman's foot.

Thus equipped, the six of them mounted – for they were taking one of the men-at-arms to take care of the horses – and rode over to Glen Rosa. The lower glen was pleasantly wooded. They crossed the still-swollen river by a ford near some standing-stones, the water almost up to their horses' bellies, the track being on the west side. Soon the valley began to narrow in to what was practically a deep gorge, with the mountains growing ever steeper and taller on either side, so much so that the narrowed sky seemed able to let in but little light. Soon there was only scanty room for the track beside the drumly water; indeed, from the debris, it was evident that this would have been impassable the day before. Some three miles up from the ford they passed a sizeable waterfall, its thunder all but shaking the gorge.

The glen was in fact remarkably straight and, Patrick said, probed for over five miles directly into the heart of the mountains, as though making for the pointed peak which was James's chosen objective. This apparently was named Cir Mhor, the great crest or coxcomb; and although it was not the highest, Goat Fell, nearer on the right, being this, it was certainly the most scenic and dramatic. Actually it was possibly the most easy of access too, since this Rosa's headstream rose right up on its east flank, in almost a straight line, all they had to do was to follow the waterside up. What the going of the upper reaches would be like remained to be seen, and would determine how far they could get the horses. Thereafter, it would be just steep climbing, for about five hundred feet, and by curving round a little it ought to be possible to avoid scaling the summit cliffs. If they had been climbing Goat Fell, or almost any other of the peaks, they would not have been able to get the horses nearly so far.

The river forked some four miles up from the ford, and the track deteriorated with its branching. They took the central burn, and could now see it running almost directly ahead of them, right up into a corrie scooped in the side of the pyramidical peak, an exciting prospect. How far would they get the horses?

The melt-water had left very soft and muddy ground, over which their mounts had to pick their way carefully. But the higher and steeper they went, the more firm was the surface, this because it had been washed down almost to the grey granite bedrock. It was scarcely ideal terrain for horses' hooves, but it made possible riding, and they in fact got their beasts almost another mile up before it would have been dangerous to go further.

Dismounting, they left the animals in the care of their groom, and started to climb.

After a reasonably moderate start, it became quickly steeper, so that soon hands as well as feet were brought into action. The girls found their borrowed brogans were very effective, indeed more so than the men's boots, since they were softer of sole and this allowed the toes to play their part. When James found his sister actually ahead of him in the climb he was distinctly put out, and Mary began deliberately to hold back. The two young men, perceiving the situation, also restrained themselves, for this was to be the monarch's day. Patrick found much opportunity to assist Anna, who laboured rather more than did her mistress, being shorter in the leg and plumper about the middle.

Nevertheless, soon Mary was panting, as indeed were they all – only the girls' physique made this the more apparent. James seemed to require, or at least take, fewer rests than did the others now, which allowed him to get satisfactorily ahead. They were getting into patches of snow and ice, very slippery.

There were cliffs around the summit, and the boy was for scaling these also, but Mary insisted that this was highly dangerous and to be avoided. He grumbled about feeble females, but allowed himself to be diverted round to the right, where there was a gap in the cliffs with a steep crevasse between. Normally this would be scree-filled, loose small stones, but it had filled likewise with snow, which at this height had not all melted away. So the scree was covered with semi-frozen snow, into which they had to dig their toes to gain footholds. Now the men's boots proved a deal more effective than the girls' brogans, and much assistance and hoisting ensued, amidst gasps, slippings and clutchings.

Eventually this was surmounted however, and now there was only the final pinnacle, largely bare and broken rock, demanding more clambering. James was, of course, first on the top, shouting and gesticulating his satisfaction, pointing at all the peaks around, monarch indeed of all that he surveyed. And it was, by any standards, a tremendous prospect, a world apart, of aloof crests and crags and ridges, rearing above deep, shadow-filled troughs and valleys, tier upon tier, daunting in its so utterly impersonal-seeming preoccupation with only space and sky.

But almost equally daunting was the cold wind up there, and they did not linger. It had taken them less time than anticipated, and James was eager for more, to go on and climb other mountains now that they were here. His companions were less keen, and it was pointed out to him that getting back to their horses from other peaks might well be very difficult, with all these gorges and cliffs. Patrick, as a compromise, suggested that they might make a traverse of the mighty ridge which stretched southwards from this summit for well over a mile, a lofty, narrow, roof-like feature flanked by tremendous precipices on both sides of a very narrow spine. It was called A' Chir, from the same derivation of Cir Mhor, and merely meant the comb, rather than the coxcomb; and certainly the serrated escarpment could be said to resemble a great comb.

Mary was a little concerned for her impetuous brother as they proceeded along that dizzy ridge, so narrow, with awesome drops on either side, a fall down which could result only in death; and by pretending that it was for her own safety, she clung to him. The knowledge that they had to retrace their steps along this, for there was no other way down, save by climbing another great mountain ahead, did not help. But the sights and vistas were so enthralling, breathtaking, that it was probably worth all the dreads, however thankful the girls were when at last they won back to Cir Mhor.

There was still the descent to the horses, a slipping, sliding progress with much disarray of Meg Fullarton's skirts, short as these were, in consequent hilarity.

They returned to Brodick well pleased with themselves, despite a certain amount of minor bruising. Some limbs might be a little stiff on the morrow.

The morrow saw them heading northwards again, but this time along the coastline, and mounted all the way. Thomas wanted to see this Lochranza Castle, which he looked upon as filched from his earldom, and to be regained if possible. The road thereto clung to the shoreside's low cliffs mile after mile, passing the small, isolated community of Corrie, and at length, after six or seven miles, at Sannox Bay, swinging inland up Glen Sannox. As well that it did, they perceived, for the coast directly ahead now looked grim indeed, all broken precipices and great rocks, with foaming reefs below, which Patrick declared extended all the way to the very northern tip of the island, known as the Cock of Arran, a headland of fierce challenge, like a fist shaken in the face of all the Highland west.

This Glen Sannox, probing westwards, was itself long and rather featureless, rising after about three miles to quite a high pass, with a drop thereafter, another three, to a sea-loch which they could see gleaming ahead. That was Loch Ranza, a remote and difficult place to reach indeed. Tom wondered why anyone had ever built a castle here; and Patrick said that it had been a hunting-seat for the Menteith earls, on the site of a more ancient fort no doubt so placed to protect the north of the island from Viking and other invaders. Mary suggested that it was hardly worth Tom approaching Lord Montgomerie about.

However, when they reached sea-level and found a small scattered community, with the fortalice sitting on a spit of land jutting into the loch, they perceived it to be a more attractive place than they had assumed, however isolated. The castle itself they found to be all shut up, and looking as though it had been that way for long. It evidently did not have a resident keeper; but Patrick took them to a rather larger house amongst the cottages of the castleton, where an elderly man greeted them respectfully enough, and on learning that he was in the King's presence, hastily escorted them down to the castle, with the keys, they being followed by a small crowd of staring folk to whom strangers were obviously a source of excitement. Their guide admitted that he had not seen Lord Montgomerie there for three years. He was getting old for stalking the stags perhaps; and that was Lochranza's principal attraction apparently. When he did come, it was by boat from Ayrshire, north-abouts. There was a jetty near the mouth of the loch.

The visitors explored the quite large castle, with its tall square tower and L-plan, and found it sparsely furnished and chilly, but with its own interests and possibilities. All agreed that it could be made into quite a comfortable house. James had pricked up his ears at the mention of stags and hunting, and had to have it explained to him that this mountain terrain, although good for the deer, meant that they had to be *stalked*, not hunted on horseback as he was used to doing. Stalking had to be done on foot, or even on bellies, by individuals, not parties, armed with cross-bows, to get close enough to the wary deer to be within arrow-shot, a very different proceeding from horsed huntsmen with hounds chasing the game. They *could* be killed in deer-drives, but this took much organising, many men and massed marksmen, not easily achieved in a place like this. The monarch's interest waned.

Thomas wanted to see the extent of this Lochranza property and its possibilities, so they did not return as they had come but continued on round the coast westwards and then southwards, with the mountains rising close on their left. One brief gap in that mighty wall Patrick called Glen Catacol, and then the hills closed in again and they were pressed almost to the shore, mile after mile. The new Earl of Arran recognised that this northern half of his territory was a deal less valuable than the rest, however fine its scenery. But he was still determined not to let it belong to someone else if he could help it, even an uncle.

Eventually they won back to the more populous and fertile areas of Dougrie and Machrie Bay, and thereafter returned across the String Road to Brodick, after a total of some thirty miles' riding.

That evening, Tom declared that they could not stay on Arran for very much longer. His father had made it clear that a week or so away would be the limit, not so much on account of his own, or Mary's, absence, but because the King was needed in fairly constant attendance with the Regent, in order to sign documents and give royal assent to edicts, charters and other measures of government. Actually Lord Boyd had been loth to let James go with them at all, but the boy had been insistent. Now Mary said that she hoped that they would not leave the island without making the visit to Kildonan Castle at the southern end, which meant more than all the rest in Scotland's story. Tom promised that they would go the next day. Meanwhile he would get Fullarton to send one of the Invercloy fishing boats over to Ayr, to have their ship come for them two days hence.

Windy again, and threatening rain, they rode south next morning, by Lamlash once more, and another great but shallower and unprotected bay beyond called Kiscadale, to the very southern coast, different again from all the rest, all cliffs and reefs and skerries, with offshore islets, one of these quite large, apparently called Pladda, where Patrick said another saint had had his hermitage or diseart, St Blaize. With Kildonan itself called after one more, St Donnan of Eigg, Anna remarked that the Arran folk must have been especially wicked – and possibly still were – to have acquired so many missionaries sent by Iona to save their souls!

Past the impressive Dippin Head they came to Kildonan Castle on its clifftop site beside one more stone circle – no doubt why it was there, for the Celtic saints, following Columba's own example, were apt to use these sun-worship circles as sites for their own cells or little churches, continuing the theme of worship but making it Christian to replace the unknown god represented by the sun; and the castle had been built nearby by the Lords of the Isles. It proved to be abandoned now, indeed part ruinous. But the visitors explored it interestedly, trying to decide out of which east-facing window the great Bruce had watched for the fire on the Ayrshire coast fifteen miles away, in 1307, with arguments about who would be with the King at that time.

The rain developing and looking as though it would continue, they proceeded no further along the south-coast cliffs but turned back for Brodick. It was on the way there that Anna came out with her proposal – which no doubt she had been hatching in her mind these last days. Why not take the good and useful Patrick Fullarton back with them tomorrow, to Dean and Stirling? If he would come? As an earl, Tom should have at least one attendant always available. And they got on very well together, did they not?

Her brother, eyeing them both, grinned. *He* would be glad of Patrick's company, yes. Perhaps that fine fellow would not want to leave Arran, however, and his father's house? He had a full life here, did he not?

By the speed with which the other young man answered this it was fairly evident that the suggestion had not come as a complete surprise to him. He promptly asserted that he would be glad to join his lordship's household in whatever capacity, and would be honoured to be so appointed.

Mary caught Anna's eye and wagged her head, but not censoriously. James obviously approved, and said that he would teach Patrick how to fly hawks, spear flounders and joust at tourneys. It was all as easy as that.

So the next day, when they took leave of the senior Fullartons, it was to relieve them of their son's presence meantime. If the parents were displeased they did not show it; John Fullarton was not one for showing his feelings anyway, and his wife was proud that her son should be thus raised in stature and move into the royal household.

When the ship, in due course, was reported as having entered Lamlash Bay, the party collected their men-at-arms, useless as these had been – and who seemed quite reluctant to leave Invercloy, getting their own appreciative send-off from the villagers, especially the womenfolk – and rode off southwards to embark, promising that they would be back. Oh yes, they would be back.

All sailed for Ayr well pleased with the Arran situation.

10

Tom and Mary found themselves in a rather strange situation when they returned to Stirling. The King's presence was necessary – but theirs seemingly was not. Lord Boyd was ruling Scotland almost single-handed, although of course he had the advice of such as Avondale the Chancellor, Somerville, Livingstone, Hailes, Bishop Graham and other lords temporal and spiritual. But basically he was a loner, and kept all the reins of power in his own hands, a strange man. He seemed to have little need for his son. And yet it was that son whom he had elevated to the rank of earl, married to the King's sister, and endowed with vast lands, while he remained only the Lord Boyd. It was as though he intended the House of Boyd to be amongst the most illustrious in the land hereafter, but he himself was quite content with *power*, as Regent. After all, he could equally well have had himself appointed an earl, and taken over all these properties, for he could get James to sign anything. But that did not seem to be his way. The future might be his son's; the present was his alone.

So Tom and his wife found themselves in little demand at Stirling, save for occasions when a show was to be made, banquets for ambassadors, visiting papal representatives, feast-days and the like. They were neither of them of the sort who could appreciate inaction, a lazy acceptance of life or continual pleasure-seeking. Hurly-hackit, hawking, hunting in season, and exploring the countryside were all very well, but such an existence palled, especially for Thomas. So, fairly soon after their return, they set off again on a series of visits of inspection to the other properties which his curious father had incorporated in the earldom – and these were many indeed, former crown lands, the estates of forfeited families such as Douglas, Dunbar, Menteith and the like. In Ayrshire alone there were Dalry, Noddsdale, West Kilbride, Monfodd, Stewarton, Terrinzean, Turnberry and Rosedalemuir. There was another offshore island, smaller than

Arran, called Meikle Cumbrae, in Buteshire. There was Nairston in Lanarkshire, Caverton in Roxburghshire, Teiling in Angus and Polgay in Perthshire. All these fell to be visited sometime, and with nothing else apparently required of him, Thomas might as well see to it now. They represented much wealth, undoubtedly. Anna and Patrick, now a firm friend of them all, accompanied them, and sometimes but not always James – for on the longer trips, it was the Regent's preference that the King was not far from his side for more than a few days; and when James was with them, an armed escort was obligatory, just in case some other ambitious lord or group thought to copy the Boyd example and stage an abduction.

So passed the spring and early summer, with much travelling and seeing places new, interesting enough usually but scarcely satisfying the Earl and Countess of Arran.

On their return to Stirling from a visit to the former Douglas property of Caverton in the borderland, they discovered that the two earls, Crawford and Argyll, had at last returned from their prolonged survey of the princesses of Christendom seeking a possible bride for King James. They had been thorough enough in their search, it seemed, but were not too happy with their findings. They had been to France, Spain, Flanders, Burgundy, Savoy and, of course, England. Young women they had seen and inspected, tactfully of course, but without conviction that they had found the right one for James Stewart – or at least for his realm. After all, the boy was still only fifteen, which meant that the suitable age bracket was very restricted. Someone even three or four years older would scarcely be apt, and bairns younger than, say, twelve likewise. And it so happened that there was a dearth of available princesses within the twelve-to-seventeen age group just then. They did bring back the names of one or two possibles, but these were of ducal rather than royal rank, and probably a little below the standard felt suitable for the King of Scots, on the most ancient throne in Christendom.

And the English situation, which might have been best in the national interest, was still complicated by the Yorkist and Lancastrian dichotomy, two men calling themselves King of England, and the outcome by no means certain, although Lancaster was supreme at the moment. It would be unwise to plunge for a daughter of either house until the position was assured.

138

A council was held to consider the earls' reports. Also to decide upon another matter. King Christian of Norway had sent another envoy, none other than the now-freed Bishop of Orkney, William Tulloch, to demand the payment of the Orkney Annual, as it was called – although annual was scarcely an apt term for the rental to Scotland of the Northern Isles, since no payment had in fact been made for over twenty years, and the arrears now amounted to an astronomical figure. The bishop, on release by St Clair, had apparently gone to Norway and Denmark to complain, and to ask for financial help for his ill-used see from his Metropolitan, the Archbishop of Nidaros at Trondheim. And now he had been sent back by King Christian, to Scotland, with this demand for payment of the Annual and at least some of the arrears. It seemed that Christian, never rich in moneys, was himself in dire financial straits, owing to the heavy costs of bringing the rebellious Swedes under his control.

At this demand, the Council was in fact more concerned than in finding a wife for young James. Thomas, who as an earl now automatically sat on the Privy Council, was discussing all this with Mary that evening, declaring that it was a pity that they had ever got the wretched Bishop Tulloch released, to cause all this trouble. But the young woman looked thoughtful.

"Perhaps the good bishop is doing us none so ill a service?" she suggested. "Good might come of this. If we Scots were to use our wits."

"What do you mean?"

"I mean that your Privy Council might solve both of its problems. See you, King Christian of Denmark – or Norway, I never know which he should be called – has a daughter, I am told. Young. He might like it well to have her a Queen."

"Marry *her* to James?"

"Would she not be as good as any?"

"She would bring no fine dowry, that one, such as is always looked for. Christian is always short of moneys. Always has been – why he wants this Annual from Scotland so keenly. *His* treasury is as empty as is ours. He has to keep a large army always in Sweden, to put down rebellion. The Swedes and Goths want independence . . ."

"I know all that. It is why I say this. Send him a token payment only. Not all the arrears, but this year's Annual. *Take* it, rather than send it. And see this daughter, Margaret. I think that she is of twelve years, perhaps thirteen. If she seems suitable, propose possible marriage with James. And her dowry – the Orkney and Shetland Isles!"

"Lord!" He stared at her. "Save us – why, oh why, did I not think of that? The Northern Isles. To become part of *this* realm, not Norway's. Here is a wonder, yes. What a head you have on that lovely neck, lass! *You* should be James's regent, I swear! But – would Christian agree, think you?"

"Offer a treaty of mutual support also. That would tempt him. And could help Scotland too, on occasion. But not against the Swedes, or we could be called upon over often. If the English, these Lancastrians, become too powerful, they may come to assail Scotland again, as they have done in the past. We have been spared that for some time. Then the Norse, with their great fleets, could be useful allies."

"Ye-e-es. That too. Here is notable thinking. Why has it been left to a young woman to think of it?"

"Women are none so lacking in wits as often men assume! And we so often have more time left us to think! But this cost no great cudgelling of brains. It is but dealing, trading. What each has and each wants. You Boyds were traders once, were you not?"

"Aye. I will put this to my father. There is one matter that may halt him, I think. The Annual. You say make one payment, for the Northern Isles. This realm's treasury is almost as empty as is Christian's, I fear."

"The realm's perhaps. But what of others? The Boyds'? Yours, my good Earl of Arran? Other lords'? All these fine lands you have acquired, with your wife! Their wealth. Surely the Scots lords could dip their hands a little way into their coffers, for once? Loans to the treasury? To pay the Annual. How much is it?"

"Thirty thousand silver florins, I think."

"Is that beyond this Scotland? What of Holy Church? The Church is rich. And the merchants, the trade guilds. This is to gain a bride for their sovereign-lord. And win the Northern Isles."

Tom rubbed his chin. "We shall see. *I* would give something, yes. As a loan . . ."

Next day he took the suggestion to his father. Lord Boyd, as anticipated, saw the virtues and possibilities of the project, but jibbed at the provision of money, private moneys. It was unheard of for individual lords, or others, to pay for state requirements out of their private pockets. He would consult others, but . . . He was not paying siller out of the Boyd revenues!

Tom said that he would be willing to make a contribution. Say of three thousand florins.

His father forbade it flatly. Then it would be expected of himself. That was not the way.

But the planted seed did bear a harvest of sorts, for a day or two later the Regent announced that, having discussed the matter with others, he had decided that the general conception was a good one – the Norse match, the Orkney and Shetlands bride-payment, and the rest. As to the Annual, whilst none were agreeable to paying it from their own pockets, it was agreed that the one-year sum should be found. Since the treasury was in no state to produce thirty thousand florins, the suggestion was to make parliament responsible for it, the Three Estates each to raise ten thousand, barons, Church and burghs. This would, of course, entail calling a convention of the said Estates – and that required forty days' notice. That would take them into October; and allowing for time for the moneys to be found, after that was no time for long sea voyaging. So an embassage to Norway would have to wait until the spring. But meantime, they could send an envoy, probably this Bishop Tulloch, to Christian, informing him of what was proposed, to prepare him and keep him quiet until then. If he refused it all, at least they would be spared the raising of the moneys . . .

Told of this, Mary declared that for men of sufficient drive and initiative to abduct a King and his sister and take over the rule of a realm, the Boyds were remarkably feeble where money was concerned. Could taxation not take care of the matter, if private coffers were too closely guarded?

Tom explained that tax-gathering was a perquisite of the lords and sheriffs of counties, as commissioners – and the very word indicated that their commission was an important part of it, part of their own revenues. Why, indeed, the treasury was so empty! Besides, any increase in taxation would require the assent of parliament.

The young woman shook her head over all this folly. But she had other matters than state affairs to preoccupy her just then – for she was fairly sure that she was pregnant.

This news set Tom Boyd in a stir indeed. It seemed never to have occurred to him that this might be the result of all their love-making – not so soon, at least. But he was greatly pleased nevertheless, indeed evidently proud of himself, a begetter of offspring. And promptly he began to treat his wife as though she was a tender plant, to be protected from every wind that blew, fussing over her, concerned for her every comfort and care, and enquiring daily for her state. Mary assured him that she was no fragile flower, that this was indeed a woman's fulfilment, not some dire hazard; besides, if she calculated aright, the birth would not be until Yuletide. Meantime, she was perfectly able to lead a normal active life.

Reassured, Thomas declared that they would call his name James, after the King. Not Grizel, she asked? She had always liked that name!

So the late summer passed into autumn, the hunting season much preoccupying James at least, so that the royal group spent much of their time mounted, in the Flanders Moss, the Tor Wood or on the skirts of the Highland mountains. There was talk of making a return to Arran, for a spell, and sampling its sport, but this came to nothing, Tom worried about sea-sickness and waves upsetting his wife. They did however make the short crossing to visit the island of Meikle Cumbrae, and found it attractive and interesting, with more ancient Pictish relics – not unnaturally, since its name, originally Cymri-ay, meant the isle of the Cymric or Welsh-speaking Celts. Four miles long and half that in width, it was like Arran in miniature.

Then, in October, the necessary parliament was held, at Stirling, a brief affair, little more than a formality intended, which, with those in power making their wills very evident, duly accepted the proposal of a Norse match for the King, and acclaimed the notion of the Northern Isles as dower. The raising of the Annual was a deal less popular, but when the Primate, Bishop Graham of St Andrews, led the way by promising ten thousand florins from Holy Church, and the burgh representatives, after consultation, agreed to find the same, the lords and barons could scarcely refuse. So the thing was passed. The Three Estates would find the Annual by Yuletide, and have it available for the embassage to take to King Christian thereafter, when sailing conditions permitted.

Mary, her condition not yet very apparent, sat in the great hall gallery listening, and smiled a little. No hint was given in the proceedings that the entire project was of *her* devising.

Under other business however, there was an unlooked-for development. Bishop Graham, without actually saying so, made it evident that he looked for reward for leading the way over the Annual contribution. He, like his predecessors before him, was much concerned over the grave matter of Scotland's non-Metropolitan status in Holy Church. It was an offence, a stone-for-stumbling and a constant danger, the English in especial always using it as an excuse for their claims to paramountcy over the northern kingdom. They claimed that the Archbishop of York was the most northerly Metropolitan and therefore the Church in Scotland was subject to himself; whilst the Archbishop of Nidaros, or Trondheim, asserted that *he* was more northerly still, and that he was Metropolitan over Scotland's Church. This folly should be ended, and the Scottish Primate, himself, raised to the status of Metropolitan, the see of St Andrews made an archbishopric. He perceived the present traffic with Norway as opportunity to effect this. It would require papal agreement and authority, of course, but that might not be too difficult to obtain, if the Norse archbishop accepted. Perhaps some inducements might be offered? If Norway was losing the bishopric of Orkney anyway, some arrangement might be come to. York would never agree, to be sure, but Nidaros might.

Was all this any concern of this parliament? the Chancellor asked. Was it not merely a matter for the churchmen?

The Primate thought that it *was* the realm's concern, since the English ever used their claim to spiritual hegemony to back their claim of regal suzerainty. But no more moneys would be required from the parliament; that at least was the Church's responsibility.

Relieved, the non-clerical members concurred. Bishop Graham declared that, in the circumstances, it might be best for himself to join the prospective embassage to Norway in the spring, to negotiate with the archbishop there.

One final matter was raised by the Earl of Crawford. Suppose that the embassage to Norway and Denmark was to be unsuccessful? King Christian might not agree to the proposed match. The princess might prove unsuitable – as had others they had considered in their travels. The Norse might not agree to the Northern Isles as bride's portion. Or they might demand full payment of all arrears of the Annual – for these the envoys would have to require to be remitted. In such case, the negotiations would fail. Should not the envoys therefore be given instructions and authority to proceed further in search of a royal bride?

This was agreed – although just where the said envoys should further go was not specified or obvious, since Crawford and Argyll had already covered most of the possibilities.

That completed the business, and parliament adjourned.

Mary could not but find the next two months somewhat wearisome, as her condition imposed increasing restrictions. However, she was interested, intrigued in her state and in what was growing within her, the development of her body, the changes in its functions. She even began to feel an identification and affection for the creature which stirred and kicked within her, and duly reported progress to her husband. Thomas, for his part, continued to be almost too considerate, the proud begetter of James Boyd, Master of Arran – as he was wholly convinced was the situation. Mary gave up warning him that it might be a girl.

So the monarch had to do without his sister's company at hurly-hackit, hunting and hawking, and often his Master Thomas also. Even Anna felt that her place was at Mary's side most of the time, although she was told otherwise. So it came about that Patrick Fullarton became James's most constant companion, a strange development for the young islander of no very lofty parentage. The armed escort, of course, was never far away.

It was on Hogmanay, the last day of the year, that Mary went into labour, and there was question whether the new Boyd was going to be born in 1467 or 1468. In the end it was the latter, after a delayed and taxing travail, that birth was achieved, and James, Master of Arran did indeed appear. Happily he was a perfectly normal child, and with excellent lungs – which he soon made apparent – and Stirling Castle was set to rejoicing, bonfires were lit and the New Year celebrated even more enthusiastically than usual. Lord Boyd himself unbent sufficiently actually to commend his daughter-in-law, and assess his grandson held in Anna's arms.

Mary smiled tiredly, and slept.

11

For Mary the months that followed were a joy, the infant preoccupying her as nothing before had ever done, a wonder and a delight, a gurgling and uncomplicated little creature of wide blue eyes, quite a lot of fair hair, dimpled fists, spreading fingers and toes, and dribbles, much dribbling. He got a lot of attention – indeed, Tom became quite jealous, complaining of neglect.

They decided to refer to him as Jamie, which meant that Mary had to stop calling her brother that; anyway, the monarchical dignity was now beginning to make the childhood name unsuitable. The King too found his little namesake something of an intrusion, depriving him of his sister's company, since *he* did not want to be always playing second to the moist brat. Anna also became a devotee of her nephew and consequently was less available for expeditions and sport – which had its own effect on Patrick Fullarton. Such was the impact of the new Master of Arran.

As it happened, the Lord Boyd it was who helped to make the royal objections of less consequence, even though not deliberately. For some time he had been indicating, as the King's guardian, that James had been spending overmuch time on outdoor pursuits and neglecting studies suitable for a young monarch. He had had his tutors at Stirling, before the abduction from Linlithgow, and was reasonably well educated and well read; but these had been dismissed. Now the Regent, who hardly approved of Patrick as royal esquire, produced another young man, another Boyd indeed, named John, or Father John, recently entered into holy orders, actually a nephew in blood of his own, an illegitimate son of the Abbot of Kilwinning, of a studious and intellectual frame of mind, indeed erudite and artistic. Fortunately he was also of an equable and friendly nature and James rather took to Father John. So that winter and spring he passed more time in mental rather than physical activity, although Tom and Patrick did frequently go hunting with him.

Tom himself had preoccupations to share with his father and the rest of the ruling group, other than preparations for the Norse venture – which looked like being somewhat delayed owing to the slow accumulation of those thirty thousand florins. This was because of trouble in the north, and worrying. Admittedly clan feuds and internecine fighting were endemic in the Highlands and Islands, and did not normally greatly concern the rest of Scotland. But this outbreak was different. It was the Lord of the Isles again, and his behaviour outrageous.

John MacDonald, Lord of the Isles and former Earl of Ross, had always been a wild and uncontrollable character – and possessed, of course, of vast manpower and a great fleet of galleys, the greyhounds of the sea; and with royal blood in his veins. As a young man he had been ambitious indeed, actually entering into a private treaty with the English Yorkist Edward the Fourth, whereby he would aid Edward to conquer Scotland and thereafter he would have all north of Forth and Clyde to rule as independent prince, this he considering himself to be already. Fortunately the Wars of the Roses had intervened and the House of York had come down, so that Mary's father had been able to subdue the Islesman in some measure, although not having large fleets at his disposal, had not been able to take over the Hebridean seaboard and isles. He could and did deprive John MacDonald of the Ross earldom but the Lordship of the Isles was different, a hereditary style and title, not a lordship of parliament, and this remained with the awkward John. He had since lain quiet, as least as far as the rest of the kingdom was concerned, although he made his presence felt all over the Highland west and over into Ireland. But now, he had, for reasons unknown, suddenly led an expedition of armed Islesmen far from his own fastnesses and down into Atholl, there to storm and take Blair Castle, capture the Earl and Countess of Atholl and take them off prisoner to his island of Islay.

This extraordinary assault could not be ignored by the crown authorities, not only because Atholl, in Perthshire, was only seventy miles as the crow flew north of Stirling, but because John Stewart, Earl of Atholl, was in fact closely linked with the ruling house, his mother having been Joan Beaufort, widow of James the First, who had married the famous Black Knight of Lorn after the King died.

Yet, what was to be done? The realm had no fleets of galleys, and without such the Western Isles were safe from any Lowland attack – always one of Scotland's great weaknesses. So they could by no means hope to overcome John MacDonald by force and thus rescue Atholl and his wife. If anything was to be achieved it would have to be by negotiation or guile. But what had they to offer the Islesman? To give him back his earldom of Ross, now merged in the crown, would be to ask for further trouble. What else?

It was Mary again, with wits presumably inherited from the longest line of kings in Christendom, who suggested the answer to that, to Tom. The small but ancient kingdom of Man? It had long, in theory, been part of the realm of Scotland, ceded by Norway in 1266; but situated where it was, not far off the Lancashire coast, and nearer Wales and Ireland than Scotland, without the required fleets and shipping to maintain the connection, the island kingdom had been more or less abandoned to its fate. Invaded sometimes by the Irish, the Norse pirates, sometimes by the English, it had suffered under a variety of overlords, and was at present held by an English lord named Stanley, who called himself King thereof. But it was still Scots territory by treaty. If John of the Isles was given charter of it to add to his lordship, he might well jump at it, even if *he* thereafter called himself King of Man. After all, his great ancestor, Somerled, the first lord, had conquered Man once. And its transference would not damage the Scots realm.

This suggestion, for want of any other, commended itself to the Boyds. Mary was not so pleased, however, when it transpired that it was the Earl of Arran whom the King, or at least his Regent, elected to send north to negotiate in the matter. And on this occasion, his wife, with a new baby, could not accompany him.

Tom himself was a little doubtful; but he did see it as something of an adventure and challenge. Anyway, he could not refuse a royal command. He would take ship from Ayr, using a couple of other Boyd vessels as escort – puny as these would seem against the Islesman's galleys – and sail for Islay. It was late April, and the seas should be reasonably manageable, even the Sea of the Hebrides. Evidently John MacDonald had found them so! It should not take so very long. Once a-sail, they should be at Islay, the most southerly of the major Hebridean isles, in three days or four at most.

So it was parting, their first since the wedding. Patrick would go with Thomas. Also Andrew Stewart, Canon and Sub-Dean of

Glasgow, Atholl's younger brother, and reputed to be a persuasive negotiator and no humble cleric. Mary realised that she was going to miss her husband, young Jamie notwithstanding.

In the event, she did not have to suffer Tom's absence for long, for he was back in just twelve days, with extraordinary news. According to Sub-Dean Stewart, God had taken over the situation, as the result of his prayers, no doubt. All was well, and his brother and sister-in-law released and indeed by now back in Atholl. Apparently, after immuring the earl and countess at Finlaggan on Islay, John of the Isles had sailed off with his galleys for Ardtornish Castle on the Sound of Mull, for purposes unknown. And off Jura and Scarba, where the Atlantic winds swept through the gap where lay the notorious Gulf of Corrievreckan, a most violent storm had struck the fleet, with disastrous results, sinking most of the ships, and with them all the rich plunder stolen from Blair-in-Atholl. The chief's own vessel had foundered, but John had unfortunately survived. He was now somewhere in the more northerly Hebrides licking his Heaven-dealt wounds. The visitors from the Lowlands, landed on Islay, had had little difficulty in freeing the captives. And all at no cost to themselves. A miracle indeed.

None disputed that.

Now all efforts were concentrated on completing the raising of the thirty thousand florins for Norway. The Church, with its traditionally full coffers, had paid up promptly in full; and the merchant and trade guilds of the cities and towns were well ahead with their collections. It was the lords and barons who were delaying and grumbling, and Thomas was now despatched on a series of visits, to collect, no very enjoyable task, and by no means entirely successful.

There were other problems. The Primate fell ill, and clearly could not face a long sea voyage and a stay in a foreign land; so a substitute prelate had to be found, to negotiate with the Archbishop of Nidaros. In the end Andrew Durisdeer, Bishop of Glasgow, was selected for this delicate duty. Then suitable shipping had to be arranged and prepared, quite a squadron, for it was recognised that this must be an illustrious and numerous embassage, to impress the Norsemen that Scotland was a realm worthy of having their princess as its Queen. These vessels were to be assembled in Leith, the port of Edinburgh; and this involved visits of commissioning and inspection.

148

It was strange how, without any real debate on the matter, it was assumed almost from the first that Mary would accompany her husband on this great expedition. Even the Lord Boyd saw that it would be advantageous to have the King's sister as one of the envoys – and, to be sure, it was her idea in the first place. For his part, Thomas was not going to be parted from his beloved wife for weeks, possibly months. Moreover, her wits in matters of statecraft had been proved, and might well be very useful in dealing with the Scandinavians.

It was the parting from the infant Jamie which troubled Mary, of course. For she could by no means take the baby with her, she had to admit. So the child had to be weaned at seven months – for it was July before all was ready – and a kindly nurse found for him. Anna would accompany her mistress; but Tom's other and older sister, the Countess of Angus, promised to look after her small nephew, at her husband's seat of Tantallon Castle on the Lothian coast near North Berwick. She had had babies of her own, and so was to be relied upon. But it was going to be a wrench . . .

At length, all was ready, and on 27th July the large concourse set out from Stirling for Leith, the King and a lofty entourage accompanying them to see them off. Mary had had her fraught private parting with little Jamie earlier. It rained, to the disadvantage of all the fine clothing.

After spending the night in Edinburgh Castle, they rode the two miles down to Leith and boarded the five vessels awaiting them in the haven there, where the Water of Leith entered the Forth estuary. James, coming aboard with the voyagers to inspect his sister's ship, declared not for the first time that he wished that he was going with them. This, of course, was not possible, for if King Christian proved uncooperative, or his daughter turned out to be unsuitable for any reason, the presence of the Scots monarch would complicate matters direly.

The vessel, the *Tay Pearl*, from Dundee, although sizeable and stout enough, and cleaned and furnished to best effect, would provide scarcely palatial quarters for a lengthy voyage; but Mary for one did not complain. It was the best, and largest, of the five, at least.

The Arrans' fellow-passengers on this vessel were the Chancellor, Lord Avondale, and the Bishops of Glasgow and Orkney, the latter's position somewhat equivocal since, although he was a Scot, he ranked as a Norse citizen, and paid allegiance to King Christian as well as being a prelate of the Norse Metropolitan, a position all hoped would shortly be amended. But he ought to prove a useful go-between.

James would have lingered aboard, but learned that even kings had to pay homage to tides, and the shipmasters were anxious to be off. So farewells were said, the first time the young monarch had been parted from this sister for any length of time, mooring-ropes were cast off and sails hoisted. That Mary was, in fact, going off to try to find him a wife, hardly seemed to interest him.

For better or for worse, Mary's notion, that time, was being put into practice.

12

Watching the Bass Rock, North Berwick Law and, more important, Tantallon Castle where little Jamie was going to be cared for in the interim, fade from sight, Mary Stewart realised that she had never actually been out of sight of land before, and found it a strange experience, so much that was familiar left behind, so much unknown lying ahead. Not that she in any way dreaded what was to come, indeed she looked forward to it, in the main; but with so much that she held dear left there in Scotland, and always the possibility that she might never see it again, it was a sobering thought. Jamie? Ought she to have left him, have come on this venture . . . ?

Tom, Anna and Patrick seemed to have no such wonderings – whatever Avondale and the bishops might have – their thoughts, questions, hopes, all ahead; although the present featured too, especially for Anna who, as they left the comparatively sheltered waters of the Scotwater, or Firth of Forth, for the wide ocean of the Norse Sea, passing south of the Isle of May, and the ship began to roll and heave, wondered whether her stomach was going to let her down, together with hopes that the ship itself would not do so either.

The shipmaster, a rugged Dundonian named Rob Carnegie, seemed entirely confident at least, his only concern that the present prevailing south-westerly wind, helpful for their sailing, might change into the east and so delay them and entail much tacking to and fro. He was not a little impatient too with one of the other vessels of the little squadron, slower than his own *Tay Pearl*. They had over six hundred miles to go to Copenhagen – where Bishop Tulloch said King Christian would probably be found – and he had reckoned on averaging one hundred miles each twenty-four hours, provided no real storm blew up. But if the ships had to keep together, and some lagged . . .

That first evening, in the low-ceiled stern-cabin which was to be their one public apartment, seeking to adjust their interiors to the

151

motions of the vessel, and none save the much-travelled Bishop of Orkney eating much, Tom sought that prelate's guidance on the strange diversity of the triple Scandinavian kingdom, with its three capitals, and where lay the priority? After all, it was usually called Norway, at least in Scotland, and its inhabitants Norsemen; and this was the Norse Sea. Yet apparently they were heading for Copenhagen, which was the capital of Denmark. Also sometimes Christian was referred to as King of Denmark. And presumably he was King of Sweden also. All very confusing. What was the King's true and preferred style? And where did Finland come in?

Bishop Tulloch agreed that it was difficult. Actually Christian, as former Duke of Schleswig-Holstein, part of Denmark, preferred to be called King of Denmark. Yet Denmark by no means included Norway. And Sweden insisted that it was a separate realm. All making for difficult governing. The terms Norsemen and Danes had been used loosely down the ages to describe the same people, although in fact they were different, but both sea-raiders with, as was to be expected, the more southerly Danes raiding in England and southern Scotland, as well as on the Continent, and the Norse northern Scotland, Iceland, the Isles and Hebrides and Ireland. Yet even so, there was this curious mix-up of names – scarcely to be wondered at perhaps, in that the two nations' warriors looked and sounded so similar, and behaved almost identically. At least the term Jutes had faded, although most of the raiding Danes came from Jutland. Probably the most notable and long-established confusion of the names was that of the Normans. These were not Frenchmen, although they soon adopted the French language, but Norsemen, so called, who had invaded and settled in northern France, yet in fact were Danes from Jutland. So, many of Scotland's leading families, claiming to be of Norman descent, were really of Danish extraction, including the royal Stewarts themselves who, before they came from Normandy and in due course became High Stewards of Scotland and married into the Bruce house, had been Stewards of Dol in St Malo.

The bishop's hearers pondered on all this but were not greatly the wiser.

When they sought their bunks that night, Tom was concerned to find that their vessel did not rise to double beds, with consequent necessary adaption of his nightly procedures, somewhat cramping his style. Mary was patient, even helpful.

The wind, fortunately, stayed in the south-west and the weather was on the whole kind, so that the ships made good time and the passengers could stroll the decks or sit on the sheltered sides of the upper-works. That other vessel, from Dysart in Fife, proved to be something of a laggard, and the *Tay Pearl*'s master frequently had to order shorten sail to allow it to catch up. But otherwise the voyage proceeded uneventfully and pleasantly enough, and stomachs soon accepted the motions of sea and ships, as they sailed into August. There was, of course, an insufficiency of matters for active folk to attend to. Mary was probably the only one embarrassed thereby, in that her husband found love-making a very constant preoccupation.

On the fourth day out there was considerable stir at the sight of land ahead, with congratulations to the shipmaster on the short time taken. But Rob Carnegie was less impressed. Had it not been for the Dysart lugger they could have been this far the day before, he asserted. That was Skagen Head, or the Skaw, the most northerly tip of Denmark. Despite that, they had a long way to go yet, and probably the worst part of the voyage, for round that headland they turned southwards into the Kattegat, the narrow sea between Sweden and Denmark, down which the tides raced as through a funnel, and strewn with islands and reefs, no mariner's delight, one hundred and fifty miles; and then through the tortuous Oresound before they could reach Copenhagen in Zealand.

Indeed, when they rounded that long pointed beak of the Skaw, they felt the difference very promptly, the ships beginning to pitch fore and aft in short, steep seas, with the wind no longer consistent but sweeping this way and that between the land-masses. They were told that in some measure the Kattegat resembled the Hebridean seas, only the land on either side was not mountainous and so there were fewer down-draughts and tidal overfalls; but because this overgrown sound entered the shallow Baltic Sea at the other end, the tidal forces themselves were greater, a deep sea linked with a shallow one.

They had to tack their way down this, winds now less favourable, and, such being the dangers of the waters, they anchored for the night in the sheltered lee of the island of Anholt, till daylight. From there on, the land drew ever closer on each side, and passing the famous Elsinore, at the tip of Zealand, by midday they were in the narrows of the Oresound, now with the Swedish coast as close as the Danish. Through the throat of this, they swung westwards into the bay, really a sea-loch, of Copenhagen, journey over.

If the visitors expected their arrival to cause any stir in the Danish city they were disappointed. No doubt groups of ships were for ever entering Copenhagen harbour, a notably lengthy one, the capital of a great seafaring nation and the principal centre of Baltic trade. They were more or less ignored, even though the *Tay Pearl* flew the royal standard of Scotland at its masthead, until, seeking berthing accommodation amongst the host of shipping already harboured there, a harbour-master's barge came out to enquire their business and docking requirements. The announcement by Bishop Tulloch, in Danish, that they had come from Scotland to visit King Christian, did not seem to make any major impression either, but they were guided through what almost seemed to be the streets of the city, penetrated by the elongated series of docks and basins, to tie up eventually amongst tall warehouses, and there left. A less splendid reception to the sea-king's domains would have been hard to imagine.

Bishop Tulloch was nowise put out, however – presumably ceremony was not a Danish, or Norse, preoccupation. Taking Patrick Fullarton with him, they set out on foot, necessarily, for the Christiansborg Slot, or palace, the King's favourite seat, no great distance off apparently.

The others had some considerable time to wait. And when their emissaries did reappear, it was not on foot or as they had gone, but from behind as it were, and by water. They came in a handsome, long-oared barge, colourful with gold and black paintwork, and in the company of a soberly dressed individual who proved to be the palace chamberlain.

He welcomed them in his King's name, but only briefly, for he did not speak any tongue that they understood, and the bishop had to translate. They were to leave most of their people in the ships here, and only the principals to go, in the barge, to Christiansborg Slot, until accommodation was prepared for the rest, possibly elsewhere.

So there were some decisions to be made as to who should go and who should stay, with certain feathers tending to be ruffled. Eventually a party of about one dozen embarked on the barge and were rowed by a narrow lane-like offshoot, a canal evidently, between two churches and various other buildings, to a suddenly opening area, with its own pier, which proved to be the gardens entrance to a long and massive edifice, somewhat featureless but obviously strong, which appeared to be their destination, Christiansborg Slot, or castle, quite unlike any Scots castle or palace. However plain, and not unlike some of the warehouses they had passed, it was commodious enough and no doubt defensible.

Here the chamberlain led them to a rear wing, facing another canal which acted as a moat. They were shown into a number of rooms, linked by a central passage, all fairly sparsely furnished, the walls hanging with the skins of animals rather than tapestries. They seemed to have these premises to themselves. Servants came with hot water, cold meats and some sort of fiery and potent spirits. They were told that King Christian was to house and would grant them audience in due course.

They were still settling in, awaiting their baggage being brought from the ships, when a big, burly individual, reddish-fair of hair and with a shaggy beard, appeared unannounced, shouting greetings. He came on the two young women first, partly unclad as they were and washing themselves, but seemed no way abashed at that. He hooted laughter indeed, and seemed almost as though he was going to advance and assist at their ablutions, addressing them in a tongue which they did not understand.

Mary was not the one hastily to cover herself up in maidenly modesty and blush, but nor did she flaunt herself.

"Whom do you seek, sir?" she asked. "My lord Earl of Arran is in another chamber." She pointed along the corridor. "With my lord of Avondale and the bishops."

"Ya! Ya!" the big man all but roared. "Beeshops. Lords. From Schottland. Goot! Goot! Womans. Schottishe womans!"

"Yes, sir." Mary gestured along the passage again. "They are there, the lords from Scotland."

But the visitor showed no inclination to leave them. "Goot womans!" he observed appreciatively, observed in more than speech. "Most goot womans."

Anna giggled, following Mary's example and covering up somewhat.

Their approver was only partially distracted by the arrival in the doorway of Tom and Bishop Tulloch. He waved a hand towards the girls, and said something vehement in his own language.

It was the bishop who answered, and bowed low as he did so. It dawned on Mary that this was evidently someone very important.

"His Majesty of Denmark," the prelate added.

Blinking, the young women curtsied.

Christian chuckled and launched into a peroration, pointing at the girls separately, back and forth, apparently comparing attributes. Clearing his throat, the bishop gave an approximate translation, most obviously embarrassed.

"His Majesty declares you beautiful. Both. Variously. He, ah, welcomes you to his realm. I will tell him who you are, Highness . . ."

The King, learning Mary's identity, was but the more appreciative, striding forward to clasp her to him in what amounted to a bear's hug, but an exploratory bear, and planting smacking kisses. Then he did the same for Anna, in slightly lesser degree, as was suitable. Clearly the Danish monarch, whatever else, was not concerned with protocol and keeping royal distance, perhaps a hopeful sign for their mission.

Tom and Avondale were then presented, and Bishop Durisdeer appearing, likewise. The King was affable, but less demonstrative than to the young women. He came back to them, now approximately respectable as to dress, to pat their shoulders with lingering caresses. Then laughing heartily, he headed for the door, shouting back something which Bishop Tulloch said was the command that they would all dine at his table that evening and drink their fill – this last the prelate adding with a little cough.

Thomas declared that he reckoned it as well for Scotland's cause that he had brought his wife along – but that it looked as though he would have to watch the said wife as keenly as any hawk, in this Denmark. Perhaps that was to be his only role.

Later, in a vast dining-hall, they found conditions to be very different from those at home on such an occasion. There was no dais, for one thing, and no waiting for the monarch to appear for, although it was not evident at first in that crowded noisy gathering, Christian was already present, not sitting at any especial top table but at one part way down the hall, amidst a group of almost equally shaggy and hirsute characters, all singing loudly and beating tankards in time on table-tops, whilst three women danced and down the said table-tops, as others were doing at adjoining tables, skirts lifted high and white legs flashing. There did not seem to be a great many other women present.

When servitors with laden trays apprised the King of the newcomers' presence, he rose alone and came to greet them, just a little unsteady on his feet, and bearing straight, or fairly straight, for Mary. He threw an arm around her and all but lifted her off her feet, to propel her onwards to the table he had left, while with the other arm he waved the others on behind him, to thread their way through the seated throng, which was now bellowing acclaim. No standing when the monarch stood here, it seemed, no signs of awe or reverence, but much hearty approval, the table-dancers for the moment neglected.

Mary was carried along to where Christian had been sitting, and there his table companions, right and left, were cheerfully waved up from their benches to go and seat themselves elsewhere, to leave vacant places for the new arrivals. Mary was sat down on the King's immediate right, and turning, he beckoned Anna, not Thomas, to sit on his left. The others could place themselves where they would. Stentorian roars demanded fresh supplies of meat and drink – the which was already, in fact, appearing behind them.

What had been a whole wild boar, roasted, tusked head still attached, was set before them, and with his own knife Christian cut a thick slice from the haunch and presented it straight to Mary's lips on the knife-point, with voluble if unintelligible comments. She dealt with this as best she could, and then, knife transferred to the other hand, she was given the King's slopping tankard to take a drink from. Wary of this last, for she had already sampled the Danish schnapps and found it potent indeed, she took only a sip, to her host's manifest disappointment. But he managed to pat her leg with the knife-hand nevertheless. Then he turned to deal with Anna in similar fashion, if with slightly less large a piece of boar. That one pleased him by gulping a considerably greater mouthful of schnapps.

A roasted goose was then presented to them, and again Christian insisted on dismembering it for them and feeding them portions personally, each bite with the tankard in support, as it were. Now Anna grew more discreet, as she perceived where this could lead.

One of the female dancers came to cavort in front of and above them, skirts kilted, and the monarch, peering upwards, gestured, and to emphasise his point, ran his hand down Mary's thigh. When it came back upwards and seemed to be going to linger, she reached down gently to remove it, but smilingly, one royal hand upon another. The king laughed, and fed her more goose.

That meal lasted a long time, with supplies by no means running out. When the dancers tired, having ever increasing difficulty in stepping amongst the accumulating platters and dishes – and avoiding the clutching hands of admiring diners – they were replaced by jugglers and tumblers, which some of the company sought to emulate disastrously, to produce the greatest hilarity of the entertainment. It was that sort of evening.

With Christian becoming ever more affectionate, Mary, noting that others were rising and leaving the hall intermittently, whether departing or merely going to attend the calls of nature, decided that, since the King had been here before they arrived and did not seem to demand any permission to leave, enough was enough for one night. She told Christian that she was tired, after their long voyaging; then, realising that he had no notion of what she said, reverted to sign-language and, releasing one of her hands from his, put her two palms together, laid her cheek against them in the gesture of sleeping, and closed her eyes. Then she took a quick breath as she recognised that he might well take this as an invitation to join her in bed, and somewhat hastily rose to her feet.

Perhaps the monarch was in fact feeling the effects of the enormous amount of schnapps he had drunk, for he only grinned, put his own hands in approximately the same position, sought to rise and sat down again heavily. Curtsying, Mary signed to Anna to follow, and moved off to pick her way through the throng to the door by which they had entered – having to elude sundry kindly hands in the process, Anna, not entirely sure of her steps and the less elusive, behind. Thomas would no doubt find his own way, in due course. The bishops, she noted, were already gone.

That night the two girls slept together for the first time since Mary's marriage – and if Thomas had any objections, when eventually he arrived back at their quarters from the banquet, he did not voice them, possibly was in no state to do so.

While it might have been expected that the Danish monarch and his advisers would have been disinclined for any early prosecution of business after that evening's entertainment, in fact Bishop Tulloch came to inform Thomas and Avondale in mid-forenoon that King Christian awaited them, to hear the

Scots envoys' proposals. Tom, with a sore head, was scarcely ready for this, Avondale likewise; but they could nowise delay. In the circumstances, although it was unusual to say the least, they both felt that Mary should accompany them, her head undoubtedly being clearer than theirs – whatever Christian's reaction might be to a woman's attendance at a council.

In the event, the King clearly approved of a female presence, on this occasion at least when, after a wait outside the council-chamber, the Scots envoys were admitted, to find the Danish councillors not only already assembled, with the monarch, but, having half-empty tankards of schnapps in front of them, looking as though they had been there for some time. Mary recognised some of the revellers of the previous night in the dozen or so men therein. Clearly these Danes had strong heads.

Christian, at council, was not so very different from his normal outgoing and hearty self, hailing Mary with evident satisfaction, although on this occasion he fell short of having her to come and sit beside him at the table. But almost ignoring the men, he shouted welcome and appreciation – at least she assumed that was the case without understanding a word that he said.

This language problem the envoys had insufficiently considered hitherto – save for Bishop Tulloch no doubt. It seemed that none there, save he, knew the other's tongue. So everything would have to be translated by the prelate, with inevitable delays and possible misinterpretations.

Seated round the bottom end of the table, the Scots found brimming tankards placed before them, while their opposite numbers' were refilled. The newcomers were cautious now about schnapps, and merely moistened lips with it.

After a general and somewhat rambling introduction by the monarch which, according to Tulloch thereafter amounted merely that his council was prepared to listen to the Scots proposals, all eyes turned to Thomas, who, as earl and senior envoy, had to lead off. And that man was in something of a quandary. For, so far, they had seen no sign of the Princess Margaret, nor of any of Christian's family – and he was said to have a German wife, Queen Dorothea of Hohenzollern, who indeed had been the widow of his predecessor, King Christopher, and three young sons by her as well as this Margaret. The trouble was, of course, that if the girl was found to be unsuitable, for any reason, to be wed to the King of Scots, misshapen, ugly, lacking in wits or otherwise, these negotiations should not be begun; or at least should be confined to matters financial concerning Orkney and Shetland. But this condition was a difficult one to announce to the princess's father. Tom required a clear head this morning. They had scarcely expected the negotiations to commence quite so soon as this.

So he began by saying that they looked forward greatly to meeting the Princess Margaret of Denmark and, if all was to their mutual satisfaction, returning to Scotland with news of her and of possible marriage settlements, for King James's decision. Whereafter, a second embassage would no doubt come to complete the arrangements. That was the best that he could do at this stage.

The bishop translated equally carefully.

Heads nodded portentously round that table, and Christian looked assessingly, but at Mary rather than at the prelate or Thomas.

A grave-faced elderly individual, the most soberly dressed there, and possibly a cleric, raised voice. He wanted to know, Tulloch said, whether the Scots had brought with them the Northern Isles Annual and arrears? That was sufficiently blunt.

Thomas said that they had brought this year's Annual, yes – thirty thousand florins. Arrears were another matter, and this would require time and consideration.

Features lightened around the table at the mention of those thirty thousand florins, the King nodding his satisfaction. But the grave man lifted a finger. The arrears were of the greatest importance, he insisted, a vast sum now owing. This would have to be dealt with if negotiations were to go ahead. Possibly this individual was Christian's chancellor.

Bishop Durisdeer said that this inherited debt was grievous to both realms. But since it would take considerable time to raise the moneys, it would be most unfortunate if the proposed royal match was put off until further payments were made.

That might be so, the other agreed. But some substantial part of it would be required before decisions could be made.

King Christian caught Mary's eye and grinned cheerfully.

There was a pause. It had not taken long to reach apparent deadlock, despite the apparent amiability of the monarch.

Mary, encouraged by that look, spoke up, quietly but not in any way diffidently. "A wise merchant accepts a fair price for what he has to sell, rather than demanding more than the buyer can pay," she observed. "We are not merchants here, but the principle is sound, is it not? My brother's realm shows its good faith by bringing here the Annual, the first such payment for many years. Even if your princess is not to become Queen in Scotland, the Annual stays with you. That is our pledge. For your part, do you not make some such pledge?"

When that was translated, Christian thumped the table. "Goot! Goot!" he exclaimed.

Most there nodded, but the soberly clad man was not impressed. Thirty years of non-payment of thirty thousand florins amounted to nine hundred thousand florins, he declared flatly.

At mention of such all but astronomical a sum, all present blinked and eyed each other.

Mary mustered a smile. She addressed the King, not the last speaker. "The heavens are high, Sire, and the multitude of the stars uncountable. As is the total of these arrears. And one as unreachable as the other. Such moneys are not to be found in all Scotland. Are they, here in your Denmark?" She did not wait for that to be answered. "There is surely more to this match, this league of the realms, than gold, silver, moneys, to count? Good-will between the kingdoms. Alliance against the enemies of both. And Orkney and Shetland themselves. These are as a running sore on your realm, Sire, are they not? How much tribute does the Earl St Clair send to you? He imprisoned your bishop, here. Your Majesty could not free him. Or did not. Without warfare and armed men and ships. And have you not other needs for such? Would you not have *that* running sore healed, at the least?"

When Christian got the gist of all that, the effect seemed favourable, however little impact it appeared to make on his evidently principal adviser.

Avondale, the Scots Chancellor, took the matter of the Northern Isles further. "Orkney is a *Scottish* earldom, Your Majesty," he said. "The Earl William St Clair is . . . difficult towards you, as has been said. If, Sire, the earl was deprived of his earldom by our King James, and given another on the Scottish mainland, then would that not much comfort you?" This had been mooted by the Lord Boyd.

The monarch nodded vigorously, but the awkward member of the council looked severe. They required silver florins, not styles, titles, allegiances, he asserted.

Looking from one to the other, Mary, weighing the differences in character which she perceived between monarch and adviser, and making her choice of approaches, produced a tinkling female laugh.

"The Swelkie!" she observed, into the silence.

All eyes turned on her questioningly. That was a Norse word, *svelgr*, even if she pronounced it slightly differently. It meant whirlpool. No translation was needed.

She had these seafarers' interest at once, as she had guessed. "You will all know of the great Swelkie off the island of Stroma, in the Orkneys," she went on. This story she had heard often as a child. "It is famous. There was once a Swedish king named Frodi. He possessed a magical quern, a great hand-mill, which he had found. He called it his Grotti, for groats, grain, which he ground in it, amongst other things. But groats are also coins, are they not? Here, as in Scotland." She waited, while the bishop translated that.

"This Grotti ground silver, gold, as well as grain. But it also brought, or bought, peace for King Frodi, which was indeed its magic. But another sea-king, Mysing, of Denmark, envied Frodi and stole his Grotti. He used it for his own ends, but decided that it would also grind salt, and salt could be sold for much money in lands which had no salt seas. So he took his ships to Orkney, where as all know the sea is more salty than is the Norse Sea, from the Atlantic tides. And there he worked the Grotti. But that man did not know when, or indeed how, to stop it working, on the seas. And the Grotti ground salt in such quantities that it made a great hole in the sea-bed, and the salt filled his ships until they sank and the Grotti with them. They were never seen again. Thus was formed the Swelkie, the famed whirlpool. All because this King of Denmark knew not when to stop, when he had gained a sufficiency."

When the translation ended there was a great shout of acclaim and appreciation from around that table, Christian's the loudest, as he slapped the boards time and again. Mary had calculated aright. These Danes were a race of storytellers as well as seafarers, saga-makers. And here was a telling saga indeed.

The grave-faced cleric looked at the young woman hardly, recognizing that he had lost this battle.

Christian rose, announcing that they had debated sufficiently long for this day, and would consider well what had been said.

162

Then he came round to Mary, to clasp her to him, chuckling, patting, all but shaking her.

"Swelkie!" he cried. "*Svelgr!* Goot!" He reached down for her still-full tankard, raised it and took a draught, then presented it to her lips, evidently a mark of royal favour in this land, possibly a gesture similar to kissing. She sipped, but only a little, smiling and shaking her head. He emptied the remainder in one vast swallow.

They must all come and eat and drink with him, he declared. In one hour. This as the Scots party left the council-chamber.

"You have that great bear of a king eating out of your hand!" Thomas declared, as they went back to their own quarters. "Only – so long as that is *all* he does! That one would take you, if he might, I swear! You gain us much with him, yes, but do not let him go over-far, wife of mine! Or I see myself as wrecking this mission, and war between Scotland and Denmark!"

"Never fear, jealous one! I think that I have the measure of Christian of Oldenburg. He may be the sea-king here, but I am the daughter of kings also, the Brucc amongst them! I can look after myself. *You* remember that, husband."

"I never forget it, nor am I allowed to." He squeezed her arm. "That of the Swelkie was a notable notion. How thought you of it, lass?"

"I was fond of the story in childhood. And reckoned that these are folk for stories. The Norse sagas, Bishop Tulloch says, mean more to them than Holy Writ! And Christian, whatever his name, is of the saga sort, that I am sure. So . . ."

"It served, indeed. And as did the other about merchants and prices to pay. You could be the Scots envoy here, on your own, Mary!"

"Me? A weak woman! Amongst all these fierce sea-rovers?"

"You are a match for them, I say, even though you have belike made an enemy of that man whom Tulloch says is the Danish chancellor. A match – whatever match we reach over Christian's daughter! Which, my dear, I think *you* may be best to enquire of him. When are we going to see the girl? All this may be but wasted effort if she is no worthy bride for James. Where is she? And her mother? This appears to be only a man's court."

"It is difficult to enquire of him when I do not speak his language. Bishop Tulloch would have to be beside us."

"Surely that can be contrived. Perhaps Christian himself would

163

wish him near – some of the time! So that you could know what he says to you, as well as feeling his hands! Ask you when we can see his daughter."

In the lesser hall, and with many fewer men present, again no women save Mary and Anna and no entertainers, they had no difficulty in getting Bishop Tulloch seated close to the King – although the latter still had Mary on one side of him and Anna on the other, so that he could pat and fondle both; but the prelate placed himself at Mary's right and Thomas on Anna's left. So that, in the absence of music, singing and dancing, all in the monarch's group could hear what was said. Schnapps was as much in evidence as heretofore. The Danes seemed to be able to swallow it more or less *ad lib*, largely without effect – unless of course they were all somewhat under the influence of it throughout.

They ate various cold meats, and a sweet which seemed to be composed of almost equal quantities of honey, cream, ground meal and some kind of wine which, potent enough as it tasted to the visitors, evidently required a lot of schnapps to wash it down. Mary again had to do a fair amount of gentle hand-removing and, by her giggles, Anna also.

Choosing her time, Mary asked, through the bishop, when they would have the pleasure of meeting the Princess Margaret? And, to be sure, the Queen Dorothea? She was told that this could be arranged at any time, almost as though it had hardly crossed Christian's mind. His wife and children were presently up at their summer palace of Helsingor, little more than thirty miles to the north – which they would have passed on their voyage here, where the Kattegat narrowed to the Oresound. They could sail there in a few hours. Mary said that they were all eager to see the possible future Queen of Scotland – assuming that all the moneys problems could be settled in mutual acceptance. To which Christian shouted, "Swelkies! Swelkies!" with roared laughter. Which seemed hopeful, at least. He also announced that there would be another banquet that night – which Mary heard without elation. If this was going to be similar to the previous one, she reckoned that the Scots party was going to require a little sleep that afternoon. Although bedding down with Thomas might not be so very restful, even so. Did all these Danes do their sleeping in the afternoon?

All agreed that the sooner they could persuade the King

164

to take them to Elsinore, or Helsingor as he called it, the better.

After only fairly brief love-making, the Arrans slept – but not before Mary suggested that, to abbreviate the royal advances that evening, if possible, they ought to contrive it so that there was not too much sitting at table for her. Suppose that they offered to demonstrate Scottish dancing to Christian and his folk? Demonstrate, and then perhaps seek to teach? That would get them up and about. Thomas wondered murmurously whether it would not result in still more clutching and fondling, but his wife pointed out that such ought to be spread amongst others, at least.

So, when the Scots presented themselves at the great hall again, and found all approximately as it had been the night before, eating and drinking already started and table-top dancing again in progress, with the addition this time of dwarfs, both male and female performing antics, Bishop Tulloch, somewhat stiffly, informed the monarch that the visitors wished to contribute to the evening's entertainment by exhibiting Scottish dancing, which might well be rather different from Danish. Christian applauded, indeed seemed as though he could hardly wait. That did not prevent him from showing his usual appreciation of femininity throughout the meal's many courses, however.

When Mary, and even Anna, had had enough of this, she signed to Tom, who rose, and announced the Schottische dance, making an up-arm gesture and jigging his feet. Intrigued, all exclaimed and clapped.

There was a problem, of course. Typical Scots reels demanded multiples of four, eight, or even sixteen. Eight was the usual number, but since it was normal to have male and female partners interchanging, the female quotient here was inadequate. The embassage had brought many lesser members with them to Denmark – indeed, over-many, for it proved difficult to know what to do with them at Christiansborg Slot, and most were still using quarters in the docked vessels and sampling the attractions of Copenhagen otherwhere. There was sufficient here at the palace to provide an eightsome, to be sure, but only Mary and Anna female. It was decided that they should first demonstrate with a foursome, the two young women with Thomas and Patrick; and when the rudiments of the reel were perceived by the audience, some of the female table-dancers would probably pick it up quickly and join in.

Then there was the matter of musical accompaniment. There were fiddlers present, but these would not know the Scots tunes. No doubt these also would pick up the rhythms in due course; but at first there was nothing for it but for the dancers themselves, and their compatriots watching, to hum and sing the appropriate airs, however inexpert might be the vocalists. So the Scots, even the two bishops, about one dozen of them, were assembled in a cleared space, and Mary chose the best repetitive tune for them, having to sing it solo for the first few bars, her efforts nearly drowned out by King Christian's huzzahs of approval. Fortunately, Patrick Fullarton had a strong and tuneful voice, and quickly joined in, Tom's contribution vehement but less melodious. The others, with varying degrees of embarrassment, added their voices, a little raggedly at first, but soon settling to a rousing, sprightly rendering, the beat more important than the melody.

Mary, whose idea all this had been, had come prepared with belts for Anna and herself to hitch up their long skirts, as was necessary – this being greeted with enthusiasm by the onlookers. Then curtsying and bowing to partners, the four timed their start to the appropriate beat of the singers, and commenced their reel, circling first, then toe-and-heel skipping, arms held high, facing partners then linking arms and birling round, before exchanging partners in a figure-of-eight movement abbreviated into four, themselves chanting the tune as they danced, with the two men interspersing their contributions with high-pitched heuchs.

They repeated this sequence twice, with considerable energy displayed, the girls graceful, the men vigorous, until they had to give up their singing for lack of breath. But now the Danes were joining in vocally and beating tankards to the rhythm, so that the Scots singers and hummers were all but eclipsed and the actual air suffered although the beat strengthened and indeed quickened so that the dancers were forced to ever speedier exercise, the young women's bouncing breasts much admired, their hitching up of skirts likewise.

At length, panting, Mary called a halt and found much of their audience now on their feet, laughing and shouting and jigging in all but elephantine fashion, King Christian foremost. He came to Mary to hug her to him, kiss her comprehensively and seek either to still or to encourage her bosom, which was not clear.

Enthusiasm reigned.

Some of the table-dancers had now descended to the floor and were skipping about, and Mary managed to detach herself from the sea-king to beckon these to her and, still distinctly breathless, demonstrate the footwork involved – which they speedily picked up. Selecting two of them, she beckoned forward two more of the Scots party, to make up an eightsome. At the same time, Tom was guiding the fiddlers to produce an approximate version of the tune.

Out of all this the largest, longest and most detailed reel was attempted, distinctly chaotic as it proceeded but enjoyed by all, impromptu copies of it developing all around, the heuching yells in especial being highly popular.

This effort did not so much finish as deteriorate into a laughing, stumbling riot of limbs and persons, the schnapps undoubtedly contributing. All but exhausted, the original four gasped for rest.

But they reckoned without the monarch. Christian was agog to try his footwork and, more especially, his handwork, and nothing would do but that a number of eightsomes should be formed up, with himself, Mary, Anna and two of the table-dancers added to Thomas, Patrick, and of all individuals, Master Martin Vanns, Grand Almoner to King James, one of the deputation, a middle-aged but nimble cleric. Four circles were contrived – the available space would not hold more – and the fiddlers and singers ordered to strike up.

What followed all but beggared description: enthusiasm, Danish spirits of both sorts, and lack of room contributing to produce uproar, pandemonium and turmoil. Yet joy of an utterly uninhibited and deafening variety prevailed, whilst all semblance of eightsome reels disappeared, and whirling, leaping, tripping bodies gyrated, males clutching females to them, often with the latter's feet off the floor and clothing apt to become distinctly disarranged. Mary, seeking to keep Christian from complete possession of her person, wondered whether *this* notion of hers had indeed been a good one. Anna, with commendable self-immolation, did come to her aid, to Patrick's concern.

But even sea-rovers can tire, especially after a heavy meal, and these two young women managed to abstract themselves, and all but collapsed back at their places at table, restoring their clothing as best they could – not that the Danish ladies seemed to trouble themselves about that. They were even glad to gulp down some schnapps.

Schottische dancing was everywhere voted a major success.

The Scots party, or the loftier section of it, effected their escape shortly afterwards when the King left without any announcement, no doubt for the relief of nature. Moving off, Thomas observed that his wife was better at devising statecraft than evening entertainment. Mary rather agreed, but did not admit it. This night's cantrips would do their negotiations no harm, she contended, the Scots' popularity enhanced. There were more ways of winning their way than by bargaining over florins.

13

Whether out of this appreciation for the Scots or otherwise, they did not know; but Bishop Tulloch informed next morning that King Christian had to perform some duty that day at the town of Roskilde, some twenty-five miles to the west, but would take them to Helsingor the day following to meet his wife and children. They would sail there in the King's own ship. So they had a free day, and the bishop suggested a tour round Copenhagen. Mary was relieved to hear that there would not be another banquet that night.

They went exploring the city therefore, on foot and in holiday mood, walking its narrow streets, many of which were in fact also quaysides, for the town was honeycombed with docks and mooring-places, ships' masts and spars being as much part of the skyline as were tall gabled buildings. They crossed its canals by bridges, examining the traders' stalls and booths and sampling their wares, the bishop a competent guide. Meeting the people interested them, their interest obviously returned. Their identity presumably would be known, as some of the Scots from the five vessels which had descended upon their community. It was good to have a day free of responsibilities.

The following forenoon they were led down to board the royal ship, flying all sorts of flags and banners, something between a galley and a galleon, two-masted with great decorated sails but also with banks of long oars or sweeps. King Christian was already aboard, and welcomed them with schnapps, loud salutations and cries of "Swelkies!" Mary suspected that he might indeed think of her under that name, and was doubtful of being identified with any sort of whirlpool – although Tom made the inevitable comment about deep women in whom men could founder and drown.

It was the oars which had to be used to get the vessel out of the narrow waters of the canal and harbourage; but once the open sound was reached, the sails were hoisted and they headed almost due northwards in fine style before a south-westerly breeze.

They were never far from shores – they could not be, for this Oresound was nowhere more than a dozen miles wide, and narrowing as they proceeded. So Christian was able to point out landmarks on both the Danish and the Swedish sides, the Swedish city of Landskrona and the Danish towns and havens of Hellerup and Skodsborg and Rungsted. Then they were passing the long, low island of Ven, with the sound now beginning to close in to its bottleneck to the Kattegat, this dominated by their destination, Elsinore, on the one side and the Swedish Helsingborg on the other. It was well seen here why Swedes, Norsemen and Danes had become almost interchangeable terms.

The castle of Elsinore, really called Marienlyst, as distinct from the town, was dramatically sited on a cliff above the narrows, based on what had been a Viking fort, tall and challenging, the town a little way behind. There was a sheltered anchorage and good harbour below the cliffs, for this was a ferry terminal for one of the main Swedish crossings, the shortest, and there was much shipping. But there was a special royal quay where their vessel tied up, almost directly under the castle.

They could see a curling, round-about road to give access to the fortalice-palace; but there was also a steep flight of steps, largely cut in the naked rock, and down this, before berthing was completed, they saw two children come running, a boy and a girl, waving. The King's ship, with all its banners, would have been recognisable from up there for some time.

"Hans! Margrete!" Christian announced proudly, and bellowed a greeting.

So, presently, at the gangway-foot, the visitors made the acquaintance of her whom they had come all the way from Scotland to see, Margrete Christiansdotter, aged twelve years, standing beside her eight-year-old brother Hans – and relief was undoubted. For the girl, although not beautiful, was well built, open-featured and smiling, calling vehemently to her father, no handicaps in evidence. The boy was sturdy, stolid, unsmiling, probably shy.

The King caught them both up, one under each arm, laughing uproariously, bringing them kicking and wriggling to present them to the Scots, Margaret squealing, Hans looking away. Presumably they were used to this sort of treatment.

The envoys could scarcely pay suitable respects to the Prince and Princess of Denmark in the circumstances. They did their best.

Set down, the youngsters showed much less interest in the visitors than these did in the girl, being obviously determined that their father took the steep stairway up to the castle rather than the coiling roadway, seeking to pull him thence, Margaret laughingly. She seemed to be a normal, happy and uncomplicated creature, which was a comfort.

The monarch was evidently easily persuaded by his offspring, and the party found itself forced to tackle the taxing and dizzy-making ascent of the cliff, arriving at the top eventually breathless. Here they met Queen Dorothea, a strange, stern-faced woman to be the wife of the ebullient Christian, silent, reserved. It seemed that the daughter took after her father rather than her mother – which might be as well for young James Stewart.

This castle was nothing like so commodious as Christiansborg, nor prepared for entertaining large numbers of incomers, and it was discovered that the King intended to stay only for one night. With but two or three of his councillors with him here, it seemed that there was to be no negotiating of terms on this visit.

That evening, after a good meal but no banquet, Bishop Durisdeer reminded Thomas of the second objective of the embassage: that was to see the Norwegian Metropolitan, Archbishop of Nidaros, to seek to transfer the Orkney see to Scotland and if possible to persuade him to relinquish Metropolitan claims over the Scottish Church. This matter was very dear to Primate Graham's heart, and he had given Durisdeer authority to offer quite substantial Church moneys as recompense. Here, at Elsinore, they were only three miles from the Swedish coast, and Norway just to the north. He was not sure just where Nidaros was, but it seemed an opportunity to deal with this matter now and save time hereafter.

They debated this. Thomas was agreeable, but felt that this was a matter for churchmen, not for such as himself. He should stay with King Christian and seek to work on him to come to suitable terms for the marriage settlement, which, now that they had seen the young princess, should go ahead. And he would require Bishop Tulloch as interpreter. So . . .

Glasgow's bishop accepted that. He would go on to Nidaros on his own, and deal with the archbishop adequately enough –

for all senior clerics must have the Latin, and they could converse in that language. Only . . . He glanced over at Mary. Only – if Her Highness would be prepared to come with him, he felt that it would be a major help. She had proved her keen wits and persuasive powers, and might well be a very useful influence with the Metropolitan. Also would give himself added authority, as the Scots King's sister. Would the princess accompany him?

Thomas was not at all keen on this suggestion, but Mary was quite agreeable – if she indeed could be of any help in an important matter for Scotland. She would quite like to visit Norway, and she would be prepared to escape Christian's further attentions and banquets for a space.

Next morning they put the matter to the King. He said that they would be foolish to cross to Sweden here, and thereafter travel by land. In his realms, all journeying was done by sea, as far as was possible. Trondheim, where the archepiscopal see of Nidaros was situated, was fully five hundred sea-miles from the southern tip of Norway, Lindesnes, and there was no point in travelling up through Sweden. Besides, the Norse land was mountainous and cut into by innumerable fjords, over and round which they would have to make their way. Much better to sail in one of their own ships, from Copenhagen to Trondheim Fjord, in three or four days, not weeks.

Presently, then, they all took their leave of the Queen and her children, well satisfied with their visit, and sailed back whence they had come.

Rob Carnegie was quite happy to make a diversionary voyage to Trondheim, for he was having difficulty in keeping his idle seamen in order amongst the varied delights of Copenhagen. A couple of days later, then, the *Tay Pearl*, with Mary and Anna, Bishop Durisdeer and King's Almoner Vann, set sail once more northwards up the Oresound, now becoming a familiar waterway. They did not take any of the escorting vessels with them. Undoubtedly there was a certain amount of disappointed masculinity left behind them, also.

Through the Elsinore narrows again, and up the Kattegat, to round the Skaw into the Skagerrak they went, and there, finding themselves now facing into the prevailing westerly breeze, had to start tacking back and forth. This continued for fully one hundred miles, until they could round what Carnegie called the Naze and

Christian had named Lindesnes, the very southern point of long Norway. This, of course, much delayed them, but once round the great headland, with the wind astern, they made excellent time up the Norse coast.

And what a coastline that was. Mary had heard that it was not unlike their own Hebridean seaboard, but now saw that it was very different, mountains cut into by sea-lochs, here known as fjords, offshore islands by the hundred and skerries and reefs by the thousand, yes; but the mountains were steeper, barer, harder, the fjords narrower and darker, the islands rockier, less sand-fringed, the whole less colourful; but dramatic, spectacular. And it went on and on, seemingly endless.

For three days and nights thereafter they sailed up that extraordinary coastline, ever aware of its domination, of the effect of sun and shadow and cloud on those fierce, riven mountains and savage landscapes, where rock and sea seemed to battle eternally. They perceived no towns or settlements – presumably any such were hidden within the fjords; there appeared to be little if any coastal plain and few trees, even heather and the like, only soaring dark stone and white water and spray. Possibly some of the myriad islands supported inhabitants, but since they wisely kept well clear of these and their defending reefs and skerries, they saw no sign of humanity. The nights were short here, at this time of year, even shorter than in Scotland, for they were considerably further north now, drawing level with Iceland; so the travellers saw a sufficiency of that seaboard and wondered at it, recognising how it had produced a race of fierce sea-warriors, the Vikings.

The young women wondered also as to how Rob Carnegie knew where he was going, for this endless succession of great headlands, soaring peaks and chasm-like fjords, behind their screen of islands, was seemingly unchanging. How to know when they reached Trondheim Fjord? The shipmaster assured them that, although he had never been here before, he had had adequate directions. When the coastline eventually began to bend away eastwards consistently, they would find the mountains drawing back noticeably, and soon thereafter there would be three large islands quite close together, Smola, Hitra and Froya. Immediately beyond this last the Trondheim Fjord opened and they turned in.

It was the afternoon of the fourth day out that they came to three much larger islands than most that they had seen, and perceived the mountains indeed sinking into hills and greenery becoming evident on the slopes. The girls had not realised that the land had begun to trend eastwards, but the shipmaster had discerned it. Round the tip of Froya the *Tay Pearl* swung at right angles and faced the hidden entrance of a fjord wider than most they had seen hitherto.

Even so, that waterway was very different from most Highland sea-lochs, deep, dark and growing darker as the mountains into which it probed closed in again. It twisted and coiled also, so that it was seldom possible to see more than a mile or two ahead or behind. And it went on and on. Carnegie told them that Nidaros was said to be thirty miles up, no less, although perhaps only half that as the eagles might fly from the sea. Mary said, was it not an extraordinary place to site the ancient Norwegian capital? He agreed, but pointed out that probably defensively it could scarcely be bettered – and it was a sea-raiders' capital. In the old Viking days this fjord could be barred to invaders at a score of places. He was told that they used to have great chains across, which could be raised from under water to prevent shipping from getting past. And presumably there was some more level and fertile ground beyond these mountains.

Some fifteen miles up they found a narrow bay, at a bend in the fjord, in which to anchor for a few hours of night – for navigating these coiling straits in darkness would be hazardous indeed. After the great seas' motions of their voyage, it was strange to lie quietly in that black abyss amongst the beetling cliffs, the only sound being the faint roar of cascading waterfalls, of which they had passed dozens.

But in the morning, quite quickly they came to a major widening in their waterway, a great basin where branching arms opened into the lessening and retiring heights, and a notable river came in from the south, the Nid apparently, from which the town took its name. It would be an exaggeration to call the surrounding area any sort of plain, but it was the nearest to such that the travellers had seen since leaving the Swedish coast. There were meadowlands, low, swelling green hills, woodlands and cultivation patches, farmeries and a town of sorts which seemed to crouch under two great dominating buildings, a cathedral and a castle, the former unlikely seeming in such a situation.

When their vessel, approaching this inhabited area, rounded

174

a small peninsula, it was to find a harbour, behind a sea-wall, with jetties and quays and a neighbouring boat-strand for fishing boats. A number of ships were tied up here, but none so large as their own. Mary still thought it a strange place to be the capital of Norway.

They had some difficulty as to mooring, for the harbour-master and his men could speak only their own tongue, not being clerics. So much sign-language, gesticulation and shouting ensued; but Bishop Durisdeer, pointing up at the cathedral and pronouncing the name of St Olav and that of Magnus, which was apparently the archepiscopal name, eventually gained them permission to dock and land.

Watched by interested peasantry and fisherfolk and barked at by dogs large and shaggy, the bishop's little party started to climb up towards that extraordinary cathedral.

It was unlike any of the abbeys or churches of Scotland, massive, many-gabled, with pointed roofs and little spires. The castle was nearby, crowning another knoll, presumably the archepiscopal palace.

In some doubt as to which edifice to make for, the question was resolved for them by the appearance of a group of men coming down towards them, in no sort of style or order but looking enquiring. Foremost amongst them was a stocky, thick-set, square and elderly man, notably short of leg and long of arm, in nondescript clothing but with a silver crucifix hanging on a chain at his breast.

"Some sort of churchman," Bishop Andrew observed. "He should be a guide, if he knows the Latin." He held up an arm in greeting, and addressed the approaching party in that tongue, to the effect that they were a mission from Scotland seeking the Archbishop of Nidaros.

The answer was brief indeed, although in clear Latin. "I am Magnus," the thick-set man said. The young women, no Latinists, understood that.

They all tried to hide their astonishment. Anyone less like a prelate, let alone an archbishop and Metropolitan of the North, would have been hard to imagine; but from the way he declared it, this could be no other Magnus, common name as that was in Scandinavia.

Durisdeer and Master Vanns bowed hastily and sought to introduce themselves with suitable respect, the one saying that

175

he was the Bishop of Glasgow, before hastily amending that to mention first the Princess Mary, Countess of Arran, sister to King James of Scots, before reverting to himself and to Vanns as King's Almoner, representing the Primate of the Scottish Church, Patrick, Bishop of St Andrews. He did not trouble to introduce Anna.

The archbishop seemed nowise impressed, but smiled amiably at the ladies. He welcomed them to Nidaros, whatever the reason for their visit. Evidently he was a man of few words.

The effect, of course, was to make Bishop Andrew the more voluble. He explained that they were part of a larger embassage to King Christian, at Copenhagen, concerned with the proposed marriage of his daughter to the King of Scots; but that *his* especial mission was over the see of Orkney and the position of the Scottish Church, matters of concern for His Eminence. The bishop used that style somewhat doubtfully. It might relate only to cardinals? Was a Metropolitan archbishop of similar rank? He had never encountered one before. And Eminence did seem an odd title for this very unecclesiastical-looking individual. This as they all made their way uphill towards the castle, not the cathedral.

Where the roadways divided, Archbishop Magnus took Mary's arm, to guide her into the right-hand track – and retained his grip. That young woman was beginning to recognise that this was an effect she seemed to have on the other sex, why she was not sure; she certainly did not deliberately intend to captivate, although she liked men, or most men.

Bishop Durisdeer, who had not been notably loquacious hitherto on their embassage, now appeared to be impelled to speech, possibly on account of the need for careful Latinity. This was hardly the moment to launch into details of their mission and proposals, but he all but did so, the more so seemingly as he got little response from the other man. Mary, whose Latin was scanty indeed, did seek to help the bishop's so evident discomfort by interjecting a few halting words of goodwill and greetings of her own – which produced only a nod of the greying head and a squeeze of the arm, perhaps sufficient response. Almoner Vanns tried out a phrase or two on some of the other men there, and did get a reply in Latin – so possibly these also were clerics. Perhaps churchmen in Norway did not dress differently from other folk normally?

Thus they came to the castle on its hillock, no very palatial residence but strong enough. There the girls were handed over to a cheerful, motherly woman, presumably some sort of housekeeper, who conducted them to a tower wing of the fortalice, somewhat bare as to furnishings, but where two maids presently appeared to cater for their needs. Evidently there was no custom of excluding women from ecclesiastical establishments here. These spoke no Latin, so it was all a matter of smiles and gestures.

Mary and Anna wondered what they had let themselves in for. They had not anticipated anything like this.

They were, in fact, left to themselves for a considerable time, although log-fires were lit for them in their tower and ample food and drink provided. Eventually Bishop Andrew found his way to them, and seemed considerably more like himself. These Norsemen, although peculiar, were none so ill, he observed. They behaved very differently from the Scots clergy, or such English as he had met, and the archbishop was an oddity indeed. But they were nowise hostile and might well be prepared to negotiate. Clearly, for an archbishopric, this one was very poor in worldly goods. This castle showed it; and while he had not yet been over to the cathedral, he could even from a distance distinguish signs of neglect. So – moneys might speak quite loudly here.

He had established relations with one a deal more forthcoming than Archbishop Magnus, whom he took to be an archdeacon or the like, named Sverre. From him he had learned quite a lot, in a general way. This church of St Olav was the first Christian shrine to be established in Norway, just prior to the year One Thousand After Christ, by King Olav Tryggvesson, who adopted the faith, demoting Thor, Odin and the rest as the Norse gods. A descendant, St Olav Harroldsson, had had it raised into an episcopal see, and built the cathedral, the first archbishop being appointed in 1150. How the Norse had achieved this Metropolitan status when the Scots could not was unexplained. But certainly now there was a lack of endowments. If the country they had passed on the way here was typical of the rest of Norway, the lack of wealth was not to be wondered at. Where the other bishoprics were, how many and how rich, was not clear either. But Bishop Andrew was hopeful that what they had to offer would not be unwelcome.

Later, a visit was paid to the cathedral, the young women included. Although very different from Glasgow, St Andrews and Dunblane, the only such Mary had seen, or the great abbeys of Melrose, Dryburgh, Jedburgh, Arbroath and the like, it was a noble and imposing building in its own way, lofty, many aisled, roofing at a great variety of levels, the stonework well carved with curious effigies, gargoyles and masks, the ceilings all vividly painted. But the said paintwork was stained and peeling, the roofing leaked most obviously, and lack of due upkeep was not far to seek. The archbishop had not accompanied the visitors; they could see why.

Magnus was present at the meal in the castle which followed, no banquet but a very adequate repast of soup, venison, beef, salmon and curds, with the inevitable schnapps. Magnus did not behave as did King Christian, but he did seat Mary at his right hand and obviously approved of her. There was no real conversation, of course, but some rapport was mutual.

Instead of dancers and performing dwarfs they were entertained thereafter by grotesquely garbed skalds, reciters and singers; and although the words were unintelligible to the visitors, the scene in the torch-lit hall was memorable, strange.

The young women discussed all this that night in bed, much intrigued. But they missed their menfolk.

In the morning they went, on foot necessarily, exploring the neighbourhood, whilst Bishop Andrew and Almoner Vanns commenced their negotiations with the archbishop and his aides. The houses here were all of wood, which seemed strange in a country with so much stone available, the people interesting and interested, not unfriendly, the fisherfolk, their boats, nets and gear very similar to those of Scotland.

They were astonished when they got back to the castle to discover that all was finished, arranged, and successfully. Archbishop Magnus had been simplicity itself to negotiate with, indeed he seemed to have looked upon the Scots as a God-send. Not that he was soft or lacking in wits; but clearly he and his desperately needed money, and it had been only a question of how much. The Orkney diocese had sent him nothing for years, and was unlikely ever to do so. Lordship over it was purely nominal. So he had been quite prepared to cede it to the Scottish Church, for suitable recompense. And once that was accepted the matter of Metropolitan status lost any point. Magnus had wanted extra payment for his agreement to write to the Pope to that effect, and to suggest that the bishopric of St Andrews in Scotland be raised to an archbishopric, and its Primate incumbent made a Metropolitan. A certain amount of bargaining had ensued over that, but in the end ten thousand florins had settled the deal.

Bishop Graham back at home, whose great ambition this had been for years, would be joyous indeed. They could now return to Copenhagen, without delay, next day perhaps.

The return voyage lasted longer than the outward one, with the south-westerly breeze still prevailing and therefore almost continuous tacking necessary, but none there grumbled. They had completed their mission in much less time than had been anticipated, and achieved their ends. Not that Mary Stewart felt that she had contributed anything on this occasion.

Back at Christiansborg Slot they discovered matters to be proceeding less speedily but not unsatisfactorily. The proposal that the Princess Margaret should wed King James, if found suitable, had been more or less agreed in advance; Mary did not fail to note that her *brother*'s suitability was more or less taken for granted. These negotiations, again, were mainly about finance and material things. In royal marriages it was customary to provide substantial settlements, portions, dowries, on both sides, and such could vary greatly depending upon the wealth of the nations concerned. Clearly, however impressive the triple kingdom of Denmark, Norway and Sweden might sound, it was far from rich in money. King Christian had to spend large sums on keeping up what amounted to an army of occupation in rebellious Sweden. Moreover, he had made a policy of buying extensive lands in his native Schleswig-Holstein, to the south. So his treasury was even emptier than that of Scotland. Yet national pride and face-saving demanded a high-sounding exchange on both sides.

So while Thomas and Avondale came to agreement with Christian on principles without much difficulty, details were holding up final decisions, details of money, florins, basically, or the King's lack of these. He could nowise offer some tiny sum which would look feeble and unworthy. The Scots, being realists, did not look for large amounts, even if they seemed to do so; but they *were* interested in the ownership of the Orkney and Shetland isles, however unexpressed had to be this aim. They had got the length of agreeing to a nominal dowry on Denmark's part of sixty thousand florins, ten thousand to be paid forthwith, the rest forthcoming when possible; also the cancellation of all the

Orkney and Shetland arrears. In return, the Scots would give the palace of Linlithgow to the new Queen, with the castle of Doune of Menteith, and the revenues of all the lands pertaining – these to remain hers even if her husband should die before her. Also she was to enjoy the revenues of one-third of all the royal lands in the event of James's death, so long as she remained in Scotland and did not remarry the King of England or one of his subjects. Moreover, each monarch obliged himself to go to the aid of the other against all parties other than already made allies.

Thus far they had got, it seemed. The trouble was, it had become evident that at present Christian just could not raise the advance payment of ten thousand florins, despite the thirty-thousand Annual the Scots had brought him – and which presumably had been used at once to pay off pressing debts. Orkney and Shetland had not yet been brought up as a kind of surety, hinted at but ignored by Christian and his advisers.

Thomas was obviously very glad to see Mary back so soon, and not only for her person. He wanted her advice as to how to force Christian's hand over Orkney; it had been her suggestion in the first place, after all.

She pointed out that the Church's successful mission to Nidaros ought to help in this matter, to give Christian some saving of face, as his churchmen had already shown the way. She recognised that the actual secession of national territory was not easy for any monarch to grant; but Orkney and Shetland were far away and of little real value to Denmark. Some device was necessary to enable Christian to swallow this indigestible morsel not too painfully.

Tom impatiently asked did she think that he had not perceived this all along? But – what?

This of the ten thousand florins which Christian could not presently find, she suggested? Was he trying to raise it right away? And they waiting here for it?

Her husband agreed that this was more or less the situation. How long it would take, the good Lord alone knew.

Then, was not that the answer, she put to him? *Not* to wait; at least, not all of them. Leave quickly, before he could raise it. Say that it was necessary to return to Scotland for instructions, with even one-sixth of the dowry not forthcoming. Leave some of the party here, to show that negotiations were not actually broken off. Then come back later, with the outright request for Orkney and

Shetland as wadset and assurance of full payment? Would that not save all faces?

The man considered that, and then slapped his knee. "I believe that you have it, lass! As ever! To go home, and then back, with this demand. As though from King James himself. Keep Christian unsure meantime. Waiting. Even if he has raised the ten thousand by then, he will not have the rest, the other fifty thousand. Nothing more sure. Demand – or request – the Orkneys in pledge for that. Mary, my heart – bless you!" He hugged and kissed her.

"I serve you as best I can, husband," she observed. "Otherwise than you serve me, to be sure!"

"What mean you by that?"

"I mean that I think that I am pregnant again. Indeed, I am sure of it . . ."

"Glory be! Another of us! Here's joy. A girl, this time. When . . . ?"

"January, I would think."

"Then the sooner that we get you home, the better, lass. Before winter storms commence."

"It is only late summer, Tom. And I am no delicate creature. But, yes – for this of Christian and Orkney, yes. Soon . . ."

"Christian is going to miss you!"

14

They left Lord Avondale, Almoner Vanns and Bishop Tulloch at Copenhagen, and with Bishop Andrew, *his* duty done, set sail in the *Tay Pearl* a few days later, King Christian seeing them off amidst lamentations as hearty as the rest of him. But he would see them again . . .

The voyage home was much slower, again, than on the outward passage, heading into those westerly winds, but was otherwise uneventful, no actual storms encountered – save, oddly, when they entered the Scotwater, off the Isle of May, and there ploughed into heavy seas. This, Rob Carnegie informed, was not uncommon, with the Norse Sea's deep waters suddenly meeting the shelf of Scotland, and the tides spouting upwards.

They docked at Leith, and the Arran party went ashore, to hire horses for Stirling, while the *Pearl* took Bishop Andrew across to Fife, to report success to the Primate at St Andrews.

They all found it good to be in the saddle again, horses appearing to be but little used in Scandinavia where, like the West Highlands, most travel was done by water. They had been away little more than two months, but it seemed longer.

Their reception at Stirling Castle was varied. James and his brothers and sister were delighted to see them; but the Lord Boyd, who seemed preoccupied, was clearly disappointed that they had returned lacking final results.

No major developments appeared to have taken place during their absence. James complained that it had been very dull at Stirling without them, Lord Boyd not having let him do much hunting or hawking, indeed not allowing him to leave the castle much at all, and then only under strict and numerous guard. There had been very little interesting company, and altogether life had been dreary. He wished that he had been allowed to go to Denmark with them. They ought to have arranged it. He would have liked to have visited those lands. He asked them, now, for details as to the places and peoples visited – but Mary noted that he seemed quite uninterested as to details regarding his prospective bride.

In their own bedchamber that night, Tom told her that he was a little concerned about his father. They had never been close in any affectionate way, indeed his sire was not a man to show emotion or reveal himself. But now he was more withdrawn than heretofore, something most evidently on his mind. And clearly he was upset that they had not brought back a definite decision about Orkney and Shetland, and the assertion that it would all probably come right in due course not enough for him. Which was strange, for the matter of the Northern Isles was not, after all, of first priority for the ruler of Scotland.

The Arrans' first need, of course, was to visit Tantallon Castle, not so far from the mouth of the Scotwater where they had encountered the high seas, to see and collect the baby Jamie, whom his mother had greatly missed. They found the child well and developed notably in the interval, a joy to behold. Indeed Tom's sister Elizabeth was loth to relinquish him to his parents.

There followed, by royal command, a period of very active, almost continuous, hunting, hawking and riding abroad, in golden October weather, James determined to make up for the inaction of the summer months; and Mary, recognising that her condition would soon forbid such, prepared to humour him, Thomas, Anna and Patrick nothing loth. The Flanders Moss and the Tor Wood, in particular, saw a lot of them. Lord Boyd made no objection, so long as the King was available morning and night to sign his decrees and charters. The fact that he had not been allowed to go before, when Tom was away, looked as though he had been afraid for the monarch's safety, or at least security. An escort always had to go with them still, of course.

The first hint they had as to what was wrong with the Lord Boyd came from that man's brother – not Sir Alexander, who seemed to be acting the recluse now down on his Dumfries-shire property of Duncow in Nithsdale – but from the Abbot of Kilwinning. With Lord Avondale, the Chancellor, away in Denmark, it seemed that Boyd had had the abbot appointed acting Chancellor, so he had had to come not infrequently to Stirling – although, in fact, the elder brother was more or less governing Scotland single-handed. So perhaps his preoccupation was not to be wondered at. But possible trouble was building up, according to Abbot William, against the regime. Always, of course, there had been those hostile in some degree to the Boyd hegemony; but now there were rumours of meetings and associations, possibly indicating more positive reaction, with the King's two illegitimate uncles, the Earl of Atholl and Sir James Stewart of Auchterhouse, apt to figure the most prominently. Moreover, some who had formerly been close supporters of Boyd were now beginning to absent themselves from court, notably the Lords Somerville and Hailes. This was worrying for the Regent, and would account for much.

The abbot added that it was a pity that the Orkney and Shetland secession had not been brought to a satisfactory conclusion as yet, for the acquisition of these territories for Scotland would constitute quite a major credit for the regency, and help to damp down hostility. He, the abbot, urged Thomas to return to Denmark as quickly as possible, and bring back the good news, together with the royal bride. Such development would undoubtedly much improve his father's position.

Tom saw that, but nevertheless was not going to rush away. More important to him than any such matters of state was Mary's care and well-being. He just was not going back to King Christian until he had seen his wife safely delivered of their second child. Besides, winter was no time to make crossing of the Norse Sea. There was no shaking him on this; and Mary of course supported him.

In November they paid a visit to Arran, before the worst of the weather set in, James not permitted to accompany them on this occasion, to his vehement protests. All went well otherwise, Patrick happy to see his parents again, and with so much to tell them. That young man had developed considerably in the interim, in manners, in self-confidence, as esquire to the Earl of Arran. He had still not become any typical courtier, but association with such had given him a polish and assurance. Anna had had quite a lot to do with that also, undoubtedly. Almost certainly they were lovers, as well as firm friends; indeed Mary had more than once caught them in all but compromising situations. But it was certain that the Regent would not countenance his under-age daughter's marriage to someone as lowly as an Arran laird's son, and their association had to remain a private one. Both were of a cheerful and uncomplicated nature, however, and prepared to accept such satisfactions as were available meantime.

The Arran interlude was enjoyed by all, although Mary was suffering some pregnancy discomfort now.

On their return to Stirling and James's grumbles against the Regent, it was not long before the Yuletide preparations were afoot, concurrently with preoccupations with Mary's forthcoming delivery, which looked like happening earlier than anticipated, with more disturbance to her normal way of life than on the previous occasion. Thomas wondered whether all the voyaging might have been responsible for this?

In the event, Christmas festivities still ongoing, on the last day of 1468, the child was born, after a prolonged and difficult labour. It was, as Thomas had required, a girl, to be called Grizel. The baby was small but exquisite, perfectly formed and a delight to behold. Mary, although weak, rejoiced.

Lord Boyd was already pressing Thomas to return to Denmark without delay to finalise the royal marriage negotiations, brushing aside his son's assertions of the dangers of winter's storms for voyaging. But Tom did not lack Boyd willpower, and was determined not to leave until he was assured of his wife's full recovery and the new infant's good progress. There was no question, in the circumstances, of Mary going with him this time, much as she would have liked to do so.

It was not until the beginning of March that Thomas felt that he could put off no longer. Carnegie and the *Tay Pearl* had been on stand-by for weeks, on the Regent's orders, and this time they came up-Forth as far as Blackness, the port for Linlithgow, to collect the travellers, this to ensure a shorter journey from Stirling, so that the two young women might ride there to see them off, this even so Mary's longest spell on horseback since the birth.

The parting was not exactly tearful but reluctant indeed, much reassuring required on both sides, although it was not anticipated that the young men would be gone for very long this time, Tom's instructions being to bring back the princess quickly even though little or none of the dowry money was forthcoming. The bride, and the mortgage of Orkney and Shetland, were what was important, vital, now, for the Lord Boyd. Haste was the embassage's watchword.

They had to await the tide at Blackness, so far up Forth, so that farewells were protracted as well as exacting, at the royal fortress there, which frequently was used as a state prison, a fairly grim establishment. Thereafter, the girls waved and waved as the ship drew out into the estuary, even after they could no longer distinguish their men waving back, loth even to turn their backs when the *Pearl* was small-seeming indeed. Denmark then seemed to them a long way off, and sea-voyaging much more hazardous when they themselves were not going along. It was almost an ordeal to turn their beasts round for the twenty-five-mile ride back to Stirling.

15

In the months that followed, Mary had no lack of preoccupations
other than wondering how her husband fared. With two little ones
to nurture and cherish, and a very discontented royal brother to
cope with, as well as a distinctly uneasy air about the court, and
rumours of the regime's growing unpopularity amongst the lords
and magnates, she had a sufficiency to concern her.

James was going through a difficult stage. He was now
seventeen and beginning to wish to act the man, and, to be
sure, the King. And Lord Boyd was not in any way conceding
this, yielding no iota of his powers and authority as Regent, nor
even making any superficial gestures of subservience towards the
young monarch. Which was folly, to be sure, when others were
doing so, for it would serve his cause nothing to make an enemy
of his liege-lord who, in a year or two would be able to dispense
with a Regent's services. Mary was scarcely in a position to tell
her father-in-law so, but she did mention the matter to Abbot
William who, shrugging, declared that he had said something
of the sort to his brother but had made no evident impression.
He confessed that he was worried somewhat, in his capacity as
acting Chancellor; and other churchmen were telling him of
opposition to the Boyds growing in the realm. The Regent was,
of course, aware of this; but, ever a man alone, and assured
of his own capabilities, which indeed were not inconsiderable,
he believed that he could weather any minor storm meantime.
And when the royal marriage was brought about and if Orkney
and Shetland were added to the Scots realm by his arranging,
he reckoned that the regency, and his own position, would be
greatly strengthened.

More Boyds than these were having problems. For, some six
weeks after Tom's departure, Anna told Mary that she feared
that she was pregnant – if feared was the word. For, in a
way, she was glad to have Patrick's child. That would be
a joy, and it might well force, ensure, their marriage. But

187

meantime, with Patrick absent in Denmark, it posed difficulties indeed.

Mary was not condemnatory, but she was less optimistic than the other over this of marriage. Knowing Lord Boyd's soaring ambitions for his family, she feared that even in these circumstances he would not allow his daughter to wed anyone of such comparatively lowly status as Patrick Fullarton. He had had his son created earl, and his other daughter was a countess. He would want Anna to marry some lordling of broad acres, she was certain. But she did not say so.

What she did do, however, was to speak to James. She did not reveal to him the pregnancy, in case he told others, but she suggested, almost casually, that since Patrick was so good and faithful an esquire to Master Thomas and indeed acting as an extra envoy at the Danish court, he, James, might confer the honour of knighthood upon him. He was the King, and could do this, irrespective of the Regent's wishes. Such was the royal right. Patrick deserved it, did he not? And they were friends.

James agreed at once. He would do it when Patrick returned. He would like that. No, he would not mention it to Lord Boyd. It would be a secret, a surprise to all.

Mary hoped that this rise in rank might help the Regent to accept the young man as son-in-law, especially if some grant of royal or Arran lands was to go with it.

In early June a ship from Denmark brought a letter from Thomas to Mary. He had hoped to be home before this, he wrote, but Christian's pride was delaying things. He just could not raise the ten thousand florins token, modest sum as this was; indeed it was rumoured that he had got together only two thousand. The envoys, as instructed, were quite content to come away, with the Princess Margaret and the wadset of Orkney and Shetland, but Christian felt that would make him look foolish, impoverished. His councillors were prepared to agree to this, and almost certainly the King would do so in the end. But it might take some little time more to bring him to it. Thomas hoped that they would be back within the month, however. Tell his father so.

In this extended period of waiting, two very significant developments eventuated, one personal, one national. The first was that, unfortunately, Anna's state began to show by the end of the month. Presumably she had miscalculated the timing. At any rate, her father perceived it, to his cold anger. And more than anger; she would not marry that low-born scoundrel, son of the Coroner of Arran as he might be. But she *would* marry, and forthwith. No daughter of Boyd was going to have an illegitimate child. He would find her a husband of as suitable rank as was possible, and such would be given sufficient reward to make the cost to him acceptable. There would be no argument, no choice. *He* would decide. His fool of a daughter had sacrificed all rights in the matter.

Needless to say, this declaration threw Anna, and to some extent Mary, into dire distress, all but despair. But there was nothing that they could do about it. The Regent wielded supreme power, and Anna was still under age. Thomas might possibly have been able to effect something, but Thomas was still far away.

The second significant event was a visit to Stirling by Bishop Andrew of Glasgow. He came privately to see Mary, not the Regent. And he brought grave news, from the Primate at St Andrews. Bishop Graham was a sick man and could not travel here himself; but he was concerned for the princess-countess who, he considered, had helped him gain what he so greatly desired, rule of the Orkney diocese from Norway and the renunciation of the Nidaros Metropolitan status over the Scottish Church and the promise of support for his own elevation to archbishopric by the Pope. In return, he desired Mary, and the King, to be secretly warned. The Boyd regime was almost certainly about to fall, and bloodily. An alliance of earls, lords and barons had been formed to unseat the Regent and take over the government and the charge of the monarch, indeed to arraign Boyd and his close supporters on a charge of treason for having laid violent hands on the King at that hunt. The alliance was very strong, and included many of the greatest in the land, led by the King's uncles, the Earl of Atholl and Stewart of Auchterhouse, and had been joined by the two earls who formerly supported Boyd, Crawford and Argyll. They were almost ready to strike, and when they did, the Primate did not think that the Regent would be able to withstand. They had even arranged to call a parliament, to arraign the Boyds for treason. That, of course, would require the royal agreement and attendance to be official, so it could not be summoned as yet. He, the Primate, had been approached secretly, and to some extent he would favour the move for, as the late Bishop Kennedy's nephew, he deplored the Boyd coup, although as Primate he had had to work with Boyd in the interim. His present sickness enabled him to take no active part in the planned uprising; but he knew that many of his fellow-bishops were in favour of it. He was anxious that the Princess Mary, who was married to a Boyd, should not suffer in all this, and so he warned her. But, if she would heed him, not to warn the Regent that she knew of it all. He, Boyd, was bound to be aware of some of it, but probably not its full extent. If he did learn how close this was to fulfilment and just how strong was the opposition, he would surely summon all the armed forces which he could muster and hide the King away somewhere to secure him, and use him as a bargaining factor. There could be war, civil war. So he urged the princess to seek her own and the King's safety, secretly, on whatever pretext, possibly going to Arran or to the strong, all but impregnable castle of Tantallon belonging to her good-sister's husband, meantime.

Thus Bishop Andrew.

Needless to say, this gave Mary furiously to think. She was not entirely surprised, save in the seeming immediacy of it all. She had sensed that trouble was coming, but had assumed that it would not come to a head for some time yet, and that Thomas's return with the Princess Margaret and the Orkney and Shetland secession would much improve the situation. But now it looked as though this might not be in time. This talk of an arraignment for treason, of course, was dire indeed – for the penalty for treason was execution. And Thomas, as son and heir to Boyd, could well be included in the indictment, whatever his services in the meantime.

What was she to do? It was all very well for Bishop Graham to advise her to take James away to Arran or Tantallon, but the Regent would never let him go. *She* could go, yes – but not James. And if the whole Boyd family was to be indicted before parliament, what of her own little Jamie, Master of Arran, who was after all a Boyd also?

Mary Stewart, usually so keen-witted as to ways and means, was here at a loss. She did not debate the matter with Anna, who had enough on her mind meantime, however hard she herself cudgelled her brains.

In the event, Anna was wholly otherwise preoccupied, for only two days later Lord Boyd told her that he had found her a husband, Sir John Gordon of Lochinvar, Baron of Stichel, who was prepared to wed her, child and all, in return for unspecified benefits. The wedding would take place immediately, in a week, no more, since she was swelling visibly and days counted, or folk would be talking. The fact that Anna had never so much as encountered Sir John Gordon seemed to be immaterial.

They met only three days before the wedding, a stiffly formal occasion, with Lord Boyd very much in charge. Gordon proved to be a wary young man, slight, narrow-featured, hesitant, speaking with a lisp. Mary guessed at once that in this strange match Anna would be the dominant partner, if partnership there was to be. Why he had let himself be brought into this situation was not divulged; but his father, now dead, had been the first Gordon, from the Merse, to move over into Galloway, where was Lochinvar, and perhaps his heir had succeeded to problems there and required financial and other assistance. At any rate, here he was, confronting with no confidence his reluctant bride, and carefully avoiding looking at her middle.

It was only a brief meeting, with Mary and James present, Lochinvar looking as eager to be elsewhere as did Anna. They would wed in the Chapel Royal here in Stirling Castle two days hence, in a quiet ceremony conducted by the Abbot of Kilwinning. Anna made but one commentary – which she had discussed with Mary beforehand; she was the royal lady-in-waiting, and intended to remain so, on the princess's orders, with her duties close to her mistress always. Mary confirmed that, there and then, whatever Lord Boyd thought of it. Probably he cared not, so long as his daughter was duly married before her child-bearing was known to all.

So the wedding took place in the ancient Chapel Royal, in the presence of the monarch and royal family, the Regent and very few others, none of the bridegroom's family attending, in a service remarkable for its brevity, vows exchanged in uncertain mutters. The meal thereafter was scarcely a feast, and got over as quickly as the rest. What was to happen then had not been spelt out, and Mary wondered how Anna would cope. But that young woman, once the knot was tied, showed her Boyd spirit and decision, for she arrived back in Mary's quarters after only a short interval, to announce that she had told Lochinvar – she avoided calling him her husband – that in her condition bodily relations between them were out of the question, dangerous to her and her unborn child. This was almost certainly erroneous, but the man had not demurred, indeed had seemed almost relieved. Where he had gone to spend the night she neither knew nor cared. But for herself she would pass it in Mary's bed, if she might.

So two forced-brides bedded down together that bridal night. One of them did dissolve into tears for a while. Mary would have comforted her by declaring that her own union had turned into love and happiness now, but recognised that this might seem to imply rejection of Patrick Fullarton. She contented herself with holding the other girl close, and consoling as best she might

The very next day, as though almost to rub salt into the wound, one of the smaller vessels of the Danish embassage's squadron, able to sail right up Forth as far as Carron-mouth, and so only fifteen miles from Stirling, brought none other than Almoner Vanns to the castle, to announce that the Earl of Arran and Chancellor Avondale, with the Princess Margaret, were on their way, and had sent him ahead to arrange for a fitting reception for the future Queen. They would dock at Leith in perhaps ten days, weather permitting, when it was hoped that the King and an illustrious company would be there to welcome Margaret to her new country.

This, needless to say, much cheered all at court, although Anna's joy was shot through with regrets and exasperation that the homecomers had not been able to arrive just a few days earlier and so possibly saved her from her ridiculous and unwanted marriage. However, she placed great faith in Thomas and Patrick, and prayed that somehow they might solve her problems for her.

Mary was overjoyed, to be sure, and hoped that from now on the entire situation would greatly improve. Master Vanns said that the Danish princess was well, friendly and apparently not at all upset by her fate and her uprooting, a cheerful youngster.

Then, only a few hours after Vanns's arrival, the atmosphere of well-being at Stirling was abruptly changed by the appearance of another unexpected visitor, Archibald Douglas, fifth Earl of Angus, the Lord Boyd's son-in-law, from Tantallon, a young man not yet out of his teens but of a vehement and impetuous nature, as befitted the Red Douglas chief. He brought grim tidings and urgent advice. The rebel magnates were massing in arms no further away than St John's Town of Perth, with their thousands, practically every earl in Scotland other than himself and Arran, under Atholl, Crawford and Argyll, with most of the lords and knights by the hundred. They had approached him for Red Douglas support, but he had temporised. The Earl of Dunbar, his neighbour, was with them – he had done the approaching. They would march in only a day or two, and nothing that the Lord Boyd could muster could withstand them. Stirling Castle, besieged, might hold out for a while, but escape would be impossible. They had issued orders for the arrest, imprisonment and trial before parliament, for treason, of the Regent and those still supporting him. They had already sent south, Dunbar said, to arrest Sir Alexander Boyd in Nithsdale, and the Abbot of Kilwinning in Ayrshire. They would demand the immediate surrender to them of the person of the King's Grace and his brothers and sisters. Angus advised prompt flight from Stirling.

Consternation reigned, even Lord Boyd for once uncertain, agitated.

Mary put the question uppermost in *her* mind. What of the Earl of Arran? Was anything being said about him? He was due to arrive back in Scotland in a few days.

The earl said that the word was that Arran was to be tried for treason along with the others, since he had taken part in the royal abduction near Linlithgow those three years before. Because of his services in the matter of the Danish princess, it was possible that he might escape execution. Who could tell? But he would be arrested and forfeited, most assuredly, once he had handed over the princess to the allied lords.

In the flurry of alarm, question and debate which followed, King James himself appeared to be the least upset. He, of course, was the least threatened there, for whoever won in this contest for power, they required him, safe and not hostile. He was the monarch, the symbol of all authority and governance. And he was already hostile to Lord Boyd, although not to Master Thomas. Whatever upheavals eventuated, his position was not in question.

Angus, at distinct cost to himself, made the suggestion. Let them all come to Tantallon with him, meantime. His castle was impregnable from the land, and the rebel lords would have no fleet of warships to assail by sea – not for some time, at least. From there, His Grace and the Regent might seek terms. He did not see the Boyd regime surviving, but once Arran, Avondale and the princess arrived, there might be something to bargain with.

The Regent shook his head, decision apparently made. That

was not for him. Boyd was not so easily beaten. He would go to his own country, Ayrshire, Kilmarnock, where lay his manpower and allies. He would raise added bargaining factors to the Danish match and Orkney and Shetland, armed men. He was still the Regent, appointed so by parliament, and as such still exercised the royal authority . . .

James broke in there. *His* was the royal authority, he declared hotly. He had had enough of being ruled by others. He was the King. And he was not going to Kilmarnock with Boyd, or anyone else. He would either stay here at Stirling, or go to Tantallon with Angus.

Regent and monarch glared at each other. In that moment, Lord Boyd lost the rule of Scotland.

Mary spoke. "I have two bairns to think of and care for. Anna here is in no state to be caught up in men's struggles and warfare. We will go to Tantallon with my lord of Angus, meantime. Until my husband arrives, James, I say that you should come with us. You will be best there until this upheaval is overpast. When the Princess Margaret arrives at Leith, she can be brought to you there, but a score of miles away. Her arrival in Scotland, after all our efforts, must not be turned into uproar. Perhaps, with Douglas guard, you could go to meet her? The nation's honour is at stake, here. And we owe it to the lass."

"Yes, yes – I will go to Tantallon," the King agreed.

Without another word to any of them, and without any sort of obeisance to his sovereign, the Lord Boyd swung on his heel and strode from the room.

The others eyed each other.

"I think that the sooner we leave, the better," Angus declared. "It is near to sixty miles to Tantallon, and the Lady Anna in no state for long riding. And bairns to be taken. We can win as far as Linlithgow this night. Then to Edinburgh . . ."

"Almoner Vanns's ship will still be at Carron-mouth after its long voyage," Mary pointed out. "Your castle is near to the haven of North Berwick, my lord, is it not? Could we not go that far, to the Carron, only some fifteen miles, and then use the ship to sail down the coast?"

"Ha! That would be better, yes. Well thought of! How long until you are ready, Highness? With the bairns?"

"Give us one hour . . ." she said simply.

James Stewart actually grinned.

16

Tantallon Castle, soaring, huge, on its high clifftop headland above the boiling seas, was as secure a hold as the young earl had claimed – it had had to be, with its stormy Red Douglas history. Landward, its narrow promontory was protected by a series of high ramparts and deep ditches, to keep cannon and cavalry at a distance; and seawards precipitous rock was sufficient defence, with offshore reefs and skerries to prevent any shipping coming close enough to be any danger, save by such as knew the tortuous channel amongst the hazards. Here the royal party arrived the following afternoon, bringing Almoner Vanns with them, a possibly useful go-between. There had been no objection made to their departure from Stirling by Lord Boyd, who had been making his own preparations to leave. That man was having to adjust his priorities drastically.

Elizabeth Boyd was glad and relieved to welcome her visitors, in especial her sister, and of course concerned over her untimely and odd marriage.

Mary's concern now was Thomas's situation, what he was coming back to, and what she might do about it, if anything. Somehow he had to be warned. How? The only possibility which she could conjure up was somehow to intercept his ship as it entered the Scotwater – which entrance, to be sure, was just off Tantallon. But the firth mouth was some fifteen miles across; and the ships might enter it in darkness.

Master Vanns could not do more than guess at even a day when the little group of ships might reach Scottish waters. Perhaps two days hence, depending on the winds, perhaps three. Mary wondered whether any signalling device might be effective to bring the ships close to the castle, but Angus saw little hope in that. They would almost certainly pass well north of the Bass Rock, for the seas between it and the Lothian shore were shallow and scattered with skerries and reefs, and thus would be too far out for any effective signalling. A beacon by night or smoke columns by day would be seen, but would not hold any significance for the travellers.

There was nothing for it, then, Mary declared, but boats out to intercept. There were fishing craft at North Berwick, she had seen. Two or three of these, patrolling the area between the Bass and the Isle of May nearer the Fife shore, ought to be able to ensure making contact with the ships – by day. But, by night? At this time of year there was little real darkness most nights; but even so it would not be easy to spot or to attract the attention of vessels, or to be seen by them. Would they, in fact, enter the Scotwater in darkness, if they were making to dock at Leith? Might they not lie off until daylight?

Angus thought not. It was less than two hours' sailing up to Leith admittedly, and they would not wish to arrive there by night; but any lying-off would be likely to be done in the more sheltered waters of the port itself. Why wait in open seas out here?

Mary was determined. Somehow she had to reach Thomas and warn him. The only way to be sure, or all but sure, was to go out in a boat and wait, go herself. Sail up and down between the Bass and the May, patrol. It might take long enough, days and nights. But she saw nothing else for it.

Angus had his own boat at North Berwick – Tantallon's cliffs were no place to tie up – and he said that she could use that, something better than a mere fishing boat although not much larger. They could get a couple of fishing craft to aid them; three boats beating to and fro would ensure that the ships did not get past unintercepted. They would have to take provisions, and pray that the weather was kind. It would be dull work and scarcely apt for a lady, however.

Mary brushed that aside. She was no flighty girl, twenty years now, and mother of two. She could fish, and while away the time with needlework, storytelling, talk with the oarsmen. She would do well enough.

So, with James and Angus, she went down to the township and haven of North Berwick, there to inspect the earl's boat and arrange with fishermen that there would always be two of their craft out assisting. Since all here were vassals of Angus, owing him service, there was no difficulty about this, and with more than a score of boats available, it was agreed that they should go out in twelve-hourly relays, relieving each other, although the earl's craft would remain permanently at sea until its mission was accomplished. They would start the next morning.

There was much discussion that night as to who should accompany Mary on her vigil. She declared that there was no need for any to do so, but the others were insistent. In the end it was agreed that her friends should take it in turns to keep her company. Since the fishing boats would be relieving each other twelve-hourly, it would be quite simple for the Tantallon group individually to come and go with these.

Also discussed, to be sure, was the likely fate and future of the Boyds. None there was very hopeful. The Regent was unlikely to be able to raise sufficient men successfully to put down or nullify this major uprising, especially lacking the King's personal assistance – and James was adamant that he had had more than enough of the Lord Boyd. If this parliamentary trial for treason did eventuate, there could be little doubt about the verdict. How Thomas might fare at that was doubtful, but neither of his sisters were optimistic. They both felt that he would do better to avoid any appearance, to flee the country meantime until tempers cooled and the King was established in a position to ensure his safety. Mary was not so certain about this, believing that the Orkney and Shetland acquisition and royal marriage would tell greatly in his favour; and was not he the King's brother-in-law, his and her son third in line in the succession?

No firm conclusions were arrived at.

In the morning they all rode down to North Berwick again, laden with food and drink, blankets and other gear. It was decided that Angus would accompany Mary for the first day, Anna coming out for the first night. Then James himself for the second day – although there were some doubts as to the suitability of this for the monarch, but he was determined – and John, Lord of Douglas, Angus's brother, for the second night. It was felt that Elizabeth should have women companions for the nights. Thereafter, if it was necessary, they could repeat the sequence.

The earl's craft was reasonably convenient, for it was of a fair size and had a screen to divide the fore-part from the rest, to give the lordly ones privacy from the oarsmen. Also there was a roofed-in portion at the bows, less than a cabin but fit to sleep under, or as shelter in wet weather. A crew of four, and two manned fishing boats were awaiting them.

Hopes were expressed and farewells said, and the three boats cast off. Apart from other fishing craft dotted over the firth, no shipping was to be seen.

It had been reckoned that the best position for Mary's boat was the central one, with each craft beating up and down a three-mile stretch. That ought to cover the area between Bass and May Isle.

It was a day of breezes and sun and cloud, the sea wavy but not rough. It was quite pleasant in the boat, strange for Mary to be alone, behind that screen, with this young man whom she hardly knew, but who proved to be an agreeable companion and quite a talker. He became presently eloquent on the turbulent story of the Red Douglases, and how they differed from the Black. Mary had never quite understood how this, the lesser, junior branch, had survived when the senior had been so drastically brought low by her father. She now gained enlightenment. The Reds stemmed from an illegitimate half-brother of the second Earl of Douglas by a Stewart Countess of Angus, later married, this in the late fourteenth century. The two lines had never been friendly. Then, fourteen years ago, at the Battle of Arkinholm, which brought down the power of the Blacks, this Archibald's father, the fourth Earl of Angus, had been in command, acting for James the Second, this battle becoming known as "the Red putting down the Black". So the Reds had always supported the throne, and thus escaped the fall of the parallel line.

Mary suspected that there was more to it than that, but did not say so.

The time passed thus congenially enough. Shipping they did see, going and coming, but always single vessels, and none flying royal banners, as would be those bringing Scotland's future Queen. There was more than enough to eat and drink, and although attending to the calls of nature was less private than might have been desired, men and women used to long riding and travel were quite inured to that, and disinclined to fuss.

Rocked by the motion of the waves, they took turns at sleeping and watching during the afternoon.

When the two evening boats came out to relieve the others, one brought Anna. There was nothing to report.

Mary had slept in the afternoon so that she could remain awake much of the night, and she and Anna talked until late. The younger girl was, of course, much concerned about Patrick and what would happen to him. If Thomas was in danger, what of him? Would he not be more so, no earl or lofty one yet a Boyd supporter? Mary said that probably being less lofty would be in his favour, especially as the King was fond of him and had even promised to create him knight.

Anna slept in time, but Mary maintained her vigil, although their four oarsmen were to take turns at watching also. The eastern sky was lightening before she dozed off.

The daytime boats came out later than arranged, with James – who was no doubt responsible for the delay. There was also a relief crew for Mary's craft. Anna was taken back. It was today that Master Vanns thought the most likely for their squadron's arrival.

Mary found her brother a less interesting companion than the others, restless, quickly bored, complaining of this and that. Seventeen is a difficult age for most young males, not yet men but childhood well past, and the need for assertion apt to be evident. She would have indeed preferred to be alone, or chatting with her new crew. James's complaints against the Regent were unending. He would get free of him now, and he would show all who it was who ruled this realm. Mary warned that he had still some years to go before he was of full age, and a new regency might be little more kindly than the old one.

As the day wore on and only coastal shipping appeared, the King grew disenchanted. This was a waste of time, he asserted. Better that they should go to Leith and wait for the ships there, in comfort. If he, the monarch, took care of Master Thomas and Patrick – and the girl, to be sure – none would dare assail them. Mary doubted that, pointing out that once they had Princess Margaret and himself in their hands, the rebel lords would be concerned to make sure that the Boyd faction did not regain strength and seek the rule again, to their own hurt. Therefore they might well wish to get rid of Thomas, who could head up a resurgent regime even though his father had failed to do so.

Her brother held to his own views.

It was quite a relief when the Countess Elizabeth was brought out instead. She was of a very different nature from Anna, quieter, less ebullient and positive, but easy to get on with, the least assertive of the Boyds. They talked of babies and the upbringing of children, also men and their odd ways, and did not disagree. Thereafter they took turn about at keeping watch.

It was soon after sunrise, with the waters glittering in the level rays, and the two countesses waiting for the morning boats from North Berwick, when their oarsmen's shouts drew their gaze eastwards. Eyes shaded against the dazzlement, they took a little while to discern the sails of four ships, hull-down but fairly close together. The chances were that this was the Danish squadron at last.

The fishing boat to the south of them, nearer the Bass, came hastening to inform, in case they had not spotted the sails. The fishermen reckoned that they were still at least six miles off, but clearly approaching.

The patrolling craft to the north had seen them also and now came back. All agreed that the four ships were unlikely to be other than those they sought.

Mary was in a state of mixed emotions, agog to see her husband, now beloved, and concerned over the news she was going to bring him and the problems which would confront them thereafter.

As the ships drew near it could be seen that the largest and foremost was flying large banners, the Lion Rampant and the Saltire of St Andrew. That would be the *Tay Pearl*.

Angus had given Mary one of his own blue and white flags with the red heart, Bruce's heart, which the Good Sir James Douglas had taken on crusade and died defending, and this they now hoisted on their own short mast in case the ships treated them as mere fishing boats to be ignored. They rowed on an intercepting course, all three boats. Mary stood up in the bows of hers and waved and waved.

There could be no mistaking intentions. The leading ship hove to, and the others followed suit. Well before the Tantallon craft could draw alongside to the *Pearl* they could see Thomas and Patrick leaning eagerly over the side, waving back and shouting. Close by was Avondale and the young princess, surprise on all faces, greetings, questions being called. A rope-ladder was lowered.

An oarsman steadying this for her, Mary was first to ascend, hitching up skirts, seeking not to bark her knuckles on the timbers and to adjust to the sway of it. Before she reached the final rungs Thomas was bending over to grasp her wrists and all but hoist her over the bulwark and into his arms.

Incoherences prevailed.

Elizabeth climbed up. If Patrick Fullarton was disappointed that it was not her sister, he managed to hide it.

Greeting Princess Margaret, Avondale, the Bishop of Orkney and Rob Carnegie, Mary was inevitably delayed in explaining the reasons for this interception, Tom apparently assuming that it was merely a particularly dramatic welcome home. What she had to tell him could not just be blurted out before all.

She was about to instruct the two fishing craft to return to harbour, leaving the earl's boat, when who should appear but the Earl of Angus himself, coming out in another boat to relieve his countess. He too climbed up the ladder.

There was more delay until Mary could draw Thomas aside and indicate that she wished to talk to him alone – he no doubt assuming this to be for more intimate greeting. Nothing loth, he led the way to a stern cabin.

Within, he enfolded her in his arms, covering her face and neck and hair with kisses, hands as busy as his lips. She was far from finding this unwelcome, or lacking in response; but concern for what she had to tell him was strong. At length she sought to hold him at arm's length, and put a finger over his lips, both.

"Thomas, my heart," she got out, "here is joy, delight, wonder! But . . . pain also. Sorrow, my dear. For I have ill news for you. I bring pain and hurt, I fear. Why I am here thus. Shame it is, to spoil this our joy at coming together again. But – you must hear it, know of it."

He searched her face. "Trouble? Here? In the realm? My father?"

"Yes. Uprising. Rebellion, it might be called. A grand alliance of the lords, against the Regent. He is gone from Stirling. To Kilmarnock, to try to raise men, an army. To fight them. But will not, cannot, win in this, I think. Many have deserted his cause – Argyll, Crawford, Somerville, Hailes. Others. He has few friends now. Of all the earls, only Angus here, and yourself, are with him. And Angus has no intention of fighting, I would say."

"Fighting? War? Not that!"

"No, I hope not, pray not. But that was Lord Boyd's intention when he left Stirling. Four days past."

"I will go after him. Seek to turn him from this. Civil war, bloodshed, will serve nothing . . ."

"So say I. But, no – do not go after him, Thomas my heart. Not you. For there is worse to tell. They, the earls and lords, intend to call a parliament. Not only to bring down, change, the regency, but to indict you all, all the Boyds, on a charge of treason. For

201

the abduction of James, that time. *Treason*, Thomas! That is the intention. It must not be! *You* must not be charged with treason. Yet you were there, when we were taken, near Linlithgow. I fear, I fear . . ."

"So-o-o! That is it. Aye, they would have me, yes . . ."

"They have sent to arrest your uncles, Sir Alexander and Abbot William. They will try to capture your father. *I* came away, with James and Anna and the bairns, to Tantallon. Here. So as to warn you. They will be waiting at Leith, for you and the princess. They will take you, nothing more sure. You must not let them get you, my heart."

"No. I see that. James – where stands he, the King, in all this?"

"He is here, at Tantallon. He greatly mislikes your father, who has used and constrained him. He will, I think, do nothing to aid Lord Boyd. But you, his Master Thomas, he likes. He will not stand out against these lords, I think, but will wish to protect *you*. He will go to Leith, he says, join them, and meet you and this Margaret, his bride. Says that he can save you. But – I fear not. They will see you as the one who might raise many against them. Your father is not popular, but you are. And our son Jamie, in line for the succession to the throne. They will, I judge, see you as dangerous. Seek to get rid of you."

"Yes, you are right. Who is behind all this? All the earls, you say? But there must be some in the lead. Who seek power."

"It is my uncles, I think, my bastard uncles. The Earl of Atholl and Stewart of Auchterhouse. Or so Bishop Andrew and Primate Graham say. They will resent the Boyds' power. Oh, Thomas, you have been away too long!"

"Aye." He took a turn up and down the confined space of the cabin. "You are right. I would be a fool to put myself in their hands now. I care not about my father's regency – that can go. I would not wish to rise in arms to try to save it, whatever *he* may seek. But . . . this of treason is bad, bad. They could hang me, for that. So – I must not go on to Leith." He shook his head. "Nor, I think, go to my father at Kilmarnock, or wherever he is gone. Nor, indeed, stay here at Angus's Tantallon. For anyone who gives aid or support or even shelter to one accused of treason is deemed to be in treason also. That I must not bring upon any."

She bit her lip, eyeing him.

"What is best?" he demanded. "Anywhere I go in Scotland,

and seek shelter, help, could gravely harm others. If I thought that we, my father's regency, his cause, had any hope of winning in this struggle, it might be different. But I do not. All along he has offended others, acted alone, kept all in his own hands, scarcely rewarded those who aided him at the beginning. I have told him so, but he heeded not. He can call on few friends now. Even Avondale here will not risk his neck for him, I think. So – where do I go now? Avondale can take the princess on to Leith. But myself – where do *I* go?"

For once Mary Stewart had to fail him. She just did not know, considering it all as she had done these last days and nights. "Over the border? England?" she suggested, but without conviction.

"What would that serve? The English, if they would let me bide there, would but seek to use me against Scotland. Make a traitor of me, indeed! They are the Auld Enemy still . . ."

They heard voices outside and Avondale called, to interrupt their privacy. Thomas went to the door.

The Chancellor looked worried indeed. "My lord of Angus, here, has told me something of what is afoot," he announced. "Here are grievous tidings. And just when we have completed our mission, with success. What is to be done? The Regent has fled. All is in chaos. None in control of the realm. The young princess . . . !"

"Aye, I have heard. This changes all. But not the royal marriage. Or Orkney and Shetland. You, my lord Chancellor, are in no danger. You will have to go on to Leith, with the Princess Margaret. And, to be sure, the King. He is at Tantallon, yonder. For myself, I cannot do so – that is clear. Where I will go I know not. Probably back to Denmark meantime. Yes, back to Denmark. I can seem to go, to announce to Christian his daughter's safe arrival in Scotland. I am, it seems, to be charged with treason! So I had better be furth of the realm until the situation is resolved, one way or another. I would be arrested at Leith, my wife says. You are different. You were appointed by parliament, as Chancellor. You were not my father's appointment. Yes, it is Denmark for me, again. They do not mislike me there . . ."

They all gazed at each other, Angus and his wife behind the Chancellor.

Mary spoke. "Do not decide on all yet," she urged. "Let us go ashore to Tantallon. The ships can wait here, can they not?

Time to think. And you will wish to see your bairns, Thomas? And the King. And Anna. There is no great haste to reach Leith, is there? They do not know there when you will arrive. Any more than did we."

"Aye, that is true. That is best," Thomas agreed. "The ships can lie off here for a few hours, while we make our decisions. These small boats will take us ashore . . ."

None controverted that, and a move was made to inform Carnegie, the Princess Margaret and the others, and to summon the fishing craft alongside again. A much enlarged group descended rope-ladders thereafter, the Danish girl greatly excited by this adventure.

On the way back to North Berwick in the earl's boat, Mary spoke quietly to Patrick Fullarton. "My friend," she said, "I have ill news for *you*, also. Apart from this of my lord Earl, and treason. Anna! She is here at Tantallon with me. So you will see her. But – she is with child."

He blinked, drawing a deep breath. "I . . . I . . . what can I say, Highness?"

"Say nothing until you have heard it all, Patrick. *That* is none so very ill! It is what followed. Her father perceived her state – she is fairly large with it, and he has a keen eye. He was wrath. He had her to wed, and at once. No choice given her, no time. He would not have her with a bastard . . ."

"Wed! Anna! God in heaven – not *wed*! Not Anna, my Anna!"

"Yes, wed. He found a man to take her, as she was. No doubt at a price. Sir John Gordon of Lochinvar. In Galloway. A weakling, I judge. But they were married, without delay. They have not slept together, nor even seen each other since the ceremony. But she is now the Lady Gordon. I am sorry, Patrick. But . . ." She left the rest unsaid.

Shattered, the young man clenched fists and stared away, as they approached the haven below the conical hill of North Berwick Law.

At Tantallon Castle there was no lack of drama and emotion, the King encountering his bride-to-be, Patrick meeting Anna, Mary and Thomas agitating as to what to do, Avondale concerned for his own future; all at first, distraction, jumbled talk, uncertainty. But since so much fell to be decided, and for so many, Mary it was who presently suggested that they should all sit down round the hall table, like any council meeting, and discuss it quietly, in orderly fashion. This was accepted.

Where to begin? Thomas, rather than the King, led off, but since James was present it seemed suitable to deal with his situation first. The proposal was that he joined the ships and sailed to Leith with the Chancellor and the future Queen. But Mary queried the wisdom of this. Would it not be asked by the lords how he came to be on that ship from Denmark? That would lead to having to explain this call at Tantallon and Thomas's leaving the party. This in turn would implicate Angus. Better, surely, if James was to ride to Leith, with Angus and an escort. He would not be there so soon as were the ships, but that did not signify. He would not be expected to know when the Danish party would arrive. There he could greet the princess, who would presumably already have landed. The lords would be in some disarray, not knowing where the King was after leaving Stirling. His presence would reassure them, and at the same time avoid any suspicions over Angus.

That was accepted as making good sense, Avondale particularly affirmative. It would avoid any questions as to his own implication. But – what would he say about the Earl of Arran's absence?"

Mary said could he not declare that Thomas had received warning from his father? At sea. A fishing boat sent out to take him off the ship. Not necessarily from North Berwick. Just a fishing boat. To take him where, who knew? Possibly to join the Lord Boyd, wherever he might be. Avondale and the Bishop of Orkney, knowing naught of what was to do in Scotland, could nowise stop him, nor think to do so. They had come on to Leith with the princess.

None controverted that.

What then of Thomas himself, the biggest problem? That was answered promptly. He had decided. He would have one of the smaller ships turned around and sail back to Copenhagen. That would be best, meantime. He had made friends in Denmark, and got on well with King Christian. He would be safe there, until the situation in Scotland was such as to allow him to return home. He looked at Mary.

That young woman drew a deep breath. It had had to come to this eventually, and she had made up her mind, hard as the decision had been.

"I will go with my husband," she said simply.

They all eyed her, none forgetting her two infants.

"The children . . . ?" Elizabeth asked.

Mary inclined her head, swallowing. "I . . . we . . . must leave them behind, I fear. We cannot take little ones like that to Denmark, not knowing where we go from there. They must . . . remain here." Her voice almost broke.

Thomas reached over to grasp her wrist. "Bless you, Mary!" he said.

"I will care for the bairns," Elizabeth declared. "My brother's children."

All were silent for a space.

Then Anna spoke. "I go with Her Highness, as ever," she said. But she looked at Patrick.

"As do I, with my lord," that young man announced quickly, eagerly.

James it was who made question of these decisions, or of some of them. "I do not think that you should go, Mary," he said. "It is not . . . suitable. You are my sister."

"I am married to Thomas, James. Made one, in the sight of God. My first duty is to him. And you have another sister, and two brothers, still at Stirling."

"They are young. I say that I can save Master Thomas from any hurt. He should remain here, in Scotland. In hiding perhaps, at first. Until matters are settled. Then I will call for him."

"With respect, Sire, I will be a deal safer in Denmark!"

"You can call for him there, James, when all is settled. Better there. Here he could well be discovered, betrayed, or his father reach him and seek to use him. Denmark is best."

James scowled. "I could make it my royal command!"

"You could — but will not, I think. Not to *me*!"

Their eyes met, and he lowered his.

"You have four years yet until full age," she went on. "So another regency will be established. Others will make decisions for you. *You* may cherish Thomas, James, but others will not. If a parliament condemns *all* the Boyds for treason, as is mooted, your pleas for him will avail nothing. Better this way."

Angus, their host, accepted that as final. "When shall we leave for Leith, Sire?" he asked. But it was at Mary that he looked. "This day? Or tomorrow?"

"The sooner the better," Avondale put in. "The ships will be

206

at Leith haven in two hours or so. Her Highness, here, should be received in Scotland in due style. Some of the earls and lords will be there, no doubt. But His Grace should be present soon after."

"I agree," Angus said. "The ships can lie off here for a little longer. His Grace and I should ride almost at once. It is over twenty miles."

"Very well," Thomas declared. "All is settled, then. We can go our separate ways . . ."

"*Almost* all," Mary interjected. "His Grace may have forgotten, in all this upset. But I have not. He promised that he would knight our friend Patrick Fullarton, for his good services and lealty. It must be now. You agree, James?"

The King was nowise reluctant about this, at least, a demonstration of his royal powers and authority.

"Yes. To be sure. A sword . . . ?"

Angus could produce one without difficulty there, and amidst murmurs and exclamations and chuckles of delight from Anna, the astonished and embarrassed Patrick was ordered to kneel in front of his liege-lord, was then tapped on each shoulder with the blade, told to be upstanding, Sir Patrick, and to be and remain a good knight until his life's end – this all in something of a rush. Congratulations followed, with kisses from Anna, Lady Gordon.

Then it was partings, these indeed dire for Mary, to say farewell to her two little ones, tears flowing. The ship-party then left James and Angus to prepare for their ride to Leith, and themselves rode down to North Berwick harbour with such baggage as Mary and Anna could hurriedly assemble.

Back on the *Tay Pearl*, Thomas and Patrick transferred their belongings to one of the lesser ships, the *St Colm* of Inverkeithing. Then it was more leave-taking, from Avondale, the bishop and Princess Margaret – the last obviously bewildered by all this coming and going.

What the master and crew of the *St Colm* thought of their instructions to turn around and sail back to Denmark could be guessed at but was not expressed, in words at least. And what Mary's and Anna's thoughts and emotions were as their vessel beat round and left the other ships there, to head eastwards again for the open sea, were little more explicit – but sufficiently traumatic, for all that.

That voyage back to Copenhagen held a strange, unreal quality for them all. Behind was disaster, danger, confusion; ahead was none knew what, in the long run. But for the present, it was reunion, joy, leisure, ease and chosen company. The weather was fair, the winds light but favourable for eastwards progress, the July seas moderate. This smaller vessel provided less comfortable quarters than did the *Pearl*, but none complained.

Mary and Thomas had learned to accept happiness when it was available, not to pine for its permanency, not to look over-far ahead, love now accepted, acknowledged, trust assured, their pain at leaving behind the little ones shared. Anna and Patrick had each other, openly, at last, for how long they knew not, but to be fully savoured while it lasted, Anna's condition a bond rather than a handicap.

With westerly winds prevailing they made good time, and three days and nights after leaving North Berwick they were into the Skagerrak and rounding the Skaw, to sail southwards into the Kattegat.

They held a conference as to how much to tell King Christian. Could they pretend that all was normal and in order? That this was merely an embassage sent to inform him that his daughter had arrived safely in Scotland and would by now be married to King James? Would the Scots send an earl and his princess wife just to say that? Probably not. Should they be frank, announce the fall of the Boyd regime; but declare that this would nowise affect Margaret's position? Since Thomas would presumably not be able to return to Scotland for some time, this might be advisable, to explain a continued stay in Denmark Yet they did not want to be looked upon as refugees. It was not likely that Christian would expel them, for they had a good relationship with him. But, on the other hand, with his daughter new-married to King James, and Denmark now in treaty with Scotland, he would not wish to offend the new regency by seeming to harbour a fugitive. It was difficult.

Mary it was who again came up with a suggestion. Thomas had mentioned that, before he had left Copenhagen with Margaret, there had been word of trouble between the Hanseatic League, Christian's German mercantile friends, and England, over growing English trading with Iceland, which the League looked upon as their especial territory. Could Thomas not use this? Tell Christian that Scotland would support Denmark in *its* support of the League, against England? Admittedly there was a fifteen-year truce with England in force, with the present Lancastrian regime – but it was *only* a truce, no real peace, Border raiding still going on, and any stick to beat the Auld Enemy was not to be neglected. It would be safe to say that this would be Scotland's attitude, and it might well please the Danes.

Thomas, agreeing, took it further. He could make himself more than just a messenger, a carrier of tidings – but an ambassador. And not only to Denmark. He could offer to approach other princes of Europe in this cause. They would receive him, married to the King of Scots' sister. Supporting the wealthy and influential Hanseatic League would gain them acceptance. And Scotland would get to hear of it, and gain him credit.

This was accepted. Only Anna wondered. In her present state she could hardly go travelling around the nations of Christendom with them. Mary acknowledged it, and said that she should remain in Denmark until her child was born. Patrick could stay with her. Now, as *Sir* Patrick, he had some status, and they would be accepted as man and wife. Thomas could do without his attendance, for once.

So they sailed down the Kattegat with a degree of confidence.

This was in no way diminished by their reception at Copenhagen, Christian obviously pleased to see them back, especially Mary whom he embraced in comprehensive fashion. They had now, of course, no Bishop Tulloch to act as interpreter, but the King made his attitude, indeed his intentions, sufficiently evident – so much so that Mary was a little concerned, although Thomas seemed to consider her well able to look after herself.

They were allotted their old quarters in the Slot.

They wondered what was happening back in Scotland, and how the Lord Boyd and his brothers fared. The family at Tantallon would be safe enough, whatever transpired, in that impregnable stronghold.

They had to find an interpreter sufficiently expert in their own language before they could fully convey to Christian and his councillors what they had to tell, inform and propose – although Thomas had picked up a certain amount of Danish in his sojourning here. This took some time, but eventually they found a merchant, in the Ostergade, who had traded with Scotland as a younger man, and was able to translate with fair accuracy. In the interim Mary had to put up with much affectionate handling by the monarch of three kingdoms.

Their interpreter, Nils by name, did not seem in the least overawed by the company he now had to keep, and appeared to be able to get their instructions across adequately and to transmit reactions equally so. Christian and his ministers were clearly interested in what they had to say, and particularly so in the Hanseatic suggestion. The situation with the Hanseatic towns, Lübeck, Hamburg, Wisby, Rostock, Stralsund and the rest, was much concerning them. It seemed, in fact, that the League controlled the entire trade of Norway and much of that of Denmark and Sweden also – these Norsemen, in the past, considering that trade and industry and commerce were beneath the dignity of a warrior race such as themselves, a costly attitude it transpired in the long run. Now they were very largely dependent on the League for economic survival.

The Danish councillors were quick to perceive advantage in having a Scottish earl and princess to act as go-betweens with the Hansa leaders, who were clearly demanding much of them at this juncture. The Hansa was in a strange position, wielding enormous influence throughout Continental Europe yet having no armed force of its own. Lübeck in Schleswig-Holstein, the principal centre, ranked as a city state; but it had nothing more militarily effective than its town guard. Similarly with over one hundred other towns and cities. Now they needed men and ships in large numbers to prosecute their offensive against the English threat to their trading monopoly in Iceland, and were demanding much of these from Denmark, Norway and Sweden. Christian had men and ships a-many, of course – but he needed them nearer home than Iceland at present, for the Swedish nobles were rising against his overlordship once more, and this had to be put down.

210

He was planning a major campaign in Sweden, if possible to end the troubles there once and for all. This Hanseatic demand, which he was in no position financially to reject, came at a most inconvenient time. He was sending a deputation to Lübeck, to put this before the leaders there; but to have the Earl of Arran and his princess with it, indicating Scottish support against the English, and he now in treaty with Scotland, would be a valuable aid.

Even Mary was quite surprised at how aptly her proposal of ambassadorship had fitted into the situation here, all but heaven-sent, she felt.

Thomas wanted to know why Iceland seemed to mean so much to the Hanseatic League? After all, it was only a small outpost of the Norse domains, remote and with no large population for trading purposes. It was explained that it was not so much the size of the country that mattered but the principle which was at stake. These Hansa trading monopolies were all-important to them. Allow one to be broken or taken over, and who could tell what it might lead to? Other nations might follow the English lead, and the great trading empire begin to disintegrate. The English trade with the Low Countries was expanding; and although Hansa had no monopoly there, they did have major mercantile links. So something had to be done about this of Iceland.

And there was another point. Iceland's main wealth was in the fishing, salted fish its principal export. And the monopoly allowed the League to be sole supplier of salt, Lüneburg salt, mined there in great quantities, that city linked by canal to Lübeck. So Lübeck itself was directly concerned, the "capital" of the League.

Thomas could understand this very well, for, next to Lammermuir wool, salted fish and meat was Scotland's main export also, and the salt trade vital, although the salt was not mined but obtained from evaporation pans of sea water.

So, how soon was the deputation to go to Lübeck, for the Scots to accompany? In a week, they were told.

Perhaps fortunately for Mary's piece of mind, King Christian was to be over in Norway for the next few days, organising the mustering of men for the Swedish campaign; so that at that evening's banquet his attentions were pressing indeed, literally so, and she had to use all her ingenuity to retain approximate command of the situation without possibly offending the monarch – on whose goodwill, of course, so much depended. Thomas came to her rescue where he could.

211

In the days which followed, they made it their business to learn as much about the Hanseatic League as they could. Fortunately, their interpreter, Nils Larsen, was a great help, for, like all Danish merchants, he had to have strong links with Lübeck, and indeed had skippered one of their ships in the past. He could speak German. For a suitable fee he would be quite prepared to come with them on their visit to Schleswig-Holstein, leaving his sons in charge in the Ostergade.

He told them that the League had started modestly as a consortium of merchants in the Baltic area and the Lower Rhineland in the twelfth century, *hansa* meaning trade guild. It had quickly spread and grown, both in size and in its powers, as other merchants in neighbouring principalities and lands saw the advantage of a united front against powerful nobles, robber barons, pirates and the like, who looked upon unarmed traders as their natural prey. Soon the League had spread from the Germanic princely states to Poland, Lithuania and Russia – Novgorod being one of their main bases. The Holy Roman Emperor, Frederick the Second, saw the League as useful and gave it his protection, and other rulers followed suit. Actually one such had later chosen to renege and renounce them – and he a Dane, King Valdemar; but the League had called on others to aid them, and defeated him. That was exactly one hundred years ago. Since then, Denmark, Norway, and Sweden to a lesser extent, had adhered firmly.

There were great advantages in this, of course, especially for maritime nations. The League not only quelled brigands and pirates but built and maintained lighthouses, trained pilots for different and difficult waters to foster safe navigation, established trading and commercial bases in many lands, and gained valuable trading monopolies. They had even set up a base in London, the Steel Yard, but this had been under a cloud for some time. In Scotland, Berwick-on-Tweed served as an agency and toehold, the Flemings having established it there.

So this of aiding the League over England and Iceland was important. The English merchants could have joined the Hansa but had rejected offers and now were seeking to capture its markets, or some of them. This must be stopped. Wars had been started over less. A united show of strength was what was required, to warn the English off.

Thomas and Mary agreed that this was something which they

212

could fully support, assured that whoever was ruling Scotland now would concur – although they did not want to be advocating actual warfare.

Christian was not back from Norway by the time that the Danish deputation set off. Since Schleswig-Holstein was no great distance, and the visit not expected to last for long, it was decided that Anna could accompany them on this occasion. They would be going by sea, so she should be undergoing no risks. The leader of the party was Erik Johansen, who was what in Scotland would be called Vice-Chancellor, two other members of the Rigsraad or Council of States with him, one a bishop, together with representatives of the Copenhagen trade guilds.

They set sail on a sultry day in August, with a hot wind blowing from the south-east – which was not the best for this journey – to enter the Oresound. With a westerly or northerly breeze the one-hundred-and-seventy-mile voyage would have taken only one day and night's sailing, but thus it might take as much as three days, unless the wind changed, with constant tacking called for. This did not greatly concern the Scots, who looked upon the trip almost as a holiday. Nils Larsen proved a good companion, knowledgeable as well as friendly, and necessary of course for any communication with their fellow-travellers.

When they reached the Oresound and turned southwards, with the wind in their faces quite strong, the need for tacking became all too obvious, their shipmaster much concerned with his sails and steering. This way and that they had to turn, at steep angles, to make any progress, the navigation complicated by islands and their outlying reefs and skerries.

The channel of the Oresound widened in time to what was apparently called the Ostersoen or Eastern Sea, as they passed beyond the southern tip of Sweden. Here the going became notably rougher as they progressed, sizeable waves developing. Nils explained that this was not so much due to the wind as to currents. The waters of the Norse Sea had come racing down, channelled through the Skagerrak, the Kattegat and the Oresound, and here met a very different trend, the cold currents of the Gulfs of Finland and Bothnia sweeping down and round. The result, in this shallow Baltic Sea, was major turbulence. It would grow worse. Indeed, between the large island of Bornholm and the Lolland coast, it could be fierce and dangerous, although on this trip they would miss the worst area.

By darkness they had reached only the island of Stege, just beyond the tip of Zealand, and they put into a sheltered anchorage here to pass the night, since navigation of these waters in these conditions, and with much shipping abroad, could be hazardous.

It was good to be spared the heaving and tossing for their sleeping.

In the morning there was little change in wind and seas, and the tacking had to be resumed. But after some thirty miles of progress, however many more of actual sailing, they passed the last headland of Denmark, the Gedser Odde, and thereafter were able to steer more into the south-west. This helped considerably. Passing the first Schleswig island of Fehmarn and through what was known as the Fehmarn Belt, they progressed into the great Lübecker Gulf, now having to pick their way amongst more shipping than the Scots had ever before seen, indicative of the importance of Lübeck as the chiefest port on all the Baltic, possibly of all Germany.

At the northern tip of this vast bay was the Oldenburg peninsula, where King Christian had been count before gaining the Danish throne. This was now the Wendish coast, from whence had come the Wends or Vandals, of ancient savage reputation.

That long, wide gulf narrowed eventually to the mouth of the Trave River, which they now entered. Lübeck, it seemed, was some ten miles upstream. It was a wide river, which it needed to be to carry the amount of traffic using it. This entailed slow progress indeed; but even so they could hope to reach the city by nightfall, better timing than they had feared.

The Scots were interested in all that they saw. This was all very level, flat country, obviously fertile, highly cultivated, well wooded and populous, with villages and small towns prominent. But presently, outlined against the westering sunset, they perceived prominence indeed, the silhouette of a large city on a low ridge ahead, all soaring spires and towers and domes above long ramparts of gables, roofs and pinnacles, a dramatic sight. As Mary declared, it only required a mighty fortress-castle on a rock rising above it all to outshine Edinburgh or Stirling.

Their shipmaster nosed his vessel through a series of outer harbours on the river-banks, nine of them he said, and into the second of two inner havens directly under the massive walls and bastions of the city's defences. They could go no further because

214

of bridges across the Trave. Erik Johansen decided that they should remain aboard ship that night, the hour too late to go seeking accommodation from the Lübeckers, although the city gates apparently were not shut of a night here. Surrounded by other moored shipping, and with much noise emanating from the dockside taverns, they passed a somewhat disturbed night.

In the morning, Johansen and his colleagues went to introduce themselves to the Hanseatic senators, as they were called, as distinct from the Lübeck councillors; and Mary and Thomas, with Patrick and Anna and Nils Larsen, proceeded on a tour of inspection of the city.

The first feature which impressed them, apart from the fact that it seemed to be divided into four distinct quarters, all very regular, was that it was all built of brick, and to a lesser extent, wood, no stonework evident save for a monument or two. They were so used to stone as the building material in Scotland that all this brick, in various colours, red, yellow, brown, even black, struck them as extraordinary, the architectural effects created with it highly decorative, elaborate. The streets were wide, compared with Scottish ones, with removable market-booths and stalls down the centre, the population obviously large and prosperous-looking, no beggars or vagabonds in evidence. Lübeck was a rich community, most clearly.

Brick-built although they were, the public edifices were almost overwhelming in their magnificence, no fewer than three cathedral-like churches towering over all, as well as numerous lesser fanes. Nils conducted them around, almost as proud of it all as if it had been his own native city – the pearl of the Baltic, as he named it. The Dom, dating from the twelfth century, the true cathedral, had two lofty steeples, more than four hundred feet high, he explained, as did the even larger Marienkirche nearby, this latter filled with priceless works of art and an altarpiece by no less than Hans Memling. The visitors had none of them heard of this character – but did not say so. They were in process of realising how ignorant they were about so much of European culture and history, how far removed from all this wealth, splendour and preoccupation with art, science, decoration and lore of many sorts they were in Scotland, where all was so much more essentially basic, although they were not backward in their own forms of erudition. To some extent they were like the Norsemen, tending to look down rather on trade and industry; here they saw what centuries of trading success could result in. Not only in merchantry, to be sure, for here had been a centre of the Teutonic Knights; at least they had heard of these.

The third great church was the Petrikirche. It had only the one steeple, but this fully as high as the others. These three were all built of red brick; but nearby was the Rathaus, or council chambers, apparently only recently reconstructed, in black brick, and huge as it was handsome, with no fewer than five council halls, it serving both the city fathers and the Hansa senators. Presumably here would be the scene of the visitors' meetings.

On their return to the ship they found themselves to be instructed to transfer to a senate guest-house adjacent to the Rathaus, where quarters were awaiting them. Arrival there revealed accommodation more luxurious and commodious than any they had yet experienced, with attendants a-many. These merchant princes, since that is what they appeared to be, knew how to use their wealth, and to impress others.

Erik Johansen came to tell them that there would be a council meeting the following forenoon, which they were invited to attend. Meantime all the facilities of the city were theirs to use and enjoy. The Princess of Scotland was to be made especially welcome.

The visitors from afar were further impressed.

Next morning, when along with the Danish deputation they were ushered into one of the handsome halls of the Rathaus, it was to find a gathering of about a score awaiting them, mainly elderly men of prosperous appearance, of a quietly confident bearing and tending to be shrewd of eye, clad equally quietly but on the whole richly, all a deal less ostentatious than leaders of nations were apt to be. All stood to welcome Mary – Anna and Patrick remained behind for this meeting. Clearly princesses were unusual attenders here. Thomas was respectfully greeted also, but the King of Scots' sister was the magnet for all eyes, her good looks as obviously appreciated as was her status. Only German was spoken, and Nils sought to convey the exchange of compliments and courtesies as best he could. The spokesman for the senators was introduced as Wilhelm Schoenbach of this city, a portly individual of middle years, wearing a gold chain of office on which hung a handsome jewelled medallion.

When they were all sat round a great table, the Scots couple placed on the chairman's right, he made a more formal speech of welcome. In translation it was evident that although he was announcing the Danish envoys as having come in response to the Hansa's request for assistance and co-operation, his primary interest this morning was in the princess and earl from Scotland, and in what they had come to say and propose.

Johansen gestured to Thomas, who rose.

Speaking slowly and in brief sentences, to give time for translation, he declared that he and his royal wife were glad to be here, appreciative of their kind reception and hopeful that they had something to offer the esteemed Hanseatic League, famous in all lands and providing notable service to all nations' trade, England's less than some, perhaps – but who knew if this might be amended? They had come, on a visit to the King of Denmark, to offer their services in any way possible, to the Hansa Senate, in especial in this matter of English infringements of the Icelandic trade monopoly.

That drew approving nods, but alert waiting as to more detailed proposals.

This, of course, was the difficulty. In his position, Thomas was only capable of uttering generalities at this stage, not knowing what he *could* offer, with any likelihood of fulfilment, an exile from his country and possibly by now a condemned man. All that he could say meantime was that he and his wife were prepared to act as ambassadors elsewhere in Europe, emphasising that the Scots were always concerned, as a matter of national policy, to limit English aggression whether in armed alliances or in trade. They had suffered the said aggression for centuries.

This, while well enough received, obviously did not greatly excite his hearers. Making an almost deliberately queenly gesture of the hand, Mary sought to come to his rescue.

Asking if she might be permitted to speak in this august company, she declared that although her husband, the Earl of Arran, was perhaps too modest to mention it, he was notably well placed to be an envoy to the princes of Europe. For he already knew many of them, and had established good relations. This was because, two years earlier, he had been empowered by the Scottish regency and parliament to visit the courts of most of the great nations – France, Brittany, Spain, the Low Countries, Burgundy, Saxony and the rest, as well as Denmark – to seek a suitable bride for her brother King James. In the end he had chosen the Princess

Margaret of Denmark; but on his questing tour he had made many friends amongst the highest in Christendom, including the Emperor himself, Frederick the Third, and so was admirably placed to help advance the Hansa cause.

This took Nils a deal of translating, but it was evident that she was making an impression. Thomas endeavoured to look suitably modest. Being so handsome a young man did no harm.

Mary went on carefully. There were, it seemed to her, two important aspects of Scottish trade which could possibly be used to assist: the great wool trade with the Low Countries, their nation's chiefest; and their major export of salt to England. Even when at active war with that realm, this export of salt went on, for the English needed salt and the Scots needed the English gold in return. If they were to halt that salt trade with England, this would gravely trouble that nation. And if they could persuade the Low Countries to halt their export of cloths and the like to England also, the English might well decide that their new efforts at Icelandic trade were scarcely worthwhile.

That had heads nodding approvingly. But would the Scots be prepared to do that? Schoenbach wondered.

Mary said that she would approach her royal brother, to urge it. Some inducement would be necessary, of course. For instance, if the League made some adjustments to its own export of salt, to allow the Scots to replace the English market? She understood that Lüneburg, near to here, a Hansa city, was the greatest exporter of mined salt in all Europe!

The senators eyed each other, and some smiled faintly. There were no head-shakings.

She went on, encouraged. The wool and cloth trade of the Low Countries could surely also be re-directed? Possibly only for a short time, until the English learned their lesson.

Her hearers looked more doubtful about that.

Thomas added his support. Surely this sort of damage to English pockets and purses would be better than enlisting armed forces from rulers for possible war?

Senator Schoenbach agreed that this last was so. But there were problems, especially with the Low Countries. Unfortunately, of recent years, a division had developed in the League. The western German states, the Low Countries and Burgundy had come to consider that the eastern cities based on Lübeck were gaining overmuch of the benefits of the League's activities. Bruges in especial was vaunting itself, with the support of Charles the Bold, Duke of Burgundy. So much so that these Hansa traders were now being called Westerlings and naming the Lübeck-based members Easterlings. This was of course a grave weakness for the League, and complicated the present situation anent England, for the English merchants were seeking to exploit this rivalry, making offers to the Westerlings and even seeking to establish trading centres at Calais and Antwerp. So some sort of show of strength on Lübeck's part was called for, not only against the English but to remind these Westerlings that the League must remain one, united.

Thomas leant forward at the mention of the Duke of Burgundy, eager now. Charles the Bold and he had become particularly friendly, he declared, on his bridal-tour. Indeed he had been able to aid the duke, by recommending his daughter, Mary, as bride for the Emperor's son Maximillian, she being a year or two old for King James.

This information commended itself to all present, and it was accepted that the Earl of Arran and his princess were most suitable ambassadors for the League – which would show its appreciation in due course.

With the senators moving on to the matter of King Christian making a formal declaration of war against England, and a demonstration expedition of his ships to Icelandic waters, as warning, the Scots recognised that their presence was no longer relevant, and excused themselves, departing amongst expressions of goodwill, and instructions to consider all Lübeck and its province at their disposal.

Thomas, once again, had occasion to compliment his wife on her wits. She certainly was a worthy daughter of a long line of kings, he declared.

They filled in the next few days, until the Danish deputation had completed their negotiations, by exploring the great city, the largest in all Germany next to Cologne, they were told; but also the surrounding countryside and territory, all of which they found interesting, Mary especially so, her first real opportunity to observe closely how the people lived in a foreign land, and to compare all with Scotland – not always to the latter's advantage. Hers was the sort of mind which was intrigued and concerned.

Most of both Schleswig and Holstein consisted of low, heathy moorland, with the population mainly concentrated on the coasts,

219

although great use was made of canals to lead into the interior, something never done in Scotland, too hilly a country for the like. These canals linked inland towns with the sea and with each other, with much barge traffic. Most were maintained by the League. They had assumed that Lübeck was the capital of Schleswig-Holstein, but found that the much smaller town of Schleswig itself was, a quiet, old-fashioned place. From there they visited Kiel, inland from its bay, where was the university and the ancient fortress-castle of the Dukes of Holstein. The interior was all very evidently cattle-country, with the slow-living peasantry which went with stock-raising; whilst fishing was important around the extensive coastline on both east and west. The travellers had heard of the Jutes, Saxons, Angles and Wends, early invaders of the Celtic lands of Britain, followed by the later Normans, Norsemen at only one remove; now they were discovering where all these had come from.

They sailed back to Copenhagen in due course, the Scots at least satisfied with their visit.

18

Now more journeying was to be planned, major travel indeed. The League would provide the means, shipping and horses, with introductions to useful contacts in sundry lands, burgomasters, aldermen, rich merchants, senators, churchmen, well-disposed nobles. It all ought to be a notable experience, and Mary and Thomas looked forward to it.

Not so Anna, and therefore Patrick. For that young woman was in no condition to set out on prolonged and extended travel; and Patrick was torn between the desire to accompany Thomas and to remain with her, having duties towards them both. Thomas said that he must remain with Anna at Copenhagen, at least until the child was born, and rejoin him later perhaps. Nils Larsen, who agreed to accompany them again, at League expense, was no lord's esquire, however worthy a character. They certainly would miss Patrick, not only for himself but as attendant, to see to much that an earl and princess could not suitably do for themselves in visiting the courts of Europe. Anna said that she would be well enough here; and once the infant was born, if she could find a wet-nurse, she might even come to rejoin them herself.

There was endless discussion about this, while the preparations went on. That is, until one day, soon after King Christian's return from Norway, when all was abruptly changed. A ship, their old *Tay Pearl*, arrived from Scotland, bearing the Chancellor again, Lord Avondale, supported by the Lord Haliburton of Dirleton, a member of the Privy Council. If supported was the right word; supervised might be nearer it. For Avondale had grown to friendly terms with Thomas and Mary on their embassage; and his mission now was less than friendly. He came with King James's orders that his sister was to return to Scotland immediately, with or without her husband. There was to be no question about it, no delay – this was a royal command. And King Christian was directed to ensure it, under the terms of the treaty between the two realms.

Mary, appalled, scarcely believing her ears, drew a great

221

breath. "No!" she exclaimed. "'I refuse! I will not do it. *He* cannot do it. My brother cannot force me to leave my husband. I, his sister, do not recognise his royal command. This is not to be considered."

"Not only the King's command, Highness. But the Council's . . ."

"No, I say! A wife's first duty is to her husband. And Thomas most certainly is not going to return to Scotland in present circumstances. That is the end of it. I . . ."

It was not Avondale who gave her pause.

"Highness," Lord Haliburton said grimly, "His Grace's and those of the Council's instructions are that should you make refusal, we are to take the Earl of Arran along with you. King Christian to be charged to enforce this."

Mary stared. "But . . . this is beyond all! It is outrageous. You cannot do this . . ."

"It is a royal command, lady." Haliburton was a stern-faced, hard man of middle years, no doubt chosen as apt for this duty. "His Grace has been as kind as he might be towards my lord Earl here, since he is Your Highness's husband. He has made it possible for *you* to come back to Scotland, alone, leaving my lord at liberty here. Only if you *refuse*, are we to take you both. That is the kindest that His Grace could command, after the parliament's decision."

"Parliament . . . ?" That was Thomas, thick-voiced.

"Aye, parliament, my lord. You, along with your father and your uncles, have been condemned for high treason. By parliament. The Lord Boyd is fled to England. Sir Alexander Boyd is already taken and executed. The Abbot of Kilwinning is gone, none knows where. So – if you return with us to Scotland, my lord, it is to your death!"

Mary and Thomas looked at each other, wordless now.

"So, Highness, how say you?"

Mary found voice. "I say . . . I say that King Christian cannot force this on us. Will not. He is our friend. This is *his* realm, not my brother's . . ."

"He has no choice in the matter, lady. The terms of the treaty which both kings have signed declare that each will support the other in all things. This is the first demand under that treaty – and in King James's own written word and seal, which we carry. And you are His Grace's own sister. Refusal by King

Christian to accede would be to refute and negate the treaty, injure King James's marriage and endanger relations between the realms. King Christian cannot but agree, however he may feel towards you."

"I am sorry," Avondale said. "But that is the decision of King, parliament and Council."

"You must go, my dear. Alone," Thomas got out.

"No!"

All considered each other.

"I think that you should well consider the matter. Together," Avondale went on, unhappily. *"Before* we seek audience of King Christian. Tomorrow. With our royal letter."

Thomas nodded. He took Mary's arm to lead her out of the room, without another word, leaving the two emissaries standing.

There was no lack of words thereafter. Indeed, far into the night Mary and Thomas lay awake, going over and over the situation, agonised, undecided – or, at least, each decided, but differing, he that she must go, she that he must not and she *would* not.

It was the young woman who, at length, in desperation, came out with the suggestion. "Thomas, let us slip away. Both of us. Alone. From here. From Copenhagen. Try to get a ship back to Lübeck. Nils would aid us. There, the League would look after us. This of your troubles in Scotland would not hurt their cause, nor what you could do for them, as envoy. Let us flee Copenhagen. Secretly. They would never catch us, from here."

"We could not do that, my heart. Without harming Christian. He has been good to us. That would grievously injure his position. He would be held responsible. Forby, it would turn *you* into a hunted fugitive – and that I will not have. I have brought sufficient trouble upon you already. If you were so deliberately to disobey a royal command, even you would be held guilty of high treason. They might not hang you, but you could be imprisoned, if captured. So, a fugitive always. No, not that, my dear."

"I will go throw myself on Christian's mercy. He likes me – likes me overmuch indeed! He will not let them take me away, if I go and plead with him."

"He cannot help himself, in this. He is a king, a monarch, in treaty with another king. *You* know his position, lass, if any does,

223

you a king's daughter and sister. Where are your famed wits, my dear? Use them."

She knew in her head if not her heart that he was right.

"Oh, Thomas – to leave you! Leave you, an outlaw. Condemned. For how long? Before I can win back to you? I think that I *hate* James! To do this to us. He is weak. But he need not have done this. They could not *make* him do it . . ."

"Weak, yes. But, I think, lost without you. He relied on you, Mary. Lacking you, he has not the strength to withstand harsh men, our enemies. And he is young . . ."

"Not so very young, now. He will soon be of age. To rule as well as to reign. Then, perhaps, I can convince him, work on him. Yes, then I could sway him to grant you pardon. My father was but nineteen years when he took over rule. James will be nineteen in less than two years . . ."

"That is it, yes. Since it seems that you must go back, then prevail on James to remit the sentence of death passed on me. Pardon me, and allow me to return to Scotland. Two years is not so long to be parted – although I shall grudge every day of it. That is best, lass. And there are the children to think of . . ."

"The children, yes. Do not think that I ever forget them. Our little ones. Perhaps that is best. All that we can do . . ."

They left it at that, meantime. But still they found that sleep eluded them.

In the morning they had thought of no better solution, and had to convey their sad decision to Anna and Patrick. These two had not failed to hear of the situation, of course, and were equally unhappy, but had come to their own conclusions and decisions. If, as they had anticipated, Mary elected to go back to Scotland alone, then Anna would go with her. Nothing else was practicable. Patrick would go journeying with Thomas. *He* dare not go back to Scotland, either – he would be condemned along with his master, nothing more sure. It would be a sore parting, but needs must.

The other couple were in no position to refute that.

Christian sent for them after his interview with Avondale and Haliburton, less than his usual hearty self. He put the best face on it that he could, but it was obvious that he was embarrassed and unhappy. He took the attitude that all was settled, however unfortunate it was, that the princess was going back to her royal brother's care and that the earl was going on his travels for the Hanseatic senators. Nothing was said of treason or death sentences. He was grieved to be losing them – and he gripped Mary to emphasise it – but they would assuredly meet again one day. Meantime they would have a farewell banquet, two evenings hence, for today he had to visit his wife at Helsingor, and the Scots lords wished to be away as soon as possible, with winter conditions coming to the Norse Sea.

So they had two days only.

Avondale and Haliburton, evidently taking it for granted that the pair had come to the only conclusion possible, now kept out of their way. Decisions taken, the two couples were not going to moon about in gloom, so that day they went to the Ostergade to get Nils Larsen to find Thomas a Hansa ship to convey him to Lübeck – for Thomas would not wish to linger here after Mary had gone. Then they wandered round the city and pretended that they were interested and enjoying all they saw, even buying keepsakes from the stalls.

That night they slept little more than on the previous one. As Mary said, hereafter they all would have plenty of time for sleeping. Every waking moment was precious.

Next day they hired a fishing boat, since Anna found much walking tiring, to take them through the intricate network of waterways which linked Copenhagen's docks area, and down the Inner Haven to the Killebo Strand, a great sheltered bay to the south-west, which they had been told of but had not yet visited, with the large island of Amager on the east, the most fruitful and densely populated rural area of Denmark reputedly, known as Copenhagen's kitchen-garden. This, then, they dutifully explored, even though their attention to all they saw was less than concentrated.

King Christian had, it proved later, gone to great lengths to make their last evening a memorable one, his way of expressing his regrets and inability to help. The feasting was beyond all previously offered, in richness and variety, the entertainment as lavish, singers, storytellers, dancers, acrobats, performing bears, even a troupe of dwarfs who posed, acted and mimicked naked, a highly suggestive presentation. Christian's own contribution, at least towards Mary, was in keeping, and grew the more so as the evening wore on, that young woman loth to repulse him in the circumstances and enduring as best she could. The unlimited schnapps, however, did come to her aid eventually, and before the evening was out the monarch had fallen asleep, admittedly a-lean against her, the arm which had been encircling her bosom dropped to her lap. Even when his guests, or some of them, made their escape, he did not awake.

Mary and Thomas were again distinctly less soporific, for who could tell when next they would lie in each other's arms – the *Tay Pearl* was to sail next day. They passed a bitter-sweet night.

In the morning, still abed, they said their private farewells, for the eventual leave-taking would inevitably be in front of others. Holding each other, halting words were the least of their exchange.

"Who would have thought that it would come to this, my dearest?" the man got out. "Parting, in a foreign land. Constrained by others . . ."

"Not truly parting, Thomas – only our bodies moving in different directions meantime. Ourselves, our love, our spirits, inseparable always, wherever our persons. Constrained, yes, but only our outer shells, these poor bodies. They can never separate *us*!"

"Lord, you name this dear, lovely body, this adored delight of mine, a poor shell! This, which I swore before God to cherish and protect, till the death. Aye, and beyond! Which I would indeed die for – may yet have to! But now I leave it . . . !"

"Hush, you. You are not leaving it. Others are taking it. But they cannot take *me*, the true me, the reality which is yours, for ever. This body – you love it, yes. And I rejoice that you do. But one day it will grow old and wither. Nothing more sure. But *I* will not. The part you love and hold. Wherever you are. The constraint is only for the body – and even so, only meantime. Who knows how soon we may come together again, in person as in love?"

"Aye. No doubt but you are right, lass. Would that I had your faith, your certainty. But . . . man's constraint is hard, hard to accept."

"And yet, was it not constraint, men's constraint, which brought us together, in the first place?"

"Dear God, yes, it was! My father's constraint of you and James. Aye, who am I to complain of constraints! We took you by force. I was wed to you by force – or, at least, against *your* will. Never mine. My father was a master of constraint, I cannot deny. For that I beg your forgiveness, Mary."

"No need. Not now. See how fair a flower has bloomed after so odd a planting, out of that constraint. It took time. Who knows what, in time, may come out of *this* constraint?"

"It did not take time, for me. My heart lurched at the first sight of you, that day near to Linlithgow. I loved you from the beginning. Not as I do now. My love grew, yes. But you smote my eyes and heart from that first meeting . . ."

She mustered a little laugh. "As you scarcely did to me! Oh, I saw you as a handsome, personable young man, a man to take the eye, a man to watch. Aye, to watch! You were *forward*, no? Assertive. Bold. And I was young, and a king's daughter . . ."

"Sakes, yes – I was over-eager. In too great a haste. But . . . I *had* to win you, see you. Myself win you. I knew that my father intended to wed you to me, from the first. Part of his plan. For power. Constraint again. And I did not want to wed a woman reluctant. In especial such a woman as I found *you*! So I had to press my cause, my own cause, not my father's. However much I seemed to be spurring ahead."

"And you succeeded. However much *I* fought you off. And I did seek to smother my dawning love for you. I confess it. I tried – and failed!"

"When did you realise it, lass? Realise that I meant something to you?"

"In my heart, if not my head, fairly soon. Or so it comes to me now, looking back."

"Before that wedding?"

"Oh, yes. I think that it may have been Anna who opened my eyes to it. That first day at Kilmarnock, at Dean Castle, when we went to collect her. Do you remember the matter? No – you will not, for she said it to me when you were not present. In her bedchamber, which I shared with her. When I told her that you were over-urgent towards me, she answered that I would be a match for you! Hastily she pointed out that she did not mean a match as marriage. Only that I could perhaps *out*match you, in my, my attitudes. That opened my eyes, I now think. Made me to realise that I did not *want* to outmatch you always, that I could accept you as leader. Not master, no. But to lead. And that a match between us, marriage, might be none so ill. Yes, I think that it was then . . ."

"So! That other night, that wedding night, you were not having

to steel yourself? You were not abhorring it? It was not just a
matter of needs must?"

"Did I act, sound, look as though I was?"

"No-o-o. But, myself, I was so beside myself that I knew little
save my own hot need and desire for you. And my resolve, such
as it was, not to hurt you if it was possible. A battle within
me . . ."

"Perhaps your battle, then, was greater than mine, husband!
Who knows? But, an inexperienced girl, I knew so little."

"You did not fail to act the woman then, Mary my heart!"

"Perhaps. But it was no great trial!"

"It, your beauty, overwhelmed me. Beauty of body, as beauty
of feature. That I, Thomas Boyd, should have been so blest. My
pride and joy, pride in your person and your looks and your spirit.
Aye, and your wits. You, with the mind to outwit so many, in
affairs of state as in lesser matters . . ."

"But not sufficient to counter my royal brother, it seems!"

"His is not wit, but weakness. James allowing himself to be
forced by others. Using me, my life or my death, to constrain
you. No wits in that. Only yielding to the wishes of hard men
who seek power and advancement. None could take pride in that.
My pride in you, lass, is otherwise . . ."

"All the pride is not yours, my love. I am proud, also. Proud of
you. Proud of what you have done. You won Orkney and Shetland
for Scotland. You were so good to James – and he repays you thus!
You shone at the tournament. And you taught me much about
my own body, kindly, patiently. I am proud to have borne your
children, a great joy to me. Those bairns, Thomas. Young Jamie.
And Grizel. They will link us always, part of each of us. We are
blest in them."

"I scarce know them, to my sorrow. And they will grow without
knowing *me*. That is hard . . ."

"Part of the price that we are having to pay for our love. A great
price. But . . . perhaps the greater the love, the greater the price?
If we loved less, how much less heavy the cost? We must hold on
to that. But, who knows – it may not be for so long."

"Even two years could seem an eternity."

"It is only so many months. We have been parted before, for
months, have we not? And even eternity is ours, for love is
eternal. That is our sure anchor. Since God Himself is love,
and His eternity ruled by love. Unlike this sorry world of men.

So, we cannot lose, Thomas – we cannot lose! Absence, here or hereafter, is no barrier to love, I do believe."

"You believe – then so must I, my heart. There is no more to be said, is there?"

So they held each other, silent now, until he rose to throw off the bedcovers.

King Christian himself came to escort them down to the dockside, a notable honour. He was excessively hearty, although not towards Avondale and Haliburton. He presented Mary with an ancient golden torque, a former Norseman's arm bracelet, as token of his affection and esteem; also entrusted her with a letter for his daughter. One day, he declared, he would come and see them in Scotland. He had chuckles and smiles for Anna too, patting her swelling frontage. He conducted them up the gangplank on to the ship.

There all was in readiness. Rob Carnegie greeted them with a sort of gruff but warm respect. The two lords took formal leave of the King, and Avondale had the grace to lead Haliburton below fairly promptly.

Their promptness seemed to communicate itself to Thomas Boyd also, for having got thus far, he appeared to be concerned to get the parting over as quickly as possible, Mary understanding all too well. Possibly Anna and Patrick felt the same.

Gripping his wife's hands in his, Thomas gazed into her lovely eyes, and for long moments his lips were tight as though sealed.

She helped him, as always. "Only a turn in our road, my love," she whispered. "That road has had many turns – but the end, the destination, is sure. A bend in it, only."

"God help us, yes! But – why?"

"He knows, if we do not. But . . . I will be waiting for you, husband. Whenever. Wherever. Waiting."

He nodded, then shook his head, wordless, features working. Fiercely he shook her, then all but flung her from him, there on the deck, and turned about to stride back to the gangway, and down, his bearing stiff as any ramrod.

She gulped and swallowed – and him safely gone, the tears welled out, hot.

Anna and Patrick were undergoing their own bitter ordeal. There it was the girl who broke away and ran, clumsily, for the companionway, sobbing.

Mary stood her ground.

For it was not over yet. A large ship cannot leave a quayside in moments, however ready and skilful the skipper and crew. Whether or not Thomas and Patrick would have departed forthwith, King Christian did not, and so they must wait there on the jetty also, endlessly it seemed, while the gangway was run in, the mooring cables loosed, the towing-barge manoeuvred into position to pull them down the canal, commands shouted.

So they stood, only some fifty yards apart still, although it might have been an endless yawning gulf already. And near as they were, Mary did not see him very clearly.

At last the *Tay Pearl* began to move, slowly, so very slowly, drawn by the barge's oarsmen away towards the Inner Haven. Thomas's arm rose, then, not to wave, not to salute, but to reach out towards her, hand open, cupped as though in mute appeal.

It was almost too much. Mary turned away for a moment, but forced herself to face him again. She spread her arms wide, and so remained. But her eyes were shut.

Fortunately Copenhagen itself came to their rescue, in this at least. Those narrow waterways amongst the docks and warehouses ensured that no lengthy views were possible. Quite quickly the quayside was hidden from the ship.

It was done.

Historical Note

Mary Stewart never saw Thomas Boyd again – not in this life, at least. Brought back to Scotland and reunited with her children, she was kept under strict guard and surveillance – as indeed, then, was King James – by a strong regency council determined that never again should one up-jumped family take over the rule of the realm and the control of a weak young monarch. She was not imprisoned nor maltreated, but was no free woman.

Thomas duly went journeying amongst the princes of Europe, and with some success, especially with Charles the Bold, Duke of Burgundy in the Low Countries, with whom he struck up a notable friendship, becoming that vigorous ruler's favoured representative, actually visiting England on his behalf, where he was recommended to the influential, by a letter which has survived, as "the most courteous, wisest, kindest and most bounteous knight, my lord Earl of Arran, clever, most perfect and truest to his lady of all knights". Whether he recognised himself in this description is not recorded. Nor is it recorded by what cause he died, five years later, in 1474, at Antwerp, whether by sickness, plague, poison or sharp steel. Duke Charles erected a handsome monument to his memory.

On the information of his death reaching Scotland, Mary was forcibly married, for the second time. This to James, first Lord Hamilton, he who had sought to halt the royal abduction at Linlithgow, if ineffectually. Sixth Lord of Cadzow, he had helped to pull down the House of Douglas, and in consequence gained great lands and possessions formerly belonging thereto. One of the new Council, he was also one of the greatest lechers in the land, and old enough to be Mary's father. He had innumerable bastards but only one legitimate daughter; but managed to produce a son and another daughter on his new wife – that son destined to create considerable upset in the Scottish crown succession, as giving the Hamilton family a claim to the throne by the Earls of Arran and Dukes of Chatelherault. Mary long survived this second husband, and as widow became a force to be reckoned with during the reign of one of the weakest of Scots monarchs, James the Third.

Of the Lady Annabella, wife of Sir John Gordon of Lochinvar, we hear no more.

Denmark never managed to redeem the Isles of Orkney and Shetland, which were incorporated in the realm of Scotland.

Lord in Waiting

Book Two

List of Principal Characters

In Order of Appearance

John Douglas, Lord of Douglasdale: Younger son of 4th Earl of Angus.

Archibald, 5th Earl of Angus: Head of the Red Douglas house.

Elizabeth Boyd, Countess of Angus: Wife of above.

John Stewart, Earl of Atholl: Uncle of King James the Third.

Annabella Boyd, Lady Gordon: Sister of the late Earl of Arran.

Princess Mary: Elder sister of King James, Princess Royal.

James the Third: King of Scots.

James Stewart, Earl of Buchan: Uncle of the King.

James, Lord Hamilton: Great noble, married to Princess Mary.

John Laing, Bishop of Glasgow: High Treasurer

Andrew Stewart, Lord Avondale: Chancellor.

William Sheves, Archdeacon of St Andrews: Astrologer and alchemist.

Alexander Stewart, Duke of Albany: Brother of King James.

Patrick Hepburn, Lord Hailes: Great noble.

Abbot Henry Kerr of Cambuskenneth: Influential churchman.

William Tulloch, Bishop of Orkney: Envoy.

Colin Campbell, Earl of Argyll: Great noble, chief of Clan Campbell.

David Lindsay, Earl of Crawford: Great noble.

John Stewart, Earl of Mar: Younger brother of the King.

Sir Robert Douglas of Lochleven: One of the Black Douglases.

Patrick Graham, Archbishop of St Andrews: Primate.

Isabel, Lady Douglas: Former Countess of Angus, the brothers' mother.

Alexander, Lord Home: Great Borders noble.

John Macdonald, Earl of Ross, Lord of the Isles: Great Highland chief.

Robert Cochrane: Master builder and mason.

George, Lord Seton: Great noble.

Queen Margaret of Denmark: Wife of the King.

James Stewart, Duke of Rothesay: Son of the King. Later James the Fourth.

William, Lord Crichton: Great noble.

Princess Margaret: Younger sister of the King.

Sir Patrick Fullarton: Son of the Coroner of Arran.

Richard, Duke of Gloucester: Later King of England (Crookback).

John Douglas was fishing. He enjoyed fishing and spent much
of his time at it – too much, according to his brother Archie,
whose was a different nature, urgent, active, headstrong. John
was otherwise, quiet, contemplative, a little reserved, but by
no means shrinking or dull – Douglases were seldom dull.
Fishing seemed to suit him, an activity which permitted his
mind to journey off on its own for much of the time – and he
had an active mind. Sometimes, of course, he had to keep his
attention very much on what he was doing, especially when in
his boat, for it was sea-fishing which he pursued, sometimes
afloat, sometimes, as now, from ashore. Tantallon was not
much of a place for river-fishing; and the nearest fishable loch
was miles off in the Lammermuir Hills.

Not that the description "ashore" was very apt for John's
present stance, for he was sitting on a jutting slab of rock some
one hundred and twenty feet above the surging tide, a dizzy
perch on which his sisters would nowise join him, and Archie
did not. Casting his line down there, duly weighted, hooked
and baited, required a certain skill in itself, for the wind, on
that long drop, was all too likely to make it sway and swing
and divert, often to catch the hook on projections or sea-pink
clumps growing out of the cliff-face, or, lower, seaweed and
the like, which in a more impatient young man would have
been found off-putting. So the control as well as the aiming
of his line was all-important, not only for that reason but
also to ensure that it fell eventually into a selected spot, a
restricted area of sand amongst the rocks, reefs and skerries
down there, this no easy open patch but a twisting, turning,
narrow channel, a channel which had to serve another purpose
than just John's fishing, for this was the only means for boats

and shipping, of necessarily modest proportions, to approach the castle above, and this only at high water and when the seas were not too rough. But that sandy bottom below the waves, winding as it was, was a notable haunt of flounders, sole, rock-cod and suchlike. And if Archie thought that his brother was wasting his time, a strangely feeble Douglas in stirring times, and his sisters, all seven of them, were afraid that he would fall over and kill himself at this ridiculous ploy, they none of them refused to eat and enjoy the fruits of his labours — if labours they could be called.

But perhaps, labours, yes. For part of him was labouring the while, after a fashion, or active at least, purposefully active much of the time. More than just contemplating. He was summoning up pictures, faces, emotions, actions, words, and seeking for due words of his own to describe these adequately; and more than adequately, vividly, dramatically, resoundingly. And sometimes in rhyme and rhythm. For John Douglas was a storyteller, and sometimes a poet. Not that, at twenty years, he claimed to be the latter; but he did frequently entertain the family and retainers with his tales and compositions, of an evening — and even Archie did not find fault with that.

Waiting for that long, long line to jerk, at a bite, and interrupting his picture-building process to deal with an already caught flounder which he had thought was suitably dead but which had now started to flap on the rock at his side amongst others of his catch, to the danger of it and them falling off and over, his attention was further distracted by a call from behind him which jerked him round, in the circumstances to his distinct danger, since his legs below the knee were already dangling over into nothingness. If he had been impatient, like Archie, he would have cursed and exclaimed. But, turning, he merely raised his eyebrows.

"Johnnie! Archie says to come," his sister Alison called, from the ultimate outer parapet-walk on the north, seaward, side of Tantallon Castle. "A messenger has come. From Stirling. It is important, he says."

John could have answered let him come to see me, then.

But he forbore, not because Archie was the elder and an earl to boot, fifth Earl of Angus, but because he was that way inclined, an even-tempered young man, not exactly placid but normally prepared to please other folk if he could – although, given sufficient cause, he could be otherwise. He waved a hand, dealt with the flapping flounder and proceeded, but unhurriedly, necessarily careful, to raise and neatly coil that lengthy fishing-line, taking heed to keep it free from the rock-face hazards. The ballad of Baldred of the Bass which he was composing would have to wait; after all St Baldred had been waiting for a long time, since the seventh century, seven hundred years.

All in order on his rock-slab, John gathered up his catch so far, four fish – if he left them there the swooping gulls would have them – put them in a canvas bag and clambered up from the lip of the precipice and along to the flight of steps cut out in the naked rock which led up to that outer bastion of the castle where the girl stood, and also down to the dizzy platform from which a rope ladder could on occasion be lowered, to give less than easy access to any boat in that twisted channel. Tantallon was that sort of castle, perched high on a narrow promontory of a cliff-girt, iron-bound coast, impregnable seat of the Red Douglases.

Alison, the youngest of his seven sisters, was aged fourteen, and bonny, a sparkling-eyed, laughing girl, everyone's favourite. She took the bag of fish and peered in, to count.

"Only four?" she complained.

"If *you* had been with me, fishing also, we could have doubled that," he told her easily. "What messenger is this? From Stirling, you say?"

"Yes. From the Princess Mary, I think. A friar, from the Abbey of Cambuskenneth. Archie seems much put-about. I do not know what brings him, but it must be important."

"Not necessarily," her brother observed, with a faint smile. "Archie being Archie! But – we shall see."

From that sea-facing bastion they stepped down into the wide open courtyard of the stronghold, partly paved, partly living rock, to move over towards the mighty keep and

3

its flanking towers linked by lofty walling and parapets enclosing lesser buildings, all in the rose-red stone typical of this knuckle-end of Lothian which shook its fist in the face of the Norse Sea. Tantallon was an unusual castle, in more ways than one, basically a vast wall of masonry which shut off this narrow peninsula's tip, so that it was defended on three sides by sheer cliffs, and on the fourth, landwards, by a series of moats, deep ditches and ramparts, contrived to keep attackers at a distance and cannon well out of range. That giant stone curtain held the huge keep-cum-gatehouse tower, six storeys high, with drawbridge and portcullis, and almost equally high flanking towers at each end of the fifty-foot-high and twelve-foot-thick linking walls. In Scotland's turbulent history, it had never been taken by assault. The blue and white banners bearing the Red Heart of Douglas flew from the three tower-tops.

Passing the deep well sunk from the courtyard, necessarily deeper than the cliffs themselves, and leaving the subsidiary buildings of kitchens, barracks, chapel, stabling and store-houses on the right, they entered the main keep, to climb a straight stairway in the thickness of the walling to the first floor, where girlish laughter sounded from six other sisters in the great hall, and on up to the next floor, now by a circular turnpike stair, to the private and lesser hall. Alison opened the door.

Within, two men sat at a table, one young, red-headed, hot-eyed, squarely built, not handsome but eye-catching, of very different appearance from his brother who was slender, fine-featured, dark of hair and grey-eyed. The other man was middle-aged, spare, tonsured and clad in black, travel-stained monkish garb. He was eating from a platter.

"John, here is Brother Anselm, from Cambuskenneth. He comes from Mary, the princess, Countess of Arran, with tidings," the younger said. "Ill tidings. Thomas Boyd is dead. The Earl of Arran."

"Dead!" John stared. "They . . . they caught him, then? At last. You mean . . . ?"

4

"Not caught, no. He died in the Low Countries. How, it is not clear." The earl looked at the friar.

"We have no sure word, my lord. Save that the Lord Arran is dead. How he died we have not heard. The word came to my lord Bishop of St Andrews from the Vatican. But with no details. Save that the Duke of Burgundy, his friend, is desolate. And is building a great monument to him. Whether he died of a sickness, or . . . otherwise, we know not. But the death is sure, I fear."

"Here is sorrow!" John said. "He was a good man – despite being a Boyd! This will be sore news indeed for Mary Stewart. And . . ." He left the rest unsaid.

"Aye, sore news in more ways than one!" his brother exclaimed. "This is why Mary sends this messenger. She is to be married again, no less! Now."

"Married . . . ?"

The friar gulped, to avoid speaking with his mouth full. "The Princess Mary asked my abbot to have the word sent to you, my lords. She is as good as a prisoner in Stirling Castle. But she sees my abbot frequently. Whenever the tidings of the Earl of Arran's death reached Stirling, the Secret Council decided that the princess must remarry. She is to wed the Lord Hamilton."

"Hamilton! That lecher!"

"That is what she has told my abbot. She is much distressed. And asks that you, my lords, her friends, come to Stirling and seek to persuade the King otherwise. To forbid this forced marriage of his sister."

"James!" Archie cried. "He will never do that. Outface the council. He is craven, weak . . ."

"We might persuade him."

"That, my lords, is what Her Highness hopes. Why I am sent to you to seek your aid. The King might listen to *you*, heed you. If you will come to Stirling . . ."

"We could come to Stirling, yes. If you consider it worth the doing," the earl agreed. "How say you, Johnnie?"

The other nodded, if a little doubtfully. He was not one for Kings and courts and great affairs.

5

"When?" Archie asked.

"Soon. The sooner the better, my lord. For there is need for haste, Her Highness says."

"Tomorrow, then. Eh, Johnnie?"

"Should I go, also?"

"Yes, yes. Better with us both. For James. He likes you."

"Very well . . ."

The friar, fully fed and refreshed, was sent on his way. The brothers eyed each other. Here were problems indeed – and not merely problems of state and court, for there was a very personal side to it all. This man who had died abroad, Thomas Boyd, Earl of Arran, a banished exile, was in fact brother-in-law to the Earl of Angus. His sister, Archie's wife, Elizabeth Boyd, was upstairs in the East Tower, with her three children. She would have to be informed.

Arran's wife, or widow now, was the Princess Mary, elder sister of the monarch, James the Third, King of Scots. Theirs had been a forced marriage. James and Mary, when out hunting, had been unlawfully kidnapped and thereafter held captive by the Lord Boyd of Kilmarnock and his brother, Sir Alexander Boyd. Lord Boyd had thus been able to rule Scotland, for three years, as Regent, in the young King's name. He had had his son and heir marry the Princess Mary. But Thomas, whom he had had created Earl of Arran, and Mary Stewart, however inauspicious the start of their marriage, had grown to admire and love each other. After those three years the Boyd regime had fallen, whilst Arran was in Denmark arranging for the betrothal of the King of Denmark's daughter to King James. Jealous and resentful nobles, led by the King's uncles, had combined to topple the Regent; and a parliament had declared the Boyds guilty of *lèse-majestè* and high treason, and condemned them to death. Arran, bringing home the royal Danish bride, had, in his ship, reached as far as the mouth of the Firth of Forth, here off Tantallon, when, with Douglas help, Mary had managed to get out to intercept and warn him of his impending fate; and she and her husband had left the bride-to-be and both sailed back to Denmark. But weak young King James, on the orders of his new governors, actually his

6

uncles the Earls of Atholl and Buchan, had sent and had his sister brought back, by royal command, although her husband had contrived to make his way to the Low Countries. That was four years ago, in 1470, and husband and wife had not met since. Now he was dead, and the new widow calling for help.

Mary Stewart's call was not to be ignored. As well as being kin by marriage, the King's sister, and possibly the most beautiful woman in Scotland, she was the Douglases' friend, well loved.

Archie, impetuous, always for immediate action, was already preoccupied with practical details. They would go by boat, of course, up-Forth, not consider the sixty-mile journey on horseback. His galley would serve. They would get as far as Airth, up the river, only nine or ten miles to ride to Stirling, hiring horses there. A score of men would be sufficient as escort . . .

John was otherwise concerned. Elizabeth! How were they to tell her, to least hurt? Her own brother . . .

Archie shook his head and shrugged one wide shoulder. "The girls . . . ?" he suggested.

"No. You are her husband. It is for you to do it."

"You come with me, then, Johnnie."

The brothers did not have to go down to courtyard level again to reach the East Tower, for those enormously thick curtain walls on either side reached higher than this level, and contained linking mural corridors on each floor, with secondary staircases, a major convenience. Along the topmost of these passages they went, silent.

They had some two hundred feet of corridor to cover, for these walls were lengthy as well as tall, actually the greatest man-made stone barriers in the land. They heard the children before they got to the East Tower, squeals and cries. This castle, grim as it looked, was full of young people.

At the tower they had to climb a further storey; but before doing so, at this level they passed an open doorway, from which the juvenile vociferation issued. At sight of the young men on the landing, two children, a boy of five and a girl of four, came

7

running out, in loud acclaim, to hurl themselves bodily on father and uncle, clutching and demanding. After them came a nursemaid, to restrain them, comely and smiling.

Archie, fond of his children, patted their heads, but when they showed every intention of climbing the stairs with them, told them to stay below meantime, and signed to the maid to detain them, reinforcing his wishes with another pat, this time on the young woman's shapely bottom, to giggles. The men climbed on.

On the next floor they entered another room, five storeys up, a light and airy chamber with surpassing views, untidy with clothing and scattered gear, in the centre of which was a huge canopied bed, and beside it a little crib or cot. On the bed, half sitting, half lying, was a young woman, flaxen hair loose, an open bedgown around her shoulders. In the crib was a tiny baby, pink, blue eyes open.

Elizabeth, Countess of Angus, opened her own eyes, and turned head to consider the newcomers. Obviously she had been dozing. The infant had been born only the day before, after a difficult labour, and the mother was still exhausted. And clearly she was surprised to see her husband and brother-in-law coming thus in mid-forenoon. But she raised a smile.

"Both of you!" she said. "What have I done to deserve this?"

Archie cleared his throat and went to peer down at the baby, leaving his brother to do the news-breaking.

John and Elizabeth were good friends. He went round to the other side of the bed, to reach out and take her hand – and she made no attempt to cover up the bosom which her bedrobe left exposed.

"Ill tidings, Liz, I fear," he said. "We are sorry to be the bearers of it. But . . . you have to hear it. And you are sufficiently brave."

"Ill? It is not the children, at least," she answered. "I can hear that they are all too well! What is it, Johnnie?"

"Your brother," Archie jerked.

"Tom? Is it . . . do not tell me that they have got him? At last! They have not captured Thomas . . . ?"

8

"Not captured, no. But . . . he has died, Liz. Died. How, we know not. In the Low Countries. Antwerp, we think. I am sorry, lass." That was John. "This is a sore blow to bring you. And at this time, when you are in weak state . . ."

"We have just heard. A messenger from Stirling. From Mary Stewart."

She looked from one to the other, and then shut her eyes. But it was John's hand which she gripped, tightly. She said nothing.

The men eyed each other across the bed, Archie looking helpless, John compassionate. He it was who spoke their thoughts.

"You have had so much to bear, lass. And now, this. You and Tom were close, I know . . ."

She nodded, silent, as tears oozed from beneath closed eyelids. The Boyds had suffered for their deeds, indeed. Her uncles had been caught and executed, her father had escaped to England and died there. Now her brother.

Archie had to get the rest out. "Mary is in trouble. With more than the death. She is to be wed again. And to Hamilton, of all men! Old enough to be her father, and the greatest lecher in the land! Atholl and Buchan would have it so. And James – he will do nothing to spare her, his own sister, that feckless halflin. She calls for us to go to Stirling. To aid her, if we can. We go tomorrow . . ."

John held up his hand to halt his brother. Elizabeth's own loss was what was of first importance here, not Mary Stewart's. She was still gripping his hand.

"Thomas will do better where he is gone, than in exile, I think, Liz," he said, seeking to be helpful. "An outlaw no longer."

She nodded again.

Archie gestured towards the door. "We will leave you, Liz. I will be back." He patted her head. He was good at patting, but found action a deal easier than words.

John could scarcely linger when the husband left. He raised her hand, pressed it, and brushed his lips over it, before following Archie out.

9

They had to stay with the children for a little, making a gesture at play, before heading back to inform their sisters of the situation, these receiving it variously but all six distressed. Should they go to Elizabeth, to comfort her?

John was unsure about this, but Archie said yes. *He* would ride down to North Berwick harbour and see that his galley was readied for the morrow.

His brother went back to his cliff-top, whether to fish again or just to sit and consider remained to be seen.

In the morning the brothers rode the two miles from Tantallon to the town and haven of North Berwick, leaving Elizabeth calm, her grief contained, the girls saying that they would look after her, and wishing their brothers well. Two dozen armed retainers rode behind their lords; it would not do for the Red Douglas, the Earl of Angus, to appear in public with a lesser "tail" than this.

The road to the town followed roughly the cliff-tops, which sank gradually, with the dramatic conical hill of the Law soaring ahead, and the island-dotted Scotwater, the Firth of Forth, stretching westwards to the limit of sight, the still more dramatic Craig of Bass, that extraordinary, precipitous rock thrusting out of the waves, to the north, all a fair prospect indeed, however familiar to the Douglases.

The town, not large but pleasingly situated, sent horns round its two sandy bays but clustered most of its red-roofed houses about the area of the harbour and church – for the latter seemed to act almost as guardian and gateway for the former. Perhaps this was the intention of the builders, long ago, before ever the Douglases came to Tantallon, and this harbour was the southern terminal for the ferry of the ancient Celtic Earls of Fife, linking their northern and southern territories, as Earlsferry across Forth, in Fife, was the northern one; fair sailing and weather conditions had been all-important, and these being in the hands of the Almighty, Holy Church had its part to play. Still, to be sure, prayers for seafaring were much in order, for North Berwick was a fishing haven as well as a Douglas fief and castleton, and these seas could be dangerous, for nearby, off the Bass Rock, there were underwater cliffs, where the land shelf met the ocean floor, and tidal commotion could be as dramatic as the views. Moreover, the harbour itself was tidal, all but drying out at low water, which could complicate life for the fishermen.

Tantallon residents were ever well aware of the state of the tides, and Archie had ensured that his galley was moved for this morning to just outside the harbour and moored to the far side of a breakwater, where it could not be grounded. The vessel was not truly a galley, although Archie liked to call it that, in salute to the fierce sea-greyhounds of the old Highland chiefs. It was really a sea-going oared barque, low-built, half-decked, with two masts and great square sails, suitable for open sea voyaging but also commodious and useful for estuarine journeying.

The travellers embarked, to much interest of the townsfolk, and two of the men-at-arms were sent back with the horses, the others now having to change character from armed escort to oarsmen – another reason why so sizeable a party was advisable. The Red Heart banner of Douglas was hoisted to the mast-head and the eight long sweeps were pushed out to manoeuvre the craft away from the breakwater, to cheers from the watchers. The Douglas brothers, standing on the stern platform, were popular as well as all-powerful in North Berwick.

It did not take long for the rowers to get into their swing and pull the long oars in unison, this aided by Archie's rhythmic beating of a gong, kept aboard for the purpose. John played his part by raising voice, and he was a good singer, to start a steady, pulsing chant which the oarsmen took up, an endless melodic beat which rose and fell, rose and fell, to the pull of the sweeps and the drawing and exhalation of breath, a strangely stirring accompaniment.

Thus they proceeded up Forth, at quite impressive speed, although they could not have the help of the sail since they were heading due westwards into the prevailing westerly breeze. They passed the islands of Craigleith, Lamb and Fetheray and the dangerous reefs of Eyebroughty or Ibris, to cross

11

the wide mouth of Aberlady Bay, with the towering peak of Edinburgh's Arthur's Seat now beckoning them on, and the long range of the Pentland Hills superseding that of their own Lammermuirs on the skyline. Although the landward journey to Stirling, where the Forth dwindled to a river possible to bridge, was over sixty miles, going thus directly by water was considerably shorter, some forty-odd to Airth and then less than ten to their destination. Even with a head-on breeze, they would do that in five or six hours' rowing, if Archie had anything to do with it, instead of a long day's riding.

With two men to an oar, and regular changes of rowers, they kept up a good and steady progress, to pass the large island of Inchkeith on one hand and Leith, the port for Edinburgh, on the other, in something over two hours. Then on to the narrows of Forth, at Queen Margaret's Ferry, where the firth made its brief closing-in to merely a mile's width, and the galley, avoiding the midway isle of Inchgarvie, was as near to the Fife as to the Lothian coast. Now they had only a score of miles to go, Archie told the perspiring and tiring oarsmen, and beat his gong the louder.

They passed, presently, the royal fortress and state prison of Blackness Castle, and then the Avon-mouth port of Borrowstounness, noted for its trade with the Low Countries. Here was the eastern start of the Roman Antonine Wall, although they could not see it from their ship. But they could see the castle of Kinneil, on the higher ground – and this drew the brothers' frowns, for it was a seat of the Lord Hamilton who, it seemed, was being chosen as new husband for the unfortunate Princess Mary.

Airth was now only a few miles ahead, beyond the flat lands of the Carron mouth. They could, to be sure, have rowed this shallow-draught vessel much further up the narrowing river to considerably nearer Stirling. But they had to consider the hiring of horses for this large party, and Airth was the best, indeed the only place for this, for here was the terminal of another ferry across from Fife, from Kincardine, which was the shortest route for travellers from all the Fife lands and burghs to Glasgow, and so the site of hostelries and stabling.

So into Airth Neuk, as the ferry port was called, they at length drew in, to thankful grunts from the oarsmen.

Although a ferry-boat had evidently just pulled in, from Kincardine a mile away, and horses were in some demand, with such as the Red Douglas himself requiring them their party had no difficulty in gaining preferential treatment and hiring a sufficiency of animals, although some were scarcely of the quality an earl might consider suitable for his train. The rowers were rewarded for their efforts with ample ale and provender at the hostelries, and by mid-afternoon, less than seven hours after leaving Tantallon, they were mounted and on their way over the levels of Dunmore Moss, by Cowie and the plains of the Pools of Forth, to Bannockburn, with Stirling Castle now prominent on its rock-top before them and the blue background of the Highland Line beyond. The talk was all of Robert Bruce and the great battle for Scotland's freedom won here one hundred and sixty years before, and how feeble a descendant of the hero-king was the realm's present monarch, six generations on.

Mounting the ridge above the battlefield, at St Ninian's, they trotted on to the outskirts of Stirling town. There were fortified gates to be negotiated, but these stood open, and the Douglas banner, transferred from the galley's mast to fly above the riders, got them past the guards without further declaration. There were undoubted advantages, as well as demands and duties, in being who they were, John had to admit.

The royal burgh of Stirling mounted by narrow streets and wynds the steep lower slopes of the mighty rock on which perched the castle, the principal seat and most secure stronghold of the Kings of Scots, a fortress since Pictish times. Climbing these, their beasts' hooves striking sparks from the cobblestones, the horsed party had to string out, however close they tried to keep, owing to the constriction of the ways between the tall buildings, tenements, warehouses, churches, monasteries and barracks. The citizens were little impressed by the Douglas party and banner, for the town was ever full of the retainers of a score of lords anyway; so they were scarcely

13

accorded a glance, although they did receive some doubtful looks from idling men-at-arms.

Up at the approaches to the castle's gatehouse and draw-bridge they were halted by guards demanding identities and their business.

"The Earl of Angus and the Lord of Douglas to see the King's Grace," Archie called back strongly.

John always was apt to wince rather at the announcement of his title, Lord of Douglas. He was all too well aware of the part their father, and the Red Douglases generally, had played in the bringing down of their senior line, the Black Douglases, some thirty years before, a sorry episode in the story of a great family. Admittedly the Blacks, the Earls of Douglas, had become almost too powerful, and marrying into the royal family, rivalling the authority of the crown; and their bloody downfall had been a shameful business. Their own father, fourth Earl of Angus, always a little jealous of the others' pre-eminence, had aided James the Second, the present monarch's father, in contriving it, and had gained much thereby, large portions of their vast lands, including Douglasdale itself, in Lanarkshire. And it was this style and title, Lord of Douglasdale, more commonly just of Douglas, which he had obtained for his second son, the first of course being Master of Angus, his heir Archie.

The Captain of the Guard went to obtain permission for them to enter the fortress, which delay had Archie frowning, for it was prolonged. When at length there were calls from the gatehouse parapet, it was not the guard who spoke.

"I am Atholl. What does Douglas seek here?"

"Audience!" Archie barked back. "Of the King."

"Many so seek, my lord."

"Angus is not many! Tell His Grace."

"Even Douglas cannot command the King! Or his uncle!"

"Douglas can command others! Many others, I'd remind you, Atholl. Many!"

John laid hand on his brother's arm. "Let *me* speak," he murmured, and raised his voice. "My lord of Atholl, here speaks Douglasdale. The Princess Mary is kin to us both, you and us. We would speak with her over her husband's death. His sister, the Countess of Angus, had word for her. His Grace will not keep us from seeing his own sister, I think. And proffering him our loyal duty."

There was a pause and then the answer came. "Very well. I will go inform the King."

Archie spluttered, "Do that! But we are not to be kept waiting here, outside, like packmen, Atholl, while you do so, by God! Douglas!"

"Very well," the other repeated. "Enter. But leave your men."

Snorting, Archie led the way in over the drawbridge timbers and under the gatehouse arch, John signing to the escort to dismount and wait.

Inside the outer bailey of the citadel they found that Atholl had disappeared.

"Where are the Princess Mary's quarters, fellow?" Archie, dismounted, demanded of one of the guard.

That individual shrugged. "In the West Tower, my lord. Beyond the pits. The Bear Pit and the Lion Pit, yonder."

John had never been in Stirling Castle before, but his brother had. Archie gave the guard their horses' reins to hold and strode off up the slope, largely naked rock worn smooth by the tread of generations, to the central courtyard. This was flanked by high buildings, the royal block or palace, the governor's tower, the Chapel Royal, the council hall and the rest. Archie marched past all.

"Should we not await word from the King?" John suggested.

"Wait? I await no man's permission. In especial one so feeble as Jamie Stewart!" They passed the parapets of two well-like shafts, from the first of which arose a strong animal smell. Peering down they could see two black bears, pacing, pacing. The other pit appeared to be empty. Beyond rose two more buildings, one of which was obviously a storehouse, the other, higher, a tower. They entered this unchecked.

They heard juvenile voices at once, and climbing to the

15

first floor found three children at play with a young woman, all turning to stare at the newcomers.

"Anna!" Archie exclaimed. "Here's fair meeting. So you remain with Her Highness! That is well."

"My lords, my lords!" The girl started forward to them. "Oh, how good to see kenn't faces! And kindly ones. It has been so long, so long. Praises be! This – this will be the Lord Johnnie? No? A man, now. And a bonny one!"

John bowed. It was four years since he had seen the Lady Annabella Boyd, the princess's lady-in-waiting, and he had been only sixteen. She had not changed much, apart from no longer being pregnant; but no doubt *he* had changed. She was a comely, spirited creature, sister to the late Arran and to Archie's wife, forthright, outspoken always.

"Have you no such praise for me?" Archie demanded. "*You* look fair enough – for what could be named a prisoner!"

"Oh, I make do, yes. We . . . survive. Unlike, unlike . . ."

"Aye, your brother. I am sorry, lass, sorry. So grievous." Archie looked at John, whom he recognised was better at this sort of thing than was he.

He went to clasp her arm, but this time said nothing. She turned, and for a moment or two buried her face against his shoulder. Then, gulping, she swung round, to hold out her hand to the youngest of the three children, who were watching this exchange great-eyed.

"Pate, come and greet the great lords of Douglas," she got out, thickly. "The Earl of Angus and the Lord of Douglasdale. I have told you of the Red Douglas. Here they are." She swallowed again. "This, my lords, is Pate."

"Your son? A fine boy . . ."

"My son. And Patrick's!" That was almost defiant.

They nodded. Anna's love had been Sir Patrick Fullarton, son to the hereditary coroner of Arran, and gentleman attendant to the earl thereof. But her father had loftier aims for her, and when she had grown big with child to Patrick, the Regent Boyd had had her forcibly married to a supporter of his own, Sir John Gordon of Lochinvar, in Patrick's and Arran's absence in Denmark. So she was, in name at least, the Lady Gordon of Lochinvar, although the marriage had not been consummated, Where, and in what state, was Sir Patrick Fullarton now, was not known.

"And here are Jamie and Grizel." She signed forward the other two. They were the children of the princess and Arran, the boy, who should now be earl, aged six, his sister a year younger. What were they to say to these?

John smiled but said nothing. His brother asked, "Their mother . . . ?"

"Upstairs. She writes letters, I think."

They climbed to the next floor where, in the anteroom of a bedchamber, they found another young woman, quill in hand, sitting at a table. At sight of them she rose slowly, and stood, one hand out, silent.

They both bowed low, but not sufficiently so as to prevent them eyeing her. As well they might, for she was the most beautiful and attractive woman either had ever seen, still only in her mid-twenties, dark of hair, fine-featured, tall and lissome but splendidly built and bearing herself with an unassumed dignity suitable for the daughter of the longest line of kings in all Christendom.

She it was who spoke. "How good, my lords, that you have come. I thank you indeed. I was loth to trouble you. But . . ." She made an expressive gesture with her hands, pen and all.

"Highness, we could do no other," Archie declared. "Your wish is our command. We came at once."

"Your sorrow and hurt and pain, Princess, must be beyond all words," John said. "In especial, *our* poor words. But . . . we are sorry, sorry . . ."

"I know it, my friends, my good friends. You, then, are John, a man grown. Five years, is it? No, four. Long, sorry years. And now . . . !" She shrugged and mustered a smile. "Here I cause you more upset and concern, as I did then. Is it the role I have to play in life?"

"Never that, Highness!" Archie exclaimed. "Tell us what we must do. What we can seek to achieve on your behalf."

"Achieve? That is very doubtful, I fear. That you may achieve anything in this of hateful marriage. But if you can

17

try, I am grateful. But come, sit. Anna will fetch wine and sustenance. At least they do not starve us, here!"

"Your husband, Highness – this grievous blow. Sorrow must desolate you. Without this added trial of marriage." That was John. "Have you had further tidings as to my lord of Arran? How he died?"

"Nothing, no. Save that he is . . . gone. To a fuller, kinder life, let us believe. But how, I know not. That is what I am writing here. To Charles, Duke of Burgundy, his friend it seems. Asking for word of it. Aye, and also for him to use his influence to halt this folly of a marriage to James Hamilton."

"Can *he* do anything? Far distant?" Archie asked.

"I think that it could be so. Charles the Bold is very strong now, and not only in the Low Countries. And his Low Countries are Scotland's greatest partners in trade. Most of our wool goes there. And hides. Scotland needs that trade. The duke, and the Hanseatic League together, could make the regency council think again. If they act quickly. My Thomas was acting envoy for the League . . ."

"And the King? What of King James?"

Mary Stewart pursed lovely lips. "James does what his uncles tell him, I fear."

"But – he is of full age now. But a year to go, no? Then he can dismiss the regency. He has a mind of his own, the monarch. And you are his sister." Archie was vehement. "Your royal sire, at his age, was acting otherwise, as Douglas knows!" He did not pursue that. "Does King James *want* you to wed Hamilton?"

"No. But he will not go against the others. He is very different from his father, yes. If Alexander – that is Albany – if he had been the older brother, it might have been different. He is more like his father, stronger . . ."

She paused, as voices sounded from below, not children's voices but men's.

"I fear that we are to have visitors!" she observed. "They would know of your arrival . . ."

Steps on the stair, and three men entered the room, without any knocking, two of early middle years, one young. The Douglas brothers rose to their feet, and bowed.

"James, here are old friends," Mary Stewart said, and coolly. "My lords, you may enter!" That to her uncles. She did not rise.

Stewarts and Douglases eyed each other.

"Our loyal duty, Sire," Archie jerked.

"Your Grace's true servant," John said.

The young King looked uneasy and did not answer.

The elder uncle, John, Earl of Atholl, he who had spoken with them from the gatehouse, was frowning, a handsome man, slender but tall, with a curious stoop to his shoulders. "My lords, you said yonder that it was His Grace that you came to see!" he rasped.

"To be sure," Archie returned. "We sought *audience*. Until it was granted, we came to see His Grace's royal sister, our good friend."

"It would have been better to have awaited His Grace's permission," the other uncle, James, Earl of Buchan, put in loudly, almost with a guffaw. A little younger, he looked older, inclining to stoutness, hair and beard greying. He was a great laugher, although not always with humorous intent; indeed he was known as Hearty James. These two, although Stewarts, were not of the royal line. Their father, the famous Black Knight of Lorn, a brilliant mirror of chivalry, had married Queen Joan Beaufort, the widow of the assassinated King James the First, and these were the progeny, half-brothers of James the Second, who had created the elder Earl of Atholl and endowed him with considerable of the forfeited lands of the Earls of Douglas. The younger, Hearty James, had until recently been just Sir James Stewart of Auchterhouse, of which lands he had married the heiress.

Mary considered them. "These friends rightly came to console me over the death of my husband. Do you find fault with that, Uncles?" She paused. "And even if you do, is that of moment?"

Atholl stiffened the more. "Highness, His Grace's permission should have been sought . . ."

"Permission! Am I a prisoner, my lord? I am the Princess

Royal of Scotland, I would remind you. James, you hear that? To your sister. How says the King?"

The monarch was actually older than John, but looked a deal younger, hesitant, awkward in his movements although quite good-looking, but with a weakness about mouth and chin. He was nibbling his lip.

"They . . . they represent the council, Mary," he got out.

"The council is there to counsel you, their sovereign-lord, James. Not to order you, like some infant. Nor myself!"

James, glancing unhappily at his uncles, said nothing.

"The Secret Council has the duty to guide His Grace, Highness. And hold responsibility for the realm," Atholl said sternly. "That is our duty. But we are not here to chaffer words, see you. The Earl of Angus and the Lord of Douglas sought audience of the King. His Grace is graciously granting it."

Archie looked at John – who himself was not too sure how best to proceed. Probably, at this juncture, there was nothing to be gained by temporising.

"Sire," he said, "as well as coming to express our regrets, our deep regrets, to Her Highness over the death of the Earl of Arran, we came because of concern that there is word that there are plans mooted to marry her to the Lord Hamilton. This against her wishes. We of Douglas would much deplore that."

"What concern is that of Douglas?" Atholl snapped.

"Friendship. Esteem. Respect, my lord. We – "

Archie interrupted him. "We address the King!" he asserted. "Not . . . others. As is my right, as an earl of this realm."

"It is . . . for the best," James said unhappily.

"If against Her Highness's wishes?"

The King did not answer.

"Hamilton is a notable lecher. I know of seven bastard sons of his, and by different women. God alone knows how many others, and daughters! What sort of match is that for Your Grace's sister?"

Hearty James spoke. "Your right, as an earl, is to *address* the King, Angus. Not to put His Grace to the question!"

"For so new an earl, *you* speak loud! To tell Douglas what he may say!"

John intervened less hotly. "Sire, and my lords, let us consider this matter with more of reason and patience. Tell us . . ."

"It is not for you, young man, to consider the matter at all!" Atholl declared. "It is the decision of the council. And for the realm's good. That is sufficient."

"The council! That is yourselves, and one or two of your friends – including no doubt the Lord Hamilton!" Archie gave back. "No *parliament*, I swear, would so consider and decide!"

That word parliament produced indrawn breaths. Parliament, the supreme authority under the crown, could do great things, even dismiss a regency.

Then, "This is no matter for parliament."

"Yet you say that it is for the nation's good. If it is the realm's weal, or otherwise, then it is parliament's business."

"This is folly!" Buchan hooted. "A parliament called over a marriage! Which the King has sanctioned. Have you lost your wits, Angus?"

"Far from it. I tell you – "

"Only the King can call a parliament," Atholl reminded.

"If one is requested by a sufficiency of the earls and lords, the King can scarce refuse. And Douglas could see that it was so requested!"

John tried again. "If you will but inform us. Why? Why this of the Lord Hamilton? What benefit for the kingdom? Your reasons, Sire and my lords. When it is to Her Highness's hurt?"

"It is of no avail, John." Mary Stewart had remained quiet throughout this exchange. "They will not heed you, any more than myself. The Lord Hamilton is rich, one of the richest in the land. He has *bought* me, I think! It is as simple as that. The treasury is, I am told, empty again."

There was a moment's silence at that, before Archie burst out, "This, this is an outrage! If true. Shameful, above all! Is it true? Is this the truth of it?"

"Not so," Atholl jerked. "Her Highness but dreams. The Lord Hamilton is the crown's good and loyal friend and strong supporter. As the King's good-brother he will greatly strengthen the throne. A widower, and a man of parts. He has been the realm's ambassador to England. And to Rome. He will make Her Highness a good husband." Abruptly he turned. "Sire, I think that Your Grace has had a sufficiency of this! It is . . . unsuitable."

"Yes, let us begone," his brother said loudly. "Your Grace has been very patient. Too patient, I judge!"

James nodded, glanced almost furtively at his sister, and made for the door, followed by the others.

This time, the Douglas brothers did not make the required obeisance.

Alone with Mary they eyed each other.

"I am sorry, my good friends, that it had to be thus," she told them, sighing. "I might have hoped for better, but scarcely expected it. This has been the way of it since the word of Thomas's death. I see no remedy."

"There *must* be!" Archie cried. "This of a parliament? It came to me. I swear that I could rouse sufficient support to demand one of the King. And lead an assault against the marriage.'

"I doubt whether you could call a parliament merely to do with the wedding of one young woman!" she said, shaking her head. "It is good of you to think of it – but I fear that it would not be sufficient to bring out the attendance necessary, even if James could be prevailed upon to call it."

"We could think of some other cause, also. Something concerned with the realm's needs. You spoke of the Duke of Burgundy, your husband's friend. Could we not use him? There is this man Monypenny, who calls himself the Sieur de Concressault, King Louis of France's envoy, new come. He seeks to enrol Scotland in France's cause against Burgundy. Could we not have a parliament called to decide on that? And also on your marriage?"

"That is possible, I suppose. But a parliament requires forty days of notice. That is the rule, that all may have time and

22

opportunity to attend. Forty days. And delay there must be, while you raise support. And my good uncles would seek to hold back James."

"Yes. But . . ."

Anna Gordon appeared with a serving-maid and a silver tray laden with food and drink, the three children in train; and for the moment debate was superseded by chatter, Anna making forthright and uncomplimentary comment on their recent visitors.

Then, with the brothers doing justice to the fare, and after no long interval, the maid came back.

"The Captain of the Guard is below, Highness. He waits to escort these lords to the gatehouse," she announced.

"Dear God – *escort*! He does? We are to be sent off!" Archie all but choked on his oatcake and honey. "These upjumped placemen think to tell Douglas that he must go! By the Rood, we will see about that!"

John looked doubtful. "Is there any point in outfacing them, Archie? It will but make them the sorer against us. And will not help Her Highness's cause, I judge."

"Have some pride, man! We are not to be ordered about by such as these."

"I think that John could be right," Mary said. "In Stirling Castle you can do nothing to effect. They could always have James to issue a royal command for you to leave. Which you could not refuse. And that would serve nothing. I fear that you should go, my friends."

"Satan roast them! The Red Douglas will not forget this!" But he rose.

"You must not let my sorry affairs bring you troubles and upset. That would but add to my woe. Best to go now, with my warm gratitude for the coming, and so swiftly. And for your support and care, which I shall cherish." She rose also, with a faint smile. "I will survive, see you! We Stewarts are good at surviving. I have had . . . some practice!"

John went to take her hand, and kiss it. She raised her other hand, to run her fingers lightly over his head and brow, and

23

meeting his intense gaze, so that for a moment or two their eyes, grey eyes both, locked. Neither spoke.

Archie, perhaps emboldened by his brother's favourable reception, went to clasp the princess to him in something of a bear's hug. She gasped a little laugh.

"Douglas's motto is *Jamais Arrière*, is it not?" she exclaimed.

Anna chuckled.

They bowed themselves out, in very differing style, to go down and meet, and ignore, the Captain of the Guard.

2

Back at Tantallon, John had little time for fishing or for ballad-composing. Almost at once he set off journeying, on a lengthy and round-about tour, to cover as much of Lowland Scotland in as short a time as possible. His task was to call upon as many barons, lairds and prelates, such as were entitled to attend a parliament, to urge them to request the calling of a session thereof, and promptly. Archie would do the same for the greater magnates, where they had some influence, such as the Earl of Morton, formerly Douglas of Dalkeith, the Earl of Crawford; married to a Douglas, the Earl of Erroll, the High Constable, similarly, the Lords of Annandale, Erskine, Cathcart and Hay of Yester, with sundry bishops likewise.

John, escorted by just two servitors, made his first call at nearby Kilspindie Castle on the shore of the great bay of Aberlady, eight miles to the west. This was a seat of their uncle, William Douglas of Cluny. The barony of Cluny was over in Fothrif, the west part of Fife, near Auchterderran; but he spent much of his time at Kilspindie, more conveniently placed. As well as being their uncle, he was their good friend. Indeed he had been Archie's guardian and tutor when their father had died a dozen years before, leaving a ten-year-old as heir. All the Douglas family were fond of him.

Uncle William, at home, received John warmly and listened to his account and request with sympathy and understanding. He was a big, burly man of high colouring and outgoing personality, but who could be sternly authoritative when necessary. Now he readily agreed not only to press for a parliament but to set off himself for Fife, Perthshire and Angus, even further north, to urge others in those parts to do likewise, using the France–Burgundy situation as main reason but prepared to contest the princess's marriage once they got there.

Well pleased with this, John rode southwards for Whittinghame, in the lap of the Lammermuirs, a dozen miles. Douglas of Whittinghame was younger, of more distant kin, and not in the best of health. But he was quite ready to co-operate in this matter and add his voice to the call. As always when friends came to Whittinghame, John was taken to see the place's speciality, the ancient yew tree nearby, an extraordinary and gigantic feature. How old it was none knew, but down the ages it had sent out innumerable branches which, in time, had rerooted themselves in the ground, to form a strange, arched and arcaded green enclosure, a sort of cathedral of boughs and verdure, a secret sanctuary in which, as children. the Douglases had loved to play.

These two calls did not take long and John decided that, instead of returning to Tantallon for the night, they would ride on southwards, through the Lammermuir Hills, for Bonkyl and Preston, another Douglas barony, only some fifteen miles as the crow might fly but a deal more than that by the twisting hill-tracks and valleys they must take.

It made a pleasant enough journey, by climbing burn channels and grassy ridges, sheep-strewn – most of them indeed Douglas sheep – over escarpments, gorse- and hawthorn-scattered, and up to the high heather-clad summits where the deer drifted, the blue hares loped and the yittering curlews called, hunting country although still sheep-dotted. They called in at Stonypath Tower, where there were more Douglas connections, the nunnery of Garvald and on, beginning to climb consistently now.

Through the fifteen-mile belt of Lammermuir, twenty-odd miles long, and so producing some three hundred and fifty square miles of the best sheep country in all Scotland – whence indeed came much of the Red Douglas wealth – they climbed and dropped, climbed and dropped, the names of all they passed, from that of the range itself, bespeaking sheep: Rammerscales, Wedder Lairs, Wether Laws, Hog Rig, Ewelaw, Tuplaw, Lamblair, Sheeppath Glen and so on. In time they came to the upper reaches of the Whiteadder, or White Water, and followed this down, past Cranshaws and the fords at Ellem and Millburn and Cockburn Mill, to Preston. It was evening now, and they were tired and hungry; but they had only two more miles to go to Bonkyl Castle, where they were assured of welcome, by another distant cousin, married to a Home.

Douglas of Bonkyl was not only a notable baron in his own right but his links with the Homes were important. For that great family largely dominated the Merse, Central Berwickshire and the East March, the more so since the downfall of the Earls of Dunbar and March, another of the victims of James the Second's policy of getting rid of great nobles capable of endangering the crown by their power. The Homes had profited, and were now on the way to becoming almost as powerful as Dunbar had been. If they could be enrolled into the parliament-demanders, that would be a major help.

Bonkyl promised to do what he could in that direction, but suggested that the present and newly created Lord Home was much influenced by his uncle, George, Prior of Coldinghame. If the Lord of Douglasdale was to call upon the prior, much might be achieved. The Priors of Coldinghame were always Homes, and their influence greater than that of many abbots and even bishops.

So next day John went on to Coldinghame, only some thirteen miles to the east, and at the great priory near the fierce coastline of St Ebba's Head and Fast Castle, made himself pleasant to the gaunt and cadaverous, irascible-seeming prior, much more like a warrior-chieftain than any cleric. His initial reception was unpromising, but when John mentioned the Lord Hamilton, that produced a very positive reaction of hostility, and anything the prior could do to counter Hamilton, he would – why was not explained.

Thereafter much longer journeyings were involved, for now John had to cross the entire borderland westwards, calling at the Douglas fiefs of Bonjedworth, Jedburgh Abbey, Cavers Castle and Hawick, then over the very spine of Lowland

Scotland, the watershed where the Teviot, the Ettrick, the Ale, the Ewes, the Esk and the Liddel Waters were born, and so down into the West March and Dumfries-shire and Galloway, lands formerly belonging to the *Black* Douglases but now many of them to the Reds. Then north, by Drumlanrig into Ayrshire and Lanarkshire, the Douglas calf country as it were, John able to visit his own lordship of Douglasdale in the by-going. The Abbot of Crossraguel promised support; these mitred abbots had seats in parliament.

Then back to Lothian, by Abercorn and Alderston, after two weeks of travel and persuasion. He had not particularly enjoyed the latter, not being of an assertive character, but he had been sustained all along by the recurring vision of Mary Stewart, her loveliness of feature, form and manner, and in especial that last long look they had exchanged on parting at Stirling.

Back at Tantallon, he learned that Archie's briefer visiting had been on the whole successful, and that Uncle Willie had sent word from Kilspindie that reactions to his appeals had been favourable. It looked as though King James and his advisers would be so bombarded with demands that they could nowise refuse to call a parliament.

And then, two days after John's return, Friar Anselm arrived again from the Abbot of Cambuskenneth, with the word that they were too late. The Princess Mary had been married to the Lord Hamilton four days previously, alas.

Distressed, angry, resentful, they heard the news, Archie in a rage, John sad, sad.

When Archie was in a fury all were left in no doubt about it, and for a while all Tantallon quivered with it. But eventually they were able to hear details. The wedding had been held in the Chapel Royal at Stirling Castle – where, ironically, Mary's other forced marriage had taken place seven years previously. On that occasion, the Primate, Patrick Graham, Bishop of St Andrews, had conducted the ceremony; but this time, oddly enough, the celebrant was a comparatively humble cleric – if humble was the word for a character who was anything but humble-minded, according to Friar Anselm, who declared the Abbot of Cambuskenneth to be much offended. The Douglases had not heard of William Sheves; but they would, their informant told them, they would! Sheves was a curiosity indeed, a hitherto obscure priest but a noted astrologer and magician, as well as a physician and purveyor of herbal medicines. King James suffered from pimples, possibly acne, and this Sheves had been called upon to treat him. He had cured him, it seemed, and a bond had developed between the young monarch and this oddity, so much so that James had had him promoted to the influential position of Archdeacon of St Andrews, this while the Primate was himself away in Rome. Bishop Graham had gone to the Vatican, although a sick man, two years before, in order to try to persuade Pope Sixtus to elevate the Scottish Church to Metropolitan status, and St Andrews to an archbishopric – this in order to end claims by the Archbishops of York, England, that they were the most northerly Metropolitans and therefore overlords of the Scots Church. This was a cause in which Princess Mary and her husband, Arran, had been much involved, in Denmark and Norway, since the Archbishop of Trondheim there had made similar claims, as a still more northerly Metropolitan. In that they had been successful, and now Bishop Graham, at Rome, had been finally so. The Scottish Church was now declared independent, and Graham an archbishop. But, his sickness continuing, he had remained at the Vatican meantime, and there were those at home, ambitious men, who claimed that he was but malingering, quite useless as head of the Church, and should be replaced, despite his achievement there. And amongst these, Archdeacon Sheves was one of the loudest, and apparently swaying the King. That James should have chosen him to perform the wedding ceremony of his sister to Hamilton was significant indeed.

The Douglas brothers were not uninterested in all this; but they were more concerned over the fate of Mary Stewart. What now, they demanded? Where was she? And in what state? Was it but a marriage of convenience, a gesture to appease Hamilton's desire to be linked with the royal house? Or was it . . . ? They left the rest unsaid.

The friar shrugged. Who could tell, as to that? But Hamilton had taken her away to his castle of Cadzow in Lanarkshire – and he was noted for his desire for women, especially beautiful women.

The brothers eyed each other.

"What is to be done?" Archie demanded. "What can we do?"

John repeated that last, but with the emphasis on the word "can".

The friar had no suggestions for them. "The marriage is accomplished. Only His Holiness at Rome could undo it – and then only for reasons of consanguinity. I do not think that there are any such."

"Poor Mary!" John said, although poor was a description which somehow nowise fitted that young woman in any respect.

"We can go to see her at Cadzow. Hamilton cannot forbid us to see her. Tell her that we have tried. This of the parliament. Discover her state, what she would have of us. That, at least . . ."

"Yes, let us do that. Go to Cadzow. Show her that she still has friends. Even though the parliament will serve nothing now."

"Aye, that parliament. We could have spared ourselves the trouble. But it will have to go ahead now. We cannot abandon that. Not when so many will have demanded it."

"If the King *does* call it . . ."

With Archie there was no delay – there never was, once he had a course in mind. Not that John was for putting off either, on this occasion. Countess Elizabeth and their sisters gave their varying views as to what to say to the reluctant bride.

They would go the very next day.

So it was more riding the country for the Douglases, due westwards this time, much of it over ground John had just recently covered on his return journey, almost seventy miles, by the northern flanks of the Pentland Hills, after Edinburgh, over the bleak uplands beyond the Calders, and down to the great Clyde valley. Cadzow was in north Lanarkshire, some ten miles south-east of Glasgow.

The castle was a strong and extensive place, picturesquely situated on the lip of a ravine, and overlooking the wide plain of Clydesdale. With their escort, the visitors arrived at sundown, and found all looking very lovely in the golden light, looking west as it did. They had some difficulty in gaining access, which was not unusual on such occasions, shouts from the gatehouse declaring that the Lord Hamilton was not there meantime. But when Archie declared haughtily that it was the Earl of Angus come to see the King's sister, Princess Mary, on the realm's business, this could hardly be refused, with the guard conceding that Her Highness had not gone to Glasgow with his lordship. The drawbridge came clanking down.

Within the main keep, who should come running down the stairs to enquire their business but the Lady Anna, all smiles and exclamations, clearly as delighted to see them as she was surprised. Amidst a great flood of chatter she conducted them upstairs. The children were just being put to bed, she announced. John managed to insert a query as to how was the princess and how taking her dire situation, to be told, with a half-shrug, half-grimace, that Mary was Mary, no great clarification.

Up on the third storey a different kind of chatter prevailed, young voices upraised in anything but sleepy fashion. At Anna's introductory cry, Mary Stewart, stooping over a bed, straightened up to turn and gaze. Then her hand came out, open, eloquent, without any words.

Archie strode forward, to clasp her, ejaculating incoherences. His brother was less impetuous, but no less moved.

She stood there looking calm and beautiful, as it were contained, but her welcome of them none the less evident for that. When John came up, she again touched his cheek gently – and he knew a great upsurge of feeling, which itself precluded words.

Archie was producing words sufficient for them all, in a spate of enquiry, assertion and declamation, Anna adding her

31

quota from the background, the children not to be outdone. Noise prevailed – but also quiet.

With Anna presently left to finish the bedding process, the princess promising to come back and kiss all three goodnight shortly, she led the two men down to her own chamber.

"My very good and dear friends," she said to them now. "To come all this way! How kind, how very kind. It lifts my heart."

"We would have come further than this!" Archie declared. "We came whenever we heard of, of this. We were wroth, hot! When we had been getting all to demand a parliament. To protest . . ."

"Yes, I heard of that. My thanks. Heard from . . . him! From my husband. Yes, I must name him that, for I am now indeed his wife. And in more than name! Someone told him of your moves for a parliament. But *after* the wedding! It, your call and claim, is being spoken of."

"He knows, then? Hamilton?"

"Oh, yes. Not much escapes that one. He knows. And who is behind it."

"And we are too late. Too late! They moved over-fast for us."

John spoke. "Highness, we grieve for you. It is . . . damnable! Your state, now. Is, is . . . ?" He could not go on.

"Is he acting the husband?" she completed for him. "Oh, yes, he is. From that first night. James Hamilton is no laggard, especially where women are concerned! Despite his years."

They were silent.

"I was . . . prepared, to be sure. Expecting no less." She spoke quickly, evenly, not making drama of it. "He is not a, a savage! Much experienced! And I, mother of two, am not some shrinking virgin. I can endure."

John, who had no least call nor claim on this young woman, princess or none, and who was restrained by nature, found it hard to restrain himself now. He bit his lip. "I, I could slay the man!" That, coming out, surprised even himself.

Archie stared, knowing his brother.

32

Mary did not comment, in words, but her look was warm, kind, understanding, even though she shook her head.

"What is to be done?" Archie asked. "Something we must do."

"You can do naught, I fear. None can. But – it is none so ill. Once I had accepted it. That was the trial, the test. But I am in some measure favoured, see you. In that my new husband is so much concerned with other women, he requires me the less! He has them a-many. Two or three in this castle itself. Others near and far. So – I am spared much.' Her faint smile was not reflected in the men's faces.

"At his age he may not live overlong, in that case," Archie suggested hopefully.

"Fifty-two is no great age. But – enough of this. Tell me of all at Tantallon. Elizabeth? Your children? Your sisters . . . ?"

"They are well enough." Archie dismissed that, with a wave of his hand. "Could not there be a divorce? Or annulment? The churchmen can usually find grounds for such, to put before the Pope in Rome. Some grounds, some pretext, some device . . . ?"

"I know of none. I thought of that, before the wedding. Put it to my friend, the Abbot of Cambuskenneth. But we could think of nothing. No sufficient reason. A man may have many mistresses, but that gives no ground for divorce. And there is no near blood relation."

"Some powerful cleric? Such need but little excuse . . ."

"Bishop Graham?" John put in. The Primate. Or, Archbishop, now. He is in Rome still, is he not? And has the Pope's ear, or he would not have accomplished this of raising St Andrews to be independent. Would not a plea to him perhaps have results? He owes you much, does he not, Highness? You went to Norway, to this Trondheim to aid in his cause. To win that archbishop's agreement to renounce claims on the Scottish Church. He, Graham, might persuade the Pope to annul the marriage, Highness."

"You must stop calling me Highness, John. I am Mary. Besides, my highness is scarce in evidence now, is it? But I fear that our new archbishop would be unable to serve, in

33

this. Even if he could. Or in much, indeed. For I deem him a broken man."

"Broken! The Primate? When he has just won to be Metropolitan of this Scotland?"

"Even so. For he has enemies, high-placed, here at home. Men who aim to bring him down. And may well succeed."

"But . . . this is folly!" Archie cried. "If he has the Pope's blessing, the Vatican's support. Who can bring him down?"

"The Lord's Anointed can! My brother! With urgings from others. You see, the archbishop is a sick man. Has been for long. It was a great effort for him to go to Rome. While he is there, his enemies can do little, no, for the Pope sees him, is aware of his state. But when he comes home, it will be different. If the King of Scots petitions the Vatican to have him replaced, as unfit for his duties, in mind as in body, and this is supported by some of the bishops and senior clergy, then the Pontiff will have little choice. And this is what is intended, I understand."

"Lord! They would do that?"

"*He* would."

"King James?"

"Not so much James. Although he would sign the petition, I have little doubt. But . . . another. You have heard of William Sheves?"

"The astrologer? The purveyor of magic? We were told of him only yesterday."

"Well, you will hear a deal more of that one, I think," she told them. "Sheves is, I judge, going to be the new power behind the throne."

"But — an upjumped nobody? A mere interloper, of no standing!"

"But of wits and cunning. Aye, and of ambition! William Sheves is only the second son of a poor Fife laird, yes. But he is a clever man, and without scruple. He knows where he is going, that one. He has wormed his way into James's silly favour. My royal brother ever lacked judgment. Sheves cured his spots and back pains. He has prophesied all sorts of splendours and achievements for James, the stars telling what

34

to do, he says. James ever needs a strong man telling him what to do – women he despises. My Thomas served for that, for a while. But now he has this William Sheves. And James is of full age in only a month or two now. Taking over the rule, as well as reigning. So . . ."

"And this Sheves is working against Archbishop Graham?"

"Yes. He has got James to appoint him Archdeacon of St Andrews, the Metropolitan see, in the archbishop's absence. Which puts Sheves in a very influential position. And the man is working on sundry of the bishops, who would seek to replace Graham. Blackadder, Bishop of Aberdeen. Treasurer Laing, who is the new Bishop of Glasgow. Others. But, if I know Sheves, he intends that great office for himself!"

"Sheves! Archbishop and Metropolitan! A mere lowly priest and magician!"

"Lowly, but with the King of Scots at his back. He will, I think, use the others to bring down Graham. Then himself slip in above them. I may be wrong – but James himself told me that his good soul-friend William would make an excellent archbishop! So I do not think that we can look to Rome, at this time, for aid in *my* affairs."

"This is damnable!" Archie exclaimed. "Such as this creature to be head of the Church! How can this be stopped?"

"The parliament," John suggested. "It may be too late to save this of the marriage. But could it not be used to seek to aid Archbishop Graham? And put some restraint on the man Sheves? Can a parliament deal with affairs of the Church? I have never attended one, not being of full age. But bishops and mitred abbots are there. If they can discuss and vote on affairs of state, may not others do as much for Holy Church? We are all its members."

"I have heard Church matters spoken of in parliament, yes," the princess agreed. "Something might be achieved there. If a parliament *is* assured. Sheves might well prevail on James not to call one."

"With a score and more lords and barons demanding one to deal with this of France and Burgundy? Can the King refuse?"

"I am unsure. If advised against . . ."

"Your uncles, the Earls of Atholl and Buchan?" John queried. And added, "Mary," somewhat hesitantly.

"They have been losing power over James for some time. This of a parliament may indeed suit James. In that it could be used to mark the end of regency and set the nation's seal on his attaining full powers as monarch. He may see it as that, and so be prepared to call it. Even Master Sheves might see it as to his advantage."

"Then *we* must see that it is not!" Archie said. He turned on a new tack. "Your brothers, Mary? The Duke of Albany and the young Earl of Mar. Albany is now reaching manhood is he not? Almost Johnnie's age. We have heard that he is very different from the King. More spirited. Could he not help to clip the wings of this Sheves?"

She considered that. "He might, yes. Alexander is already chafing at the bit, at his lack of any power or authority. Since James and his Margaret have had their little son, Alex is no longer next heir to the throne, and feels himself to be ignored. He is a very different character from James, vigorous, eager. And James seeks ever to put him down. He will resent Sheves, yes – that is sure."

"Then we must try to work on him. He could be useful."

"How to do that?" John asked. "We will scarcely be welcome at Stirling Castle, now that Mary is no longer there. And where else can we see him?"

"Would you invite him here, Mary? Your brother. Would Hamilton have that?"

"I do not see why not. The question would rather be – would *you* be welcome again? When my husband hears that you have visited me, and then you came again, shortly, he might wonder. When he knows that you judge this marriage a mistake."

"Somewhere other, then?"

"Perhaps. But I am not always going to stay here, at this Cadzow. As the King's sister I can claim to be with him frequently. That cannot be denied me. So I will be at Stirling, at times. And you can come there then . . ."

Anna arrived, to announce that if Mary did not go upstairs to bid the bairns goodnight and tell them their story soon, they would all three be down here in a riot of protest.

So affairs of state were superseded by more urgent matters. Indeed, with the youngsters excited by the visitors and demanding more attention and stories, John volunteered to help out, and gave them the ballad of St Baldred of the Bass and his friends the seals, if after that they would go to sleep. This went down well, especially with Mary herself, who said that it was fascinating and that she had never heard of it previously. When John admitted that it was in fact his own composition she was greatly interested, saying that she had had no idea that he was a poet and balladist, a sennachie indeed, and clearly a notable one. Nothing would do but when they went downstairs again, he must give them more of his compositions, with the young women presently picking up lute and lyre to put his words to music, and with considerable success. Archie was less enthusiastic, but put up with it all nobly.

So that evening passed pleasantly, scarcely what the visitors had anticipated at Cadzow Castle.

In the morning, Mary took them down to the town on the lower ground, which in the past had been called Netherton of Cadzow but which its present lord had got elevated to the status of burgh and called Hamilton. Here they were inspecting, considering and admiring when the clatter of hooves drew their attention, as a party of riders came trotting through the streets.

"Ha! My lord returns sooner than looked for," Mary said. "This will be . . . interesting!"

The newcomers reined up, and a big floridly handsome man doffed his bonnet gallantly to the two young women, at the same time eyeing the two young men keenly. James Hamilton had a personable presence, although slightly overweight, with an air of complete self-confidence and a ready smile. Only those searching eyes rather qualified that smile, weighing, assessing.

"Whom have we here, my dear lady?" he asked.

"Friends of mine, good friends," Mary answered. "My

lord Earl of Angus and my lord of Douglasdale. Come visiting."

"Ah! A Douglas visitation! We are . . . honoured! Friends of yours are friends of mine, to be sure – if they will have it so. I have heard that these are not . . . uncritical of our felicity, my dear!"

"Let us say that, being friends of my late husband, indeed his kin, they did not look to see me wed again so speedily. As did not I!" She waved a hand, to change the subject. She could be very much the princess, on occasion, if it was called for, that one. "Your errand to Glasgow was successful, my lord?"

"Moderately so. Churchmen are never easy to deal with. This new Bishop Blackadder is not unconcerned with *this* world and its goods, as well as the next! But, heigho, I should have expected as much." He nodded to the brothers. "I will, no doubt, see you anon, my lords." And he rode on.

"James Hamilton is a man to be reckoned with," Mary observed simply, and led the way down to the stalls and booths of the market-place.

Returning to the castle, Archie declared that they would not linger, now that Hamilton was there. It would only make for discomfort, and no gain, to have words with the man. John agreed, saying that he would have difficulty in keeping his feelings in check, and so had better be gone – a statement which earned him a touch on the arm from Mary and a nod of approval from Anna.

Hamilton, however, thereafter did not prove awkward, indeed was fairly evidently endeavouring to be affable, although admittedly he did not press the Douglases to stay. In the circumstances there was not much that they could do, to any effect. Archie did get out, somewhat abruptly, that the princess's well-being and happiness were very much his concern, as kin to his own wife; to which Hamilton returned that, needless to say, his concern was even greater.

They made shift to depart fairly promptly, saying that they would be halfway home before nightfall. Unfortunately Hamilton played the good host and accompanied them to their horses, so that they had no last private word with Mary. Their farewells therefore were stilted, constrained, and eyes rather than lips had to say it all. But such can be eloquent enough – and not the least eloquent were James Hamilton's, warning, whatever his words. They left in no doubt that here was a dangerous man to cross.

3

This parliament was duly called for late May, important as the first after King James's coming-of-age and assumption of full powers as sovereign. It was held at Edinburgh, not in the Tolbooth as was sometimes done, nor in the Abbey of Holyrood, but in the great hall of the citadel-fortress itself, to emphasise the importance of the occasion – and perhaps to ensure that there could be no unsuitable demonstrations by ambitious or hostile lords and their armed followers, as could and did happen on occasion.

Archie and John arrived in good time for the noon opening, to have opportunity for word with the various Douglas kinsfolk and supporters. There could be no value now in protesting against the Hamilton marriage, since the deed was done and could not be undone by any parliament. Any hopes in that respect would rest on Archbishop Graham at Rome. So it was important that any moves against the Primate should be countered – and these, apparently, were anticipated. And the matter of who would be best to try to counter the unending threat of English aggression, Charles Duke of Burgundy or King Louis of France, would come up for decision. The Douglases were to support Burgundy.

Unfortunately Archie and John could not sit together. The earls had special seats just below the dais, whereas the lords-of-parliament, of which John was one, were seated in rows behind them, the holders of territorial baronies, commissioners of the shires and representatives of the burghs further back still. The clerics, bishops, mitred abbots and special officials of the Church sat across a central aisle.

There was a good attendance on this occasion, unlike some when many entitled to be present did not trouble to come from their faraway lands. John found himself seated between the Lords Hailes and Livingstone, while Archie sat with the fairly newly created Earl of Morton, formerly Douglas of Dalkeith. Up in the minstrels' gallery, where distinguished visitors sat, John could see the Princess Mary and her sister Margaret, amongst foreign ambassadors, sheriffs of counties and officers of state who did not have the right to vote. The young Queen was not present, despite the importance of the occasion for her husband.

Trumpeting heralded the opening of the proceedings, with the Lord Lyon King of Arms entering with his heralds and pursuivants from the dais door, colourful in their red and gold tabards. Lyon thumped on the floor with his staff, for silence, and announced that His Grace by his royal command, ordained that this parliament was now in session. All to be upstanding.

A further thumping ushered in two individuals, a gorgeously robed cleric, John Laing, Bishop of Glasgow and High Treasurer of Scotland, who, in the absence of the Primate, represented the authority of Holy Church; and Andrew Stewart, Lord Avondale, the Chancellor, who would chair the proceedings, under the presidency of the monarch. Avondale, a middle-aged scholarly man, went to the Chancellor's table in mid-dais, where monkish clerks already stood waiting, while the bishop moved over to a single fine chair at the far side.

More trumpeting, and from the dais doorway emerged none other than James Hamilton, bearing the sword of state held high, followed by the Earl of Buchan, carrying the royal sceptre, and his brother, Atholl, with a cushion on which lay the Scottish crown. These three items were placed on the Chancellor's table, and their bearers went to stand behind the empty throne.

John frowned. He had understood that it was the duty of the Earl of Erroll, the High Constable – who had married a Douglas of Dalkeith – to bear the sword of state; this of Hamilton carrying it looked ominous, a sign of increasing influence. There was no sign of Erroll.

A long and resounding flourish of trumpets all but shook

the hall, and the Lord Lyon raised a hand instead of thumping.

"Hear ye, hear ye!" he cried. "This assembly of his realm greets its liege-lord and sovereign, James, third of his name, by God's grace High King of Scots."

There was a distinct pause and then James appeared in the doorway, looking almost apprehensive, hesitant, eyes searching the thronged hall before seeming to summon up courage to enter and make hurriedly for the throne. Despite the splendid finery of cloth of gold and crimson velvet, he looked uncertain and younger than his years, clearly in a state of alarm.

Everyone bowed.

Behind came three others, two young men and one of early middle years, this last bringing up the rear. The pair in front were very different, one tall, well-built, head high, carrying himself with assurance, Alexander, Duke of Albany, until recently heir to the throne; the other, slight, head down, looking no more at ease than his eldest brother the King, John, Earl of Mar. Behind was a slender, almost thin, hatchet-faced man with hooded eyes and a pronounced stoop, which gave him a distinctly vulturine aspect, plainly dressed in clerical garb.

These three went to place themselves, the two royal brothers to stand immediately on either side of the throne, and the third, undoubtedly William Sheves, to station himself behind Bishop Laing's chair, from whence he surveyed all keenly, calculatingly.

The King sat, so all others might do the same save for Sheves and the group around the throne.

Lord Avondale, the Chancellor, picked up his gavel and beat on the table. "By order of the King's Grace," he called, "I declare this parliament in session. I, Chancellor, remind all present of the importance of the occasion. His Grace, having attained full age, as is his royal right, takes over the rule and governance of this realm. None here is called upon to make sanction of this. But it is usual and suitable for the Estates of parliament to acknowledge so notable an occasion, and to express its congratulation and goodwill. I therefore call upon my lord of Atholl, representing the former regency council, to lead in this."

Atholl, whose declension in importance all this represented, was understandably brief. "I wish His Grace well, and hope that I may still be able to advise him on occasion," he declared stiffly.

"Holy Church."

Bishop Laing stood. "I rejoice to add my blessings and good wishes, representing that other realm, Christ's kingdom upon earth, whose vassal James is. May he reign and prosper, assured of the support and guidance of Holy Church, for his own weal and that of Scotland."

"The earls."

The Earl of Fife, Coroner or Crowner of the realm, stood, his the most ancient as to creation. "We, representing the *seven* earls, do offer our devotion and allegiance." He distinctly emphasised that numeral. There were now many more earls than seven, more than double that number indeed, but the original seven had represented the seven *ri* or sub-kings of Celtic Scotland, who had elected the High King; later they were called *mormaors*, then earls after the Norse *jarl*, all these earldoms north of Forth and Clyde, the old Alba – Fife, Angus, Mar, Moray, Strathearn, Atholl and Ross. "We salute our High King!" Again that *our* was emphasised.

Something of confusion ensued as the three who were not already standing, there or beside the throne, rose, Moray, Strathearn and Archie – Ross, as Lord of the Isles, was in rebellion as usual; but this call had been addressed to the earls of Scotland, not just seven of them, so some of the others began to stand also – to the frowns and head-shakings of their seniors and the grins of lesser men.

Avondale moved swiftly to resolve this. "Lords of Parliament," he called.

Before anyone else could respond, James Hamilton spoke from behind the throne, only first Lord Hamilton as he was. "We, who represent the ancient noble houses of this land, do hail and salute our royal James, whom we shall

43

cherish and sustain whilst life is in us!" he declared strongly.

John wondered sourly who gave *him* authority so to assert.

"Commissioners of the shires."

An elderly man but solid, massive, Sir Walter Scott of Harden, rose to bow silently. The Borderers had their own priorities, allegiances, even laws – and anyway preferred actions to words.

"The representatives of the burghs."

It had to be the provost of Edinburgh, Sir Alexander Napier of Merchiston, who answered, since the assembly was being held in his city. "Your Grace's most humble and devoted subjects," he said. "We pledge our fullest service and devotion, and that of all your leal lieges, the true backbone and sinews of your kingdom!"

That drew some scowls from the higher-born, who reckoned that the commonality ought to know their place.

That over, the Chancellor rapped for the next business. "The matter of the Archbishop of St Andrews," he announced.

There was a notable stir in that hall as men eyed each other and murmured. Bishop Laing rose at once.

"Your Grace, although decisions on the rule and appointments in Holy Church are in the main for the decision of the College of Bishops, there are some which call for the consideration of Your Grace and parliament, where these may affect the well-being and good name of the realm at large. Such is here the case, I do judge. The Primate, Patrick Graham, now domiciled in Rome, is, I say, beyond all doubt unfitted to occupy the position of Archbishop of St Andrews and Metropolitan of Scotland. This by reason of failing health, both of body and of mind. It is my contention that the College of Bishops should be urged to effect his replacement by a more worthy successor, for the good of both Church and state."

"If that is a motion, my lord Chancellor, then I second it." That was Bishop Blackadder of Aberdeen.

A considerable volume of acclaim arose from all over the hall.

"*Can* you?" Archie Douglas jumped up. "Can you, we, or

44

any other, replace the Primate? Was he not made archbishop and Metropolitan by the Pope? And may be unmade only by the Pope?"

There were a few supportive shouts.

"It was not His Holiness who made him Prelate," Bishop Laing countered. "The College of Bishops so appointed him."

"No College of Bishops could make him archbishop and Metropolitan!" Archie insisted. "If it could, it would have been done long since. For this has been the need of this realm for centuries. In order to prove the folly and insolence of the English Archbishops of York, who have claimed that since there was no Metropolitan north of York, *they* should rule over the Scottish Church. And the Kings of England have used this against us time and again, in *their* efforts to gain supremacy. Not until Your Grace's royal sister, the Princess Mary, and her late husband the Earl of Arran, my own good-brother, persuaded the Archbishop of Trondheim, still further north, in Norway, to withdraw any claim *he* had, was Bishop Graham able to win from the Pope this great blessing and achievement for Scotland. And now you would pull him down! Why? Out of envy?"

That was a long speech for Archie, and becoming a little incoherent towards the end. Unfortunately those last four words were clear enough. John, for one, would have preferred them unsaid, for the sake of their cause.

There was near uproar in the hall, so that Lord Avondale had to bang his gavel loudly for order.

"My lord of Angus," he said severely, when approximate quiet was restored, "that is unworthy language to use in parliament. You stand reproved."

Muttering, Archie sat down.

John was somewhat reluctantly coming to his brother's aid when another Douglas did that, the Earl of Morton.

"My lord Chancellor," he said, rising, "the fact remains that Bishop Graham, *Archbishop* Graham, has served Scotland notably well in this. He has been a sick man in body for long. But that did not prevent him from going all the way to Rome,

45

to win this victory for Scotland. Yet now there is this move to unseat him and reduce him. Is this right, proper?"

"Patrick Graham, whatever he has been and done, serves Scotland nothing now," Laing asserted. "The Church needs a Primate, who *acts* the Primate. Not a sick man in Rome, wandering in his mind!"

A new voice spoke, and a strange one, light, almost musical – and the stranger to come from whom it did, the man standing immediately behind the last speaker, William Sheves, that intimidating figure. "May I speak, Your Grace?" he asked. It was noticeable that it was the King he addressed, not the Chancellor, and that he had chosen to stand where he did, rather than sit amongst the Church dignitaries down the hall.

James nodded.

"It is important, Sire, that this assembly recognises the true situation regarding the Primate," he said, in almost conversational tones. "What he has done, to gain Scotland Metropolitan status, is commendable, to the realm's great advantage. But *how* he has done it is less so. It is like to cost the realm dear. Has already done so. He has taken to the Vatican no less than three thousand one hundred golden florins from Scotland, the revenues of innumerable parishes, benefices and religious holdings, which he has been accumulating for years. This is part of the price he has paid for this privilege and his archbishopric. The rest, however, is still more costly. And to all here." He paused – and had all present hanging on his words, clearly a born actor as well as all else.

"Graham has had himself appointed by Pope Sixtus *legate a latere*, to Scotland, as well as all else, and with a special purpose. He is to come back to this land to assess and list all lands and properties due for tithe, to upgrade them for higher tax, and to send the moneys so collected back to Rome, large monies indeed. That is the price. I need not tell you . . ."

He got no further, the din drowning his voice. None there failed to perceive and assess personal impact. Few landholders were exempt from tithe, in theory, however little they actually paid in fact. This of assessing anew,

46

upgrading and actual payment, and to Rome, was anathema.

"Only a man not in full command of his wits could have so committed the nation," Sheves went on, and the comparative mildness of his tone but added to its impact. "As Archdeacon of St Andrews I have had to find large sums – above what the Primate has already paid. It will cripple the archdiocese. I am . . . concerned."

A score of voices added their own concern.

John's spirits sank. It looked as though this cause was lost.

Then another voice arose, James Hamilton's. "My lord Chancellor, I have heard, from a reliable informant, that the sum of twelve thousand merks, no less, has recently been offered to the treasury for royal help to bring down the archbishop. Can I ask my lord Bishop of Glasgow, the Treasurer, if this is true?"

Absolute silence greeted that.

"My lord Bishop . . . ?"

"All questions, observations, motions, must be addressed to the Chancellor," Avondale reminded.

"Ah, yes. But . . . perhaps His Grace, my good-brother, may choose to inform us?"

That skilfully outmanoeuvred Avondale.

The King looked embarrassed, shook his head and said, "No, no." Which did not greatly help.

"Since His Grace is uninformed, may I put forward a motion, Chancellor? That this parliament asks the Treasurer to state whether that account is true? And if so, where the moneys came from?"

The bishop spoke up, at last. "I have received no such sum," he said.

"Ah – but my information was that it was *offered*, not necessarily given. If so, there must have been an offerer. And it is a large sum. Who?"

Silence again.

"This is a motion," Hamilton reminded. "That parliament be informed who offered twelve thousand merks, for help to bring down the Archbishop. And why?"

"It has not been seconded," Avondale also reminded.

Almost without conscious volition, John Douglas found himself on his feet. "I, Douglasdale, do second," he declared. It had certainly never crossed his mind that in his first parliament, his first contribution would be to support this man who had contrived to gain Mary Stewart as wife.

"Is there any contrary motion?"

Since anything such would have been almost an admission of implication in the matter, there was no response.

"Then the motion stands, and – "

Sheves intervened. "Your Grace and my lord Chancellor, perhaps I may somewhat elucidate this matter. It was felt, I am told, by certain clerics in the diocese of St Andrews, that the absence of their bishop, first through long sickness and then for two years in Rome, bore sorely on the diocese. Much which should have been attended to and done was not. There was much neglect. They decided that amendment was required; but also that the amendment could come only from the incumbent himself, in Rome. Or from His Holiness the Pope. None other was sufficiently senior to achieve anything. So Rome it must be. But who to send to Rome, with sufficient weight to approach the Pope? They came to my humble self, as archdeacon, and I advised that only the King in parliament had the necessary authority so to do. Hence this present matter up for debate. As I told the assembly, I had already had to find large sums from the diocese. I could not do more. The said clerics recognised that for parliament to send a mission to Rome would be costly, and that since it was to improve conditions in the diocese, the diocese should contribute. So they raised this sum, and offered twelve thousand merks."

There were sounds of approval, now, from many.

"Are you sufficiently answered, my lord of Hamilton?" Avondale asked.

That man shrugged. "May I ask to whom the offer was made? To parliament? To yourself, as Chancellor?"

"No."

"Nor to the King's Grace?"

James shook his head.

All looked at Sheves.

That man smiled. "It was, I understand, made to the College of Bishops. As was suitable." John could have sworn that answer had a trace of exultation in it, as the man looked down on the mitred head of the prelate sitting in front of him. Were these two enemies, then? For Laing was acting chairman of the College of Bishops, in the Primate's absence.

The bishop rose, face expressionless. "An offer was made. To be considered," he said briefly. "But the affairs of the College of Bishops are no concern of this parliament." He sat down.

John looked from Sheves to Hamilton. Both looked well satisfied. Yet these two were enemies, he reckoned. Here were currents and undercurrents as complicated as any which the tides produced below Tantallon Castle's cliffs. Was this what a parliament was all about? The working out of enmities and plots and ambitions? What now?

The Chancellor it was who had to decide that, and to control the proceedings – for there was now considerable noise in the hall. He banged for quiet.

"Has any other aught to add to this matter of the Archbishop Graham, in Rome?" he asked, and in a voice which fairly clearly indicated that he discouraged anything such. Almost before anyone had time to rise, he went on. "In such case I refer further consideration to a committee of parliament, to be chosen by His Grace, myself and my lord of Atholl. To report and act." He brought down his gavel. "The next business." He consulted his papers. "The question of alliances. With France or Burgundy. To contain the English threat. Sire, you would guide parliament in this matter?"

It was surely time that James, in this his coming-of-age parliament, did more than sit looking uneasy. He nodded, seemed about to rise, recollected that he alone did not have to, and cleared his throat.

"I . . . we . . . are concerned," he began hesitantly. "The English make trouble. Again. We have had some respite these part years. While they warred with each other. What they called the Roses Wars. But now the Yorkist Edward has gained the power, and they grow in ill-will towards this realm again. It is . . . I have agreed . . . there is suggested by, by my advisers, that my son, the Duke of Rothesay, should be betrothed to Edward's daughter Cecilia. For the peace of the realms. When first put forward Edward seemed well pleased. But now – now, he has refused safe-conduct for our envoys to travel through England. So . . ." The royal voice trailed away.

Most there undoubtedly were as confused by this statement as was John Douglas. Was this what was meant by alliances – the marriage of a three-year-old boy and a five-year-old English princess? What of France and Burgundy? What was the English threat?

The Chancellor sought to make the situation more clear. "His Grace's concern is that King Edward grows warlike now that he has full power in England. This of the marriage was to seek to ensure good English relations with Scotland. But now he, Edward, appears to question it, although he agreed before. Which is no good omen. Forby, he is seeking an alliance with the Duke of Burgundy, hitherto his enemy. And is said to be contemplating an invasion of France. Therefore, it behoves us in Scotland to consider the situation well."

This explanation was not of very great help to most there as to what they were to debate and decide upon.

The Earl of Strathearn spoke. "What is proposed that we should do? To whom are we to ally ourselves? I thought that it was to be to Burgundy. But now, it seems, France would be better. If either! If English Edward is considering invading France, need we fear his invasion of Scotland?"

Strangely enough it was not any warrior but the churchman Sheves who answered him. "It is not *invasion* by armies that is feared, my lord, but these constant raids over the border by English bands. Which King Edward does nothing to stop, indeed seems to encourage. Also his failure to grant safe-conducts to His Grace's envoys. And failure to pay agreed compensation for the loss and plundering of the St Andrews Barge, at Bamburgh – that is the fine ship, the *Salvator*, which the late Bishop Kennedy built and which went aground on the Bamburgh coast. All these point to

Edward's ill-will towards Scotland, and represent threat, the age-old threat of England towards this kingdom. Parliament's concern in the matter requires to be expressed." He bowed towards the throne. "His Grace calls for guidance."

Called upon again, His Grace wagged his head. "Something must be done," he said lamely.

There was a hoot from his side. "Done, indeed!" young Albany cried. "I tell you what to do! Invade *their* borders! Teach the English their lesson. An army into Northumberland or Cumberland. *I* will lead it, if need be!"

Cheers rose at such spirited and uncomplicated talk, after all the confused detail.

"Your Highness may be right," Avondale said carefully. "But this for debate now is over alliance. To contain the English threat, not to encourage it. By policy. Alliance with France, Burgundy or other."

"France is Scotland's ancient ally," John's neighbour, Lord Livingstone, asserted. "Why change now to Burgundy? France's rebel."

"The Duke of Burgundy is a warrior, whereas King Louis is not," Hamilton pointed out. "He is much more likely to take action for us than is France."

"But if Edward is himself seeking alliance with the duke . . . ?"

"*Seeking* – but I think not yet gaining! Duke Charles is carving out a kingdom for himself in the Low Countries. And he has the support of the Emperor, who does not love France."

Archie jumped up. "The Earl of Arran was a good friend of Duke Charles. He worked on him in Scotland's favour, over the Hansa League. Against the English. I say that he will serve us best."

"If the one does, the other will not," Buchan emphasised. "Nothing more sure. Which will have the greater effect on England? I say France. France is ten times the size of Burgundy."

"I agree," his brother said. "And if Burgundy did attack England, might not France take opportunity to attack Burgundy?"

51

"Then might not the Emperor attack France?" That was Hamilton.

So it went on, for and against. John, like others, was not a little bewildered. But he did recognise that once again James Hamilton, the man he looked upon as an enemy, seemed to be on *their* side, pro-Burgundy. It was all very difficult.

Albany was speaking again. "I say that while we argue and debate, and then send envoys, whether to Edward, to Burgundy or to France, the English remain untouched, free to assail our borders. They will laugh at us. And foray the more, to our hurt. I say, let us wipe the smiles off their insolent faces! Give me a thousand men, and I will make Edward of York think again!"

Again there were cheers. Undoubtedly this line of thought appealed to many there, in especial amongst the younger men.

Archie rose. "We could do both," he exclaimed. "Send the envoys. But – I will bring five hundred Douglases to aid His Highness cross the borderline!"

John, for one, gasped. Archie was ever the enthusiast, emphatic, headstrong. But this was a bolt from the blue, battle, war. And their Douglases involved.

"I agree with my lord Duke and my lord of Angus," the Lord Hailes, at John's other side, declared. "They can count on two hundred Hepburns, at the least."

After that it was a matter of competition, lords and lairds seeking to rival each other as to the numbers of men they could contribute to a raiding force, the matter of alliances all but forgotten, despite Avondale's attempts to reintroduce it. Eventually he had to revert to the solution of a committee to work out priorities and details, on the assumption that parliament approved in principle that an alliance was probably advantageous. The Duke of Albany and his supporters could forgather, after the session adjourned, to make their own plans.

Meantime, Avondale announced, a final item fell to be considered, the matter of false dooms. These were appeals from sheriffs' and justiciars' decisions at justice-ayres up and down the land, on which the high court of parliament could be called upon to reconsider, and if they thought fit here, overturn or amend. There were three such appeals to be dealt with now, one from Teviotdale, one from Fife and one from Aberdeenshire. Members always tended to find these tedious, and usually left it to the High Justiciar, presently the Earl of Argyll, to advise them. Thereafter there was an officer of the court, the Dempster, to see that their decisions were carried out. On this occasion the Campbell chief, Argyll, made fairly short work of it, urging dismissal of all three appeals. This was duly accepted and the Dempster instructed.

Amidst sighs of thankfulness and renewed professions of loyalty and regard towards the monarch, the Lord Lyon King of Arms announced the adjournment of the session, and King James departed promptly, clearly nowise the least thankful. To be born a ruler and yet to be no born ruler was obviously a trying fate.

Actually, quite a proportion of the company remained in the hall, to cluster round young Albany and Archie, and to offer men and discuss strategy and tactics, their sovereign-lord a notable absentee, as was John, Earl of Mar, the Stewart family evidently divided on this matter as on so much else. John Douglas, being little more enthusiastic over the raiding project, but realising that he could not seem to speak against his elder brother in public, whatever he might say in private, chose to go in search of the Princess Mary.

He found her, with her sister Margaret, on their way to the palace block of the citadel, where it seemed they had quarters. She greeted him warmly.

"How did you enjoy the parliament, John? Your first, was it not? Here is the Lord of Douglasdale, Meg, of whom I have told you."

The other princess was only eighteen, quite pretty but scarcely appearing characterful. She simpered a little as he bowed.

"I cannot say that I greatly esteemed all that went on," he said. "There were . . . surprises!"

"There always are," she conceded. "I have attended many parliaments, and know. What surprised you, may I ask?"

"Much. This of marriage for an infant prince, not yet of three years. That of plotting to bring down the archbishop. Payments offered. The man Sheves – I had not thought of him so. I see him as dangerous, indeed. And, and your husband's part. His . . . attitudes."

"Ah, yes. You did indeed second one of his motions. That surprised *me*!"

"It surprised myself!" he admitted. "But what he said was sound. On both issues – the archbishop and that of Burgundy."

"Oh, my husband does not lack wits. Nor judgment . . . in some matters! I learned that quickly enough!"

"M'mm. He does not like Sheves, I think?"

"He does not. In some degree they are rivals. They both seek to sway the King, who is all too easily swayed, at least in some directions. You would think that my husband, a lord of great lands, and now married to myself, would have the advantage over an illegitimate clerk of no lofty blood. Yet I think that William Sheves will win."

"You do, Mary? Yet he is a man of baleful looks. Cruel-seeming, like some bird of prey. Despite his soft voice. And the other lords will not esteem him, I think. Nor the bishops, *especially* the bishops, the princes of the Church! He and Bishop Laing are not friends, by the sound of them."

"Further rivals, although for a different end."

"Yet, with so many against him, you think that Sheves will rise still further? Prosper?"

"He has won greater influence over James than any other I have known. With his physics and alchemies and astrologies. And with his supposed divinations as to James's future. Our poor silly brother has come to believe in him entirely. James, you see, has always lacked confidence. Sheves indeed does not give him it, but guides him as to what to do and say and think. As does none other, myself included. For James has come almost to despise women. I fear for James, I fear indeed. And now that he *rules* as well as reigns . . ."

They were at the royal quarters now, and John was doubtful about entering, but Mary insisted. She would send a servitor to the hall to fetch Archie – when he was ready. This of raiding into England? That *had* been a surprise, now!

He wagged his head. "What made Archie propose that, the good Lord knows! It is folly, surely. Will but make matters worse. Bloodshed and rapine. The English will but further retaliate."

"They may – but there could be worth in it also," Mary said. "King Edward might take heed. If it was a sizeable force, not just a small raiding party. Archie said five hundred Douglases, did he not? Although that may have been but a flourish. Others will join. Hailes, for one, can field many."

"Yes, for sure there will be no lack of men. Back there they compete with each other. But think you that it is right, wise?"

"Yes, yes!" Princess Margaret exclaimed, surprisingly. "I hope that they go."

"As to right, what is right and what is wrong, where nations seek to serve their ends?" her sister asked. "Statecraft is, I fear, judged by its success or failure. But, wise? Yes, I think that it could be no unwise move. If it is well done. Using wits, not just cold steel and vengeance. A demonstration of strength rather than any mere border foray. Since our father died, there has been no show of Scottish strength – perhaps nothing ill in that. But Yorkist Edward clearly deems us weak. His brother Richard, Duke of Gloucester, he has made Lieutenant of the North, and he is a fighter. He encourages English raiding over the border. So, this of my brother Alex's devising, and your Archie, may be of some value."

John marvelled to hear a young woman, beautiful, gracious, talking thus. He knew, of course, that Mary had shrewd wits, and took a great interest in affairs of the kingdom, indeed had been so largely responsible in winning Orkney and Shetland for Scotland, much of the wits behind her late husband Arran's successes. If only her brother James had had a similar endowment.

The Lord Hamilton arrived, to eye John with his usual penetrating glance shot with something like amusement.

"Ha! The young supporter, not only of Her Highness but now also of my poor self, it seems! Do not tell me that I am earning Douglas approval?"

"Your policies, my lord, seemed to me worthy." There was a slight emphasis on the word policies, perhaps.

"I am flattered."

"Let us say that he preferred you to William Sheves," Mary said.

Margaret giggled.

"As to policies, I do not know that *I* approve of this of raiding into England, which seems to appeal to the Douglases! Young men's enthusiasms may cause others suffering."

This, too, was John's view, but he could hardly say so in the circumstances.

"So long as it is well devised and well controlled, there could be good in it," Mary observed. "Give King Edward pause. He appears to believe that the Scots are feeble, cowed, ripe for dominance. And if his daughter is betrothed to the heir of Scotland, he may well see himself as becoming Lord Paramount, as others have sought to become since the first Edward Plantagenet two centuries ago. A Scottish army, parading English soil, but not devastating it, might well serve as warning."

"It is not Edward of York, woman, that I fear, but his brother of Gloucester. That Duke Richard is like your own younger brother, Albany, a hot-head. And he is now made Lieutenant of the North, which gives him control of the English borderlands, and of their Wardens of the Marches. How think you Gloucester will take invasion of his territories and authority? And he can raise many thousands more than can we."

"I think that he will not invade Scotland without King Edward's permission."

"Do not be so sure. Richard of Gloucester, Crookback, is a man to act first and seek permission after! I tell you – "

He was interrupted by the appearance of Archie Douglas,

56

loud with enthusiasm for their project, and for Albany. They had over six thousand men promised already, and more to come undoubtedly. They would teach the English their lesson.

"At whose cost, my lord Earl?" Hamilton asked interestedly.

"Eh?" Archie stared. "Theirs, to be sure!" he jerked.

"Ah! Not Homes, Kerrs, Elliots, Turnbulls, Hoppringles and the rest? Border folk. I think that you will have few offers of support from these lords and lairds. When Gloucester strikes back and harries their lands, burns their houses and crops, slays their men and rapes their women. Douglas, of course, is not a middle march house!"

"Cavers is, in Teviotdale," John mentioned.

Archie frowned. "We will set good guard on the borders. But, 'fore God, if we made such reckoning before we moved, never would we Scots move at all! And the English would have been ruling Scotland long since. Is that Hamilton policy?"

"Hamilton has fist and steel – but prefers to use the head!"

Mary sought to cool the atmosphere. "My lord of Angus and my brother Alexander will no doubt also use their wits. Hold their people back from unnecessary violence and ravagement. A show of strength, not of force . . ."

"If the hot-bloods will heed!"

"Why then do *you* not go with them, my lord? With some of your many Hamiltons. To . . . advise!"

That set all three men eyeing her and each other.

"Would not your presence and guidance be valuable? To these *younger* lords?" That was said coolly, reasonably – but there was challenge in it nevertheless.

Her husband stroked his chin. "M'mm. I will think on it," he said.

Archie looked doubtful, to say the least. "Time we were off, Johnnie," he said. "If we are to reach Tantallon this night . . ."

They said their farewells, John reluctantly, Mary nodding understandingly, unanimity less than evident amongst them all.

57

4

Despite all the enthusiasm and martial fervour amongst the younger magnates, it took some considerable time, many weeks indeed, to assemble their force. Lords and lairds and chiefs from all over the land were involved, and their men had to be collected from wide distances before being brought south. That this all coincided with the hay harvest complicated matters, for cattle-raising was the mainstay of much of the rural economy and the hay was essential for winter feed. So it was July before the great muster could take place.

Choosing the assembly point held its own problems, for numbers promised had risen to approximately ten thousand – and ten thousand men and as many horses required a deal of space, feeding and forage; and having to wait for latecomers meant that many were marshalled for some time. Moreover, there were the matters of co-operation and of territory. As Hamilton had foreseen, certain Border chiefs were less than supportive of this initiative, the newly created Lord Home in especial. And the Homes controlled most of the East March. No help nor supplies would come from there. The same applied otherwhere. Fortunately the Kerrs, based on Ferniehirst and Cessford in the Middle March, were more co-operative, possibly because their various fortalices and houses had been burned down or sacked so many times by the invading English already that once more would make little difference. So the town of Jedburgh was chosen for the muster, where there was ample accommodation and provender to be had and townsfolk who would do approximately as they were told by their Kerr lords. Ferniehirst himself was in fact providing over one hundred of his own mosstroopers, who would undoubtedly be very

useful as guides over on the English side of the borderline.

John Douglas was learning much which was no doubt good
for him – mainly how to control men who suddenly found
themselves freed from their duties as farmers, cow-herds,
shepherds, millers and the like, provided with horses, jacks
and helmets, swords and lances, and, however serious the
intent, looking on the entire proceedings as a holiday, and one
with the prospect of booty, unlimited English booty. Third in
command of the Douglas contingent – not second, since the
Earl of Morton had joined them with three hundred – John
had a personal "tail" of two hundred to lead, and found it
occupying most of his time. He felt that he was perhaps not
a born commander of men.

The Duke of Albany, of course, was in supreme charge,
youthful as he was, with Archie his chief lieutenant. Albany
was a commander, or at least esteemed himself to be so,
and was now in his element. Undoubtedly he would have
made a more suitable king than James, although he might
have required restraint. He at least made a splendid figure
in gold-inlaid half-armour, organising, detailing, planning.
Some of the older lords were a little critical.

James Hamilton almost certainly was that way inclined, but
was too clever to show it. He had surprisingly joined the array
with a troop of over one hundred from his Lanarkshire lands,
presumably to exercise a moderating influence; and a number
of others clearly looked to him as leader. He had brought along
with him no fewer than four of his illegitimate sons, John,
Patrick, David and James, all in their early twenties. So there
was something in the nature of two camps at Jedburgh, largely
representing age-grouping, although presumably the Hamilton
bastards would support their father. John's own inclination
was undoubtedly towards the older men, but he sought not
to show it.

Tactics, of course, loomed large. Ten thousand men was
a major force and represented problems in management and
feeding and control not only here, at assembly, but on the
march. It was accepted that some split-up was advisable, the

question being into two or three? Albany was for two, one to be sent to the West March. Others pointed out that there were three Marches, and therefore there should be three divisions. The duke rejected this, possibly because it would reduce the size of his own command. But eventually it was decided that while the main thrust should be here on the Middle March, a detachment should be sent off later, to deal with the eastern English sector.

At length patience was exhausted and a move was made, any latecomers to follow on. They divided up approximately seven thousand and three thousand, with Morton , one of the only two earls present, given command of the latter, for the West March, Morton being a Dumfries-shire fief. He would strike up Teviotdale, over into Eskdale and so down into England in the Cumberland Bewcastle area. The two forces would keep in touch thereafter, using scouts, mainly Kerr mosstroopers.

John went with the main body, up Jed Water to the actual borderline at the Reidswire, high in the Cheviot range, everyone in good spirits. Cheers resounded down the long line as they crossed into England, with scores of banners and pennants fluttering, colourful heraldic shields, armour and lances gleaming, a gallant sight. Since the roadway was not wide they could ride no more than three abreast, so seven thousand made a lengthy column indeed. John hoped that word of their coming had not been carried southwards from Jedburgh by travelling packmen or wandering friars, to enable them to be ambushed by the English, thus strung out, for they could be cut into segments and annihilated. He mentioned this to Archie, who scoffed, but said that if he was so concerned he could use his two hundred, with some Kerr guides, to act as scouts ahead and on each flank, to ensure safe passage through these hills.

That is what they did. Splitting his Douglases into three parties, they went down Redesdale, himself taking some four score a mile or so ahead, with Kerr guides. The upper area of the dale, amongst lofty Cheviot summits, was all but unpopulated, barren hillsides and all too near the borderline for safe living; it was some three miles down that they came to their first settlement, at the foot of a small lake, called Catcleuch. It was no part of John's duty to deal in any way with this, unless they were assailed. But the River Rede flowed out of this lake and soon became deep enough to form a major barrier, with the drove-road following the eastern side. So only a few men were detached to cross and proceed down the western slopes, while John sent probing parties up the many side glens and hollows opening to north and east, with instructions merely to watch for possible hostile activity and not to initiate any, or to attack any remote houses and farmeries they might find.

A mile or two on they came to their first little community, scarcely a village, at Byrness, where they were eyed askance by the inhabitants, such as were about, but offered and suffered no confrontation. John felt oddly miscast in the role of advance guard leader, his of anything but a belligerent nature.

With no problems reported by his flanking parties, in a few more miles they reached the former Roman Camp area of Bremenium, at a widening of the dale, where there were two peel-towers and the nearby village of Rochester, their first possible opposition. But no challenge developed. John rode up to both towers, to announce that a large force of Scots was approaching and that the owners and local inhabitants might be wise to absent themselves into the surrounding hills until all was past. Whether his advice would be followed, and whether the Duke of Albany would approve of this interpretation of his duties, he did not know. Leaving alarm behind them, they rode on.

The next community, three miles further, was Elishaw, but before they reached this they could see clouds of smoke rising behind them – which seemed to imply that Albany was using fire if not sword to announce his message to King Edward, thus early. Since there were four columns of the brown smoke mounting high, burning thatch and straw no doubt, John reckoned that this would indicate approaching menace far ahead of them, and warning. Was this the intention? Or had Albany just not considered that?

At Elishaw they had come some thirty miles from Jedburgh, and here the drove-road forked, one route to go on due southwards to Tynedale, at Corbridge and Hexham, another twenty-five miles the Kerrs said; and the other to swing eastwards through the fells for Newcastle, almost double that distance. Newcastle was, of course, a major walled city, and Albany had agreed earlier that they could scarcely assail such without siege-engines, and it would be foolish to waste time there when there was so much else which could be done more profitably. But presumably here at Elishaw would be where the detachment would strike off for the East March demonstration. So, discovering that there were three peel-towers or bastle-houses in the vicinity, John took his men to warn their occupiers to lie low or vanish. But he found them all already shut up and deserted, although there were signs that the owners had not been gone long, livestock and poultry still in evidence. Those smoke clouds, it seemed, had already conveyed their message. He decided to wait here for the main body.

As expected, although it was only late afternoon, Albany decided to camp for the night at Elishaw, before the force split up. Also, there was a special interest hereabouts, for the Douglases in particular. The site of the Battle of Otterburn, which the English called Chevy Chase and had made a ballad about, was only a couple of miles to the east. This was the occasion, almost a century before, when a dead man was said to have won a battle, the dead man being in fact William, second Earl of Douglas, who, stabbed in the back by his own armour-bearer, Bickerton of Luffness, before ever the real battle began, cried out that he was a dead man, a dead man, but for his esquires to carry his body forward, upright, shouting the dread war-cry of 'A Douglas! A Douglas!' This they had done, and the battle against Hotspur Percy of Northumberland was fought and won. Few of the present array, save the Kerrs, had ever seen this famous place. So, whilst cattle already captured from Byrness and this Elishaw were slaughtered, cut up and cooked for their dinner, the leadership rode over the hill to Otterburn to inspect

In fact, there was not a great deal to see in the shallow valley, for the site was no typical battleground but rather a camping place by the burn, where Percy and the English had stolen up on the Scots bedded down for the night – hence the hasty donning of armour in the dark and Bickerton's opportunity to dispose of his master, against whom he held some grudge. Needless to say, the assassin did not live long thereafter.

Back at Elishaw, they all dined well on Redesdale beef and other local provision, with hay-barns full for the horses. John told Archie about the warning effects of burning homesteads and towers, but was assured that this did not matter. Soon much of Northumberland would be ablaze, and the message made the more clear for King Edward.

For Richard of Gloucester too, John reminded.

Sentinels posted, they settled down for the night. They were not disturbed, save by some of their own folk who discovered wines and ales in one of the peel-towers, and celebrated the fact noisily.

They were winning clear of the major hills here, and John told Archie that he did not see his role as leader of an advance guard of an army. Some much less onerous position for him. He was told to please himself, do what he wanted. Clearly his brother judged his attitude feeble. John said that probably he would be best acting rearguard, and this was accepted.

So, when a move was made, with the Lord Hailes and some fifteen hundred leaving them to ride off eastwards, John's company remained behind while the main body moved on due southwards. George, Master of Seton, was now given charge of the advance party.

They left a suitable gap of some two miles behind the army before proceeding. Fairly quickly it became apparent that this duty of rearguard was going to present problems not anticipated – mainly in the matter of *keeping* in the rear. For now that they all were out of the close confines of the Cheviots, the main force changed formation from column-of-march to spreading out in groups large and small, to left and right, to advance southwards on a very wide front, indeed no real front at all; and keeping to the rear of this was difficult, occupied in sundry activities as all ahead became. By the time that they got as far as Bellingham – which quite large township they found in flames – John reckoned, from his outriders' accounts, that the advance was now on fully a five-mile front. Smoke arising far to left and right indicated as much, and also that the policy seemed to be to burn as they went, a delaying process, whatever the wisdom or rights and wrongs of it. Moreover small parties kept coming back northwards, herding cattle and horses homewards, which added to the confusion. It might be typical cross-border usage, but if this continued it was going to reduce the size and effectiveness of the army. Booty, clearly, was what not a few of the participants had come for.

From Bellingham the rearguard progressed slowly down to Redesmouth, where Rede joined North Tyne, and here, as well as burning houses and barns, trampled corn and damaged mills, they saw their first bodies. Whether these represented casualties killed in fighting, or merely slain whilst protesting about their properties being ravaged, was not to be known, but none were in armour, although this *might* have been stripped off by the winners as useful.

John grew the less happy.

By now the entire sky, east and west, was largely hidden behind a pall of smoke. This would be seen for scores of miles, and must surely provoke some major English reaction. Where was Richard of Gloucester likely to be based, as Lieutenant of the North? Newcastle? Carlisle? Or further south, at Durham, or York even? If indeed he was the fiery character alleged, he would not be long in coming to discover and amend the situation.

At Humshaugh, near the ancient Roman Wall of Hadrian, rearguard or none, they came up with quite a large section of the army, stationary. This proved to consist of Hamilton and sundry other lords, with their contingents, who had been the least enthusiastic of the invaders – and who were now still less enamoured of the venture. John was treated to a chorus of complaints and criticisms as to the folly of the proceedings so far, the dangers involved and the lack of control; it was these, rather than moral scruples, which appeared to preoccupy the protesters, he noted. As the Earl of Angus's brother, he seemed to be considered, if not partly responsible, at least in a position to influence Albany and Archie for the better. He was doubtful about how to disillusion them.

It seemed that the main leadership, with the major portion of the army, had gone on to Hexham, another nine miles or so. Hexham, with its great and renowned priory, was the chief town of upper Tynedale, and seat of the ancient lordship and Liberty thereof, an independent ecclesiastical jurisdiction under the Archbishop of York. Also it was the messuage of the smaller but rich county-palatinate of Hexhamshire, under the prior thereof. It was therefore an important place, very much in the possession of Holy Church. Even so, it would not be capable of providing for over five thousand armed men; so Hamilton and his critical friends, with some two thousand supporters, had been left here at the Humshaugh, Chollerton and Chollerford vicinity, to fend and forage for themselves.

John, not only at their urging, but seeing no point in himself waiting here, and no need for any rearguard in the present circumstances, decided to go on to Hexham also. He and his men crossed North Tyne and the Roman Wall at Chollerford, and across level, fertile lands now, by Acomb, where the North and South Tynes joined. Devastation was evident all the way.

Hexham, ahead on slightly rising ground, at least was not burning. Walled, and dominated by its splendid cathedral-like priory and tall castellated Moot Hall, it made an impressive sight in the early evening light.

They found most of the army encamped on the common land between town and river. Leaving his men there, John rode on into the town itself, where he was told that the leaders had installed themselves. In the streets he saw surprisingly few people; perhaps not so surprising, with an invading army on their doorsteps, and wise folk best behind the locked and barred doors of their houses.

John had no doubts as to where to look for Archie and the Duke. They would be in the finest quarters available, and that would be the prior's palatial establishment; for this prelate was known, even in Scotland, to rival most bishops in wealth and magnificence. Up the slope to the Moot Hall he rode, and sure enough, all around it were the horses and attendants of the Scots leadership.

As brother of the Earl of Angus he had no difficulty in gaining admission, through sumptuous apartments and anterooms, to a second-floor hall where he found the Scots lounging at a table strewn with the remains of what had been evidently little short of a banquet. There was no sign, however, of the host prior or any clergy.

Archie hailed him, and made room for him on a bench at his side. "My cautious brother!" he exclaimed. "You see, Johnnie, that we have fared well enough. Despite your fears. We have made our mark on Northumberland this day."

John sketched a bow towards Albany nearby. "A mark, yes. Or, shall we say . . . a stain!"

"Call it what you will. We have shown the English that we Scots are not to be tampered with. Come, eat and drink, man. The good prior provides liberally! With a little persuasion! When last did you feed?"

"This morning . . ."

"Aye, they say that a hungry man is an angry man. Or a sour one!"

John was indeed hungry, and glad to accede. Albany eyed him.

"You find our demonstration not to your taste, my lord? Like your friend Hamilton?"

"The Lord Hamilton is not my friend, Highness," John answered, mouth not quite empty. "But I agree with him, and with others, that your demonstrations should be . . . less violent. Less of burning and destruction. More of what Your Highness's sister called a parade. A *show* of strength rather than a harsh invasion. I have seen slain men . . ."

"If these English oppose us they must take the consequences," Albany returned.

"Men will seek to protect their own houses. As would *you*, Highness. And this widespread burning. All the miles of it . . ."

"John is a poet and a ballad-monger rather than a warrior, Highness," Archie pointed out.

There were growls from around the table.

"I agree that I am no warrior," John said. "But I hope that I do not lack wits of a sort. Even poetry demands such! And I am a Douglas!" That came out strongly, almost surprising the speaker himself. "I see that these great smoke clouds, whether justified or not, are as good as fast couriers sent to warn the Duke of Gloucester of our presence. And he cannot fail to respond."

"Let him!"

"We will give him welcome!"

"Who fears Richard the Crookback!"

Challenge came from all around.

"We have learned that Gloucester is presently with his archbishop at York," Archie interposed. "This man they call the seneschal, here, the archbishop's representative, told us so. Some matter to do with rents, they discuss."

"He will not have left the north defenceless. And he could be here in three days. There are English Wardens of the three Marches, all fighters necessarily – the Earl of Northumberland, the Lord Dacre and the Lord Scrope. Think you that they will sit idly by, watching your smokes until Gloucester arrives? They will be marshalling men, many men. And could raise their tens of thousands. Many times your numbers."

"Do not forget Morton and Hailes," Albany reminded.

"Their numbers small by comparison, Highness. And if *their* men behave as do some of yours, their numbers will be smaller still! For not a few are already heading back to Scotland, droving cattle!"

That did make some impact. Evidently these great ones had not been informed of this.

"If that is so, it must be stopped," Albany jerked, his handsome features dark. "All of you, see to it. Time enough for cattle and the like on our return home."

"If that return is not too hasty for anything such, my lords," John observed. "Cattle make slow droving. And you may well have Gloucester on your heels."

"You have a doleful brother, Angus, by God!" the Duke

67

exclaimed, and John realised that he was perhaps overdoing it. That would not help.

"My regrets, Highness. But perhaps being the rearguard makes one thus? Lacking the, the flourish of those in the lead! May I ask where you lead, hereafter? Your plans now?"

It was Archie who answered. "We think to make a still wider front of it. Across the very width of this land. To link up with Morton and Hailes. Then head southwards. To Weardale and even Teesdale."

"If my lord of Douglasdale approves!" Albany put in sarcastically.

"You go *further* south, then?"

"To be sure. We have but started." Archie gave his brother a warning frown. "We may reach to Durham."

"It was reaching Durham, and further, if I mind aright, which brought disaster to the two Kings David. The Battle of the Standard, and that of Neville's Cross. It is a long way back to Scotland from there, Archie." He made that as though it was a personal exchange between brothers. "Douglases died at both!"

There was silence in the hall.

Albany rose. "We will go visit this prior and the seneschal. See what they can tell us as to Gloucester's position and forces. In exchange for some remission of our wrath upon their lands!"

John was left to finish his meal in solitude, if not in peace of mind.

He returned to his company at the riverside camp, and finding much revelry going on there, and no one apparently responsible for security, reckoned that this perhaps might be one of the duties of the rearguard commander. He organised some of his people, in relays, to go to nearby viewpoints to act as sentinels, before composing himself for sleep.

In the morning, seeing little use for a rearguard behind a line which stretched for a score of miles, especially with Hamilton's force in reserve behind, he went back to the Moot Hall for instructions from Archie. His brother had no real guidance to offer – save that he would in future watch his tongue anent complaints and criticism, especially in Albany's presence. They were not all complete fools, and John could hardly claim to be an experienced campaigner anyway. The best service he could provide, probably, was to linger behind and turn back any parties proceeding homewards with captured cattle. Scarcely relishing this as a worthwhile task, John suggested that, since apparently their long line was continuing to head due southwards, and danger presumably would be apt to come from that direction, he and his might profitably go well ahead, not as an advance guard this time but as scouts, to watch and warn. This was accepted as possibly useful. There was much high ground to the south, and they would start by going up the two parallel valleys of the East and West Allen Waters, which led over into Weardale. If Johnnie's party went up these, they could act scouts well enough.

So, dividing his company into two, John set off early to take one hundred up the East Allen, and the rest to go on to the West valley. There were a number of Allan Waters in Scotland also; he supposed that the name was but a corruption of the Gaelic *abhainn*, meaning a stream – which indicated that the Celtic people had originally occupied this land also.

The two valleys were only about four miles apart. Moreover, the South Tyne itself eventually took a major turn southwards, so that much of their army would presently have to turn up all three valleys. John decided to take half a dozen men with him to act as couriers, and left the eastern river to ride over the intervening heights westwards, and then over the western Allen likewise, up to the still higher ground beyond. Up here he would be in the best position to oversee all three valleys, especially the larger Tyne one, and still be able to observe the wide lands ahead.

This programme involved much rough riding, as he and his little group patrolled the high ground, negotiating outcropping rock, screes, corries, bogs and the like. The land carried sheep and a few rough cattle, but was devoid of human habitation – that is, until they came across a shepherd's cabin in a lonely side valley, where they learned that this was Whitfield Moor,

69

common land for the township of Alston which they would find on the lower ground some seven miles ahead.

Looking back from summits they could see more smoke arising, but not nearly so much as on the day before. John did not flatter himself that this was the result of his warnings, but rather that there was just precious little to burn in these hills.

No messengers came looking for them from the Allen valleys.

Having covered some twenty difficult miles, in late afternoon they came to Alston, near the head of the South Tyne. John had an idea that they were over into Cumberland here, and so perhaps on Morton's line of advance. It seemed to be a sizeable community, and with only half a dozen men he was in no position to go riding in and warning the inhabitants that a large hostile force would be coming up Tyne presently, possibly to pass the night here. But he did speak to a couple of cowherds idly watching their charges on the common land, and told them of the situation. Whether they would do anything about it John could not be sure, for they listened, looking more uncomprehending than alarmed. But it was the best that he could do. He pressed on, by quite a fair drove-road now, south by east, which would presumably bring them to the West Allen Water again.

Soon they were entering a major east–west vale, which could only be Weardale. There were no signs, as yet, of any opposition materialising from the south, or from anywhere else for that matter. Were Archie and Albany right in anticipating no real challenge?

They duly came across their West Allen company, awaiting instructions at what appeared to be the head of that river, now a mere burn which dwindled into little headstreams. This detachment had nothing to report of any import, only the small community of Whitfield passed and no trouble. A herd there had told them that the *East* Allen had its source only some three miles away, where there was a township, suitably called Allenheads, where they might pass the night.

This seemed a sensible suggestion, and they all moved on

eastwards. How far behind were the various sections of the main army they could not tell – with nothing worth burning, there were no visible signs. But presumably they would not be too far off by now.

At Allenheads they found the rest of their scouting group already having taken over the village but, knowing their lord's views, they had not acted aggressively towards the inhabitants. So there was little difficulty in settling in, with John declaring that he would pay for provender used.

It was some time later that they saw smoke mounting up to westwards, at no great distance. That almost certainly would be Alston. Evidently their successors arriving from the north held different views as to procedure.

No further Scots appeared down *this* Allen Water before they bedded down for the night, guards posted.

Next day they were off early, still southwards. John reckoned that they were now over into County Durham, none so very far from that city itself – which must be given a wide berth.

With no sign of the main army yet, save for smoke, they had gone only some four miles across Middlehope Moor when they gained their first intimation of danger. They entered Weardale and turning eastwards along it necessarily, came to the township of Stanhope, quite large. Having all two hundred of his men with him now, John was not precluded from entering. And there he found alarm prevailing ahead of their arrival, the place seemingly all but deserted save for barking dogs. But they noted faces peering at them from around corners, mainly women's faces and children's. Dismounting, they made enquiries.

John found the parish priest less fearful than most, in his conviction that Holy Church was sacrosanct, and from him learned much. Word had come to Stanhope the day before, of invasion – come not from the north but from the south, from Darlington. The Duke of Gloucester was there, it seemed, and ordering mobilisation of a great assembly of armed men at Durham, for this day. All able-bodied men to report, under their lords, squires and leaders, horsed as many as possible,

71

where the duke would join them to repel and punish the invaders. Thomas Stanhope, son of Sir Richard, had taken one hundred and twenty from hereabouts. So – let the rascally Scots beware!

Since it was more or less what John had been anticipating, he was not surprised; but he did seek details from the confident cleric, or such as the man might guess at. Was Gloucester actually going to Durham himself? Numbers possible? Was a day set, to march?

He was told that the duke might well be at Durham now. Darlington was only twenty-five miles away, and the word had come yesterday. All North Yorkshire, County Durham, Northumberland and Cumberland were being mustered. There would be scores of thousands, more when the Yorkshiremen arrived. The Prince-Bishop of Durham himself could field twenty thousand, the Earl Percy of Northumberland still more. If Stanhope could raise one hundred and twenty, Weardale alone could produce twenty times that.

John grimly decided that he had sufficient information here. He and his men remounted, to turn back.

Where was he likely to find Albany and Archie? The Allen valleys were fairly narrow and devoid of large settlements, whereas the South Tyne was larger, wider, and dotted with villages, he had been told. So, since the Scots had to move southwards by one of these, it would almost certainly be Tyne for the main body.

Back up Wearsdale they rode, fast now. At Nenthead they came on a party under the Master of Montgomerie, burning thatches and hay-barns, and warned them not to proceed further south or east. Beyond, they found Alston a smoking ruin, with Lord Cathcart's company ranging far and wide around, spreading destruction. Cathcart John told of the situation, and headed on, in the Tyne valley now. The heavy smoke palls ahead told their own story.

It was at a village called Knarsdale that he came up with Albany and the main force, the leaders actually holding something of a council of war. It seemed that word had reached them from Lord Hailes, relayed by Hamilton in the rear, that the Earl of Northumberland, Warden of the East March, was marching south-westwards in strength, with a force estimated as at least fifteen thousand. He, Hailes, was retiring before it, in this direction. There seemed to have been some thought, in this council, of turning back to face the Earl Percy, Archie strong for this, with the long standing Douglas–Percy feud not forgotten. And Albany and the lords, evidently rather tiring of burning, were inclined to favour this.

However, John's news of the great English muster at Durham, less than fifty miles away, changed views considerably, even Albany looking thoughtful. To be caught between two major forces, one under Gloucester himself, altered the picture undoubtedly. To go on then, the army scattered and split up as it was, would be folly, all agreed.

There were various alternative suggestions. Reassembled, the force might be able to defeat Northumberland, especially if they could collect Morton's West March array. If they could get the Hailes force to circle round *behind* the Percy one, and themselves attack from the front, with Morton threatening from the side, that would give the Scots much advantage; this was Archie's proposal and it gained support.

John was not the only one to express doubts. *If* they could line up with Morton? *If* they could get Hailes to circle back – if he was able to do so? Even if these moves were possible, they would take time. Had they the time? Gloucester could move fast. He might even now be advancing. All the smoke would guide him as to where to march. It could be themselves who were trapped between major armies.

Albany's youth showed now, in indecision. What could they do, then? They could not go scurrying back to Scotland like whipped curs!

John braced himself to say what was in his mind, recognising that he was scarcely popular. "Highness, we cannot challenge Gloucester's great muster, even if we were all ourselves assembled together again. And he could be upon us tomorrow. No time to draw in Morton, Hamilton and Hailes. But we *have* one advantage. We are, here, well over to the west, a deal nearer to Carlisle than to Durham or Newcastle. Alston is in Cumberland, I am told. So – use that. Have it that you have made your gesture, your warning to King Edward – as indeed you have. You entered England from the east, cut a wide swathe southwards, and ended up here in the west. March home from here by the West March, picking up my lord of Morton, credit nowise lost. Send Hamilton and Hailes back by the way we have come, up Redesdale. It will look as though that was always the intention. Move so, while you still have time, and it will preserve our honour and save us from sure defeat."

That was quite a lengthy contribution, especially from such as himself, but it was listened to without interruption or frowns, indication of the quandary in which all found themselves, a quandary which ought to have been foreseen.

Albany, who had been nibbling his lip throughout, seemed to perceive it as a solution indeed. "North from here, how far to the border? And where?" he demanded.

There were no West March lords present, these having gone with Morton. But Kerr of Ferniehirst, himself a noted raider over the borderline, was still with them, and appeared to know their whereabouts well enough. By Gilsland and the Bewcastle Fells they could be into Liddesdale, Scotland, in about thirty miles, he opined. Empty country most of the way.

That sounded hopeful to most there.

"But what about the others?" Archie demanded. "Morton, Hamilton, Hailes? They must be told."

"Morton will be between us and Carlisle," Ferniehirst asserted. "Keeping Scrope contained – the West Warden. He will be covering the Walton, Lanercost, Brampton, Geltsdale area. Easy to send riders west to warn him. Tell him to retire by Bewcastle."

"*I* will ride back to tell Hamilton, and try to find Hailes," John volunteered. "Tell them to retire up Redesdale."

The thing was accepted. Homeward it would be, honour and credit preserved. John got his first approving glances of the expedition.

* * *

Actually, his own self-appointed task proved to be comparatively easy. He found Hamilton and the other reluctant ones still at Hexham, which had remained unburned thanks to the arrangement with the prior and seneschal. These had had word from Hailes that he was coming up Tyne fast, hoping to reach the main army again, keeping ahead of Northumberland; and they had thought it best to wait for him there. He should arrive at any time now.

It was later afternoon by this time, and, sure enough, in mid-evening the East March fifteen hundred came hastening up Tyne, as if it were looking over their shoulders. They were obviously relieved to find their friends at Hexham. They declared that Northumberland was no more than ten miles behind, in the Belsay area. Fortunately, more than half of his force were foot, and this was slowing him up. But even so, he had sufficient horse to more than deal with themselves.

When Hailes heard John's account of the position he was further relieved. But he insisted that they must not linger here, nightfall or not. The Percy cavalry could be upon them in an hour or two. Darkness would be to their advantage. Let them all head north for Redesdale forthwith. They would find their way easily enough. They had come this way, after all.

Hamilton and the others were nothing loth. Orders swiftly were given to move.

So it was quite a large force which rode northwards into the half-dark, putting the South Tyne valley behind them, thankfully still with no sign of Percy of Northumberland's army, presumably the foot delaying it. No doubt the earl was assuming that he would probably have to face the full Scots strength, with Hailes rejoining Albany, and so was meantime keeping his cavalry back with the rest. How much the English knew, or guessed, as to Scots total numbers, none could judge.

They crossed the Roman Wall area at Chollerford, and felt the better for that, to make for Bellingham and so to Redesdale. There seemed little likelihood now of any pursuit, or at least any which might catch up with them. They reckoned that they had some thirty miles to go to the border at the Reidswire.

75

Weary as Hailes's people and their horses were, they thought that they ought to be there by sun-up.

And then, what? John, for one, was concerned about what might follow. Would Gloucester and Northumberland, united, invade Scotland? Having such a large force mustered and on the march, they might well do so by way of retribution. But Hamilton and Hailes thought not. They might well make some brief token sally over the borderline, a gesture; but they thought that full-scale invasion was improbable. That sort of action called for advance planning and careful provision. These hastily gathered English thousands would not be prepared for that. Also, as the experienced Hamilton pointed out, Gloucester would probably assume that the Scots Borderers would all be on the alert, ready, waiting, supporting Albany. Moreover, he, the Duke, was unlikely to attempt full-scale war without King Edward's express permission.

The others there agreed with this judgment; and who was John Douglas to say otherwise?

Nevertheless, when all but exhausted, the company passed Catcleuch's wan lake, in the dawn, and climbed over the final ridge to the Reidswire and into Scotland by the Jed Water valley, John announced that he was going to halt, with his two hundred, just in case. None of his colleagues thought that this was necessary, nor offered to wait with him – and what could a couple of hundred do anyway? But there was a stubborn Douglas streak, and a little way down towards Jed, where by a burnside there was scrub woodland and shelter, they parted company, John's group to camp, the other to proceed on to Jedburgh and thereafter back to their own various territories, Hamilton in especial shaking his head almost amusedly over the younger man's decision.

Posting lookouts on eminences nearby, the Douglases thankfully rested themselves and their tired beasts.

John spent two days and two nights on the high ground above the Jed Water, waiting, watching, his men glad enough to idle after all the riding and activity, able to provision themselves adequately from the Kerr communities nearby without making themselves a nuisance. In that time they experienced no alarms, no enemy came up Redesdale, no sighting of armies or even scouts were discerned by sentinels and look-outs. That is, until eventually a sizeable company was reported as coming, not from the south but from the west, from the Southdean and Bonchester area. Watched cautiously from hiding in scrub woodland, this proved to be none other than Ferniehirst and his Kerrs returning home to Jedburgh. Much greeting and news-exchange followed.

John learned that Albany's main force had duly contacted Morton, and together they had made their way through the Bewcastle Fells without incident, to Liddesdale and safely into Scotland. In fine style, banners flying, they had covered the last of English ground, without any burning to draw attention from a distance, but also without seeing anything of pursuit in flank or to rear. Where Gloucester was none knew, nor North-umberland now, neither. They had ridden up Liddesdale and over the Wauchope passes to the upper Rule Water and Bonchester, into Teviotdale, where Ferniehirst had left the army, on its way up to Edinburgh and Stirling. Whether there would be retaliation by the English, who could tell? But meantime, Albany was making a triumph of it, a successful invasion of England carried out without loss, all objectives achieved, policy vindicated. They were the heroes!

John wondered.

However, now that Kerr of Ferniehirst was here, back on his own ground, there seemed no need for the Douglases to remain on guard. They had served their turn, even though James Hamilton had been proved right. It was home to Tantallon for them, scarcely pretending triumph but in fact with no worse casualties than saddle-soreness.

Thankfully they rode northwards.

5

John was back at Tantallon, and glad to be so, for some days
before Archie came home. His brother was in high good
humour. He was a hero, it seemed – although not quite so
much so as was Albany apparently. They had been hailed as
such by all at court, and allegedly by the nation at large – or
almost all, William Sheves and therefore the King excepted.
The warriors had succeeded, twisted the English leopard's
tail, demonstrated that the Scots were to be reckoned with.
Edward must now think twice before making his alliances and
betrothing his young daughter. The next parliament would
publicly thank them, without a doubt.

The Douglas sisters and Archie's countess were not a little
confused. For John's account to them of the expedition had
been rather different. Whilst not actually dwelling on its
follies and excesses, he had indicated that there had been
mistakes, errors of judgment, grievous risks taken, to his mind
inadvisedly. Archie of course pooh-poohed all that. However,
he was good enough to accord Johnnie some credit for having
discovered and brought word of Gloucester's alleged muster at
Durham – whether this had in fact occurred – enabling Albany
and himself suitably to adjust their triumphant sweep; which
was one way of describing the situation. He confided that they
had been able to correct the man Hamilton's report of the
proceedings to the Princess Mary, and had made something
of John's contribution.

As a result of all this, it seemed that Archie's reputation
and position at court was much enhanced; indeed Albany
was insisting that he should become a frequenter of the
court and be his lieutenant and supporter in more than
armed expeditions. With Albany's own stature increased,

of course, this meant something. King James's attitude was less clear.

John was not enthusiastic. He enjoyed his own quiet life at Tantallon, well content with his poetry and ballads, his fishing and hawking and wildfowling in their seasons, also the company of all the young women there. Court life, no more than martial adventures, did not appeal to him – save in that Mary Stewart was known to be fairly frequently at her brother's court.

It was Mary Stewart indeed who did fetch them to Stirling, and before long. No counter-invasion of Scotland had developed, rather surprisingly, although such might be in preparation. Harvest-time was upon them, a little late this year – the same would apply to the English, of course – and the Douglas brothers were by no means too grand to shun work on the corn-rigs, with their people; for Tantallon was sited beside some of the most fertile and productive land in all Scotland, and its crops contributed not a little to the earldom's wealth. But when Friar Anselm from Cambuskenneth arrived at the castle one busy day, with a message from the princess, there was no hesitation about downing scythes and donning finer clothing, and having the castle barge readied. For this was a call for help.

It transpired that Archbishop Graham had arrived back from Rome, and had promptly been arrested, scarcely believable as this seemed. On the King's orders, he was confined to quarters in his own city of St Andrews – although not in his episcopal palace – to await trial by a joint court of the Privy Council and the College of Bishops.

The friar was clearly much upset by this extraordinary development, as was his superior the Abbot of Cambuskenneth, who it seemed blamed most of it on William Sheves. It appeared that, as now Archdeacon of St Andrews, he had prevailed upon a majority of the bishops to charge Graham with a lengthy list of offences – heresy, simony, misuse of Church funds, even blasphemy, misleading the Pope, to whom they had written, making complaint and requesting deposition from the archbishopric, and even excommunication. He, Sheves, had indeed persuaded the bishops to offer the King twelve thousand merks to order this arrest and imprisonment. They were jealous of the new Metropolitan's powers over them, powers which as mere Primate the Bishop of St Andrews had never possessed; Bishop Laing of Glasgow, the Treasurer, especially. They claimed that he had only won the primacy, first among equals, because he was a nephew of the late Bishop Kennedy, that he had never been a satisfactory prelate, quite apart from continuing ill health, and was indeed losing his reason.

The princess, who had always liked and supported Patrick Graham, was much distressed, and urged that Archie and John should come to court and use their influence, especially with Albany – who seemed to be uninterested, one way or another – to have this great wrong righted.

The very next day the brothers were on their way up Forth, even though John, for one, doubted his ability to achieve anything of value in the matter.

At Stirling, John was surprised to find himself all but a celebrated figure, as having led the advance guard of the famous army, his rearguard activities apparently forgotten. Evidently the late demonstration against England was being used by what had become an Albany faction as a credit-raising factor, and John was the all-unexpected recipient of some of it.

Mary Stewart received them, as ever, warmly, John particularly so – or was that just in his imagination? Her husband, needless to say, was less warm, but even he was not unfriendly – again, more so towards John than towards Archie, presumably judging him the least foolish. It was unclear where Hamilton stood in this matter of the archbishop.

Mary contrived to be alone with the brothers that evening, in her quarters in the palace wing of the castle, with a banquet being given by Sheves for a delegation being sent to Rome – presumably out of the archdiocese of St Andrews' funds – and the newcomers not invited, the princess herself calling off at the last moment for alleged feminine reasons.

She was not long in broaching the subject of Patrick Graham. "It is shameful. He is a good man and has done much for Scotland. He has delivered us from the age-old threat of domination of the Scots Church by the archbishopric of York, which the Kings of England have used to better their claims of overlordship. Thomas and I aided him in that. And now – this! Envious men lacking all scruple bring him down. And use my weak brother, foolish James, as their tool!"

"What would you have us to do?" Archie asked. "We have no pull with the churchmen – a plague on them!"

"No, but you have now, on my other brother Alexander. And those who favour him. He, Albany, cares nothing for religion, or clerics, and is not interested in this matter. I have sought to show him that it is important. He but shrugs. You two, however, he likes and admires. He would wish to have you on his side."

"Scarcely *me*, I think," John put in. "He sees me as feeble, lacking in spirit. Archie, yes . . ."

"I think not. He has spoken well of you, John. Says that you rendered him good service in England, ahead of his array. My husband says the same – although in different regard, it seems!"

"Johnnie is no dashing leader, nor yet a hero!" Archie declared. "But has his uses as information-gatherer!"

"You said, Mary, that the duke wanted us on his side? What side is that? What mean you – his side?"

"It is a strange matter. For some time now Alexander has been turning away from James, seeing *him* as feeble – not you, John! He judges James a poor King, mistaken in his policies and of course sadly influenced by William Sheves and other favourites. In this I agree with him, to be sure. But not to the extent of setting up an opposing faction. As a woman, I could scarcely do so anyway! Alexander can see no good in anything that James does. And he hates Sheves. So, since this of Archbishop Graham is Sheves's policy, Alexander and his supporters could be brought to oppose it. Actively. But, as I say, he despises all churchmen, and calls down curses on them all! Like Archie, here! I have tried to persuade him that this matter is important, for the whole realm. But he does not have much respect for women

81

and their wits either! But you Douglases he does think much of. So . . ."

"Your husband, Mary? How does he see all this?"

"He does not approve of Sheves, no. But nor does he approve of my brother Albany. Considers him a hot-head, rash. So there is no unity, as is needed."

"I will do what I can," Archie said. "But it does seem to be a matter for churchmen. And I have no pull with them, whatever I may have with the duke."

"The Abbot of Cambuskenneth," John put in. "*He* clearly condemns this move against the archbishop."

"A mere abbot! What could *he* do?" Archie objected.

"There might be others . . ."

"That is true," Mary agreed. "There *are* others, I know, who feel as he does. It is their superiors, the bishops, who are determined to bring down Patrick Graham. The abbots, to be sure, are on a different level from the bishops – not only in rank, status. They represent the monastic side of Holy Church, not the governing side. Important in their own way, but without the influence of the bishops. Very few of them ever become bishops, however senior they are; that has come to be reserved for the sons and bastards of great lords, more's the pity!"

"*Holy* Church!" Archie snorted.

"Yes, but if they acted together, could not the abbots achieve much?" John asked. "There are abbacies in every diocese. They are in touch with the people. They possess lands. Much of the Church moneys must come from, or through, them. If they could be mustered against Sheves – whom they must look upon as an upjumped clerk – might not they be able to sway even the College of Bishops?"

"John is right," the princess said. "Something might well be gained there. Many of the abbots, I know, resent their bishops. After all, they are often much more experienced, senior, wiser in the faith. I have heard of bishops who cannot even recite the Lord's Prayer! Many abbots will conceive that *they* should be bishops, the leaders and spokesmen of the Church. If they could be brought to speak with one voice, against Sheves and all his works, this of the archbishop in especial, lead a revolt in the Church, it could serve. Unfortunately they tend to shut themselves up, each in his own abbey or monastery . . ."

"Broken reeds, I say!" Archie declared. "We need *men*, fighters, not suchlike church mice! *I* will try to bring the duke round to it. And other lords. You can forget your abbots."

"No, not forget them. We need all the help that we can gain."

"If I went to the Abbot of Cambuskenneth, and urged some counter-action, think you that he would heed me?" John asked her.

"Would you? Yes, I think that Abbot Henry would respond. He is a fine man. He acts my confessor on occasion. Would you do that, John? And go round other abbots? Try to win more support?"

"If you think that it might help."

"Why not? The abbots are next in rank to the bishops. If they spoke with one voice, or many of them. Do that, John."

"You are welcome to your task!" Archie exclaimed. "Going round these sainted clerks! Although it may not be so ill for you? I have often thought that you should have been a priest, Johnnie! With all your wordcraft and writing – not Lord of Douglasdale! You go see your clerks. I will go to the men who matter."

"Between you, we will see what can be done," Mary said, smiling at John. "And I will seek to work on my husband – who has his own strength."

So it was decided.

Next morning, then, John went down to the Abbey of Cambuskenneth, sited on a great bend of the meanders of the River Forth just before it opened out to its estuary, little more than a mile from Stirling Castle. It was a splendid place, extensive, its large church surmounted by a lofty square tower, famous as the scene of Robert Bruce's reception of the many surrendered English lords immediately after the victory at Bannockburn, a spectacle unparalleled in Scotland's story. John had seen the abbey from the castle but never visited it.

He found Abbot Henry to be a spare, elderly man of stern, bony features but with a sudden warm smile to lighten them. With an introductory message from the Princess Mary, he was assured of a good reception. He was informed that the abbot had heard of his prowess on the recent expedition into England.

Assuring that this was much exaggerated and not important anyway, John worked round to the object of his visit, via Friar Anselm's couriership. He declared confidently enough that he and his brother were concerned over Archdeacon Sheves's activities, and over the shameful treatment of Archbishop Graham.

"You are not alone in that, my lord," Abbot Henry told him. "Many are."

"How many, my lord Abbot?" Henry was entitled to that honorific, Cambuskenneth being a mitred abbacy, carrying a seat in parliament.

The other raised grizzled eyebrows at this rather abrupt response to his statement.

John, coughing, added, "I ask for good reason. It is the princess's belief, and our hope, that there are many indeed, and that these, or some of them, can be united to speak out against this wickedness. In especial the abbots of Holy Church. How think you on that?"

He was eyed keenly, searchingly. "That is a large question, young man."

"I know it. But we think that it could be answered, and profitably. And that you might help in this."

"How might I help, my lord?"

"You are a senior churchman, a mitred abbot. You will know others. Many of whom may well resent William Sheves, his sudden rise to power, his influence with the King, and the policies he advocates. Especially this of Archbishop Graham. If they would speak out, join in making their feelings known, perhaps sign a petition, some betterment might result."

"I see. A petition? To whom?"

"To the King. And to the College of Bishops. To parliament itself, indeed."

"M'mm. Carefully worded, *I* would sign such a petition, yes."

"It is hoped that many others would. And that you would help in this. You will know the other abbots, who they are, where they are. As we do not."

"You wish me to name you names? I could tell you of a score, thirty perhaps, abbacies in Scotland, my son. But the views of their abbots – who knows?"

"That is the task. To see them, or many of them, *learn* their views, seek to persuade them, if necessary."

"You set yourself a large project, young man! I could name you abbacies from Ferne, in far-away Ross, to Dundrennan in Galloway; from Melrose and Kelso and Dryburgh in the Borders to Saddell in the Highland west; from Arbroath in Angus to Paisley in Renfrew and Kilwinning in Ayr. Do you think to travel to all these?"

John blinked. "I could scarcely do that. It would take months. But some, yes. There must be many nearer at hand? Perhaps enough for our purposes. Without going great distances."

"There are some, yes, none so far off," the abbot admitted. "Lindores and Dunfermline, Balmerinoch and Culross, in Fife; Scone at Perth, and Inchaffray in Strathearn; Arbroath and Coupar in Angus, Holyrood at Edinburgh, Newbattle in Lothian; and in the Borders, these others, with Jedburgh . . ."

"Enough there, surely? That must be over the dozen. And those near to Glasgow?"

"You would visit all these? You are much concerned, it seems, my lord!"

"*Somebody* must do something. If we have the matter at heart."

The older man smoothed his chin. "Yes. I commend your resolve. Does Archbishop Graham mean so much to Douglas?"

John hesitated. He could hardly say that he was willing to do it for Mary Stewart's sake. "He has done a great service to Scotland, has he not? We all owe it to him, I think."

85

"Indeed you are right in that. So you would take a petition round all these abbeys and seek the abbots' signatures?"

"I see no other way. You abbots do not meet together? No College of Abbots, as of Bishops?"

"Unfortunately not. Our tradition is monastic, seeking to work God's will within our own abbacies, priories and collegiate churches."

"So there is no way to get the abbots together? Or some of them?"

"Only at a diocesan synod, and then only perhaps two or three. And mitred abbots at a parliament. I fear that you have much riding ahead of you, my friend!"

John took a deep breath. "I had hoped, my lord Abbot, that *you* might come with me. At least to some of them. Your position and authority would carry much more weight than would mine."

There was a long pause as the older man took that in. "Have you considered what you ask, young man?" he said at length. "I have an abbey to manage and guide. Many friars and monks and lay-brothers to control, their work and their worship. We are an enclosed community of the religious, seeking to serve God in this place. Not to travel the land proclaiming causes, however worthy. There are travelling friars, yes – but not travelling abbots!"

"I understand, yes. But this is a matter touching on the well-being, honour and esteem of Holy Church, is it not? Must you leave it to . . . others?"

It was certain that Abbot Henry had never been spoken to like that, at least since he became an abbot, and by one young enough to have been his son. His stern features reflected that for a moment or two – and then his smile broke through.

"You do not lack spirit, my lord of Douglasdale, I will say that for you! I have heard that the Douglas motto is *Jamais Arrière*, Never Behind! You are sufficiently forward, I think! But . . . perhaps you are right, and you shame me into my wider duty."

"Then . . . you will come with me, my lord Abbot?"

"Some of the way, perhaps. I do not promise to visit any

great many of my fellows; but some, yes. It is as well that I have a good prior, Adrian, to be my deputy here. When do you plan to start your . . . crusade?"

"The sooner the better. The archbishop is a sick man, I understand, and should be being cared for, cherished, not imprisoned."

"That is true. Then give me two days to set my house in order. And I will be ready to ride, my son."

"You . . . you are a fair horseman, my lord?" That was put a little anxiously.

"I was reared on the Middle March of the Borders, where all are born to the saddle. I am a Kerr of Altonburn."

"Kerr! I rode with Kerr of Ferniehirst on the English expedition. A good man to have as friend, I judged."

"But not as enemy? He is none so distant kin of mine. Now – this of the petition? How do you think to word it?"

"I, I fear that I have not thought of that, as yet," John confessed.

"Then – leave you that to me. The shorter the better. The fewer words to any petition, the more impact it has. And the fewer objections to signing it! Two days, then, my friend, and I will be ready to ride with you."

"Thank you! Thank you!"

"No, no. Perhaps it is I who should be thanking you? For showing me my duty . . ."

Much enheartened, John rode back to Stirling Castle. Mary would be pleased.

With two Douglas men-at-arms to act as escort and grooms, they were at Cambuskenneth early, perhaps too early for an elderly abbot, to discover that the monastic discipline had all the monks up by five o'clock, the abbey fully into its daily routine, and Abbot Henry ready and waiting with a fine white mare saddled. The petition was likewise ready, a scroll headed "To the King's Grace, the College of Bishops, and the Estaits of Parliament: we, the undersigned, declare . . ." What followed was brief and to the point, with no names mentioned other than that of the archbishop, but little doubt as to who were the villains of the piece and what were the objectives. It already held one signature: "Henricus, Abbate de Cambuskynneth".

Clearly, when the abbot took on a task, he did it well. He had made out a proposed itinerary. They would go eastwards, firstly, to Fife – to Culross, Dunfermline, Inchcolm, Lindores and Balmerinoch, Fife being particularly rich in abbacies. Then westwards to Scone and Inchaffray. After that, they would reconsider. He pointed out that *mitred* abbots' signatures would carry the most weight, as parliamentarians. And three of the Fife ones happened so to be – Culross, Dunfermline and Inchcolm – this last strangely enough, since it was sited on an island in the Scotwater or Firth of Forth, and inconvenient to reach; but it was one of the most ancient and renowned, dedicated, as its name suggested, to St Columba.

They set off on a golden October morning, in good spirits. John decided that he liked Abbot Henry Kerr. Avoiding the Forth's extraordinary and complicated windings, they headed due eastwards along the foothill country of the Ochils, by Tullibody and Alloa and Clackmannan on its hill above the now widening estuary, and so into Fothrif, the westernmost portion of Fife, coming back to the waterside at the little port of Kincardine. Here they were only four miles from Culross.

John had never visited this quite famous community, renowned as the birthplace of St Mungo, founder of what became Glasgow. His Celtic princess mother, Thanea, daughter of King Loth, who had given name to Lothian, had come drifting up Forth in a coracle, banished by her father because she was pregnant, to ground at St Serf's Columban monastery here, back in the sixth century – a strange and romantic story, which John could make into a ballad perhaps? The present abbey, founded by an Earl of Fife in 1215, rose on the high ground above the tight cluster of the little town's houses, almost certainly a different site from St Serf's more modest establishment. It was still a less fine place than Cambuskenneth, but extensive, with a handsomely towered church, all surrounded by orchards on the south-facing terraced hillside below, trim trees in rows everywhere.

They found Abbot John, a plump, rubicund character, superintending the pressing of the pear crop for the making of perry, a beverage for which this religious house was famed apparently, as it was for its cider, this taking place in a long barn-like structure, filled with presses, vats, casks and long shelves of fruit. Obviously surprised at the quality of his visitors, he seemed just a little embarrassed to be discovered at this commonplace task, but made up for it by quickly launching into a dissertation on the qualities of different varieties of pears for this excellent liquor, and the stages of production, from pressing, fermentation, racking, and the manufacture of by-products such as pear cheese, and its comparison with cider cheese. It took the newcomers some little time, and tact, to transfer the conversation to the matter of Archbishop Graham and the man Sheves.

Even when they had achieved this, Abbot John dealt with the situation briskly, briefly, almost as a tiresome distraction, declaring Sheves to be a scoundrel and the archbishop a wronged man, then reverting to perry-making and the differences from cider, taking them over to his own quarters to sample the product. In the midst of this, Abbot Henry produced the petition, which the other signed without any discussion, "Johannes Abbate de Culrose", suggesting that his unexpected but welcome guests stayed on for a meal in due course. Exchanging glances which mutually indicated that they should be on their way to Dunfermline, avoiding any further enlargement on the subjects of pears and apples, perry and cider, the pair took their leave, John for one somewhat bemused.

They agreed, as they rode on eastwards, that if the other abbots' signatures were as easy to obtain as this one's, then their pilgrimage might not take as long as they had anticipated.

Dunfermline, the capital of Fothrif, and one of the richest Church properties in the land, lay a further eight miles, well back from the firth, on much higher ground. They went by Torry Bay, where they turned inland, by Cairneyhill and Pitfirrane, and could see the great abbey and its neighbouring royal palace rising above the town long before they reached it.

This was clearly a very different proposition to Culross, and Abbot Henry said that it might well offer them a very different reception. For, because of its wealth and status, Dunfermline was a sought-after prize in the Church and, rather like the bishoprics, was looked upon by lords and great men as a desirable haven for their younger sons. The present abbot, he was told, was of this sort, Henry Crichton, kin of the late Lord Crichton, who had ruled Scotland during James the Second's minority. He had formerly been Abbot of Paisley, and now was preferred to this richer and more prestigious seat, during the present monarch's minority. He might well be reluctant to seem to move against the monarch and his present advisers.

Dunfermline Abbey was certainly magnificent, more so than the royal palace which stood nearby. They approached it past a deep ravine which cleft the town's terrace, and on the edge of which perched the ruins of Malcolm Canmore's castle, a modest and simple structure by comparison. The mighty fane of the abbey had been built by Canmore's queen, the celebrated St Margaret, as almost the first great stone religious edifice in Scotland, cathedral-like, after she had managed to put down the ancient Columban Church, which did not go in for such splendours, and which she considered heretical.

The travellers had some difficulty in interviewing this other Abbot Henry. He was reported to be out inspecting new lands he had bought in the Saline area to the west – which, Henry Kerr murmured to John, ought hardly to have been necessary, since the abbacy of Dunfermline already possessed most of the half-county of Fothrif, as well as great other lands including, strangely enough, the quite major town of Musselburgh in Lothian. So they had to wait, in the luxurious abbatial quarters so far removed from monastic simplicity – but at least they were provided with an excellent meal by an individual who seemed more like a lord's chamberlain than any monkish brother.

When eventually, in late afternoon, Abbot Crichton arrived, he proved to be a tall, handsome man of early middle age, with a limp but a lofty bearing. He showed no joy over his visitors but seemed just a little more impressed with John than with his fellow-cleric. For his part, John did not forget that the Lord Crichton, as Chancellor and adviser to the late King, had been largely responsible for the policy of putting down the Black Douglases – but sought not to think of this now.

At least there was no problem here of enduring lengthy enthusiasms and preoccupations, as at Culross, with Crichton almost curtly enquiring their business. The callers therefore came straight to the point, neither of them really hopeful of a successful outcome. But in this they were surprised, for hardly had they mentioned the name of William Sheves when their host interjected with a spate of distinctly unclerical eloquence, denouncing upstart schemers and malevolent practitioners of satanic rites, who swayed their young monarch and sought thereby to raise themselves above their betters. This went on at some length, and only ended with the declaration that scoundrelly Sheves clearly intended to get himself hoisted into the position of archbishop, utterly deplorable, intolerable and indeed ridiculous as this would be, with others more worthy and suitable. The impression given was that the speaker himself would not be the least of these.

Abbot Kerr promptly took the obvious opportunity to observe that his fellow-abbot therefore would not be averse to adding his name to a petition to the King, bishops and parliament, which sought to limit Sheves's ambitions and support the ailing Archbishop Graham?

The other scarcely bothered to read the words put before him, concerned rather with finding a pen and ink to dash off his signature with a flourish. He offered no single word as to Patrick Graham.

A further denunciation of William Sheves followed, with condemnatory references to astrology, witchcraft, magic and diablerie, Crichton pacing his chamber with its rich carpeting. Although the visitors had thought of spending the night here, it now occurred to them both that they would prefer to be elsewhere, having got what they wanted and present company being scarcely to their taste. Nor, when they indicated departure, were they pressed to linger.

Glad to be on their way again, they headed eastwards still,

the abbot pointing out almost apologetically that all his kind were not like that.

John had remembered that there was a Douglas castle at Aberdour, not so very far away, indeed he imagined one of the nearest points to the island of Inchcolm. It belonged to the Douglases of Dalkeith, the Earl of Morton's line, and would probably provide them with a more congenial night's lodging than would Dunfermline Abbey.

Although it was almost dark before they reached Aberdour, above its silver sands, the lights of the small community and its castle looked welcoming – and not only these, for out in the firth a larger light burned which, Abbot Henry declared, would be Inchcolm itself. Holy Church had a care for mariners, it seemed, and this abbey kept a beacon burning of a night to guide seamen, as did the Priory of Pittenweem, much further east, this on the Isle of May. All monastic establishments provided shelter and sustenance for travellers; and such island ones could best serve thus.

At the castle, despite the hour, they received a friendly welcome from none other than the Master of Morton, son of the earl, whom John had briefly met at the start of the late English adventure. A cheerful young man, he was interested to hear John's side of the story after their parting at Jedburgh. The Master had a pleasant, laughing wife, and there was an amusing interlude when, telling of their experience at Dunfermline, it transpired that she was herself a Crichton and kin to the abbot there, whom she did not greatly like.

The Master told them that they were fortunate in being able to see Abbot Michael, for it might well have been otherwise. He had been on a visit to Berwick-on-Tweed, in the spring, with others, sailing there in the late Bishop Kennedy's fine barge, when a storm from the north had driven the ship southwards and wrecked it on the Northumbrian shore near Bamburgh. Some of the passengers were drowned, but Abbot Michael had survived; but, despite the truce, had been taken and held by the English, and forced to pay a ransom for his release. St Colm, or Emonia, as some called the island, not being a rich abbacy, he had had difficulty in raising the necessary moneys, and was not long back from his imprisonment. He was a quietly pious elderly man and appeared to be not greatly concerned over his misadventures, save in that it cost his abbacy the moneys, but was more upset in that he had been unable to continue with his great preoccupation with illustrating the abbey's breviary and missals. The Master did not think that they would have any difficulty in persuading him to sign their petition, for he was a quietly saintly man who would grieve over corruption and plotting in high places, especially in Church matters.

It was late before they were bedded down in an attic room within the parapet-walk of the tower. The Master himself would take them out next day to the island in his own boat.

So in the morning the three of them went down to the little haven where, amongst fishing-boats, the Master had his own craft moored, smaller than the Tantallon barge but seaworthy enough. Four fishermen were found to row it out, John and the Master glad to lend a hand. The island was plainly visible, less than two miles offshore.

They were told the story of the abbey. Alexander the First, no very notable monarch, a son of Margaret, out from Dunfermline, had almost drowned when his boat capsized in a sudden storm, but had managed to reach the island, whereon was only a hermit-monk of the old Columban Church, who nursed the injured King until signal-fires eventually brought aid from the mainland to rescue him. In gratitude for his delivery, he endowed this abbey, dedicating it to St Columba, one of the few of his line who had any care for the ancient Celtic Church. As abbacies went, of course, it was one of the most modest; but the hermit's cell had been there since the seventh century, which few of the others could rival, and it was considered an especially holy place. Needless to say, it was scarcely sought after by more ambitious abbots.

The island was fairly low-lying, crescent-shaped and only half a mile in length, the monastic quarters neither extensive nor imposing. But the visitors' reception was warm, indeed a party was waiting for them at the sheltered cove, less than a harbour – for, of course, any approach to the isle could be observed, and callers would not be frequent. Half a dozen monkish brothers greeted them, hailed the Master of Morton, and were much impressed by the identity of the Abbot of Cambuskenneth. They said that the Abbot Michael would be at his chosen duties of illustrating missals.

They found the old man in stained, indeed ragged, robes, busy amongst his paints, pens, brushes and parchments, but delighted to see them. They duly admired his artistry, noting the prevalence of seabirds depicted, terns, kittiwakes, eiders and the like, entwined amongst Celtic interlacing and symbolism. Abbot Michael claimed to be all unworthy of the holy subjects illustrated; but God had given him only a small talent in this respect, although a great sense of the need. Perhaps with constant practice he would improve? He did not ask the reason for their visit.

They spoke to him about his ordeal in the shipwreck and capture by the English, and the shame of demanding ransom in time of truce – although John admitted that the recent expedition into England, in which he had taken part, was also an infringement of the truce. But the English had to be taught a lesson. This brought them to current problems of state. When Abbot Henry broached the subject of the petition, the other could not have been more eager to support their cause in any way that he could, claiming that a mere signature was inadequate indeed. Anything further that he might do to help the good archbishop, he would. He did not presume to condemn William Sheves, the man; but if his policy was to unseat the new Metropolitan, then might God forbid it, and all the faithful offer their aid.

He signed "Michaelis Abbate de Insule S. Columbe".

Invitation to partake of refreshment, humble as it might be, was appreciated but refused, on the excuse that they had a long ride ahead of them that day, right across the width of Fife to Balmerinoch. But beakers of wine they accepted, before being escorted down to the boat by Michael and the entire company of the abbey, with urges to come back on another occasion. Wavings followed them much of the way back to Aberdour.

Mistress Janet had a meal waiting for them on their return to the castle, so they were somewhat delayed after all in their further journeying. But they eventually left for the north, well pleased with this stage of their mission.

Their route now entailed some climbing, for the great peninsula of Fife and Fothrif, between the Forth and Tay estuaries, consisted, apart from the coastal plains, of two fairly lofty ridges of high ground, known as the Rigging of Fife, that is the roofing, and a wide trough of low and fertile land between known as the Howe. Balmerinoch lay on the Tay coast, so all of this had to be crossed, very much slantwise, some forty miles, a fair day's riding which they hoped to cover in half a day. Abbot Henry proved to be entirely up to it however. But again it was dusk before they were able to look down on the narrow coastlands and the wide Tay firth, from the shoulder of Ardle Hill, and see the lights of their destination winking, practically on the shore, a lot of lights.

When they reached the abbey they were not long in discovering the reason for the lights, or at least the excuse therefor. This establishment had its own speciality – as, it seemed, most of these enclosed monastic houses had – in this case, bees. The manufacture of candles from beeswax was its main preoccupation, apart from daily worship, this together with the by-products of honey and honey wines. The illuminations were presumably something in the nature of a demonstration of their wares.

Balmerinoch's Abbot Walter had been at St Andrews University with Henry Kerr, and they were on friendly terms. This did not necessarily imply agreement of views on affairs of Church and state; but as it turned out their host did accept that the archbishop was being shamefully ill-treated, and that Sheves was a menace, so was prepared to endorse the petition, and further action, without any major discussion. So now they had five signatures, three of them mitred abbots.

They ate well and, weary, slept well. But in the morning they were not permitted to depart without an inspection of the candle-making process, a seemingly valuable industry and trade, for of course candles were in great demand in ordinary homes as well as in churches and castles. The honey wine-making was also explained and sampled, and the great walled gardens with their bee-skeps inspected amidst buzzing hordes of insects, John wondering rather alarmedly how often the monks were stung – to be informed reprovingly that God's bees did not sting God's servants.

They proceeded on their way.

Lindores lay comparatively near at hand, a mere dozen miles to the west, skirting the coastal plain by Creich and the famous hill of Norman's Law with its Pictish remains. The Abbey of Lindores was another rich one, which Henry had some doubts about, for its abbot was young, a Stewart, and related to Lord Avondale, the Chancellor, and so might possibly be unwilling to appear to go counter to the ruling interests. In fact they caught him just as he was about to ride off to visit two of his many granges, or abbatial farms, and his impatience to be on his way was evident. But his attitude to Sheves was in line with all the others interviewed, resentment at such a nobody being elevated to such power merely because of foolish and unsuitable influence with the King. He added the superscription "Andreas Abbate de Lindorus" almost without remark. He did declare that his prior would give them sustenance, if they so desired; but they said that they had got to reach Scone as soon as possible. So they rode off simultaneously, themselves still westwards, the other southwards down the side of Lindores Loch.

Henry Kerr dryly asked what John thought of Scotland's abbots? He was answered, carefully, that like its lords they seemed to be of varying character – which raised a thin smile.

Their journey now took them along the levels of the narrowing Tay estuary, to pass the weaving village of Newburgh, properly the New Burgh of Lindores and belonging to the abbey, where they turned aside to see the famous Cross of MacDuff, a curious monument within a circle of stones, no doubt of Pictish origin, pitted with nine holes. This figure of nine was significant, for here any member of the Clan MacDuff who had the misfortune to have slain anyone in hot blood could find sanctuary, so long as he touched one of these holes nine times, washed nine times in a nearby spring called the Nine Wells, and paid nine cows, presumably to the abbey's Celtic Church predecessor. Whether the MacDuff Earl of Fife who slew King MacBeth did this, is not recorded.

The ancient town of Abernethy, also of Pictish importance, with its renowned Round Tower, overlooked the plain where the River Earn joined Tay and where MacBeth had won the bloody Battle of Black Earnside. Thereafter they forded Earn under Moncrieffe Hill, where the Stone of Destiny was said to have been hidden temporarily to save it from Edward the First's clutches, and so came by Tarsappie to St John's Town of Perth, where Tay was bridged. They had come nearly forty miles that day, but Scone was only two miles or so further on, at the other side of the river, so they pressed on.

Scone was one of the most famous shrines in the land, scene of the coronations of the Scottish kings, sacred even in pagan Pictish times as the point where the kindly fresh waters of the river overcame the salt tidal waters of the ocean. Here, after the Viking raiders had so often worked destruction on the still more sacred abbey on Columba's Isle of Iona, Kenneth MacAlpin had brought the Stone of Destiny for safe-keeping, the coronation seat which was probably Columba's own portable altar.

The abbey stood above the river beside the extraordinary Moot Hill – extraordinary in that it was allegedly wholly artificial, created by soil brought from all over the realm. This was because, at coronations, the landholders of Scotland came to pay their oaths of fealty to the new monarch, and tradition had it that they should stand, and then kneel, upon their own soil whilst doing it, in token that all the lands were held of the king. So generations of lords and ladies and chiefs had brought pocketfuls of earth to empty here before the coronation seat on which the monarch sat, and this had built up and up. John, who had never attended a coronation, somehow doubted this, but did not say so.

Abbot Alan was a spritely character of middle years, slight of build, birdlike in bearing, with a humorous, almost mischievous glint in his eye. But there were no smiles or twinkles when William Sheves's name was mentioned. Pursing his lips, he declared that man to be a rogue and charlatan, who deserved the utmost condemnation and retribution rather than this latest preferment. When the visitors asked what he meant by preferment, they were told that Sheves had just been appointed Dean of Dunkeld, as well as being Archdeacon of St Andrews, to the resentment of all the clergy of the diocese. Scone was in that see. The implication was, of course, that the Bishop of Dunkeld, who must have agreed to this, was one of these who were working with Sheves for Archbishop Graham's downfall. Abbot Alan added his name to the petition gladly.

They spent the evening with this cheerful little cleric who, while deploring much that went on in Church and state, did not let this unduly affect his high spirits. They went to their beds well content. Seven signatures, four of them mitred abbots, and only one more to visit before their return to Stirling.

Inchaffray lay in mid-Strathearn about a dozen miles to the west. So it was back through Perth next morning, and on, by Tippermuir and Cultmalundie and Williamston, in the fair and wide vale on the skirts of the great mountains, most of the way to Crieff where the Highland cattle trysts and sales were held. The abbey stood on low, level ground at a bend of the Pow Water, a bend which had once been an island in undrained marshland, as the name implied. It was not large, but wealthy, endowed with large lands in this vale, with no fewer than six churches under it in this fertile strath, with their villages. Abbot George was old, reserved, silent – save on the subject of glass-staining and window-decoration, they discovered. Abbot Henry suggested that he came to Cambuskenneth one day, with a view to designing a suitable addition to the church there. John suspected that this was in the nature of a bribe for his signature, but if so it turned out to be unnecessary, for this abbey was also in the diocese of Dunkeld and its incumbent likewise offended by the elevation

98

of Sheves to be their dean, over their heads as it were. The superscription "Georgio Abbate de Insule Missarium" which seemed to be the original name of the establishment, meaning the abbey of the island of offerings or mass, was added to the others.

They left Inchaffray fairly promptly, after admiring much stained-glass artistry and processes, calculating that they could get back to Stirling that same night, some thirty-five miles. They had done well, eight signatures and no refusals. Surely this must have some effect on the situation? Even before other abbots might be approached.

They rode back due southwards across the strath, by Trinity Gask and the Roman signal-stations along the Earn, crossing that river at Kinkell and thereafter following the line of the old Roman road itself, by Machany and Braco, to cross Strathallan, another vale, and over Sheriff Muir to Airthrey, where they looked across the Causeway, scene of Wallace's great victory of Stirling Bridge, to Stirling Castle, towering on its rock. They had been five days away, with much achieved, including John Douglas's education, both in matters clerical and in the better appreciation of his native land. And the princess ought to be pleased.

Five days was no long interval, but much seemed to have happened at Stirling in the interim. An embassage had arrived from King Edward of England, consisting of the Bishop of Durham, the Lord Scrope and the Lord Russell, all notably from the northern parts of that kingdom, Scrope actually Warden of its West March, the area so recently invaded by the Scots. They came seeking to settle and confirm the betrothal of his three-year-old daughter, Cecilia, to the two-year-old Duke of Rothesay, heir to the Scots throne – this allegedly to ensure lasting peace between the two realms, but undoubtedly to enable Edward to invade France without fear of a Scottish attack at his back. No counter-invasion by Richard of Gloucester had eventuated in the meantime, and the Scots expedition into England was not so much as mentioned; it appeared that this last had fully achieved its object and was therefore a still greater success than hitherto assessed. So Albany's star was in the ascendant, and Archie Douglas's with it – to the effect that the former had there and then been made Lieutenant of the Borders and the latter Warden of the East March. All this, together with news from the north-west Highlands that John of the Isles, Earl of Ross, had invaded Argyll and Lochaber in strength, and created mayhem which demanded retribution, had rather put the plight of Archbishop Graham into the background, it seemed.

But not in Mary Stewart's mind. She welcomed John back with a warmth which rejoiced him, praising his efforts and delighted with the results. She was greatly distressed over a dire new development in this situation, however.

"The man Sheves has further demonstrated his spleen and cunning, also his power over James," she declared. "I learned of this only yesterday, from one of my brother's clerks, a monk who favours the archbishop, and who helped to write out the letters to the Pope which James signed, at Sheves's behest. They went off to Rome three days ago, by the hand of the Official of Lothian, one of the St Andrews archdeaconry's officers. What is written therein is scarcely believable. It is to inform Pope Sixtus that Archbishop Graham is now completely a madman. That he has proclaimed *himself* Pope, having been commanded to do so by an angelic messenger from God, and crowned by the angel!"

"Lord save us!" John exclaimed. "Madness! Here is madness indeed! But not the archbishop's . . ."

"None so mad, by Sheves's wits. For he adds that Patrick Graham has revoked all papal indulgences granted from Rome, which could cause chaos in the Scots Church. And has even appointed his own nuncio, unnamed. We may conceive this crazy; but nothing is more likely to alarm the Vatican. And since these charges are endorsed by the King of Scots, he will almost certainly accept them as truth, or enough so to take action. Utter folly as it is."

"But this is beyond all belief, even at Rome's distance. The Pope must be told otherwise. Somehow."

"I agree. But how? John, this petition, signed by your abbots. That, revealing Sheves's pretensions and plots, might help. If we sent that with a letter, explaining all. The pity of it, but Sheves is backed by most of the College of Bishops. They do not want to become mere suffragans to a Metropolitan. Before, the Primate was merely the most senior of them, the chairman of the college, not their master. They resent the change, especially the Treasurer, the Bishop of Glasgow, who considers himself to be an all but independent prince of the Church. Moreover, the archbishop had brought a demand from the College of Cardinals for contributions from all Scots dioceses for a new crusade against the Turks, and this they do not want to have to pay. So they are supporting Sheves meantime. Fools, I think, for he will use them and then reject them."

"Can he do that? Even though he has now become Dean of Dunkeld, we learned. He cannot overrule bishops . . ."

"Ah, but he intends to! This message he has sent to the Pope, backed by James, asks that he, Sheves, be appointed Bishop-Coadjutor of St Andrews, until this trouble in the Scots Church is put to rights. You see what that means? If the Vatican agrees – and I understand that a large sum of moneys has gone with the Official of Lothian – he will be a bishop himself, and acting in the name of the primacy, thus claiming seniority over them all. He is a clever man, is William Sheves. These others, in their envy of Graham and pride in their independence, do not realise the lion which they have unleashed!"

"Then – would the signatures of eight mere abbots serve any purpose at Rome?"

"They might, I think. Abbots can offer a truer picture of the Church as a whole than may ambitious bishops, who are largely in their sees not because they are holy men but because they are the scions of lordly families. The Pope must know that – even though he himself is no doubt of the same sort! If the petition was sent with a letter explaining the true situation and supporting the abbots, it might serve to halt Sheves's designs. Or delay them, until the truth be established."

"Who would send that letter? Or sign it? To counter the *King*'s signature."

"Only one, I can think of, who would carry sufficient weight – since a woman's would be scorned! The King's brother. Alexander of Albany. He hates Sheves and his power over James. Even though he cares nothing for churchmen and their affairs. I think that I could have him sign such letter."

"You would write it? Archie and I would get other lords to add their names, if that would help? Although the Pope may not be greatly concerned with such."

"It might add weight. But what *would* carry weight, I think, would be who carried the message and petition to Rome. If a bishop was to take it . . ."

"Is that possible? Would any of them do it? Against the others."

"I can think of one who might – Bishop Tulloch of Orkney. He is different from the others. And friendly towards myself. We worked together in winning Orkney and Shetland for Scotland. He accompanied Thomas and me to Norway and Denmark. His diocese used to come under the rule of the Archbishop of Trondheim, you see, the only Scots bishopric so to do, so he did not sit in the College of Bishops. He will do so now. But he is not as the others."

"Where is he? In Orkney?"

"Yes, I think so. He is no courtier. He takes his diocesan duties seriously. If he would do it . . ."

"To ask him to leave his islands? Go away to Rome. That is a lot to ask."

"I know it. But I can think on no other, as suitable, or who might do it. And he has one great advantage. Being bishop in those islands amongst the stormy northern seas, he has to have a good sea-going ship. He used it going to Denmark. So he could sail to Rome without seeking aid from others."

"Aye, that would greatly help. What, then? Orkney is far away . . ."

"John, would *you* do it? You, who have done so much. Would you go to Orkney, with a message from myself to William Tulloch? Help persuade him to take the petition to the Pope. It is a great matter to ask. But, it could be so important. Would you?"

"I would do a lot. If you asked me!" he said simply.

"My dear! Bless you, John! I do not know who else I could ask. And it is urgent. Can you go soon?"

"I am my own master as to time. And the Tantallon barge lies at Airth Neuk. Archie will not be needing it, I think."

"You would go by sea? All the way? Is your vessel sufficient for that?"

"To be sure. It was built for Norse Sea waters. Tantallon requires that. To ride up to Caithness and there find ship could take weeks. I have never been so far, but I would think that I could be at Orkney in three days and nights' sailing. If the winds were not unfavourable. Three hundred miles?"

"I know not. But we went to Denmark in four days. And it

103

will not be so far, surely? Oh, John – you are good! If there were more like you!"

John did not want more like him – where Mary Stewart was concerned. He looked away. "Your husband?" he asked, at less of a tangent than it might seem. "The Lord Hamilton. Where stands he in all this?"

"He is over on Arran, seeing to our lands there. Or mine. For the Arran lands were royal, and part of my dower, for Thomas's use. When he was forfeited, the earldom remained with me. James Hamilton now gains the rentals from it, but he is not Earl of Arran. He would *wish* to be! This much affects his behaviour towards the King, who alone can make or break earldoms. So he does not show frank opposition to Sheves, for fear of offending James. I fear, strong enough man as he is, in this matter he is of little use."

"You . . . you find him . . . none so ill, Mary? He is not . . . unkind?" That was hesitantly put, but urgent nevertheless.

"He is my husband now," she answered quietly, flatly. "Not of my choice. But he does not mistreat me. Nor make many demands on me. On my person! He has a sufficiency of other women. And he needs me, you see. Over this of the earldom. And in other ways, as the King's sister. So – we must be husband and wife. But we go our own ways in many matters now I am very pregnant. In this of the archbishop, however, I think that we can seek no help from him."

John pondered the various aspects of that statement, the archepiscopal side of it not foremost in his mind perhaps, silent.

She went on. "John, haste is required, if this matter is to be righted and a great injustice avoided. But, I think, where *you* are concerned, haste for another reason also. This of John of the Isles, Earl of Ross. He has made serious inroads into the mainland of the north and threatens more, threatens royal and Stewart lands, in Lorn and Lochaber and Atholl, even Arran itself. After all, his own lands of Knapdale and Kintyre reach within sight of the Isle of Arran. So there is great alarm. An army, and ships also, will have to be sent up to deal with him. They say that he has contracted his own private treaty with

Edward of England – which of course is treason. The northern earls, Atholl, Argyll, Buchan and Huntly, demand action. My husband is likewise concerned. There will be mustering of men, many men. And soon, before winter snows close the Highland passes. And *you* have won a name for yourself in that sally into England, reluctant warrior as I know you to be! Archie also, of course. My brother Albany has been given command of the Borders, as Lieutenant, so he may not have to go north. But *you* might well. It would be as well if you were gone elsewhere before such call reached you."

"M'mm. I see. Yes, I will go to Orkney forthwith, then. I will have to have Archie's permission to use the barge. I have not seen him yet. He is still here at Stirling?"

"Yes. He goes hunting daily with Alexander. They are closer than ever, it seems. James hunts on occasion also – but not with Alexander. They are all but enemies now. My sorry family! Each night they feast apart, almost hold separate courts."

"And you, Mary? Which do you attend?"

"Sometimes one, sometimes the other. I seek to mediate between them, where I can, but to little good. More often I dine alone with Anna and my children. My other brother, John of Mar, keeps his own company, a secret young man. *Your* family is different, I think? All good friends."

"Yes. We suit each other very well. I am sorry for you, in this. As, as in much else . . ."

"We are our strange father's children. Mother's also, to be sure, but she was less strange! Well, John – tonight I will dine with Albany and you can come with me and see Archie there . . ."

So that evening John sat between Mary and Archie in Albany's wing of the great palace block, and listened to an account of an encounter with a wild boar during a deer-drive that day in the great floodlands of the Flanders Moss to the west of Stirling, and Archie's pride in managing to kill the brute with his throwing-spear – to Mary's reproval. Did he not remember that the wild boar was the ancient symbol and standard of their early Celtic royal line, before ever William the Lion, David the

First's son, changed it, for some reason, to the Lion Rampant – he who was no lion, ramping or otherwise. Boars should not be slain by men proud of their ancestry – and the Douglases had royal blood in their veins, had they not?

That set Archie and John off into discussion, almost argument, as to how many times the Douglases had intermarried with the royal family, down the various branches of the house, four or five, altercation developing as to whether the Fair Maid of Galloway could truly be called royal.

That led to Border matters and Archie's satisfaction at being appointed Warden of the East March, and his plans in that regard. The Homes would be very jealous, undoubtedly, for they looked on the East March as all but their own property. He might have more trouble with them than with the English raiders. Fortunately Home was to take a contingent of his mosstroopers on this Highland expedition against the Lord of the Isles, which ought to give him a chance to settle in as Warden. Who knew – Home might even get himself killed by the wild Islesmen!

That allowed John to raise the subject of the barge. Archie would not be needing it for the borderland. Here was a way that he could serve the ill-used archbishop's cause, by letting himself take it to Orkney to seek to enrol Bishop Tulloch in their design. He explained about the petition situation and the Rome proposal, Mary adding her pleas.

Archie at first took it that the ship was required to take the bishop all the way to Rome, and looked doubtful about that, thinking that it might be away for many weeks; but when he heard that it was only to go to Orkney and back, he agreed that Johnnie could have it. He admitted that, with all the other matters on his mind, he had not been able to do anything to help Patrick Graham. This at least he could do.

So it was settled. John could sail next day, since he said there was need for haste. And after he got back from Orkney he could come and help rule the East March of the Borders.

During all this discussion, Albany, at the other side of his sister, and somewhat the worse for liquor after a tiring day's hunting, had been plying an unidentified lady with

106

refreshment, in between fondlings, and had now actually fallen asleep, one hand still within the female bosom, head on her bare shoulder. Mary shook her own head over this, and rose, observing that if sleep called, she for one preferred her own bed. John promptly declared that he would escort her thereto – and then, blinking, sought to amend that proposal to a less suggestive and more formal reference to quarters and apartment, which, of course, only served to emphasise the previous offer's implications. The young woman only smiled and patted his arm.

They had to go out into the chilly October night, and round the block to the further wing of the building, and Mary took that same arm companionably as they went.

"You and your brother are very different, Johnnie," she said – and he noted with pleasure that it was the first time that she had called him Johnnie, as distinct from John, as did all his own family. "Almost as different as are my own brothers. I like you both, but feel more sure of you!"

"Sure . . . ?" he wondered. "What mean you by sure, Mary?"

She gurgled a little laugh. "Does that sound . . . unsuitable? Like your own remark back there at table! It is not meant to be. I feel sure of your, your reliability and constancy. Yes, and your caring. I can feel safe with you, you see."

John was not sure that he wanted this woman to feel so safe with him, in his heart. But he rejoiced in her trust and recognition of his caring, and in her saying so.

"I am glad that you trust me and find me reliable," he said, as they turned in at the outer door. "I hope that you may always do so. But" – as she let go of his arm, to climb the narrow, twisting turnpike stair – "I am a man, as you know. And you are a very beautiful woman!" That came out in something of a rush.

They went up the two floors thereafter, one behind the other, in silence.

But at the upper doorway to the first of her three intercommunicating apartments, she turned. "Johnnie," she said, "I know that you are all man. And that perhaps I may cause you

107

stress, trial, holding back, at times. But *I* am all woman also, you see. I am sorry if I seem heedless on this, even heartless. I am . . . far from it. But, placed as I am, I cannot fully please myself. I am not truly of a discreet nature, but discretion is required of me. You do understand?"

He swallowed. "I understand, yes."

"But we can be close friends. We *are* close friends. And may . . . gain much from each other, despite, despite the discretion. No?"

"I . . . hope so."

"Yes. We must help each other, Johnnie. For I need help also."

That made him less hesitant and doubtful. "Yes," he agreed. "Help."

"We will do that. Knowing what we do." She gripped both his arms. "Johnnie, this of your going to Orkney is a great matter. And done more for me than for poor Patrick Graham, I know well. I thank you. I will have the letter for the Pope written, with Albany's signature, sent to you in the morning, when he is sober enough to sign it! And another from me to Bishop Tulloch. Go now, Johnnie – while I am still strong enough to send you away!" She pushed him off, quite forcibly, with both hands – and then suddenly, without loosening her grip, changed direction to pull him to her, to kiss him full upon the lips, before wrenching free and turning to enter the doorway at a rush. Without looking back, she slammed the door shut behind her.

The man stood there for long moments, biting those lips so generously used, and seeking to order his seething wits. Out of their turmoil he managed to salvage two thoughts. One, that he had somehow succeeded in controlling his arms, his whole body – or most of it. And two, that those lips of hers had moved against his own.

Presently he turned and went downstairs slowly, a man possessed by surging emotions.

108

7

The Tantallon barge was a useful vessel – a barge they called it, although barque or bark would have been more apt, for it was no flat-bottomd scow, but wide and open enough amidships to take horses, very necessary where Douglases were concerned, two-masted and sufficiently strongly built and high-sided to face Norse Sea storms. It used oars, long sweeps, as well as its square sails, something like an Islesman's galley – on which indeed it was modelled, together with a Norseman's dragon-ship, a mongrel craft indeed but sturdy, effective.

Its crew numbers varied, depending on length of voyage and waters to be sailed. Coming up Forth they had needed only a minimum, eight men; but for a voyage to northern seas they would require more. So John called in at North Berwick, *en route*, to inform the Countess Elizabeth and his sisters of the situation, and to collect the sea-going crew. All the North Berwick and Cove fishermen were retainers of the earl, their services always available when required.

The regular and prevailing south-westerly winds were reasonably favourable for this voyage, and having made good time down Forth, after leaving North Berwick in the early evening, provisions aboard, they did even better, heading north by east, this without using the sweeps once they were into open sea. John reckoned that they should be able to average fully eight miles in each hour, so long as this wind lasted, and practically no tacking was required. They could hardly expect such conditions to apply all the way to Orkney; but at any rate they were making a good start. Before turning in, around midnight, to his bunk, he calculated that they would be some fifty sea miles on their way, and possibly opposite Montrose.

Sun-up saw them another fifty miles to the north, past

Aberdeen, some two miles offshore, with the levels of the Ythan estuary discernible to the west. Now the wind was veering somewhat nearer due west, which was a little less in their favour, entailing occasional tacking; but still they would be making six miles in the hour. Their skipper, Dod Baldie Douglas, said that unless the breeze dropped altogether, or changed into the north, they ought to be level with Duncansby Head, the final tip of mainland Scotland, in twenty-four hours.

The wind did not drop, but freshened from the west, and by the time that darkness began to hide the coast they were following, they were passing the mouth of the Dornoch Firth, at Tarbat Ness. John went to bed well satisfied.

Next morning dawned wet and unpleasant, with choppy seas, and found them closer to land than expected. This, Dod declared, must be because he was steering only a little east of north, and he had heard that the very northern part of their land thrust out considerably eastwards. So they altered course a little in that direction – in which the wind aided them. How far to Duncansby Head? Another fifty miles? The coastline here was unknown to them, and seemed to consist of almost solid medium-high cliffs, with no outstanding landmarks.

Soon after noon, they learned what they wanted to know, and in no uncertain fashion. None aboard had ever had occasion to be as far north as this, and they were unprepared for the conditions applying once they passed the mighty cliffs of Duncansby and entered the waters of the Pentland Firth, which separated Orkney from Scotland. Here the great Atlantic tides were funnelled in to meet those of the Norse Sea, with dramatic effect. What had been choppy seas before became as a mill-pond, compared with this. And the westerly wind, now untrammelled by the landmass, developed into almost a gale. The barge took it all stoutly, but progress dropped notably, all Dod's seamanship called into play.

How far to Orkney now? Or to Kirkwall, rather, for these isles were said to cover an area of hundreds of square miles, possibly thousands, with Kirkwall, the bishop's seat, fairly central, allegedly. This travel into the unknown was exciting, challenging, but exacting also, full of questions. Moreover, Mary had warned John about the roosts, which Bishop Tulloch had told her of, and for which the Orkney waters were apparently notorious, whirlpools and great turbulences in the sea, caused by those battling tides circling round underwater prominences, mountains even and valleys. These could capsize a ship, even suck it down, it was said. They were, however, said to roar, which should give some warning. Clearly these Orkney isles were not advisable to thread in darkness.

They had some six hours of daylight, which, in these conditions, might let them cover thirty miles, no more. How far to the shelter of the first isles? None knew for sure, John wishing that he had been able to consult a knowledgeable shipman. Mary had said that she thought the Pentland Firth hereabouts was little more than ten miles wide – but that was scant comfort.

They could only sail on hopefully. Visibility was fairly good, and presently, from wave-tops, they could see land ahead. Which of the isles that might be they could not tell; but at least it might afford shelter of a sort, if not a haven possibly some cove or cranny on the leeward side of cliffs.

In mid-afternoon on their zigzag course, amidst the wind howling and the clap of sails and protesting creaking of timbers, they thought that they heard a deeper roaring ahead and half-left, which they assumed would be one of these roosts. They promptly veered well to the east to avoid it. Whether it was or not they did not learn, but their change of course did reveal that there was nearer land ahead, still further eastwards.

Lack of knowledge of the geography of the islands – and John understood that there were scores of them, great and small – was a major handicap. Kirkwall, their destination, was on the largest, and fairly centrally placed. This land ahead almost certainly could not be that on which Kirkwall was sited. Presumably it was the southernmost isle. So they might be still a day's sail, at least, from their destination. With darkness not far off, it would be dangerous to proceed, in island- and reef-strewn waters. They should make for the leeward side of this first island and try to find a sheltered anchorage, to lie up for the night.

Their near approach to land was not comforting, with the white of breakers and spray screening dark precipices and outlying skerries. But they could see that the coastline swung away sharply to the north not far to their right, eastwards, and in this wind that would be the sheltered side. So they steered in that direction and presently were into calmer waters, with cliff-girt land towering above them. This at least was a relief, even though the land looked inhospitable, to say the least.

After about three miles, however, a bay opened, with a light or two twinkling at the head of it. It was small and not deep, but they turned into it thankfully.

Coming to a stone jetty, where three fishing-craft were moored, larger than their Scottish ones – they would require to be, in these seas – they tied up alongside, and John and Dod went ashore. There seemed to be five low-browed cottages here, with drying nets nearby, also a group of men coming down to meet them, in the half-dark, showing enquiry but no obvious hostility.

John hailed them. "Friends, we come from Scotland, from Lothian. We seek the Lord Bishop of Orkney, William Tulloch. I am John, Lord of Douglasdale, this is my ship-master. We would shelter for the night."

The men, six of them, digested that, nodding. They conferred briefly. One spoke, with a strange accent, but clearly enough.

"You are welcome, lord. But the good bishop is not here. This is Windwick. On South Ronaldsay. He is on Pomona, at Kirkwall.

"Yes. We guessed that this was not the right island. We but seek a night's shelter, not to sail these waters in darkness. May we remain?"

"To be sure, lord. We will give you food. But we have no dwellings for lords. We are but fishers . . ."

"We seek no quarters. We will sleep on the ship, as we have done. And we will pay for what you give us, gladly."

112

All the Orkneymen declared that there was no need, that they had plenty. But John insisted.

They were as good as their word, bringing down cold mutton and fish, coarse oaten bread and honey, with jars of some strong, home-brewed ale. No women appeared.

Well pleased, the travellers spent a peaceful night.

In the morning more provisions appeared, and they were told how to get to Kirkwall. This island of South Ronaldsay was about seven miles long apparently, and there was a smaller isle immediately to the north called Burray. Beyond this, to the north, was a long south-stretching arm of the main island, Pomona. Keep on up the east side of this, avoiding the dangerous islet of Copinsay and the thrusting headland of Point of Ayre, to its northern tip, Mull Head. Then due west across a wide bay past another two headlands, beyond which was Kirkwall's own bay. This was repeated for them. A score of miles, no more.

They parted on excellent terms.

The wind this morning was still westerly, but less strong, and at first they were sheltered behind land. When eventually they rounded Mull Head however, they had to get out the long oars, going almost directly into the wind, strenuous work for seven miles. Once they had turned the final headland of Car Ness they could turn south, and raised sails again.

Kirkwall, at the head of its bay, proved to be quite a busy port, with a town set below rising ground, all its quays, warehouses and buildings of stone, no wood, indeed no trees anywhere to be seen. On landing, none asked their business, as they tied up at a vacant berth – clearly the inhabitants were used to much coming and going of shipping.

At least there was no problem as to where they should go now. Up on the high ground above the huddled town reared a magnificent redstone cathedral, quite the finest John had ever seen.

Up to this they climbed through narrow crooked lanes – they could hardly be called streets, so close-packed were the houses, no doubt as protection from these prevailing strong winds. There were many people, all seeming friendly enough.

113

The cathedral, which Mary had mentioned was renowned, and dedicated to St Magnus, of whom John knew nothing, was even more impressive near at hand, hugely towering yet strangely delicate in its lines, a master-builder's masterpiece. Close by, one on one side, one on the other, each across a cobbled street, were two castle-like buildings, one long and lofty, one longer and lower. That on the south side was entered by an arched gateway in a high wall. Over the gate was carved a heraldic shield, richly painted, with crossed pastoral staffs. This would surely be the bishop's palace.

Leaving his companions in the courtyard, John sought admission to the house, asking for Bishop Tulloch. He was told that the prelate was in his garden and orchard, of which he was fond, and was led out thereto, noting the first trees he had seen in Orkney.

He found a spare, grave-featured man of later middle years, clad in no fine episcopal garb but down on his knees, not worshipping but tending plants with a trowel — although perhaps there could be worship of a sort in that also. He looked a little annoyed at this interruption of his activities, remaining kneeling. But when, introducing himself, John declared that he had come from the Princess Mary, Countess of Arran, the other's expression changed and he stood up and offered a cordial enough welcome, asking heedfully after the princess's health and well-being, clearly her friend.

"She is well, and making the best of her marriage to the Lord Hamilton," John told him. "Less happy than she deserves to be, I judge — but she does not make complaint. A very noble lady. She seeks your help, my lord Bishop. Not for herself but for another. The Archbishop Patrick of St Andrews."

William Tulloch looked at him keenly and stroked his chin. "I had heard that the new archbishop had his enemies," he said carefully.

"He has indeed. All too many, shamefully. And highly placed."

"And have you come all this way to Orkney, my lord, to tell me that?"

"I am the bearer of a letter. From Her Highness. She has

114

given me sundry instructions." He produced a sealed paper from the pouch at his belt.

The bishop took it, unopened. "Perhaps we should go within," he said.

John followed the other into the long house, less than palatially furnished but warm with peat fires – he had been aware of the peat-reek ever since he had landed. He was conducted upstairs and into an untidy study, littered with papers and documents, where Tulloch tinkled a silver bell to summon a servant to bring refreshments, and sat down to read Mary's letter. John could not yet feel entirely optimistic over his mission.

Wine and oatcakes brought, John sipped and nibbled while he watched the other's strong features as he read. They revealed only gravity.

At length the bishop put the paper down. "This petition?" he asked, briefly.

John drew the so precious second paper out of his pouch and handed it over.

The other read it as carefully, scanning the signatures one by one. "Did any refuse to sign?" was his only comment.

"None. We had no time to travel further seeking more. That is, Abbot Henry of Cambuskenneth and myself. No doubt we could have gained others, but for the need for haste."

Tulloch nodded, and folded up letter and petition, and laid them on his table amongst all the other papers. "I will consider this," he said.

John took a deep breath. "Yes, my lord Bishop. But . . . you understand? This need for haste? Sheves's approach to the Pope, carried by a royal envoy with the King's signature, and with considerable moneys to support it, has been gone now for two weeks at least. Whatever is to be done, requires to be done quickly."

"I understand the situation, young man. I have said that I will consider. Now – I see that you have men out there. My servitors will attend to their comfort and take you to your chamber. I have the office of nones to take, over in the cathedral, my daily service. You may attend if you so wish." He rose.

115

John could do no other than accept this part-dismissal, part-invitation. Less than enheartened, he bowed, and moved over to the door, where he found the servant who had brought the provender waiting, more handsomely clad than was the bishop. He was shown to one of many rooms along a lengthy corridor on the same floor, where a steaming tub of hot water awaited him beside a bed, the chamber plainly but adequately furnished.

He was glad, at least, to attend to his ablutions in more thorough fashion than had been possible on shipboard. He was still unclothed, and washing comprehensively, when a pealing of bells from across the roadway indicated, he assumed, a summons to the service of nones. Hastily he dressed again. He felt that he had better go over, as invited, anxious to appease the prelate rather than the Deity. John was a God-fearing young man rather than a religious one, more concerned with personal worship than with dogma and forms of observance — even though his brother often said that he should have been a priest or a monk, Archie being Archie, presumably because of his concern with words, poetry, songs and the like. He had never attended a service of nones, nor indeed any of the monastic canonical hours, only the usual Sunday celebrations at the church in North Berwick or the very occasional special devotions in the little chapel in Tantallon Castle.

Now, on entering the cathedral, he decided that probably he would have been better to have stayed away, for the service had started, and he received some critical glances from the few worshippers in a side chapel in one of the vaulted aisles. However, he quickly forgot that in his awe and delight over what he saw, a sort of excitement born in him by the sheer beauty, sublime, of line and form and artistry of the great building in which he found himself, its soaring height yet perfect proportions, its serene and simple certainty, with nothing of fuss or over-decoration such as he had seen in some churches.

It is to be feared that John paid but little heed to the proceedings, which the bishop, now in full canonicals, was conducting in person, so lost was he in his own admirations.

116

This wonderful shrine certainly changed his opinion of the Norsemen, those Vikings whom he had been taught to look upon as cruel and savage warriors, if they could produce such an achievement as this.

Whether nones was always brief he did not know, but this service did not last long, and soon the more conventional worshippers were filing out, giving him odd looks in passing. He rose and went forward to examine the ranked pillars, the clerestoreys and the transepts of the cruciform building, staring upwards into the soaring central tower, trying to calculate the height of this, and to note that the choir and nave were vaulted but the transepts were not, when he found Bishop Tulloch at his side, minus his splendid vestments again.

"You inspect, my lord," the other asked, interest in his voice now. "You admire? Or otherwise?"

"I am *lost* in admiration! I had no notion that men, mere men, could raise such a noble pile as this. It is the finest building that I have ever seen. Its proportions are a, a hymn of praise in themselves!"

"Ha! So say I. It is good that you should so perceive it, my son." This was a different William Tulloch from the reserved and deliberate man revealed hitherto. "It is my joy."

"That I can understand. To be part of this . . . !"

"So! You see it, you feel it also. *Part!* That is the truth. Part, yes – part! You are a worshipper, then?"

John coughed. "I, I cannot claim to be that. I am no churchman, I fear. No heretic, but less religious than I ought to be, no doubt . . ."

His companion snapped episcopal fingers. "That is not what I meant. All that is often not true worship. But seeing God's hand and will and love in all things, and responding in your heart – that is worship. Being *part* of God's purpose and acknowledging it, however modest a portion as we may be. So much of the rest is mere custom, ritual, gesture."

A little embarrassed, John changed direction somewhat. "This great cathedral – how old is it? Who built it?"

"The Earl Rognvald built it, or had it built by one Kol, a master-mason, in memory of his sainted uncle, the Earl

117

Magnus. In 1137. Magnus was murdered by his own cousin Hakon. Come, I will show you his tomb. And that of Rognvald also. Beneath these massive piers . . ."

"Hakon? That was the King who invaded Scotland, lost the Battle of Largs, no?"

"No, no. That was a later Hakon, a century later. But another sinner and man of blood. The miscreant took up his quarters here, in this sacred place, with his warriors and minions, before going on conquest, going to his ravaging of the Hebrides and Highlands, before his defeat at Largs. That was in 1263. Then he came back, a broken man, to this cathedral, on his way to Norway again. And here he died. He was buried herein also, for a time, until his body was disinterred and taken back to his own country. God is not mocked, see you."

"I think that William Sheves should be brought here!"

The bishop shrugged. "He will face his Maker one day, wherever. As will we all."

John was shown other features of the great fane, to his wonder, before, bowing towards the high altar, they went out.

"That was good for me," he said. "I have felt that way watching a glorious sunset. Or looking up at the host of the stars. Or even at a tiny, perfect flower. But never in a church before." What made him confess to this to the older man he did not know.

"Yes. I can understand that also, my son. *I* will miss it all, myself. I think that nothing that I shall see or experience in Rome will outshine this."

It took a moment or two for John to realise the significance of what he had just heard. He drew a deep breath.

"You mean . . . ? You will go? To the Pope? You will do it?"

"Why, yes. I have considered it well. And prayed. It is my duty, as I see it. I shall go. Give me two days to put affairs here in order, and I will sail. My vessel is always readied, for I have to do much travelling around these islands and the Shetlands."

"This is good, good. The princess will be pleased, much heartened."

"How successful I may be with His Holiness, who knows? But I will do what I can, with God's help." He nodded. "Now, my friend, I have much to see to. Since the St Clair Earl of Orkney has been given the earldom of Caithness, and these islands have become a Church fief held direct of the crown and no longer Norse, I, as bishop, am responsible for all their governance. My absence will call for much arrangement, much deputation. That is why I had to consider well. I must instruct others meantime. But . . . you will dine with me this night, my lord. And tell me of this William Sheves and his doings, all that I should know . . ."

So the thing was done, mission accomplished. John would sail for home on the morrow, and face those daunting seas again. He wondered whether the bishop would encounter as chancy waters on all his voyage to Rome?

8

After a safe but slower journey back to Tantallon, for now the south-west winds were almost consistently against them, entailing continual tacking, John continued up-Forth to Airth, and on a-horse to Stirling. There he found all in commotion, ferment and noise, with much of the army still assembling there for the expedition against the Islesman Earl of Ross, and due to march any day. It seemed that he had returned a little too soon.

Mary had had her child, another boy, and all was well thereafter, it seemed. She was delighted with John and his news, of course, but had to express her feelings more discreetly than he might have wished, for Lord Hamilton was back from Arran and residing in her quarters in the castle. But even he was glad to hear of this endeavour to clip the wings of the man Sheves, and congratulated John on his efforts. Mary managed to convey her appreciation and gratitude in some degree, nevertheless.

Archie, it transpired, had gone with Albany to Dunbar Castle, on the south-eastern edge of Lothian, where the latter intended to make his base for the control of the Borders, not too far away from the vital centre of the land to be out of touch with national events. It was the seat of the earldom of March, or Merse, which was one of Albany's secondary titles. Archie, it seemed, had left instructions for John to come and join them at Dunbar. But Hamilton had other ideas and declared that the younger man's services would be much better employed on the northern expedition. He appeared to consider John a born leader of scouts, ridiculous as this seemed, and was being backed up by the Hepburn chief, Lord Hailes. And to emphasise this conviction, mistaken as it might be, these two had gone to the King and persuaded him to make a royal command of it. So, willy-nilly, the reluctant warrior was to be part of this Highland venture. Perhaps he should have lingered on in Orkney for a while?

He had no Douglas men-at-arms to form a cohort this time, of course; but Hamilton and Hailes between them said that they would provide four score seasoned horsemen for him. So there was no way out. Mary was concerned for him, but could not in this case change matters.

According to Hamilton, disgustedly, the chaos and commotion in and around Stirling was duplicated in the castle itself, as far as the expedition was concerned, muddle prevailing. King James was wholly inexperienced in military affairs, and in such Sheves could not competently advise him – although some even suggested that it might have been better if he could, for the man, whatever else, was efficient. The leadership situation typified the confusion. At first, the Earls of Atholl and Crawford were to be in command. Then two other earls, Argyll and Huntly, made claim to lead, and with some reason. Since the rebellious Earl of Ross was also Lord of the Isles and apt to make his headquarters in the Hebrides, however much mainland raiding he did, clearly shipping was going to be important in any attempt to subdue him – and the Campbell chief, the Earl of Argyll, was the only one who could provide a galley fleet of sufficient numbers to be in any way effective. But as Earl of Ross, John of the Isles' principal stronghold was at Dingwall, on the eastern side of the land; and here the Earl of Huntly, chief of the Gordons, could field the greatest force, with the Earl of Buchan next in strength. So with five earls vying for command, strategic planning was difficult, to say the least. Probably Albany should have been recalled to take charge, however rash a general he made, but James would not hear of it, jealousy and Sheves's spleen forbidding it.

John, for one, doubted whether, in the circumstances, this northern venture could ever be successful. Sorry the realm with a weak King.

In the end it was decided that there should be three distinct thrusts: the main force under Atholl and Crawford up by

121

land into the Highland west; the sea approach under Argyll; and an eastern assault under Huntly and Buchan. All three might well have to link up eventually. Just to complicate matters, however, it was arranged that, to spare them the slow and weary march north by land with the army, Atholl and Crawford should go as far as The Oban, in Lorn, in one of Argyll's galleys, sailing from Dumbarton.

John was thankful, in all this, that his instructions as leader of scouts were to go on ahead of the main force.

There was fretting and fuming at delays, especially by Argyll and Huntly, the one because every week now in late autumn could worsen the weather for his galley fleet; the other, used to mountain conditions, warning that the passes could soon be closed by snow. But the full complement of troops was slow in assembling.

At length it was agreed to wait no longer. Any further contingents must follow on. November was upon them. John, with almost one hundred mixed Hamiltons and Hepburns, was the first to move off, one day ahead of the rest, this unlikely soldier spearheading the advance.

Presently, he began quite to enjoy this part of the proceedings. He saw that he would have to keep the peace between the Hamiltons and the Hepburns, who had little in common; but Hamilton of Innerwick was a Lothian laird, and seemed to get on well enough with Hepburn of Beanston, almost a neighbour; and these two should be able to control their respective westland and eastland parties. Either of them would have served well enough to lead the scouting group instead of himself, John recognised – but he was a lord, and such rank appeared to be the deciding factor.

The weather was kind, crisp, with morning frost and only a thin haze of cloud. There was no question as to route, for they had to go where a large army would be able to follow, even though by not the shortest road, through mountainous country that was apt to be less than straightforward since it meant using more settled land and populous glens where provisions and forage could be obtained. John's English experiences helped in this, to be sure.

So they rode by the Teith valley north-westwards past Doune and Callander, and into the mountains by the Pass of Leny and Strathyre. There was no need, at this stage, for any great haste, for they would move much more quickly than would the main force behind, and they must not get too far ahead. They need hardly look for any enemy presence for a long way yet, indeed probably until they were out of the Campbell country of Lorn itself – although John MacDonald of the Isles, when he heard of this challenge, might well descend on the territory of his hereditary enemies the Campbells in a pre-emptive strike. John saw his duties meantime as mainly to seek out camping places where there was water and food to be purchased and hay for the many horses; also, perhaps, to warn the local inhabitants of what was approaching so that they might hide their poultry and womenfolk from predatory fighting men.

That first night they halted at Balquhidder, some thirty miles from Stirling, where there was ample space for the host, and the MacGregor and MacLaren clansfolk would sell provisions. Then on next day to the head of Loch Earn and up Glen Ogle to Glen Dochart, and so westwards to Crianlarich in the mouth of Strathfillan, MacNab country. There John sought out the former house of the Dewar of the Coigreach, the ancient Celtic Church's keeper of St Fillan's relics, who had conferred the blessing of that Church on Robert Bruce at one of the lowest tides in the hero-king's career when he had been excommunicated by the Pope in Rome and had just suffered his first major defeat at the Battle of Methven. This gesture had much enheartened the newly crowned but unhappy monarch. At the head of Strathfillan, at Tyndrum, they passed the second night, another thirty miles on. John reckoned that this was as far as the mounted army behind could expect to cover each day.

Now there was different, wilder country to traverse, the land of Mamlorn of Breadalbane, literally the high pass into Lorn over the central spine of Alba, the ancient Pictish name for this Scotland. Here they had to climb from the fork of glens at Tyndrum and up over a lofty gap beneath Ben Lui, to enter the long and distinctly downward-sloping bare valley of Glen Lochy, for the foot of great Loch Awe, mile after mile, passing the incoming Glen Orchy. This would be no territory for the army to linger in, so they pressed on along the loch, one of the longest freshwater lakes in Scotland, below the mighty mountain of Cruachan, in Campbell country now. They threaded the daunting Pass of Brander, a deep trough cut by the River Awe, where Bruce had at length turned the tables on his Comyn-linked enemy Lame John of Lorn in a notable battle, the beginning of his long haul to eventual victory and freedom triumphant. At Taynuilt, on the shore of the sea loch beyond, they passed the third night, John setting sentries now, for they could look for an enemy presence any time hereafter. They were only about a dozen miles from The Oban, his destination.

John was here much intrigued. This was like being in another land altogether, this Hebridean seaboard, a land which was indeed less land than water – although what land there was was impressive enough, and beautiful, great mountains of heather and rock, sloping woodlands of scrub-oak and birch and alder, green islands everywhere, with headlands and peninsulas, skerries and reefs decked with multicoloured seaweeds so different from the dark green Norse Sea variety. But it was the water itself which most impressed John, so translucent, reflecting the skies above and the seabed below, in every shade of blue and green from palest amethyst over white cockle-shell sand to deepest azure. Here, he felt, despite its bloody story of feud and war, was the Creator's painted masterpiece.

The Oban, next morning, he found to be a crescent-shaped port at the head of a great bay, this latter sheltered, all but landlocked, by the island of Kerrera, less than a mile out. Beyond was the glittering Firth of Lorn, backed by the blue mountains of the Isle of Mull, by Morvern, and the fair and fertile Lismore of St Moluag, Columba's disciple, the name meaning the Great Garden. John loved his own Lothian and the Borders, but found all this a joy to behold.

He knew about that sheltering isle of Kerrera, at least, for it was there that Alexander the Second had died, two centuries before, leading an expedition to repel Viking invaders of the Hebrides, and left a seven-year-old child as heir. Alexander the Third, he whose death without male heir precipitated the Wars of Independence, Wallace, Bruce and all. Kerrera, small island as it was, like similarly sized Iona, had played a large part in Scotland's story.

The Oban, the name meaning merely the sheltered and peaceful bay, lived up to its style that morning, revealing no hint of strife, war or armed threat, John's own troop representing the only martial sign. So far no ships had arrived from Dumbarton or elsewhere; and of any MacDonald threat there was no hint. John and his men camped at a beach a little way north of the township, to wait, uncertain what to do next.

The galley fleet began to appear that afternoon, in single and small and larger groups of ships, their sails mainly painted with the Galley of Lorn device. All these came to anchor in the bay, and soon that township and vicinity was alive with men, in kilts and plaids, armed to the teeth, no doubt to the alarm of the inhabitants. These, questioned, proved to have come from Campbell, Lamont, MacAulay and MacMillan lands all over Argyll and Cowal and Bute, in answer to their earl's call. They were not the leadership vessels from Dumbarton.

There was much roystering at The Oban that night, some of it developing into fisticuffs and minor clan fights, John determinedly keeping his people out of it, to some small resentment.

Fortunately, Argyll and the other leaders appeared next morning in half a dozen ships, and took up their residence on Kerrera itself, where John got a fisherman to row him. He found rivalry and altercation going on here also, of a different sort but sufficiently vehement, mainly and inevitably concerned with who was in supreme command, and priorities as to procedure. Atholl, as the King's uncle, considered himself to be the obvious choice, although Crawford, with more distant royal connections but at least legitimate, thought otherwise. And Argyll himself, of course, in his own Campbell country

125

and master of the shipping, saw the situation very differently. Hamilton, Hailes and most of the other lords were with the main army, due to arrive at any time.

Questioned as to enemy activity or presence, John said that he had seen none nor heard of any – and found himself all but criticised for this, Atholl indicating that he ought to have been out scouting the glens ahead to north and east. This was enough for Crawford to declare that a waste of time and energy meantime until the main force came up and they could decide on lines of advance. Argyll pointed out succinctly that any advance northwards from here would have to contend with lengthy sea lochs probing deep into the mountains, and the area would best be explored by scouting galleys; moreover John of the Isles was unlikely to waste *his* time and energies on marching men round all these lochs and over those mountains but, if he was going to attack, do so by sea in galleys.

So the disagreement went, and John was rowed back to his men a little depressed.

Next day the army made its appearance, weary but in good heart. John accompanied the other lords back to Kerrera, where a council of war followed. In the interim, Argyll had sent out ships to north and west, and these had reported no sign of enemy war vessels in neighbouring waters.

The council did at least reach some sensible conclusions. If the enemy was not seeking to challenge them, that was a good sign. They must do the challenging, therefore. They could not be sure where John of the Isles was, of course, which complicated matters. He might be in his Easter Ross domains, or up in wild Wester Ross. He might be in mainland Lochaber, Morvern, Moidart or Glengarry. Or in his island strongholds on Islay, Mull, Eigg, Rhum or Skye. The man controlled all the north. If he did not advance against them when he heard that they were here, all that they could do was to make sallies against his various territories within reach, with fire and sword, and hope to provoke a reaction in which they could come to grips with him. If he was far away in the east, then Huntly and Buchan would have to deal with him; but at least their own efforts ought to reinforce the message and teach him a lesson.

Thus the broad strategy. More detailed tactics called for local knowledge, and sundry Campbell chieftains were summoned. Their information led to plans being made, tentative as these might be, must be. Argyll would take most of the galley fleet, with many extra men, and make for the large island of Islay, the most southerly of the major isles, on which the MacDonald judgment-seat of Finlaggan was sited. A devastation of Islay ought to be a telling blow. But he would seek to keep in touch the while with the mainland forces, and the residue of the galleys, in case hostilities developed elsewhere. This was accepted by all as valid.

The land-based situation was much less clear, thousands of men mustered and waiting, and no very certain views as to what to do with them. The nearest MacDonald mainland territory was at Glen Coe, none so far away as the crows flew but across high mountains, difficult to reach from The Oban. Further north was the Keppoch area of Lochaber, but that involved the negotiating of many sea lochs. Other MacDonald lands such as Moidart, Garmoran, Morar, Knoydart and Glengarry were further north still, and best reached by water. It seemed to John that Argyll had been right all along, and that dealing with John of the Isles, Earl of Ross, and his son Angus Og, called for ships and a seaborne force, not any horsed host.

This of the son, Angus Og, produced discussion. Illegitimate, but with no lawful brothers, he was forceful and aggressive apparently, ambitious and a born rebel, and known to be at odds with his father frequently. He it was, in fact, who had taken by force the royal castles of Inverness, Urquhart and Ruthven. It was now suggested that, if a wedge could be driven between father and son, then their task might be much aided. Various proposals were put forward as to how this might be done, the most ambitious being that if Angus could be persuaded to claim the lordship of the Isles, as distinct from the earldom of Ross, and claim it now, this might tempt him to rebel against his sire, with his lust for power, and so greatly weaken the latter. Only the King could offer to authorise this division, of course; but the suggestion could be made to Angus to see how it might appeal. How this might be achieved was another matter. None knew where to look for Angus Og, any more than for his father.

Into this discussion John Douglas raised his voice. Only one of the MacDonald chiefs would be likely to know where the earl and his son were, he said – if such could be persuaded to tell. The nearest, it seemed, was at Glen Coe. If MacDonald of Glencoe could be approached and not exactly threatened but given to understand that there was an important message for this Angus Og, to be delivered on behalf of the King, then he might give them the information they required – especially if this spared him and his from attack by this King's army.

This suggestion was hailed by all as excellent, even by Argyll. He said that Hugh MacDonald of Glencoe was probably the least powerful of the Clan Donald chieftains, unable to raise more than a couple of hundred broadswords, and so would be reluctant to confront any larger force. He, Argyll, proposed that the Lord of Douglasdale should forthwith lead a party of perhaps three hundred to Glen Coe. If that chieftain gave him the information required, then to go on to wherever Angus Og was to be found, and make the proposal to him, as it were coming from the King. He thought that there would be no difficulty in getting James to approve of it all.

John was somewhat taken aback by this so personal an application of his suggestion, and protested who was he to act as envoy to the MacDonalds – but had it pointed out to him that he was a Lord of Parliament and a brother to the Earl of Angus, Warden of the East March of the Borders. Undoubtedly he was suitable enough for the part. No refusal was to be considered.

It was decided, therefore, that while Argyll took his fleet off to Islay, the other two earls should lead the main army northwards round all the lochs to Lochaber, to lay waste and challenge Keppoch. John should be given an extra hundred men and a Campbell chieftain to guide him through the mountains to Glen Coe. The council broke up in more agreement than had seemed likely at the outset.

John, with little more in the way of instructions and guidance, was rowed back to The Oban with a dark-avised young man, Dugald Campbell of Dunstaffnage, who had orders to detach one hundred miscellaneous Campbells, Lamonts, Buchanans and MacAulays to add to his nearly two hundred Hamiltons and Hepburns, to make up the Glen Coe party. They would set off first thing in the morning, their appointed leader doubtful in the extreme as to his capabilities for this mission which he had so rashly suggested.

It was not long after sun-up, and the three hundred on their way, before John discovered what Argyll had meant as to the difficulties of negotiating sea lochs. A mere four miles north of The Oban, and having Dunstaffnage Castle pointed out to him by its captain, Dugald Campbell, where the fabled Stone of Destiny had been hidden for a period, they came to the mouth of Loch Etive, down which of course John had ridden on his way here. This mouth, at Connel, was only a quarter-mile in width, but it represented a major problem nevertheless, thus early. There were two ferry-boats admittedly, but these were small, and scarcely suitable for transporting three hundred horses. Added to this was the hazard of the crossing itself, for here were the dangerous Falls of Lora. These resembled, to some extent, the roosts of the Orkney seas, overfalls in the loch's waters which were quite dramatic and which at certain stages of the tides could be highly dangerous for craft. Presumably these were caused by underwater cliffs. The ferrymen treated them with great respect. They declared that while they could possibly get some of the horses and men across, nothing like half would be over before the tide turned to menacing, and they would have to wait for hours to complete the crossing. This of course had John in a quandary, and demanding whether they could not instead ride round the head of the loch? Dugald Campbell pointed out that it was a long loch, fully eighteen miles – although admittedly it did turn, halfway, northwards in the direction of Glen Coe; but

129

there was only the roughest of roads for much of the way and mere deer-tracks thereafter. So John had to make a decision. To hang about here was hardly to be considered – and the Douglases had a reputation for rough riding, like so many Border families; they could not let difficult conditions deter them, he decided. The Campbell shrugged, but did not make protest. John did wonder what Atholl and Crawford would do with the main army, when they reached these Falls of Lora.

So it was eastwards now, back along the winding shores of Etive which they had followed westwards, from Loch Awe and the Pass of Brander those days before. For the first ten miles it was not difficult, that is as far as Taynuilt, where the short River Awe came in to join Etive. But after that, with the long loch bending away northwards into empty, fierce country, with the mountainsides coming down steeply to the water's edge, cut by deep glens with rushing torrents, it was a deal less easy, the horsemen having to string out along the roughest of tracks. However, there was the occasional house even here, with a small laird's establishment at Inverliever seven miles on, and the track did continue, after its fashion. But beyond Glen Kinglass, quite a sizeable valley with a foaming river to ford, the prospect became challenging indeed, with practically no level ground along the loch shore and the hillsides abrupt, often sheer, rocky and broken, bad for horses' hooves. Such tracks as there were twisted and turned, rose and plunged, sometimes amongst slippery seaweed, sometimes hundreds of feet above the water. But they did see half-wild cattle now and again, so all the tracks were not those of deer, and men must come here on occasion, even though probably not on horseback. Dugald Campbell admitted that he had never actually ridden here, but had sailed in a boat as far as the head of the loch, landing only here and there.

Frequently now the riders had to dismount, to lead their beasts over dangerous stretches, and their rate of progress dropped drastically. There was much muttering and cursing from the men. But, according to Campbell, there was only another five or six miles of it to the loch-head, where conditions changed, and a road of sorts came in from the north, down wide Glen Etive, from the mouth of Glen Coe.

It took them all that day to cover the score of miles, dusk finding them at Kinlochetive, with a green vale opening before them, this seeming like a garden after what they had traversed. Vast and spectacular mountains still rose left and right, but back somewhat now, Ben Starav to the east and mighty rugged giants to north and west, which Campbell said were Glen Coe's serried peaks – for the head of that glen was only some eight miles ahead. But even so it was no country to ride in darkness, especially as, their guide said, MacDonald's house was down near the foot of the ten-mile glen, and they could cut a useful corner by traversing a high pass on their left, called the Lairig Eilde, the pass of the roe-deer, saving fully a dozen miles' riding. So, tired, they camped on riverside meadows near a little community of cattle-herders' huts. At least there had been no casualties amongst their mounts. MacDonald land as this was, John decided that he need set no sentries here.

They passed a chilly night.

In the morning there was a powdering of snow on the high tops surrounding them, something of an ominous sign. But cold as it was, the sun shone, and with its light and shadow threw into dramatic relief a scene of extraordinary splendour, grandeur, these mountains more fiercely challenging than any John had ever seen. He felt an urge to climb at least one of them – but this was no occasion for such foolish notions.

Five miles further up the cattle-dotted glen was another little community, Dalness; and soon thereafter Campbell pointed out a gap in the mountain wall to their left. This he said was the mouth of the Lairig Eilde. And uninviting as it appeared, a well-defined track certainly led up into it. Since the place looked like merely a steep corrie cleaving the peaks, and rising to a great height obviously, John wondered what was the point of the track, to be told that this was in fact a drove-road for cattle. Still bemused, he asked who would want to drive cattle down this, into the wilderness, to be informed that the beasts were not driven down it but up it, and that the cattle they had been passing yesterday, and from other

131

high grazings over a vast area of more or less empty land to south and east, were herded this way northwards into Glen Coe and so to Loch Leven-side, to centres in Lochaber, from whence they were passed on across the spine of the land, Mamore, eastwards to the great trysts and markets at Perth, Crieff and even Falkirk. When John wondered at the extraordinary distances these herds were made to travel, it was emphasised by the Highlander that cattle were in fact the life's-blood of the Highlands, and since winter feed was always in short supply in these uplands, large numbers of beasts had to be disposed of before every winter set in, and distance to markets just had to be covered. Droving was an important and quite skilled occupation, and the drovers' services vital for the Highland way of life. The herds did not cover many miles in a day, to keep them in good condition, and the routes, these drove-roads, selected carefully to provide adequate grazings. A drove could be a month or more on the hoof, and the beasts, hardy as they had to be, reared as they were, usually arrived in good enough shape for the merchants. October and November was the droving season, so they might well see some of the herds on this journey.

When they started up the Lairig Eilde, although they did not come across any droves, they did see much dried cattle dung on the quite wide track, indicating that herds had passed not so long before. This heartened the horsemen, facing that fierce-looking climb. If cattle-beasts could surmount it, they could.

There were four miles of the pass, and it rose up and up to a great height, none able to estimate how high, but sufficient for the travellers to gain tremendous views to south and west over far-flung land to the distant isle-dotted sea, with all the seemingly endless mountains of Lorn, Argyll and Cowal. Ahead were only jagged savage peaks.

When they reached the *bealach* or lofty head of the pass, the vista became different indeed, enclosed now, high as this was, with only fierce towering giants and serrated rocky ridges hemming in the narrow deep and broken valley immediately below, as enclosed a declivity as it was possible to imagine.

If this was where a sept of MacDonald clung, its members must be tough indeed. Dugald Campbell mentioned the names of some of the most dramatic summits, but these meant little to John, however affected he was by their dominance, almost threat.

Down the cleft of the glen itself they had to cross a rushing, foaming River Coe, at a bend where there was a shallowing formed by an underwater causeway of stones, for the cattle-droves. Then they turned down westwards, to follow the river. Seven miles or so, Campbell said, was MacIan's house, near the mouth of the glen. When John asked who was MacIan, he was told that this was MacDonald of Glencoe's especial style, to distinguish him from all the other MacDonald chieftains.

Three miles down that barren, shut-in valley they came to a slight widening wherein was a small loch. There were some stunted trees and bushes now, and shaggy, long-horned cattle grazing, little pasture as there seemed to be. Low-browed, reed-thatched cot-houses now began to appear. And where, at length, the blue waters of a wider loch began to show, the sea-loch of Leven, a long, low hallhouse stood on a mound above a cluster of shacks, huts and barns, destination reached.

Clearly their approach had not gone unnoticed, for quite a crowd of wild-looking Highlandmen stood awaiting them below the hallhouse, wary but less than welcoming, arms much in evidence. But three hundred horsemen were not to be challenged lightly, even in Glen Coe, however much of a threat they represented, and no swords were actually drawn.

A stout and thick-set elderly man, grey-bearded and high-coloured, stood in front of the throng, his bonnet distinguished by two eagle's feathers. Him Campbell of Dunstaffnage addressed in the Gaelic language, in a strange mixture of respect and defiance, gesturing towards John. He spoke at some length, the other silent.

There was a pause when the Campbell ended. John broke it. "I have not the Erse tongue," he said. "I am John, Lord of Douglasdale, brother to the Earl of Angus. Do you speak *my* tongue, sir?"

"Yes, then – I do. Och, yes. Glad I am to hear that you

are no Campbell, whatever!" That was said in a softly sibilant voice, almost musical, odd to come from so formidable-looking a character. "You do not keep the best of company, lord! I am MacIan."

John cleared his throat. "I come in King James's name, MacIan. As indeed does Dunstaffnage here. We bring you greetings."

"Is that so, then? And all these, whatever?" A wave of the hand at the ranked mounted men. "They also are after bringing greetings to MacIan?"

"They act my escort. For our further journeying."

"Och then, you are to be greeting more than MacIan?"

"That is so. And seek your guidance, sir."

"Indeed and indeed! And how am I to be guiding one of the King's Southron lords, where the Campbell can not?"

John shook his head. "It would be better, I think, if we were to speak more privately, my friend."

"As you will, young lord. But you only, whatever. I will have no Campbell to enter my house, at all!"

"M'mm." A glance and shrug at Dunstaffnage. "Very well. But all here are not Campbells. Here are Hamilton of Innerwick and Hepburn of Beanston, Lothian lairds."

"Then these may cross my threshold, if you require attendants."

Nodding, John and the other two dismounted, leaving a tight-lipped Campbell in charge of the party. The ranks of the MacDonald clansmen parted to allow the trio to follow their chieftain, who had turned and was stalking back to his house, broad back scarcely friendly.

Nevertheless, on entering the building, MacIan was shouting, in his own lilting tongue, commanding women, who came hurrying with flagons of what proved to be a very potent whisky and platters of oaten scones. The visitors were led into a large, high-raftered hall, the walls draped with tartan hangings, the floor strewn with deerskins, great fireplaces burning logs at either end. Taking up his stance before one of these, their host hoisted his kilt to warm his backside, rounding on them and waving a filled goblet in their direction.

"You will be from The Oban, then?" he declared. "Sent by the man who names himself Argyll? Hoping that you can be finding some way to prevent Clan Donald from driving you all into the sea?" That sounded interested, rather than aggressive.

Blinking at this, and wondering at the other's sources of information, John shook his head. "The Earl of Argyll is gone to Islay with his galleys," he amended. "I come from the commander of the royal host, the Earl of Atholl, His Grace's uncle. With the King's message."

"And what would one of the King's bastard kin want with MacIan, at all? Drink, lord – drink up!"

"Guidance, as I said, sir. We desire that you should tell us how to reach Angus MacDonald, the Earl of Ross's son. *Bastard*, son," he rather emphasised. "We think that you may know this."

"Hech, hech – is that it! You seek Angus Og. For why, at all?"

"For the good of all. Your good. Mine. The good of the realm. Of Clan Donald most of all."

"Clan Donald can be seeing to its own good, young lord! We need no Southrons telling us, whatever."

"I think that you do, MacIan. Or many of Clan Donald will die. Much of your lands be wasted. Sorrow in the glens and hills. Which all could be avoided. And should be."

"Och so? You do not want to fight then, at all? You have not the belly for it, no?"

"If fight we must, we will. And *win*, see you! For we can. But the better way is . . . otherwise. After all, we are all fellow-subjects of the King's Grace."

"And the better way?"

"That is what I have to put to Angus Og. We think that you will know where to find him, MacIan."

The chieftain went to a table, to refill his goblet – and seemed surprised that his guests were not similarly needful.

"What want you with Angus Og?" he asked.

"My message is for him alone, sir. Do you indeed know where he is to be found?"

"I know, yes. But I will not be after telling you without you tell *me* what you will be wanting with himself."

"I think that we could *make* you tell!" Hamilton of Innerwick put in tersely. And the Hepburn growled agreement.

John waved a hand at them. "Tell me this then, MacIan. All know that Angus Og and his father are at odds. They see matters differently, to the hurt of Clan Donald. They favour opposing policies, shall we say. Which of them do *you* favour?"

The other stared at him. "Are you thinking that I will answer that, Southron?"

"I think that you should. For your own sake, but also for the clan's." He took a chance. "And for Angus Og's."

Silence.

"The message I have for Angus is important. Very important. How good a Lord of the Isles, think you, would Angus make?"

"Good, yes. He is a fighter, whatever."

"Better than his father?"

Silence again.

"It is not only fighting which counts. Has Angus a head on him? Can he think what is best for all the Isles? A great heritage and responsibility. Could he *rule* the Isles well?"

"Well, yes."

"Better than the father, the Earl of Ross?" John persisted.

Again there was no answer.

Satisfied, the younger man nodded. "So be it. What I go to see Angus for is to offer him, in the name of the King, the lordship of the Isles. Now. To separate it from the earldom of Ross, by royal decree. If he will halt this raiding and ravishment of the lands of others, keep the King's peace. Rule the isles independently of his father, who has all Ross and the northern mainland. Angus to be Lord of the Isles. As was another Angus Og, in the Bruce's time."

The other drew a deep breath.

"Now, will you tell me where I may find him, MacIan?"

"This is the truth, whatever?"

"On my honour, yes. I am sent by the Earls of Atholl,

Crawford and Argyll, in the King's name, to offer it. If Angus agrees, the King's forces will withdraw to the south again. Leave you in peace."

"So-o-o! Yes, then, I will tell you, lord. Angus Og is in Ruthven Castle, in Badenoch. He will be there for the winter."

John let out a long sigh. "I thank you. That is . . . well. You serve the Clan Donald well, MacIan, in this. I must now go to this Badenoch."

"It is a long road, see you."

"No doubt. But it is my mission. You could, I hope, tell me of the best routes?"

"I could be doing better than that. I will be giving you a guide, to be leading you. You will, I think, be needing him, indeed and indeed!"

That sounded distinctly ominous. "Then, I thank you further, sir . . ."

So, after no lengthy delay, they set off again, now with a young man of about John's own age, personable, cheerful and seeming not in the least daunted by the duty thrust upon him nor the company he had to keep, however much he looked askance at Dugald Campbell of Dunstaffnage. He was, it seemed, Alastair MacDonald, a younger son of MacIan himself, mounted on a shaggy garron.

They rode down to the shore of Loch Leven, John interested that there should be another loch of that name to the one he knew near Kinross in Fothrif, where there was a Douglas castle. Alastair MacDonald explained to him that the name, like so many another – Avon, A'an, Almond, even Devon and Deveron – all derived from the Gaelic *abhainn*, meaning merely running water, river. Here they turned westwards for the head of the loch, seven miles to Kinlochleven. Across on the other side was the great territory known as Lochaber, they learned.

Staring this way and that, John asked how long was it, this sea-loch; and was told thirteen miles from mouth to head. So, he wondered, if Atholl and Crawford were to invade Lochaber,

137

as planned, they would have to come here, all this way, round this Loch Leven? As well as get past Loch Etive?

"And Loch Creran between the two, ten miles," Dunstaffnage put in grimly.

Shaken, the Lowlanders considered the problems of campaigning in the western Highlands.

They halted for the night at Kinlochleven, where they were scarcely welcome but accepted on account of MacIan's son. Ahead of them was the great central mountain watershed of Mamore, part of the main spine of the Highlands, a vast empty tract of heather, peat, rock and scree; but at least there would be no more sea lochs to negotiate.

In the morning, they began their climbing almost at once, into a daunting prospect of steeply uptilted land, west by north. Due west and south the territory looked somewhat easier, but Alastair said that there lay illusion, and danger, for that way spread the impassable extensive Moor of Rannoch, endless waterlogged desert and swamp. Hereafter they would climb by many twisting valleys through the hills, making for Loch Treig, a great water, passing many lesser ones, and from there over to Glen Spean, a major strath leading northwards, which would bring them up to Laggan, in Badenoch and so to the Spey, halfway across Highland Scotland. If the Southrons were fit for it, and their spindle-shanked horses, they might do it in three days – this declared conversationally, affably.

That, then, was their route and programme. How many rough miles altogether they had no idea, for miles in such wild, up-and-down, twisting and trackless wilderness meant little. Sometimes they were in deep, dark chasms, sometimes up at snow levels, sometimes circling lochs and great bogs, sometimes seeking fords over torrents.

The first night they passed uncomfortably camped at the head of Loch Treig; the second, rather better, at the foot of Loch Laggan in Glen Spean; the third, after easier going down Strathmashie, near to Cluny, with the wide strath of Spey beginning to open before them, backed by the mighty blue mountains which formed a distinct barrier to the east, and which Alastair called the Monadh Ruadh, or Red Mountains.

In the morning they rode down to the River Spey and turned northwards into a comparatively populous land after what they had travelled, Macpherson country apparently, with their MacDonald careful now to shout out *his* identity at every township and community they passed. Even so, the company was left in no doubt as to danger and vulnerability. But the name of MacDonald clearly carried enough weight, especially when that of Angus Og was added to it.

This Strathspey, wide and level as it was although flanked by such lofty ranges, was much flooded, even though the foothill slopes were so populated. And quite soon after passing the quite large township of Banchormore, they began to see, rising out of the waterlogged levels, a prominent mound topped by the towers and high walling of what appeared to be a fortress of sorts, the first that they had seen on their journey. Ruthven Castle, they were informed.

Long before they reached this they were challenged, and in no minor way. A large band of armed men came at a strange loping run towards them, in ranks around a single mounted man clad in half-armour part covered in plaiding, a fierce-seeming individual this with long down-turning moustaches. Alastair MacDonald was urgent to cry that he was son to MacIan of Glencoe, bringing notable messengers to see Angus Og of Islay.

This seemed to be approximately acceptable to the horseman, who reined round and left his aggressive-looking company, to ride back to the castle.

The visitors waited, watchful.

When this individual returned, after some considerable interval, he brought a group of others with him, all dismounted now, most of these tending to wear eagle's feathers in their bonnets. One, sporting three, a tall, hot-eyed and saturnine-featured young man, addressed the travellers.

"Who claims to come to Badenoch, uninvited, in King James's name, to Angus of the Isles?" he demanded.

"I do – John Douglas, Lord of Douglasdale. Come at some cost and labour, sir. To your advantage – if you are Angus Og."

139

The other barked a scornful laugh. "What advantage could I gain from the feeble youth James Stewart?"

"Not a little, I think. But . . . I would prefer to tell you what more privately. I judge that you would have it so, also!"

"You would? And did you require all these men to bring me this word?"

"I have covered half of Scotland to bring it, the unruly half as you will know! If the King's peace was kept better in these Highlands, I would not have required so many!"

"Ha! And you think to be after blaming *me* for that, lordling?"

"I blame whoever claims to be master in these parts." John said that levelly. "Can I now speak with you privily, Angus, Master of Ross?"

"I do not name myself that, whatever!" the other jerked. "I am Angus of the Isles. But come you, then. Leave your men here."

"The lairdly ones come with me, Angus Og."

"One is a Campbell!" Alastair MacDonald announced, grinning. "Dunstaffnage. I am MacIan of Glencoe's son."

"Any Campbell is fortunate to be in your protection, Douglas. But he comes no further."

John glanced at Dunstaffnage and shrugged. With Hamilton, Hepburn and the MacDonald he dismounted, to leave their party and walk behind the Ruthven group towards the castle, each party keeping very much to themselves.

The fortress was much larger than most Highland castles, as befitted a royal stronghold, completely covering the flat top of its steep, regular mound which was obviously man-made, this rising out of the wetlands which formed an effective moat, across which was the only access, an easily defended, narrow causeway – a place of strength indeed. Yet Angus had captured it, presumably without cannon. No signs of damage were evident about the high walling.

"Who was captain here?" John asked Alastair.

"This is Macpherson country. It would be Cluny, just."

"Then Cluny Macpherson is either a weakling or played false!"

They were led across the causeway, and up the abrupt climb by a long series of steps, to the courtyard gateway, and within. At the guardhouse, Angus turned and, waving away the others, gestured John inside.

"Your word for me, Douglas?" he demanded shortly.

"If you are Angus of the Isles, I am Douglasdale, a lord of parliament." That was said as shortly. "But, then . . . you are *not* indeed Angus of the Isles, are you! Only son to the Lord of the Isles and Earl of Ross. And illegitimate, no? Scarce even Master of Ross!"

The other's hot eyes flared and his fists clenched. "Watch how you speak to me, Douglas!"

"I say the same, MacDonald! But . . . you have more to gain than I have by keeping a civil tongue. And I have come many miles to tell you so."

"I wait."

"Hear me, then. This is the message of the commanders of the King's host, and in the royal name. Your father, the Earl of Ross, is in rebellion against His Grace, and must pay for that rebellion. Moreover, he is in a private treaty with King Edward of England. This is known — and is high treason. You also are in rebellion, and have taken the royal castles of Inverness, Urquhart and this Ruthven. But, we judge, in your father's name." That might not be strictly true, but it served John's purpose to put it so.

Angus waited, tight-lipped.

"His Grace and his councillors, for the sake of the realm, and of Clan Donald itself, for peace, make offer to you, Angus Og. You are known not always to agree with your father. Perhaps in this of treason with England? So the King makes you generous offer. Come you into the King's peace, return these royal castles to His Grace's officers, and he will separate by royal decree the Lordship of the Isles from the earldom of Ross. Your father will still be Earl of Ross, yes, and have to repent of his deeds. But *you* will be Lord of the Isles. Angus of the Isles, indeed!"

His companion drew a long, quivering breath, but for the moment found no words.

"It is a fair offer, is it not? You have the isles and the Hebridean seaboard – your ancient heritage. He keeps the mainland earldom, enough for any man. If keep it he can! You Lord of the Isles, with your own seat in parliament. Somerled's successor. How say you?"

"This . . . this is truth? No deception? No cunning falsehood to ensnare me?"

"I have not come all this long road to tell false tales. It is a true offer. You have my Douglas word."

Angus took a turn or two back and forth in the limited space of the guardroom. "Why this? The reason?"

"I told you. Your peace, and the well-being of the realm. Your father has proved no worthy ruler of Clan Donald and all its lands and isles. You, it is hoped, will do better, as Lord of the Isles."

"And Argyll? He ravages Islay, in our lordship. I am preparing to go deal with him. What of the Campbell, Argyll?"

This was indeed the weak link in John's chain, and he was the less happy that Angus knew of Argyll's present invasion by sea; news must travel faster in these Highlands than would be expected.

"Argyll will withdraw from Islay as soon as *you* withdraw from the three royal mainland castles," he said.

"If he does not, then, this compact is finished, over. You understand?"

John understood indeed, with a quickened pulse. The thing was accepted, then! Angus Og had taken the bait. He tried not to let his satisfaction show.

"I do," he said. "It is agreed. Argyll retires from Islay and any other MacDonald lands. And you become Lord of the Isles."

"I must have that signed and sealed, Douglas. By the King."

"You shall have it. Where to send the papers? Since you will not remain here, at Ruthven."

The other produced a twisted smile at that. "I will go to Ardtornish, in Morvern. But, no – send them to Finlaggan on Islay. There is the judgment seat of the lordship of the Isles. I will look for the proof there."

"Very well. Finlaggan on Islay." John nodded. "That, then, concludes my mission."

"As you say, whatever."

They eyed each other, no love lost between them. There was no invitation from Angus to enter the castle proper, no offer of hospitality, no suggestion that the visitors should remain in the vicinity before turning back on their return journey. It was only midday, to be sure.

So John nodded again. "I will go whence I came, then. A long road."

"Yes."

Thus, without further ado, much less civilities, the mission left Ruthven-in-Badenoch and started on their return southwards, mixed feelings prevailing, John at least satisfied that he had achieved what he had set out to attempt, however unimpressed he might be with Angus Og MacDonald. As they camped for a chilly night near Cluny in Laggan, he considered calling upon the Macpherson chief there in his stronghold, to urge him, if he was indeed the captain of the royal castle of Ruthven, to go there and resume possession – but decided that this was really no concern of his, and forbore.

Next day, climbing over the high ground of the Lairig Leacach between Glen Spean and Loch Treig, they ran into a snowstorm, warning that winter was coming to the mountains, and no time for armed campaigners or even wise travellers, a recognition reinforced as they continued on their difficult way.

It was back at Kinlochleven, two days later, that they were confirmed in this judgment, and in major fashion. For here they came upon chaos and turmoil indeed, with the royal army come only thus far – or part of the army, for a large proportion was apparently still strung out all the way along the south shore of the loch from Ballachulish at its mouth. They had found a ferry there, it seemed, but only a single modest scow, laughably inadequate to transport any large force and its horses across the quarter-mile narrows, and so the host was having to make its weary way round the twenty-six-mile circuit, to the frustration of the leadership and the grumbles of the rank and file. With snow-showers threatening, all were in a state of low morale indeed. The Earls of Atholl and Crawford were, in consequence, happy at John's arrival with his news, interpreting it as justification for them to turn and head for home, an end to this folly and misery, even though they had not as yet begun the actual invasion of Lochaber nor struck a single blow against Clan Donald. They could return now, declaring duty done, the royal flag shown in these benighted parts and the enemy, if not conquered, at least satisfactorily divided and so weakened. John was, if not the hero of the hour, at least a popular figure.

His popularity was by no means lessened by his urgings, almost insistence, that Argyll, on Islay, must be informed and must withdraw therefrom at once; for this gave the other two earls excuse to leave the army to make its own slow way back to the Lowlands as best it might, under lesser leaders, whilst they, with some of the more senior lords such as Hamilton, Hailes and Home, set off from this godforsaken spot by boat for The Oban, and from there to take ship, first to Islay to inform Argyll, and then home by Dumbarton to Stirling, with speed and a degree of comfort. They agreed that John, with his party, should make his own way southwards as quickly as possible, to inform King James and get the royal edict separating the island lordship from the Ross earldom sent promptly to Angus Og at Finlaggan. They gave him a paper bearing their signatures and seals to this end, as authority.

So it was a parting of the ways, the great ones off by boat down Loch Léven, the army beginning to straggle back along its south shore, and John's much-travelled three hundred to head up Glen Coe and over the western edge of the great Moor of Rannoch to Glen Orchy and Strathtay, for Perth, and so to Stirling by the quickest route, Alastair MacDonald still acting guide. They had all become quite fond of him.

The hill-tops were all snow-covered now. None would be sorry to leave the Highlands behind, lovely as they could be.

9

Thankful as he was to reach Stirling four days later, and so seek an audience with King James, John became promptly concerned with other matters, and demanding ones, Mary Stewart, as usual, being the source. Glad as she was to see him back to safety, and successful in his endeavours, she was nevertheless distressed. It was once again over the issue of the unfortunate Patrick Graham, the archbishop. Sheves had had him lodged in the island abbey of Inchcolm, supposedly for his own safety, as insane, but actually as a prisoner; now he had had the poor man taken from there to that other Loch Leven, in Fothrif, to be confined, allegedly in a dungeon, as a dangerous menace to Holy Church in Scotland and a rallying figure for disaffected abbots and the like. Mary feared greatly for him there, for he was in ill health anyway, and undoubtedly conditions would be rigorous indeed. They must try to help him, somehow.

"Loch Leven!" The man stared, drawing a deep breath. "There!"

"Johnnie," she said, "I am told that the castle there belongs to a Douglas. Sir Robert, is it not? So he will be gaoler of the unhappy archbishop. I fear that we will not be able to win him release. Not with Sheves so set against him and contriving his ruin. But we can try, to be sure, to gain some betterment of his state, some easement and comfort. I have spoken to James, seeking release, but he is wholly under Sheves's sway, my wretched brother, and will do nothing. So we must attempt this, at the least."

John swallowed. "This is . . . a little difficult, Mary," he said.

"But – is this Douglas of Lochleven some kin of yours? That should help, no?"

"Far-out kin indeed. Of the Dalkeith and Morton line, *Black* Douglases, not Red. But, that is not the problem. It is . . . my mother!"

"Mother? What mean you?"

"My mother is at Lochleven Castle!"

She stared. "What are you saying? That you have a mother? Alive?"

"Alive, yes. I have not seen her for years, none of us have. But she has not died, I think. She is no old woman, yet."

Mary shook her head, wordless.

"It is a sorry tale," he went on. "Our father died twelve years ago. And after bearing nine of us children to him, he was dead only months when she left Tantallon, and us all, and went to wed this Sir Robert Douglas of Lochleven. Extraordinary! To abandon nine of us, the youngest, Alison, still an infant. And not to come back. We assume that she had never loved our father. They were wed very young, an arranged match. It may be that she had always wanted this Robert. She cannot have greatly loved any of us, to be sure. We saw but little of her, reared by others. A very handsome woman. She will still be under forty years . . ."

"Johnnie, how strange, how very strange! To bear, and then leave, nine children! Even if she did not love your father, to leave all her own bairns! Has she, has she all her wits?"

"Indeed she has. Or had. We none of us have seen her for long. Scarce think of her as mother. A succession of aunts came to Tantallon to look to us. I have never been to Lochleven Castle. Archie went once, over some matter of lands . . ."

"Then, then you will not wish to do so now. Reopen an old sore . . ."

"I will go, yes. Do what I can. Perhaps it is good that I *should* go?"

She searched his face. "It could be so, yes. Perhaps. I go also. We go together. But – it is much to ask of you." Abruptly she came to him and flung her arms around him. "Oh, my dear! How good you are. How kind. Ever you help me, do what I ask. Always I am calling upon you, seeking your aid. And you never fail me. And now, at this such cost to you . . . !"

He had difficulty in speaking now, as once before, overcome by her warm gesture of affection, the feel of her lovely person against him – for he automatically encircled her with his own arms, pressing her closer.   ·

"I will ever . . . . do anything that I can," he got out thickly, lips in her hair.

They stood in the grip of emotion, as well as of each other; and, by the heaving of her splendid bosom, Mary's emotion was as evident as his own.

He was hoping for a repeat of that wonderful kiss he had gained on the last occasion of togetherness, when she gently released herself.

"Johnnie, Johnnie, we must restrain ourselves, I fear," she said. "I am sorry. But – if I do not, how can I expect *you* to do so? Sorry indeed. Or, no! Not sorry. But, but . . . I but apologise!"

"Lord!" he gasped. "Apologise! You." He wagged his head, words quite inadequate.

She managed a smile then. "I have my responsibilities, have I not? Over-many. Am less strong than I ought to be, as I have told you. And you are so patient, so understanding. I use you shamefully, I fear."

"I would be used by you, always, Mary." That at least was not hesitant, breathless, but was deep-voiced.

"My dear! But let us avoid – no, suspend – this dangerous talk meantime. Speak of what must be done. Safer, perhaps! So, you will take me to this Lochleven Castle? Despite the cost to you. In the matter of Patrick Graham how think you this Douglas kinsman will heed?"

"I know not. Nor . . . his wife! But . . . can you indeed come with me?"

"You tell me that my husband is gone to Islay? He will not be back here for some time, then. I am scarcely a free woman, but yes, I will go with you. And soon, Johnnie – it must be soon."

"To be sure. But first I have to see the King. Over this of

Clan Donald and the Isles. Could you arrange an audience, without Sheves's presence?"

"That will be easy. For Sheves is gone to St Andrews. More and more he is there now, as Bishop-Coadjutor. Acting the archbishop indeed! He went two days past, and will not be back yet awhile. We can go seek James now. He will not be hunting in this weather." Sleet was falling, this first day of December. They had some searching to do before they found the King in that rambling rock-top fortress, for he was not in his own quarters in the palace block. Eventually they ran him to earth in a range of workshops in the northern wing, where he was actually working with his hands, under the direction of a craftsman, fashioning woodwork for the furnishing of a new great hall for the castle which was being designed by the master-mason here guiding him – a strange preoccupation for a monarch. Not that John Douglas thought any the less of his liege-lord for this, although others might.

James eyed their arrival without favour. No doubt he looked upon his elder sister as something of a nuisance, always troubling him with pleas and urgings for this and that cause, and criticising his decisions and friends.

"James," Mary said, "here is the Lord of Douglasdale new come from the Highlands. With excellent news for you."

His sovereign looked at John warily. He was a strange young man, quite good-looking but with an aspect of almost perpetual suspicion about him, as though ever expecting trouble, his features not so much weak as set already against persuasion, as though he felt that the world was against him. He had no love for the Douglases, of course, seeing them as in his brother Albany's camp.

"Sire, your humble servant," John said, bowing briefly. "I have a letter here for you, from my lords of Atholl and Crawford." He drew out the sealed paper from his doublet pocket and handed it over.

James laid down his chisel and hammer and took the missive almost gingerly, distastefully. He did not break the seals.

"What is it? Where are they? Why send *you*? Have they taken that John of Ross?" he asked jerkily.

"No, Your Grace. The Earl of Ross is believed to be far north, in his Easter Ross castle of Dingwall. This paper tells you of his son, Angus of Islay."

"What of him? A bastard and ill-doer." James had left the letter unopened on the workbench.

"Yes, Sire. But powerful. And a stronger fighter than his father. *I* bring the news to you, since it was I who went to him. Won his agreement. At Ruthven in Badenoch."

"Where is that? And where are my uncles of Atholl and Buchan?"

"The Earl of Atholl, with the Earl of Crawford and other lords, is gone to the Isle of Islay, to bring back the Earl of Argyll from his invading there. My lord of Buchan has gone with my lord of Huntly to confront the Earl of Ross in the north-east. Badenoch is in Strathspey, some fifty miles south of Inverness, and Ruthven there a royal castle which Angus Og had taken, in his father's name. There I was sent to seek him out and make him the council's offer."

"Offer? What offer?"

"Should you not read the letter, James?" Mary suggested.

The other ignored that. "What council and what offer? I know naught of this."

"A council of your earls and lords, Sire. Held at The Oban, in Lorn. When it was learned that the Earl of Ross and his son were not together, were, indeed, at odds. It was decided that this could be to Your Grace's and your realm's advantage. If father and son could be separated, then the Clan Donald and its septs could be greatly weakened. And Ross brought low. Without great battle in those difficult Highlands and Isles. It was agreed that if the lordship of the Isles could be divided from the earldom of Ross and given to Angus, then Your Grace's cause would greatly benefit – for the Islesmen are the fiercest of the Clan Donald warriors, and with their ships, galleys, can threaten all Scotland's coasts. So – I was sent to Angus to make him that offer." John cleared his throat. "In Your Highness's name."

James scowled. "I knew nothing of this."

"Your Grace had put the command of your army and

149

expedition in the hands of my lords of Atholl and Crawford and Argyll. They acted in your name. And for the nation's weal, Sire."

"James, this is excellent news," Mary interjected. "You should be glad indeed. Grateful. Especially to John of Douglasdale here, who went, at great risk and danger to himself, to win the son Angus's agreement. And gained it. As this paper will tell you."

"Yes, Sire. Angus of Islay has agreed to become Lord of the Isles in place of his father. And will enter into your peace, and vacate the royal castles taken, greatly weakening John of Ross, if Your Grace will sign the necessary decrees. Thus saving war and much bloodshed amongst your subjects in which your forces might well have come off worst, in those so difficult mountains and loch-divided uplands. And lacking a sufficiency of ships."

James, who had never visited the west Highlands, looked doubtful. But he picked up the letter, broke the seals, and read. Finished, he laid it down, silent.

"Are you not happy with this, James?" Mary demanded. "You and the kingdom are greatly advantaged, and at no cost to yourself. You should thank this my lord in especial – for I judge that it was his notion in the first place."

"I should have been consulted," the monarch said.

"Sire, that was understood by all. But with time against us, the winter storms already upon us . . ." John gestured at the sleet outside. "The passes, blocked by snows, there was no time to send back to Stirling for your royal authority. The army was held. Never reached Lochaber and the MacDonald lands. Here was the best way out."

A monarchical shrug.

"You *will* sign a decree separating the lordship of the Isles from the earldom of Ross, Sire?" John asked, a little urgently.

"I will discuss the matter with Bishop William."

"James, William Sheves is at St Andrews. Haste is required, if this is to be achieved. And it has nothing to do with churchmen. You are *Ard Righ*, High King of Scots, and

150

your earls are the *ri*, the lesser kings. This is between you and your earls. These earls, Atholl, Buchan, Crawford, Argyll and Huntly, seek to bring the rebel Earl of Ross to his due allegiance, guilty of treason as he is. This can help to do it. Are *you Ard Righ*? Or is William Sheves!"

Listening to her, John found himself wishing that Mary Stewart had been Queen of Scots, on the throne, instead of this so uncertain brother. Then he recognised that had she been, she would have been still further out of his reach than she was at present.

James was glaring. "He is my friend, my good friend. As are few who, who ought to be! As is Robert, here." He gestured towards the master-mason, Robert Cochrane, who watched them from nearby, a dark-avised, tall man, with a strangely thrusting lower lip.

"Your friends are your own concern," his sister acceded. "But as *Ard Righ*, these cannot be your advisers. As High King you must deal with your lords. And this of Ross and the Isles is of the first importance. Clearly, if the Earl of Ross is no longer Lord of the Isles, his power to make trouble is halved, more than halved."

"And his bastard son? What trouble will he make? With his savage Islesmen?"

"Since he *is* bastard, Sire, he cannot claim to be of the royal house," John put in. "And is therefore a deal less of a menace to your throne." The Earl of Ross was a descendant of Robert the Second, and therefore could make a distant claim to the succession, as his father had done at the great Battle of Harlaw.

That seemed to reach the King, who pursed his rather slack lips. "If I make this decree will he abide by it? Not return to his father's side? And nothing gained."

"I think not. He and his father are ill disposed anyway. Angus mislikes being treated as illegitimate. This will give him standing, status, Lord of the Isles, a great and ancient title. And will not make either love each other the more!"

"He could still rise against me, use his new power to my hurt. I would have no hold on him. Any more than the crown has

151

had over other Lords of the Isles. They consider themselves independent princes!"

That was true, and John had thought on it in his long journeyings. "Your Grace, the lordship of the Isles is a style, a great one but only a style and title. If you were to make it a true lordship, a lord of parliament, then you would have some hold on the bearer. You can summon lords of parliament *to* parliament. They are responsible to parliament and to Your Highness in parliament. His father, as an earl, has a seat in parliament. Give Angus Og one also, and their clashing could be the more guided and . . . manipulated."

Mary actually clapped her hands at this suggestion, and even her brother looked impressed.

"There is sense in that," he admitted. "Yes, if he was in parliament, we could have some grip on him. I could do that."

"Your royal decree and edict could change the entire situation in the north, Sire. A simple writing on paper, with your signature and seal. The work of mere moments."

"M'mm. I will consider it."

John was greatly daring. "I think, Sire, that there is something further to be considered. That is, my lord Earl of Argyll. *He* will not esteem this so well perhaps. The seeming raising up of his hereditary enemy. The Campbells and the MacDonalds are ever at feud. Argyll could work against this. But, if it was done, the decrees signed and despatched to Angus before Argyll returned from Islay, then he could do nothing."

"Argyll could not overturn my royal will and signature, Douglas."

"No, Sire, but he could make trouble. And the Campbells have many friends, as well as enemies. So I would humbly counsel haste. Send the decree by especial courier to Finlaggan on Islay, before the earl's return."

"That might be best, yes . . ."

"Are you not grateful to my lord for all this, James?" his sister asked.

"Does he seek some reward?" That was grudging.

"No, Sire." That was hasty. But a glance at Mary changed

152

his tune a little. "Not for myself, that is. But . . . for Arch-bishop Graham. If his sad lot could be bettered a little . . ."

"The man is insane. And evil. Setting himself up to be Pope, claiming that angels appointed him. No, no – he is a heretic and idolator. He should indeed be burned at the stake!"

"All that is but hearsay, Sire. He is a sick man, but in body, rather than mind, I think. And he gained Metropolitan status for Scotland, a great service to the realm. Freeing our Church from English claims of domination."

"No, I say! Graham is infamous. I will hear no more of this."

Recognising that he might endanger the other issue, John held his peace. Although Mary did not.

"I say that you are very mistaken in this, James," she asserted. "You believe only what William Sheves tells you. And he is determined to bring Patrick Graham down. Because he wants his place and station. You should heed others, your many abbots . . ."

"I trust Bishop William's judgment before that of any abbot. And certainly before any woman's!" The King picked up his chisel. "This audience is closed!" he said, although he did not look at his sister, only at John.

That man bowed, and backed out of the workshop. After a moment, Mary followed him, head held high.

Next morning they were on their way to Loch Leven. Fortu-nately the sleet had gone and been replaced by quite a hard frost. Despite the sad and sorry nature of this venture, John could not but feel elated. joyful at this his first expedition alone with Mary – or, not exactly alone, since he felt bound to take three of his men with them as escort for a princess; but these rode well behind and knew their place. He recognised that it was unusual, to say the least, for a married woman, let alone a princess, to go riding in the sole company of a man not her husband.

They crossed Forth by Stirling Bridge and covered the mile-long causeway beyond, where Wallace's great battle had been won, to the beginning of the Ochil foothills, along which they turned eastwards, their route to follow this line immediately below the steep green slopes for some twenty-two miles, by Menstrie, Alva, Tillicoultry and Dollar, hillfoot villages, to the widening at the mouth of Glen Devon, where the hills receded. It made a pleasant ride, nowise tiring. They chatted companionably however much neither actually looked forward to what lay ahead.

But, after some three hours' riding, and they left the hills to enter the great basin between the Ochils and the Fife and Fothrif hill masses, a level, fertile plain at the centre of which lay Loch Leven, they fell silent, preoccupied. Whatever was the outcome of this visit, it could not be other than stressful, especially for the man. Presently, with the smokes of the little town of Kinross rising before them and they saw their first blue glimpses of the loch in the clear, sharp air, Mary shook her head.

"Johnnie, I should not have brought you on this mission," she said, urgently. "It is too, too sore on you."

"You could scarcely have come alone," he pointed out. "And I would do more than this. It . . . may not be so ill. For me. And for her. Who knows? It could be that she will not be so displeased. You are a mother. How think you that a mother will feel? After all these years."

"How am I to enter the mind of a woman who has acted as she has done? I could never leave children of mine abandoned. And nine of them! Think you, did she perhaps *mislike* your father? Resent all the bairns he burdened her with? Could that be it? And when he died, she cut adrift. Back to her early love? Yet – surely she must have had some love for her own children? A mother must have."

"I do not know. I was too young to understand – we all were. I was but nine when my father died and she went. She was only sixteen years when she was wed, I think, and to a much older man. A mere girl, the daughter of a Fife laird, Sir Andrew Sibbald of Balgonie. She had us all in very quick succession. Too quick, probably. It may be that our father was . . . over-hasty! Too eager, hard on her. Ten years of constant child-bearing. Then release! And she fled. It could have been

154

that. She would still be under thirty years. Even now she will be but thirty-eight years or so . . ."

"Poor woman! Poor woman! I thought that I must hate her. Now, I am not so sure . . ."

They realised that they had almost forgotten the real object of their visit, the unfortunate Patrick Graham.

They came to Kinross, and threaded its narrow streets, down to the waterside – and quickly they saw why William Sheves had selected this prison for the man he wanted to be rid of. Loch Leven was large, unlike most Highland lochs almost as wide as it was long. There seemed to be two islands in it, one quite near and the other at the far southern end, possibly three miles off. The one nearby was small and perhaps a third of a mile offshore, its surface almost wholly occupied by a castle and its courtyard, walls rising high. Despite the little town's proximity, only two very small boats were tied up at the lochside jetty here, where a large bell hung from a gantry. Clearly that bell was to attract attention from the castle, when necessary; and equally clearly, no one would be able to approach the castle unawares or unwanted – nor to escape therefrom.

There was a cot-house sited near the jetty, and the riders saw themselves being watched from the doorway. John hailed the man standing there.

"Here is the Lord of Douglasdale and the Princess Mary, Countess of Arran, come to see Sir Robert Douglas. How do we win out to him?"

The watcher, expressionless, walked forward to the gantry and rang the bell, which clanged out loudly. Three or four times he repeated the ringing, wordless. Then, from across the water came an answering tolling. The man, still unspeaking, got down into one of the little boats, pushed out the oars, and pulled away to row towards the island.

"No warm welcome!" Mary commented. "But clearly the customary one."

They waited.

Developments took some time. The small boat disappeared round the further side of the island. When it eventually reappeared, it had company. A larger craft, a flat-bottomed scow with four oarsmen, came pulling shorewards.

"At least we are to be permitted access!"

"Perhaps. Or perhaps not. That young man in the stern is not old enough to be Sir Robert. Who might have come himself, hearing who visits. If he is at home."

Nearing the shore, the said young man stood up. "What, sir, is your business at Lochleven Castle?" he shouted.

"We are from the court of King James at Stirling," John called back. "And our business is with Sir Robert Douglas. Himself."

The other seemed to consider that. Then he waved the oarsmen onwards, and they pulled in for the jetty.

John aided Mary to dismount and told their escort to remain with the horses. There would be an inn in the town.

The young man bowed briefly to Mary as he handed her aboard. He did not offer any identity, nor indeed any remark. And John was certainly not going to question him.

So in silence, save for the creak and splash of the oars, they headed out to the island.

Round on the southern side they came to an inlet where, under frowning walls, they found a number of craft moored, including a quite handsome small barge. Landing here, they were led up through an archway below a gatehouse, and into a courtyard.

The castle appeared to consist of a square keep, with parapet and defensive rounds, plus a linked wing of apparently somewhat later date, the whole surrounded by a high courtyard wall topped by a wall-walk. Men watched the newcomers therefrom.

Another man stood in the arched doorway of the keep itself, arms akimbo. Strong featured, well-built and of middle years, he had a formidable look about him. He also did not speak. They were a silent lot at Lochleven Castle.

"I am John Douglas of Douglasdale. Are you Sir Robert Douglas of this hold, sir?"

"I am, yes."

"Then, kinsman, make your due duty to the Princess Mary, Countess of Arran, the King's sister."

Smoothing a hand over lips, the other bowed. "Highness," he jerked.

Mary smiled. "We greet you, Sir Robert. I have met many Douglases – but not yourself. In your stronghold, so heedfully guarded!"

The knight inclined his head again. "You will, no doubt, have reason for visiting my poor house, Highness?"

"We have, yes. We have come to see the Archbishop of St Andrews. Who is lodged here, we understand."

The other's voice was expressionless. "The former Primate is placed in my care, yes."

"Good. Then we would have word with him."

There was a brief pause. Then, "My instructions are that he is to be held unvisited."

"Your instructions from whom, Sir Robert?" That was John.

"From the acting Primate, the Bishop-Coadjutor, my lord."

"And you, a Douglas, take your order from an upjumped cleric, sir?"

There was no reply.

"At least, you will not forbid us entry to your house, kinsman," John went on carefully. "We have ridden all the miles from Stirling."

"No. No – come within, Highness and my lord. I regret it if I seem lacking in civility. That is not my wish. Come, you."

They were led within, past vaulted basement chambers and up a narrow turnpike stairway to the well-furnished, first-floor hall, where a well-doing log fire blazed in a great heraldically decorated fireplace. As they entered, a door at the further end closed quietly.

Inviting the visitors to sit, their host rang a hand-bell, and when a servant appeared, commanded refreshments to be brought.

"How distant kin are we, Sir Robert? Apart from . . . marriage connections!" John asked.

The other eyed him levelly. "Far out, I judge, my lord. *We*

157

are Blacks. Whom you Reds helped to bring low! The ends of the Earls of Douglas."

"Yes. That was ill-done, even though it was at the King's command. By my father, before my time."

"That was *my* father," Mary put in. "We have to live with the strange actions of parents, have we not? Forgive, if we can!" That was significantly said.

Robert Douglas cleared his throat. "No doubt," he said shortly. "Kings have their policies. As has your royal brother, Highness. I understand that it is on his command, rather than on Bishop William's, that the former archbishop is to be held thus."

"Say on William Sheves's advice! He uses my brother's name. And the archbishop is still archbishop. Sheves is not so high-grown yet that he can cancel the Vatican's appointment, sir. May we see him?"

"He is . . . unwell, Highness. In no state to receive visitors."

"You mean that you keep him in such conditions that he must not be seen!" John charged him.

"Not so . . ."

"Then, if you have nothing to hide, let us visit him. We but wish to speak kindly with a sick man, a wronged man. In *your* house, is that forbidden us?"

The knight hesitated, he who was clearly no hesitant man. "Does His Grace know that you come here?"

"His Grace knows that I am concerned for the archbishop's state, yes, Sir Robert," Mary said.

"Very well. I will take you to him. But only for a short time. And it may be to your . . . distress. Come. This way."

Exchanging glances, the visitors followed their host, just as the refreshments arrived, back whence they had come, downstairs and across the courtyard to the separate wing, which was in the nature of an angle-tower. Entering this, Sir Robert took a key from a hook on the stone walling, to unlock the massive door of one of the basement vaults. Standing back, he ushered them inside. He left the door open.

"He stinks!" he observed, curtly.

At first, even with the door wide, it was difficult to see inside that stone-arched cell, lit only by the narrowest of slit-windows. The smell caught their throats, Mary all but choking. And it was cold, cold – where the stench would seem to have indicated otherwise. There was no fireplace here.

When their eyes adapted to the gloom, they saw a low plank bed, a wooden form and a pail; that was the entire furnishings. On the form lay a tray with untouched food. And on the bed lay what looked like merely a heap of blankets or rugs. There was no stirring.

"He seldom speaks, seldom moves," the laird said. He sounded almost apologetic, now.

"Dear God!" Mary exclaimed. "Do you wonder? In this foul sty!"

"It is clean enough. He was in a better chamber above. But Bishop William put him here. As heretic and blasphemer."

"The Metropolitan of Scotland!" John accused. "And a poor, sick man. The nephew of the great Bishop Kennedy, who ruled the realm for James the Second. Come to this, from the envy of a charlatan, a sorcerer!" He pointed. "This a Douglas should not have done!"

Mary moved over to the bed, to gaze down. She spoke. "My lord Archbishop! Patrick. Patrick Graham. Here is . . . a friend."

There was no response, no movement from the pile of blankets.

She bent, to touch the heap, to try to grip something more firm under it. "Lord Patrick, hear me. It is Mary Stewart, your friend, the King's sister. Hear me."

Whether it was the touch or the woman's voice, there was a stir, and slowly, tentatively, some of the covers were drawn aside, and white hair, wild and shaggy, of head and beard appeared.

The young woman gently stooped to draw back the coverings further, to reveal haggard, grey features amongst all the unkempt hair, great lacklustre eyes and trembling lips – but no speech.

"My lord Archbishop. You remember me? Mary. Come to, to visit you."

She gained no reply other than a stare – although it was scarcely that, so dull were those watery eyes.

John came forward. "My lord, I am John Douglas, Douglasdale. Brother to Angus. We come seeking to bring you our goodwill, hope, possible betterment."

Still no answer, although those eyes turned on him.

"Speak to us, my lord," Mary besaught him. "We wish to aid you. To tell you that you still have friends."

The pale lips moved but no words came.

"He speaks to none," Sir Robert said, from the doorway. "Has not done for days."

"The more shame on his captors!" John jerked. He reached down to try to grasp something of the frail body beneath. This produced some reaction, something of a convulsion indeed, although a feeble one, with movement and stirring of the blankets, which ended in them being drawn back to cover the face and head as before. That was all.

The visitors eyed each other helplessly in the gloom.

"It is ever thus," the other man said.

"In God's good name . . . !" Mary got out.

"That is Scotland's first archbishop and Metropolitan," John repeated. "The leader of Holy Church in this nation. Brought to this, by evil, by envious men!"

"Here by the King's royal command, my lord. Who am I to disobey it?"

"*I* will give you another royal command, Sir Robert!" Mary said. "You will move the archbishop from here. You say that he had better quarters upstairs. Then move him back therein. Forthwith. That is *my* command. In my brother's name!"

The other shrugged. "I did not wish to put him here. That was the Bishop-Coadjutor's orders."

"Then you have had other orders. From a higher source than William Sheves. Move him."

"As you will, Highness. On *your* responsibility!"

"On mine, yes." She looked back at the pile of bedding. "My

lord Patrick, you will be moved. Bettered. You hear? Back to a kinder place."

There was no least reaction.

"It is of no avail, Mary," John said. "He is scarcely conscious. Perhaps the move will aid him, in some measure. We can do nothing here."

Sadly they left that cell, the knight closing the door behind them – but significantly not locking it.

They went back to the castle's hall in silence, where the neglected refreshments awaited them, Sir Robert obviously ill at ease.

They were sitting at the great table, eating and sipping and scarcely realising that they did so, when John, facing down the hall, noticed the far door opening slightly and remaining just a little ajar. On impulse, biting his lip, and without a word to their host, he rose and strode over to that door, and flung it open.

A woman stood there. She blinked at him, opened her mouth to speak, and then shut it again, her eyes searching his face. She was tall, proudly built, fine-featured and of early middle years.

"I wondered . . . !" he got out, gazing.

They stood, wordless, eyes locked. Behind them the other two sat watching, as silent.

"Mother!" Somehow John got it out.

The woman swallowed. She nodded, features working. "You will be . . . John!"

"John, yes. Your son."

Slowly a hand rose and reached out to him, quivering. "Johnnie!" she whispered.

He took that hand, and found his own fiercely gripped. Neither could speak.

Mary rose and came to their rescue. "Lady Douglas! Or do you still use Countess of Angus? My husband's sister – my first husband – Elizabeth, is wed to your son Archibald." It sounded banal, of course, but perhaps that was what was needed at this juncture. "We hoped that we would see you."

The older woman drew herself up. "Ah! You are kind,

161

Highness. Yes, kind." But she looked at her son as she said it. "I judged . . . that you would not wish to see me."

"That would have been unkind, I think."

"Unkind!" The word burst from the other's lips. "*You* speak of unkindness! To me!"

It was John who answered her. "Mother, the past is past. Let us forget it. We see each other again. That is enough."

"You *wished* to see me? Who deserted you all. I, who bore you!"

"That was long years ago. No doubt you had your reasons."

"Oh, I had, I had. But . . . what I did was unforgivable, nevertheless. Can you, in truth, forgive?"

"Who am I to forgive, or not forgive? God, they say, forgives. So – may you not forgive yourself?"

"Never!"

"Yet . . . you have never come back to Tantallon. To see us. I would have thought . . ."

"I dared not. I have been too ashamed. Once I came to my senses. Oh, you will not understand! I had a new responsibility, see you – to Robert here. If I had once returned, to you all . . ." She shook her head helplessly.

His name raised, her husband came over to them. "It is an old story. Better buried – with George Douglas! Your father." He looked at John. "She, my wife, has suffered enough. We both have. Can you not let it be?"

"Can we not amend it, in some measure?"

"How? It is done, past."

"The pain of it, for us all, could be lessened, taken away. We, the children, are grown now. Can see matters better, no longer bairns. Come to understand your . . . needs. And stress. Aye, and pain. Our mother, wed almost as a child herself."

"I was always . . . rebel!" the woman exclaimed.

Sir Robert mustered a grim smile. "And that she has remained!"

She touched his arm. "You, at least, are good."

It was evident that these two loved each other.

"I cannot speak for my brother and sisters," John went on.

"But I, for one, would wish old sores healed, and end to blame and ill judging."

"Your brother, Archibald, came here once. Some years back," his mother said. "With papers to sign, over lands. He was less forgiving."

"Archie is headstrong, hot-tempered. Something of a rebel also! But he can change in moments. I know. His heart is warm enough. And the girls are kindly."

"My brood of daughters! How fare they? Women, now!"

"All well, and fair. Even Alison, the youngest, is near to sixteen years . . ."

"Nearly as old as I was when I was wed to your father! Nearly as old as when I bore Archie!"

"Yes. And, and against your wish?"

She nodded, tight-lipped.

He went on. "Isabel is to marry Sir Alexander Ramsay of Dalwolsey. And Elizabeth, the eldest, is being courted by Graham of Fintry. Kin to the unhappy archbishop here."

That caused intakes of breath and an exchange of glances.

"They are happy in these matchings?"

"Both, yes. They were not . . . arranged."

"Praise God! If *I* may invoke his name!"

"The forgiving one," Mary reminded.

"So you say. Well, give them all . . . what can I give them? To talk of love makes me hypocrite, to add to all else! But I wish them very well. All. And you, John. What am I to say to you? Or them? You, who have come to me."

"You *can* do something for me, yes, Mother. You can show some kindness to Archbishop Graham, there. He needs it, deserves it. Do not believe that man Sheves. He is a rogue. Unfortunately he has the King's ear. *You* are a rebel, you say. Then rebel against Sheves's wicked orders. And you, Sir Robert. He, the archbishop, will not live long now, I think. Let him have a little kindness before he goes."

"I have been saying that, these many days. We shall do that, Robert." That was scarcely a question.

They all eyed each other. There did not seem to be anything more to say.

163

Mary nodded. "If we are to win back to Stirling before darkness, we should be on our way, Johnnie."

"That is true. Three hours' riding. More."

The others made no attempt to detain them.

The parting was no more easy than the rest, emotions held in check, mother and son fearful of words but very much aware of each other.

"You will come to Tantallon one day?" he said. "To see us all."

She spread her hands. "All may not be . . . as you are."

"I think, when I tell them, you will not be unwelcome."

"I wonder!"

John turned to the other man. "Bring her, Sir Robert."

"We shall see." That was doubtful. "Sleeping dogs . . . !"

"This dog is not asleep. Only broods, see you. Better wakened, I think."

Neither answered him, and Mary touched his arm.

"Yes. We go then. To the boat. I . . . we wish you well. Very well."

Lady Douglas looked away, to hide her working features.

Mary raised a cupped hand, and turned to move off from that courtyard gate. Then looked back. "See well to Patrick Graham," she urged.

Shaking head, John followed on.

They were silent on that boat's return trip.

But presently, mounted and on their way, Mary summed it up. "I think that it was worth the coming. In both respects. We did what we could. I, I would wish to have a son like you, Johnnie!"

"I would wish something very different!" he exclaimed, turning in the saddle to face her. "But . . . !" He left the rest unsaid. There had been enough emotional talk for one day.

She reached out to squeeze his arm, but wisely said nothing.

10

In the great hall of Tantallon Castle, Yuletide celebrations were in preparation when John got home from Stirling. Archie had arrived back from the Borders only the day before, as full of news and views as an egg of meat: the depredations of the cattle thieves on both sides of the line; the feuding between the great families; the uselessness of the other two wardens, Middle and West – his was the East March; Albany's forceful measures but the problems of enforcing them; and so on. His wife and sisters were not greatly interested in all this; nor indeed was John, who had other matters on his mind, even though, it appeared, he was destined to become assistant Warden of the East March himself.

It was not until they were all sitting around the tables for their evening meal, with a great fire blazing nearby to counter the booming of the winter seas which battered themselves into spume at the foot of the castle cliffs, that John found suitable opportunity to tell them all of his own doings. They were, of course, sorry for the archbishop, and saddened to hear of his present state; but clearly it was the name of Lochleven Castle which was their principal preoccupation. There were indrawn breaths and searching glances when he pronounced it.

Accepting their priorities, he fairly quickly transferred to the subject which concerned them all. "I saw our mother," he said. "Talked with her."

Silence.

"It was difficult. But . . . none so ill."

"None so ill for whom?" Archie demanded. "You? Or her?"

"We both were . . . troubled. But it was worst for her, I think. She is so much unhappy over it all."

"As well she might be!"

"No doubt. But she is a woman stricken with guilt and sorrow for what she did to us, blaming herself sorely. And yet, at the same time, believing that she *had* to do it."

"Had to desert her family for a paramour!"

"For the man she truly loved. And still does love, I believe. She never loved our father."

"Poor woman!" Archie's wife said.

"What is she like? Our mother?" Isabel asked.

"She is handsome. Still young-seeming. In good health, by her looks. But . . . sad. At least with myself before her."

There was a battery of questions from the sisters, oddly enough mainly to do with their mother's appearance, manner, dress, bearing and the like – which drew snorts from Archie.

"What signifies is what she has *done*, not what she looks like!" he declared.

"She is concerned for you all," John reported. "While nowise forgetting her own fault in leaving us. She asked after your matchings, Elizabeth and Isabel. Glad that they were not forced on you, as hers had been. She did not fail to point out that she was little older than any of you are now when she was given to our father, a much older man."

"None of which excuses her desertion of her children!"

"No. But I found her a woman that I could like, all but admire. I was sorry for her. For she had suffered, I think, greatly more than we have, by her action all those years ago." He spread hands. "She said that she does not want to be a hypocrite, to add to the rest. But . . . she cares."

"Yet she has never come near us," Archie objected. "If she had been as sorry as she says, would she not have visited us here? That at least."

"She was too ashamed, she said."

"I can understand that," Johann accepted. "I would have felt the same."

"This man that she married, Douglas of Lochleven?" Anne asked. "That she left us for. What of him? You say that they still love each other. How saw you him?"

"I found him none so ill. He is strong, well-featured.

A man of parts, I would say. But in a difficult situation."

"Why does he act gaoler to the archbishop?" Archie demanded. "Mistreat him so? Why choose *him* to do it?"

"He obeys the King's orders, he says, conveyed to him by the man Sheves. Sir Robert would have treated Patrick Graham better. Did do. But Sheves ordered this worsening. And Lochleven Castle is as secure a place to hold him as any in Scotland, as you well know, Archie. On its island and midway between St Andrews and Stirling, where Sheves passes often. But he, Sir Robert, will better conditions for the poor man, I think. With our mother's urgings. She has her own strength. She told me that she was ever a rebel."

"There are rebels and rebels!" Archie said darkly.

"Which sort are you, brother?"

They all laughed at that.

"Archie rebels when he does not win his own way!" his wife observed. "Quickly I discovered that."

"But you as quickly learned how to get round me!"

In this kinder climate, John added his final item. "I asked her to come to us here. Asked Sir Robert to bring her to Tantallon."

They all considered that, eyeing each other.

"Why not?" Elizabeth asked.

"I would like to see her," Alison said.

All the girls agreed. Only Archie felt it incumbent upon him to express doubts.

"They may not come," John pointed out. "They did not promise . . ."

They left it at that. And Anne went on to tell her brothers that when visiting Sir Robert Graham of Fintry, with Elizabeth, she had met the most wonderful man, so handsome, the Lord Graham himself, Robert's half-brother. Archie must invite him to Tantallon after Yule. Did John know him? About the court? He would be some kin to the poor archbishop . . . ?

John was in touch with his mother again, sooner than he

167

had anticipated. For, only three days after the new year commenced, a messenger arrived from Mary at Cadzow Castle, the Hamilton seat in Lanarkshire, with news that Patrick Graham had died two days before Hogmanay. Shamefully, he had been buried, on Sheves's orders, in unconsecrated ground in a corner of the castle islet, as infidel and heretic. This must be rectified, went the message. Would the Lord of Douglasdale be good enough to meet the Princess Mary at Stirling as soon as possible hereafter, to seek to right this wrong?

John, despite the wild weather, was not one to hesitate over this request. In fact, distressed as he was by this latest example of Sheves's spleen, he rejoiced that he would be seeing Mary again so soon, and that she so consistently turned to him for help and company. The only flaw was that, when Archie heard of it, he decided at once that he would go also. It would be an opportunity to see their mother and make his own judgments. And, since it seemed that he was going to be allied by marriage to the Graham family, it was suitable that he should help further in the matter of the archbishop. John could scarcely seek to dissuade him, however much he would have preferred to go alone.

There was one advantage in this, however. John had been prepared to make the long ride of some sixty miles to Stirling, whatever the weather conditions. But Archie declared that they would go in his barge again. The seas in the Forth estuary would not be so rough as out here, and it would halve the time of their travelling. Moreover, from Stirling, they could sail down Forth again to Queen Margaret's Ferry, near to Dunfermline, and ride due north by Benarty Hill, and so again almost halve the second part of their journey, up through Fothrif instead of along the Ochil foothills. This was undeniably so.

The next morning, therefore, the brothers started out from North Berwick haven, the fisherfolk crew of the Tantallon barge apparently nowise concerned over the prospect of the voyage – which undoubtedly would be apt to be much less uncomfortable than their normal winter-time fishing trips out into the Norse Sea. It was the horses which would be least happy.

In the event, it proved to be a bumpy and chilly sail, but fairly expeditious, with the south-easterly wind to aid them. Even so it was nearly dark before they reached Airth, and were able to land and ride the few miles up to Stirling.

They found Mary installed in her usual quarters – and minus her husband, as also was becoming usual. Lord Hamilton was, of course, still reputed to be the greatest womaniser in the land, and was probably quite grateful when his wife betook herself off, which, as the King's sister, she was entitled to do. If she was surprised, now, to see John's brother with him, she did not show it. And she perceived the advantage of having the earl's barge to take them part of their way.

She was much angered and upset over Patrick Graham's death, although she conceived him as better off where he had gone by far; but this of burying him in unhallowed ground was beyond all in savagery. They must put that to rights.

But, over a meal, Mary revealed that she had more than the late archbishop on her mind. Had they heard of the Sieur de Concressault? John had vaguely heard the name somewhere, but that was all. Archie, however, had a notion that it had been a French title conferred on one of the Stewarts of Darnley as reward for aid given to the French King at the Battle of Baugé. Mary agreed with this, but said that Stewart had died, and now the lands and style were bestowed on another Scot in the French service, William Monypenny of Pitmilly, a Fife laird. Now Louis the Eleventh was using this Monypenny as an envoy. He had come back to Scotland, to urge King James to aid the French in their warfare against the Duke of Burgundy.

"Burgundy? Charles the Bold?" Archie exclaimed. "Who is, or was, your husband's friend, no? Thomas's friend. Whom he went to when he was forfeited, and could not come home to Scotland. Burgundy, Arran's, my wife's brother's friend?"

"Duke Charles, yes. Now the King of France is at war with him and seeks Scots aid. And my foolish brother is minded to give it. And to take the aid, himself!"

169

"What! James? Thinks to go to France? The King!"

"Not only to go, but to take thousands with him. An army. Louis, you see, is offering him two baits. The earldom of Xaintonge, which was to have been granted to my grandfather, James the First, as part of the dower for his daughter, who married the Dauphin. But was never actually given. Now offered. And more than Xaintonge – the whole of Brittany! If he can take it from Duke Charles the Bold!"

"Lord! *James*, go to war, against one of the greatest warriors of all Christendom! To aid the crooked Louis of France."

"Yes. Folly! But this Monypenny is very persuasive. He has won over Sheves. And therefore James. He has already ordered the mustering of men. And, as I say, he talks of leading the venture himself. James, who has never seen swords crossed in anger!"

"But this is crazy-mad!" Archie cried. "I know of this Monypenny. He it was who acted envoy to France for your father, a cunning talker. And was given Douglas lands in reward! *Black* Douglas lands. Those of the last Earl of Douglas's brother, the Earl of Ormond. And he has turned Frenchman! And is given Concressault."

"He has got more than that. For James is so taken with him and his mission that he has created him a lord of parliament. So he is now *Lord* Monypenny!"

"Save us! Has the King lost his wits altogether? A small Fife laird . . . !"

"William Sheves is also the bastard of a small Fife laird, I would remind you! They know each other. And I think that Monypenny has brought Sheves moneys from France to aid his cause."

John spoke up. "Why is the King thinking to lead this expedition himself, Mary? He, who has no experience of war. And done nothing of the sort before."

"It is jealousy, I think. Of our brother Alexander, Albany. *He* has gained the name for being a warrior. James has come almost to hate him, fear him. The lords look to Albany for leadership, not James. So, he will lead this army. Win Brittany for Scotland, and become the hero-king! That is it, I judge."

"The fool!" Archie gulped a little at what he had blurted out about his sovereign-lord, all but treasonable as it was. Not that the princess looked offended. "When is this to be? This muster. And campaign."

"It will take time to mount. Shipping to carry the army will be the greatest problem. That must limit the numbers, for the vessels are not easily come by. Such as Argyll's galley fleet are well enough for raiding in the Hebrides and the like, but to carry an army to France, and in winter seas, no. It will be spring before all can be ready. But James has already issued orders. He is asking my husband for four hundred Hamiltons! Others also, to be sure. And so soon after they have got back from that Highland venture. There is much grumbling, I am told . . ."

"There must be more than grumbling! This must be stopped." Archie thumped the table, something that John would never have thought to do. "The earls and lords must be roused to halt it. Albany! I will go to Albany at once. He will come and put an end to this folly. He is still at Dunbar Castle."

"That might help, yes," she agreed. "If the lords will unite, and deny James their men, he can do little. It will not increase the love between him and Alexander – but it might well put an end to this French nonsense. I have talked with my other brother, John of Mar. But he is no more strong of character than is James. He is against the venture also, but is ignored. Albany is otherwise. It might serve."

"I will go to Dunbar tomorrow. The Border Marches can look after themselves for a space! You will have to go to Loch Leven on your own, Johnnie. First things first!"

John made no objection.

So, in the morning, there was a change of plans. They would all ride to Airth and board the barge, which would take them down to Queen Margaret's Ferry. There Mary and John would land, but Archie would proceed on by sea to Dunbar, which was serving as Albany's headquarters although it was scarcely in the Borders, but convenient and only some ten miles south of Tantallon. He would hope to bring the duke

171

back to Stirling forthwith, to seek to rouse the lords. This would be the speediest course of action.

In a drizzle of cold rain the trio set off, cloaked against the weather. The wind still easterly, when they reached Airth it had to be oar-work in the barge – but at least that kept the rowers warm, so that the Douglas brothers themselves elected to take a hand at the sweeps, dignity in abeyance. Mary could hardly do that; but she made no complaint at the cold, under three cloaks.

Queen Margaret's Ferry was situated some twenty miles down Forth, at the sudden and brief narrowing of the estuary where Malcolm Canmore's Queen had established a ferry four centuries before, to carry pilgrims over from Lothian and the Borders to her splendid new Romish abbey at Dunfermline, in Fothrif, where Malcolm had his palace. Like the abbey, the ferry still existed, even though pilgrims were now scarce indeed, but as a great convenience to less worshipful travellers.

The barge pulled in to the northern terminal and Mary and John disembarked, with their mounts. Archie forgot to wish them well on their, to him, scarcely vital mission, urgent to be off on his own.

"Your brother is very different from yourself, Johnnie," Mary observed, as they commenced their ride northwards. "Yet you seem to get on well together. Unlike *my* brothers!"

"Archie is the man of action, always. Sometimes he acts first and thinks afterwards! Whereas I think first – and do not always act at all! But we are good friends, even though he thinks me feeble at times. And says that I should have been a priest!"

"I am glad that you are not," she said. Which pleased him not a little.

They had a score of miles to go, passing east of Dunfermline town and on by Hill of Beath and Blairadam, heading for the gap between the Cleish and Benarty Hills, to the foot of Loch Leven. Fortunately the rain had ceased, so the riding was not unpleasant, especially in their own company, despite splattering mud and overflowing burns to

172

splash through. They were able to talk, although with interruptions.

What were they to do about Patrick Graham, needless to say, was now uppermost in their minds, a difficult problem indeed. It might, in theory, be possible to pronounce Christian burial over an already interred corpse, using some local priest; but even if this could be arranged and effected, it seemed to them a very feeble and unsuitable gesture towards Scotland's wronged first Metropolitan. Surely they could do something better than that?

"Would the Kinross parish priest do it, anyway?" John wondered. "After all, he will know that it was done thus on Sheves's orders. So no humble priest is likely to risk the wrath of whatever Sheves now calls himself, Bishop-Coadjutor of St Andrews. And be unseated in his parish, for his pains."

"True. Yet whatever is done will require a cleric's aid."

"Yes. I was thinking of this last night, before I slept. All the vicars and priests of this area will come under the diocese of St Andrews, I fear, so none will dare to offend. But . . . abbots are different. I discovered that when we went round them all with our petition, now of none effect. They are largely independent of bishops and diocesan clergy, monastics. One of them might serve our purpose, if we could persuade him. They none of them professed love for Sheves."

"To be sure. I should have thought of this earlier. My mind has been so full of this French foolishness. I should have asked my friend, Abbot Henry of Cambuskenneth, to come with us. He would have done it, I think. But we can scarcely turn back now . . ."

"No. But there are other abbeys nearer. Lindores, in north Fife, is probably the nearest. Balmerinoch a little further."

"Dunfermline, which we have not long passed? But, no. Dunfermline is an especial case. It is in the crown's gift, attached to the palace. Its abbot would never think of offending James and possibly losing his abbacy."

"Lindores? As I recall it, the abbot there was a proud and distant man. He signed the petition, but showed us no favour. Was scarcely courteous. But Balmerinoch was different. Friendly. We spent the night there. He was greatly concerned with bees, I remember. *He* might do it."

"How far away is Balmerinoch, Johnnie?"

"From here? A fair distance. Say . . . let me think. Say nearly forty miles. It is on the south shore of Tay. A dozen miles, perhaps, east of Lindores."

"Could we ride there now instead of on to Loch Leven? We could reach there before nightfall, no? We could not do that *and* get to Loch Leven this day. But one day will not signify, now. If you think that this abbot might do it."

"Who can tell? But he was a simple, honest man, as I recollect him. And glad to sign in the archbishop's favour. I think that he might well be prepared to afford Graham Christian burial."

"Let us go there, then. Where shall we turn off?"

"As I judge it, fairly soon. At Blairadam. We did not come this way, after Lindores and making for Scone, near to Perth, but went by Tayside. I think, from Blairadam, if we rode by Hilltown of Beath to Loch Ore and north from there to Leslie, in Fife. Then north to Falkland and on over the gap between the Lomond Hills, we would come to Auchtermuchty and so to Lindores. A lengthy ride, but . . ."

"We can do it. Better than sitting working with a needle at tapestry in Stirling Castle! I wish that I knew my Scotland better . . ."

They pulled off their northerly route, then, at Blairadam, and headed through rolling and fertile country with woodland, to pass the small loch of Ore and on by the township of Ballingry, where John reined up to ask directions for Leslie. They talked now mainly of the national, wider situation, and how the King's mistaken plans could best be amended.

"It is all very well for your brother to bring back mine, Albany, to Stirling, to rouse the lords," Mary observed. "But, however much the said lords may be against James's French expedition, they cannot actually *stop* him, even though they deny him the men he needs. Somehow he will be able to raise men. Especially if Sheves gives him Church moneys to hire them. He is the King, and a group of lords, even led by the King's brothers, cannot overrule the monarch. Only parliament can do that, in some measure."

"Parliament, yes. You think a parliament will be necessary? But . . . it is the King who must call a parliament. He will not do that if he thinks that it will overturn his plans."

"I realise that. We will have to use our wits. Show the need for a parliament to settle other issues than this one. Issues which James will accept. Then, when these are dealt with, raise the French matter. And have many prepared to speak, and vote. That way."

He nodded. "Good. But what could we put forward as requiring a parliament which the King would accept? It would have to be a major issue. Or more than one. And a parliament calls for forty days' notice."

"See you, we can always rely upon relations with England to make a major issue for parliament. And that should not be too difficult to raise. You know that James has proposed that his infant son should be betrothed to the Princess Cecilia, child-daughter of King Edward? Parliament has not been consulted on that. And there is now talk of my sister Margaret being offered as wife for the Duke of Clarence, Edward's brother and heir. If that was agreed, it would bind the two nations more closely."

"And would *you* be for that?"

"I think so. We have been enemies for too long. Better that we be friends – if that is possible. Such ties could help. And England sides with Charles of Burgundy. Margaret says that she has been told that Clarence is a personable young man and has no other hopes. You have doubts?"

"No-o-o. Save that I do not see Scotland gaining much by such ties. It would suit Edward well if he could be assured that Scotland would not attack his rear when he goes campaigning in France. But what do we gain? If we could win something in exchange . . ."

"Such as?"

"Well – Berwick-on-Tweed! Archie is for ever complaining about Berwick being in English hands, since he is Warden of the East March. It is the cause of constant trouble. The

175

English raid from there. And our Scots Border scoundrels and law-breakers, when they are all but cornered, flee into Berwick, and they are safe from him. Berwick is a Scots town. It was, and should be, the capital of Berwickshire, and one of our greatest ports. From that port is exported most of the wool from the Lammermuirs, our greatest sheep-rearing territory – and it is the English merchants who gain. Berwick was stolen from Scotland. Parliament could demand it back as price for these royal betrothals."

"Johnnie – splendid! That would make an excellent excuse for calling a parliament. James could not object to it, might well see it as to his own advantage, a feather in his bonnet! Yes, that would serve. A treaty to win back Berwick. The English may not accede to it. But it is worth the attempt, and gives the excuse we would require . . ."

Crossing the high pass between the Paps of Fife, as the twin Lomond Hills were called, Mary had another notion.

"The matter of the errant Earl of Ross. If he was ordered to appear before this parliament and make his obedience to James before all, that would much please my brother, raise his pride. Make him the more ready to call the parliament. Even if Ross, in the end, did not come."

"He might not, no. But I think that his son Angus Og would come. He has been made a lord of parliament, and this would be his first chance to show himself as such, to demonstrate his new standing as Lord of the Isles. And if his father came also . . . !"

On into northern Fife they rode, as the afternoon wore on, and by the time that they had passed Lindores Loch such sun as there was was setting fast; and they had still another dozen miles to go. John felt that it had been too lengthy a ride to impose on the young woman, but she would not hear of it. She had ridden further than this in the past, although perhaps not in January conditions, and so soon after giving birth.

It was almost dark before they reached Flisk, where there was a chapelry of Balmerinoch Abbey, and here they halted to seek a guide for the remaining miles. Abbot Walter's name was sufficient to gain them a young monk's aid, who, somewhat overawed by having a princess to escort, assured them that it was only another couple of miles to the abbey, and he would have them there before vespers. Mounted on a shaggy garron, he led the way.

They were glad of the guidance, for there was much woodland hereabouts, which made track-keeping difficult in the dark. But in fact the last half-mile required little leading, for an abundance of lights ahead proclaimed the abbey's situation – and, as John observed, proclaimed also its denizens' preoccupation with bees and wax-making; candles and lamps were very much in evidence, every window appearing to be lit up. Their guide declared that Balmerinoch was the Lamp of Fife in more respects than one.

Unheralded as they were, the visitors were kindly received by Abbot Walter, who well remembered John and was much impressed by the identity of his companion. He however knew nothing of the death of Archbishop Graham, nor indeed that he had been at Lochleven Castle, the last that he had heard being that he was staying at Inchcolm Abbey. He was much shocked.

Over a simple but adequate repast the abbot expressed his shame over Holy Church's treatment of its foremost divine and true leader, and his horror at the denial of Christian interment. When asked if he would come with his guests to rectify this grievous wrong, he showed no hesitation. Yes, he would go with them, the least that any humble servant of God could do. They would go in the morning, after prime and sunrise.

Thankful indeed for this, the visitors attended the service of compline, the last of the day's offices, and were thereafter conducted from the chapel to the abbey's guest-house, young as the evening was, monks being early bedders. Ushered into what looked like a small hall, sparsely furnished, but with a good fire blazing on the hearth, they were bidden goodnight, and left.

Looking around them they saw that this apartment had unusual features. Along the opposite lateral wall from the fireplace was a series of five open cubicles, each provided with a bed, folded blankets and a *prie-dieu* chair, that was all. The

177

sixth cell had a door, and opening this they discovered that it held a table, two basins and two pails, one with steaming water, the other empty. There was also a bar or narrow bench, behind which was another pail, obviously for sanitary purposes.

John cleared his throat. "This is not where Abbot Henry and I were lodged when we bedded down in Balmerinoch. We were in the abbot's quarters. This is . . . less than adequate for such as yourself, Mary. Clearly they are not used to entertaining women!"

"We will do very well here, never fear," she said easily. "It is warm, we are well fed. And we have gained what we came for."

"Yes. But here is scant privacy!"

"We are not halflins, Johnnie, not bairns either. I am a married woman, much married! And you? No prudish and guarded lordling, I think?"

"That was not what I meant," he said, and left it at that.

They sat by the fire for a while, and although they had a sufficiency of issues to discuss, they also found that they could sit in companionable silence, which was pleasing. But they had had a long and tiring ride, and presently Mary was yawning frankly.

"Yonder couch calls me, Johnnie," she decided. "Have you any preference which? They all look alike to me."

He shook his head dumbly.

"That water in there will still be warm," she went on. "Perhaps we should have had it here by the fire? But it will serve. I feel in need of a washing, after all the horse-work."

"Yes."

"I will leave sufficient for you. How far have we ridden today? Fifty miles?"

"More."

"As well that we have sturdy mounts. How far tomorrow?"

"To Loch Leven, perhaps thirty miles."

Rising and patting his shoulder, she went over to one of the cubicles. There were no curtains or hangings to enclose their fronts.

He heard her humming some melody to herself over there for a little, but kept his gaze firmly on the fire's blaze.

The humming changed to a tinkling laugh. "These monks do not favour bedrobes, I see," she called. "A blanket must do instead."

"H'rr'mm. Yes," he said, without turning his head.

He heard her pad over to the end cell, open its door and then close it behind her. Thereafter there were sundry clangings of pails and splashings. He fed logs to the fire.

Then the door opened again. "Johnnie, I fear that I have used more than my share of the water," she announced. "Will this be enough for you? Or do you wish to go out and seek more? Where from, I do not know. They will all be abed by now."

That, with more pail-clanking, more or less compelled him to turn his head. Mary was standing in the doorway, pail in hand, draped in a grey blanket, its inadequacy as a covering entirely apparent. Although she held it approximately in place with the other hand, long white legs were inevitably evident, as was one shoulder and arm.

He rose. "I need little water," he jerked. "What is left will serve."

She smiled. "You have not seen how little there is!" A laugh. "You could always use some of what I have washed in? Or would that be quite unsuitable for a man so heedful of what is proper? Yet, you have seven sisters, have you not? You must be well used to females' persons."

He swallowed, but moved over to the cell door. "You are different," he got out, that was all.

"Not so very different, surely?" She turned back and put her pail down beside the other. "Male and female created He them! Do I . . . incommode you, Johnnie?"

"No. No, not so. It is but that I feel that I, I intrude here. On your privacy."

"We have no choice. Do I intrude on yours?"

"With a man, it is . . . otherwise."

"Very well. I leave you to your so scanty washings. But you will come and bid me goodnight thereafter, privacy or

179

none." That was in the nature of a royal command. Hitching up her blanket, she turned and left him to the candles and pails, closing the door behind her.

His ablutions were indeed and necessarily brief, although he did use the young woman's water, and not with any reluctance. His use of the further-back pail was somewhat preoccupied. Still fairly well covered, in shirt and breeches, he emerged. He went to extinguish the room's candles, although the fire still provided its own flickering illumination.

"I like the firelight," Mary declared. "Companionable. Friendly. This is pleasant, is it not?"

He could by no means disagree, but was concerned that his so pleasurable excitation was not too evident. "It is more than that," he exclaimed.

"Ah. You enjoy the firelight also? Better than all Abbot Walter's candles! This bed is hard. But it will not prevent me sleeping, I think."

He went over to her cubicle. She was sitting up under one blanket, still with the other draped round her shoulders. She patted the bed.

"Sit here," she said.

He obeyed. Even the patting gesture had disturbed that blanket a little, and disturbed the man further, since it revealed more white flesh, and the deep shadow of the cleft between her breasts. She hitched it back again, but easily, naturally.

"You are . . . beautiful!" That came from him involuntarily, but heartfelt.

"You think so, Johnnie? You are kind. Although, perhaps, *I* am not? Putting you to something of a test, in this? Your manhood. Yet I am woman, too. And cherish your regard. Am I lacking in consideration? When, when . . ."

"When we both know that you are not for me!" he finished for her, more harshly than he intended.

Biting her lip, she reached out to touch his arm, to further blanket-disarrangement.

"That is not *quite* true, Johnnie," she told him. "We cannot be each other's, no, while I am a married woman, however little I love my husband. But we can be, we are, for each other, close, in friendship and understanding and trust. We have much, together."

"Trust!" he interjected. "Trust, yes! There you have it. You trust me. So . . . !"

She searched his face in the firelight. "Oh, Johnnie, Johnnie – what am I doing to you? In trusting you so. Do you wish that I did not? We would not be here, thus, if I did not."

He spread his hands. "No. I am a fool! I should not have said that."

"You think . . . that if I did not so trust you, you would feel more free? Your own man. To do . . . what?"

"There you have me! To do what! I would not offend, hurt, misuse *you*, even if I was not trusted. I told you – I am a fool, Mary."

"Perhaps we both are foolish in this. And yet – there is caring and joy in it also, is there not? Which we would both be the poorer without?"

"I would not be without it, without *you*, for, for aught else in this world!"

They considered each other there, silent, words quite inadequate, and so sat. Then she leaned over towards him.

"Go to your own couch, John Douglas. While we still have our wits and wills. Better so. Still able to rejoice in what we *have* – and not weeping for what we cannot have."

So near to him now, her face upturned to his, and that blanket falling away, he had to take her in his arms, nothing else sufficed. They kissed. Inevitably one of his hands moved down to cup and fondle one of her full breasts. Nor did she shrink back nor push him away, responded rather in her own feminine fashion.

For long moments they remained thus. Then, sighing, he it was drew back, and rose, stepping away, to look down on her. She did not replace the blanket.

181

"Oh, Mary!" was all that he could say.

"Goodnight, my dear," she answered. "I shall not forget this night. Goodnight. But – do not go far from me. The next cell. And we can still talk . . . ere we sleep."

"Talk!" he ejaculated, but recovered himself. "Yes, talk." Swinging round, he strode over to the fire to feed it with more logs. "We will be warm *thus*, at least!"

Turning back, he saw her still sitting up watching him, a lovely picture of womanhood indeed. He did not pause, however, but went straight to the next cubicle next to hers, to spread the folded blankets there. He threw off his clothing almost urgently, feeling that the sooner he was under those blankets the better, pointless as this was.

Mary did talk, and wisely on subjects which would not add to present stresses. She wondered whether the Earl of Ross would come to the projected parliament, and how he and his bastard son would behave if they both did; telling of a new oddity whom James had added to his increasing entourage of low-born intimates, introduced by Sheves, one Doctor Andreas, or Andrews, a Flemish astrologer who specialised in prophecies and the like; word circulating at court that Pope Sixtus, Sheves's friend, was enhancing Vatican finances by instituting and registering brothels in Rome, which were alleged to be bringing him in eighty thousand ducats yearly; and Sheves poisoning James's mind against Albany, suggesting that he was failing in his duty as Lieutenant of the Borders by encouraging Liddesdale and other West March clans to raid into England, this harming relationships with England and King Edward, when these were being improved. This last produced a reaction from John, to the effect that the possible sources of these allegations were the Lords Home and Hepburn, of the East March, who both resented Albany's lieutenantship, and indeed Archie's wardenship also, the Homes considering the latter position to be almost a hereditary right of their chiefs. Archie was in constant dispute with them over their own depredations in the borderland. John quoted some examples, and getting no response, wondered whether his companion was feeling sleepy? No answer convinced him that she was, indeed.

It took the man, however, considerably longer before he could sufficiently drown that evening's experiences in slumber.

In the morning the abbey was astir long before sunrise, and the travellers were off westwards in good time – which was as well, for Abbot Walter proved to be no fast rider, and his mount placid rather than spirited. So it took them until early afternoon to cover the thirty miles, by Lindores, Strathmiglo and Milnathort, to Kinross and Loch Leven.

There, out on the castle island, they were greeted with surprise but no hostility. And when they explained the object of their mission, Lady Douglas declared her support.

"I consider it shame indeed, to bury the archbishop so," she declared. "Robert was also against it. But Bishop Sheves was determined on it. He indeed insisted on it being done, and there and then, in his presence. I, at least, sinner as I may be, said a silent prayer over the grave, if that was the only one! Robert, I fear, is not a great one for praying!"

Her husband shrugged. "There are prayers and prayers," he said.

"Well, we are here to rectify that wrong," John declared. "Abbot Walter will give Archbishop Patrick due Christian burial."

"How?" Sir Robert demanded. "Since he is already under the sod."

"Where is that?"

"In a corner of this island. It is rocky, so there is little soft ground for burying."

"We shall have him up, then," the abbot said. "With all reverence. The grave will not be deep. Then inter him again in more worthy fashion."

"In the same place?" Mary wondered.

Lady Douglas spoke up. "I would have had him buried on

St Serf's Isle. A suitable resting-place, a holy spot. Why not there, now?"

The visitors eyed her questioningly.

"I have heard of it," Abbot Walter said.

"It is an island at the other end of this loch. Small but fair. Larger than this, indeed green not rocky. The Columban St Serf, from Culross Abbey, had his hermitage there, for retreat and contemplation. Nine hundred years ago. They built a shrine and a chapel, and later a monastic house, a priory. Small but ancient, now deserted. St Serf is buried there, it is said. Also other early saints. Ronan and Moak and more. So – why not the archbishop?"

"Oh, that would be the answer!" Mary exclaimed. "Splendid! Who does it belong to, this isle?"

"I would think that it is mine, now," the laird said. "It was the property of Holy Church, of St Andrews indeed. But it is no longer used, and I have sheep on it. All around this loch is mine. So why not this island?"

"Then we must do it. With your permission, Sir Robert?"

"If Bishop Sheves found out . . . !"

"He need not. He thinks it all over, done with. Who is to tell him? Only ourselves will know. Until it is safe to speak of it. How say you, Abbot Walter?"

"That would be fit and meet, worthy, Princess. Where St Serf himself lies, and these others of the ancient Celtic Church. Yes, let us take the good archbishop there."

After refreshment for the visitors, there followed the grim business of disinterring the remains of Patrick Graham. Two of Sir Robert's men, actually the same who had done the burying, were employed to dig up the pathetic corpse, which was not difficult, the grave being very shallow, while the others watched, unspeaking.

The frail body was wrapped in old blanketing, and stank only slightly, the cold weather helpful in this. It was then raised and laid on a sort of pallet or stretcher, used for carrying the fishermen's nets, and carried down in a sad little procession. It was carefully placed in the laird's barge, the shovels added, and the five mourners embarked. The two diggers now commenced their quite lengthy row, of almost two miles apparently. Apart from the heavy breathing of these, the creak of the oars and the splash of water, that was a hushed passage.

There were five other islands in the loch, they were told, but these were small indeed. As they drew near the priory isle they could see that it was very different from the one that they had left, perhaps three times as large, triangular-shaped, fairly level, grassy, with a few small hawthorn trees. Sheep grazed. There were buildings at the southern end, few and nowise impressive, and a little jetty at the tip or point nearby.

They landed here and went to prospect. There was no indication as to where the burial ground might be, but almost certainly it would be fairly close to the abandoned priory buildings. No headstones were evident. Anywhere there, then, would do. Even on a grey winter's day it was a lovely and peaceful place.

They let Abbot Walter choose a suitable spot, and set the two oarsmen to digging again, hoping that they would not disturb the remains of others. No depth of grave was necessary.

Whilst the diggers worked, the others examined the little monastic establishment, not so much ruined as abandoned, deserted. It had obviously always been modest, functional, never a major establishment. Abbot Walter told them it could not have been so very long thus, for Andrew Wynton had retired here to write his famous *Original Chronicle of Scotland*, towards the end of last century. He deplored the fact that it was now deserted. But John, and Mary also, were otherwise minded, and said that they liked it as it was, with its aura of peace and quiet, its activities past, its present gentle solitude. Let it remain haunted only by the spirits of good men who have passed on to better things. Sir Robert coughed at that, while his wife looked at her son and the younger woman thoughtfully.

It did not take long for the shallow cavity to be dug – and no other bones unearthed. Then they all moved down to the barge again, the diggers to lift out the shrouded body and carry it reverently up to the open grave and place it therein, the others following silently, to gather round.

The abbot fulfilled his part admirably thereafter, not hurrying over it nor yet going on overlong, saying a prayer of thankfulness for the life of the departed, declaring him now in God's nearer presence and spared the further pains and trials of this life, whilst savouring the joys of the next. He declared that Scotland was his debtor, however ill it had treated him. But he also asked the Almighty's forgiveness on those who had, in their misjudgment and error, brought sorrow on one of Christ's humble and faithful servants. Then, with the sign of the cross, and a sprinkling of holy water from a little phial he produced, he committed the earthly parts of Patrick Graham to his Maker, in the sure and certain hope of final resurrection, assured that his more important part, his eternal soul and spirit, was already on its way, joyfully, to bliss in a much more rewarding and challenging life.

That left them all wordless, to add, if they could, their own incoherent contributions. Mary squeezed John's arm.

The sheep nearby watched, and grazed and watched again.

Then a token sprinkling of soil, and the men took up their spades to cover all and replace the turf. So they left Scotland's first archbishop, in good hands.

There was little more talk on the return sail than on the outward one.

It was dusk by the time that they reached the castle isle again, and clearly all three visitors would have to spend the night there. Isabel Douglas proved to be an excellent and careful hostess; and the castle was large enough to provide them all with separate rooms, no remarks being passed about the previous night's accommodation.

After supper, Mary declared fairly soon that she was tired and would seek her couch, Abbot Walter having already retired to his devotions – which enabled John to have a talk alone with his mother before the hall fire, Sir Robert tactfully absenting himself.

It was difficult and jerky converse at first. But as her son warmed to his theme, telling her how all at Tantallon would welcome a visit from her, and urging her to it, his mother did react less diffidently, less guiltily, and ended by promising to come and see them all, in the spring. Thereafter they got on more easily, naturally, with even stirrings of affection, the woman telling him of her years of sorrow and shame, yet of knowing that somehow she had had to do as she did – and indeed, to be honest, would do the same again. Did John understand what love, deep love, between a woman and a man could engender? Not just affection, esteem, attraction, but the love which was more strong, more important than life itself? And Isabel Douglas searched her son's face.

Gulping a little, he said that he thought that he might understand it.

"That woman? The princess? Another man's wife. With children by two husbands!"

"We are . . . good friends. That only. She cannot be for me."

"No, I fear not. And yet . . . ?"

"Friends," he reiterated. And rose. "I go to my bed now, Mother."

"Yes. Your own? Or hers?"

"My own. I told you, friends only."

"But, you do favour women? Not like . . . some men?"

"Oh, yes. I sufficiently favour women! But . . ." He left the rest unsaid.

She accompanied him up to his room door. "I would wish you to be happy, John, my son," she said. "And happiness is not always easily come by!"

"I know it. A man must be content, it seems, with less than his desires!"

"And a woman also! That one cares for you, Johnnie. Go kindly with her, but heedfully. Although – who am I to counsel you?"

Nodding, he kissed her forehead, and said goodnight.

Again he had sufficient to think about, before sleeping.

Next day, Sir Robert solved a problem for his visitors by

providing his useful couple of men to escort Abbot Walter back to Balmerinoch, which allowed Mary and John to head straight for Stirling, all parting on good terms, with a feeling of duty done.

11

That parliament did eventuate, but it took until mid-March to assemble it, by which time there had been developments which added to its drama and significance. And these, in turn, assured a good attendance.

In the meantime, John had been sampling his new duties as Warden-Depute of the East March, and finding them scarcely to his taste. Archie, being Archie, saw to all the more interesting and exciting tasks himself, leaving the humdrum and routine ones to his brother, too many of which consisted of sitting in judgment on Border thieves, reivers, ravishers and the like, and seeking to settle disputes between unruly neighbours, not his choice of activity, especially the superintending of hangings ordered by Albany or Archie. This he found taxing in the extreme, and frequently and shamefully he deputed to underlings, to his own self-judgment – although, where at all possible, he sought to commute to sentences of imprisonment. He was not cut out for magistracy, he quickly recognised.

He was glad, therefore, when the summons to parliament had to be obeyed, and a return made to Stirling – and not only because of business of state.

He found Mary, with her husband and family, the Lady Anna in attendance, in the princess's wing of the palace block; so on this occasion it was unlikely that there would be any problems of an intimate nature. But the castle was overcrowded, so that Archie and John were given a room to share in Mary's lodging, which produced satisfaction and frustration both.

Rumours abounded at Stirling on the eve of the parliament. The Earl of Ross was said to be in the town but not parading his identity. The Lords Home and Hailes were going to make a charge against the Duke of Albany. A papal nuncio had arrived from Rome, and William Sheves was in smiling mood. The astrologer Andreas had prophesied alarmingly that the lion would be attempted to be devoured by its whelps, and King James was taking this personally. And so on. Lord Hamilton declared that the morrow was going to be lively. Mary was anxious. Much would depend on Albany, inevitably, and she did not altogether trust that brother's judgment any more than the others'.

Archie said that all would be well. The right would triumph. But John did not fail to share Mary's forebodings.

With much business to be enacted, the parliament was to start earlier than usual, in mid-forenoon. So the less important lords, clerics, commissioners and burgh representatives had to be up betimes and taking their seats, John amongst them. He sat between the Lords Seton and Livingstone.

Presently he saw Mary and her Anna come to occupy the minstrels' gallery, amongst the illustrious visitors, and they exchanged looks. Shortly afterwards a senior cleric ushered in a red-robed portly prelate to the gallery, presumably the papal nuncio.

After the Lyon King of Arms, to trumpet-call, made the announcement that this parliament, called by royal command, was now going into session, the earls filed in, followed by the bishops and mitred abbots. John noted that William Sheves was not amongst these clerics.

Another trumpet blast ushered in Lord Avondale, the Chancellor, looking his age and frail, who went to his table in the centre of the dais and remained standing, which was unusual. He was followed by Bishop Laing, of Glasgow, the Lord High Treasurer.

There was a pause and then more trumpeting had Lyon ordering all to stand. The assumption was that this would herald the bringing in of the symbols of state, borne before the monarch. But no, it introduced Sheves by himself, and most gloriously attired, from jewelled mitre downwards. He paced over to take up a stance, not amongst the other bishops but behind the throne. None there failed to recognise the significance of this.

The sword, sceptre and crown were then carried in by Hamilton, Buchan and Atholl, followed by the Duke of Albany and his brother John, Earl of Mar. The symbols were laid on the Chancellor's table, whilst the royal brothers went to stand behind the throne also, glaring at Sheves who was already there. The enmity between these three could not have been more evident.

Then Lyon was announcing the presence of the high and mighty James, by God's grace High King of Scots, and the sovereign hurried in, looking anxious, wary, more unsure of himself than any other who had preceded him. He went to sit on his throne, and Sheves bent to murmur something in his ear and even patted the royal shoulder.

All sat down, save for the Chancellor, and the three standing behind the throne.

Then Avondale turned to face the King. "Sire, with your royal permission, I declare parliament, duly called, now in session. But before we proceed to business, have I Your Grace's authority to make an especial announcement of great importance and significance, to all present and to all your realm?"

James nodded.

"This announcement emanates from Rome, the Vatican, in a letter from Pope Sixtus, brought by His Excellency Monsignor Prosper Camogli de Medici, his nuncio. It appoints the Bishop-Coadjutor of St Andrews, Master William Sheves, to be Metropolitan of Scotland, Archbishop of St Andrews and Primate of Holy Church in this realm. He will be consecrated hereafter at the Abbey of the Holy Rood in Edinburgh."

There was silence in the hall.

"It need not be emphasised how much this of Metropolitan status means to the nation," Avondale went on. "No longer may the English Archbishop of York claim spiritual hegemony over us. Nor the Kings of England use such claims to support their own of paramouncy. Which claims have plagued us for centuries. Great is our gain. We hail

191

our new Metropolitan!" No mention was made of Patrick Graham.

One or two voices were raised in acclaim, but only one or two – and none from the ranks of the bishops.

"With Your Grace's permission, the Archbishop of St Andrews will now address the assembly."

William Sheves stepped forward, bowed to the King and raised a high hand. "I greet all, in God's holy name!" he announced sonorously. "A new day dawns for His Grace's realm of Scotland. All must contribute to it, all!" He paused there and looked around him, almost challengingly. "His Holiness the Pope sends greetings to all the faithful. It is our great blessing to have thus gained his favour." Another pause, that all might recognise whom they had to thank for that. "We are grateful, Sire, my lords spiritual and temporal and commissioners of parliament. And in token of which, my first act as Metropolitan and Primate is this. I hereby appoint to the vacant see of Caithness the bearer of these most welcome tidings, His Excellency Monsignor Prosper Camogli de Medici." He looked up to the minstrels' gallery, and beckoned. "Come down, Prosper, Bishop of Caithness, and take your place in this assembly."

There were gasps from all around as men stared at each other. Never had such a thing been heard of, a foreigner being made a Scots bishop, Italian or other. Was it possible? How could it be? Would he stay on in Scotland? Work in his diocese? Or would it be purely a nominal position? In which case who would serve Caithness, the land's most northerly bishopric short of Orkney?

Men had time to ask each other such questions before the Italian got down from the gallery, to come and bow to the King, to Sheves, to the gathering and, saying no word, walked over to the bishops' benches and sat down. He received no welcome smiles from those already there.

"I have one matter further to declare to you before my lord Chancellor resumes," Sheves added. "Bishop Prosper has brought information from His Holiness which is of much import and which was not known to us here. Charles, Duke of

Burgundy is dead. Slain in battle with the Switzers. Defeated twice and slain. God's hand justly against him. This event alters all." Nodding to the Chancellor, he turned and went back to stand behind the King.

To say that the company was thunderstruck would be little exaggeration. Here was an astonishment, a development scarcely conceivable, an event to change the face of Christendom. For two decades Charles the Bold had been the greatest warrior of Europe, holding the balance between the Empire, France and Spain, expected to be about to set up his own central kingdom. Now – dead! And defeated. Slain by that small folk, the Swiss!

Archie Douglas turned round in the earls' benches to stare at John. This, of course, as Sheves had said, altered everything. There would be no call now to go to the King of France's aid, no opportunity for James to act the commander. Albany's projected rallying of this parliament against that folly was now unnecessary. In a moment, all was changed. Exclamation, talk, filled the hall.

Avondale banged his gavel for quiet. "Hear me. I also have tidings which concern this parliament and the royal house. His Grace has been informed by King Edward of England that his brother, the Duke of Clarence, formerly English Lieutenant of the North and who was to be betrothed to His Grace's sister, the Princess Margaret, has been found guilty of treason against his brother, and has been executed. Drowned. In wine. In a butt of Malmsley wine! So . . ."

Again noise erupted, drowning the Chancellor's further words, at this third announcement of the scarcely believable.

John looked up at Mary, who shook her head, clearly at a loss.

When he could make himself heard, the Chancellor added the obvious. "So the proposed marriage of the Princess Margaret is annulled. But the betrothal of the child James, Duke of Rothesay, heir to His Grace's throne, to the Princess Cecilia of England, is not altered. Peace with England remains His Grace's firm policy, as agreed by his Privy Council and parliament."

None sought to comment on that, there and then.

Avondale sat down now, and made pretence at consulting his papers. Turning in his chair, he glanced at James, and then Sheves. The latter nodded.

"The first business to put before parliament, for consideration, is a charge laid by the Lords Home and Hailes. They claim that the Duke of Albany is misusing his position as Lieutenant of the Borders. I call upon the Lord Home to speak to this charge."

That produced not uproar but a hush. To accuse the King's brother before parliament was almost unheard of. The fact that it was being done, that James was allowing it to be done, spoke for itself. Albany, it seemed, was more or less condemned in advance. There were indrawn breaths and grim faces. And many there, to be sure, felt that not only was this not the time and place for such confrontation, but also that time should have been given for discussion of the previous momentous issues, even though they were not apt for any action by parliament.

Lord Home, a spare, stern-faced man of middle years, rose. "My lord Chancellor," he said, "we in the Borders live on the edge of a sword, a sharp sword! We are at constant risk from breakers of the King's peace, from outlaws and thieves and from English raiders. The Lieutenant's duty is surely to guard honest men from all such, and to lead the Wardens of the three Marches to put down all such evil-doers. We say that the Duke of Albany has not been doing this. Indeed he himself has been leading forays into England, the which but invite further raids in retaliation. Forby, his own tenants in his lordship of Annandale are amongst the worst offenders of His Grace's peace, their hership and ravishment notour. We have protested to the duke, but to no avail. We claim parliament's aid." He sat down.

From behind the King, Albany hooted a laugh. "There speaks the man who thinks that *he* should be Lieutenant! And himself one of the most arrant leaders of reivers and despoilers of others' goods, gear and women, in all the Borderland!"

194

Avondale coughed. "My lord Duke, all remarks, all statements in parliament, should be made to the Chancellor, and in the form of motions or answers thereto."

"Tell that to Home and his friends!"

"My lord of Home, you seek parliament's aid. Do you wish to put a motion for the assembly to debate and vote upon?"

"I do. I move that the Duke of Albany be deprived of the office of Lieutenant of the Border. And another appointed in his place."

"And I second that," Lord Hailes, chief of the Hepburns, declared. "I support all that Lord Home has said, and more. The Borders need and deserve better rule than this."

"Hear a Hepburn say that – who lives on stolen cattle and robbery!"

"My lord Duke! A motion is before parliament and has been seconded. Is there any counter-motion? You may make it, if so you please."

"I will not so waste my time! And yours. How dare such as these raise voice against me, Albany?"

"As you will, my lord. Does any other wish to move on this issue?"

Archie jumped up. "I do, my lord Chancellor. I, Angus, am Warden of the East March. I know what goes on in the Borders, all too well. I *know*! I know that these lords who complain do so out of envy and spleen. Know that they themselves are the greatest law-breakers. I know that my lord duke well serves His Grace's realm in these parts. I move that this charge be dismissed as it deserves. Aye, and its movers condemned as trouble-makers!"

Next to him, Lord Seton rose. "I second that."

"So! We have a motion and counter-motion before parliament," Avondale said. "Does any other wish to speak, for or against?"

There was a pause. Most of the lords and commissioners undoubtedly favoured Albany, as a vigorous, strong and outgoing character, as against the introverted and suspicious James, who had few real friends amongst his nobility and gentry, however many low-born favourites; and clearly this charge could not have been brought thus without James's agreement. Yet he was the monarch, the source of power, to whom they all owed allegiance, however others might manipulate him. There was no eagerness to offend their liege-lord in public, although none to support Albany's enemies.

Sheves spoke. "My lord Chancellor, I hesitate to make allegations against His Grace's royal brother. But representations have been made to me that there has been a proliferation of the so-called courts of war in the Borders since the duke took over as Lieutenant. These are occasions where, instead of a due and lawful trial of offenders or contestants before a lawful court, the contenders are offered the alternative to fight it out, with swords or dirks, before the justiciar, the winner to be considered as having the rights of the case. Such duels are clearly a mockery of justice, and if the duke encourages them – "

"The litigants are given the choice," Albany interrupted. "These are no new issue, courts of chivalry. Many so choose, rather than have to attend justice-ayres with long pleadings and debate. The Borderers are warlike folk, and can so prefer. You, a clerk, may not find it to your clerkly taste! But others do." A bark of laughter. "And provide excellent sport, at times, in the doing of it!"

There was a mixed reception for that, many of the lords and knights expressing agreement, the clerics showing disapproval.

Sheves was frowning now. "I say that the duke's reply sufficiently supports this complaint. These duels are a mockery of justice, and encouraged for the entertainment of spectators! If such represent the Lieutenant of the Borders' behaviour, then there is ample cause for enquiry into the rest, I say."

Avondale, uncomfortable obviously, seized on that. "Yes, my lord Archbishop. Due consideration must be given to these complaints and charges, details produced and reasons put forward on both sides. This cannot be done here and now. A committee of causes and complaints can attend to this hereafter, to hear all, and report to the next session of parliament. Is it agreed?"

"It is not!" That was Albany strongly. "I will not stand here behind my brother and be insulted by clerks and robberbarons! Nor my affairs debated by any committee of upstarts appointed by them. I, Albany, Earl of March, Lord High Admiral of Scotland and Lieutenant of the Border, will not!" And without so much as a nod at James, he stepped out from behind the throne, all but knocking Sheves over in the doing of it, and strode to the dais door and out of the hall. After only a moment's hesitation, John of Mar followed him.

There was uproar.

It took some considerable time for order to be restored, with Avondale's gavel bang-banging. This parliament was not going to be forgotten in a hurry, little as it had produced in debate so far. James, sitting tensely on the edge of his throne, looked agitated indeed, turning to Sheves for help. That man seemed unsure of himself, for once.

It was the Chancellor, experienced as he was in coping with parliament's problems, however extraordinary this one, who effected a return to at least superficial order. He rose and managed to make himself heard. Turning to the Lyon King of Arms, he commanded, "Bring in my lord Earl of Ross."

That certainly had the company gripped, all falling silent and remaining so for long moments until Lyon returned and ushered in a fine-looking man in Highland tartans, who stared straight ahead of him, expressionless.

"John MacDonald, Earl of Ross and Lord of the Isles, to submit himself to the King's Grace," it was announced.

The earl did not look submissive. After a distinct pause, glancing neither right nor left, he paced over to the throne, bowed briefly and went down on one knee before the King, two hands out, palms apart in the traditional gesture, not of submission but of allegiance.

James cleared his throat. "Aye, then," he said. "Aye."

Sheves murmured something inaudible.

Avondale left his table to come and stand beside the kneeling man. Even he seemed a little uncertain as to procedure. "You, John of Ross . . . you have come to make your submission and humble duty to the King's Grace before this parliament,

197

as commanded. After long insurrection and treasonable acting. You have, in the past, called yourself King of the Isles, rejected the crown's authority, entered into private treaty with the King of England, and risen in arms against His Grace's forces." Launched into this, the Chancellor's voice grew stronger, more confident. "You, an earl, one of the *ri*, have rebelled against the *Ard Righ*, the High King of Scots, to your shame and *his* hurt. Can you deny this?"

Silence, but Ross remained half kneeling.

Perceiving that apparently he was going to obtain no further or spoken recantation, Avondale went on: "The penalty for treason is death, as all know well. Have you aught to say why such sentence should not be pronounced against you?"

Again no word answered him.

The Chancellor looked at the monarch and then at Sheves, but got little help from either. He continued: "Your presence here speaks for itself. And His Grace is merciful. It is his royal decision that you should be spared the full penalty of treason. You will not die. You will not even lose all your lands. But the earldom of Ross will be taken from you, and invested in the crown for all time coming. You will forfeit the lands of Kintyre and Knapdale. But, since you represent a large people, Clan Donald and its septs, subjects of His Grace, he will permit you to retain the style and title of Lord of the Isles. And that you may hereafter serve him, and them, better, he hereby creates you a lord of parliament. I repeat, a lord of parliament. For the good of this his realm. You, John, Lord of the Isles, may now take His Grace's royal hand in due token of allegiance."

James held out his hand. The kneeling man took it between his own, and then stood up. He had not spoken a word throughout.

That could not be said for others all over that hall, where further astonishment reigned. John Douglas, for one, would have been bereft of speech anyway.

"You may now take your seat amongst the lords," Avondale ended, and turned back to his table.

The Lord of the Isles nodded rather than bowed, and went to descend from the dais to go and seat himself not far from John. There had been no sign of his bastard son, Angus Og.

John, biting his lip, was staring up at Mary Stewart in the gallery, so he did not see his brother Archie turning to gesture to him from the earls' benches. Mary was leaning forward, looking distraught.

With Avondale banging for quiet again, John jumped to his feet.

"My lord Chancellor," he cried, "here is mistake, error, a grave miscarriage. The lordship of the Isles was promised, with a seat in parliament, to the earl's, this former earl's son, Angus Og MacDonald. I, John of Douglasdale, was sent to offer it to him. In return for his adherence to the royal cause, his yielding up of the royal fortresses of Inverness, Urquhart and Ruthven of Badenoch, and his denunciation of his father's treasons. That cannot now be refuted and the lordship given back to the father."

Avondale held up his hand. "My lord, you may not say 'cannot' to any action of the King's Grace. None may. It is done."

"But . . . here is a great wrong! An injustice. I went in the King's name to far Badenoch with this offer. Which was accepted. Honour is here involved. *My* honour. Yes, and the King's! Sire, hear me. This is wrong. And, if not righted, nothing is more sure than that there will be trouble in the north, dire trouble . . ."

"My lord, address me, the Chancellor, not His Grace."

"My lord Chancellor, *I* will speak," Sheves interrupted. "This young man is headstrong, but no doubt honest enough. He it is who is mistaken. He went to visit the bastard son of the former Earl of Ross, yes. But not with the King's consent nor even knowledge. He was sent by . . . others. They, no doubt, also intended well. They may have been acting *for* the King, using His Grace's name. But they were not, are not, the King! None may make nor break an earl or a lord of parliament save the King's Grace. And this is His Grace's decision."

"His Grace can unmake a decision, can he not? This will mean war, I tell you."

199

Once more there was uproar in that parliament, men shouting for and against John's stand, Avondale's banging of no avail.

Abruptly James rose, and without a word to anyone, even Sheves, hurried from the hall. After a moment or two of hesitation, Sheves followed. That parliament was ended – for without the monarch's presence it was no parliament.

The assembly broke up in disorder.

Later, in Mary's apartments, there was discussion, question, concern, exasperation, spirited indeed if permeated with a feeling of helplessness. Unfortunately the Lord Hamilton was present, and not only he but three of his older illegitimate sons, for all of whom he had obtained knighthoods – Sir John Hamilton of Brumehill, Sir Patrick Hamilton of Kincavil and Sir James Hamilton of Finnart – there because of the dire overcrowding of castle and town.

With such a variety of issues to preoccupy them, and differing attitudes thereto, inevitably the exchange was somewhat incoherent and less than orderly. But the most pressing, all came to agree, was the situation concerning Albany. What was to happen now?

Lord Hamilton was grim. "Here is a pretty pass indeed! Folly! The royal house split for all to see. James is clearly against him – this charge could not have been brought before parliament otherwise. Albany should not have walked out. He should have stayed, to put his case. Parliament would have found for him. Shown the King, and Sheves, that toad who guides him, whom the nation supports."

"I agree," his wife said. "But Alexander lacks patience. What will happen now, only the good Lord knows. John favours Alex. As do I. And our sister Margaret. James stands alone in the family. Yet he is the King, with the ultimate power. That man Sheves has him. And now that he is archbishop, and undisputed head of the Church, his influence will be the stronger."

"That man is evil!" Archie declared. "A curse on him! What

now, as to the Borders? Will Albany still remain Lieutenant? Can Sheves get him unseated there?"

"I fear that he can," Hamilton said. "At least, the King can, at his direction. This of a committee of complaints is but a screen. Had Albany waited and fought his cause, then parliament would have appointed a fair group to consider it. Now, Sheves, Home and Hailes will nominate whom they choose, and Albany will be found at fault. And dismissed, by royal command. Nothing is more sure."

"Damn them!"

"Alex will not take that lying down," Mary said. "There will be great trouble, I fear."

"What can he do?" John asked. "Lieutenant means the *King*'s lieutenant. If the King dismisses him . . . ?"

"*I* care not whether he is Lieutenant of the Borders, or not," Mary asserted. "He is Earl of March, and has the castles of Dunbar and Hermitage and Caerlaverock, in the three Marches. His style of Duke of Albany means little. But the earldom of March is different. What matters is the clash between my brothers. What it will lead to? The one headstrong, the other fearful, envious, and therefore dangerous."

They considered that with head-shakings.

"And myself?" Archie demanded. "What of me? Am I still to be Warden of the East March? All know that I am Albany's man. No doubt, whilst Home will be seeking to be Lieutenant, Hailes will be wanting my wardency."

None could answer that. The position was also a royal appointment.

"You will remain Warden until you are unseated," Mary said. "Does the position mean so much to you?"

"No-o-o. But I have unfinished business there. And I would not wish to see that rogue Hailes in my place."

"You may be otherwise occupied!" John put in. "We all may. For there will be war in the north. Angus Og MacDonald is not going to accept this of his father being given back the lordship of the Isles after the bargain struck. He was to have a seat in parliament. This was base, a treachery. He will fight.

201

And the Islesmen are fierce and have galley fleets which we, or the King, have not."

"That was ill done," Mary agreed. "And folly indeed. After all your good work, Johnnie."

"We will put down the Highland cateran," Sir James Hamilton averred. "Easily enough. That is the least of our troubles."

"Be not so sure, boy," his father told him. "*You* have not seen these Highlands and Isles, these long sea lochs and savage mountains. They are a plague to any armed host. Only ships, galleys, can prevail there. And these Islesmen are in treaty with the English, do not forget."

"But the English are now tamed, for us, are they not? This of the betrothal of the King's son to Edward's daughter."

"They are both but children. Much can happen before they come of age. I do not trust that Edward. These English leopards do not change their spots! He will do anything which will further his immediate needs and interests. Even slay his own brother Clarence . . . !"

"To drown him in wine!" Sir Patrick exclaimed. "That was dastardly!"

"That is Edward the Fourth! Remember it when you talk of the English being tamed."

"At least there is no longer the need to dissuade the King from leading an army to France," John said. "This of the death of Charles the Bold is beyond all strange. Scarcely to be credited. Defeated by the *Swiss*!"

"He was my husband's friend." Mary did not qualify that, there in front of her present husband. "Aided him when James abandoned him. I grieve for Duke Charles. Nevertheless, this of the ending of the French venture is the only good to have come out of this parliament, I do judge."

All acceded to that.

The archbishopric situation, and the astonishing appointment of the Italian to the See of Caithness drew some comment. But as far as Mary and John were concerned, it was the complete silence over Patrick Graham, his gaining of the Metropolitan status, his death a prisoner, and his

202

shameful burying, which most distressed them. But in this company they did not know whether they could altogether trust these Hamiltons with the secret reinterment, and did not divulge it.

Archie, eating over, declared that he was going in search of Albany. He was soon back, distinctly bemused, not to say somewhat offended. The word was that the duke had already departed from Stirling, presumably for his castle of Dunbar, without apparently any message left for Archie or other. What now?

Bed, John suggested. Enough for one day. Mary had already gone.

12

At Tantallon, John was almost thankful that the wardency situation was so uncertain meantime, since it meant that he was not required for duties as depute – and he had more than sufficient to keep him busy nearer home, without that. The fact was that Archie left more and more of the duties and responsibilities of lord of his broad acres to his brother, seeing his own role as an earl of Scotland as more concerned with national affairs. This was, in a way, somewhat amusing, in that, because of his continuing association with the Princess Mary, John in fact probably played the larger part in such affairs, although usually in a covert, unproclaimed fashion, not exactly secret. And there was much which required to be seen to at Tantallon and its wide domain, which included large stretches of the green Lammermuir Hills, whence much of the earldom's revenues came. These grassy and heathery hills, rounded and bare, in the sense that they were little wooded save in their secret valleys, quite lofty but not rugged like the Highland mountains, were the main sheep-rearing area of Scotland, hundreds of square but very curving miles of high pasture, ideal for the hardy native black-faced sheep. The wet winter had engendered much liver-fluke amongst the flocks, and this was the death of many, entailing much work for the shepherds just before lambing-time, for the ailing beasts had to be killed off and skinned for their wool, wool being the single greatest money-earner for the Douglases. There were also the mills to keep an eye on. The earldom had many constituent baronies, and amongst the profitable baronial privileges was ownership of mills at which the grain of the farmers, tenants and crofters must be ground, at a percentage commission for the barony. The allocation of rigs for growing crops, narrow strips of land, had to be changed in rotation annually, so that no holder got all the best ground, and frequently there were arguments about this, and authority had to be exercised, human nature being what it was. The far-flung common grazings, too, could be a source of dispute, especially with neighbouring landowners. With all this, and much else, the stewards could usually deal; but not infrequently the lord's own decision was called for. The new Border duties had meant that the brothers had rather neglected these at home.

So John was kept busy, but was glad to be at Tantallon, with his sisters, and to have some little time for what Archie called his ballad-mongering, but little practised since he had become so friendly with Mary Stewart. Not that the princess did not arouse poetry and romantic urges in the man, but her interests in the realm's affairs tended to have him preoccupied.

And this involvement again interrupted, when less than a month after the parliament, another message arrived from Stirling, with a plea for John's presence and help. Details were not sent, but a note of urgency was.

He was on his way next morning, local duties or none, and far from annoyed or depressed by the summons, however disturbing the cause might well be.

He found Stirling Castle in a very different state from when he had last been there, no longer crowded or busy, indeed all but empty of great ones. The King and court, it appeared, were gone to Edinburgh, to the Abbey of the Holy Rood there, for the consecration of Archbishop Sheves. Mary, however, had excused herself from attending.

John could not complain about his reception. She clasped him to her in frankest affection and warmth, even though Anna and the children were watching, exclaiming her joy at seeing him and her gratitude at his so prompt coming.

"Oh, Johnnie, Johnnie – your heart must sink when my monkish messengers arrive at Tantallon!" she told him. "Always I am calling upon you. And always it is trouble. But who else can I turn to? Who else *would* I turn to?"

"I would not have it otherwise," he declared, and with entire conviction.

"You are good, kind. But I fear that you must tire of it. And nothing in it all to your own advantage. The reverse, it may be."

"I am advantaged by your trust and presence." He could not say more in this company. "What is the trouble you speak of, Highness? In this ever-troubled realm."

"Johnnie, you need not Highness me, here. Anna knows of my regard for you. The trouble is John, the other John. My brother. John of Mar. He is taken, imprisoned. At the castle of Craigmillar, near to Edinburgh."

"The Earl of Mar? Imprisoned! The King's own brother! Here is madness!"

"Aye, well may you say it. But it is true. James, on the urging of Sheves and that man Cochrane, his craftsman friend, crafty indeed, has ordered it."

"But why? The prince has done no ill. Commits no offence against the King, or other. He may not love Sheves – but who does?"

"They have hatched a plot, such as only James would heed. I think that it is to get at Alex, at Albany, whom they do fear, using poor John as bait for their trap. You remember that canard which the astrologer Andreas invented about the so-called divination that the whelps would devour the lion? At Home's and Hailes's bidding. Cochrane contrived that for them, and got James to listen, to esteem it as referring to himself as the lion and his brothers as the whelps. It stems from that. Now they have produced another alleged prophecy, this time by a witch whom they have brought into this castle, who says that her familiar spirit informs her that John has been employing magical sorceries against the King, and that James was intended to be laid low by his nearest kindred . . ."

"Save us, how crazed can the King be? To believe such tales! Witches and warlocks, sorcerers and astrologers! He is not a child . . ."

"He believes what Sheves and Cochrane tell him. They say that Andreas foretold the death of Duke Charles of Burgundy. Whether he did or not, I know not. But James accepts it.

And accepts this latest charge. And has locked up John in Craigmillar."

"Why imprison him? What threat could John of Mar be to the King? Or to Sheves?"

"I think that it is not so much John as Alex, whom they fear. Alex is strong enough, vigorous enough, and ambitious, to think that perhaps he might unseat James and have himself proclaimed King. That might just possibly be so. And by imprisoning John, they think to bring Alex hastening back from his strong fortress of Dunbar, to win his freedom. A trap to lure Alex into their clutches."

"Lord! You think that? And then . . . ?"

"Then, I believe, it will be Alex's turn to be imprisoned. So both the 'whelps' will be caged! I fear for him. I fear for them both."

"Albany will not be so easily taken."

"I am not so sure. They will coax him to come to John's aid. Perhaps even say that John is sick, asking for him. It is horrible, shameful. My own brothers! And I greatly fear. For they are saying that the matter of the Duke of Clarence, Edward of England's brother, was of a like sort. That his alleged treason was foretold by another astrologer, who also prophesied that he would die drowned in wine! So James, poor, superstitious, foolish James, is the more concerned."

"This is the Devil's work indeed!"

"Yes. But I must save my brothers from the Devil if I can. So I turn to you, Johnnie. Will you go hot-foot to Dunbar? To warn Alex not to come to Edinburgh or Craigmillar. Not, at least, without a strong force to protect him. He *will* probably come, being Alex. But if he is sufficiently escorted they may not be able to harm him. Your brother Archie will be with him at Dunbar? Tell him. Alex is headstrong, impulsive. He may dash off, with few to guard him. Archie could use his Douglas men-at-arms. I do not altogether trust my present husband to do anything which may be against his own interests. He is at Edinburgh, with James."

"I will do what you say."

"How soon can you be at Dunbar?"

"I came in the barge, to Airth. By water, I could be back at Dunbar in six or seven hours. Or a little longer, depending on the winds. It is but ten miles beyond Tantallon. But they may not be there. They could be anywhere in the Borders."

"Well, if they are not, it will also be harder for James's call to reach them. There is that to it. But haste is essential. I would come with you, but Baby James is sick. Anyway, I might but delay you . . ."

"I can ride for Airth at once. Late April light lasts long. Sail at dawn. So long as the wind does not turn easterly I could be at Dunbar by soon after midday."

"That gives you no peace, no rest. You must eat . . ."

"Food, yes. Anything will serve. I would wish to linger — but time could be all-important."

"Yes. I would accompany you as far as Airth. But it would mean riding back alone in darkness."

"Not to think of it . . ."

Anna was seeing to food being brought for him, cold venison, bread, cake and wine.

John left without delay, swallowing his disappointment over the brevity of his visit. He rode into quite heavy April showers, unpleasant — but at least the wind was still in the west, to speed his voyage.

Dunbar Castle was as unusual as was Tantallon, perhaps more so, for not only was it built on cliffs above the sea, not so high as were Tantallon's, but it also extended out into the sea itself, on rock stacks, these separate towers linked above the tides by covered stone bridges, themselves fortified, under one of which was the entrance to Dunbar harbour, a useful arrangement which allowed the lord thereof to close the haven at will by letting down a timber barrier, thus enabling him to exact his tithe of all the fishing-boats' catches. The castle was all but impregnable from the land, deep ditches keeping sows, mangonels and battering-rams at a safe distance; and from the sea any attack against those tall perpendicular stacks all but impossible. Starving out would be the only way of winning the place.

Approaching in the barge from the north, the Bass Rock now far behind them, open sea here, not the calmer waters of the firth, John saw the great wooden boom or barrier come down from the second bridge as they drew near. The guards there presumably had not recognised the device of the Douglas arms, embellished by the Bruce heart, which flew from the craft's mast-head, although he would have thought that it would be sufficiently well known here. John had been to Dunbar often of course, but never come by sea.

At the boom, which closed the harbour, oars shipped, he shouted up to men peering down from an open gap in the bridge.

"The Lord of Douglasdale to see the Duke of Albany."

"His Highness isna here, lord," a voice told him.

Cursing beneath his breath, he asked where Albany was. It was important. To be told that the duke did not inform the likes of them what he was about.

"Then, my brother, the Earl of Angus. Is he here?"

"He's gone to Eyemouth, lord. To hang wreckers."

"Eyemouth." That was another score of miles down this Berwickshire coast. "Is the duke with him?"

"They didna gang thegither. The duke rode off yestreen."

What to do, then? Best to see Archie as quickly as possible. The barge could be at Eyemouth in a couple of hours. Better that than landing and borrowing a horse. He waved to the guards and ordered his oarsmen to get their sweeps out again. They were not finished their labours yet.

The coastline south of Dunbar soon became very different from heretofore, after some low-lying ground and shelving beaches, quickly beginning to rise dramatically to vivid red cliffs and scars, heuchs as they were called, almost bright scarlet in colour, these presently giving way to enormous craggy and savage precipices, hundreds of feet high. This was, indeed, the knuckle-end of the Lammermuir Hills abruptly reaching the sea, and shaking defiant fist at it, a coast well known and feared by mariners as one of the most dangerous in all Scotland, the cliff-foots strewn with reefs and fangs, amidst which the tides boiled and surged in breaking spray

209

even on calm days. And its reputation was not enhanced by a feature which stood out, halfway down one of the beetling cliffs, a castle perched incredibly on a spur of the precipice, reachable only its occupiers knew how. This was Fast Castle, a Home stronghold, notorious as a wreckers' hold, from which ships were lured to their doom on the rocks at night by clusters of lights carried along the cliff-tops to give the impression of safe harbourage and population. Once wrecked, the crews and passengers were slaughtered and cargoes of any value stolen. The name Fast was a corruption of *faux*, false – False Castle.

The Tantallon barge gave it a wide berth.

Soon thereafter they were passing still higher cliffs, seamed with yawning crevasses and caverns, known as St Abb's Head, named after St Ebba, a Northumbrian princess who had established a nunnery on the rock-top, of all places, allegedly to escape the attentions of Norse sea-raiders. Whether she was successful in this is in doubt, for her women were reputed to have cut off their breasts further to discourage the Vikings.

It was that sort of seaboard.

Thereafter there were slower, less spectacular shores and bays, until something of a creek opened, wherein was Eyemouth harbour, where the Eye Water entered the sea.

Eyemouth, originally only a fishing haven, had risen in importance with the English occupation of Berwick-on-Tweed less than ten miles away. Berwick had been Scotland's most valuable port, for the export of wool, hides, salt-mutton and the like, from the Lammermuir Hills area and the lands of the Merse of Berwickshire. Now much of that trade went through Eyemouth instead, as a free port for independent dealers, whereas Dunbar, seat of the earldom of March, or Merse, could and did exact tolls.

John had no difficulty in locating Archie, who was dining and wining in the harbour-master's house after his wardency duties – the which were indicated as accomplished by four figures who dangled from a gallows nearby. Wreckers these might well be, but John would wager that Home of Fast Castle, king of wreckers, would not be amongst them.

210

Archie, surprised to see his brother, was outraged when he heard of the reason for this visit – and much upset, in that Albany had received a message from the King telling him that John of Mar was sick, and requesting his brother's presence at Edinburgh. He had set off forthwith, and with no large escort. What would be his reception at Edinburgh? The brothers eyed each other.

At least Archie had no indecision as to what should be done. The Douglases would ride for Edinburgh likewise, and in strength. They might be in time to prevent any serious trouble.

Archie kept some fifty of his men-at-arms with him at Dunbar, for wardency duties, and he had a score with him here at Eyemouth. They would hasten back to Dunbar, pick up the rest and then on to Tantallon for more. One hundred or so Douglases arriving at Edinburgh, with more to follow on if necessary, ought to make a major impact on the situation.

With the men gathered in from their various recreations in the little town, the brothers sent them off northwards whilst they themselves embarked on the barge, with a relief shift of oarsmen to give some respite to the weary ones. They ought to be at Dunbar before the horsemen.

They were, but did not delay there for long. Giving orders for the rest of his men-at-arms to assemble and come on with the group from Eyemouth, the brothers re-embarked, with the setting of the sun. It had been a long day for John and his crew.

Dusk at Tantallon did not prevent the summons from going out for near-at-hand tenants, fishermen, farm-workers and supporters to be ready, armed and accoutred, to rise at sunrise.

Then it was blessed sleep for John.

It was up betimes, necessarily, with twenty-four miles' riding to Edinburgh, and a tail of over one hundred less speedy than any small party. The girls wishing them well, they set out.

Behind North Berwick Law, by Sydserf and Fentoun and Ballencrieff and Longniddry they came to Seton Palace where,

211

at John's suggestion, they halted to rest their mounts and recruit the young Lord Seton, a friend of John's and one of the richest lords in the land. He loathed Sheves and all his works, and could prove a useful ally. Unfortunately he had no men assembled, and at short notice could mount only a dozen. But many more could follow on, and he himself was happy to join the Douglas band. He was an admirer of the forthright Albany.

By Salt Preston and Musselburgh they came to Edinburgh in the early afternoon and made their way through the scattered woodlands of the great park of the Abbey of the Holy Rood, beneath the soaring lion-hill of Arthur's Seat. When in Edinburgh, the monarchs almost always lodged in the monastic quarters of the abbey, so much more comfortable and convenient than those in the royal fortress up on its rock-top, so like Stirling's but lacking its accommodation.

The arrival of so large a body of armed men under the Douglas and Seton banners did not fail to attract considerable attention from the crowds around the abbey precincts, attendants at court, the servants of prelates and lords, and citizens of Edinburgh. All eyed the cavalcade doubtfully.

In the abbey forecourt the horsemen reined up and the three lords dismounted. They went to present themselves at the door of the abbot's quarters, the most splendid John had seen. Their arrival here also had not gone unnoticed, and a sub-prior awaited them.

"Angus, Douglasdale and Seton to see the Duke of Albany," Archie announced briskly.

The other blinked. "The, the duke is not here, my lords," he said.

"Where is he, then?"

"He is . . . up at the castle."

"Is the King there also?"

"No, my lord. The King is here, within the abbey."

The trio eyed each other.

"What does the duke at the castle?" Archie demanded.

"That is not for me to say, my lord Earl."

"No? Did he go . . . willingly?"

"You must ask others that."

"We will!" That was grim. "Inform His Grace that we are here."

The sub-prior hesitated, bowed and left them standing.

That was no way to treat the Red Douglas. Archie snorted and marched inside, the other two following.

They waited, sundry monks and servitors watching but keeping their distance.

After some considerable interval, the sub-prior returned. "My lords," he said unhappily, "His Grace is . . . occupied."

"Occupied! What mean you – occupied?"

"He is in conference. With the archbishop. And others."

"Then we will join his conference! Lead us there."

"My lord, I cannot do that. I was told that, that you should not come to them."

"Who told you that? The man Sheves?"

The other was silent.

"Conduct us to the King," Archie ordered, peremptorily. "I am one of the *ri*, the earls of Scotland. It is our right, the lesser kings, at any time to enter the presence of the *Ard Righ*, the High King of Scots. See to it, clerk."

Looking still more unhappy, the cleric turned and led the way.

They had not far to go. Along a corridor and through an anteroom they came to a closed door. The sub-prior knocked and opened to enter. He was closing the door behind him when Archie strode forward and pushed it wide again and went in. His rather less forceful companions followed.

Four men sat at a table, drinking – the King, Sheves, Robert Cochrane and another. They stared at the newcomers.

The three lords bowed briefly to the monarch. James did not speak.

Sheves did. "What is this!" he demanded. "You were told. His Grace is in privy session. Not to be invaded thus! Begone!"

Archie flicked a dismissive hand at him. "Sire," he said, addressing James directly, "do you permit the bastard of a small Fife lairdie, however upjumped, to speak to one of your

213

earls thus? And the Red Douglas, at that! We come into Your Grace's royal presence, as is our right."

James looked uneasy, positively alarmed. "I do not . . . he is archbishop now. He . . ." His voice tailed away.

"Who did he steal the archbishopric from? A better man, of better blood! An honest man betrayed. But that is not why we come here today, Sire. We seek the Duke of Albany."

"He is not here . . ."

"We are told that he is in Edinburgh Castle. What does he there?"

It was Sheves who answered. "He pays the price of his treasonable intentions towards his royal brother."

"Treasonable intentions! What folly is this, Sire? His Highness the Duke intends no treason. Nor would. He is your brother. He – "

"We have sure word of his treasonable intent. And that of His Grace's other brother, the Earl of Mar." That was Sheves again. "But they will not perform it. They are both safe prisoners, and awaiting His Grace's royal decision and pleasure."

"Prisoners! The duke a prisoner! In Edinburgh Castle! You lie!"

"Why should I lie? He is imprisoned on His Grace's orders. Is it not so, Sire?"

James nodded, tight-lipped.

"This is beyond belief . . . !"

To John Douglas, at least, it was not beyond belief. He made his first contribution. "Your Grace's mind must have been poisoned against your brothers. They are your loyal subjects as well as your kin, the duke serving you well in the Borders, despite the accusations of envious and self-seeking lords. Do you accept the tales of sorcerers and witches against your own family, Sire?"

"Who are you to speak of self-seeking lords, my lord?" Sheves asked. "All know you as ever working against His Grace's policies."

"Against some of *your* policies perhaps, my lord Archbishop! Never against my liege-lord's."

"My sister ever questions my acts," James said. "And you do her bidding."

"Her Highness seeks only your good, Sire. And the weal of your realm – "

Archie interrupted. "We will go speak with the duke. And bring Your Grace his assurances of loyal duty. That he may return to your side and your support."

"No."

"But, Sire, it is to your advantage, great advantage. And I must see him, the Lieutenant of the Borders, in my role of Warden of the East March . . ."

"Alex is no longer Lieutenant of the Borders."

"You will not go see the Duke of Albany," Sheves persisted. "He is to be held secure and alone, until His Grace's pleasure in the matter is known."

"Not see! Me!"

"None to see him. By royal command."

"*Your* command, usurping witch-master! Sire, this cannot be! Your own brother . . ."

"You, you have my permission to retire, my lords. My, my royal command."

Archie drew a deep breath, but John touched his arm and gestured towards the door. After a pause, they bowed themselves out.

Spluttering with rage, Archie stamped off, and back to the horses.

"What now?" Seton asked. "What are we to do?"

"The castle," Archie jerked. "We ride up to the castle."

"Is that wise?" John said.

"Wise? It is *right*."

"But what point? If we cannot see Albany . . ."

"Whoever keeps that hold will not prevent the Earl of Angus from seeing Albany! Come, you."

So the cavalcade moved off, to clatter up the Canongate and under the Netherbow Port into the High Street of Edinburgh. The files of horsemen filled the narrow streets, forcing aside the citizenry into the still narrower close mouths and wynds, urchins running after them, barked at by dogs, pecking poultry

215

flapping and squawking. They passed St Giles High Kirk and the Mercat Cross and so into the Lawnmarket, and from there into the tourney-ground before the castle gatehouse, with the towers and battlements of the fortress soaring behind.

The drawbridge appeared to be down and the portcullis up as they approached.

"Can we risk riding in?" John wondered. "We could be trapped inside, if the governor so wished. He will have his orders."

"Trap all these?" Archie gestured at their following.

"The bridge is narrow. No more than two or three at a time can cross. They will not let six score men inside, I think."

"We shall see."

As they came to the bridge-end a voice shouted from the gatehouse parapet, "Who comes in such force to the King's citadel?"

"Do you lack eyes, sirrah? Can you not see the Douglas and Seton colours? I am the Earl of Angus. To see the King's brother, the Duke of Albany."

"You should not have said that," John murmured.

"I will inform the governor . . ."

"No need," Archie cried. "I will inform him myself!"

"I have my orders, my lord . . ."

Archie's answer was to turn in his saddle, wave the front ranks of his men onwards, and then to spur his mount towards the bridge. Doubtfully John and Seton followed.

Their beasts' hooves made a hollow drumming beat on the bridge timbers. Then that noise was suddenly joined by another and very different sound, the creak and clang of iron chains and the roll of metal drums from above their heads.

"The bridge!" John shouted. "They raise the bridge. Quick! Back!"

Sure enough, the timbers began to lift beneath them, and immediately the horses felt it and commenced to sidle and toss uneasy heads.

"On!" Archie bellowed angrily.

"No – back! We will be trapped inside. Quickly! They might let down the portcullis!"

That thought, the massive iron gate weighing tons slamming down on top of them, restrained even Archie Douglas. With the slope steepening below them and the three horses rearing in alarm, they reined round and part-slithered back to firm ground. And only just in time, with the bridge, drawn up by its pulleys, rising to leave a great gap below, the water-filled moat.

Beside himself with fury, Archie shook clenched fist. "Dastard! Spawn of Satan! I'll have your head for this, I swear! By all the saints, I will! You scum . . ." The rest was lost in the skreik and grinding of a new noise, as the massive iron portcullis began to come down, once the bridge timbers were high enough not to be struck by it.

John had never seen Archie so enraged, beside himself, by no means speechless but his words incoherent, jerked out, breathless.

"At least they did not let it down on top of us!" Seton said. "We would have died."

"He . . . will . . . die!" Archie got out. "That guard."

"Aye, but see you, there must be another behind him," John pointed out, his own words a little uneven. "He would not do that lacking orders. To an earl and lords. The governor must be there, and obeying royal commands. Do not wholly blame the guard captain."

They considered the situation. It was frustrating indeed to have over one hundred armed men at their command and to be unable to use them to affect the issue in any way. That fortress was impregnable save to the heaviest artillery.

"Nothing that we can do here," Seton declared. "Or elsewhere, I fear."

"Something must be done!" Archie grated. "That rogue Sheves is not to have his evil way. *He* accuses the King's brother of treason! A parliament? That could put a stop to this folly."

"It is the King must call a parliament," John reminded. "Would he? And it requires forty days of notice. Six long weeks."

Archie smashed fist on saddle-bow. "We must act! You,

217

John – you are the one for devising and plotting. Think of something to get Albany out of here."

His brother wagged his head helplessly.

At any rate they could not sit there in front of the gatehouse, all their men-at-arms noting their rejection. Reining his mount round savagely, Archie led his company back down into the town.

There was no point in going back to Holyrood Abbey, even if they would be admitted therein. If anything was to be done, it would not be done there. Archie was now talking about rousing other sympathetic earls and lords, although to do just what was not specified. But John had made up *his* mind.

"I will go to Stirling to see the princess," he announced. "If anyone can see what can be done, she can. She has the wits of that family."

His brother was not impressed by this decision but did not seek to dissuade. It was back to Tantallon for Archie. He would see what might be contrived from there.

Seton had no practical suggestions, but he would aid in any way possible.

So down at the Grassmarket they parted company, there and then, John to go westwards, to the West Port of the walled city, the others eastwards for Arthur's Seat and its parkland. John took no escort; he would ride faster alone, with thirty-five miles to cover.

Mary Stewart, recognising that whatever brought John back after so surprisingly short an interval must be serious indeed, scanned his face after their warm embrace.

"You bring ill tidings, I think, Johnnie? Is it . . . John, my brother?"

"Not the Earl of Mar, no – although I have indeed no tidings of him. It is Alexander of Albany. He is imprisoned in Edinburgh Castle. Held fast and alone. None to see him or speak with him."

"A-a-ah! Alex himself, now! I feared something like this. A prisoner! They coaxed him to come? To John?"

"Yes. I was too late. The duke had left Dunbar the day

218

before. He is to be charged with treason. They both are. It is vile. But . . ."

"Treason! They will have difficulty in proving that!"

"Need they prove it? So long as the King declares it. It is all this of astrology and witchcraft which Sheves has conjured up. With the man Cochrane and that Andreas. James is wholly under their influence, I fear. We, Archie and I, tried to reason with him. At Holyrood. But to no effect. We were forbidden to see the duke. But we went up to the castle despite that. We were denied entrance, the drawbridge raised against us. We cannot think what to do. So – I came to you, Mary!"

She stared at him and past him. "Oh, Johnnie, what am I to say to that? What to advise? We must think. Think. But . . . not now. You must be weary – I see it in your face. Hungry. You must have ridden sixty miles this day, at least. Come. Anna will get you provender. Since last I saw you, you can scarcely have drawn breath!"

John did not deny that he had been busy, if with scant results.

After a suitably restorative meal for the traveller, they sat themselves down on a cushioned settle before a log fire, the Lady Anna tactfully retiring early. For long they were silent, before somehow John's arm came to rest around the young woman's shoulders. She did not draw away.

"I have been thinking," she said. "I will go to Edinburgh to see James. He cannot prevent *me*, his sister, from seeing our brother Alex, surely? Sheves can scarcely prevent that."

"I would not wager on it, Mary."

"I must try, at any rate. Will we go tomorrow?"

"To be sure. But what would you think to achieve? *Seeing* Albany may comfort him, I agree. But that will not win him his freedom."

"No. But if I can but get them together. See each other, James and Alex. I am their elder sister. I acted almost mother to them, for long, when our true mother, the Queen, died young. James *must* heed me."

"Sheves, Cochrane and the others may claim divination

against it. Say that they have been warned by ghostly powers. They have that wicked hold on the King."

"I must seek to controvert that. At least as far as my brothers are concerned. I cannot remain here and do nothing."

"I see that. It is why I came. I but spell out the difficulties. Sorry as I am to do so."

"Oh, I see all the difficulties, yes. Oh, Johnnie, why has this evil befallen James? And therefore his kingdom? It is all so wrong, so *devilish*! James is not really wicked, only weak, weak. Why does God allow it, in His anointed and crowned monarch?"

John could not answer that, save by the pressure of hand and arm. She laid her head against *his* shoulder and he kissed her hair.

So they sat, for how long neither really knew, time being scarcely valid to them then. They watched the flickering flames, content to be silent however much they might lack contentment in other respects, the scope of their own association perhaps equally with their feeling of helplessness over the royal family's situation.

It was the sinking down of those flames which eventually altered the pattern of the evening. John, disengaging himself, was rising to put more logs on the fire from the wood-chest opposite, when Mary halted him.

"Do not feed it further, Johnnie," she said. "It is late, and you are tired indeed. You need your sleep, especially if we ride again in the morning. Besides, this, although more than pleasing in one fashion, is trying in another, is it not? Trying ourselves! When it is profitless to do so. As we both know well. I love to feel your arm around me, and more, even though I should not perhaps. And know how you restrain yourself. But the fates have ordained it so, it seems. If we cannot have each other as we would wish, at least we need not so *test* each other. No?"

He looked down on her, lovely and desirable as she was — and he was in two minds as to whether or not he could agree with her on this. But he recognised that hers was probably the wise decision – he who was apt to talk about wisdom to Archie.

220

So he nodded, if no more vocal about it than had been the last part of their evening.

She stood. "Take me to my room door, Johnnie Douglas," she said.

Arm-in-arm they went upstairs, that far. Servants had lit lamps, to sit in alcoves. At her door they came into each other's arms and kissed deeply.

"Goodnight, my dear," she murmured, lips against lips. "You know how I feel. About this door. But . . . let it be no barrier to our minds, at least, our inner selves. As it is to our bodies."

He kissed again, and left her, wordless. It had been a remarkably ineloquent night for him. Or had it?

She watched him stride along the corridor, hand up to those lips.

In the morning, Mary let him have his sleep out. She had her children to see to and bid farewell to. Fine horsewoman as she was, those thirty-five miles to Edinburgh would not take more than five hours, so immediate haste was not essential. Despite the stresses of the evening, John had slept soundly and long.

After a hearty breakfast and prolonged leave-taking with the youngsters, they set off, with two of the castle's royal guard as escort. It was the first day of May, and already cuckoos were calling.

They discussed procedure as they rode. Mary would go alone to Holyrood Abbey, since John would certainly not be welcome there. He would put up at a hostelry in the Canongate, where she could contact him. Probably when she went to Edinburgh Castle – and she was determined so to do – she had better go alone. At this stage, undoubtedly, John's attendance would be no asset. Until James's reactions were ascertained, there was little more that they could decide.

With the countryside burgeoning green and the sun shining, in that company it would have been a pleasing journey had their thoughts not tended to dwell on what lay ahead.

They entered the city in the early afternoon, and made

straight eastwards from the West Port, through the Grass-market and down the Cowgate, for Holyrood. John, telling Mary that he would be at Lucky Brown's hostelry – he would have preferred the monkish hospice of St Michael's but recognised that monkish tongues might wag in the direction of the abbey – held back from the Holyrood forecourt until he saw her admitted to the abbot's quarters. Then he went to seek lodgings in rather humbler quarters, which seldom had lords as patrons – although actually, at this time, with the court in town, this tavern was fairly full with the followers of the great men. He hoped that he would not be recognised. Fortunately, he was not a grand dresser.

He settled down to wait, after a meal, listening interestedly to the chatter and gossip of his fellow-guests who, with little to do but sit, eat, drink and talk, were an education for him. He could not recollect ever having been in such a situation before. He learned not a little about a different world from his own, but also something of his fellow-lords and lairds which he had not known, and also their ladies – although all he heard might not be gospel-truth. What interested him most, however, was the scorn and hostility of almost all there towards Sheves, Cochrane and the others, indeed in some degree to the King himself. If these were typical of the monarch's ordinary subjects, then Scotland was in no very happy state.

Despite the noise around him, presently he fell asleep at his table.

Oddly, some indefinite time later, it was silence which awakened him, and not because the premises had emptied but because talk had died away as men stared. As well they might, for it would not be often assuredly that ladies, save such as were commonly called of the town, entered, and alone, richly clad and bearing themselves with such calm assurance. Mary was there, scanning the company.

John started up almost guiltily and apologetically; but there was nothing remotely critical about her greeting. Smiling, she waved towards the door, and went out. The buzz of talk rose again, as he followed her.

In the yard of the inn, amongst all the tethered horses,

she turned to him. "Johnnie, I disturbed your rest, your well-earned rest. But, see you, we cannot talk here. Let us go riding in the park yonder."

They mounted and rode out of the Canongate towards the green slopes of Arthur's Seat.

"What happened?" he asked. "Did you see him? The duke?"

She nodded. "I saw him. After a fashion. Not alone. And not with James. My foolish brother did not want me to go. But I insisted. In some degree he is a little afraid of me, I think, strange as that may be. I pleaded with him to come with me, but he would not. He sent his creature Cochrane with me, however – can you believe it! That . . . craftsman! He never left my side . . ."

"The shame of it! You, a princess, to be put in the charge of such as that. He was not insolent . . . ?"

"Not in his words. But his manner. Of mocking and amused play of respect. Showing who held the reins!"

"Damn him! But – you did see Albany?"

"Yes. But only for a very short time. Cochrane clearly had his orders. And Alex did not improve matters by cursing Cochrane to his face, ordering him out of the cell he is in, threatening him. Which, I fear, shortened the visit still further."

"Aye . . . I can understand that. He is well enough? Alone. In a cell, you say!"

"Held like any felon. But he is fit enough, yes. And angry. So angry that we could say little of worth to each other. And with Cochrane listening. As a visit it was scarcely a success."

"How could it be? Was anything decided? To any effect?"

"I fear not. I wished that the brothers might meet. But neither would have it. Alex would talk only of making James pay, of raising the realm against him, of having Sheves and all his low-born crew, including Cochrane there, accused of *lèse-majesté*, and hanged! It was not the meeting that I aimed for!"

"I see it all. You can scarcely blame Albany. But it would have been wiser to have kept his wits, in the circumstances.

223

Wiser! *I* am ever counselling wisdom in others – and showing little of it my own self!"

"What is wisdom? I wish that I knew. In especial, in this coil of my brothers."

"Aye. So you gained nothing out of your journey and efforts?"

"Nothing from Alex or James. And I have not seen John. I will ask to go see him at Craigmillar tomorrow. But something I did learn, which could have its uses. I met the governor of the castle and his deputy. They were unhappy, both of them, with the situation. The governor is Sir David Falconer of Halkerton. He was carefully correct towards me, and I sensed sympathy in some degree. But his deputy was less careful, more openly friendly, and glaring at Cochrane. I did not know who he was until he told me, in an aside while the governor was speaking with Cochrane. He is William Graham, kin to your sister's Lord Graham, and nephew to the late Archbishop Patrick Graham!"

"Sakes! I have not heard of him."

"Nor had I. But his father, another William, was younger half-brother of Patrick's."

"So-o-o . . . !"

"So he hates Sheves and all his works. Told me so. As well he might. He will do what he can to ease Alex's position in the castle."

"That is good, yes. But . . ."

"But yes, Johnnie. It has occurred to me, as perhaps to you, that we might possibly be glad to have a friend in such position in that castle. Who knows – it might have to come to escape!"

"That thought had come to me, earlier," John admitted. "But this of a Graham there makes it the more worth considering. If Albany's imprisonment continues for any time."

"That is what I feel. If so, this William Graham might help. As to Falconer, I know not . . ."

"As governor, he could scarcely knowingly allow a prisoner to escape, even the King's brother. He would pay the penalty. But if he could be coaxed away for a time, somehow . . ."

No lengthy riding desired after their journey from Stirling, they turned back presently, Mary to return to the abbey – where she said that she was scarcely welcome but where she could hardly be excluded, she admitting that she had not so much as enquired where her husband might be lodging meantime – and John back to Lucky Brown's. She asked if he would accompany her to Craigmillar Castle on the morrow? Since James had been against her visiting Albany, he would probably be the same about her other brother, so she would not ask permission but just go. It was agreed that she would call for him in the morning.

John was not long in seeking his couch in a bare attic room of the hostelry, leaving a roistering company below.

Next day, in mid-forenoon, Mary arrived, with the two Stirling guards who, clad in the royal livery, might serve to reinforce her authority at Craigmillar.

That quite large castle crowned a low ridge a couple of miles to the south-east of Edinburgh, on the far side of Arthur's Seat. It was unusual in that, although it was a private establishment of the Preston family, it had long been accepted as a sort of temporary harbour for royalty when, for one reason or another, they did not want to occupy either Holyrood Abbey or Edinburgh Castle, but desired to remain in the vicinity – usually when one of the periodic outbreaks of the plague, or other epidemic, smote the city. What successive Preston lairds thought of this arrangement was not to be known; but it no doubt had its compensations.

So the escorted couple rode round the west perimeter of the majestic hill mass, so extraordinary a feature for the outskirts of a city, and below the curious red columnar cliff formations known as Samson's Ribs, and thereafter round Duddingston Loch, haunt of wildfowl and favourite royal hawking area. Craigmillar Castle dominated the ridge in front of them.

They had no difficulty in gaining entry to this stronghold, at least, being civilly received by Lady Preston. However, she informed them that they were too late to see the Earl of Mar, for on the King's instructions her husband had taken him to some apothecary's premises in the Canongate of the city that very morning. For treatment, it seemed, although he had not appeared to be a sick man, save for some earache. Mary said that her youngest brother had suffered from earache since childhood.

So, after refreshment, they turned back for Edinburgh, Mary wondering what all this meant, and whether in fact Mar was now to be confined in Edinburgh Castle with Alex, presumably for added security.

Rather than returning immediately to the abbey, the princess reluctantly decided that it might look better if she went to inform her husband of her presence in the city. She had learned that he was lodging in the town-house in Niddry's Wynd of the Earl of Atholl. John, with no especial desire to see the Lord Hamilton – whom he recognised that he should not hate nor resent – excused himself. He would be at Lucky Brown's, when Mary needed him.

Understanding each other's positions and problems, they parted at the Cowgate-foot, the princess retaining her escort. He could hardly tell her that he hoped that Hamilton would not be seeking his marital rights from his wife out of this unanticipated reunion.

Finding time to hang heavily, John went up to his attic chamber in the hostelry, and there sought to school his mind to the sorely neglected ballad of St Baldred of the Bass.

It was mid-afternoon when Lucky Brown herself, who proved to be a large motherly female, came panting up the stairs to announce the princess-countess, Mary just behind.

At first glance John perceived dire trouble. The younger woman's features were set, drawn, etched with distress. Pushing past Lucky Brown, she flung herself into the man's arms, gulping. The other woman backed out, closing the door behind her.

Mary burst into tears.

Seeking to soothe her, to comfort her, John held her close. He stroked her hair, kissed her brow.

At length she got words out, breathlessly. "He is dead! Dead! John is dead. They have killed him. Oh, poor young John! Slain! Murdered! My brother . . . dead!"

Speechless, he stared, clutching her to him.

"Vile! Vile! They bled him to death. Drowned him in his own blood! They declared that he was sick and should be bled. They put him in a bath of hot water. To increase the bleeding. Cut his veins. Held him down in the water. Long, while the blood drained out of him, all his blood. Till he died. At the behest of those astrologers and witch-masters. They said that only so would the curse be lifted from him, the everlasting curse of treason, of plotting his own brother's death. James's death! Oh, God in heaven . . . ! John, poor, innocent John, my brother!"

He held her quivering, heaving body. What use were words? Patting her hand, almost as though she was a child, he sought to console, utterly inadequate as he knew it to be.

At length she stilled her person somewhat and raised head to scan his face from tear-filled eyes. "It is scarcely to be believed," she said thickly. "Tell me that I but dream, Johnnie! That this is but a nightmare. Not the truth!"

He shook his head. "Would that I might, my dear. But . . . who told you of it?"

"My husband. Hamilton. He had just heard. Even he could scarcely credit it."

"The King? Did *he* order this? His own brother!"

"James must have sanctioned it. Sheves and Cochrane would contrive it. But they would not dare do it unless James allowed it."

"No. It is appalling. But . . . it is almost a copy of the death of that other royal brother, the Duke of Clarence. Drowned in wine. At the bidding of these satanic sorcerers."

"You think so? Yes, it could be. But, Johnnie – Alex! If they could do this to John, what of Alex? Now, I am terrified for Alex."

"Aye, well may you be. Albany is their main prey. Him they fear. We must get him out of this castle, if it is at all possible. And quickly. By all the saints – we *must*!"

"Quickly, yes – quickly. Before, before . . . !"

13

Urgently they discussed and debated, weighing the possibilities and probabilities, the means and the consequences, the risks involved for any and all. Desperately aware of the almost certain need for haste, they reached conclusions, John at least recognising that this preoccupation was probably good for Mary in her present state of shock and sorrow.

They decided that to win Albany out of the fortress they must get Sir David Falconer, the governor, decoyed away for a spell, in the hope that William Graham would co-operate. That man would not be able to remain at the castle thereafter, they judged – but he might be prepared to go along with the duke and share his fortunes. After all, if this attempt was successful, Albany would most certainly seek to establish himself as an alternative power in the land, and would be grateful towards those who had aided him.

So – the procedure? Mary to go back to the castle with the royal guards whom she now thought that she could trust entirely. Ask for the governor, saying that she came from her brother the King. Tell Falconer that James desired his presence forthwith down at the abbey, for further instructions as to the duke's security and treatment, a royal command. Then, when he was gone, and surely he must go, persuade Graham to bring Albany out of his cell, still very much a prisoner – bound wrists if necessary – and with Mary and the two guards lead him down, out of the fortress, allegedly to take him to some new place of confinement. It was highly unlikely that the gatehouse captain would question his deputy governor. Once out, they would hasten to disappear amongst the wynds and closes, and seek to flee Edinburgh before the city gates were closed for the night.

It would mainly depend on William Graham of course. If he refused to co-operate there was little that they might do. But being a Graham, the Graham links with the Douglas family and his own anger at Sheves over the shameful treatment of his uncle ought to tell. And if Albany promised his favours hereafter, that would help. The fact was, of course, that if the duke did obtain his freedom, James's reign might indeed be of limited duration thereafter – and Scotland be the better therefor.

John suggested an adjustment. If he was to change places with one of their Stirling guards, wear his livery, he might be able to assist in it all, both with Graham and Albany. Nobody at the citadel was likely to recognise him in that disguise.

This was agreed.

Timing was the question now. This day, or tomorrow? The city-gates would shut in about five hours. Although it might be possible to win out of one thereafter, it would attract attention and add to risks. But Mary was loth to wait until the next day. Having murdered John, their enemies might not delay in seeking to dispose of Alex. She was for getting him out just as soon as possible. She thought that they might just have time, that evening.

Mary's guards would still be downstairs waiting. They could be brought up here. Mary wondered whether John would mind changing outer clothing with one of them – to be told that this was the least of their problems.

So he descended to the noisy premises below, where he had no difficulty in finding the two guards drinking ale amongst the throng, their scarlet royal tunics, with the Lion Rampant emblem on breast and back, making them sufficiently conspicuous. He led them upstairs again.

Mary explained the situation to the pair. They were obviously shaken by the account of the Earl of Mar's death and what it implied. At Stirling they had served Mar, as well as the princess and Albany, on occasion. They had attended on the brothers in many a hunting expedition, and although in theory part of the King's guard, almost certainly felt much more loyalty towards Albany and Mar and the princess. They did not require much convincing to assist in this attempt, assured that the duke would look after them hereafter.

The exchange of outer clothing was effected without over-much embarrassment, size dictating which was most suitable. The different bonnets were the most difficult. Then they all went downstairs.

There another decision faced them – horses. Mounts would be required for Albany and Graham, assuming that all went well. Presumably Graham would have his own beast in the fortress, but would there be one for the duke? John solved that problem by simply taking an extra mount from the many tethered in the yard – first things first!

So they rode off, up to the castle.

There was no hold-up at the gatehouse, with Mary declaring that she had come from the King to see the governor. They found Falconer at table in his own quarters beside St Margaret's Chapel on the crown of the rock, his deputy with him, Mary having left the guard dressed in John's clothing outside, advisedly. She wished it to appear purely a visit from the King's sister, and two members of the royal guard sent with her.

Surprised to see the visitors, and at this hour, the pair at table rose respectfully, bowing.

"Sir David," Mary said, "His Grace sends me, on a matter of some delicacy. He fears that there may be disturbances in the city. He will tell you why, no doubt, when you see him. But he requires your attendance forthwith down at the abbey. It is to give you instructions regarding a change in the custody of our brother, the Duke of Albany. James, and the archbishop, have decided that this is necessary. He wishes to inform you and arrange for a second move for the duke."

"Disturbances? In the town? How should this be, Highness?" Falconer wondered.

"It is grievous." Mary sought to keep her voice under control. "The Earl of Mar is dead! My other brother. A, a tragedy. In the city. Brought from Craigmillar. When the people hear of it, there may well be trouble. With the duke imprisoned here. Or so His Grace fears. So you

230

are to attend on him, Sir David. For instructions. And at once."

"The people, the city crowds, could not win into the castle here, Highness."

"Not the people, no. But – the lords and earls. *They* could be . . . difficult. Suspicious. Raise the mob. Rouse the city. Better if the duke was no longer here. Or so they consider in the abbey. It is not for me to question their decisions. The word will soon get round. So, haste you, Sir David."

Falconer looked unsure, perplexed, but he did not argue further. "How did the Earl of Mar die?" he asked.

"His Grace will tell you himself. With your permission, sir, I will go and tell my other brother, Albany, the sad news. And to be ready."

"Yes, Highness. Gartartan will take you." His deputy was Graham of Gartartan, in the Carse of Forth.

John heaved a sigh of relief as the governor bowed himself out.

They followed Graham thereafter down to the prison cells.

Mary was careful not to inform him of the true situation too soon, until she was fairly sure that the governor had left, in case Graham proved to be uncooperative. But on their way to Albany's lowly quarters, the man proved to be so upset and alarmed over John of Mar's death that she felt convinced that he could be trusted to aid them.

"Did the earl truly die of a sickness, Highness?" he asked, low-voiced, so that the guards did not hear. "So suddenly! Or – is it more of the wretched Sheves's wickedness?"

"You are right, it is," she told him. "God forgive the King for allowing it. His own brother. Murdered. So I greatly fear for Albany."

"Aye. By all that is holy – so must all! Dear God, to murder a man's own brother! And for what? The earl was no plotter, I swear."

"No, he was not. But he much preferred Albany to James. And that was enough for them, third in line for the throne as he was. What, then, will they seek to do to Alex, my other brother? If they can."

231

"Moving him from here, then, is but a device, you think, Highness? To have him slain elsewhere, also."

"The device is ours, mine, my friend. To get the governor out of the castle. James did not send for him. Here is the Lord of Douglasdale. Clad thus. We wish you to let us take my brother away to safety. Now, at once. Before Sir David learns the truth and gets back. Will you do it?"

Graham halted in his tracks, to stare, almost at the prison block door. "Take him . . . ?"

"Yes. Only so, I judge, will we save his life. You must see that. Oh, you must do it, sir. My brother's life."

"It . . . would mean, for me . . . death also!"

"Not if you come with us. With the duke. He would be everlastingly in your debt. And if he escapes, he will not become any mere hunted fugitive, of that you may be sure. *He* has the spirit of the family! Whatever the future, he would reward you well."

"If I know Albany, he will himself make a bid for the throne, Graham," John told him. "We will flee to his strong castle of Dunbar. He could rouse the Borders. Most of the lords, I think, would support him. You would be in no poor company."

"And you would help to avenge your uncle, friend," Mary put in. "For if James has to yield the crown, Sheves is finished, archbishop or none."

"Aye. There is that. By God, I will do it! Yes. We will free the duke. I have pitied him here. But how to effect it best . . . ?"

"We will tell him," John said. "We will tie his wrists, very much still a prisoner. Then all mount and ride down with him in the midst, to the gatehouse. The guard there will not halt *you*, the deputy governor. Say that he is to be taken to the King. Then, once in the city, we make for the St Leonard's Port and out, before the gates shut. But hastily, before Falconer can get back. We have not long . . ."

"I see that, yes. But I must gather some gear . . ."

"The less the better. You have a horse here? We have one for the duke, waiting. And bring rope, that we may bind him.

232

Let us into his cell. We will tell him all, whilst you go prepare. But swiftly, Gartartan."

The guard on duty at the prison block made no bones about unlocking the door of Albany's cell, and the three of them went into the dark, stinking confines. The duke lay on the bare boards of a bed, staring. Graham hurried off."

Mary ran to embrace her brother, to his incoherent exclamations and questions. Royalty as they were, John broke in on them.

"Highness, talk can wait! We have little time to effect your escape. When Graham, who is in this with us, gets back we will tie you, like the prisoner you are, and get you out, on to a horse, and away. Falconer, the governor, is decoyed hence. But not for long. He will be back. You can ride?"

"By the Rood I can! And will. Here's a wonder! How was this contrived?"

"You will hear. Is there aught that you have to take with you?"

"In this filthy hole? Nothing. Save my hatred of my brother James!"

"Yes, Highness. But meantime it is flight."

"John is dead, Alex," Mary told him, level-voiced. "Slain."

"John! Dead? You . . . this cannot be!"

"It is true. Murdered. Why we must get you out of here quickly. Lest they serve you likewise."

"God! This is Sheves and Cochrane?"

"Yes." She was telling him the manner of Mar's death, John fretting, when Graham arrived back. He brought a satchel of clothing, a rope for the duke's wrists and also a cloak for him. Having tied the prisoner, they went out to the horses, Albany scarcely able to take it all in. John reckoned that they had an hour until the city gates closed.

Riding down the quite steep and rocky slope, they picked up their other guard and came to the gatehouse. There, as anticipated, the presence of Graham gained them passage without question. Out into freedom, they trotted over the drawbridge timbers, tension, they hoped, disguised, the built-up anonymity of the city beckoning.

233

John's feared reappearance of Falconer did not materialise, and Edinburgh swallowed them up blessedly.

Avoiding the main streets, they made eastwards for the St Leonards Port, attracting little attention. The gates still open, although the town guard looking eager to close and be off, they rode out, into the parkland under Arthur's Seat.

"Dunbar, Highness?" John asked. "You can ride that far?"

"Dunbar, yes," Albany answered, although it had been to Mary that the question had been addressed. "I could ride further than that, this night – in especial if it was to Sheves's hanging!"

"It is near thirty miles, Alex. And you have been close in a cell all these days."

Her brother's response was to spur his mount into a canter.

All settled down to hard riding.

As it happened, the only real problem of that long May night's journey came at the end of it, when the travellers had difficulty in gaining admittance to Dunbar Castle on its series of rocks, the night guard suspicious indeed. It was, of course, the early hours of the morning, and although not really dark, sufficiently so to make the identity of the party of six hard to prove. Albany's cursing rage eventually did convince, with his threats of dire consequences for the culprits.

Archie Douglas, who was in the castle, was rudely aroused from his slumbers, and heard all with sleepy astonishment. Thereafter, weary indeed, the travellers gulped down some food and drink and sought their respective couches, Mary making no complaint at quarters found for her scarcely suitable for a princess. John saw her to her door, and there obtained some slight reward for his efforts on the Stewart family's behalf.

At a late breakfast, they discussed the future. John was worried about Mary, who was for going back to Stirling. He held that when the King heard of what she had done, he would be very angry and, with the sort of advisers he had, would be set on punishing her. And such punishment would be dire indeed. Would she not be better either staying here at Dunbar with Albany or else coming back to Tantallon with him, both strong places where she could remain secure?

She demurred. With Albany escaped and strongly placed here at Dunbar, set to avenge his brother's death – and of course his own shameful imprisonment – James was now in a very different position. He would be angry, to be sure; but he would also know that his position on the throne was now gravely endangered. Albany would almost certainly make a bid to dethrone him, and, after the murder of John of Mar, a great many of the lords and magnates would be apt to turn against him – if they were not already so over Sheves and his like. James would now have to walk warily, to keep his crown. However angry he might be with herself, it was unlikely that he would further endanger his position by attacking his elder sister, wife of one of his great lords and friend of the Douglases. Her place was with the court at Stirling, where she might just possibly help a little in the realm's affairs, and seek to counter the evil influence of Sheves and the others.

John was not wholly convinced, but bowed to her conclusions.

They decided that they would ride to Tantallon right away, and from there take the Douglas barge to Airth. When James and the court would go back to Stirling they did not know, but it probably would be fairly soon.

John went to see his brother, elsewhere in that odd, rambling castle of the bridges, to discover Archie's intentions now. He found that not usually uncertain man in two minds as to his own best procedure in the present extraordinary circumstances. Albany was already talking about putting the fortress in a position to withstand siege, and at the same time calling on the nation to rise in support of himself as replacement of James on the throne. Also intending to raise the Borders in his favour, and this at once. Archie was, in the main, in favour of this; and of course as East Warden – if he was still that – could play a major part. On the other hand, he did not want to get shut up here in Dunbar Castle under siege, if that developed. Nor to become something of a fugitive, hiding in the Border hills. After all, he had an earldom to consider and manage. And his family to think of. Was there going to be a civil war?

John told him of Mary's attitude and anticipations. He thought that at this stage Archie should keep his options open, not commit himself too deeply to Albany's cause until the situation was a deal more clear. The King was still the King, and as one of his earls he had to beware of any suggestion of a charge of treason and its consequences. Wait until they knew James's reactions. And how the nation responded, its lords in particular. No harm in testing the feelings of the Border clans, although, who knew, he might no longer be Warden; James could have cancelled that. Also, to remember that the Homes and the Hepburns would be against Albany, and no doubt would seek to persuade their neighbours in that. It was all in the balance at the moment. John advised caution. Archie would, he judged, be better at Tantallon than here meantime, until they saw how matters evolved.

Archie was not the cautious type, and all too apt to blame his brother in that respect – however positive John's activities had been since he became involved with Mary Stewart. But on this occasion he listened and nodded. He would make a quick survey of the borderland, test out feelings there, commending Albany's cause, then return to Tantallon rather than here to Dunbar, to await developments.

So Mary and John took their leave of Albany, leaving William Graham and the two former royal guards with him, and wishing them all well, Mary promising to send her brother word from Stirling as to James's reactions and plans. The duke expressed his gratitude for all that they had done for him.

Then the pair rode the ten miles north to Tantallon.

John would have had Mary to stay on at that cheerfully female-oriented house on the cliffs for a day or two at least; but she wanted to get back to her children, whom she was seeing too little of these days. Also she had her husband's attitudes to think of. Lord Hamilton's views on the current situation could be important. The court might have returned, or it might not; but she would prefer to be there.

So she stayed only the one night among the Douglases, wife and sisters, a pleasant interlude wherein they tried to forget the nation's problems and uncertainties for a little while in an evening of music and chatter, John persuaded to recite some of his balladry, to considerable acclaim. He had ordered the barge and crew to be ready for the morning, at North Berwick.

Next day the voyage up-Forth to Airth was uneventful; and riding to Stirling thereafter they found that the court was not yet back from Edinburgh. Amidst vociferous greetings from the children, the Lady Anna told them that the castle was buzzing with excitement, rumour and speculation, accounts, stories and assessments competing with each other. It was known that the Earl of Mar was dead, whether dying of sickness or murdered was in doubt, debate. And Albany said to be at large and about to raise the standard of revolt. What would happen? The part played by the princess in all this did not appear to be known.

The newcomers did not enlarge on that aspect, meantime. But the word of Mary's arrival was soon learned – and produced one unexpected happening, a visit from the Queen. This was unusual, for James's wife was a very retiring person, keeping herself very much to herself, and seldom being seen outside the confines of the royal quarters, diffident and very unsure of herself – perhaps scarcely to be wondered at with the husband she had. She came now to Mary's apartments, young, plain-faced and very pregnant, daughter of King Christian of Denmark. She brought with her the child James, Duke of Rothesay, now three years old, heir to the throne.

What of James, she wanted to know, in her heavily accented voice. Where was he? Was he safe? How had John died? Where was Alexander? Would there be war? She wished that she was back in Denmark. This was a bad land.

Mary sought to soothe her, whilst her son played with the other children. James would be safe, she was sure. He would be coming back to Stirling soon, no doubt. She did not think that it would come to war. Their brother John was dead, yes – horribly murdered. That would be the man Sheves's doing, with his sorcerer friends; she prayed that God would punish them, and that James would be rescued from their wicked influence. She, Queen Margaret, could help in that, to be sure, if she would?

There was no response to that plea.

Mary was concerned to see the other Margaret, her sister, she who had been betrothed to the drowned Duke of Clarence. It seemed that while the court was in Edinburgh, she had gone down to lodge at Cambuskenneth Abbey with their friend Abbot Henry. A religiously minded young woman, who would have liked to become a nun, she did not enjoy court life and was glad to escape when she could, often spending periods at the abbey, a very different character from her elder sister. So that evening Mary and John rode down to Cambuskenneth, amongst the Forth's meanders, near where the Battle of Bannockburn had been fought.

John scarcely looked forward to the meeting, in the circumstances, feeling that the sisters should see each other alone, at least at first while Mary broke the grievous news, which possibly Margaret would know nothing of. He was glad, therefore, to remain with Abbot Henry when they arrived, while Mary was conducted to the Princess Margaret's modest apartment.

The abbot proved to know more about current events than they had anticipated, churchmen being frequently the best-informed in the land, thanks to the news-bearing of so-called wandering friars, who performed such useful services for remote communities seldom reached by parish priests. Abbot Henry had heard of the death of Mar and the escape of Albany that very day, but had no details. He said that the Princess Margaret was indeed prostrated with grief.

John was able to inform him more fully, to the older man's horror and distress. The abbot said that he feared that their land was accursed indeed.

John did not disagree with him, but held that since most of their fellow-countrymen were honest and decent, it was up to them to bring down the evil-doers and self-seekers. In this regard, he had a question to put to the abbot, as a senior cleric. Where lay his, John's, duty as a lord of parliament who had

238

necessarily had to swear an oath of allegiance to the monarch when that monarch was so evidently acting unworthily, to the extent of allowing his own brother to be foully murdered, and was in the hands of an unprincipled scoundrel like William Sheves? If Albany raised the standard of revolt, as seemed almost certain, what then? Could such as he support such revolt against the monarch? As he would feel inclined to do.

The other, never a man of hurried words, took his time to answer that. "My son," he said, at length. "You set me a sore problem and a difficult decision. But, as God's humble servant, I can, I think, give only one true answer. King James is the Lord's Anointed. As such, he is accountable for the rule and governance of this land to God Himself. Not to us, his subjects. We are not to be his judges. Yet *he* took vows also, at his coronation and anointing. To rule justly, by God's guidance, and to heed the advice of his due counsellors. Which means, I judge, parliament. So if he fails grievously to do so, parliament may seek to correct him, has the duty to do so. Parliament, not individual subjects, however high-born. Advise, correct, seek to restrain if need be – but not to rise in arms against him."

"But it is the King who must call a parliament! If he refuses . . . ?"

"A convention can then be summoned, by his earls. It is not a parliament, without the monarch, but it can present the will of parliament."

"And if the King does not heed it?"

"Then it is in God's hands."

"M'mm. You will pardon my doubts, but that seems to me scarcely adequate!"

"I know it, my son. But it is the answer to your question, as best I may give it. I well understand your doubts. But if vows before God, and holy anointing, mean anything, that is what I must tell you. God forgive me, I have similar doubts! Not only over the King, but over William Sheves. I find him hateful, as you know, a wicked man. Yet he has been consecrated and made Metropolitan and Archbishop of St Andrews by the Holy Father in Rome, whatever his faults. And as such

239

I, like all other clergy, owe him allegiance, difficult as many of us find it . . ."

"Archbishop Graham was also so appointed and consecrated. Yet the Scots clergy did little to save him from Sheves's machinations!"

"That is true, to our shame. So – who am I to counsel you? But you asked me . . ."

It was at this juncture that Mary and her sister came to join them, the latter red-eyed.

"We have decided, my lord Abbot, that Margaret should return with me to the castle this night," Mary announced. "For our mutual comfort. She is distressed. That will be best, I think."

"I understand, Highness. God Himself console you both . . ."

So the three of them left the abbey. John, whilst sympathising with Margaret Stewart, tried to smother his own disappointment that it looked unlikely that he would have the evening, or any part of it, alone with Mary as he had been hoping.

And so it proved, Margaret showing no inclination to seek an early bed, and Mary eventually declaring that the sisters should share *her* couch that night, in the interests of mutual consolation. He had to be content with the briefest of goodnight salutations at their bedchamber door; but he did receive a vehement and significant pressure on his arm as they parted.

In the morning he was on his way back to Airth and the waiting barge. What he would be returning to at Tantallon and Dunbar, what decisions fell to be made, he did not know.

240

14

Strangely enough, after all the excitements and apprehensions, there followed a notable lull in events, at least as far as John Douglas was concerned, indeed the nation at large. Albany remained secure in Dunbar Castle, while reaching out feelers all over the land to try to gauge support, active support, amongst the lords and magnates. Archie canvassed the Borders, as Warden, although doubtful whether he still held that position, sounding out opinions there. The King, with his court, returned to Stirling, but took no more dramatic measures meantime. Undoubtedly James and his close advisers recognised that the realm's opinion was almost wholly against them over the treatment of Mar and Albany, and that the latter, if he raised revolt, would almost certainly have major support from the nobility. So no steps were taken against Mary, even though James shunned her company. And Archie was not officially unseated in his wardency. An uneasy calm quivered over the land.

Friars from Cambuskenneth came periodically to Tantallon bringing messages and information from Mary to John.

So passed May and June and July, with little to report. John, who was not really a man for excitements and flourishes, was glad to live quietly at home, managing the properties for Archie, fishing, and getting on with his neglected writing of ballads and poems. He greatly missed seeing Mary, of course, but felt that in the circumstances he would be unwise to appear at Stirling Castle for the time being.

There were domestic developments within the Douglas family. In late June sister Anne married the Lord Graham, in the chapel at Tantallon, amid much festivity; and at the same time Elizabeth announced her betrothal to Sir Robert Graham of Fintry, the half-brother. The nuptials were attended by Albany himself, from Dunbar, coming with Archie for the occasion – and surprisingly, with the new Lord Monypenny. Enquiries from Archie as to what this last signified elicited still more surprising information. Monypenny who, as Sieur de Concressault was in effect Louis of France's ambassador, had become convinced that King James was an ineffective ally for France and was less interested in maintaining the Auld Alliance than in forging closer links with Edward of England, whom he now seemed to see as a fellow-target of the satanic powers. So he, Monypenny, had come to the conclusion that Albany would make a better friend for King Louis than was James – and anyway, with some help, might soon become King of Scots in his place. He was urging the duke to go back with him to France and there raise a French army to come and assist in effecting his bid for the throne – and Albany was seriously considering doing so. When John, concerned, doubted the wisdom of this, his brother pointed out that some such development was called for to bring matters to a practical conclusion and to end this period of inaction. The nobles were being slow in actually committing themselves to armed rising, however sympathetic towards Albany, and talking about a parliament to have the sentence of treason lifted from the duke rather than taking to arms – which would undoubtedly be necessary eventually. Better if a French army came, to bring matters to a head. Parliaments, however high-sounding, were really all talk and no action, a putting-off device. Besides, there were rumours emanating from Stirling that Sheves and Cochrane were urging the King to send a force, with cannon, to besiege Dunbar Castle, and the last thing that Albany wanted was to be trapped therein, even though it probably could hold out more or less indefinitely.

When Join pointed out the value of a parliament, if James would indeed call one, to advise and correct the monarch in his policies, as Abbot Henry had explained, Archie pooh-poohed that as just more talk. What they required were swords and lances, not speeches. What heed would Sheves and the King's other low-born cronies pay to such strictures? If they allowed a parliament to be called at all. No, better this way – a French force to arrive, and the Auld Alliance invoked and seen to be supporting Albany. That way they would soon have an Alexander the Fourth, King of Scots! Johnnie should be less cautious, less feeble.

The wedding and betrothal festivities were barely over, and Albany, Archie and Monypenny gone, when another monkish courier brought dramatic information from Stirling, in early August, in the form of a letter from Mary this time, quite a long letter. Its content, besides affectionate greetings and esteem, included four main items of news. One, that James had actually created the man Robert Cochrane, the master-builder and mason, Earl of Mar in his brother's room, to the outrage of all other earls and lords. Two, that the King was indeed going to send an army to besiege Dunbar, under Lord Avondale the Chancellor, and had already begun to call for armed men from his loyal supporters. Three, Edward of England was now proposing the matching of his new favourite and brother-in-law, whom he had created Earl of Rivers, to James's sister Margaret. And four, James Lord Hamilton had fallen suddenly and seriously ill, and was abed at his seat of Cadzow Castle in Lanarkshire, where she felt it had to be her wifely duty to go attend on him, but where she would be happy to see Johnnie if and when he might be able to visit. In the meantime, it might be more difficult for her to communicate with him at Tantallon, lacking Abbot Henry's so useful messengers.

Needless to say, all this set John urgently to think, to cudgel his wits – at the same time seeking to smother the hopes which immediately leapt to his mind that Hamilton might not recover from his sickness, unworthy reaction indeed, which had him debating the rest of the news the more concernedly. First things first: Albany must be warned, Archie also, as to the impending assault on Dunbar, if they had not already heard of it. So, he must get a courier off to Dunbar forthwith. Then this of elevating Cochrane to the royal earldom of Mar, though scarcely believable, would do more to make the nobility unite against the monarch than even the murder of the previous

243

Earl John – and to that extent was perhaps to be acclaimed, if secretly. It was unheard of in all Scotland's long story for such a thing to happen: Robert Cochrane was a master-mason, and good at his task and trade, able to design fair buildings as at Stirling Castle itself; but to create him not only a lord of parliament but an earl was unthinkable, indeed as most would aver, impossible. The earls of Scotland, unlike those of England, were the successors of the *ri*, the lesser kings of Alba who were the deputies and semi-royal colleagues of the *Ard Righ*, the High King, in the ages-old Celtic polity. There had originally been only seven of them, but there were now a dozen; but all were nobly born or of royal blood, legitimate or otherwise. So this was totally beyond credence. James must indeed be out of his mind. But it ought to ensure nationwide condemnation. If a parliament was indeed called, then indubitably there would be major outcry.

The matter of the Princess Margaret was offensive, in a different way, if James agreed to King Edward's proposal. This new Earl Rivers, Edward's brother-in-law, brother of Queen Elizabeth Woodville as he might be, was also low-born, son of a small squire, and of a bad reputation – as indeed was his sister – unsuited in every way to be the husband of a princess of Scotland, the suggestion an insult to the northern kingdom. If James even was considering it, as Mary more or less inferred, then there would be further trouble concerning the throne.

All in all, it much added to the seriousness of the present situation. John decided that he would go in person to warn Albany, and at the same time consult with Archie. Thereafter he was for Clydesdale and Cadzow Castle, even though it was harvest-time for the lands around Tantallon. Mary had invited him, had she not?

At Dunbar, he was surprised to find Albany already gone, the news of intended siege having reached there, from his own Stirling sources, two days previously. He had departed the very next morning for Eyemouth, where he had word that one of the many wool-ships sailing for the Low Countries would be leaving *this* day, and so was on his way to France. He had taken the Lord Monypenny and two or three others with him, and left two of his vassal Merse lairds to hold the castle in his name, no pleasant task – Ellem of Butterdean and Home of Polwarth. John was interested to see the latter there, for the Home clan, taking their lead from the Lord Home, were in the main hostile to Albany. This one, however, a man of middle age and strong views, had gained Polwarth and half of Kimmerghame by marriage, and these were in the earldom of March belonging to Albany; he had evidently thrown in his lot with the duke.

Archie was not at Dunbar but gone on a roving commission in the Borders, none knew exactly where.

John could scarcely contemplate searching all the wide borderland for his brother. But he could plan a route westwards through a swathe of it, on his way to Lanarkshire at the other side of Lowland Scotland, a road he knew well, most of the length of the River Tweed and over to upper Clydesdale, the way he had to take occasionally to visit his own lordship of Douglasdale. He might be fortunate, in hearing of Archie somewhere therein.

As it fell out, he was not, no single word did he hear as to his brother's whereabouts.

He had a lengthy journey ahead of him, perhaps one hundred and twenty miles, at least. He rode by Duns and the Merse, to Kelso and the Tweed. Then westwards up that great river, getting as far as Melrose, there to spend the night in the abbey's hospice, weary after some sixty miles. The abbot and monks were loud in their fears over what was to come in the kingdom.

On to Tweed in the morning he passed Innerleithen and Peebles on his way to where, at Broughton, the river took its sharp southwards bend towards its high source on Tweedsmuir, wherein, as it happened, Clyde also rose. But he cut through green hilly country, to Biggar and thence to Lanark, in Clydesdale now, passing none so far from Douglasdale. From Lanark he followed that other equally great river down to Cadzow, near Blantyre, fully another sixty miles. As well that he ever ensured that he had excellent horseflesh.

At Cadzow Castle above its ravine, his arrival had to be somewhat muted, inevitably, with its lord stricken and sinking fast, a clutch of his illegitimate children there to watch and wait, as well as Mary, her offspring and Anna. Mary was delighted to see him but had to keep her welcome moderated, even though Anna hugged him warmly.

John was in due course taken to the sickroom – and was shocked by what he saw, a suddenly old man, not exactly gaunt but flesh hanging loosely, body limp, eyes lacklustre and wandering, lips dribbling. Whether Hamilton recognised his visitor was uncertain, but his reaction was slight. They did not linger there long. Mary said that the physicians insisted on bleeding him, far too much in her opinion, adding to his weakness. His condition had deteriorated greatly these last few days, but still they were bleeding him.

Their father obviously dying, certain of his bastard sons had arrived, not so much out of filial duty, Mary thought, but to ensure that they were left their due share of his estate – for Hamilton all but rivalled Seton as one of the wealthiest lords in the land. So the atmosphere at Cadzow Castle was not all one of hushed sorrow and caring, but not a little tinged with enmity, jealousy, suspicions and downright greed. John knew some of the sons, in especial those he had met at Stirling; but others he had not heard of. Presumably there were daughters also, but these were not so evident – and presumably not so expectant of inheriting largesse. Mary likened the brood to a flock of kites hovering over a carcase-to-be. For herself, she cared nothing as to this husband's properties. The rich earldom of Arran was safely invested in her little son by Hamilton, and a sufficiency hers until he came of age, her other children provided for. The great Hamilton lands could be squabbled over by his unlawful progeny at will.

The castle thus full, it was difficult for John and Mary to have private converse, much less any affectionate exchange. It was not until her children's bed-time that they managed to gain some privacy when Anna, smiling, withdrew – and even then the youngsters were slow indeed in falling asleep, with their mother remaining so pleasingly nearby. And, to be sure, the couple were inhibited by the presence of the dying man below, although Mary had never so much as pretended any love for him.

They did hold each other's hands, presently, as they talked low-voiced, there in the children's bedchamber, high within the parapet-walk of the fortalice overlooking Clydesdale in the August sunset, eyes saying something of what lips could not. After the Hamilton situation, they discussed the nation's affairs. Mary was, of course, concerned over Albany's flight to France, although glad that he had not got shut up in a besieged Dunbar Castle.

"Bringing in the French, or seeking to, may not be the right course," she declared. "The Auld Alliance can be useful, yes – but I do not trust that King Louis. Any more than Edward! Kings can be utterly without scruple – as we know to our cost! And that one less honest than most, I judge."

"So I said to Archie when he spoke of the possibility. A foreign army on Scots soil could offend more than it aided. But there is nothing that we can do about that now."

"No. But what will be James's reaction? Or that of his wicked advisers? The more apt to turn to Edward of England, I think, for help. Poor Margaret. This of Edward's good-brother, Woodville, whom he has made Earl Rivers. That must be stopped! He is a notorious loose-liver. Old enough to be her father. Like, like . . ." She left the rest unsaid, as they considered the man who lay low downstairs.

"Princesses' lots can be sorry ones," he agreed. "But how can this one be spared, if James is agreeing?"

"Something must be done. Margaret was weeping on my shoulder over it when I left her. She is appalled. Pleading with me to help her, somehow. She turns to me, always, in need. Me! And I could not save my own self!"

"What could you, or other, possibly do?"

"I have been thinking long on this, Johnnie. It is no easy matter, no. But I believe that it could be done. If Margaret would consent. Which she might not, indeed." She paused. "Johnnie, do you know the Lord Crichton?"

"William Crichton, grandson of the famous one? Yes, I

247

have met him. A well-favoured young man, despite being lame."

"Well, he has been paying some attentions to Margaret, these last months. I have noted it, twitted her on it. She does not rebuff him, quite likes him, I think. There is nothing serious between them, at least on her part. But . . ."

"You think . . . ?"

"I think that something might be made of it. Scarcely pleasing, but possible. It would have to be swiftly done."

"What have you in mind, Mary?"

"Something very simple. Basic, indeed! Pregnancy!"

"What!"

"The one matter which would prevent any marriage with this Rivers would be if Margaret was already pregnant. Or alleged to be."

"But – save us! You mean . . . ?"

"I mean that it could be put to her. For her choice and decision. And to Crichton, to be sure. If she declared herself pregnant to Crichton, and he would marry her, then this English match would be impossible."

John stared at her. "You are an extraordinary woman!" he got out. "I vow, there is little that is beyond you! Could this be effected?"

"I see it as the only way out, for Margaret. If she will accept it. I think that she just might."

"And he? Crichton?"

"To win her, I think that he would agree. Would not you, in like case? If he truly loves her."

"M'mm. Yes, I suppose it. But it would put him very wrong with James."

"He favours Alex, anyway. And he was a close friend of John."

"There is that . . ."

"Would you do it, Johnnie? Do this, for Margaret. And for myself."

"Me? Do what?"

"Go to Stirling. See them both. From me. Tell them what they must do, and say if Margaret is to be spared being given

248

to Edward's favourite. *I* cannot go, myself, my husband here all but dying. But you, Margaret would accept and heed!"

"Lord, what a task!"

"I know it. But who else could I send? To attempt a great mercy. You have done so much at my bidding, Johnnie. Will you do this?"

He swallowed. "I, I must try, yes. But . . ." He wagged head helplessly.

She gripped his hand tightly, but said no word.

"When?" he asked.

"As soon as possible, my dear. This, if it is to be done, must be done quickly. It cannot wait. An English dower payment is being discussed, for Margaret. Her price!"

"I will go tomorrow, then . . ."

They discussed other matters, the widespread fury at James's creation of Robert Cochrane as Earl of Mar, and demands for a parliament; but with that dramatic decision about the Princess Margaret preoccupying their minds, they found the rest difficult to concentrate upon.

Thereafter it was Mary's turn to escort John to his chamber door that night, for she herself was going to pay another visit to her husband's bedside before retiring, inadequate wife as she was. She did not hate James Hamilton; indeed she admired many of his qualities, and recognised that he could have treated her a deal worse than he had done. He had got what he wanted, to wed a King's daughter and sister, and to have an heir by her; and in return, he had granted her much of freedom. She owed him something for that.

The castle being so full, and Mary not wishing John to have to share a room with a miscellany of Hamiltons, she had found him a small chamber amongst the servants' quarters across the courtyard, beside the stable block. Unfortunately the said servants were very much in evidence, and it would not do for the princess-countess to be seen entering therein with a male guest. So they had to perform a fairly hasty and discreet leave-taking at the outer door.

John's visits to Mary, so important to him, so looked forward to, tended to produce almost as much frustration as they did satisfaction.

In the morning he was on his way to Stirling, in no state of elation or confidence as to his mission. Of all the projects which he had undertaken, this was surely the most delicate and embarrassing. How to go about it? Should he seek to see the princess first, or Crichton? Probably the latter, since if *he* would not co-operate, there was no point in approaching Margaret, with all the discomforts involved. If he was admitted to Stirling Castle at all. In present circumstances, the guards might be instructed to exclude all but known friends of the King and his advisers. And Crichton himself might not be there.

John rode north by Bothwell and Coatbridge, avoiding Glasgow, and thence to Kilsyth to reach the Campsie Fells. Thereafter through those green hills, across Strathcarron and into the great forests of the Tor Wood, so prominent a feature in the campaigns of Wallace and Bruce. It was not nearly so long a journey as the day before, some forty miles, and he was at Stirling by early afternoon, still in doubts as to procedure.

At least he was not debarred from the castle, the guards knowing him well and showing no hostility. Enquiries as to the King revealed that he had left the day before for his hunting-palace of Falkland in Fife, with the archbishop and Earl of Mar, but no great train. Relieved at this, and also that seemingly the whole court had not gone with him, which meant probably that the Lord Crichton would still be hereabouts, John went in search of the latter.

He found his quarry engaged in the sport of hurly-hackit, that is sledging down the steep, grassy slope on the north side of the castle rock which descended to the terrace called Ballengeich, sitting on oxen's skulls and using the horns as handlebars, a favourite diversion of the castle's inmates. Crichton's lameness, born one leg shorter than the other, did not seem to debar him from this strange but exciting pastime. Amidst the shouts, jeers, tumbles and high spirits, John managed to detach the other, a couple of years younger than himself but still boyish, and lead him apart to a spot overlooking all the flooded Carse of Forth, known as the Flanders Moss, and backed by all the blue Highland mountains.

"I come from the Princess Mary, Countess of Arran, at Cadzow," he said. "I have a message for you, from her, Crichton. A, a difficult message."

"That princess is ever friendly towards me, Douglasdale," he was answered. "Why should her message be difficult?" He paused. "Ah – is it her husband? Is the Lord Hamilton dead?"

"No. But very sick. Princess Mary is friendly towards you, yes – hence my mission. But it concerns the other princess, her sister."

Crichton's features stiffened. "What of her?" he questioned, defensively, immediately on his guard.

"This is where the difficulty lies, my friend. For me, at least," John said, picking his words. "I am but the messenger. Your concerns are not for me to discuss. But the Princess Mary *is* concerned. For her sister."

Silence.

"She believes that *you* may have a fondness for the Princess Margaret, my lord. If that is so, then you will wish to hear what I have to say."

The other did not commit himself. "So?"

"It is about this proposed betrothal to the Earl Rivers, of England. Do you approve of that?"

"It is not for me to approve or otherwise."

"I think that it is. Or the Princess Mary does. She sees it as a tragedy, to the hurt and humiliation of her sister."

"As do I, by God!" That was anything but non-committal, suddenly. "But what can be done about it, if it is the King's will?"

"Much, I think – *we* think! If you are prepared to do it."

"Me? I am the last man James will heed! He does not love me."

"James may not heed you. But Margaret may!"

"What do you mean, man?"

251

"Here is the difficult part. Would you wed her, the Princess Margaret, if you might? And she would have you?"

"Why do you ask that? When it is impossible."

"Not impossible, her sister thinks. If you will play your part."

"You are not cozening me, my lord! For some purpose of your own?"

"I am not. But it is no light matter that the princess proposes. Would you think to wed Margaret?"

"I would next to give my life to do so!"

"Ah!" That came out as a sigh of relief, at least. "That is what I wanted to hear. We do not suggest that you give your life. But you could risk the King's displeasure."

"That I have already, I think! Over Mar and Albany."

"Perhaps. But this would be more . . . personal. If it halted this Rivers betrothal. And the English dower moneys which would come to James therefor!"

"How in heaven's name could I do that?"

"Simply. If you would. And if Princess Margaret would. It is really she who must take the great step, if she will. But *you* have to play your part. She will have to declare herself pregnant! And by you! Now."

"God Almighty! Pregnant! By *me*! The princess!"

"Yes. Her sister says that only so can this betrothal be stopped. Never would Edward of England agree to his good-brother and favourite wedding an already pregnant woman. If you would so claim, and marry the princess, then all could be saved. So says the Princess Mary."

"But . . . but, man – what of Margaret? She does not love me, as I love her. She smiles on me, yes – but that is all. She can smile on others. She has indeed said at times that she might take the veil, become a nun. She would never agree to this."

"Be not so sure. Her sister, who knows her best, thinks that she well might. She is devastated at the thought of being wed to Rivers. And Mary says that she likes you well. Put at its worst, if she has to wed, you would be better than the Englishman! But it is not so bad as that. If she has any fondness for you . . ."

The other eyed him, bewildered, speechless now.

"Will you do it, friend? Or seek to?"

Crichton moistened his lips. "If, if Margaret will have it, have *me*, yes! But I cannot believe that she will consider it."

"That we shall see. I go to her now. I had to see you first. Will you come with me?"

"To tell her that! To have her announce to all that she has bedded with me! When we have not so much as kissed! Save on her hand . . ."

"Nevertheless, it might save her a great sorrow. A lifelong one. And you would entreat her well . . ."

"Save us, I would! I tell you, I would die for that one!"

"Very well. Come, you . . ."

On their way to the princess's quarters, John, much less confident as to what lay ahead than he had sounded, decided that he must see Margaret alone, first. To announce it all to her with Crichton present would be too embarrassing for all concerned, especially if the young woman chose to refuse. But he should be nearby, to be brought in to say *his* part in confirmation. This was essential if she gave any sign of acceptance, or if doubtful, to seek to persuade. So he should wait in an anteroom until called for.

That was agreed.

Far from sure of themselves, the two men entered the palace block, and asked for the princess. Both were known, of course.

When John was ushered into Margaret's tower room, it was to find the young woman stitching needlework with one of her ladies, and looking anything but cheerful. Bowing, he announced that he came from her sister, from Cadzow, with private word for her ear alone. Looking at him almost alarmedly Margaret, after a moment's hesitation, dismissed the other girl.

"Mary – is she well, my lord?" she asked. "And the Lord Hamilton – how does he?"

"She is well, Highness. But he is not. I fear for him. She sends her loving greetings. Owing to her husband's state she cannot leave his side meantime, so she sends myself. With, with important message."

She waited, eyes to the window. She was fair enough, plump, but not nearly so attractive as was her sister, in that man's eyes at least.

"She is greatly concerned for Your Highness. Over this grievous matter of the Earl Rivers of England, as proposed. She declares that it must not be. You must be spared that."

"How? How?" Suddenly she was urgent. "*Could* that be? Oh, could it be?"

"It could, she believes. But . . . it is difficult. It would require some, some distress on your part, Highness. If you would do it."

"What would I *not* do, to escape this vile fate!" she cried. "Tell me."

"It is . . . not easy. For me to tell you. Any more than for you to agree to it. But it could be done." He took a deep breath. "If Your Highness was to declare herself pregnant, with child!"

Her eyes widened. "Pregnant! Me?" She half rose from her seat by the window. "You, you jest, my lord! And, and shamefully . . ."

"Hear me, Highness. Here is no jest. Only so, only pregnant, or claiming to be, can you escape from this betrothal. Neither English Edward nor this Rivers would consider you as bride, in such case. You must see that . . ."

"But it is a lie! I am *not* pregnant, nor will be. All would discover that soon enough. I am virgin, as all know. To propose other is, is shame, I say. My own sister – she did not say this? I cannot believe it of Mary!"

"She did, Highness. It is the only way. And it would not be disbelieved. Not if you wed. And at once."

"Wed! Wed whom? Ah, to wed *you*, my lord! Is that it? I am to wed you, to escape the Englishman!"

"Saints above, not that! Not me, of a mercy! No, no – wed the Lord Crichton."

"William? Willie Crichton! Wed him . . . ?"

"Yes – if you would. He favours you greatly. Says that he would die for you! And Mary believes that you think not unkindly of him."

"But . . ." She was standing now. "He . . . would he do

that? Wed *me*? Say that . . . say that . . . that he . . ." Her voice died away.

"Yes, he would. He would. He is here, outside. He would, I think *rejoice* if you would have him. A good man, and kind. He would make a better husband, I swear, than Anthony Woodville, Lord Rivers!"

"Willie!" Abruptly, she was a different woman. "Willie Crichton! Yes, yes – oh, yes. I would wed *him*. Of all here he is – " She cut herself short. "But, but . . . pregnant!"

"Only saying so, Highness." He could not keep the relief out of his own voice. "Or *you* saying so. None could say that you lied. Say it, then be gone. To marry. Before His Grace returns."

"Yes, yes."

"I will get him in, Highness. He waits." Thankfully John turned to the door and went to hail Crichton within. It had not been nearly so bad as he had feared.

William Crichton came but hesitantly, even though he must have seen from the other's expression that the signs were good. It was a fraught moment for him. Recognising it, John actually took him by the arm to all but propel him forward.

Margaret, lips parted, took a step or two towards them, then halted. This was not easy for her, either.

When neither spoke, John did. "You both see this as . . . good? For the best. Strangely brought about as it is. The Princess Mary's doing, not mine. Shall . . . shall I leave you?"

"No! No!" Two denials, one each, and both definite. But it was at each other that they stared.

At something of a loss himself, now, John felt that probably a brisk attitude was called for. He could not push them into each other's arms, but he had to help them bridge the gap somehow.

"You will have much to say to each other, much to decide upon," he went on. "I will help, where I can. Delay clearly is to be avoided. The sooner that you are both away from this Stirling, the better. Have you any notion, Highness, for how long your royal brother is gone to Falkland?"

She shook her head.

"You, my lord, you will take Her Highness to Crichton? Your castle?"

He nodded also, neither of them vocal at this juncture.

"Good. Then it had best be quickly. If you wish it, I will come so far with you. See you safely on your way, before I return to Princess Mary at Cadzow to inform her that it is well. A letter, Highness, I think. A letter to the King, to await him here. Telling him that . . . this of pregnancy. And that you are wedding Lord Crichton. That will put an end to the Rivers matter. Tell him that you are happy."

She nodded again.

"Can you be ready this day? It would be best. We would ride by devious roads, lest by any chance there could be pursuit. You, my lord, agree?"

"Yes. If, if Margaret so wills . . ."

"Oh, I do, I do . . ."

On that note John decided gratefully that he could leave them to it, make his escape.

"I will be waiting," he said. "Do not think to carry much with you. This is an escape which must be successful." Bowing briefly, he got out of that room, closing the door behind him. He signed to the lady-in-waiting there to leave the pair alone. How trustworthy she was he did not know.

A couple of hours later they were on their way southwards, just the three of them. How the eloping pair had got on in the interim John did not enquire; but they seemed happy enough in a sort of dreamy way, with much clutching of hands but few words. Margaret was a fair horsewoman, not so good as her sister but able for reasonably long journeys. They had about forty-five miles to cover to Crichton, also in Lothian but much nearer to Edinburgh than was Tantallon. John hoped that they would get as far as Linlithgow that night. Not that he thought that they should seek lodgings in the royal palace there, as the princess could have done; there was a hospice of the St Lazarus brothers nearby, called St Magdalene's, originally established for lepers, but now that leprosy was happily less prevalent the Lazarites made it available for travellers. Since his aim was to make themselves as inconspicuous as possible meantime, this ought to be the sort of place for them that night.

They covered that nearly twenty miles without incident, and certainly no signs of pursuit. Not that they really anticipated to be followed; but it was always possible that James or one of his friends might return to Stirling sooner than expected, and word of Margaret's sudden departure, with two lords known to be critical of the King's policies, might cause apprehensions.

It was dusk before they reached Linlithgow, where, just outside the town's gates, the Lazarites made them welcome in a quiet way. John had been wondering how his two companions would elect to spend the night. Together? Or would that be too sudden? In the event there was no question, for the brothers proved to have a separate building for women. It was the two men who shared a cell, after a better meal than they had looked for. John left Crichton to say his goodnights out in the early autumn night. That did not take long, he noted.

In the morning, it proved that both the elopers had been thinking, and coming to conclusions, on their single couches. They divulged, as they rode on eastwards now, that they had decided that they ought to be married at the very soonest possible. There was a church at Crichton, built by William's grandfather, the first lord, a fine place apparently, near the castle; and the parish priest could wed them at shortest notice. Then there could be no way James could cancel what was done, even with an archbishop's assistance. Any requested papal annulment would take a considerable time, by which time . . . ! So, a brief ceremony soon after they arrived at Crichton would be best. Would John come with them there, and assist?

He could scarcely say no to that, little as he had envisaged himself as bridegroom's assistant, however responsible he was for the nuptials.

That day's journey took them to within sight of Edinburgh under its lion-hill. But they avoided the city, passing well to the south of it, between the Braid Hills and the higher Pentlands, going by the Douglas town of Dalkeith, Black Douglases not Red, and on by Cranstoun and the ford of

Tyne at Pathhead. They were coming into low hilly country now, outliers of the western Lammermuirs, and following the Tyne valley upwards. John pointed out to Margaret, to whom all this was new territory, that this River Tyne actually entered the sea between Tantallon and Dunbar, some twenty-five miles to the east. For his part, Crichton pointed out some notable local features, but went on longest about one that they could not actually see – this because it was underground, a splendid example of a Pictish souterrain or earth-house, into which one had to crawl but could walk upright once within, its walls decorated with Celtic carvings. He would take her there one day, he promised. He knew no other so good.

Soon thereafter they came suddenly on a deep wooded valley up which the river turned and out of one side of which thrust a high bare bluff or shoulder, abrupt and steep, on top of which soared the walls of a courtyard-type castle, dramatically sited indeed, its red stone glowing in the afternoon sunlight. And as they turned in towards this, there in the castleton village in the valley's mouth stood a very handsome church of the same red stone, its square tower as stoutly battlemented as was the castle, an unusual place of worship to see in such a rural location. Crichton was no minor lordship, obviously, apart from the other lands it comprised at Sanquhar in far-away upper Nithsdale. William's noted grandfather, another William Crichton, had built this church, for the glory of God no doubt, but also of himself; he had been Lord High Chancellor and Master of the Household to James the Second, more or less Regent of the kingdom during that young monarch's minority.

They rode up to the castle where, it transpired, there was not a little explaining to be done. For William had a mother only in her early forties, and two brothers and a sister in their teens. For Willie to arrive home unexpectedly, with a bride-to-be, and the King's sister at that, engendered some astonishment.

However, the Lady Janet, a pleasant and characterful woman, was understanding and helpful, the reverse of critical. She had had ample experience of family crises, being a daughter of the last Dunbar Earl of Moray, whose earldom

258

had been forfeited and given to a Black Douglas, brother of the eighth Earl of Douglas, he whom the new bride's father had stabbed to death, the earldom again forfeited and given to a Stewart. She had had two husbands, both dying young, and had had to bring up this family alone. If she had doubts as to the wisdom of this marriage, she did not express them. Her children saw it all as a sort of adventure, exciting.

Margaret and John were cared for, whilst, without waiting, William and one of his brothers, Gavin, limped off in search of the parish priest.

Despite the Lady Janet's good reasons for not loving the present royal house, and the fact that she was thus going to be abruptly superseded as chatelaine of Crichton by Margaret Stewart, she treated the younger woman kindly, and sympathised with her in the working out of this predicament. There was much discussion in the great hall of the castle that evening, and a certain amount of good advice given. The parish priest, his orders received, would marry the couple an hour before noon next day. It would be a very modest wedding for a princess and a lord of wide acres, just the family and some of the local retainers present; but its effectiveness none the less for that. The early timing of it was chosen so that John might thereafter get off on his long ride to Cadzow at a reasonable hour.

So before a very small congregation in that large church, John played groomsman for the first time, and wondered whether he himself would ever be in the position to require a groomsman? The priest, an old man and much overawed by the lofty status of the couple before him, made a somewhat halting job of it, repeating himself once or twice and coming to a sudden end with the all but breathless announcement that William and Margaret were now man and wife, in the sight of God and man. Which was, to be sure, all that really mattered.

Thereafter John did not wait for any sort of hurriedly improvised wedding-feast, pointing out that he had fully seventy miles of riding to cover, across the width of Lowland Scotland, from Tyne to Clyde. Crichton offered him a change

259

of horses, but he declared that his fine animal, rested again even thus briefly, would serve him adequately he was sure. Wishing the newly-weds well indeed, amidst their incoherent thanks, he took his leave. Lady Janet added her own measure of appreciation.

Then it was just prolonged and steady riding, south and west, by Borthwick and Balintradoch, Penicuik and The Carlops, Dolphinton and Elsrickle to the Clyde again at Lanark and so to Cadzow. So much had happened since he had come approximately this way before.

Mary Stewart, of course, was delighted to see him back, with his news, and could not sufficiently commend him for his efforts and achievements. She had scarcely expected all to be done so speedily, desirable as this was, to be sure. She enquired closely after Margaret's reactions and behaviour, and was relieved by what she heard. One day, she hoped that she would be able to reward Johnnie Douglas as she wished, for what he had done. That was quietly but carefully said.

James Hamilton seemed to be neither better nor worse, a man now little more than existing, with some of his numerous offspring beginning to show signs of impatience.

In the circumstances, John felt that he should not linger at Cadzow, where his presence at such a time could look unsuitable. He was worried about Archie's situation still and was urgent to see his brother – if he could find him.

So next day he was for the saddle again, to head back eastwards, on the first day of September, in drizzly rain. His regrets at leaving Mary thus were tempered by the presence of a gold chain and Celtic cross, within its circle symbolising eternal life, which now hung round his neck. It was the first token she had given him, and was the more precious in that hitherto it had hung habitually on her own bosom.

15

There were two surprises awaiting John at Tantallon. Archie
was home, so he did not have to go seeking him all over the
Borders; and their mother and Sir Robert Douglas had arrived
on their long-awaited visit from Loch Leven. The pair had
been there for a couple of days, and seemed now reasonably
at ease in their association with the family, whatever had been
the case when they had first appeared. Archie, who might have
been the awkward one, had only turned up this same morning,
from Dunbar, and no doubt the girls had received their rather
difficult guests kindly enough. John wished that he had been
there in person to, as it were, break the ice; but as it was,
all seemed to be well, Archie so full of the current national
situation and its likely effect on him and his, that such as
mere family disharmonies paled into insignificance. Indeed he
was deep in discussion with Sir Robert when John arrived, on
what was to be done about this utterly absurd and disgraceful
elevation of the man Cochrane to be holder of a royal earldom
and the late John of Mar's at that. Something *had* to be done.
If only Albany had not departed for France, he could have led
immediate revolt. The whole land would have risen against
the King in outrage. The older man, while agreeing that it
was a dire scandal and misjudgment on James's part, was
less sure about rebellion; but he declared that a parliament
must somehow be held to consider Mar's death and Albany's
imprisonment and flight, with the realm's security in general;
and this matter of the master-mason could be dealt with then.
If the King refused to call a parliament, it would have to be
a convention, but that would be less decisive. How was a
parliament to be achieved?

John left them to it, and went to seek out his mother.

He found all the women in equally animated discussion – and it amused the man to discover that it was on a subject of recent relevance to himself: pregnancy, and its joys and problems. It seemed that the Countess Elizabeth was now pregnant again, this the fourth time, and hoping for a daughter; and word had just come that Anne, now Lady Graham, was likewise in the family way, notably expeditiously. There was much exclamation, postulation and enquiry from the unwed girls, with Elizabeth acting as the instructress and bringing in her mother-in-law prominently to the lively talk – as was suitable indeed, with the former countess having given birth to all but one there present. Clearly Elizabeth was acting link and bridge to good effect. John's appearance by no means curtailed the conversation, and he was able to add to it by his description of his recent mission. All were intrigued, and much commended the entire project. He received a warm pressure on his arm from his mother. John's new gold chain and cross drew some interested comment.

Thereafter the evening meal brought them all together in an association become cordial and easy, Archie apparently having jettisoned any lingering hostility in his approval of Sir Robert Douglas. He now declared that he would be off next day to try to contact as many of his fellow-earls as he could reach, in order to demand, as the *ri*, the calling of a parliament. John might come with him? John declared firmly that he would prefer to stay at home. He had had a sufficiency of traipsing the country, for the moment. He did not add that he wanted to be at Tantallon in case the so significant message arrived from Mary Stewart. And he suggested that Archie might be wise not to appear too visibly against King James at this stage, with Albany absent – or he might not be available to assist the duke when he returned! Sir Robert backed him in this, as did all others present.

For all that, Archie was off next day, in the Tantallon barge, heading north. It so happened that the majority of Scotland's earls resided north of the Forth and Clyde estuaries, the most important being the Stewart ones – and likely to be most outraged, as semi-royal – Atholl, Buchan, Strathearn and

Lennox. Few of these were now frequenting the court. If he made for the port of Dundee, at the mouth of Tay, he ought to be able to reach some of them, if not all, including Crawford and Huntly.

Thereafter, with the Lochleven Douglases departing the day following, a kind of peace descended on Tantallon Castle for the meantime, welcome indeed to John.

That feeling of peace did not survive for long unfortunately, estate management, fishing and poetry composition having to retreat in the face of what amounted to warfare, national warfare. For only a few days later, this eastern part of Lothian became the scene of active hostilities, with the threatened army under Chancellor Avondale arriving to besiege Dunbar Castle. Suddenly the entire coastal area between the Lammermuirs and the sea was alive with armed men, and these tending to behave in undisciplined fashion well beyond the bounds of Dunbar, as is the way of armies. John, although thankful that Archie was not there, and possibly thinking of trying to aid the Dunbar garrison, had to muster the Douglas strength, in some measure, to protect their own properties and people as far as possible from cattle-stealers, looters and ravishers. The booming of cannon-fire from ten miles away emphasised the end of peace at Tantallon.

John was uncertain as to what he ought to do, he who was so good at advising Archie. While in favour of Albany's cause in general, that was in abeyance meantime. And there was nothing that he could do about the siege of Dunbar. On the other hand, Archie, having been the duke's deputy, was bound to be suspected by James and his advisers, and they might turn a hostile eye on Tantallon. He had to protect the womenfolk here, hardly prepare for siege likewise, but do something. He decided to go and see Avondale, that unlikely warrior. He had never had any personal disagreement with the Chancellor, whom he judged to be honest enough, and who indeed he felt should be supported where possible, as a more wholesome influence near the monarch than was Sheves and the others. Mary had always spoken fairly kindly of him.

So, with a score of Douglas men-at-arms, he rode south to

263

Dunbar amidst the roving bands from the besieging army, up to mischief in their idleness.

He found that the Chancellor had taken over the house of the provost of Dunbar, in the town, and was doing his besieging as comfortably as possible from there. The comfort was physical, however, rather than mental, as John quickly discovered. Avondale greeted him doubtfully at first but, assuming that he came in a helpful capacity, enquired whether he had any useful and effective cannon at Tantallon. Unfortunately those he had been given to bring with him from Stirling were useless. At best, cannon were unreliable and difficult, as he was sufficiently old-fashioned to believe – and as the King's father had discovered to his cost – but the four he had here were valueless, indeed a menace to themselves rather than the enemy, two unable to fire at all, and the others feeble in the extreme and erratic as to aim. Dunbar Castle needed powerful artillery to breach its thick and islanded walls. What made the situation worse was that the castle's own artillery appeared to be in a much better condition, keeping the besiegers at bay. Indeed, only the day before, there had been an appalling incident. A single enemy ball, at long range, had ploughed into a group of his waiting knights and lieutenants, and killed three of them at a stroke – Sir John Colquhoun of Luss, Sir Adam Wallace of Craigie and Sir James Schaw of Sauchie. He was short enough of well-born leaders as it was; this was disastrous and ill-omened.

John expressed sympathy, but hastily declared that there were no effective cannon at Tantallon. Only two old pieces which had been there all his life and which he did not know whether had ever been fired; he rather thought not. The old Chancellor, disappointed, said that he had sent to the Lords Home and Hailes to see if they could produce artillery, but was not hopeful. It looked as though Dunbar Castle would have to be *starved* into submission. He wished that King James had never allotted him this task. The siege was premature, and unpopular anyway, he felt. With Albany gone, it was no longer an essential measure. Better to have waited until parliament arraigned the duke on a charge of high treason, when a much more effective assault could have been authorised. The King, unfortunately, had little notion of practicalities, and those closest to him had no experience in such matters. He had sought to dissuade him, but . . .

John sympathised further. It was obvious to him why Avondale had been chosen to head this attempt. The fact was, clearly, that none of the warrior earls and great magnates was prepared to do so, in their offence against the King's follies, and the faithful old Chancellor was the most senior figure available. John had not failed to note the implication that a parliament *would* be held, and asked about that, to be told that James had indeed bowed to pressure from the lords, and had reluctantly issued the required summons. Parliament would assemble at Edinburgh towards the end of October.

To make his visit to Dunbar seem of some point and reason, John told the other that if indeed this siege was going to be prolonged, Tantallon was only ten miles away, and the Chancellor would be welcome to come and lodge there for some of the time, if he felt so inclined, in probably more suitable quarters than in this small townsman's house. Avondale thanked him, but said that in the event of a lengthy wait for surrender, he was not going to remain sitting here indefinitely. As Chancellor of the kingdom he had other duties elsewhere, especially with a parliament to prepare for, so the King would have to find some other commander.

On that note they parted. John could at least feel that he had offered a helping hand to Avondale, whatever Archie might think of it, and ensured, as far as he could, that Tantallon would not be involved pointlessly in this imbroglio. He was sorry about the three knights killed by that cannon-ball, none of whom he knew, although he had heard of Colquhoun, chief of that small clan. That was an extraordinary event, a misfortune of war indeed. James would probably declare that it was the work of satanic powers.

Archie arrived back a few days later, cutting short his mission, having heard that the parliament had already been called. But he had seen the Earls of Crawford, Erroll and Menteith, and all agreed that the situation could not be allowed to continue as it was, that James must be shown that he had lost the trust and support of his people. The parliament must assert the nation's needs. No doubt the other earls would say the same.

That was satisfactory, as far as it went. But John was concerned that Archie might think to involve himself in the present conflict here at Dunbar. Urging his brother to more cautious courses was not always an effective procedure, but in this instance he had thought up a method which might serve. He pointed out that, with a full army besieging the castle, there was nothing that he, or other, might do to relieve the place. In time, the garrison must yield, inevitably, through lack of food and gunpowder, even though it might exist on rations of fish and some supplies delivered by boat for perhaps weeks. So their own most useful part would be to organise the means of supply meantime, and then eventual escape, by sea – since almost certainly it would come to that. They would require fishing-boats to be ready to approach the castle by night, sufficient to take all the garrison; and also possibly the provision of a sea-going ship to carry the leaders, Ellem and Polwarth and the rest, off to France to rejoin Albany.

Archie had to accept this as the best that he could do at this stage. But he made a distinctly restless and caged-like denizen of Tantallon in the meantime. John was hardly at peace in himself, either. No word had come from Cadzow.

It was a poor autumn, weatherwise, difficult for the harvest and unpleasant for the besieging force at Dunbar, much of which settled in at the town for comfort – and seeking such of that as they might obtain from its womenfolk, to the resentment of their men. There proved to be more fighting in the streets and taverns than around the beleaguered fortress. Lord Avondale abandoned his command, without visiting Tantallon, and returned to Edinburgh to prepare for the parliament, leaving the Lord Home in charge.

That so important parliament should have been preoccupying the minds of all concerned with the well-being of the realm. Archie talked about it incessantly. Unfortunately, however, there were other preoccupations apparently. The lack of any firm hand at the helm of the ship of state inevitably permitted disorders throughout the land, these often involving folk who should have known better and shown fair examples. For instance, the Earls of Erroll and Buchan were all but in arms against each other; the Master of Crawford and the Lord Glamis had indeed come to blows, with their followings; the Borders were in some disarray, lacking a Lieutenant now and Archie unsure whether he was in fact still Warden, with the Maxwells and Scotts at active feud, likewise the Rutherfords and Turnbulls. And in the Highlands, Angus Og of the Isles was now in full-scale war against his father, John, and the latter's allies of MacLeod, MacNeil and Maclean.

All this, sad to say, played into the hands of Sheves and the King's chosen coterie, enabling them to declare that this was why a parliament was being called, and that it must be mainly concerned with establishing good government and control over the kingdom and a uniting behind the royal authority – which was the reverse of what the Albany faction had intended. Moreover, two weeks before the assembly, the duke was formally cited at the Mercat Cross of Edinburgh to appear before the said parliament to answer the accusation of high treason – a shrewd move, no doubt by Sheves, for failure to obey would in itself constitute treason in law, and Albany scarcely able to respond, even if he learned of it in France and had time to come.

Archie, as were no doubt others, was much concerned that the parliament might not produce all that they had hoped for.

Then, a week before the due day, at last a messenger arrived from Mary Stewart, one of the Abbot Henry's friars again, so coming from Stirling not Cadzow. The Lord Hamilton was dead. Mary would be at Edinburgh, with the court, for the parliament, and staying in the Hamilton town-house in the Cowgate. She hoped that she would see John there.

So now John's priorities were suddenly altered. He was still concerned over the parliament, but he could not accord it the prominence in his mind that the meeting with Mary, now widowed again, came to hold in his thoughts. A new situation, for them. What would be the outcome?

16

The brothers rode for Edinburgh the day before the parliament, on the last day of October. They halted at Seton, to pick up the lord thereof, and were persuaded to spend that night there – at least Archie was. He had no town-house in the city, and it would be only an hour or so's ride in the morning. John was the impatient one now, but he could hardly insist on going on alone in the hope of finding lodging in the Hamilton house. The city would be packed, he was assured, and Seton Palace infinitely more comfortable than anything that they would find therein.

So he fretted, physical comfort scarcely his consuming concern.

In the morning, as Seton had foretold, they found Edinburgh overflowing with the parliament's attenders and their retainers, rivalry and feud already in evidence, and the town guard prominent in the streets to try to keep the peace. Were other nations like the Scots, John wondered – always more ready to fight each other than the common enemy? In the circumstances, they rode directly up to the castle, where the assembly was to be held, John with vivid memories of the last time that he had been there and all that had transpired since.

In the great hall an atmosphere of excitement and anticipation prevailed. John and Seton went to their places in the lords' benches, whilst Archie disappeared to join the earls, who would process out of the robing-room for the formal opening.

In due course Mary Stewart appeared, to take a seat in the minstrels' gallery, amongst the envoys and ambassadors. They exchanged small signals.

When Lyon King of Arms ushered in the earls, all present

looked to see how Robert Cochrane comported himself with them, if indeed he so dared. But he was not present, which met with general relief and approval. Sheves led in the bishops and mitred abbots but, as before, did not sit with them but went to stand behind the throne. Avondale came to take his seat behind the Chancellor's table, looking markedly uneasy.

Then, to trumpeting, Atholl appeared bearing the sword of state, Buchan carrying the sceptre and then, bearing the crown itself on its cushion, none other than Cochrane, Earl of Mar. The hall erupted in exclamation and fury.

The noise prevailing was nowise stilled by the next trumpet blasts, which brought in the King. All must rise who were not already on their feet protesting. The Chancellor banged his gavel time and again for quiet.

James, eyes lowered, hurried to his chair, and sat, a picture of uncertainty, all but guilt mixed with a sort of defiance. Atholl and Buchan placed their symbols on the table and went to their places with the other earls, but Cochrane went to stand beside Sheves behind the throne, where Albany and his brother John had stood formerly.

The assembly positively seethed. Lyon announced that parliament was now in session, but his declaration was barely audible.

Avondale's unhappiness was obvious, but he had to keep hammering for quiet. When at length he obtained it, he announced, head ashake, that the dignity of parliament and respect for the monarch's presence must be maintained, and that the King of Arms would, if necessary, eject any who might persist in unruly behaviour or interrupt the proceedings. The business of the state fell to be conducted in orderly fashion. He would now, accordingly, move to the first issue, which was a most notable proposal of His Grace's own. The King intended to make a royal pilgrimage of great significance, for the good and well-being of his realm and them all, and leading a great train of the highest and most noble in the land. This to the shrine of St John at Amiens, in Picardy, that sacred place.

Struck dumb, now, with astonishment, the company stared,

all hardly able to believe their ears, other matters for the moment in abeyance.

Not so Archie Douglas however, dumbness not a weakness of his. He jumped to his feet.

"My lord Chancellor, I protest!" he cried. "Before we proceed to any business, I declare, as one of the earls of Scotland, the *ri*, that here is shame, error, folly! Which makes folly, false and mockery of this parliament. Indeed, is it a parliament at all, with the crown itself borne in by one who has no least right to do so? Who cannot truly be an earl, a man of no estate, or no least right to bear any symbol of state, or to be here at all. I do most strongly protest!"

That aroused varying reactions. Almost all there agreed with what he said undoubtedly, but not all that this was the time to say it, or the way to do so – which was John's opinion. And all were still bemused by the extraordinary announcement of James's proposed pilgrimage to France. Confusion reigned.

Avondale beat his gavel. "My lord of Angus, sit down!" he ordered. "You are out of order, quite. You may not interrupt the Chancellor's announcement of business. I have not finished. Sit!"

Archie did not sit. He knew that whatever the other might say, no Chancellor could order an earl to be ejected from parliament.

"I am entitled to make objection," he asserted strongly. "The symbols of state, sword, sceptre and above all crown, represent the highest authority of the realm. They give the authority to parliament. If the crown is brought in by one who has no right to bear it, then the parliament itself has no authority. It is not valid!"

James was agitatedly speaking to Sheves, half out of his throne.

"My lord, I said to sit!" Avondale commanded, his voice quivering now, an elderly man much troubled. "These may be your opinions but this is not the time to voice them. *I* am in charge of the business of parliament, in His Grace's royal name and presence. And I command you to be seated, while I continue. If you insist, you may speak later . . ."

270

A voice behind him was raised, that of Sheves. "My lord Chancellor, I myself would not here speak. But I do so at the King's own orders. The Earl of Angus is not only out of order but totally in error. Symbols are symbols only, important, but not *the* authority. They represent royal authority, yes. But when he is here present, the King himself is the authority. His Grace is the fount of honour, the only such. None can deny that. And he can make or unmake lords of parliament, even earls! Be you warned, my lord! His Grace has made Robert Cochrane here Earl of Mar. So Earl of Mar he is. And the crown is the King's. If he choses my lord of Mar to carry it, then that is in order – and my lord of Angus is not! This I declare at His Grace's express command."

There was silence now as men eyed each other. In fact, of course, what Sheves had said was true. By any and every standard the parliament depended on the King's authority. If he walked out of it, then it was no longer a parliament. However unwise, foolish or mistaken the royal behaviour, parliament had to accept it whilst in session, or cease to be so.

"I acknowledge His Grace's royal will," Avondale said. "And thank you, my lord Archbishop. The Earl of Angus will sit, to allow this parliament to proceed with its due business."

Scowling, Archie Douglas sat.

The Chancellor's hand was visibly shaking, trembling. "Further to this of the royal pilgrimage," he went on. "It is His Grace's designs that it shall be a most important event, to establish this realm's status and standing amongst the nations of Christendom and its monarch high-ranking amongst the princes thereof. Particularly to the King of France, to whom the Duke of Albany has fled instead of appearing here to meet the charge of high treason." Growling interrupted that. Hastily Avondale went on.

"This pilgrimage will also, it is intended, serve to improve relations with King Edward of England, to whom a request for safe-conduct through his realm for the company has been sent. Such improvement called for because of the unauthorised and unfortunate marriage of the King's royal sister, the Princess Margaret, to the Lord Crichton, which has incurred His

Grace's displeasure, when she was to be betrothed to the Earl Rivers, King Edward's good-brother. So this pilgrimage is a venture of much concern to all who care for the well-being of this realm. It is His Grace's wish that many here present will accompany him, with their trains, that it may display Scotland's strength and import."

None there required to be told further what was behind this surprising proposal. It was a move to counter Albany's efforts to embroil Louis of France in his attempt to unseat his brother; and at the same time to reassure King Edward that the forging of closer links with France did not threaten his own security. It could be a clever conception, probably Sheves's own, this the more likely in that it was to be in the form of a religious pilgrimage to the shrine of St John at Amiens, in which Pope Sixtus was known to be interested, and which would increase Sheves's influence at the Vatican.

While men murmured about this, the Chancellor, making play with his papers although this was clearly not necessary, almost reluctantly proceeded.

"The matter of the Duke of Albany," he said. "His Highness is known to have been plotting against His Grace, so had to be apprehended for question. He contrived to escape from royal custody, with the help of disloyal elements, in this very castle. He went to Dunbar Castle, and fortified it against His Grace, the which is still being besieged. He has been duly cited to appear before this parliament to answer charges of treason. He has not done so. This in itself is a treasonable offence. It is the royal will that parliament hereby declares the treason established, and authorises the measures of punishment."

Here, then, was the crunch. Not a sound was heard in that hall.

It did not take long for Archie to break that silence. When nobody else seemed in haste to do so, he jumped up.

"I move to the contrary," he exclaimed briefly, and sat.

That at least produced a chorus of seconders.

Avondale moistened thin lips. "Motion heard, although it is expressly against the royal will. And seconded. And counter-motion, supportive of His Grace's will?"

"I move in favour of the King's decision," Sheves said. "Albany to be declared guilty of treason. And I remind all present that failure so to support the royal will could itself be considered as treasonable!"

"I second." That was the new Earl of Mar finding voice. The growling rose in volume.

"The motion proposed and seconded. Counter-motion likewise," the Chancellor said, looking around him, a man torn. "Must I put this grave matter to the vote?" He seemed to wait for an answer to that.

Inevitably Archie gave it. "Vote!" he shouted.

Into the hubbub a new voice was raised, that of the Earl of Argyll, the Campbell chief. "My lord Chancellor, this is a matter of deep consideration, concerning the King's own brother. All must have time to take due thought. The duke has scarcely had time or opportunity to hear or to act on the summons to appear before us, from France. In these circumstances, I move that the decision on this weighty question be postponed to the next meeting of parliament."

"I second," Atholl was quick to declare.

Avondale hesitated, glancing round at Sheves and the King. But the shouts of approval from all over the hall left no doubts as to the sentiments of the vast majority present, and he bowed to the situation, and shrugged.

Sheves spoke. "No doubt due consideration will ensure a suitable decision over His Grace's erring and dangerous brother. But meantime charges of treason cannot be denied against those miscreants who still hold Dunbar Castle against the King's forces, in shameful defiance. I say that parliament has no option but to condemn for treason George Home of Polwarth, Ellem of Butterdean, and all the others presently defying the royal command to yield up Dunbar. I so move."

"I second," Cochrane said, and added, "Should not the Lord Crichton also be condemned for treason, for his deliberate contradiction of the royal will and bringing to naught the intended marriage of the King's sister, the Princess Margaret, with King Edward's good-brother. I add that . . ."

The rest was drowned out in angry denunciation that this

273

upjumped nobody could so criticise before parliament one of its own lords of ancient lineage. The new Earl of Mar's unpopularity could not have been more clearly and vehemently displayed.

The Chancellor, a realist, hastily amended the suggestion. "That would have to be a different consideration, my lord Earl," he asserted. "Whether it is treason or no is debatable. But this other, of the Dunbar defiance, is clear. It is a treasonable offence against the royal will and command. There can be no other verdict. I so declare."

Although there were murmurings, no one actually made a contrary motion, and without delay Avondale went on.

"Parliament has to consider the present state of lawlessness which prevails in the land and, grievously, involving some here present. Fighting amongst the King's subjects, against the law and the King's peace. Feud and strife, even open warfare. This must be halted. I, I need not name names, here – but all know that some lords, and even earls, are not guiltless. The King will have to take steps to halt it, if parliament's edicts are not accepted. And punish offenders. I herewith call upon parliament to condemn it, and to command that all such feuding cease forthwith."

Righteously Atholl so moved, his brother Buchan, Hearty John, being one of the prime offenders. Huntly seconded, although his Gordons were by no means guiltless of feuding. No contrary motion was raised, so the matter, a mere formality which no one took very seriously, was passed.

"The fighting between the Angus of the Isles and the former Earl of Ross, his father, has developed into full war, in the north," Avondale went on. "This is to be deplored, especially as it involves MacLeans, MacLeods, MacRaes and other lesser clans. But, short of mounting another armed expedition, in great force and with a galley-fleet, to seek to bring these Highlanders to order – which is not convenient to consider in view of His Grace's proposed great pilgrimage to France – there appears little that parliament can do to express its condemnation, other than call upon the clans to halt their strife."

"Let them fight and slay each other, to the greater peace of the rest of us!" Argyll exclaimed, to cheers and the first laughter of the session.

"Is it agreed?"

There was no dissenting voice.

That over, the Chancellor had another very difficult theme to tackle. "There is the vexed matter of law and order in the Borders also. This is not at present being preserved as it should be. The Duke of Albany was, to be sure, the King's lieutenant there and is now gone. There are Wardens of the three Marches, but none to oversee them. Is it parliament's will that a new Lieutenant be appointed?"

There was silence as men exchanged glances. None had to be informed that here was dangerous ground to tread – the Douglases least of all. Was Archie still Warden of the East March? Was the Lord Maxwell that of the West? He was one of the principal feuders of his own area, all but at permanent war with the Johnstones of Annandale. Lord Home was still presumably Warden of the Middle March; but he was the only lord known to be friendly with the man Cochrane. He might well covet the status of Lieutenant of the Border. But that would be unpopular. Moreover he could hardly be raised above the Earl of Angus. And Angus himself, so loud a supporter of Albany, would never be accepted as Lieutenant by James and his advisers. What other magnate would wish to be so, or could impose his will on the troublous borderland? In the circumstances there would be few, if any, volunteers.

When no voice was raised, Avondale looked round at Sheves. But even that dexterous plotter was unsure.

"I would propose the Lord Home as Lieutenant," he said. "But . . . there is the question of seniority. Perhaps he might be raised in dignity?"

Archie did not trouble to rise. "I would refuse to serve under Home!" he called out. "And the worst troubles in all the Borders are in the Middle March, with the Turnbulls and Rutherfords burning and slaying far and wide, each other and others. He, Home, does nothing."

Avondale tapped his gavel in required protest at this

unsuitable interjection, but spoke no reproof. Nor did anyone else.

Into the uncomfortable pause, it was a bishop who raised
voice, Glasgow, the Treasurer. "My lord Chancellor, I suggest
that until the decision on my lord Duke of Albany has been
taken by the next parliament, the matter of the lieutenancy of
the Borders should be held in abeyance. The duke *is* Lieutenant
until parliament decides otherwise. Therefore decision need
not, should not, be taken now. What is required is that the
three Wardens be commanded by this parliament to take more
strenuous and determined steps to assert their authority, and
the King's peace, in their respective Marches. And to give
account of their activities to the next parliament. I so move."

There were ample relieved seconders for that.

Sheves, knowing well that almost the entire parliament was
against him and his, did not make a contrary motion.

"To the next business, then." The Chancellor could hardly
have got that out more swiftly. "The appointment of a justiciar
for Galloway . . ."

John Douglas, for one, was all but astonished. Despite all, it
seemed, Archie was still Warden of the East March, indeed by
implication confirmed in that office by parliament and given
the greater authority to act. He could scarcely credit it.

There followed a lengthy list of relatively minor appointments up and down the land, to approve and discuss, these
requiring parliamentary sanction, all boring to most there
after the previous excitements, with recognition that the main
concerns of the parliament were over.

Not the least restless was King James, his indecision and
agitation very much in evidence, although he had not once
raised his voice throughout. He tugged at Sheves's magnificent
sleeve presently. That man nodded, and moved forward to
murmur in the Chancellor's ear.

Avondale was not loth to accede. After the Earl of Buchan
had declared that many Scots merchants living and trading in
England had had their properties confiscated, and some were
therefore applying for denization, or English citizenship, to
avoid such fate, and should not similar action be taken in

Scotland against Englishmen, to teach Edward his lesson. The Chancellor asserted that this was a matter which fell to be considered very carefully before any such action was decided upon, and therefore should be held over to the next parliament in March. If there was no other business, with His Grace's permission, he would now adjourn the session.

James got up and hurried out, before most there had time to rise as required, followed by Sheves and Cochrane. Parliament broke up in something like disorder.

Outside the hall, Archie was much elevated. There was no doubt about it, now. He was Warden indeed, and moreover, expected to act vigorously. And he would, he would, let none doubt it! Even though he had to do some of Home's work for him! That two-faced wretch!

John admitted that he was surprised. And not only over the matter of the wardenship. He had been almost fearful that James would have made the new Earl of Mar Lieutenant of the Borders – which would indeed have provoked chaos. The Albany issue had disappointed; but at least decision was postponed, giving time for positive developments. As for this extraordinary proposal of a pilgrimage, he did not see the King mustering any large train of followers, if indeed the thing ever came to pass. It would be Sheves's idea, to be sure, and aimed at impressing the Pope, for his own further advantage, as well as seeking to halt French aid for Albany.

Archie dismissed it all as nonsense, like so much else which had transpired. In especial the matter of Cochrane. Somehow that creature must be brought low. Johnnie was good at schemes and devices. He must put his mind to it. Meantime, the parliament was over sooner than expected. They could get back to Tantallon that night.

Seton, with them still, suggested that they should go only as far as his palace, to avoid a ride in darkness. They could discuss it all there, in comfort. Archie concurred. But John had other ideas. He required to have word with the Princess Mary, he said, although possibly he might join them at Seton later. He was for the Hamilton house, meantime.

Archie declared that to be a good notion. The princess

277

was clever at devices and scheming, also. They might all go to her.

That was scarcely his brother's preferred programme. He pointed out that a lot of the Hamilton brood might well be present, and he knew that Archie did not approve of them. Better that he went alone, in this instance.

Seton, a not insensitive man, smiled but agreed. They might see John at Seton later.

They rode together down the Lawnmarket and the High Street, to the Blackfriars monastery, where John turned off for the Cowgate. What lay ahead, he wondered?

There were three Hamiltons present, Sir John, Sir James and Sir Patrick, all holding baronies despite illegitimacy, and all having attended the parliament – likewise all very vocal now. Wives and offspring were also at the town-house, so the place was crowded indeed. John found Mary, Anna and the children all crowded into one room and a tiny annexe, highly disappointing as far as privacy was concerned, for him at any rate.

Mary's reception had to be moderate in the circumstances, indeed the man got more of a hug from the Lady Anna, whom he knew approved of him. Thereafter she did her best to keep the children reasonably distant from their mother for a while, without entire success. After being deprived of maternal company for hours, the youngsters were noisy now.

Comment on the parliamentary proceedings was limited therefore, and little could be said about the Lord Hamilton's death and its consequences. Mary observed that the parliament had, in fact, gone rather better than she had feared, as far as Albany's position was concerned, as well as the Borders situation. The pilgrimage notion was a folly, of course, but she doubted very much whether it would ever come to anything. Cochrane was proving insufferable in his new position, lording it over everyone and gathering his own little court of sycophants about him – indeed so much so that she wondered whether Sheves himself was not becoming doubtful.

John declared that that would be a desirable development. The more disharmony there, the better.

"Yes. If Cochrane comes to think that he can influence James more than does Sheves, then . . ." Abruptly, Mary changed the subject, as though all this had been secondary in her mind. "Johnnie, I want you to take me, to take us all, to Arran," she said.

He blinked. "Arran? The island . . . ?"

"Yes. Arran." She took his arm to move him over to the window, backs to the others. "Johnnie, I am concerned. Arran must be preserved, saved for my children. It is endangered now, now that James Hamilton is dead. It was crown property, bestowed on myself and my husband, Thomas Boyd, as my dower, when *his* father ruled Scotland for James as a boy. Tom created Earl of Arran. So I am still Countess of Arran. James Hamilton married me, and got the *revenues* of Arran, and other estates, but not the earldom. That should now come to our son. But . . . I fear for it on two counts. One, that James may think to snatch it back, for himself, the crown. It is a rich heritage. Or else that these other Hamiltons may seek to grasp it. At least while my son is a minor. There are so many of them, and all hungry for lands. So I want to go there. As is my right. Take possession. It was really *my* portion, not Tom's. And I want to ensure that my two sons keep it. Will you take me there, Johnnie?"

"I will take you anywhere that you wish to go, Mary," he said simply.

"Thank you, my dear." She squeezed his arm. "I knew that I could rely on you. When can you go? So soon as possible, if you will."

"Yes. Let me go home to Tantallon, to see to some matters there. Discover Archie's plans. Then come for you. Two days or so will serve . . ."

"I will move back to Cadzow tomorrow. That is also my responsibility now, for my son. He is the Lord Hamilton, as well as Earl of Arran. I will have to attend to matters there. Leave all in order and good care. Then, Arran. Come you to Cadzow in a few days, Johnnie, if you will."

"I will, never fear."

"I think . . . that you will not regret it, my dear!"

They eyed each other, silent.

John left soon thereafter, for Seton, there being little point in lingering.

17

Exactly a week later, in blustery weather, John reached Cadzow in mid-forenoon, after a less than enjoyable ride from Tantallon. He had been delayed by Archie, over his plans and decisions. Indeed his brother had not been pleased over this trip to Arran, desiring that he come to the Borders with him as Deputy Warden, with much to be done. But John, on this occasion, was not to be diverted.

He found Mary and quite a sizeable party awaiting him, not exactly impatient but eager to be on their way, all but ready for departure. For she was concerned to be gone from Cadzow. James Hamilton had a brother, Alexander, and there was a well-established custom where a child was left heir to a lordship or large property that he should be represented and largely governed by what was known as a tutor, not a teacher but a guardian — women being generally considered unfit for such responsibility; and word that Alexander Hamilton of Drumsargard was talking of coming to claim this position had reached Mary, who was determined that any tutoring would be done by herself. So before a horde of Hamiltons descended again on Cadzow she was anxious to be off, with her children. It was some thirty-five or forty miles to Ardrossan, where they could get a ferry-boat to Arran, and the youngsters could not ride so far in one day. But they probably could get as far as Kilwinning Abbey, *en route*, and the Abbot of Kilwinning was a Boyd, her first husband's uncle, and they could pass the night there.

So the party left Cadzow after only a brief interval: Mary, her three children, the Lady Anna and her young son, two serving-women, and their menfolk as escorts. All had been bred to horsemanship, so they should not be too grievously held up. But with the youngsters, and little Elizabeth only four, they would have to take turns at carrying her. They also had a train of laden pack-horses. John had never travelled in such a convoy previously.

But it was a cheerful company, the children at least seeing it all as a great adventure. They rode by East Kilbride south-westwards by Eaglesham and up on to the high, lochan-dotted moorlands of Craigenfaulds Moss, then along the Fenwick Water to Fenwick itself, and on to Kilmaurs. This was Boyd country now, out of the Hamilton influence, north Ayrshire. Although the children could not be other than tired, Mary sought to keep the boys at least interested in all that they saw by telling the elder, Jamie – they were both christened James actually, for family reasons – that *he* was the true Lord Boyd, even though the title was at present in forfeiture, and all this land should be his. Whereas they were heading for the Isle of Arran, where James, his half-brother, now should be earl. The chatter as to the whys and wherefores of it all occupied them for the rest of the road to Kilwinning.

That abbey was a large and rich one, William Boyd, its abbot, now an old man but still very much in charge. Although greatly surprised to see his nephew's widow and his great-nephew, there was no lack of welcome. Also no difficulty about accommodation, for the travellers' hospice here was much in use, with a special wing for women and children. The monkish larders were well stocked with provender. So the evening was spent in fair comfort, although short of duration, for these monastic establishments went early to bed and expected their guests to do the same. Fortunately they did not require the latter to rise for the early morning rituals.

Before bedding down, however, Abbot William, hearing of their destination, offered further and welcome help. They had been heading for Ardrossan, from where the regular ferry-boats made the crossing to Arran; but the abbey had its own vessel, berthed at Irvine, much nearer at hand, which was used to communicate with its daughter-houses on the island, three of them, St Molas's monastery on the small Holy Isle, and the two St Michael's hospices in Glens Cloy and Sannox. The travellers could use this craft and save trouble and expense. He would send a sub-prior with them. This offer was gladly accepted.

John, who had covered the width of Lowland Scotland in these two days, slept soundly that night.

From Kilwinning to Irvine was only some ten miles, and presented no problems, with the children excited now about the boat trip. John told them about the great Battle of Largs fought nearby, in Alexander the Third's reign two centuries earlier, when the Norse menace to Scotland was finally overthrown; but rather failed to hold their attention, despite all their ancestors undoubtedly being involved.

With the sub-prior's aid they had no difficulty about the vessel, another flat-bottomed scow suitable for transporting horses, although not the most comfortable in broken seas – and on the small side for all their livestock this day. The skipper and crew had to be routed out of their homes in the little town, which took some time; but these were all servants of the abbey, and there was no particular reluctance to set sail. The sea would be choppy, all were warned.

It was, with the winds fresh – much to the delight of the young people, if not of all their elders and the horses. The Firth of Clyde here was some seventeen miles across, and in a south-westerly wind, as now, was very exposed. Ahead Arran looked dramatic, its mountain-tops, lofty and steep, already capped with early snow, its cliff-girt coastline challenging. It was a large island, fully a score of miles long by half that in width.

The scow, propelled by both sail and oars, covered the crossing in a couple of heaving and rolling hours, John and Mary at least concerned for the safety of the horses, which might fall and be injured. They made for Brodick Bay, mid-way down the long east side of the island, where central Glen Cloy came down to salt water, and where the township of Invercloy clustered round the bay. This was not the earldom's largest community, that being Lamlash, further to the south; but it was above Invercloy that Brodick Castle, their destination, rose, on a spur of hill.

They could see this red stone pile as the boat neared land, impressively sited. Mary explained that the island had other castles, at Lochranza, Dougrie, Drumnadoon and Kildonan, but that Brodick was the principal seat of the earldom, with a stirring history, having been founded by the old Lords of the Isles. The island, in fact, had quite a large population.

Landing, and glad to, and eyed interestedly by the Invercloy villagers, they mounted their now restive horses and commenced the ascent to the castle, quite a climb of almost a mile, Mary and Anna exchanging bitter-sweet memories of their previous visit here. John had been told, of course, of Anna's romance with Patrick Fullarton, son of the coroner of Arran who managed the island properties for the earl, as steward. Patrick was the father of her eight-year-old Alexander, although never her husband. Anna, when discovered to be pregnant, and to no lofty individual, had been compulsorily married off by her father, the Regent, Lord Boyd, to Sir John Gordon of Lochinvar, a purely nominal arrangement, for the couple had not lived together; this whilst Patrick was away in Denmark, *Sir* Patrick as he now was, having been knighted by King James as a youth.

The castle, on its wide shelf of the hill, with its far-flung views, was larger than John had anticipated, two square keeps linked by an unusual pair of stair-towers, within an irregular courtyard, its shape dictated by the contours of the hill. There was no gatehouse, the approach being such that no attacker could reach the site without coming under defensive assault from the parapets of the main keep itself, sufficiently daunting. The doorway below was reached by an offset flight of steps, with a gap across which a gangway could be pushed to admit access.

Despite its obvious strength, the place had an oddly deserted look about it, no sign of life evident save for smoke rising from a single chimney. The new arrivals dismounted and John went forward to climb the steps of the forestair. There was no way that he could reach across the gap to beat on the door's timbers, so he had to shout. His men below took up the bellowing.

They had quite a wait before the shutters of an upper

window opened and a face peered out, too distant to make out features. They waited.

At length there was a creaking, groaning sound, and what had seemed to be a door turned into a small timber drawbridge which, lowered slowly, spanned the gap to the stone forestair. Behind it was a yett or gate of interlaced iron bars, and behind that the door. This opened, and a youngish man stood there.

"I am Douglasdale," John announced. "Bringing the Princess Mary, Countess of Arran, to this her castle. With her children."

The other did not look as though he was listening. He was staring beyond the speaker and down to the waiting group, wide-eyed, eager. A hand rose, to point. Then he rushed forward over the little bridge, past John, and went down the steps two at a time, to run to the still-mounted party. He shouted something incoherent.

The newcomer was not alone in his excitement. Annabella Boyd, after a moment or two of gulping surprise, hitched up her skirts and flung herself down from the saddle, to open arms wide to the running man.

"Patrick! Oh, Patrick!" she cried. "It is *you*! Dear God – Patrick!"

Astonished, John went down to join them.

Mary was now dismounted also, and patting the man's arm. She hailed John over to meet Sir Patrick Fullarton.

There followed a flood of explanation, talk and to-do, the children loud in question and demand, in especial young Alexander – for this, of course, was his father, hitherto unseen. Anna and her beloved could not let go of each other's persons.

It took them some time to get inside that cold and all but empty castle.

They learned that Patrick Fullarton had returned here to Arran, his home, almost a year before, secretly, for he was a forfeited man, along with his late master Thomas Boyd, Earl of Arran. When Anna asked why he had not let her know of it, he pointed out that he had not done so for her sake. It could have endangered her, had she sought to see him, since he was proclaimed guilty of treason by the present regime. So he had lain low, here in the island castle, helping his father to manage the Arran estates. He now lived alone in the fortalice, leaving his parents to reside down in their own house of Kilmichael.

All this came out in fits and starts, as all hands set to the task of bringing in wood and lighting fires, the children in their element. Brodick Castle had been standing neglected, save for Patrick's little chamber off the vaulted kitchen; now it was to be warmed up and made into a family home again, servants brought in from the adjoining castleton, and life restored to the historic pile.

With fires blazing in all the bedchambers and in the great hall, they ate their evening meal – adequate considering the haste with which it had been prepared – in the kitchen, for the hall would take some time to heat up, a happy repast with talk incessant. Then the excited children were packed off to bed, protesting, their parents tending them but distinctly anxious to be free of them this night of all nights.

Back by the kitchen fire again, the four adults recounted experiences, happenings, adventures and their consequences – and there was much to tell on both sides. But presently the talk slowed down, became intermittent, as they watched the flickering flames, and in time all but died away.

It was Mary who eventually made a move. Rising, she touched John's shoulder.

"The children should all be asleep by now," she said. "It has been a long and eventful day. My own couch beckons. No doubt yours do also," and she glanced at Patrick's door off the kitchen. "Come and bid me goodnight, Johnnie, in a while. But be not too long or I shall be asleep also! Your chamber is next to mine and the children's. You two – may the night be kind to you!"

John watched her go, wordless.

Anna rippled a laugh and nodded. She went to the cauldron of water which steamed on its chain above the fire, and skilfully tipped out its contents into two great jugs. One she handed to John.

"Mary will thank you for that, I think," she said, and

grinned at him. The other she took herself – and it was to Patrick's door that she carried it, and went into the smaller room. They heard the tinkle of her further laughter as the door shut behind her.

The two men eyed each other, and found nothing to say.

That steaming jug served at least part of its purpose. John did not wait for long, lest the water cool overmuch. Pointing to it, he inclined his head, said a brief goodnight, and departed for the twisting stairway.

Their rooms were on the second floor up in the easternmost keep, three in a row off a corridor, the children's first, John's at the end. No sounds came from the first, but he heard a faint lilting singing coming from the second. This was something new to the man. He stood for a moment, listening. Then he knocked.

"I have brought hot water," he called, but softly.

The singing stopped. "Come," he heard.

He opened the door. Only the firelight lit the room. She was standing silhouetted against it, near the hearth, clearly wearing a bedrobe. She turned.

"More water?" she said. "The women have already brought some. So – *you* need not wash in that I have used!"

"Think you . . . that I would object . . . to that?" he asked her. He put the jug down on the hearth, and turned to her.

Mary had turned back also, to face the fire again, and thus illumined, it was to be seen that her robe hung open, and that within it she stood naked. Searching his features in that flickering light, with a strange seriousness, she held out her arms to him.

With something like a groan, he went to her. "Oh, woman! Woman!" he got out. "At last! At last!"

Eyes still on his, she shrugged off that bedrobe, which fell to the floor, to reveal all the sheer and graceful loveliness of her for him to embrace. "I fear that I am . . . an immodest woman . . . when I, when I . . . permit it of myself," she said. "Earthy, I . . ."

She got no more uttered, as her lips were closed by his – or not entirely closed – and he clutched her to him, his hands

287

urgent over that warm and smoothly rounded femininity, firm to his touch yet yielding, yielding gladly.

In a sort of desperation John all but shook her. "So long!" he mumbled against her moist lips. "So long . . . I have waited . . . for this! So very long . . . !"

She stroked his hair. "Better . . . yonder!" she got out. "My dear."

With an access of a different kind of strength, he stooped to pick her up bodily, a well-built woman, to stride to the great bed, and fell thereon with her. She gave a little gasp as his weight crushed down on her, clad as he was – and that involuntary sound had the effect of bringing him partly to his senses. He took hold of himself, physically and mentally, raised himself and drew back, panting.

For long moments he stood there, gazing, gripping himself instead of Mary. He was indeed astonished at himself and at this fierce passion which had possessed him – and still did, even though he was mastering it. He did not know that he was capable of such behaviour, considering himself to be on the whole a moderate and equable man, not an oaf of ungovernable desires. This was not joy, delight, pleasuring, but sheer, rampant carnality, lust even. As he recognised and fought it, he was tearing at his clothing, to be rid of this unhelpful restriction thereof.

But in the midst of it all his eyes were busy; and gradually the wonder and excellence of what he saw lying there largely began to overcome the rest. She was so beautiful, so perfect in his eyes, all of her, from her beloved fair features, eyes melting towards him, hair spread over the bedclothes, the graceful column of her neck, the white shoulders above the twin enchantments of full and shapely breasts, proud-tipped, the curved belly leading to the dark triangle at the groin, the long legs outstretched, thighs inviting and calves slenderly moulded, all enticing indeed – and all his now.

"Mary of my heart, all my heart!" he declared, and it was that, a declaration of entire and all-embracing devotion, as he threw off the last of those cloying clothes.

Again she held out her arms to him. "Johnnie, take what

has been yours for long," she murmured, inviting in person as in words.

He came to her then, only a little more contained than heretofore.

There was no fumbling nor hesitation, no need for foreplay, on either part. Only one small matter came between them then – that little gold cross on its chain which she had given him and which he now wore always next to his skin. He had omitted to take it off, and now it pressed uncomfortably against the breasts between which it had formerly hung. Mary bore it for a little, then diverted a hand from elsewhere to move it to one side, quivering a tiny laugh.

"Received back . . . but not now welcomed!" she breathed.

John, in no state for laughter or other comment, put a stop to further words from her.

It did not take them long, of course, the man in especial, after so lengthy a repression – but for all that he was just in time to give her satisfaction before his fullness came, in some measure to fulfil them both, in a violent flood of male ardour and need, her co-operation less than passive, helpful indeed. All too soon over, he lay on her heavily, gasping, heaving, words now trying to come where so much else had done, prostrated.

The woman was a deal less prostrate, despite his weight on her, nor so devoid of verbal eloquence. "My dear, my dear," she murmured. "As well, perhaps . . . that I am no innocent virgin! That was . . . oh, a, a completion, my love!"

"Too soon, too soon! I am sorry . . ."

"Hush you!" She stroked his sweat-damp hair and brow. "You were sufficiently . . . masterful! It may be that I needed a master? One that I could love, not just suffer! Oh, yes – make no apologies, my dear. That was good, good!"

He raised himself somewhat to look at her. "You are . . . all in all to me," he enunciated carefully. And then, turning and twisting a little, collapsed again, at her side now.

It was the princess who presently rose from the bed and went over to put further logs on the fire. John was not so exhausted that he did not watch, and savour the comeliness of what he saw in the enhanced firelight, as she came back to him.

They lay, thereafter, holding each other, for some timeless period of peace and quiet, uttering occasional thoughts and appreciations and endearments, fingers gently roaming, communication more eloquent than it was verbal. But, after a while, Mary turned on her side, raising herself a little on one elbow, to look directly at him, seeming to search his face.

"Johnnie, my heart, there is something that I must say, that I *have* to say to you. It may . . . offend! I do not want to spoil this bliss. Yet, tell you I must, in all honesty. This may not be the time, but . . ."

"You will not marry me," he said simply.

She drew a quick breath. "You . . . knew!"

"Oh, yes, I knew. I guessed it. Thought that probably it would have to be so. Feared it, yes – but was prepared for it. I know what is here involved, Mary lass. The cost of our love. The dangers. You, the King's sister. The price that we have to pay . . ."

"Yes. James would strongly disapprove, I know. And with Sheves so close to the Pope, I would not put it beyond them to have any marriage annulled, which did not please them. But it is not only that. This Arran is a royal earldom, and rich. James regrets that it was ever separated from the crown and given to the Boyds, in his youth. I think that he would have it back, if opportunity offered. And my marriage to one he disapproved of, my becoming the Lady Douglasdale instead of Countess of Arran, could allow him to step in, belike. Either to take my son, as Earl, into his own keeping, as ward. Or just to declare the earldom itself returned to the crown. No – I must keep it for young Jamie, his rightful heritage. If I possibly can. My simple duty to him. And to . . . his father."

There was a little silence at that last. Then John nodded. "To be sure. I recognise it all, my dear one. All your . . . caring. But could not the King command that you wed someone else? As he was going to do with your sister. Use you as pawn also. Married to some Englishman or Frenchman!"

"I think not. I am not as Margaret was, an innocent, unwed

virgin. Married already, and twice, with my three children. That would not commend me to some foreign princeling or great one."

"Perhaps not. But he might seek to use you as wife for one of his friends, here at home. One of his wretched favourites. Even that Cochrane, perhaps! Give him the King's sister, as mark of especial favour!"

"Never! I . . . I would fight him with all that is in me!" Passionately she said that. "I would say that I was sick. Ill of some dread disease. Anything to have them shun me . . . !"

He stroked her so smoothly inviting person. "No. No, it will not come to that, lass. It was but a thought. Do not trouble yourself. This of the earldom I understand . . ."

She gripped his hand. "It is not only Arran, Johnnie. There is my other boy also, little James. The Hamilton inheritance. I told you, this of tutoring. For *both* the titles and lands, I must remain Countess of Arran *and* Lady Hamilton. Meantime at least, while they are young. To oversee all, for them both. Fortunately, I can do it. I was born, I think, with sufficient wits to manage properties and persons. Too much so for a woman, perhaps? But I am a mother, and love my children. I must cherish them as best I may . . ."

"They are fortunate in their mother! As I am in, in my lover!" That stroking and hand-holding had been having its own effect, on the man at least. The fondling became urgent, purposeful, with other stirrings to match. And it was not long before the woman was beginning to respond. Talk gave way to that other sort of eloquent communion.

Now it was different from before, no less eager but a deal less impetuous and hasty, more lingering, savouring, exploratory, on both their parts, each conforming and moulding to the other's movements and urges and needs, all but becoming one indeed in their compelling embrace. In sheerest physical empathy they moved onwards towards eventual entire fulfilment, even deliberately delaying the climax until at length Mary yielded wholly, in an exquisite admixture of triumph and surrender, leaving John to his own masculine victory, love and desire equally consummated.

Thereafter, with only an endearing word or two of murmured gratitude, they sank to sleep in each other's arms.

18

So commenced the happiest period in John Douglas's life to date, winter days of exploring the island, inspecting properties and farms, gathering wood for the fires, instructing the children in outdoor and indoor activities which they had not previously experienced, long evenings by the hall fire with talk, music and John's balladry. And, of course, blissful nights. These not only for Mary and John; Anna and Patrick were equally in delight, and making no bones about it. Developments elsewhere, the future, and the rest of mankind, could wait. Meantime it was happiness.

There was much to see and savour on Arran, its two hundred square miles rich in a great variety of terrain and scene, with its castles, old estates held by vassals of the earldom, including Kilmichael of Patrick's father, the coroner, Kildonan where the Bruce had waited for the fiery signal from the mainland which would beckon him to win back his kingdom from the invading English, ancient churches and shrines, communities of herdsmen, shepherds and tillers of the soil, fishing havens and boat-strands, even falconries, hawking being a favoured sport here. It was a little kingdom in itself, and much that it embraced new to John.

One activity that he sampled for the first time, under Patrick's tuition, was the stalking of red deer. He had hunted deer on horseback frequently, and had shot woodland roe-deer with bow and arrow. But this of stalking the larger red deer on high mountains was new, a Highland sport, and challenging indeed. They did not have to climb to the lofty summits, for with winter snows the beasts came lower. But even so, much clambering amongst rocks and heather was entailed, much crawling on bellies and getting wet and chilled. But it was worth it, the chase exhilarating as it was demanding and difficult. With Patrick, or later alone, he had to search the hillsides for the animals, usually in small groups and herds, then when found, seek to plan a hidden way up to them, hidden not only from their sight but from their scent, for the deer had the keenest of noses. Then crawl in such cover as he could find to sufficiently near his selected target to be able to shoot an arrow with fair hope of killing. And all this dragging with him a cross-bow and quiver, which had to be carefully protected. The odds were distinctly in favour of the deer.

Nevertheless, they ate a lot of venison during those weeks.

Yuletide passed joyfully, none recollecting a happier, the children more or less in charge.

John, to be sure, could not escape certain feelings of guilt in all this. He had, he supposed, responsibilities elsewhere, at Tantallon, and to a lesser extent with Archie and the Albany cause, which he now saw as the cause of Scotland itself. But in mid-winter he did not think that much would be going on, however much plotting there might be. And there were enough of the family at Tantallon to pass a rewarding Christmas without him. So he told himself.

They were not entirely cut off from information regarding mainland affairs, of course, for Arran had frequent links by ferry across the Firth of Clyde, especially with churchmen visiting their island houses. And Abbot William sent his kinsfolk news. The main item they heard was of the arrival at Stirling of a leading and quite celebrated cleric, a Doctor John Ireland, of Scots birth, a professor of theology in France, sent by King Louis as envoy to try to heal the breach between James and Albany, and to unite them and himself against England. King Edward was seeking to rouse the Emperor against France – the late Charles the Bold of Burgundy had a daughter married to the Emperor Maximilian – and Louis thought that the Auld Alliance was worth reviving. Whether Albany himself was behind this was not clear; but Doctor Ireland was saying that Pope Sixtus was. So that probably meant that Sheves would react favourably – and therefore the King.

John and Mary were interested, concerned even; but did

not see any immediate involvement for themselves.

There was no word of James's projected pilgrimage.

Another later item of news, which quite probably was not unrelated to the first, was that Richard Crookback, Duke of Gloucester, had been sent up by his brother Edward to take charge again in the north of England, and was already massing men near the border. Presumably Edward knew of the French approaches, and this was in the nature of a warning to the Scots not to co-operate with Louis. Certainly this could be more serious, and Archie, as a Border Warden, could be involved. And *he* wanted John as his deputy.

Discussing the situation with Mary, she said that it seemed to her that, as far as they were concerned, it would all depend on Albany. Was he in agreement with King Louis's approach? Somehow, she did not see him as desiring rapprochement with James; his aim was to supplant him, not agree with him. He might well not be in favour of this French alignment. He had gone to France to seek Louis's help in unseating James, not to get involved in war with England and the Empire. They must wait to hear what was Albany's attitude.

So further weeks passed pleasantly, although at the back of John's mind was the recognition that this happy state of affairs was unlikely to go on for very much longer, as the snows crept back up the mountains and spring's coming was heralded by the appearance of snowdrops and aconites in the woodlands – spring, when warlike men were apt to stir for action after the winter's hibernation.

Then, in March, the call came, not from Abbot William this time but from Tantallon. Archie Douglas wanted his brother back – and as Earl of Angus and head of the family, he expected co-operation. Moreover, he needed advice.

Mary agreed that John had no option but to go. But he must come back, just as soon as was possible. She intended to remain on Arran more or less indefinitely, with her children. This was the place for them meantime. John must look upon Brodick Castle as a second home. So – come back, and soon.

A few days later he was on the ferry for Irvine.

*   *   *

295

Arrival at Tantallon was pleasant too, for John was fond of his sisters and sister-in-law. He was welcomed home with enthusiasm, but also with reproaches for having stayed away for so long. There were, of course, sisterly enquiries as to relations with the King's sister. Archie, it transpired, was not at home, and not scouring the Borders this time but summoned to Stirling, to see King James.

This news intrigued John. He gathered that Archie had gone only doubtfully, reluctantly.

His brother arrived back at Tantallon two days later – and glad at least to see John. For if he wanted brotherly advice before, he needed it more now. He, Archie, was in a state of unusual indecision.

James had sent for him, to order him to lead a raid into England, of all things; this from a monarch who had only recently been eager to wed his sister to the English King's brother-in-law. It was really Sheves, of course. He was advising it, to comply with Louis of France's urgings, backed by the Vatican, the latter, as usual, at odds with the Emperor. It was noteworthy that he, Archie, was chosen to head this invasion, not Atholl, Buchan, Argyll or any of the other earls closer to the throne. Because he was senior Warden of the Marches, James had said. But he suspected that it was so that he could be blamed and disavowed if later the policy was proved to be at fault and abandoned. A warning blow to the Duke of Gloucester was to be struck. No English assaults to be made on Scotland, and a gesture to please Louis and the Pope.

Archie's trouble was, of course, what of Albany? He was unlikely to be in favour of joint action of French and Scots, which would tend to bring James and Louis closer in harmony, instead of the reverse, French support for Albany against James. He, Archie, had had no word from the duke, whom he had heard had just married Anne de la Tour, daughter of the Count of Auvergne and Buillon. What was he to do?

John said that if it was a direct command from the King to the Warden, he did not see how it could be refused. Not that *he* wanted warlike raiding. It might not grievously affect Albany's cause. The damage to that was already done, presumably, with this of Louis calling for the revival of the Auld Alliance. How soon was this raid to take place? And on what scale?

It was to be as soon as possible, and a major assault to penetrate fairly far south, no mere cross-border foray. And, could Johnnie believe it, the deplorable Cochrane had actually sought to give Archie orders in the matter, where to go and what to do – to himself, one of the *ri*!

What men? And how many?

That was left to himself, Archie said. Many would have to be Douglases of course. But they would collect a sufficiency from the various Border clans – Kerrs, Elliots, Scotts, Turnbulls, Olivers, Rutherfords, even some Homes although he was not going cap-in-hand to ask that rogue the Lord Home for assistance, as Cochrane had advised. Cathcart was now Warden of the West March, replacing Maxwell, and, with Gloucester based on Carlisle, would be told to make some demonstration over that border to try to keep that duke preoccupied and prevent him from cutting in across behind their own advance and forcing a rearguard action.

So Johnnie was to go off westwards, to Douglasdale, and their other Clydesdale lands to collect men, calling on the way on Scott of Buccleuch. At least they had the royal authority for the muster and did not have to appeal. To go forthwith.

Less than eagerly, then, John was away next morning on the now so familiar road to the Clyde valley. He had visualised some such errand, whilst in Arran – but it had been to raise support for *Albany*'s cause, not his brother James's.

In the event, his mission presented few difficulties or prolonged hold-ups, only much riding and a deal of organising of a sufficiency of horses of a sort suitable for the occasion. Fortunately the Borderers were riders almost to a man, and fonder of raiding and reiving than of humdrum daily toil. So his assembly orders met with little reluctance, even some enthusiasm. David Scott of Buccleuch was no more loth than lesser men, and said that he would have four hundred at Coldstream, chosen as the mustering place, in five days'

297

time. John reckoned on a week for his more westerly Douglas recruits.

Actually it was nine days before he reached Coldstream, with almost eight hundred men, to find Archie waiting impatiently with three thousand assorted mosstroopers, much to the offence of the Coldstreamers. John had thought to return to Tantallon before heading south, but that was not his brother's design. He had waited long enough, he said. They would be off at first light next morning, across Tweed.

His plan was to bypass Berwick and strike due southwards up the River Till, by Etal and Ford to Akeld, then to cross the shoulder of Cheviot, wild open country, to allow them unnoticed passage to Coquetdale at Rothbury. Then by more high empty country to lower Redesdale, at Otterburn, from which, by Bellingham and the North Tyne, they could reach the main and populous Tyne valley, Corbridge, Hexham, Haydon and Haltwhistle. Thus, unannounced, they would create the utmost havoc and alarm, without getting too dangerously near the walled city of Newcastle, which would be beyond their assault without artillery. But there would be sufficient rewarding targets thus, before returning by the coastal plains.

All this sounded sadly familiar to John, from his earlier days, the Duke of Gloucester then leading the opposition, as now. Did conditions never change between the nations, no progress made down the years? He was no warrior, those years had proved.

The return northwards over the fertile lower lands was so that they could collect a convenient booty of cattle, to recoup them for all their trouble.

John found himself allotted his former role of leader of the advance party, which suited him well enough since it would spare him the distasteful burning and ravaging which always seemed to be the preoccupation of invading armies. Indeed, on this occasion, he was not two hours on English soil, no further than Akeld, when he saw the great smoke clouds rising behind him. Whether or not his two hundred men felt deprived over this he did not enquire.

He and his met with no resistance, villagers in no position
to challenge troops of armed cavalry, and themselves leaving
peel-towers and castles for the attention of the host behind.
John kept small scouting parties out forward, and well to
the flanks, to warn of any enemy forces materialising; and
he sent back messengers frequently to inform his brother
of the situation as he found it. He had no knowledge as to
whether Gloucester was still at Carlisle, and if Cathcart had
indeed made his diversionary sally over the West March.

Probing carefully, not hurrying, his company divided into
three groups to cover a ten-mile-wide frontal advance, John
reached Ingram, on the Beamish Water, that evening, twenty-
five miles into England, without bloodshed or any real hold-
up. How far behind was the main body was uncertain, smoke
clouds being no accurate guide. At any rate, the advance guard
was not caught up with that night, nor did any courier arrive
from Archie.

Before noon next day they were across Coquet at Alwinton,
still in the Cheviot foothills, and into Redesdale, with Tynedale
ahead of them. This was lower and more populous country,
dotted with towns, where the great Roman Wall crossed this
land – Chollerford, Corbridge, Hexham and the rest. John
saw it as no part of his duty to make for these. *He* could
not assail them, with his numbers; and he hoped that Archie
would not do so either, and produce unnecessary slaughter.
Moreover, word of the invading presence was bound to reach
the townsfolk, and could produce reactions. Archie had spoken
of a three-day raid; and if that was adhered to, then they
were halfway now and should be considering turning back,
gesture made. So he decided not to go much further, to
line up his people on the high ground between Bellingham
and Kirkwhelpington, where they could look down on the
wide Vale of Tyne without descending into it – and hope
that Archie would be content. If indeed Gloucester did come
over from the Carlisle area to challenge them, it would almost
certainly be down Tyne that he came. The smokes behind them
still seemed a fairly long way off.

There, then, they waited, watching in all directions, no

developments materialising. And after almost three hours, John saw what he had rather hoped for, the smoke clouds beginning to rise further and further to the east, in Coquetdale, which presumably indicated the army's move towards the coastal lands, no longer southwards. It looked as though Archie was being wiser than sometimes, and recognising that, if he did not want the Earl of Northumberland, English Warden of the East March, having time to muster and march against him, whatever Gloucester might be doing, he would best be on his way back to Scotland. Moreover, if indeed they were going to collect and drive cattle in any large numbers, that would much delay them. So, thankfully, he called in his outlying scouts, and ordered a move north-eastwards back whence they had come.

In fact, they came upon the main force encamped near Whittingham on the Aln, which he felt was dangerously near to Alnwick, where Northumberland had his principal castle. But he found Archie and all the others in high good spirits, loud in their acclaim of all that they had achieved thus far, the villages burned, the barns destroyed, the mills wrecked, the towers looted, the scoundrels hanged, and suitable lessons taught to the villainous English. John noted that all the cattle-lifting had not been reserved for the morrow. Archie's one complaint was that he had not had time nor opportunity to make an example of any fair-sized Northumbrian town. He would have liked to have burned Hexham. However, if they made an early start in the morning, it ought to be possible to destroy, say, Bamburgh before crossing back into Scotland. Alnwick would be nearer, but it was possible that the Percy might be massing there if he had heard of this raid. Safer in the circumstances to avoid Alnwick.

That night, all gorged on under-hung beef, mutton and poultry, with over-much wine and ale to wash it all down.

So the dawn start was in fact a little delayed. Reckoning that they were only about a dozen miles west of Alnwick, which spelt danger to John but something like a challenge to his brother, they headed due northwards now, John again going ahead with his group.

This was very different country from the Cheviot foothills and moorlands, with much tilled land, meadows, villages, squires' houses – and cattle-herds. And this last began to preoccupy the invaders, John's men equally with the others behind. They were all Borderers, after all, and cattle for them represented not only wealth but their very way of life. Armed forays and gestures were a pleasing diversion, but cattle collection was basic. The leaders of this expedition, at this stage, were left in no doubts about it.

So John's scouting services took on a rather different aspect, with rich pastures tending to be the priority, and a general slowing down of progress inevitable. Yet they were still almost forty miles from Scotland, and Archie was anxious to leave at least one sizeable town ablaze as proof of his prowess, Bamburgh the most likely. So it became something of a battle of wills between leaders and led, all complicated by the ever-growing and slow-moving herds of beasts, expert enough as were the horsemen at the droving.

John, coping with all this as best he could, and heading north by east, by Chillingham and Chatton and Adderstone, was caught up with by none other than Archie himself, with a few men as escort, having ridden well ahead of his force, and much concerned with the prevailing situation, worried on three counts. One, that the Earl of Northumberland might well by now be coming after them from Newcastle, or Alnwick itself, in strength, and his own people so laden down with booty as to be in no condition to meet them adequately. Two, that Gloucester must surely be aware of the situation by this time, and might come over from the west in major force. And three, that the delay would give Bamburgh warning and prevent a successful descent thereupon. What was to be done?

John suggested forgetting Bamburgh, with its so strong castle nearby, or indeed other large target, and heading straight for home and over Tweed. But his brother was determined on being able to claim a notable centre destroyed.

So, little as he relished the prospect, or desired a part in it, John put forward an alternative programme. They did not require three thousand men to assail the town of Bamburgh, he claimed. Half of that would serve equally well. Why not split the force, one half to be concerned with the attack, the other to concentrate on the cattle, the collection and the droving northwards. This last could probably average about four miles in each hour, and they had still some twenty-five miles to cover. Say six hours. It was now midday. Even if they were delayed somewhat, they ought to reach Tweed by darkening. Getting the many hundreds of beasts across the river would in itself take time; but by then the other part of the force should have been able to deal with Bamburgh and to have come up behind, to form a protective screen whilst the river-fording went on. If Gloucester or Northumberland did appear on the scene, of course, they might have to change their plans and reassemble, forgetting both Bamburgh and cattle.

Archie conceded this as probably the best that could be envisaged in the circumstances. But the two sections of his force must not be caught unawares, from west or south. How was that to be ensured?

John, glad to be spared the sacking of a town, said that *he* would use his own two hundred to form a lengthy crescent-shaped watch, occupying such higher ground as was available hereabouts. Such could not, of course, challenge any large enemy strength; but they could, if necessary, give timeous warning, and even make diversionary sallies here and there, enough to give any pursuing force pause, not knowing just what was confronting them.

That very much commended itself to Archie, who thereupon reined round to ride back to his main body and organise the division of troops. John, leaving a few men to look after their own haul of livestock, set off with the rest for the nearest low ridge, that of Greensheen Hill, there to prospect, and decide on his dispositions.

Actually, on the higher ground, he perceived a much better and longer ridge, which one of his men said was known as the Kyloe Hills, modest heights as these were by Scottish standards, this between Lowick and Fenwick, which ought to give him wide vistas to west as well as south. It should serve as a base, meantime, from which to send out small parties to occupy other viewpoints covering an extensive area.

So presently, on Kyloe, he settled down to wait and watch again, with a nucleus of some fifty men, the others despatched hither and thither, with instructions to keep him informed, and not to be distracted by readily available pickings, whether bovine or feminine.

In an hour or so he was able to see a fast-moving force, unhampered by cattle, intermittently visible, indubitably Archie's contingent heading for Bamburgh. He sent down a couple of riders to intercept and inform that so far there was no sign of enemy.

Sooner than he had feared thereafter, the huge concourse of drovers and droved came into view, or perhaps only some of it. So far so good.

It was, in a way, a trying experience to sit there on their horses doing nothing but scanning the land, while others acted; but better, John told himself, than assaulting peaceful folk, enemies in theory as they might be. He was somewhat concerned for Archie's present attempt. Bamburgh Castle on its high, thrusting rock above the tideline, not unlike Tantallon, was a powerful stronghold, actually a royal citadel, built by the ancient Kings of Northumbria; but it rose some distance east of the town, and Archie would undoubtedly put a cordon between. But had it artillery? Cannon? If it had, then the position would be radically altered and Scots casualties might be high. He did not think that it was probable, but was possible. He would soon know, for if there was indeed cannon-fire he would hear it here, across these levelish coastal plains.

He heard no gunfire. But with the sun beginning to sink he saw smoke clouds rising from the direction of Bamburgh, dark, billowing clouds, and larger than any seen hitherto. That would be the town's thatched roofs burning. He hoped that casualties there would be minimal . . .

Satisfied that his own part was played, he sent to call in his outlying groups, and then to head north by west now. All this had taken distinctly longer than he had calculated.

They were making for the fords at Horncliffe, opposite Fishwick in Scotland, six miles west of Berwick, this because there were no fewer than three possible fording-places thereabouts, which would greatly simplify getting all the cattle across Tweed. Going by Fenwick and Haggerston and Unthank Moor, that would be some fifteen miles. But it was easy riding country; and assuming no interruptions, should not take two hours.

Actually it took rather longer, for in the Ancroft area they came up with Archie's fifteen hundred warriors, all very pleased with themselves. Bamburgh had been no trouble at all, its people fleeing at sight of them to the security of the castle's walls, leaving only some old folk, who presented no problems. The castle itself did not offer any attack. So all had been simplicity itself. The only disappointment for some was the few women, save for old hags, who had been available to entertain ardent and not too particular admirers. They had had too early warning.

The combined host caught up with the cattle-herders, in the dusk, in the Longridge area, without any sign of enemy forces. So it was slow progress indeed, amidst loud lowing of protesting beasts, and practically dark before they reached Horncliffe and its fords. Nevertheless the major task of crossing Tweed was commenced forthwith, however reluctant the cattle to take to the water. With what was now reckoned to be four thousand head, the business took hours, but only the animals complained. Here were riches to add to the virtue of duty done.

Lining the north bank of the wide river, to guard against any hostile attempt to cross after them, and sending parties to watch the other fords to east and west, the victorious host camped for what remained of the night, well satisfied, none more so than Archie Douglas, objectives achieved and with scarcely any losses to report. And it had been all excellent practice and experience for Albany's eventual coming.

John was more relieved than satisfied – save in that killings had been few, however many the burnings.

Back to Tantallon in the morning.

19

Much as John would have wished to return to Arran almost immediately, he recognised that this would scarcely do. He would have to put in at least some time in token duty as Archie's deputy in the East March. And apart from family concern and affection, he had overseeing responsibilities over the Tantallon lands and other properties of the Angus earldom, as well as his own Douglasdale. Archie, of course, ought to be seeing to some of this himself, but his mind was generally on higher matters. John, in fact, found such activities quite to his taste, supervising the productivity of the estates, improving the land, drainage of marshy areas, clearing scrub woodland, dealing with tenants' complaints and pleas, ranging the high sheep pastures of the Lammermuir Hills, seeing to welfare in the town of North Berwick, ensuring that all was well with the fisher-folk, their smoke-houses, salt-pans and net-works, and the like. Also of course, baronial judicial functions. They had land stewards, employed for these duties, or some of them; but the lords' own concern was necessary, and surveillance valued and appreciated.

All this had been considerably neglected while John was in Arran, and fell to be made up for now.

While these duties were being accomplished, matters did not stand still on the national front. The Duke of Gloucester initiated a return raid into Scotland over the West March, doing his best to lay waste Eskdale, Liddesdale, Annandale and southern Nithsdale, difficult country to ravage, and fierce folk therein to subdue. He was only sketchily opposed by Lord Cathcart, the new warden; and Archie, making his report to the King at Stirling, was abruptly called upon to go down to reinforce, indeed to take over from Cathcart, and to act now more or less as Lieutenant of the Border, Albany's former position, an odd development. Fortunately, perhaps, he had not got much further in calling the West March to arms than making his headquarters at Lochmaben Castle in Annandale when Gloucester retired into England. So now a state of undeclared war existed between the two kingdoms, nobody quite sure what would be the next development. John, thankfully, was not called upon to take part in all this before Gloucester departed.

From Lochmaben, Archie issued orders for all the west and middle borderland castles and fortresses to be garrisoned and made ready for war – Caerlaverock, Morton, Comlongon, Sanquhar, Threave, Buittle, Hermitage and the rest. Scotland was in a state of unease. All able-bodied men were ordered to be ready, on eight days' notice, to assemble under arms. A penalty was announced for any fighting man who neglected his duty and, strangely, whose spear was found to be shorter than five and a half ells. Axemen were to provide themselves with targes or shields of wood and leather. Weapon practice was to be pursued. And so on.

In these circumstances, John did not feel that he could disappear to Arran anyway.

So spring passed into early summer. King Edward sent furious letters, threatening all-out war. King Louis sent envoys offering benefits. The Pope issued commands and indulgences. No word came from the Duke of Albany.

During all this, Scotland's nobility and landed folk seethed with more than demanded preparedness for war. Cochrane, Earl of Mar in especial, but the other low-born favourites also, were behaving with arrogance and vaunting pride, acquiring extensive properties, dressing with magnificence, working themselves into positions of influence up and down the land, and monopolising the royal attention at court, so as to outrage the realm's natural leaders, who were now deserting the said court. This, in turn, affected the military situation, for of course it was the lords and lairds and chiefs who could produce and control the manpower which was required to prosecute warfare, the crown having no standing army. This, with little enthusiasm for aiding the French, and the fairly general favour towards Albany, tempered the traditional anti-English sentiment, so that the actual mustering and training of troops was half-hearted – save in the Borders area where invasion would hit hardest and properties and lives be at risk. So Archie had less of this problem to face than did others.

In this situation John decided that he could risk a visit to Mary, although possibly a fairly brief one. He did not think that he required an excuse, or anyone's permission; but, being the man he was, called in at the royal castle of Lochmaben, Archie's headquarters, which had once been the Bruce's, to inform him. But his brother was not there, gone somewhere unspecified in the Galloway region. So he left a message, saying where he could be found, and thankfully headed north for Irvine.

Reception at Brodick was all that he could have hoped for, despite reproaches here also for having delayed so long. Mary was all kindness, caring, delight, the children vociferous in their welcome, Anna and Patrick warm. His tidings about events on the mainland were listened to with interest – but somehow they did not seem so important here on Arran. And of course they were not entirely ignorant as to developments, the churchmen keeping them fairly well informed. It was Albany's position and probable plans which concerned them most, Mary, knowing her brother, asserting that he would not be content to bide his time. He was not the patient type, any more than was Archie Douglas.

That first night at Brodick was beyond all in joy and satisfaction, both participants eager, even hungry, for each other, the princess no passive lover. They did not do a great deal of sleeping, but there was no lack of fulfilment.

The days that followed were fulfilling also, in their own way, in the saddle inspecting, hunting, hawking, stalking on the hills, swimming on the west coast beaches of the Kilbrannan Sound, even spearing salmon from horseback in the shallows of river mouths – or trying to – being instructed by a monk from the Solway estuary where apparently such sport was popular. The evenings, once the children were abed, held their own pleasures; and the nights perfection.

And then, all too soon, the call came – and it was in the nature of a bombshell. A messenger arrived from Archie demanding John's return – and not to Lochmaben but to Tantallon. This in itself set John wondering. But what the messenger added, although short in detail, was the more surprising, extraordinary indeed. Albany was in England, rejecting Louis of France as useless to him, and turning to King Edward instead. And Edward was taking up his cause. The Lord of Douglasdale was to return at once for consultation and assistance.

Mary was as surprised as was John at this utterly unlooked for development. She had been prepared for some move on her brother's part, but scarcely the throwing in of his lot with English Edward. That was wrong surely, a grievous misjudgment, all but shameful. What could have possessed him to do it? This must be changed, somehow, put to rights, Alex shown his error and folly. She would write to him, get a letter to him somehow. Edward would use him for his own ends, and to Scotland's hurt, nothing more sure. This was not the way to gain James's crown, the last thing that Alex should have done. What would Archie Douglas do now? He was Alex's friend and chief supporter. But he must not aid him in any English-backed assault on Scotland. Johnnie must go and tell him so, in no uncertain terms. Here was madness.

John agreed, unhappily.

The messenger, young Douglas of Whittinghame, had hired his own boat from Ardrossan, and this was awaiting them. There was no time to be lost. Mary, with Anna and Patrick, accompanied the pair down to the haven at Invercloy, for an emotional parting.

20

Archie Douglas, a character normally of all too much decision, John found to be in a sorry state of indecision at Tantallon, a man torn. He had felt that he had to come back here from Lochmaben, leaving Cathcart in command there, while he made up his mind. And developments since he had sent for Johnnie had but added to his dilemma. He had had messages from both Albany and James – and astonishingly also from their distant kinsman, the forfeited Earl of Douglas, a pensioner of King Edward. Albany was naming him his chief lieutenant in Scotland, to be assisted by the Lords Gray and Drummond, and urging him to raise the land in arms in his favour – for he was coming north with a great English host to back him. And King James, impressed by the success of the recent raid into England, and his leadership, had sent word appointing him his commander meantime of the Scots forces to defend the borderline. What in God's good name was he to do?

John had every sympathy for his brother, and by no means clear in his own mind as to procedures, save in that military support of Albany, with an English army descending upon Scotland, was out of the question. The Scots would never rise for that.

Archie knew it, he knew it. Yet he was Albany's man and despised James. Albany had said that he was to co-operate with none other than Crookback Gloucester, of all people, who would command the English force – the man they had just been challenging. And James said that his brother had actually and treasonably assumed the style and title of Alexander the Fourth, King of Scots, at Fotheringay Castle, in Edward's presence; and had signed a treaty with England, acknowledging Edward as superior, Lord Paramount of Scotland. The fool, the fool! If this was true, few would ever rise for him. It might be only a lie, of course, a device made up by James's advisers, but, true or not, once this was noised abroad in Scotland, Albany's cause would suffer.

John was appalled. To admit the King of England as overlord of Scotland, in order to win his support, was beyond all, unforgivable. Could this be but an invention of Sheves? Even if it was only that, the harm done to Albany would be immense, once it was known. When was the duke intending to march north?

That was not stated, Archie said. But this asking him to raise Scotland on his behalf, indicated delay, surely. It was now late summer. A winter campaign was unlikely. So the probability was that it would be spring before there was actual warfare. What were they to do, meantime?

John informed that Mary Stewart was writing to Albany to try to dissuade him from this course, pointing out its probable consequences in Scotland. Whether her brother would pay any heed, having gone so far, was questionable; but she was the eldest and wisest of the royal family, and the others did respect her wits and judgment. They must hope. But, of course, Edward would now be for pressing on, eager to gain what his predecessors had so long fought for and failed to achieve. And what was this of the exiled Earl of Douglas?

He was supporting Albany, Archie said, and urging that he raised all the Black Douglases, in his name. They had been lying low now for a score of years, since the King's father had put them down; but they were still strong in numbers, especially in the Galloway regions, and could produce a fair fighting force. He, John Douglas, formerly Lord Balveny, had added that Edward was trying to persuade Albany to get rid of his new wife, Anne de la Tour, and wed instead Edward's own daughter, the unfortunate Princess Cecilia, who had already been so often betrothed and was presently so to the young James, Duke of Rothesay, heir to the Scots throne – clear indication that he, Edward, intended to dominate Albany as father-in-law. And he was demanding, as further reward for his aid, that Albany, or Alexander the Fourth as he now was being called, hand over the towns of Berwick, Coldinghame and Roxburgh to England for all time, together with the castle of Lochmaben and the Border districts of Eskdale, Liddesdale and Annandale. These demands Albany was secretly resisting, and almost certainly would reject once he had the Scots crown. He might also reject the lord paramouncy of Edward, under the pretext that it had been granted under duress.

So that agreement was not in fact a device of Sheves, John commented. Albany could be playing a double and dangerous game, using the English to aid his cause, and then rejecting them once safely in control in Scotland. It could be that, scarcely honourable but just possibly effective. Could King Louis have had something to do with this? He was a notorious schemer. And it was strange how Albany had so suddenly changed his sponsors. There might be more in this than there seemed.

Archie conceded that, but demanded how he was to act meantime, with both royal brothers calling on his services. He wanted to see Albany on the throne, yes – but not with Edward as overlord. And James would expect action from him soon.

John himself was in a quandary, little clearer as to the best course to be followed than was his brother. But he was fairly sure on one aspect of it all: Albany was in England, but James was still on his throne, King of Scots. Archie could nowise be seen to be in opposition to the crown at this stage – that would be treason, and he could be taken and hanged for it, that is if he did not want to become an outlaw and hunted fugitive. So he must at least appear to be doing the King's will while they awaited developments. Seen to be concerned with raising the royal army, even though in fact he was more truly testing armed support for Albany.

His brother was hardly satisfied with this rather feeble advice but supposed that it was as much as he could expect, at this stage. He would do nothing to commit himself openly meantime, and hope and pray that clearer guidance would be forthcoming soon. Inactivity was not his preferred role.

Tantallon Castle remained in a state of unease and tension.

Development there was, presently, and guidance implicit therein. An English fleet under the Lord John Howard appeared in the Firth of Forth, and assailed Leith, Edinburgh's port, doing much damage before one Andrew Wood, a Fife merchant-adventurer and shipmaster, son of the laird of Bonington, managed to assemble a motley host of shipping from the northern seaboard and came across to drive off the invaders, a feat of some considerable prowess which much impressed Archie Douglas who, from Tantallon, was able to watch much of the encounter taking place between there and the Isle of May. This had the effect of making him more violently anti-English, and therefore more inclined to hold his hand over support for Albany meantime, and seem to obey James's orders. He decided to set off on an extended tour of the Scots nobility, sounding them out as to preferred allegiances, and proposals for action when, and if, Albany arrived with an English army. This would also help to fill in the time as they awaited events, while seeming to comply with his responsibilities as army commander.

Fortunately, he did not demand that John should accompany him, preferring him to remain seeing to all at Tantallon, and to act deputy in the Borders.

So autumn weeks passed, with John kept busy but without actual invasion. Because of fears thereof, the Borders area, which would bear the brunt of any initial attack, was much less unruly than normal, preparing for major trouble, this much lightening John's duties there. At home, two more of his sisters were involved in romances, Johann becoming betrothed to Sir David Campbell, kinsman to the Earl of Argyll, and Isabel marrying Sir Alexander Ramsay of Dalwolsey, and departing to dwell at that strong castle in Midlothian, only a score of miles away. Archie came back for the wedding, and then departed on his travels again. He reported that almost all the lords and chiefs he had seen so far were, like himself, in favour of Albany taking over the throne from James, but angry at this conceding to King Edward of the style of Lord

Paramount of Scotland, and not prepared to allow an English army to come and take over. That was too high a price to pay for Albany's enthronement. It was all a highly upsetting and uncertain situation.

John would have liked to return home to Arran for Yuletide, but felt that the circumstances forbade it, and had to content himself with sending greetings and messages.

Archie came home once more for the traditional twelve days. He informed that he had felt bound to call at Stirling on his way back from Aberdeenshire and the north, to make some sort of report to the King, and had found the monarch doing carpentry and drawing up plans for the rebuilding of the palace of Falkland, rather than preparing for war, the man Cochrane more or less in charge, now almost seeming to supersede Sheves, who was apparently staying away more and more at St Andrews. He, Archie, had all but exploded at Cochrane's insolence and slighting attitude towards him, asserting that he was failing in his duty expeditiously to muster a great army, and that if he did not improve, and swiftly, he might well have the command taken away from him. While Archie would not have been sorry for that to happen, he hugely resented being told so by this upstart. At Stirling, however, he did learn that English Edward had sent another envoy, a cleric by name of Legh, to announce that he was now Sovereign of Scotland, and unless this was formally announced by James and parliament, he would unleash cruel war on the rebellious northern kingdom. Also he insisted that the young Duke of Rothesay be delivered over to him, by the month of May, to be married to the Princess Cecilia. This last at least looked as though Albany had refused to put away Anne de la Tour, if the unfortunate little princess was still available for James's son. There appeared to be no word from Albany himself. None of all this seemed to be greatly concerning the King, whose interests, extraordinarily, were otherwhere.

But May seemed to be the significant date – as indeed was to be expected, with the spring sowing over, like the lambing, and large numbers of men becoming available for a summer campaign. Although that date might be but a ruse, to lull the Scots into unreadiness for a more immediate attack.

So Archie went off to Lochmaben again, which he had been ordered to make his command-post, still unsure of what was to be done if Albany arrived with an English army without informing him of his true intentions.

Then the King called the delayed parliament for late March, to decide on measures and priorities. With no assault developing before that date, Archie and John duly attended. Comparatively few others did, in fact, and it was almost the most unrepresentative parliament on record – although John's heart lifted, at least, to see Mary Stewart in her accustomed place in the minstrels' gallery. He had to restrain himself from dashing up, there and then.

The proceedings were brevity itself. There was no contrary motion to the Chancellor's announcement of the royal order that the realm's fullest manpower should be assembled. While a western assault was probable, indeed likely, with Gloucester reputedly based on Carlisle, the signs were that the main invasion would be towards the east, possibly at Berwick, or further up Tweed, or over the Carter Bar in the Middle March. All of these could be used. So it was thought best to muster at a point midway, as it were, where the defending host could move at short notice to the most vital area, or send out divisions should there be multiple attacks. Lauderdale fitted that strategy, with easy access to lower and middle Tweed, and offered a reasonably easy route south-westwards through the hills, by Ettrick and Yarrow, to upper Annandale and Lochmaben. So assemble at Lauder.

None objected to that.

Then what all had come anticipating was raised by the less than confident Avondale. The matter of the treasonable behaviour of the King's brother, the Duke of Albany, carried over from the last parliament. All must by now be decided on the issue, for had not the duke now most shamefully compounded and increased his treason by allying himself with the King of England, declaring himself to be King of Scots and nominating Edward as Lord Paramount of

Scotland? This could leave no doubt in the minds of any that highest treason was being committed. None could deny it now.

While the Chancellor was speaking thus, a servitor came down the hall, highly unusual, in almost furtive fashion, looking left and right apprehensively, to stop at the row of lords' benches where John sat. He handed a scrap of paper to Lord Seton, who occupied the end place, and darted off whence he had come. Seton glanced at the paper, and handed it to John.

Thereon was very brief writing indeed. It read. "Hearsay evidence only. Could be English lies. Postpone. M."

John glanced up at the gallery, from which Mary nodded to him urgently. It occurred to part of his mind that it was not many women who would carry with them the small inkhorn and quill which were not uncommon amongst clerkly men and the priestly orders – he had one himself, for sudden inspirations towards balladry – but he had seen one hanging from Mary's girdle ere this. The other and more vital section of his wits was busy absorbing the message and its implications, and seeking to assemble suitable words to comply with it. He could not fail Mary in this.

When the Chancellor stopped, Sheves, behind the throne again, with Cochrane, moved forcefully a conviction of highest treason and due sentence of death therefor. Cochrane promptly seconded, while James nibbled his lips.

John waited a few moments, in case any more lofty than he wished to take the initiative. But when none did, he rose.

"My lord Chancellor," he said, his voice less steady than he would have wished. "I make counter-motion. What you have declared to be the Duke of Albany's behaviour and statements are but hearsay. Where have these reports come from? They come from *English* sources. From envoys. Couriers. King Edward's minions. They are what Edward wishes us to believe, I have no doubt. But are they true? Such sentence as is here proposed would suit the English, to be sure. But that is all the more reason to doubt their word. English Kings have been seeking to gain overlordship of Scotland

315

since Edward the First in 1296. If Edward the Fourth thinks to gain it this way, need we trust him? I say wait until His Grace's royal brother speaks his *own* mind. I propose a further postponement of decision on this issue."

All around there were relieved cries of agreement. The Lord Gray jumped up to second.

Avondale, wise in the ways of parliaments, looked round at Sheves. Clearly he had no doubts as to how a vote would go. Presumably neither did Sheves now, by his reaction. Expressionless, he spoke.

"If that is parliament's will, I accept that the matter be carried forward to the next session." He paused. "But, with the threat of English armed invasion, it behoves all to be prepared, whatever the involvement of the Duke of Albany. The towns of Berwick, Coldinghame and Roxburgh, named by King Edward, must be protected. As must be the Border dales. Moneys must be provided for this. I say that Holy Church will pay two parts of every five of the costs. Two-fifths. No doubt lords and magnates will do the like? And the burghs of the realm provide the rest. I so move."

It was skilfully done. By this gesture of Church generosity he was able to counter in some measure the hostility clearly engendered by his motion against Albany, and to turn men's minds back to the nation's peril, and to the costs to their pockets. John acknowledged it. But at least he had achieved Mary's immediate objective of having the treason conviction postponed.

The motion was agreed without division.

Cochrane now proposed another, that wapinschaws should be held fortnightly throughout the land, so that men should be fully trained for war. And that the Earl of Angus be instructed to inspect the progress of these trainings, to ensure compliance with parliament's will, and to report thereon to the King's Grace.

Whatever Archie felt over this assumption of military concern and responsibility on the part of the one-time master-mason, no one countered the proposal, and it was accepted. John noted that it was to the King that report was to be made – which meant to Sheves and himself, Cochrane – not to the Privy Council, representing parliament, which these days seldom seemed to meet. He considered putting forward an amendment to that effect, but decided it as scarcely vital and, after his earlier interjection, might, as Archie's brother, appear to emphasise hostility to the royal will.

Thereafter only one or two routine matters fell to be passed, and the parliament adjourned. However brief a sitting, it had held its own significance.

With Archie proceeding out with the other earls, John hurried round to the gallery door to meet Mary. They had to restrain themselves in front of others, but their eyes were eloquent. Squeezing his arm, Mary said how well John had taken up her suggestion as to Albany, and how satisfactory the result. For his part, he praised her quick thinking, and ability to send her message.

Making for Mary's palace quarters, she told him that she had been determined to attend this parliament, and to have some words with James, however little attention he was likely to pay. Living on Arran was very pleasant, and best for her children, but she did feel out of touch with events, and ineffective as one of the royal family. She had spoken to James privately, the day before, but was not optimistic as to any impression made. He was wholly under the influence of Sheves, Cochrane and the others. When John mentioned Archie's report that Sheves was spending less of his time at court, she agreed that she had heard the same, but that his personal hold on James was being looked after by his brother Robert Sheves, whom he had had appointed Master of the Wardrobe, and so able to keep a close eye on his interests at court and to relay information.

Despite her satisfaction over the treason postponement, Mary was much worried about Albany and his present activities. She feared that he *had* made a grievous mistake, and that it was not all English lies. Edward was too assured over it all for that – he had even written privily to James rebuking him for not yet having done homage to himself as Sovereign of Scotland. He surely would not have gone so

317

far without having some confidence that he could possibly enforce it.

John put forward the suggestion that Albany might be acting the cunning deceiver, intending to repudiate the concession once he was safely on the throne. Mary admitted that it might be so, although which would be more shameful, such false intentions or the original offer of overlordship, she did not know.

Then Archie arrived, much engrossed by the day's events and their likely consequences, praising John's intervention but implying that he had been about to do the same himself, and incensed at Cochrane's assumption of the lead in matters military, about which the man could know nothing. This of wapinschaws and inspections he was not against; but that Cochrane should have so ordered it and named himself to see to it, like some mere underling, was intolerable.

John and Mary had to spend some time in soothing him down thereafter.

Unfortunately Archie appeared to be going to spend the night with them in these quarters, which Mary could nowise refuse, however scanty John's enthusiasm. And any notion of escorting Mary back to Arran on the morrow was negatived by the brotherly decision that they must return to Tantallon first thing, whereafter Archie would set off on his rounds of inspection and enquiry – for there could be little time to spare – and Johnnie must go deputising for him in the Borders, as before. That was where attack would come, if there was an early development, and he must be kept informed. The western Border clans, Armstrongs, Johnstones, Maxwells, Elliots and the rest, would be the first to know, with their cross-border links, of any English move. Johnnie must keep in close touch with them.

So, when Mary proposed bed, all that John could do was to escort her to her chamber and there enjoy an embrace as brief as the rest of the day's proceedings, before returning to share a room with Archie – and to try to be civil about it. He wished that his brother was just a little more perceptive in some matters.

21

There followed three months of urgent activity for the Douglas brothers – even though John sometimes wondered how necessary it all was, at least his part of it, criss-crossing the borderland almost continuously, interviewing chiefs and mosstrooping lairds, seeking information, arranging meetings between them, seeking to play down feuding and rivalry, selecting watch-places and assembly points. All this with rumours abounding. Gloucester was here or there. English forces numbering unspecified thousands were mustering in a variety of locations, awaiting the arrival, one said, of King Edward himself. Nothing was certain save that war was coming and the Borders would see the first of it.

Archie's endeavours, involving even more travelling, were only occasionally and sketchily communicated to John, but the impression was that he was on the whole well satisfied. The Scottish nobility, at least south and east of the Highlands, where they were not really interested one way or the other, were ready to rise, and suitably prepared – but not to support James or his coterie of strange cronies. Almost all would prefer to see Albany on the throne. But they were considerably unhappy about the reported price to be paid to the English, and unless Albany repudiated it they would not fight for him. This was the message. Somehow, they must get it conveyed to the duke.

John despatched a messenger, young Douglas of Whitting-hame again, to Arran, to acquaint Mary with the situation and to urge her to get a letter sent to Albany if she possibly could.

Then, at the end of June, word reached John from a different source and of a different sort. The King's uncles, the Earls of Atholl and Buchan, had at last asserted themselves and taken over control of Edinburgh Castle – this without James's permission and indeed against his wishes. It was no tremendous gesture, but indicative of their will to oppose the monarch if necessary, and a signal to others, and therefore significant.

At last, a week into July, there was definite news of the invaders. Albany and an English host had arrived at Alnwick, where Gloucester had joined them. They were marching north, a great array.

The call went out, in the King's name, for Scotland's fullest power to rally, and at Lauder. Soon there would be decision, one way or the other.

John was at Dunbar Castle when he heard of it, and hastened back to Tantallon to gather the Lothian Douglas contingent. The assembly point for all this area was the traditional one at the Burgh Muir of Edinburgh. Three days later, there he arrived with six hundred men, all mounted.

Already the wide common land was a seething, colourful mass of men and horses, pavilions of the lords being erected, banners flying. John identified the flags and heraldry of Stewart, Lindsay, Leslie, Ramsay, Seton, Wemyss, Hepburn, Graham and Sinclair. Other assembly places would be at Stirling, Glasgow, Ayr and Lochmaben. The call was being heeded in major fashion. Which way would the pendulum swing?

Most of his fellow-lords, he found, were actually staying meantime down in the comfort of town-houses in the city; but such as John was able to consult were in no very confident state, for the leadership of an army about to confront the enemy. None was sure how matters would go when it came to the crunch. The crowned King of Scots? Or Albany and the English? It was a dire choice. They had all taken the oath of allegiance to James, at his coronation or later; and England was the Auld Enemy, and this King Edward a menace indeed. Yet they almost all would prefer to see Albany on the throne, and liked him. If only he had not allied himself with Edward . . .

No one was sure when they would be moving off for Lauder, or whether they would be waiting for the Stirling muster to join them here. Or when the northern forces would arrive – the Gordons, Frasers, Keiths, Burnets and the like. Seton suggested that since it did not look as though they would be going south for a couple of days more, at least, and his house was only an hour's ride away, they might as well leave their people here and go for some easement. There probably would be little of that to come hereafter, for some time.

John was glad to accede and went with his friend. His men did not require his presence on this Burgh Muir.

They wondered about Archie. Presumably he would be bringing those assembled at Lochmaben over to Lauder – or some of them, for he might well decide to leave quite a large force to watch the West March crossings from England. John also wondered whether Atholl and Buchan, now that they had belatedly shown their willingness to run counter to the King, would be prepared to serve under the command of the much younger and less senior Earl of Angus? And if they decided to take charge themselves, would they indeed openly support Albany, who was, of course, as much their nephew as was James? There were so many imponderables in this situation.

They went back to the Burgh Muir next day, and learned that a start would be made the following morning, under Atholl, Buchan, Argyll and Crawford. They would not wait for the Stirling contingent.

It was hard to assess the numbers which eventually left the Edinburgh vicinity to head for Dalkeith, Cranstoun and Fala to the great monkish hospice and camping place at Soutra Hill: possibly five thousand horse and ten thousand foot. The infantry ought to cover the seventeen miles to Soutra before darkness; but the cavalry, even in such large numbers, should make Lauder itself, in summer-time conditions, crossing the Lammermuir Hills at their western end, and down Lauderdale itself, another dozen miles. Their leaders would, at any rate.

The small royal burgh of Lauder lay at a widening of the vale of the River Leader, where the hills drew back and four tributary streams came in, about halfway down, as good a place as any for present purposes. The first of the horsed force to arrive, which included John and Seton, found the town and its surrounding levels already full of armed men, amidst much stir and bustle. Archie and the Lochmaben contingent proved to have already arrived also, and he was impatiently waiting. The Ayr grouping were expected at any time.

It was a while before the brothers were able to have a word together, alone, although clearly Archie sought it. With so many of Scotland's magnates appearing, there was inevitably a deal of talk, consultation and discussion. At length Archie got John apart and spilled out his news.

"I have word from Albany," he announced, glancing around to ensure that no one else heard him. "A messenger, none other than Home of Polwarth, reached me at Lochmaben just as I was about to leave. Come from Alnwick, secretly. Albany says that all this of telling Edward that he could be Lord Paramount is but a ruse. It was Louis of France's notion. Albany is still in league with France. But with the Emperor threatening France, he could not risk weakening his defences by sending an army to help Albany. So they drew up this plot. Albany to go to England and seek Edward's help to win the Scots crown, with the pretended offer of overlordship. This to be rejected as invalid once he has the throne, since it would require to be endorsed by the Scots parliament. And this would be denied."

"Lord!" John exclaimed. "Parliament! I had not thought of that. Using parliament as his way out. Clever – but dishonourable!"

"King Louis's suggestion, Polwarth says. He is ever a plotter. And, if hereafter Edward tries to gain his ends by force, France will threaten *him* with invasion. So the Auld Alliance still stands."

John shook his head. "I do not like this . . ."

"Perhaps not. But it is better, is it not, than we feared? So, what am I to do now? It is secret information, sent to me as Albany's closest supporter here. Am I to tell it to the others? Atholl, Buchan and the rest?"

John was apt to be amused, surprised, by his forthright and

322

impulsive brother's habit of turning to him, the supposedly feeble and clerkly one, for guidance in moments of crisis or doubt. But there was no amusement in this situation. What was he to advise?

"We have come here to fight off the English," he said. "If Albany remains with them, we must seem to fight him. He is not proposing to leave Gloucester and come over to us, is he?"

"Nothing of that was said."

"Almost all here favour Albany, as against James. But they will not quietly let an English host trample over Scotland. James has ordered this assembly and preparation for battle, yes, a royal command. We all can scarcely go over to side with the English invaders! Nobody here knows just what to do . . ."

"Guidsakes, man, don't *I* know all that! I do not need to be told it. What I want to know is, do I tell them all of this deceit of Albany's? What he intends, once on the throne?"

John had really only been thinking aloud, trying to make up his own mind. "I think, I think – yes. Yes, you should tell the lords. They largely represent any parliament. They may not approve of the way it has been done, but they will approve of Albany's recognition that the ultimate decision should lie with parliament. So this word may help to make up minds, make decisions. Yes, I think that they should be told."

"What will they do, then?"

"Who knows! But it will give all time, opportunity, for thought and decision. Our own, as well as others'."

"Aye, our own! I am the commander, God help me! Or am I? The way that Atholl was speaking back there, it sounded as though *he* would assume the command. As senior earl, and uncle to both James and Albany. Aye, and I almost wish that he might!"

"Think you that a message could be sent to Albany? To urge him to leave Gloucester? To come over to us, secretly if need be. With him at our side, we would face the English united, decided. Drive them off, it is to be hoped."

"Would he do that? *Could* he? It would unite and assure us, yes. But would Albany risk it? Putting himself into James's hands again – James who murdered his brother. How could Albany be sure that, without the English protection, he would not fall into James's clutches once more. Be slain for treason!"

"If the earls and lords sent him their assurances that they would protect and support him. A signed letter, perhaps, all signing it . . . ?"

"While James still occupies the throne, that itself would be a treasonable document! Putting the signatories' own heads in a possible noose!"

"Aye, well, we shall see . . ."

Back amongst their fellow-leaders, Archie suggested something of a conference. Hold it in the town hall of the little burgh. And since all there were in a state of perplexity and indecision as to further action, this met with no objection. It was noteworthy, however, when they all assembled, that it was Atholl, flanked by his brother, Argyll and Crawford, who seemed to take the lead, and called on the Earl of Angus to put the situation before them.

Archie did not beat about the bush. Without preamble, he announced that he had had privy word, sent by the Duke of Albany himself, that the offer to Edward was but a ruse, entered into with the agreement of the King of France, that any proposed overlordship of Scotland would have to be approved by parliament, that it would not be so. And he, Albany, from the throne, would thereupon denounce it. There was no need, therefore, for war and battle.

The little hall erupted in clamour as men exclaimed and commented. There was no doubt about the impact of Archie's announcement. The company was exercised, to a man. Questions, demands, assertions abounded.

It was the Lindsay chief, Crawford, who concentrated matters. "What of Gloucester?" he asked, after beating for quiet. "How are he and his thousands going to take this? He has come to invade Scotland. Will the duke leave him and join us?"

"I do not know," Archie admitted. "There was no word as to that."

"Gloucester will not turn back now, whatever Albany does," Atholl declared. "Not when his brother Edward is to be made Lord Paramount of Scotland."

"Be not so sure," Argyll, the Campbell chief, put in. "It is known that Crookback does not love Edward overmuch. Has not forgiven him for the murder of their other brother Clarence, to whom Gloucester was close. They say that he covets the English throne for himself. He might be glad to have Albany remain his friend, in this fankle. When he hears what is intended, he could be pressed to make a compact. No war, but an undertaking between himself and Albany, of Scottish support for *him*, should he seek to replace his brother."

They all digested that. The Campbell was a known intriguer and plotter, a clever man, indeed he was being named as likely to succeed the ageing Avondale as Chancellor. Some scoffed, but only a few.

"A letter to Albany?" Archie suggested. "Signed by all here. Urging him to come over to us. To offer his support to Gloucester if it is ever needed . . ."

"I sign no letter which could be held to be treasonable!" Buchan interjected.

There were murmurs of agreement.

"A message, then. *Telling* him. This could change all – "

Archie was interrupted. Douglas of Cavers came to the hall door. "My lords," he cried, "a host is entering the town. From the north. The royal standard flies above it."

That broke up the meeting as men hurried out. It presumably was the Stirling contingent.

It proved to be more than that. It was King James himself. None had anticipated that the unwarlike monarch would come in person to lead his defensive force. And at his side, seeming infinitely more resplendent in gold-inlaid armour and plumed helmet, rode Robert Cochrane, Earl of Mar, with a party of magnificently attired followers close behind.

In silence the assembled lords awaited their liege-lord, set-faced.

James himself was little more forthcoming, ignoring his uncles – who had to be sure offended him by taking over

Edinburgh Castle – and scanning all faces doubtfully, to see who was there and who was not. It was Cochrane who assumed the lead, declaring satisfaction with the turnout, asking for numbers so far assembled, and who were still to come. He received but brief and scowling response.

Archie, as commander designate, went forward to make his report to the King, seeking very evidently to turn his shoulder on Cochrane and the others, and being anything but obsequious towards his sovereign. When Cochrane interrupted, demanding details, there was all but an explosion.

Fortunately James, weary after long riding, was more concerned just then with rest and refreshment than with the state of his armed forces; and Cochrane demonstrated his efficiency in matters practical and structural by promptly and personally superintending the unpacking and erection of an enormous and elaborate silken pavilion, emblazoned not with the royal arms but with the colours and devices of the earldom of Mar, even its cordage of colour-entwined silk, complete with furnishings, facilities and rich provender, all unloaded from a long train of pack-horses, this on the river bank of the Leader.

The lords stared, in astonishment and resentment.

As the newcomers settled in, the nobles returned to their own more modest tents and lodgings. The Douglas brothers were, at least, glad to see, amongst the Stirling array, Sir Robert Douglas of Lochleven, who had brought one hundred men.

It was a distinctly captious and disunited Scots camp which settled down at Lauder that night, even though feasting had gone on in the Mar pavilion accompanied by music – the man Rogers was a noted musician, to be sure.

Next day, the Ayr contingent arrived, with the Lords Montgomerie, Kennedy, Kilmaurs, Somerville and Lyle. The combined force now was assessed and totalled some sixty-five thousand men, the largest army assembled in living memory. Their marshalling, and especially their feeding and horse-forage, much preoccupied the leadership – although scarcely the coterie around the King – and quite overwhelmed the unfortunate folk of Lauder, who locked and barred themselves into their houses, or fled. James and Cochrane took over the town hall.

It was there, presently, that all of importance were summoned by royal command, presumably for a council of war. They found Cochrane very much in charge. He had discarded his splendid armour and was clad now in black velvet with gold braiding, a golden locket on a heavy gold chain around his neck and, oddly, a gold-tipped horn on another chain suspended at his side, with jewels of beryl dangling from each end. His friends there were only a little less fine, although James himself, who cared nothing for appearances, was still in his travel-stained riding-garb.

Cochrane, with an imperious wave, called the gathering to order. "His Grace requires the close heed of all," he began. "We are here assembled, to repel with all our strength the threat of English invasion, shamefully supported by the Duke of Albany. The attack is expected, in the main, at Berwick-on-Tweed, but secondary assaults may be made at Norham and at the Carter Bar. So the greater part of our army will make for Berwick, detaching lesser forces to guard those crossings. Five thousand to each will serve. Which will leave me fifty-five thousand at least to confront Gloucester and Albany. His Grace has appointed me to be commander, in place of the Earl of Angus, who will command the Norham force. And the Earl of Atholl at Carter Bar. I shall appoint others . . ."

He got no further, as uproar broke out. There was hardly a man in that hall who was not shouting his outrage and fury. James actually rose from his chair in alarm. Some of his cronies likewise showed their concern. But not Cochrane. He stared around him, head high, and sought to wave down the noise haughtily, calling into the din.

It was some time before he could make himself heard. "Silence, in His Grace's royal presence!" he was repeating. "If any wish to question any of His Grace's plans and intentions, there will be opportunity hereafter. Meantime, attention to details. Consideration of our dispositions. We will march tomorrow, down this dale of Lauder to Tweed at Leaderfoot. Then . . ."

Again he got no further. Atholl raised his voice, and to some effect. "James!" he cried. "I will hear no more of this. From this, this upstart! No more! I ask your royal permission to retire!" And without waiting even a moment for the said traditional permission, he turned and pushed his way through the throng for the door.

And, as with one accord, led by Buchan, Crawford and Argyll, the entire company turned about and followed him out, in loud acclaim, leaving the hall empty save for the monarch and his group of favourites. John was one of the last to leave, much after his brother.

Outside, he found the lords congregated in noisy debate and exchange, much approval of Atholl in evidence. That man presently pointed to the nearby church, and started out towards it. All followed. Prayer was unlikely; but it was the only other large building in the little town.

Therein, the general indignation and wrath continued, with gradually the lords and knights coming round to ask what they were to do about it all, in especial of course the assumption of leadership by Cochrane, and his scarcely believable appointment as army commander. None there was in any doubt that this was utterly impossible to contemplate, none prepared to serve under him. But what to do about it, with his royal backing, was unclear.

They were looking to Atholl for a lead. And he seemed less assured than he had been in the hall. Others of the earls appeared to be equally at a loss, as to how to proceed – save Archie Douglas.

"We must inform the King that by no means will we march under Cochrane's command. Nor allow our men to do so," he exclaimed. "Appoint another, a suitable commander, or there will be no army for him to command!"

Approval was expressed for that, but doubts also. Argyll headed these up.

"And if the King refuses? As well he may."

"Then we refuse to move."

"And if he makes it a royal command? To disobey that would be a treasonable offence. When in arms, that could be punishable by instant execution."

"He could not execute us all!"

"He could execute whoever made the protest, man! Order the royal guard to seize him. Remember, we are dealing with the High King of Scots, weakling as he is. None may disobey a direct royal command, and live."

"He could not execute a host of us!" Archie repeated. "If all told him together."

"Not there and then, perhaps. But later. Any time later. Who would sleep easy, then? Named traitor. Liable when off guard to be taken and slain. Lawfully. That is not the way."

"What is, then?"

"Get Cochrane. Himself. When he is not with the King. Take him and . . . dispose of him!"

Breaths were indrawn as men eyed each other. There was considerable nodding.

"Cochrane is always with the King," Archie objected. "Always has this crew round him."

"The crew we can deal with. It is the King's presence we must avoid."

"How that? When they are always together? We cannot – "

"Are we all mice, that we dare not to tell the King how we feel? We, his lords!" Gray, a hard-featured man of middle years, interrupted. "Speak with one voice and he must hear us."

"I repeat, Gray, if the King refuses? As he will, with Cochrane and the rest present. Then we are held. Can you not see it? High treason if we refuse further."

There was silence as these men, all of whom had taken the feudal oath of allegiance to the monarch necessarily, now considered the feudal consequences of direct refusal of a royal command, outside of parliament.

"Somehow the King and his familiars must be separated," Argyll went on. "For a space long enough for us to deal with Cochrane and the rest. You spoke of mice, Gray. If mice use their wits, they can perhaps outwit the cat! You mind the fable? The mice, preyed on by the cat, decided that if a bell could be hung on it, they could hear it coming and would be safe. The mice agreed. But which would bell the cat?"

"How bell?" Gray demanded. "For us?"

"That we must decide, devise. It must be possible to attract the King away from the others, on some pretext. Some device . . ."

"Ha! The King is much diverted by pretty boys!" Gray pointed out, grinning. "if we could coax him away with promises of one? Here, in Lauder. He would not wish to have others with him then!"

There were knowing leers and murmurs at that.

"He has one of them with him now, that John Ramsay," Archie put in. "Others of them also, perhaps that way inclined! But Ramsay is especially favoured, I am told. Bonnie indeed. He has even knighted the creature, shame on him! How could we get him, James, to desert Ramsay for a space?"

"Variety!" someone suggested. "Ever a draw, they say."

"Are we to find such a youth in Lauder?" Argyll objected.

"Or amongst our great host," Gray said. "Surely, in all these thousands, there are two or three who might appeal? I am not knowledgeable in such matters, myself. Some of you, perhaps, are better . . . informed?"

There was no lack of hooting at that.

"Is there need to find another?" Douglas of Lochleven asked. "Ramsay himself will serve, no? If we can use *him* to draw the King away from the others. No doubt they both would be glad of a brief joust together!"

"Aye, perhaps. But how to contrive it?" That was Atholl. "We can scarcely suggest it to them, not before the others. It is a weakness of James, yes. But how to use it . . . ?"

"Wait you," Archie interjected. "The King has other weaknesses. We could use them. This of astrology, divinations, witchcraft and the like. Use that, along with Ramsay. All around us in this Lauderdale are the relics of the long past, stone circles, sites of pagan worship, Pictish settlements. There is one at the leper hospice of St Leonards, down the dale but two miles from here. I saw it on my way from the west.

We could use that. Tell James — or better, tell Ramsay to tell James — that it is a notable place, with legends of witchcraft and devil-worship, such as the druids who built it used. Suggest taking the King and himself to see it. Leaving the others. They would not mislike that, I think."

"Excellent!" Argyll exclaimed. "If it can be done. Who will attempt this? Persuade the King and Ramsay to go to this place, this hospice, while we teach Cochrane and the others their lesson. Who will bell the cat?"

"I will!" Archie cried. "I will bell the cat for you. If I can. Seek out Ramsay, suggest taking him and James, only the two of them, to this St Leonards stone circle. He to tell the King. While you . . ." He left the rest unsaid.

"Aye, aye . . . !" sounded from all around.

"We will ensure that your time is not wasted, Angus!" Atholl said grimly.

The cries of hearty agreement began to die away, then, as men turned to stare, the situation abruptly changed.

With warm July weather, the church door had been left open. And there, in the doorway, now stood a figure — none other than Robert Cochrane himself.

In the sudden hush, that man strode inside. "My lords," he said, "your attention. His Grace agrees with me that a probing expedition should be sent forward, over the borderline into Northumberland, to discover if possible how the English army approaches, how far it has got, its numbers, whether it has split off lesser formations, and the like. I judge that my lord of Angus, as Warden of this March, is best suited for this duty. My lord, you will see to it forthwith?" That was a command, rather than any question.

Archie, gulping down his ire, stepped forward. "*You* give *me*, Angus, orders, fellow!" he jerked. "You tell the Red Douglas what he is to do!" He pointed. "By Almighty God, you do not!"

"I am the Earl of Mar . . ." The rest was lost in hubbub and vociferation. Involuntarily Cochrane stepped back a pace at the menace implied, although he was clearly no craven. "I come in the King's name!" he shouted. "I wear the King's royal seal in this locket." And he touched the golden pendant at his breast.

"It becomes you not! Meeter that you should wear a rope than this collar!" And impulsively Archie took a couple of steps forward, to reach out and grasp the locket, and to wrench. The fastening of the chain at the other's neck snapped, and chain and pendant came away in Archie's hand.

"Is this jest? Or earnest . . . ?" Cochrane gasped.

That action, symbolic as it was, seemed to unleash the rageful anger of the entire company. Almost to a man they surged forward, fists clenched, some clenched indeed on dirk-hilts. It so happened that Douglas of Lochleven had been keeping watch at the door, and so was nearest the intruder. He leapt to follow his step-son's lead, and grabbed at the chain which carried the gold-tipped hunting horn, and tugged fiercely. It also came away in his hands.

"Nor yet this horn!" he exclaimed. "You have already hunted after mischief too long!"

After that chaos ensued. In a rush of furious men, Cochrane went down, to blows and kicks, an unseemly scene for the nobility of Scotland.

Argyll at least considered it so. Turning to take the mass bell from the altar behind him, he rang it and rang it. The thing made no very loud noise, to outdo the clamour, but its high tinkle, associated in all minds with the eucharistic sacrament, probably had a greater and subtler effect. Men started to restrain themselves and drew back. Cochrane remained on the floor.

"This is not the way!" the Campbell declared. "We must use our wits, not fists! And see you, close that door. If any of the man's friends or guards see this, and tell the King . . . !"

All saw the point of that, belatedly. The door was shut and Lochleven stood guard on it, still holding the hunting horn on its chain. Voices were everywhere raised, demanding what now, and making sundry suggestions.

John Douglas, who had been the unhappy spectator of all this, was now concerned to be out of it, and to get Archie out of it, recognising that the consequences could be dire indeed for more than Cochrane, once all this reached the King's ears . . .

"Archie, come! Ramsay, and the King. To get them away, if possible. Before they hear of this. Come!" That was almost a command to his elder brother.

Archie did not hesitate for long. No doubt he too perceived the dangers now. Nodding, he turned to wave to Argyll, who appeared best to have kept his wits in all this turmoil, handing Cochrane's gold locket and chain to Lochleven as they hurried out.

They went back to the town hall, but found it all but empty.

"That pavilion. Cochrane's," Archie jerked.

"Best to get our horses first."

Their mounts were tethered not far away. Riding down to the resplendent silken tent by the waterside, they heard the clear notes of a flute coming therefrom.

"Music!" Archie snorted disgustedly. "Bringing flutes and the like on warfare!"

"They could do worse. The least of their follies!"

At the pavilion entrance two of the royal guard stood on duty.

"Sir John Ramsay within?" Archie demanded. "Tell him that the Earl of Angus seeks word with him. Him only, see you."

One of the guards went within. The music did not cease.

It was only moments before the man was back, and with Ramsey, a slender youth with long, curling fair hair and almost beautiful appearance, superbly dressed.

Archie cleared throat. "The King is within?" he asked.

"He is, yes. What do you want with him, my lord?" There was scarcely veiled insolence in that.

Archie, well aware of it, drew quick breath. But his brother was still quicker.

"Sir John, you, like His Grace, are interested in matters of ancient lore, are you not? Witchcraft. Divinations. Signs and wonders. We have word of such, near to here. We thought, during this time of waiting, that perhaps His Grace and yourself might care to visit such a place. It is but two miles. Inspect it. There may be little to see, save a stone circle and inscribed stones, but there are legends. How think you?"

The youth did look interested now. "Where is this?"

"Near a hospice called St Leonards. Down Leader two miles," Archie declared. "Just you and the King."

"We feel that there may be little to see," John put in, hurriedly again. "So no point in any large company going, at first. Just His Grace and yourself, until you see whether it is worth showing to others. You we deem especially concerned, with the King, in this. You might wish to inspect these stones together. Especially the inscribed ones, with their ancient and strange symbols."

"Ah! Yes. Ourselves alone, to be sure. I think . . . the King and myself . . . he would be interested. How would we find this place?"

"We would take you there," Archie said.

"Leave you to inspect them. Since we are not knowledgeable in such matters," John added.

Ramsay clearly saw possibilities in the suggestion. "Yes. We would best be left to consider it ourselves. But two miles, you say, my lords? Now? I will go ask His Grace."

"Can you ensure no larger party?" John stressed. "That would be best."

"Yes, yes. James will heed."

Archie frowned at this unsuitable use of the King's name by this puppy, only great magnates like himself entitled so to do. Actually, to be sure, this youth was of much better birth than were the rest of the royal coterie, the son of a substantial laird, Ramsay of Corstoun, of the Fife house of Carnock. But still it was a liberty.

Ramsay turned and re-entered the pavilion, leaving the Douglas brothers standing by their horses.

The lute music stopped, and they exchanged glances. However, after only a brief interval it started again, to their relief. More so, when Ramsay reappeared with King James, who eyed the brothers questioningly.

Archie, more respectfully now, repeated their proposal,

emphasising that they made it knowing His Grace's interest in the occult, and believing that any large group would not be advisable to visit such a sacred place, with talk and chatter.

James seemed to agree. John had feared that he might be suspicious at this unexpected suggestion, especially on the insistence that they should go alone. But he gave no such impression. Archie, of course, was his Warden of the March and, up until a short time before, his appointed commander of the army.

While James was enquiring as to the situation and details, Ramsay went to collect the horses.

John thought it worth taking a risk, just in case the King could be doubtful as to being lured away from the others. He asked if His Grace would wish to have an escort of the royal guard accompany them? He heard Archie's intake of breath.

James declared that, if it was only two miles, that would not be necessary.

So, despite surprise by some there, only the four of them set off down Leader-side, southwards.

Archie let his brother, who was more knowledgeable about such things, tell something of what they might hope to see in this St Leonards area. John mentioned that there was a hospice there, no doubt the site chosen because it was an ancient holy place, actually a former leper community or lazar-house, that accounting for the name. It should be St Lazarus, the style of the knightly Order of Chivalry which specialised in the care of lepers; but because there was no pronouncing of the letter z in the Scots tongue, the name was commonly corrupted to St Leonards or St Lawrence. And the hospices were always necessarily a mile or two outside any town or centre of population. All of which, no doubt, His Grace knew very well. It seemed that there was a former Pictish or Caledonian settlement on the higher ground behind the hospice, with the usual stone circle as worshipping-place, and to this last legends and tales related, with symbol-stones and pagan altars perhaps. Probably His Grace would know what to look for . . .

His Grace seemed preoccupied.

The hospice proved to be set back from the river, on ground

beginning to rise, on the west side, higher slopes lifting out of scattered woodland behind. The green grass-grown ramparts of a Pictish fort and settlement were just visible, if one knew where to look. The four of them did not trouble to call in at the hospice, but turned off to ride straight uphill.

They had less than half a mile to go to the ramparts, three concentric rings with wide ditches between, enclosing perhaps an acre. This was the fort. Nearby was another and larger enclosure, with only the one turf-covered bank surrounding, the interior littered with the stony foundations of huts, the settlement. And further still, on a more prominent eminence, were the remains of a stone circle, some of the monoliths still standing.

It was towards the last that they headed. Five of the stones were approximately upright, one somewhat askew; but as they drew close the horsemen could see others fallen. They counted thirteen, forming the circle, with a more bulky one in the centre, no doubt the original altar for the sun-worshippers.

Dismounting, they went to examine the stones, James exclaiming at the significance of the numbers and siting, telling the others that the stones were all lined up astronomically and astrologically, to mark the exact positions of the sunrises and sunsets in relation to the two solstices; a matter for wonder, demonstrating the great knowledge and wisdom of these ancient peoples. He treated them to an exposition on sun-worship, fertility rites, the importance of certain given numbers, human sacrifice, and more, which John in fact found exceedingly interesting, and caused him to consider his monarch with rather more respect than heretofore, although Archie was clearly bored.

Unfortunately there proved to be no inscriptions visible on these. However, when they went over to the settlement enclosure, they discovered a single monolith, standing a little way off, on which there were lichen-covered but regular indentations. When the lichen was scraped away, quite clearly discernible were three carvings of strange symbols. These were a crescent moon with what looked like a broken arrow in the shape of a V superimposed; two linked double circles, with another arrow, or possibly a spear, broken in the form of a Z; and a single circle with a handle and below it what was obviously a toothed comb – this group James declaring with some excitement to be the mirror and comb symbol, which would represent a woman, presumably of some especial note. This could well be the tombstone of some Pictish chieftainess. He went on at some length as to the possibles.

Having got thus far, Archie was eager to be off, leaving the pair to their own devices, the object of the exercise. Ramsay seemed similarly impatient. Only John, strangely enough, would have liked to linger on and learn more from their peculiar liege-lord. But he had to recognise priorities.

His brother announced that while His Grace and Sir John would no doubt have much to discuss here, and perhaps discover more interesting relics, he and Lord Douglasdale ought to get back to Lauder where they had duties with the great assembly of men. With His Grace's permission, therefore, they would leave them. Would an escort be desired to bring them to the camp, in due course?

Nothing such was required, they were assured. They would return when they were ready.

Delighted with the success of their mission, Archie said their farewells – although John was just a little less happy about it all, for some reason.

The brothers rode back to the town, Archie speculating on how long archaeology and the like would triumph over more personal concerns, behind them.

They reached Lauder and the vast camp, to find all in a state of high excitement indeed, men everywhere loud in elation, glee and approving comment, more especially the well-born ones. All directed the brothers to the town bridge over the Leader.

Riding thither, they could not get near the riverside for the crowds of vociferous men. Archie had to shout, and threaten with the flat of drawn sword, to give way for the Earl of Angus, driving his alarmed horse right into the throng, amongst more curses than his own, before they could approach the bridge. However, their horsed arrival, in the otherwise horseless

337

crowd, drew the attention of some of the leadership there, in especial Sir Robert of Lochleven, who managed to clear a way for them. Then they discovered the other results of their mission.

The low-born favourites had indeed been dealt with.

Six of them were hanging from the parapet of Lauder Brig – Cochrane, Rogers the musician, Stobo a clerk, Torphichen the dancing-master, Leonard the shoemaker and Preston a merchant. None of them was now so much as twitching.

John was appalled, even if his brother was not. It had never occurred to him that it could come to this.

There was no lack of information and detailed description, for them, as to what had transpired. Whenever the lords saw that the King had gone, they had descended upon the silken pavilion, carrying the dazed and battered Cochrane with them, and arrested all the occupants thereof. There and then, Atholl presiding, they had held an impromptu court, promptly found all guilty of shameful treason in subverting the monarch to their wretched wills, and condemned all to immediate execution, no single voice raised in defence, save Cochrane's. Thereupon they had been brought down to the bridge here and hanged, without benefit of clergy to hear their confessions. Cochrane, it was cheerfully recounted, had pleaded not to be hanged with a hempen rope like any common cur, but, as an earl, to be at least granted a silken cord – one from his pavilion would serve – to be informed that he was no true earl, and that they would hang him with a horse's halter instead. Which they had done.

So perished all the crew which had mismanaged the ship of state for so long – or not quite all, for there was still the youth Ramsay. And, to be sure, William Sheves, who might not be so easy to bring to book, as an archbishop with papal protection.

This last, at least, John could agree with.

When he could get Archie to himself – which was not for some considerable time – he put it to his brother. The thing was done, deplorable or otherwise. But what was to happen when the King came back?

Archie shrugged. "They will take Ramsay, no doubt. As to James, what can he do? He cannot accuse *all* his lords and chiefs of treason. Most of parliament is here, save the clerics. He can do naught."

"He will be devastated! And he is still the King of Scots. And can issue royal commands."

"Perhaps. But cannot enforce them."

"He has his royal guard."

"Think you *they* will stand up against the thousands here assembled? Four score of them! No, James is helpless."

John was less sure. At this juncture he might be. But hereafter?

He was concerned about John Ramsay. That young man was scarcely deserving of this fate, whatever his weaknesses. John wondered whether he ought to go back and warn him. Archie said no – that would be also to warn the King. The pair might then avoid coming back to the town and camp, make straight north to Edinburgh or Stirling, alone, and there arouse trouble, retribution. Sheves was still a power in the land, and would undoubtedly seek to raise opposition, possibly armed opposition. And he had the wealth of Holy Church behind him, and Vatican authority. That could start civil war.

They were discussing this when James and Ramsay came trotting back, rather sooner than anticipated. All in authority there more or less held their breaths.

The pair might not have perceived that something was amiss, at first, but some of the common soldiery were not to be denied their own enjoyment of the situation. Grinning, they shouted and pointed to the bridge, eagerly but less than respectfully. James and his young friend turned their horses' heads in that direction.

Archie, John and other lords hastened back thither.

There was no lack of drama thereafter. At sight of what hung there, the King emitted a great wail of anguish, all but falling from his saddle in his shock and distress. Ramsay stared, first at the bodies and then around him, in alarm and quick fear. Horrified, they sat.

But not for long. Led by Gray, a group of the lords moved in to the couple. Ignoring the monarch, they grimly surrounded Ramsay. Seeing their hatred and intentions, the youth reined round, as they reached out to grab at him. Being mounted, he had the slight advantage, but they closed in nevertheless, and men-at-arms surged forward to assist them, shouting.

Desperately Ramsay lashed out with his riding-whip, but quickly saw that he could nowise escape them. Instead, he abruptly pulled round closer to the King's horse, with James sitting paralysed. The youth, in sheerest terror, flung himself out of his own saddle and on to the back of the royal horse, behind his monarch, to cling to the King, gulping demands for protection and saving.

Although no doubt done on unthinking impulse, it was in fact an effective move. For as long as he hung on to the royal person, he could not be detached without physical violence involving the monarch, the touching of, and roughly, the liege-lord of them all. And that was the unforgivable offence of *lèse-majesté*, laying hands on the King, worse even than high treason. The lords, at least, knew it, and restrained themselves from that dire transgression meantime.

Atholl and Buchan arrived, and John Douglas ran to grasp the former's arm. "My lord Earl," he cried, "halt them! Save the King. And this Ramsay. He is young, has done little harm. It is enough. Care for James, now. And this youth. *You* can do it."

Whether the King's uncle had required this prompting or not he nodded. He strode forward, hand raised, to wave the lords back, commanding them to desist. Perhaps in their sudden predicament over *lèse-majesté* they were glad enough to be spared decision. At any rate, they drew aside a little.

Atholl went over to take the bridle of the King's horse. "Come, Sire," he urged, all but ordered. "Fear not. *You* are safe. This other, we shall see. Come."

Turning, he led his nephew's mount and its two riders back up into the town's street, James in trembling fright, Ramsay clutching tight. Silence fell upon the watching crowd, lords and soldiery alike. None sought to challenge the premier earl of Scotland leading the monarch.

Atholl took the pair to the provost's house, which he had been occupying, and where they could be locked in, for safety.

"Thank God for that, at least!" John exclaimed, to his brother. "What now?"

Archie could not tell him that. It was an extraordinary new situation, not only as regards the King and Ramsay, but as to the army assembled, and the national threat. They at least agreed that a council be held, to bring matters into some sort of order. Archie went to urge this on Atholl and the other earls.

The town hall theirs again, the leadership gathered, in a state of considerable uncertainty, Atholl presiding. It was Argyll, however, who seemed to have the clearest ideas as to what should be done, and quickly took the lead.

"Do we wish to go on, to battle, in these circumstances?" he demanded. "The King is in no state for that. Nor, I think, are we! Certainly we would not wish to seem to fight the Duke of Albany in this upset. I say that we should return to Edinburgh, and there wait. Keep the army assembled. But seek to negotiate with Albany. And Gloucester, to be sure.

There were murmurs for and against this course, but more of the former.

"I agree," Atholl said. "We cannot take the King, now, into warfare. And we are here in his name. Nor do we wish to fight Albany. To remain here, with these large numbers of men, to be fed and kept in order, is scarcely possible. Back at the Burgh Muir of Edinburgh they can be provided for from the city while policy is decided."

"Meanwhile the English army advances over the Borders and Lothian!" the Lord Hailes objected – whose lands lay therein.

"Albany has declared himself to be Alexander the Fourth, King of Scots!" Lord Gray put in. "Can we not welcome him as such? And call a parliament to dethrone James!"

"What of Gloucester?" the Earl of Crawford asked. "And

341

this of Edward's demand for paramouncy? Would not accepting Albany, with Gloucester's very present aid, seem to accept that also – which God forbid!"

That last at least drew general acclaim.

"I say that we should send a messenger to Albany," Archie declared. "In answer to his message to myself, at Lochmaben. Seek an assurance from him that he will openly reject this paramouncy claim. Come to Edinburgh, and there reject it."

"With Gloucester and an English army standing by!" Hailes scoffed.

"Our Scots army standing by also, and very close! And larger, belike. On our own ground."

"You would have a battle at Edinburgh."

"Be not so sure. Richard of Gloucester is none so fond of his brother Edward. They say that he seeks the English throne for himself. If he was offered Scots aid, by Albany, if it came to that, he might well give up the paramouncy claim. Not to offend us. And spare himself a battle."

All considered that, and Argyll conceded it as probably the best course in the circumstances. But this would be a delicate matter to put to Albany and Gloucester. Who would do it? No mere courtier, with a letter, would serve.

"I say that my brother, the Lord of Douglasdale, would be best to go," Archie announced. "He is skilful with his tongue. And known to the duke."

Not consulted in the matter, John found it being approved by all. Without actually glaring at his brother, he did throw him a resentful look, Archie shrugging airily.

It was decided that the army would return to Edinburgh on the morrow, when the Lord of Douglasdale would set off on his errand.

The meeting broke up soon thereafter, Archie being already hailed as Archibald Bell-the-Cat. It had been an eventful and memorable, if hardly glorious, day in Scotland's story.

22

With a small troop of Douglas men-at-arms, John rode southwards for Tweed next morning, there to turn eastwards down
the great river, at Melrose. He was unsure where he would find
Albany and the English host, but assumed that Berwick was
probably the best place to make for. The invaders, coming
from Alnwick, would almost certainly cross into Scotland
there, at least their main force. They might be already
beyond it, of course, in which case he would have to follow
them up.

He was not looking forward to his mission.

The journey at least was simple and straightforward, if
lengthy, merely following the Tweed, by Dryburgh, Makerstoun,
Roxburgh, Kelso, Birgham and Coldstream, to the river's mouth.
He could have taken a shorter route, by Greenlaw and Swinton,
but had to take into consideration the fact that the invaders
might possibly come over further west, by Carter Bar and
Jedburgh. However, they in fact saw no sign of enemy all
the way until they reached Berwick.

John was unsure of the situation there, whether or not the
English army would have reached thus far. It was, of course,
a Scots town, the county town of Berwickshire or the Merse.
But it had long been, off and on, in English hands. And a
distinction had to be made between town and castle, the latter
standing on high ground some distance north of the town
walls, an unusual position, dictated by a usefully defensive
cliff. Sometimes the town itself was in English occupation
and the castle was not. Occasionally, but not often, the
reverse. The last John had heard, Berwick Castle, a very
strong place, was held by the Master of Hailes, Sir Patrick
Hepburn of Dunsyre, but the port still in English possession.

Powerful artillery would be required to capture the fortress. It was unlikely, surely, that Gloucester and Albany would burden themselves with heavy and slow-moving oxen-drawn cannon in this venture.

In fact, arriving with the dusk and the town gates shut for the night, they found English flags flying over Berwick but Scots ones over the castle. After some delay and shouting of identities, they gained admittance to the latter, to discover the Master of Hailes still in command. John knew him, as an East March notable and one of Archie's lieutenants. He was able to give him news of his father.

From Hepburn he learned that the English army had been two days in the Berwick vicinity. They had made no attempt to assault the castle. He reckoned their numbers as between twenty-five and thirty thousand. They had moved on northwards only that morning. Probably they would be at Dunbar by this time, to pass the night there.

John decided that a very early start in the morning would enable him to catch up with the invaders before they had progressed much further than Dunbar itself, large armies moving comparatively slowly. They would not be concerned with taking strong castles, and would probably bypass Hailes and Tantallon. So he spent a brief night as the Hepburn's guest, and was off northwards with the dawn.

In fact, they covered the thirty miles to Dunbar in time to find the last of the English rearguard leaving that town's common land, and had been glad to note, on the way, no signs of devastation or burning, only the inevitable large amounts of horse-droppings and other debris which went with an army's passage. The arrival of so small a troop of Scots aroused no alarm. Albany was presumably endeavouring to ensure that the minimum of hostility was aroused in Scotland, a wise precaution.

Spurring on past the long-strung-out array, they reached the head of the column, colourful under a host of banners, in the vicinity of the Tyne ford at Prestonkirk, not so very far from the Hepburn main seat of Hailes Castle, which obviously also was being bypassed. John had no difficulty in identifying the two dukes in the crowd of English nobles. But he also saw there amongst all the standards, the Red Heart under Blue, of Douglas. That must be the Black Douglas himself, the earl, formerly Lord Balveny, the only one of the ill-fated and betrayed brothers to survive. His own Red Heart pennon would proclaim who *he* was.

Raising hand in salute, John, leaving his men behind now, made his way through the throng of interested Englishmen to their leaders. He had expected Gloucester, from his by-name of Crookback, to be a deformed, hunched figure, but he was not: a slightly built man of thirty, with one shoulder rather oddly higher than the other but no other oddity, thin-featured, keen-eyed and dark, the youngest of the Yorkist brothers. At his side, Albany recognised John right away, and hailed him in friendly fashion. At the other side was a grey-bearded, sober-looking individual, who would be the rightful Earl of Douglas, although that title was forfeited in Scotland.

"Douglasdale!" Albany exclaimed. "Come to welcome me back, I hope?"

That made a difficult start for the reluctant courier. "I come as envoy from my brother and the other earls and lords, my lord Duke," he answered carefully. "Greetings!" he bowed, but only slightly, in the direction of the tip-shouldered man.

"This is His Highness of Gloucester. And this, Richard, is John, Lord of Douglasdale, brother to the Earl of Angus."

"Ha – another Douglas!" Gloucester jerked. "I am lost amongst them!" And he glanced at the older man at his side.

"I am the *Black* Douglas," he was told briefly. "Chief of the name. They are Reds." That was enough. There was no love lost between the two.

John nodded again. "My lord," he said.

"Have you come from Lochmaben?" Albany asked. "That is where I heard that your brother was based. I sent word to him there."

"I come from nearer than that, my lord Duke. From the King's army, in Lauderdale." He judged that to be the best line to take at this stage.

It gained some sharp glances.

"You refer to James Stewart?" Gloucester asked pointedly.

"The King, yes, Highness. I left him, and the army, yesterday, at Lauder."

"Army?" Albany said. "At Lauder. What does James with an army, at Lauder?"

John had been debating with himself as he rode here how he should try to conduct this difficult interview, and get over his message. This was not the way.

"My lords, I have much to tell you," he said urgently. "Much to ask and make known. For this I was sent. It is scarcely meet that we should talk of it here, in the saddle. My home, my brother's house of Tantallon, is but a few miles from here. Might I suggest that you leave your host to make its way onward, up Tyne, perhaps to Haddington, to camp. And you, with whom you will, come to Tantallon, where we can speak at our ease. And spend a comfortable night?"

"Have you so much to say to us, at ease or otherwise?" Gloucester asked. He had a notable air of authority, and a tight mouth.

"I think that I have, yes. Although *I* am only a messenger. My mission is from others a great deal more important than myself." And John looked at Albany significantly.

The duke nodded. "I think that we might accept your offer of hospitality, my lord, at Tantallon," he said. "A change from the camp?" And he looked at Gloucester, who shrugged. "How many of us can you house?"

"As many as you please. In reason."

"Half a dozen would serve, I think. You have your Douglas guard, I see!"

While the others decided who was to come with them, and gave orders for the host to proceed on to Haddington town, six miles, and there camp, John sought to arrange his thoughts. This prolonged interview and exchange was not going to be easy; nor was the five miles they had to ride to Tantallon. He hoped that his sister-in-law and sisters were not going to berate him too sorely for landing this visitation upon them.

Fortunately, the half-hour's trot, by Tyninghame and

346

Scoughall, was less difficult conversationally than might have been expected, for Gloucester let Albany go ahead with John, while he and Douglas rode behind with a few of the English lords. Albany asked about James and his deplorable favourites, and John had to tell him about the latter's fate at Lauder Brig – which seemed much to please and divert the duke as well as filling in what could have been an uncomfortable little journey.

The appearance of Tantallon Castle, towering high and dominant on its peninsular cliff-top, duly impressed the visitors, even Gloucester remarking that it looked a difficult place to take.

The young women received the invasion well, all things considered, obviously intrigued to be entertaining the royal dukes, two such renowned and controversial figures. Producing the necessary provender was not difficult in an establishment accustomed to catering for a large company; and the Englishmen were, in return, duly appreciative and attentive to the ladies, more elaborately so indeed than was the normal Scots fashion. Oddly Gloucester himself proved to be quite a ladies' man.

After the meal, John suggested that Albany and Gloucester should come with him into the withdrawing-room off the main hall, where they could discuss necessary matters in privacy – and as an afterthought included his namesake John of Douglas, as a civility. Servitors brought them wine to assist the deliberations.

Gloucester took the lead from the first, obviously a strong and assertive character which, with Albany similarly inclined, made for an interesting situation and possible clash.

"Now, my lord, your message?" he demanded of John. "Which you seem to make much of!"

"My message, Highness, is mainly for the Duke of Albany." That was firmly although not provocatively said. "It comes from the lords, in council, the Earls of Atholl, Buchan, Argyll, Crawford, Erroll and Angus, and many lords of parliament, including Gray, Seton, Hailes, Home, Kennedy, Montgomerie and Somerville. . ."

347

"A resounding roll, perhaps," he was interrupted. "And from James Stewart?"

"*Not* from King James, no."

"After the deaths of his familiars, James will be . . . stricken?" Albany said.

"Yes, stricken indeed. He is in the care of his uncles, and yours, my lord Duke."

"And your errand, man?" Gloucester sounded impatient.

"My duty is to tell you of the feelings of the lords. Strong feelings. Of much importance to your present situation and hopes, my lords." John was speaking very carefully, as well he might. "Almost all, I am to tell you, are in general favour of King James being superseded on the throne by you, my lord Duke. But all are very much against any claims to paramouncy over Scotland by the King of England."

There was silence then, for seconds on end.

It was Gloucester who broke it. "Are *their* feelings on this issue of any vital importance? My brother Edward's, and Alexander's here, are what signifies, I say!"

"I think not, Highness. No such decision could be effective without the express agreement of parliament. And these lords and chiefs represent the major voice of parliament."

"Parliament!" Gloucester scoffed. "A playhouse of talk! No more."

"Your English parliament may be that. But ours in Scotland is otherwise. The King in parliament rules the land, as my lord of Albany knows well. Without parliament's approval, the King is held. Save in small, personal matters. And parliament will not approve this of English overlordship, that I can assure you!"

Albany drummed fingertips on the table but said nothing.

The other duke looked at him. "How say you to that, Alexander?" he asked.

"It, it can be got over, I hope. I judge."

"We must ensure that it is! It is the price of Edward's aid, the price of this expedition."

"I know it. But . . ."

"A few Scots lordlings are not going to tell my royal brother

348

what may or may not be! Or any parliament of speech-makers! Swords will decide this, if necessary. And we have thirty thousand of them, to hand!" That was harshly said.

John sought to keep his voice even. "That would be . . . unfortunate, my lord Duke. For we will have *sixty* thousand assembled on the Burgh Muir of Edinburgh, by this night. With cannon from the castle!"

So there it was, down to the basics it had to come to.

For a little none spoke.

The Earl of Douglas made a contribution. "What of the Church? The Lords Spiritual? How say they? And the burghs?"

"All are at one in this, at least. No paramouncy."

Albany was looking not so much unhappy or surprised as uncertain, uneasy. And it was at Gloucester that he tended to look, not John. Yet he was namely as a man of decision. "What now?" he wondered.

"What indeed! We put the matter to the test," Gloucester declared. "We have not come all this way, with our thousands, to turn back now, because of a mere message. On to your Edinburgh, I say."

"Yes. But there?" He turned to John. "How united are the earls and lords in this?"

"Wholly, my lord. In this matter, there is no dissenting voice. As to the throne, there are some who remain loyal to King James. Especially the churchmen. Whom Sheves greatly controls."

"That clerk!" Gloucester barked.

"What, then, do *you* advise?" the Earl of Douglas asked.

John hesitated. He could hardly suggest that they turned back now, after what Gloucester had said. That would be ignominy, unacceptable quite. To wait at Haddington would serve no purpose.

"I would go on to Edinburgh," he said, but without great conviction. "Not in war. But to talk. To negotiate. Not with the King, but with the lords. Leave your English army well back from the Burgh Muir, that there be no clashes. In the great park of the abbey of the Holy

Rude, probably. Try to come to some agreement with the earls . . ."

"Agreement as to what?" Gloucester demanded.

"As to the throne. Not any paramouncy."

The others eyed each other, unspeaking.

Not himself perceiving anything more usefully to be said, John suggested a return to the others in the hall.

There he had a quiet word with his sisters. Where was Albany to be bedded down? Alone? He was told yes, in the South Tower's first-floor chamber. Gloucester in the room above.

When, eventually, their guests sought their couches, John waited for some time to elapse before making his way, with a lantern, to the South Tower, perched so dramatically above the waves. There, at the first-floor doorway, he paused to listen, in case there were voices from within. He heard none. He tapped quietly, and opened the door a little way.

"It is John Douglas," he announced, in little more than a whisper. "May I enter?"

"Ha! Come," he was told.

By the lamplight he saw Albany sitting up in bed. Closing the door, he went to him.

"My lord Duke, I think that a private word with you is in order," he said. "I am your friend, as are others. We would support your bid for the throne. But cannot stomach English overlordship, even in name. Why did you offer it? You must have known?"

"Louis of France advised it, man. Only so, he judged, could I gain Edward's help. For Louis himself could not spare an army. I was not sure how much support I had in Scotland. But James had to be dethroned. He murdered my brother. Would murder *me*, if he could. I needed armed support. This way I could have it. And reject the paramouncy when I was safely crowned. Not the most honourable course, I admit. But he who begs may not choose. And Edward is a rogue, another murderer of brothers. He deserves no better."

"Perhaps not. But this has gravely injured your fame

in Scotland. Done your cause harm. Aye, and what of Gloucester?"

"Richard is a hard man. But I think that he will accept this. For himself. Although he may not be able to say so, without offending Edward. He himself seeks the English crown. But is not ready yet to make a try for it. He has to seem to play Edward's game meantime."

"Will he turn back from Edinburgh without this assurance of paramouncy? Indeed assured that they will *not* get it!"

"He will have to have something to take back to Edward, from this expedition."

John shook his head. "We do not want war, outright war, with Edward. But, see you, the first matter is *your* position. Rejection of this paramouncy will not itself win you the crown. Especially with an English army at your back. You are still forfeited by parliament. Sentence for treason is only postponed, not lifted. In law you are an outlaw, crazy-mad as this may seem, my lord Duke."

"Yet you say that most lords are for me!"

"True. And the position can be righted, I judge. But only by a parliament. And a parliament demands forty days of notice, to call. And the *King* must call it!"

"The folly of it!"

"The folly, my lord, is otherwise, I fear! Did you not get a letter from your sister, the Princess Mary?"

"I did." Albany did not elaborate on that. "What is my best course now, then?"

Why did others keep asking *him* that sort of question, John wondered? "I am no sage," he said. "But I would think that your best course is to go on to Edinburgh, withdraw the paramouncy offer, before all, seek to come to some sort of terms with your brother the King, so that he can be persuaded to call a parliament, and so get the forfeiture and outlawry cancelled, your position and honours restored. And only after that make a lawful claim for the throne, on the grounds of James's inability to rule and govern the realm. Something of that order."

"That would take weeks, months!"

351

"I fear so. But what else can you do? With any hope of success?"

"I would call a rising against James, in my favour, here and now. The earls and lords supporting me. *Take* the throne. That is what I came to do."

"With an English army at your back? Here in Scotland! Gloucester and his thousands are your *weakness*, not your strength! I do not see many backing you, in arms, while Gloucester remains here."

The other remained silent.

"Think well on it, my lord Duke. Sleep on it. Either you turn back now, I think, or you go on to Edinburgh prepared to face the situation that I speak of. What you can offer Gloucester, I do not know."

John went to his own bed, and did not sleep easily.

In the morning, Albany gave no signs of indecision or doubt. Certainly there was no suggestion of turning back. Gloucester it was who was the silent one. They left Tantallon to rejoin the army at Haddington, six miles away.

It was a further sixteen miles to Edinburgh, and the leadership of the strung-out host covered it in under two hours. The abbey-park, below the soaring Arthur's Seat, lay east of the city walls, and when they reached the start of it, it was to see many flags flying over the abbey itself and its monastic premises, which was unusual. Admittedly the abbey was frequently used by monarchs as residence, being a deal more comfortable than the grim fortress of Edinburgh Castle. So perhaps they had brought the King here? Leaving Albany and Gloucester to mark out camping places for the following host, John rode forward to investigate.

Well before he reached the abbey he came up against a barrier of armed horsemen, waiting, watching. No doubt the progress of the English army had been under observation all along. Fortunately there amongst the company he was able to pick out his friend, the Lord Seton, who indeed spurred forward to greet him and grip his hand.

Briefly told the situation, Seton for his part informed that most of the lords, from Lauder, were now here, quartered in the abbey. But not King James. Atholl and Buchan had taken and locked him up in the castle, allegedly for his own safety. The army was encamped, as had been agreed upon, up on the Burgh Muir, over a mile away. Archie Douglas was up at the castle now, conferring with the other earls. A force of about ten thousand had been detached and sent off eastwards, to get behind the English host, and to assail it from the rear and cut off its retiral if it came to battle.

John said that, as he saw it, the best course now was to bring Albany and Gloucester here to the abbey, and send up to inform the earls, who could come down to confer with them. He hoped, indeed believed, that there would be no battling necessary.

So while Seton sent a messenger up through the city, John went back to the English camp-site.

He had no difficulty in persuading Albany and Gloucester to come back with him to the abbey, with a group of English lords. Their reception there was wary, to say the least, but that was only to be expected. The Holy Rude, one of the largest abbeys in the land, had extensive monastic and hospice wings, and even with its present influx of Scots lords, accommodation was found for the newcomers, even if there was little actual association.

It was not long before a troop of earls and magnates arrived down from the castle, including, John was surprised to see, Sheves and another bishop, Dunkeld. Archie came, and sought out John for information. For his part he said that Sheves was being unusually co-operative. No doubt the deaths of his odd friends at Lauder was having a salutary effect. And the King was now wholly in the grip of his uncles, in effect a prisoner in the castle here; and Sheves's influence, save in Church matters, was exercised only through James. So his authority was suddenly much limited. As Archbishop of St Andrews and Primate, of course, he could still wield considerable power, acting in the name of the Pope, speaking for the bishops, appointing to or removing from ecclesiastical office, restricting the sacraments, even excommunicating; but without virtual control of the monarch, he was a much reduced figure.

Archie had further news for his brother, even more to his satisfaction. Atholl and Buchan had sent for their niece, from Arran, to come and try to bring her brothers to some understanding, possibly the only one who could, as they both had some respect for her. This had been decided upon as they were leaving Lauder. If Mary came at once, as they urged, she ought to be here by the morrow, or the day after. Mary! At once all became brighter for John Douglas.

The meeting, part confrontation, part conference, held in one of the abbot's primary chambers, was inevitably a strange and difficult one. The numbers attending were deliberately restricted, not even all the earls being present, John only there because of his prior association with the two dukes. Atholl, Buchan, Argyll, Crawford and Archie took part, with Gray and Hailes representing the lords, and Sheves and Dunkeld the Church. Apart from the dukes, the other side had only the Earls of Douglas and Northumberland. Oddly, of them all, Albany and Gloucester seemed the most assured, their royal blood and upbringing perhaps responsible.

Albany from the first adopted the leading role, declaring that he rejoiced to see his friends there, and that he had come back to his own country in order to seek to restore and rescue it from the misgovernment and follies of recent years. He brought the good wishes of King Edward of England, who was represented by his royal brother, Richard, Duke of Gloucester, whom they all should welcome to Scotland.

There were pursed lips and grunts at this last. It was Sheves who found words first.

"His Highness of Gloucester is, to be sure, welcome. And in the name of Holy Church, I greet him," he said smoothly. "But the thousands that he has brought with him are . . . otherwise."

Gloucester shrugged that upraised shoulder, with a thin smile. "My good men are here in support of my friend Alexander," he said. "Not as any threat to Scotland. We have

354

been most careful to avoid any hurt to people or property on our long journey here."

Atholl spoke. "Highness, my lord Duke of Albany did not require any such support on his return to his friends in Scotland."

"The friends who deprived him of his offices, and forfeited and outlawed him?"

Throats were cleared at that. Argyll raised his softly lilting Highland voice, so deceptive as to his character.

"Mistakes have been made," he admitted. "On all sides. We now must remedy them. Without recourse to armed force, it is to be hoped.

"Yet you have, we are told, large armed force assembled nearby!"

"When invasion is threatened, Highness, precautions have to be taken."

"This is not invasion," Albany asserted. "We come in peace. But . . . in strength."

"English strength!" Gray growled.

"May we ask why His Grace of England sent these thousands, in peace or otherwise?" Sheves asked. "Was it to seek to enforce his claim to overlordship of Scotland?"

Breaths were held.

"Enforce, no. There was no need," Gloucester answered. "The Kings of England have always rightfully held such paramouncy. Since the days of Edward the First, our ancestor. Claiming it is nothing new. The force we brought is not to enforce *such* claims, but to support Alexander's claim to the Scottish throne."

"Unnecessary, I fear, since the duke does not require such foreign aid," Argyll said. "A pity, Highness. that you have been put to the trouble and cost!"

There were approving murmurs.

John fidgeted. He supposed that all this was bound to be voiced, but it gained nothing, got them no further. He looked meaningfully at his brother, at his side.

Archie cleared his throat. "We all here accept that this realm has been mismanaged. That the King's Grace has been ill-advised." And he glanced at Sheves. "We have taken steps to right that, in some measure. Further steps will be required, and will be taken. But, so long as this issue of overlordship or paramouncy is put forward, we are tied. The realm will not accept it. Nor will parliament."

"Accept or protest does not alter it," Gloucester said flatly. "The fact remains. The Kings of England are superiors and suzerains of the Kings of Scots."

The angry chorus of denials left no doubts as to the impasse.

Albany catching his eye, John decided to speak up. "My lord, we are here, surely, on the nation's behalf. To try to find some common ground. To better governance. And, indeed, better relations with England. Positions have been stated. What we need, I now humbly suggest, are not statements, but discussion of steps to better the situation. To move *towards* each other, not further apart. No?"

Strangely it was Sheves who first took him up. "And your suggestions to that end, my lord?"

"I hesitate, with so many more senior to myself present, to offer them. But it seems to me that steps *can* be taken to improve the position. First, surely, is to make lawful and effective the Duke of Albany's state here. At present he is forfeit and outlaw, the treason charge only postponed, not quashed. *We* cannot alter that. Only a parliament can. So a parliament must be called. Which requires King James's agreement."

Silence.

"Any gesture towards England will also require the authority of parliament," he went on. "What that might be, it is not for me to say. But nothing to effect can be done without a parliament."

"All very well," Gray grated. "But that will take time. Meantime, two armies gaze at each other!" He did not add that to hold together the huge Scots host, idle, for six weeks, and at harvest-time, would be impossible – he did not need to. Nor would the English force remain quietly camped there.

"I know it. But we must find a way to win round that.

Round this table, surely, there is a sufficiency of powers to do so?"

"The King will not call a parliament. Against his own interests."

"He must be . . . persuaded!" That was Archie.

Men eyed each other. Particularly they eyed William Sheves, who could be relied upon to seek to dissuade James from signing the necessary papers.

Atholl summed up the general feeling that enough was enough, meantime. "I say that we must consider. Consider well. All here. And meet again."

There were nods. Gloucester had the last word.

"Alexander, as King, could call your parliament," he pointed out. "Perhaps you overlook that!"

None answered him, as they dispersed.

John found that Archie was lodging up in the castle, and that he could share a room with him. As they rode together through the city streets, he spoke of Sheves in especial.

"That one may seem to be less ill-favoured towards us. But he should not be allowed to see the King. Assuredly he will seek to dissuade him from calling a parliament."

"I know it. But James may not require his dissuading."

"Yet a parliament is essential. All hangs on that. Without one, I do not see this coil unravelled. Where is Sheves biding?"

"As Archbishop of St Andrews he has a house in Edinburgh. Much of Lothian is his, to be sure. I will tell Atholl to order the castle guard not to admit him, Sheves."

"How *is* James? Has he recovered from Lauder?"

"No. He keeps his room. Will speak with none, even his uncles. Sore stricken. Is like a man wishing to die. Would that he might!"

"Almost we should be sorry for him. If he was not the King! Any other, and he would be entitled to such friends as he chose."

"No doubt. But he *is* the King, still. Suppose he *was* to die?"

"Men do not die of heartbreak."

"He might die otherwise! After all, he deserves to die. He had his own brother, Mar, foully murdered."

"No, no. Not that, never that! Mary – she could be here tomorrow, you say? That is good. Perhaps she could reach him, persuade him. If anyone can."

"That is our hope. But if not . . ."

At the castle, later, Atholl sent for the Douglas brothers. Buchan, Argyll and Crawford were with him. They wished to question John.

Albany, he was asked, how had he seemed? Did Douglasdale see him alone? Apart from Gloucester? Was he willing to heed them? Listen to reason? Wait for a parliament?

John answered that he thought that probably he was. But Gloucester was the problem. He would not go back to England empty-handed. But what could they offer him? They had heard him on this state of paramouncy. He was as strong on it as was his brother, it seemed. With that not to be considered, what could they offer him. Moneys were of little use, England being so much richer than Scotland. What else was there?

None there had an answer. They could only hope that his English army, faced by twice their numbers of Scots, with more available, might soon wish to go home. And Gloucester perceive that he could not gain his ends . . .

Not very hopefully they left it at that.

It was agreed that Sheves should not be allowed to enter the castle.

In the morning, John and Archie, with others of the lords, rode up to the Burgh Muir to keep an eye on their forces, and to impress on all that there should be no clashes with the Englishmen camped on the other side of Arthur's Seat. They must keep out of the city streets meantime, also – the town guard was instructed to deny access. The situation was like a powder-barrel which required only a spark to blow up. The Douglas contingent was given the role, under Whittinghame and Lochleven, of sheepdogs, to try to ensure that the vast flock did not stray.

Returning, with Archie heading for the abbey to see if he could have a private interview with Albany, John elected to leave him to it and make for a different destination, the Hamilton town-house in the Cowgate. His heart lifted as, entering the gateway, he saw four hard-ridden horses being unsaddled in the little courtyard. He hastened within.

Upstairs, he was met with a squeal of excitement as the Lady Anna emerged from a doorway to discover him, hurling herself into his arms with typical enthusiasm. In only moments, Mary herself was standing in the same doorway, less ebullient but warm-eyed, smiling. The man found himself disengaging from the one lady rather more hastily than was perhaps courteous, to go to the other.

No words were needed, nor forthcoming, as they held each other, Anna doing the talking. But presently that lively creature almost reluctantly took herself off, and Mary led John into the room and closed the door. This time they came into each other's arms gladly indeed.

It was some time before there was any semi-coherent talk, and longer still before, personal matters dealt with after a fashion although with promise of fuller, more comprehensive dealings to come, they got round to what had brought the princess from Arran. She knew the general situation, but not the details. John told her what he knew, what he feared, what he judged was needed, and what *she* might possibly be able to achieve. If she could prevail on James . . .

"He is so low?" she asked. "Broken, quite? Refusing all speech? Stricken by the deaths of his friends. These hangings – that was ill-done, however wretched and vile they were. It was too much . . ."

"Yes. Yet he also had your brother, and his, as shamefully slain! Was that not at their behest? Or Sheves's?"

"No doubt. But that scarcely excuses it. But . . . it is done, now. And we must seek to better the situation. I will go to James, yes. Although he may not heed me either."

"I think that only you *can* reach him. Since we must not let Sheves get to him. If you could prevail on him to see Albany. Bring them together, even in some small degree. That is vital.

But even more so, to get him to call a parliament. Only so can we win out of this pass. A parliament to restore Albany to his proper status and offices, possibly appoint him as Regent or governor for James meantime, James sick and unable to rule. After that, the crown itself would not be so hard to win. Lawfully."

"I can try, yes. But, Alexander? Will he accept this? He is headstrong. And Richard of Gloucester? He is proud, a fighter, all know. No easy man to deal with. And having come thus far . . ."

"Alexander, I think, sees what is necessary now. But Gloucester – there is the rub. He will not withdraw without some sure gain for England. Since he cannot have any consideration of paramouncy, what can he be given? I have thought and thought. *You* have the wits of us all, Mary. Set them on to this. You won Orkney and Shetland for Scotland. What can we offer Gloucester?"

She shook her lovely head.

Anna evidently considered that she had given them long enough alone, for she arrived to announce that a meal of sorts was prepared and that they must be hungry. *She* was, having ridden far. John's hunger was otherwise just then, but he did not say so. They went below.

Over the repast he told the young women of his adventures since last they were together.

It was while he was recounting his catching up with Albany at Dunbar and first meeting Gloucester, that Mary interrupted.

"Johnnie – Berwick!" she exclaimed. "Berwick-on-Tweed. Is that not a possibility? You say that the town is still in English hands, as it has been so frequently. But that the castle is not. Would Scotland lose much by letting Gloucester have Berwick? It is a fine port, I know. But we have not had full use of it for many a year. Withdraw from the castle and let the English have that. Berwick Castle is little use to us, always in a state of near-siege. If Gloucester could go back to his brother and say that he had won England Berwick, then that might serve. At little cost to us."

John blinked. "Berwick!" he said. "Berwick – there is a thought! But . . . the East March lords, Hailes, Home and the rest, would not like that. Nor Archie."

"If they misliked it so much, they could try to take it back, in the future. But it would be a small price to pay for getting rid of Gloucester. One castle! Would it not? If he will take it."

"Aye, you are right. As ever, you have the answer. Or a possible one. If parliament would agree."

"Parliament need not be asked, at this stage. It takes six weeks to call a parliament. Gloucester will not kick his heels here for six weeks. We want to be rid of him and his army at the soonest, not wait until late September. If a parliament decided that this was a mistake, it can order recapture of Berwick. But that castle has been strong enough to withstand the English. In English hands it will be no less strong. Gloucester will know that."

He nodded. "We can suggest Berwick, then. Now, when will you see James? Or would you prefer to see Albany first?"

"No. James first, I think. Until I have seen him, talked with him, I have little to tell Alexander. It is not late, yet. I will go up to the castle now."

"I will accompany you . . ."

So they rode up by the Blackfriars monastery to the High Street, and on to the citadel, where John's identity ensured no difficulty of access with the guard. They found Archie back there, eating with the other earls; and there was much satisfaction and welcome at the arrival of the princess. John was interested to discover another of her illegitimate uncles with Atholl and Buchan, their half-brother, Andrew Stewart, Bishop-Elect of Moray. He looked intelligent, but scarcely the typical cleric. He it was, indeed, who presently took Mary to the chamber where the King was as good as a prisoner, all wishing her well.

Andrew Stewart was soon back; but it was a long time before his niece reappeared.

She looked, for that woman, a little strained. To the volley of questions which greeted her she answered, level-voiced, "I

361

spoke with him, yes. And in time won some response. He is
. . . not far from deranged. Is blaming *himself* for the deaths
of his friends. Says that God has abandoned him. He is lost,
lost. But he will see Alexander. If *I* bring him. I – "

Murmurs and sighs of relief interrupted her.

"I do not say that he will agree to anything else. That he
will call a parliament. I put that to him, but he did not say
yea or nay. It was . . . difficult . . . All of it . . ."

Praise was showered upon her, but she was obviously only
anxious to be away from them all. John announced that
he would escort her back to Hamilton House. He hoped
that Archie would not expect him back to share his room
that night.

Mary was very silent on their way down to the Cowgate, and
the man respected her feelings and did not further question
her. But when she said that she was going to her bedchamber
almost at once, she clearly assumed that he would come
with her.

Mary Stewart was no temperamental or posturing character,
no creator of scenes. But after only a few moments standing
gazing out of the window, she turned and threw herself into
John's arms, to burst into deep sobs.

"Oh, Johnnie, Johnnie!" she panted. "My poor, poor,
unhappy brother! Cursed by fate and his own nature! Why,
oh why was *he* born before Alexander? It is all so wrong, so
utterly wrong. Has God indeed abandoned him?"

Holding her close, he stroked her hair. "I think . . . that
He does not . . . abandon anyone," was all that he could say.
"James will come to know it."

She shook her head under his hand, but said no more.

She remained in his embrace for a while, breathing deeply,
her breasts rising and falling against him; then straightened
up and moved over to the bed, to sit and start to remove her
riding-boots.

"Do you wish . . . that I leave you . . . tonight, my dear?"
he asked.

"No, Johnnie, no! I think that I need you more tonight
than, than even I usually do. Stay with me."

He forbore to help her to undresss, as he would have wished to do.

In bed she came to him, not hungrily but with another sort of urgency, seeking comfort, clinging to him.

"Am I a fool, Johnnie? To be . . . thus? I, who have been long so critical, ashamed, of James. *You* have sisters. If one sinned, grievously transgressed, you would still feel for her? Love her, in your heart?"

"I would, yes. It is not foolish, lass. Never think it. You helped to rear him, did you not?"

"Aye, and cannot think that I did it well, by the man he has grown into! But we were close, then . . ."

"You helped rear the other two brothers. And your sister. With none so ill results. Do not blame yourself, my heart." He was stroking her person gently, which became less than soothing for himself, whatever the effects on her.

They talked off and on for some time, John seeking to turn her thoughts away from James to Albany, whom he would take her to see in the morning. And whether it was his words or his strokings, gradually the tension and distress sank away, and Mary's body began to assert itself. Presently he progressed to actual making love, in a gentler, quieter fashion than sometimes – and was not disappointed with her response.

Thereafter kindly sleep took over, with its peace.

23

Although John went with Mary to the abbey, he could not of course remain with her for her interview with her brother. Nor did he see Gloucester, who apparently was with his troops in the park. He passed the time with Seton, that hospitable man who, as usual, suggested that they would be more comfortable at his palace, ten miles away, than up at that grim castle or in this overcrowded abbey. John reserved judgment.

When Mary came back to him she was fairly satisfied. Alexander, she said, had proved reasonable. He was prepared to wait, if Gloucester could be persuaded to depart. He had been quite taken with the idea of handing over Berwick Castle, and thought that it might just serve to save Richard's face. And he had a suggestion of his own, not in itself enough, but if added to Berwick might tip the scales. This was to give back the instalments of the dowry moneys which had been sent by Edward for his Cecilia's betrothal to the young Duke of Rothesay. Edward had sought to persuade him, Alexander, to wed that much-bargained-for princess; but he was not going to give up his wife, Anne de la Tour, of whom he had grown fond. Cecilia was mighty plain; and he did not relish Edward as father-in-law. So this might be an acceptable gesture.

John was relieved thus far.

Mary was going to conduct Alexander to see James that afternoon – and she was not looking forward to the occasion. But it had to be attempted, and she judged that only she could bring them together, however partially.

Wishing her well, John returned to his preoccupation with a parliament. On that all depended, he thought. One signature on a paper, by James, was all that was required. And of course the King's agreement to attend, when it took place, since it would be no parliament, only a convention, otherwise, and lack the necessary powers.

Mary acknowledged that this was important; but thought that the forthcoming meeting of the brothers would be difficult enough without trying to persuade James that far, in his present state.

They went back to Hamilton House.

In the afternoon, Albany arrived, alone, strange as it was for a prince to ride unaccompanied through the city streets; he did not think that he had been recognised, however. He appeared to be in fair spirits, indeed tickled a little by the notion of seeking entry to Edinburgh Castle on such a mission, to the brother who had had him imprisoned there, and from which he had made his dramatic escape, in present company, last time he was in Scotland.

John went with them up to the fortress, and wished brother and sister well in what lay ahead of them.

Archie had news for him. It had been agreed amongst the earls that Sheves must be disposed of, somehow, not only because of his baleful influence on the King but because he controlled the great revenues of the Church, which the realm needed, and to such a large extent swayed the bishops, since he could promote and demote. But they could not hang the Archbishop of St Andrews over a bridge, much as they would like to, or they would have the Vatican outraged, damning all to excommunication, and commanding all the princes of Christendom to unite in punishing Scotland. Subtler means were called for. Some had suggested poison; but, with the man disappointingly healthy, that could arouse suspicion. Since, at least on the surface, he was seeming to be more co-operative than heretofore, it was felt that they should play on this. Archbishop Graham had been got rid of by slow degrees, by Sheves himself; now they should give him some of the same treatment. Seem to accept him, but never let him be alone with the King. Pope Sixtus was reported to be seriously ill, Sheves's friend. If he died, his successor might well not be so interested in the man. And if Albany became King, or even Regent, he might well be in a position to petition the Vatican for Sheves's replacement on some ground or other. Actually, Andrew Stewart was ambitious to be Primate, and as the brother of Atholl and Buchan, uncle of the King, and a man of sharp wits, he would be a good choice. But meanwhile Sheves could well influence the churchmen's votes in parliament, which could be dangerous. So it had been decided that Argyll, who was the most wily of the earls, should be deputed to work on and with Sheves, as necessary link. Was that not a wise policy?

John was distinctly doubtful, but could offer no better suggestions at the moment, with too much other on his mind.

When, after over an hour, Mary and her brother emerged from James's room, both looked worn, unusual with Albany. But they were not despondent. However difficult their task had been, something had been achieved, it seemed. John had to wait, until Archie took Albany off to confer with the other magnates over Berwick for Gloucester, to hear details, as he escorted Mary back to the Cowgate.

At first, she told him, James would scarcely look at his brother, and Alexander had been stiff and cool; so she had had to work hard to try to establish any sort of contact between them. They never really came to address each other, although Alexander did make some attempts. Any exchange had to go through herself. It was as though John of Mar's ghost rose between them. But eventually she had got Alexander to concede that their brother's murder had been mainly the doing of Sheves and Cochrane, which James seemed prepared to accept; and after that all had been a little less difficult, although there was no real coming together. James had, at the end, agreed that Alexander should be restored to his former position, and the outlawry cancelled; and since a parliament was needed to effect this, indicated that such parliament should be called. Which implied that he would sign the necessary summons. That was as far as they had got, and it had taken a deal of reaching.

John was much heartened, and greatly praised her efforts. What now, then?

Mary assumed that her uncles would draw up the paper to summon the parliament without delay, present it to James for signature, or even perhaps get *her* to do so, then have it sent out all over the land, speedily. Even so it would be late September before an assembly could meet, which would have the advantage of harvesting being over, always important. It was to be hoped that by then James would have recovered sufficiently to attend. He was, to all intents, her uncles' prisoner here, although at present he might not fully realise this. But when he did, he might well refuse to appear at a parliament unless he was freed. In which case Sheves might be able to take him over again. There was that danger.

John shook his head over all the problems and difficulties of this involved situation. How grievous was the state of a nation with a weak King. But at least a parliament would probably be summoned. And if Gloucester accepted the Berwick offer, and returned thither, then there was progress.

Mary said that Alexander would put it to him at the earliest, and was hopeful. Another notion had come to her. If Alexander was somehow to gain the crown, or even the regency, James had to be convinced that he should abdicate, or at least retire from rule meantime. So to convince him would be difficult probably. Although it might not, in his present lowness of spirit. He had never been proud to be a monarch, she thought. And there was another problem. There was James, Duke of Rothesay, lawful heir to the throne. What of him? If Alexander replaced James, arrangements must be made for his young nephew to succeed him. Fortunately, as yet, Alexander had no children. But that might well change. So here was something else that had to be dealt with. Another decision for parliament.

John had to admit that he had rather forgotten this other James Stewart – as probably had most. Because the King and his wife saw little of each other, the Queen and her children were seldom seen, she being of a retiring nature anyway. Margaret of Denmark had her own dowry palace of Linlithgow, midway between Edinburgh and Stirling, and lived quietly there, almost like a widow. It was an odd situation, like so much else about James Stewart.

Mary now explained her notion. She would go to Linlithgow and see Margaret. Try to get her to come to Edinburgh and talk with her husband. Urge her to persuade him either to abdicate or retire, for the sake of the realm and them all. Bring the boy James with her. This might well help to further matters. Margaret was anything but the eager Queen consort, and was reputed often to have said that she wished that she could go home to Denmark. A quiet life was her desire. She might even prevail on James to take her to Denmark for a spell – which would solve a lot of problems. Although that perhaps was too much to hope for.

John acclaimed this idea. He would gladly escort her to Linlithgow.

She added that if she could persuade Alexander to go with her, and to assure Margaret that her son's eventual succession was not in doubt, whatever happened to his father, then this might greatly assist. She would put it to him. But first, if possible, they must get rid of Gloucester.

John greatly approved of Mary's choice of residence on Arran, and the opportunities that provided for himself; but he was thankful, as he judged all Scotland should be, that she had come back from her island, in the present situation. A pity that she herself could not be Regent. Although – no, that would not suit *him*, at all!

That night they spent together in considerably less stress than the one before.

It was good news. Richard of Gloucester, while reserving his position, or at least his brother's, on the issue of paramouncy, was prepared to accept the Berwick offer, plus the dowry repayments, and to retire to England, conflict avoided. He stipulated, however, that Albany himself, with other suitable representatives of authority, should accompany him, in order to ensure that the castle was handed over to him by its keeper, the Master of Hailes, without any difficulties. The obvious authority was, of course, the Warden of the East March,

Archie Douglas, or as he was now universally being called, Archibald Bell-the-Cat. And Archie insisted that John, his deputy, came too.

This seemed rather to interfere with Mary's proposed visit to Linlithgow, and she felt that the sooner Queen Margaret's influence was brought to bear on her husband, the better. However, as Linlithgow was only eighteen miles from Edinburgh, they could go there and back in one day, although it might take longer for the little Queen and her son to follow on. Albany agreed to come with them there for, after all, it would take Gloucester some time to have his army pack up and return to Berwick. So he could make both journeys.

John suggested that, in fact, it would be better if the duke and Archie did not actually *go* with the English force. Better if they could arrive at Berwick first, and prepare Hepburn and his men for the very surprising exodus, which could hardly be popular – although Hepburn might be glad enough to be relieved of his tedious duties as keeper, more or less confined in his stronghold. This was accepted, and Albany said that he would suggest to Gloucester that he delayed his departure for another day or two.

The following morning, then, the three of them, with a small escort, set off westwards on the well-trodden Stirling road, Albany in good spirits. Gloucester was co-operating and would not start for the south for a couple of days. He, Albany, was quite prepared to accept young Rothesay as eventual heir to the throne. He would do all that he could to persuade Margaret to adopt helpful attitudes, even to suggest that she took James off to Denmark for a prolonged visit "while he recovered". If *he* was Regent in the meantime, it should not be difficult to take the next step to the crown itself.

This was good, John felt, to be riding free, after so much otherwise of talk and planning, and in Mary's company. Their journey, straightforward, through the August countryside, took them just over two hours, and they were at Linlithgow's red-stone palace, above its loch, by noon. The traditional dowry place for Scots Queens, it was quite a

369

large quadrangular pile, not a castle, with its present occupant using only a small part of it, her household as modest as the rest of her.

Margaret was surprised to see them, visitors being few indeed here. But she liked Mary, although she was shy towards Albany. That could not be said of the eldest of her three sons, James of Rothesay being a lively, spirited and attractive youngster of outgoing, friendly character. It occurred to John that, in due course, he might well make an excellent monarch for Scotland. The middle boy, oddly, was another James, this because Sheves or some other astrologer had prophesied after the eldest son was born that the child would bring sorrow to his father. Assuming that this meant that the boy would die, the King, concerned that the royal name of James would go on as King of Scots, had the next son called that also.

John Douglas in fact spent the next hour or two unexpectedly. He could not include himself in the royal family discussion, and found himself adopted as playmate by young Rothesay, who no doubt suffered from a lack of male visitors and too much female and infantile company. So he seized the opportunity to show this visitor his little house which he had constructed on a small island in the loch, this involving a distinctly hazardous voyage on a raft, also of his own building, John more than once fearing that he might have to swim for it before making a landfall, in especial with the boy's vehement demonstrations with his oar in all directions. And once on the islet they had to make a fire, with a certain lack of suitable tinder for their flint and steel. For his part, John recited his ballad of St Baldred of the Bass, after describing that other island, the Craig of Bass, rather more dramatic than this one. He found himself having to promise to take the boy there one day. They became good friends in the space of that hour or two.

It was Albany's hallooing which fetched them back to the palace, to find a meal awaiting them, and the older duke anxious to be off back to Edinburgh. He and Mary seemed reasonably satisfied with their mission. The Queen gave no indication as to her reactions, a markedly undemonstrative mother for her eldest son.

They left soon after, saying that they hoped to see Margaret and Rothesay in a couple of days, the boy demanding to be taken to the Craig of Bass and wondering whether they would see any of the seals St Baldred used to feed?

Thereafter John learned that the Queen had been helpful, although doubtful as to her influence with her husband, one way or the other. But she was in favour of a retiral by James, would accept a regency by Alexander, and glad of the assurance that Rothesay would remain heir to the throne. She had shown a gleam of enthusiasm over the suggestion of a visit to Denmark, with or without her husband.

It was a fairly satisfying outcome for their journey, if not necessarily productive of major results. For John Douglas, in fact, it held a significance which he could not guess at.

Next day it was more riding, not for Mary this time, with the plan for a warning for the garrison of Berwick Castle being proceeded with, Albany accompanying Archie and John in order to bolster their authority, and to ensure that Gloucester behaved properly when he and his army arrived.

They decided that, in the circumstances, a small force of men-at-arms and mosstroopers should go with them just in case of unforeseen and difficult developments. There was a sufficiency of men assembled up on the Burgh Muir, with nothing to do, so six hundred, mainly Douglases, could well be detached.

With the English force preparing now to move off, with presents from the provost and guild-brothers of Edinburgh for their good behaviour – another idea of Mary's – the warning party, not to get involved in this movement, chose to head for Berwick not by the usual coastal route but inland through the Lammermuir Hills, by Yester and over to the Whiteadder valley, by Cranshaws and Cockburn to Chirnside and the final eight miles to the Tweed's mouth, more or less following the course of the Whiteadder all the way, some fifty-five miles in all, much of it over difficult upland country. With this hard-riding company, however, they reckoned that they could cover it in one day. They took with them a letter from the Lord Hailes to his son, the master, giving his rather dubious parental blessing to the yielding up.

They encountered no problems on their journey, even though six hundred men do not cover the ground so swiftly as do half a dozen, even mosstroopers. They reached Berwick by sundown. The Douglas banners ensured no trouble in gaining access to the castle, for the leaders at least, at this hour. Their men camped out between castle and town walls.

In the event, they experienced no difficulty in getting Sir Patrick Hepburn and his men to evacuate their stronghold, where they had felt themselves to be penned up for overlong. The master had a wife and family at his own seat of Dunsyre, and he would be glad to win back to them; no doubt his men would be happy to get home also. As to the policies of it all, he made no comment.

So next day was spent by the garrison in packing up for departure. The problem was horses, there having been no accommodation for more than two or three of the leaders' beasts in the castle, so that forty or so of the men were without transport for themselves and their baggage. Archie solved this difficulty by detaching sufficient of his hundreds to take the others up pillion behind them, and some to carry their gear. By mid-afternoon they were all away northwards, leaving the castle empty save for the newcomers.

When Gloucester and his force arrived the following forenoon it was merely a question of handing over, a very bloodless conquest of a notably strong place. It was strange that, throughout, there had been no least communication with the walled town and port so close at hand, in English hands although the population was Scots. Gloucester would probably change that.

There being nothing to detain Albany's party now, they took their leave without undue delay. The parting with Gloucester and his lords had an atmosphere of unreality about it, but no ill-feelings were in evidence. The rather sad Earl of Douglas remained with the Englishmen.

So it was back to Edinburgh. They would go by the coast road, over Coldingham Muir, and spent the night at Tantallon.

24

They found the Queen lodging with Mary in Hamilton House rather than in Edinburgh Castle which, unlike Stirling, did not run to very comfortable or commodious quarters, especially for women. Some progress had been made, they learned, in the interim. James had accepted his wife's and son's visit, if scarcely enthusiastically at least without rejection. He had more or less conceded that he was a sick man and not fit meantime for the problems of running a divided country and exercising rule. Without actually saying it, he seemed to be prepared to accept his brother in the role of temporary Regent – which implied a parliament to restore Albany's status. So the parliament summons ought to go out any day now. Mary would have liked to see this issued at once; but her uncles, and Argyll, pointed out that with the Scots army still assembled nearby, and so many of its leaders involved in a parliament, they must be given time to go to their homes and see to their affairs, especially at harvest-time, before returning here for the session, since they could hardly be expected to hang about Edinburgh for six idle weeks. So the intention now was to call the parliament for the beginning of December.

Mary and John thought that this was a mistake, but Albany did not seem to see it so. It would allow him to canvass all necessary support for his cause before the parliament.

Mary decided to return to Arran once the Queen went back to Linlithgow. John would wish to go with her, but Archie was adamant that he should remain at his side during this hanging-fire period, when who knew what might happen. William Sheves could not be written off as no longer a menace. And the East March required a Warden's attention, and he himself wished to stay close to Albany and the King's uncles until matters were stabilised. So John must fulfil his role as deputy.

Meantime another demand arose for John Douglas. James, Duke of Rothesay required to be taken to see the Craig of Bass, and was urgent about it, finding this hanging about his depressed father's room dull work indeed. So, with the Queen's permission, it was decided to have a brief trip back to Tantallon, and John had no great difficulty in persuading Mary to come with them. Thereafter the Queen and her son would return to Linlithgow and Mary to Arran.

If it had been good to ride free to Linlithgow, how much better this escape with the boy, to his own cliff-top home above the Norse Sea waves. Rothesay scarcely drew breath throughout the twenty-mile ride, exclaiming at all that he saw, demanding what this was and that, declaring that this East Lothian was much more exciting than was the West wherein was Linlithgow. Traprain Law drew admiring comment, and when they reached North Berwick with its spectacular conical hill rising over it, he would have climbed it there and then had this been permitted. But when, only half a mile further on, he suddenly came in sight of the Craig of Bass out in the sea, the boy was for once all but struck dumb with wonder. Not for long, of course. Soon he was explaining that he had thought that it was an *island*. This was not an island, it was a rock, a great big, mighty' rock rising out of the waves. He had never seen the like. Could they go out to it? When?

Tomorrow, if the weather remained kind, he was promised.

Their arrival at Tantallon produced more exclamation, with its enormous curtain walls, great gatehouse keep, tall towers and multiple moats. Their welcome was, of course, joyous. Mary was fond of the place and its occupants – Elizabeth was her sister-in-law and good friend. She was delighted with Archie's two very small sons, whom she had never seen. Her own nephew was made much of, and started to explore right away, the cliffs in particular fascinating him. Could they climb down to the water? A rope, perhaps? And these birds circling around? The ones that dived into the sea?

And the ones that seemed to float about without flapping their wings? Could they see any seals from the cliff-tops? And so on. John perceived that he was going to have a busy couple of days.

Although it was late afternoon, activities started right away. The heir to the throne would have been for the Bass there and then – after all, it might not be good weather tomorrow. But John pointed out that that trip would take most of the day. The next demand was for St Baldred. Did he feed his seals out on the Bass? How could he, with its great cliffs dropping sheer into the sea? It fell to be explained that the seal-feeding took place nearer at hand, that the saint did not actually live on the Bass but used it as his *diseart*. That, it had to be explained, was the term for a Celtic saint's place for occasional retirement for peaceful renewal and repair – they all had them. His Highness would know of the town over in Fife called Dysart, quite a big port these days but once the *diseart* of a St Serf; not the only one, for he had one in an islet in Loch Leven. This irrelevant information was impatiently dismissed. Where, then, did Baldred live? His ballad had said something about a cradle, did it not? Did that mean that he had a baby. No, it was acknowledged gravely, that was a rock, not a big one, about four miles down the coast. Perhaps he fed seals there, at the mouth of the River Tyne. But there was another one, near at hand. They could actually see it from the castle here, known as St Baldred's Boat. It was a sort of a knob of rock at the end of a reef, reachable at low tide, a skerry where the saint used to go, supposedly to commune with God and the seals, for which he seemed to have a great love. Did he see it? Just beyond a lumpish green mound, which looked like an island but was not, called the Gegan, which meant a dwarf, probably the Bass's dwarf child! And below this there was the smallest harbour in all Scotland.

Nothing would do but that they must go at once and see all these wonders. Female preoccupation with a meal could wait. They could eat at any time, could they not?

The pair set off.

John took the boy to see the small priory of Auldhame, home

of a few monks, less than a mile south of the castle, on another and less steep cliff-top, with a magnificent sandy beach below, which drew more cries of appreciation. The priory was alleged to be built on the site of Baldred's original cell, this back in the eighth century. This did not greatly interest the boy, who wanted to see the seal-rock and to race along the splendid beach. Could they go swimming? Not today, he was told, not if they wanted to visit Baldred's Boat, the Gegan and the little harbour.

Fortunately the tide, although coming in, was two-thirds out. Finding their way down the steep slope to the shore, they were able to pick a slippery route over the seaweed, mussel-beds and rock-pools of a lengthy reef which extended seawards to end in a slightly higher hump, flat-topped, which was the Boat. Sadly not a single seal was to be seen, much to the prince's disappointment. They did see great solan geese, or gannets, diving for fish, however, quite close at hand, and even one rising out of the water with a flapping fish firmly in its beak, which much enthralled the youngster. He was told that there were thousands of these birds out on the Craig of Bass. They were not really geese, of course, but certainly large enough to be so, with a six-foot wing-span. All the whiteness that they could see on the cliffs out there was their droppings. This compensated for the sad lack of seals. They returned to the shore before the tide cut them off.

Northwards along the beach, back towards the castle, they approached the curious lumpish mound, red stone below but grass-grown on top, which was in fact linked to the land by a neck of rock, although it had looked like an island, the Gegan or Dwarf. But before they reached this there rose an isolated little stack of the same red rock, tall as three men but only a few feet wide, which of course had to be climbed, a challenge. John had so frequently been impelled to do this himself, as a lad, that he could by no means prohibit it now; indeed they both clambered up, to balance precariously on the summit, clutching each other, amidst laughter. Then down, and on to the next challenge of the Gegan, when the boy was distracted by an extraordinary feature close by. This was a deep oblong basin or trough cut in the sheer rock, obviously by human hands, straight-sided and angled, water-filled and containing two boats. There was no room for more. This was the smallest harbour in the land, John asserted. How the rock had been cut away so sheerly, cleanly, was a mystery. Nor whether it had been there in St Baldred's time, although there were stories that he had made it miraculously to keep his coracle in for his voyages out to the Bass. The monks used it now for their fishing trips. The curious dog-legged entrance made getting in and out of it difficult, although there was a knack in it; but it did protect the little haven from heavy seas. And the seas on this coast could be heavy indeed.

After that, climbing the Gegan was rather tame. But a slab of rock which projected over the waves at the far end provided the required excitement, and John had to hold his breath, and grab for the boy's hand, as Scotland's heir started out to dance a jig thereon.

Chatter on the way back to the castle was incessant. Nor did it stop there.

The evening by the hall fire was pleasing relaxation, with Rothesay's yawns fairly quickly enabling his aunt to pack him off to bed without too much protest. Tomorrow, the Bass!

That night was bliss for at least two of the company.

Blessedly the August day dawned calm and fair, although overcast. No delay was permitted, the prince having been up and clamorous from an early hour, even breakfast considered an irrelevance. So it was off to the North Berwick harbour for a boat, Mary and Alison, the youngest sister, coming with them.

With the sea comparatively calm, and only a couple of miles to go, there was no need to use the Douglas barge and its crew, an ordinary fishing-boat being adequate, with a couple of oarsmen, these being much amused by the boy's excitement and questions. He found a long-dead and flattened flatfish on the floorboards of the craft, and was for taking this back to eat, but was persuaded to throw it overboard instead.

The gannets were circling everywhere, and diving into the sea with innumerable small waterspouts, this producing queries as to how they did it. Could they see the fish under water? How deep did they go? And would not the fish have swum away some distance from where they were when the dive started? None of which the boy's elders were really competent to explain, although John tried, saying that if they counted the seconds that the birds remained under water, they could guess that some swimming was also entailed.

As they neared the Bass, with the sheer size of it becoming ever more apparent and awesome, the legions of the circling fowl, the screechings and smells preoccupying all, even though John and his sister were used to it. The different types of birds had to be identified and their names spelled out – cormorants and shags or black doukers, fulmars, gulliemaws, kittiwakes or tarrocks, puffins or sea-coulters, and the like.

They rowed close in under the soaring precipices, which John declared to be nearly four hundred feet in height, and there, on the north side, he was able to point out the entrance to a great cave – although that was through the rock, with another mouth at the other side. The inevitable demand that they should sail through this had to be refused. It was pitch-dark in there, the passage twisted, narrower and wider, and the tide surged. Boats *could* navigate it, it was declared, but lights, torches, would be required, and very calm waters. In storms they could hear the hollow booming of it even away at Tantallon.

Disappointment was forgotten, however, when, on ledges near the tunnel mouth they saw no fewer than five seals basking, which only flapped their way into the water when the boat drew very close, and even then two of them bobbed up to examine the visitors interestedly, like round-eyed and mustachioed, plump old men, to Rothesay's delight. Could they not feed them, he asked, like St Baldred did? Unfortunately they had brought no suitable food with them. They should have kept that flatfish, he declared.

Rowing clockwise round the rock, they came to the southern, landward side, where they passed the yawning jaws of the other end of the tunnel. Soon thereafter they came to the landing-place, if so it could be called, consisting only of weed-hung ledges and a ladder-like ascent of the rock face, which had Mary pretending to be scared, although she jumped ashore nimbly and, hitching up her skirts, clambered up after the boy effectively enough. Alison Douglas was no less agile, much to the approval of the boatmen.

This south side was, indeed, less sheer than the rest. They came to a sort of terrace part-way up, where it was said that Baldred had his tiny shelter, although they could trace no sign of it. Further up they reached a fair-sized slantwise apron of grass dotted with a plant which John named as mallow, saying that he did not know of the like growing anywhere else. Then on, the prince away ahead despite calls for care, right to the summit of the rock, now amidst screeching, protesting fowl swooping around them, the smell all but overpowering.

Up on that dizzy platform, the boy had to be physically restrained from going too close to the edges, with that breathtaking drop to the waves, especially with birds all but buffeting them at this invasion of their kingdom. The vistas held the adults' eyes, not so much straight downwards, like Rothesay's, but far and wide, out to the Isle of May, eight miles to the north-east, but seeming so much nearer from this viewpoint, up Forth to its scattered islands and the far-away cone of Arthur's Seat, southwards to the great headland of St Abbs and the eagle's-nest wreckers' hold of Fast Castle and, of course, due landwards to Tantallon, which looked a comparatively modest place from here.

It was Mary who drew attention to something much nearer at hand, the seaweed scattered about in quantities here on the rock-top. She asked whether this could have been brought up by the birds and dropped here; but John said that he did not see why the creatures should do so – they did not eat seaweed nor use it for their nesting. No, it was the waves which were responsible. Hundreds of feet up as this was, in winter storms, especially easterly gales, the seas could break right up here in clouds of spray, bringing the weed with them.

They stayed up there, savouring it all, for some time. Rothesay went to see if he could pat one of the multitudinous solan geese roosting on the cliff-top ledges, but came back presently with a bleeding finger, saying that he had been pecked, but nowise concerned.

They returned, carefully necessarily, to their boat, where the oarsmen had filled in the time line-fishing, with half a dozen flatfish to show for it, which they presented to the young prince to compensate for the one he had had to throw overboard. He said that he would see how many of these he could eat for his supper.

It was back to North Berwick, all well pleased with themselves. The boy declared that there was still time for a swim on that splendid beach. He was good at swimming, doing a lot of it at Linlithgow, out to his island. The ladies, urged to participate, declined gracefully. Enough was enough, for one day. In the morning, perhaps.

But the morning was wet, and although the prince was nothing loth, his elders were not tempted. And when the rain cleared, at midday, a ride down the coast to see St Baldred's Cradle and other features at the mouth of the Tyne took priority.

Even though the cradle itself was a little disappointing after all the other wonders, James of Rothesay announced, when they left for Edinburgh next morning, that he wished that he could persuade his mother to come and live at Tantallon instead of Linlithgow.

Two days later, John, with Mary, Anna and escort, accompanied the Queen and prince back to Linlithgow, and an almost tearful parting with the latter, the man having to promise that it would not be long before he returned, to take the boy on further expeditions, Margaret obviously grateful. Thereafter the Arran party started on their long ride south by west, hoping to reach Hamilton, thirty-five miles, by nightfall, and on to Irvine and the sea crossing next day.

At the pier at Irvine, John said his reluctant farewells. He would come to Arran again just as soon as he could contrive it, he hoped before the parliament in early December which Mary would endeavour to attend.

25

John spent a rather frustrating autumn, in the Borders most of the time. He did not enjoy being Deputy Warden, seeking to settle disputes, acting the judge, investigating unlawful activities, mediating in feuds – and all in the name of his brother whom he seldom saw and who probably would have acted differently anyway. He could have refused to do it, of course, and have Archie appoint some other as deputy; but he supposed that it was some sort of duty he owed, just to whom he was not sure. And admittedly he could return to Tantallon fairly frequently, if only for brief visits. He would infinitely have preferred, needless to say, to have been in Arran.

It was on one of these visits home, in late October, that he found Archie there, and from him learned something of events on the national scene, however many rumours he had heard circulating in the borderland.

Albany was behaving well, showing himself around the country, being gracious, making friends amongst the provosts and royal burgh representatives who would have a voice in parliament, carefully cultivating Provost Bertram of Edinburgh, an influential and wealthy merchant. This they all conceived as necessary, for William Sheves was seeking to stir up the churchmen against Albany, and the bishops and mitred abbots had votes in parliament also. Bertram was induced to gather quite a substantial sum from his own and other burghs and guilds to add to the moneys being sent to the Curia at Rome to further Andrew Stewart's application to replace Sheves as archbishop; also to help repay the dowry moneys for Edward's Cecilia. They were hopeful about the archbishopric, for Pope Sixtus was failing fast and the Vatican was being ruled by a committee of cardinals under Giovanni

Battista Cibo who would almost certainly be the next pontiff. So the money was directed there. If Stewart was Primate, it would make a vast difference, and the money shortages would be at an end, with the Church's riches available again. Another excellent move was that they had got the King to sign a document limiting the attendance at this parliament to commissioners whose annual income from lands was over one hundred pounds. This would greatly lessen the number of lairds, knights and lesser barons attending, the votes of many of whom were doubtful. Also Avondale, a weary old man now, had been persuaded to resign as Chancellor, and Bishop James Laing of Glasgow, a resenter of Sheves, appointed in his place. All of which was excellent – even though John doubted the legality and probity of much of it, especially this of limiting parliamentary attendance.

James himself, it seemed, was being less difficult, not exactly co-operative but accepting meantime that he was in his uncles' care and lacking friends, however humiliating a situation for the King of Scots. He had even agreed to sign a letter to Sheves urging him to consider resigning the primacy – not that that man was likely to do so. All would depend on this parliament.

John agreed, but somehow returned to his duties in the south less than assured.

The great day duly dawned, and John made his way to Edinburgh the previous evening, heading of course for Hamilton House to see if Mary was there. She was, without Anna this time, and they made a joyous reunion, problems of state for the moment in abeyance. They did discuss the situation of course, with Mary uneasy about the way things were going; but it was all very much subordinate to more personal matters. They were blest in each other, and they had had three months and more of parting, John's apologies for not having been able to visit Arran in the interim accepted. There were other Hamiltons using the house, but John managed to make his discreet way to Mary's room when the others were abed.

The parliament, it appeared, was to be held in the Abbey

383

of the Holy Rude, not as usual in the castle's Great Hall, this as a gesture towards the Church and also because there would be fewer attending and in order to make this less evident. Also, a special demonstration had been organised, to engender popular feeling and support. James and Albany were to ride together in splendid procession through the city streets, from the castle to the abbey, with a train of nobles and led by Provost Bertram and his bailies, with the deacons of the various trade guilds and the Town Guard. This, the first appearance of the sovereign in public since Lauder, and with his brother at his side, ought to soothe the populace's fears and doubts, and further Albany's acceptance back to grace and favour.

John did not join in that procession, preferring to escort Mary to the abbey in person. They went first to the foot of the Canongate, however, there to wait amongst the noisy crowd and duly watch the spectacle, the like unseen in this reign. The cavalry, when it arrived, certainly drew the cheers of the citizenry, resplendent indeed, although James looked tense, almost furtive again and made no response to the plaudits. Albany, magnificently attired, was all smiling gallantry and flourish, making very obvious who should be the monarch.

Thereafter John led Mary not to the great abbey-church itself but to the smaller Lady Chapel which opened off the east transept, and which would not look half empty as would the vast cathedral-like fane, with the present modest turnout. There was, of course, no minstrels' gallery in the chapel, so the few selected onlookers, ambassadors, distinguished visitors, and Mary, had to occupy the choristers' seating, which made them seem more prominent than usual, or was apt. John left her there, to take his own seat, beside Seton, in the body of the chapel.

When proceedings started and the earls made their entry, it was noticeable that Argyll was not amongst them. He had been less evident of late, to be sure, having been given the duty of keeping an eye on Sheves. The latter did not appear, either, to take his preferred stand behind the throne, did not come at all. And there were a number of other notable absentees. But Argyll's non-appearance was strange.

The new order was emphasised when James Laing, Bishop of Glasgow, came in to take his place at the Chancellor's table at the front of the chancel. And the trumpeting of the Lord Lyon's herald did sound over-loud in this smaller space, as the monarch entered, last of all, to make for his throne-like chair before the altar. He looked no more at ease, nor happy, than usual. There was no sign of Albany yet.

The Chancellor, a heavily built, stern-faced prelate, himself opened the proceedings with prayer, and besought the Almighty's blessings and guidance on their deliberations and decisions. Then, declaring that all rejoiced that His Grace, a sick man, had made this effort to be present in order that the important assembly should indeed be a parliament and no mere convention, he urged all concerned to keep their motions and remarks as brief as possible, so that His Grace should not be wearied unduly, and able to remain with them – a subtle touch.

Livingstone, Bishop of Dunkeld, rose to say how rejoiced all loyal subjects were to see their sovereign-lord present, and at least somewhat improved in health, this to polite murmurs of approval. It set John wondering, however, for Livingstone had been in the Sheves camp, indeed promoted by him. Was this perhaps a move to indicate that James was sufficiently well not to require any regency or governorship? It could be.

The Chancellor went on without delay. The principal business of parliament on this occasion, he said, was the position of the King's royal brother, Alexander, Duke of Albany. As all would recollect, he had been accused of working against His Grace, had been taken into custody and had made escape therefrom and fled to France, being thereupon accused of treason by some. Parliaments had twice, wisely, postponed making any such condemnation, for lack of due evidence, but in the interim had ordered forfeiture of positions and lands, together with outlawry, until the duke should return to Scotland to answer such charges. As they all knew, His Highness had now done this, refuted all such indictments and returned to the affections of his royal brother. Consequently, it was the concern of parliament to consider the lifting of the charges and reinstatement of the Duke of Albany in his due positions and offices.

Almost before he got that out, Atholl was on his feet proposing it as a motion. His brother Andrew, Bishop of Moray, promptly seconded.

Bishop Laing asked whether there was any contrary motion – which was, he suggested, not to be expected.

Silence.

"I therefore declare," he intoned, "that His Highness the Duke of Albany's outlawry is banished and lifted, and his offices restored. And that he be asked to enter and take his due place in this parliament."

The trumpeter sounded and, amidst cheers, Lyon led in the duke, looking suitably modest however splendid in appearance. He bowed to the throne.

"My lord Duke, do you wish to address the parliament?" the Chancellor asked.

"Only to express my thanks and goodwill for this reinstatement. And to promise all aid in the good governance of the realm, as is my simple duty," Albany said. "In the present state of His Grace's health, the less of talk the better."

That went down well. But John was not the only one surprised, obviously, when the duke, instead of going to stand behind his brother, as he had been used to do, went to sit beside his uncles on the earls' benches.

Somehow, James seemed very much alone up there, which no doubt was the intention.

The Chancellor, who clearly had been well schooled, went on. "The offices borne by the Duke of Albany heretofore included Lieutenant of the Borders and Lord High Admiral, the former carrying with it the keepership of the royal castle of Dunbar. Since parliament has lifted all penalties on His Highness, these offices remain in his hands. Is that agreed?"

No dissenting voice was raised.

Laing resumed. "In His Grace the King's present state of

health, it is felt by his earls and councillors that he should be aided and supported in matters of rule and governance by a senior figure whom the realm will recognise and accept as suitable. The said magnates believe that none could be more suitable than His Grace's royal brother. Therefore it is proposed that the Duke of Albany be given the further task and responsibility, and nominated governor, with authority to act in the King's royal name, until such time as His Grace can resume fullest rule. Regency refers to a guardian for a young or incapacitated monarch. The term governor, indicating governance, is considered more correct. Is this agreed?"

Buchan proposed it as motion and Archie seconded.

There was a pause. This was the crux of it all. If parliament accepted this, the rest should follow. No single voice was raised, notably not the King's. John glanced over at Mary, who nodded. Then at Archie, who was grinning. After all, much of this was of his contriving.

"So be it," the Chancellor said. "These governor's duties will involve the duke in much travel and expense. And the dukedom of Albany, whilst lofty and honourable, bears scant lands and rental wealth. It is proposed, therefore, that to assist His Highness in his new responsibilities, the royal earldom of Mar and the Garioch, vacant since the sad death of his royal brother, be conferred upon him. This is in His Grace's gift, and has been acceded to."

Men exchanged glances. No mention of Cochrane as Earl of Mar, now.

The Chancellor seemed to consult his papers. "There is one last issue which may concern His Highness of Albany, Earl of Mar and the Garioch. It is on the grave matter of the realm's peace. The King of England has sent an envoy to His Grace saying that he is displeased that the fact of his paramouncy has been rejected in Scotland. He claims that he *is* Lord Paramount, whether it is accepted here or no. He is not satisfied with the ceding of Berwick-on-Tweed and the return of the dowry moneys. He demands acknowledgment of his paramouncy. Or he will take steps to assert it. He . . ."

Shouts and cries filled the chapel. Even fists were clenched and shaken.

When he could make himself heard, Laing went on. "In these circumstances, the realm must again be prepared to defend itself, forces be readied, and commanders chosen. Leadership in war, as well as in peace, may be necessary. It is therefore proposed that the Duke of Albany, skilled in warfare, be appointed Lieutenant-General of the realm, so that he can ensure preparedness and readiness in the event of war, before the campaigning season is on us."

"I so move," the Earl of Crawford cried.

"And I second." That was the Lord Gray.

That was a surprise to John, and no doubt to others. Although it made sense, from Albany's point of view, gaining him almost complete power. His surprise was furthered, as was that of all.

From the back of the chapel, a voice spoke up, a somewhat reedy and quavering voice, but not uncertain as to assertion – and well known to all there. It was the former Chancellor, the Lord Avondale, an illegitimate Stewart himself.

"This parliament is not competent to make any such appointment," he said. "The King alone can make a Lieutenant-General of his forces. All manpower of lords and feudal tenants of the crown is at the disposal of the King's Grace and him only. He alone may call upon his earls, lords and subjects to rise in arms. And he alone may appoint an overall commander for such army."

That produced a considerable stir, and no little frownings. But none was in a position to suggest that the former Chancellor, expert in matters of procedure and feudal observances, did not know what he was talking about.

Laing was clearly offput. He looked from his mentors, the earls, and round at the King.

Avondale was not finished, not quite. "My lord Chancellor – with your permission, I would ask whether His Grace does so appoint the Duke of Albany to be Lieutenant-General of his forces?"

388

James sat unspeaking, unmoving, although his fingers tap-tapped on the arm of his chair.

The moments passed, but the monarch remained silent, all eyes upon him. He looked almost alarmed, but that was all.

It was an extraordinary situation, none quite sure how to proceed. It was clear that James was making some assertion of himself and his position, at last. He was still the King. If there were protests and objections now, he could rise and walk out – and it would no longer be a parliament, and would lose its authority. The new Chancellor had been brought up sharp by the old one.

Into the awkward and prolonged pause, Albany did his best to bring the proceedings back under control.

"My lord Chancellor," he said, "His Grace's will and decision in this matter must be our law. He may wish to consider. But, meanwhile, steps must be taken, if not to call to arms again, at least to send answer to Edward of England. We cannot ignore his threats and challenges." It was strange to hear the Duke, who had allegedly offered Edward the paramouncy, speaking thus. "I suggest that an embassage be sent to England, to tell Edward that we will resist his claims to overlordship to the last drops of our blood. But there may be other matters which we can offer, to appease him in some measure . . ."

"What?" Gray shouted, ignoring the Chancellor.

"I have not answers to that here and now, my lord Chancellor. I did not come prepared for this! But no doubt it will not be beyond our wits to devise something to offer and for an embassage to take."

Laing recovered himself. "Yes, my lord Duke. And Your Grace. Is it agreed then, that envoys be sent to the King of England to seek to reduce this latest threat? What to offer him to be decided later."

None there could object to that, and hurriedly the Chancellor went on.

"His Grace's new governor is going to require moneys, considerable moneys, to order the realm, much having been neglected of late, necessarily. I have been Treasurer, and am

389

well aware of the problems and needs. But I cannot be both Chancellor and Treasurer. Therefore, I propose in this pass, that a new Lord High Treasurer be appointed. And, since it is important that he should work in co-operation with myself, as Chancellor, as well as the fact that he has had much experience in the handling of moneys, I would suggest the Suffragan Bishop of Glasgow, Master George Carmichael, at present treasurer of my diocese, for the position."

Not all there, perhaps, would perceive that this was rather more than just a convenient arrangement for the said officers-of-state. Glasgow, the largest and wealthiest single diocese after St Andrews – which was why it had a suffragan – had long sought to be independent of the latter, not to come under the sway of the Primate. Indeed it had petitioned popes more than once to this effect. Now, if both Chancellor and Treasurer were leaders of Glasgow, it must greatly strengthen the diocese's position *vis-a-vis* the primacy, and in the Church at large. And also strike one more blow against William Sheves.

No objection was voiced. There was only a moderate turn out of bishops and mitred abbots anyway. The treasurership had always been considered to be a position for a churchman, since indeed much of the nation's revenues came via the Church. John was prepared for Livingstone, Bishop of Dunkeld, to question this move, but he did not.

From the spectators' seats, near to Mary, Bishop-Coadjutor Carmichael rose, bowed, and sat again.

Looking relieved, for so stern seeming a man, the Chancellor asked if there was any other business – keeping in view the fact that His Grace's strength must not be overtaxed this day.

Barely giving time for anything such to be voiced, His Grace rose and hurried out.

The so-vital parliament was over and done with. It had achieved most of what had been hoped for; but apart from that curious non-action by the monarch, it had seemed just something of an anticlimax.

Outside the Lady Chapel, John and Mary began to discuss

it all, on their way back to Hamilton House. Although superficially it seemed to have gone fairly well, both felt a certain unease, the woman in especial. A number of points concerned them. First, of course, James's refusal to appoint his brother as Lieutenant-General, even though he had apparently swallowed all the rest. Did this indicate some stiffening of resistance? Before, he had been under his uncles' control and Albany's influence. Here, in the parliament, he had been on his own, lonely yes, but able to take an important decision. That did not bode well for the future, perhaps.

Then there was Argyll's strange absence. He was quite the most clever of the earls, and if this staying away was deliberate, then it could represent disharmony, a possible break with Albany's party. The Campbells had a reputation for side changing. And Bishop Livingstone? Had *he* changed sides? At least, this bringing forward of Laing's suffragan to be Treasurer was in their favour, for with Glasgow very much against Sheves and his primacy, to have both its leaders controlling the purse strings was advantageous.

King Edward's renewed hostility was disappointing and significant – for it would seem to indicate disagreement with Gloucester for being prepared to accept only Berwick as the price for English withdrawal. This of sending an embassage to him was all very well, but what had they to offer, since paramouncy was not to be considered, or any move in that direction? John, for one, could think of nothing. Was it to be war, then? Not just on a modified scale, as the late move, but outright full war? At this stage, with Albany still some distance from gaining the throne, war would be a dire development, quite apart from the bloodshed and turmoil.

Mary said that she too had been racking her wits for some answer. Alexander himself might have some plan, but she would doubt it. One slender notion had occurred to her, but whether it would serve was doubtful. Tynedale.

The man looked questioningly.

Did he not know the story of Tynedale, she asked? Tynedale in Northumberland. In England, yet in theory coming under the Scottish crown. Confessing ignorance, almost disbelief, John was told a strange tale.

Long ago, in the twelfth century, King Stephen of England, the Conqueror's grandson, and a weak monarch, had ceded Tynedale, west of Newcastle and over into Cumbria, not exactly to Scotland but to the Scottish crown in the person of King David the First, for services rendered. This cession had never been considered to be of much value by the Scots kings, for quite a wide belt of England separated it from Scotland, and any efforts to impose overlordship, collect rents, dispense justice and the like, would be difficult in the extreme and not worth the trouble. Mary had been told about it, as a girl, by her father, who had wondered whether he could do anything about it. There had been a famous court case, in the 1270s, when the Sheriff of Northumberland refused to give judgment in a thieving charge because the offence had been committed in Tynedale, out of the realm of England and within the jurisdiction of the King of Scots. And the great Bruce, immediately after Bannockburn's victory, had led a strange progress down to Tynedale, even taking his wife and daughter with his great train, not in war but to demand his due fealties from the landholders there, as a means of bringing Edward the Second to a peace conference. The issue had never been repealed, by any mutual consent. So . . . ?

John shook his head in wonderment. To think that he had never heard of this! So strange a situation. Probably *this* Edward had never so much as heard of it either! She meant, if James, or Albany, now offered to return Tynedale to England, it might mean something to Edward?

She did not know. He might well scoff at it. Yet his councillors might see it as of value, a lawful defect in English sovereignty, and advise acceptance. And it would be at no real cost to Scotland. It would be something for the proposed embassage to offer.

Later the pair went up to the castle to put this notion to Albany and his supporters.

They found an atmosphere of satisfaction prevailing in the citadel, their own doubts not echoed there – although there *was* wondering about Argyll. The assumption was that now all ought to go more or less according to plan. Albany was governor of the realm, and held the power of the crown. Only a matter of time until he held the crown itself. This of English Edward was annoying certainly, and unexpected, but they could deal with that no doubt, either by negotiation or by armed force. Edward was a great threatener, but less of a warrior.

When Mary asked about the proposed embassage, it turned out that this was already being arranged, and none other than Archie was to lead it, because of his links with Gloucester. So far, however, no useful bribes had been devised other than monetary ones – which, in the circumstances, despite the churchmen's generosity, could not be seen as substantial in Edward's eyes.

Mary's suggestion about Tynedale was greeted with a mixture of astonishment and approval, although some doubts were expressed as to whether the Scots tenure there still existed, by the few who had even heard of it hitherto. But it was agreed that it was worth a try; and they would seek to think up something else as well. The envoys must not delay long in departing.

John was rather dreading that Archie would require his own attendance on this mission, but was spared that, being needed to continue to deputise as Warden meantime – which in itself was less than welcome, since he had been hoping to get over to Arran for a spell.

They learned more. James was proving difficult again, still withdrawn and not keeping up any pretence of affection towards his brother. He was, it seemed, not unnaturally desirous of getting away from this Edinburgh Castle, and demanding that he be allowed to return to Stirling. Albany, anxious now probably to demonstrate his power, but also to seem not unkind towards his unhappy brother, was inclined to accede to this, although his uncles were doubtful. But Chancellor Laing thought that the King would be as well at Stirling as here, provided that Sheves was denied any access. Mary proposed that if the Queen could be persuaded to go to

Stirling with her husband, she might well be a good influence on him in this situation, and might even convince him that a visit to Denmark, with her, would provide a desirable interlude.

This was accepted, and Mary enrolled to accompany her brothers to Linlithgow, on their way to Stirling, to use her good offices with Margaret. Mary pointed out that John had made an excellent impression on the Queen and her son, and might be a valuable ally in this – to which that man made no least objection.

So next day they would head westwards with James, while Archie set off southwards for England, before the winter hard weather set in. John was surprised to learn that Bishop Livingstone of Dunkeld was being suggested as one of the envoys – so he now indeed appeared to have severed his links with Sheves. The other ambassadors were to be the Lord Gray and a Sir James Liddell of Halkerston, a noted and experienced negotiator who had served as envoy on various occasions and would act as adviser. The Stewart uncles would remain in charge at Edinburgh, meantime.

Hamilton House beckoned.

The royal party's reception at Linlithgow Palace was reasonably warm on Margaret's part and ecstatic on young Rothesay's. The Queen was not eager to leave her favoured quarters there for the very different atmosphere of the rock-top fortress of Stirling; but she could scarcely refuse to join her husband, even if he showed little enthusiasm either. But his eldest son did, at least – any change from the female-oriented atmosphere at Linlithgow was welcome, especially if Lord Johnnie was going too.

It would take a day or two for the Queen and her ladies to pack up and move. Meanwhile the others would continue on the further eighteen miles to Stirling. The boy duke clamoured to come also, not out of any evident affection for his father it might be said; John Douglas seemed to be the magnet. The Queen made no objection.

By darkening, then, the travellers were at the principal royal citadel of Scotland. It was a considerable time since any of them had been there.

Mary, back in her old quarters, with John – and her nephew, as he demanded – declared that she would wait until the Queen arrived, to see her suitably settled in to the male-dominated establishment, and would then depart for Arran and her own family. John, for his part, was left in no doubt that *his* duties would be to keep the lively and adventurous heir to the throne happy in the interim. What was there to see and do at this Stirling?

The next couple of days, then, were active ones, playing hurly-hackit – that is sledging down a steep, grassy slope on ox-skulls – visiting the sites of the great battles of Stirling Bridge and Bannockburn, where Scotland's freedom had been forged, meeting Abbot Henry at Cambuskenneth Abbey, and exploring the wildernesses of the Flanders Moss which stretched between them and the Highland foothills. Fortunately the weather for December was mild, with even blinks of sunshine. Mary came with them on the first day, but left them to it on the second. The boy, throughout, was as good company as he was demanding and tireless. It was a real friendship which developed between them.

On their return to the castle the second day, it was to find the Queen arriving and settling in – to only moderate rapture on her eldest son's part. But they had one more day's adventuring, to ride the Gargunnock and Fintry Hills, whilst Mary attended on Margaret. Then, the following morning, it was farewells, John to escort Mary the long journey down to Irvine and the ferry over the Firth of Clyde. It was quite an emotional parting, those being left at Stirling less than joyful, the Queen and her son both fighting back tears, and the King detached, seeming scarcely with them. Albany would accompany his sister as far as Falkirk, with his troop of guards, when he would head eastwards back to Edinburgh, and Mary and John continue on south by west.

The second parting, at Falkirk, was not emotional at all,

Albany, governor of the realm, cheerfully off to take up his duties. John was now the glum one, with only one more day and night with Mary to look forward to meantime, and then the Borders.

26

Winter set in in earnest just before Christmas, and although
John managed to get up to Tantallon for the Yuletide
celebrations, with Archie still absent in England, the weeks
which followed were trying for Border travel, the high ground
snow-covered, rivers in flood, fords difficult to cross, and
icy conditions hard on the horses. The Merse coastal area
was less difficult, but John could not confine his activities
to this, with the worst reiving, raiding and general Border
lawlessness tending to take place in the upland parts. He was
kept busy.

He gleaned very little news of what went on outside this
world of its own. He did learn that Albany was occasionally
at Dunbar Castle, which was his seat as Lieutenant of the
Border; but he was no doubt too busy with his other duties
of ruling the realm to venture further south.

It was not until mid-January that he had a visit, unexpected,
from William, Lord Crichton who, to escape the King's wrath
for marrying his younger sister, had exiled himself and his
Margaret in his remote northern barony of Frendraught,
but with Albany's rise to power had returned to his own
lands of Crichton, in Lothian, and kept in touch with the
Douglas brothers. He brought John news which he believed
would be significant, astonishing news. The Chancellor was
dead, poison suspected. One day he had been hale, the
next dying in agony. Livingstone, Bishop of Dunkeld, was
nominated by Albany as the new Chancellor, but was said
to be hesitant to accept the office, fearing a like fate, his
assumption that Sheves was behind it all – which indeed
was the assumption of most of Albany's entourage. After all,
it had been as astrologer and witch-master that Sheves had

first commended himself to the King; and his brother was still Master of the Wardrobe at Stirling. All the scoundrelly crew of diviners and potion-mixers had not died at Lauder Brig. Even so, John pointed out that poison seemed a large assumption; apparently healthy men did die suddenly not infrequently. But Crichton countered that by telling him that the Treasurer, Bishop-Coadjutor Carmichael, had taken ill with violent stomach pains the very same day, and it was doubtful whether he would live. That silenced John. He did not doubt that Sheves was capable of it, if he it was who had contrived the ghastly death of John of Mar. *How* it had been done was another matter which Crichton could throw no light upon. But these astrologers . . . ! If, as it seemed likely, it was poison, where was it going to end? A sobering thought indeed. They might not stop at the Chancellor and Treasurer.

Distinctly alarmed, John continued with his Deputy Warden's duties.

Archie arrived back from the south in no state of elation or confidence, his mission's success less than certain. There were going to be great changes in England, and soon. King Edward was very ill and not expected to survive. He would leave two young sons; but Gloucester was determined to succeed him, declaring that a child monarch was a disaster for any kingdom. So it had been with Gloucester that Archie had had to negotiate, which, on the face of it, might have seemed an advantage. But Gloucester, planning to become King of England, was a different man from Gloucester, the younger and jealous brother of the reigning monarch. He was, it seemed, not prepared to let the paramouncy issue go. He would not accept the award of Tynedale, claiming that it had always been part of England. He required substantial benefits from Scotland to put before the lords, to gain their support for his accession, as against the prior claims of his nephews. If Alexander of Albany wanted *his* friendship, and no warfare against Scotland, he must produce undoubted signs of service, vassalage. His suggestion was that this of Tynedale could help, not in the form of returning it to England, but that Albany should come south to *him* and pay fealty to him once he was

King, for the said lordship and honour of Tynedale. That would put the matter on a much better footing. Archie, of course, had seen the trap therein. Once a King of Scots paid fealty to a King of England, for Tynedale or any other property in that realm or elsewhere, then the latter would be in a position to claim that the former was admitting his subservience as a monarch – in other words, admission of paramouncy, even if it was on this limited scale, the first step. This was the message that Archie was to deliver to Albany as price of peace with England. Once Edward was dead, Albany was to go to Tynedale and, before the High Sheriff of Northumberland, take oath of fealty to the new King for the alleged lordship thereof.

And that was not all. The English lords were, on the whole, dissatisfied with what they considered was the tame withdrawal of Gloucester and his army from Scotland, with only Berwick-on-Tweed as gain. They were demanding some further armed move to be made against the Scots, to demonstrate who held the longer and sharper sword. And since Gloucester required their support in his bid for the throne, some gesture at least must be made. With James Stewart still King, such gesture could also help Albany unseat him completely. An English attack on the *West* March, even if only a token one, ought to serve both their causes.

John failed to see the point of this, but his brother said Gloucester was insistent.

Finally, their far-out kinsman, the Earl of Douglas, was being difficult. He was Edward's pensioner, and it was Edward who had insisted that Gloucester had brought him with him on his sally into Scotland, to recover his lands and titles. This had not been done. Now he fell to be pacified, for he had made many friends amongst the English nobility during his long exile, including Elizabeth Woodville, Edward's ambitious and clever Queen, whom, at this stage, Gloucester did not want to offend, however much he would have to do so later. She had even got Douglas made a Knight of the Garter. Needless to say, this requirement did not commend itself to Archie any more than did the rest, for of course quite a substantial part of

399

the Douglas lands had come to the Angus earldom, including John's titular Douglasdale.

The latter digested all this, with forebodings.

Archie was much exercised to learn of the deaths of the Chancellor and the Treasurer – for Bishop Carmichael had indeed succumbed. He had no doubts as to poison, and that Sheves was behind it, however difficult that might be to prove. What was Albany doing about it, apart from appointing Livingstone as successor to Laing? John did not know.

He asked, of course, when Archie would be resuming his activities as Warden of the March, and when he himself might be released from these deputy's duties, to have this brushed aside as all but irrelevant in the present national situation. More important matters were concerning Archibald Bell-the-Cat

So it was back to work for his dutiful brother. It was now late February.

Three weeks later the tidings reached John when he was holding a Warden's court at Hawick. James Livingstone, Bishop of Dunkeld, the new Chancellor, was seriously ill, few doubting that it was the result of poison. The word was brought by a messenger from Archie. He was at Dunbar Castle, with Albany. John was to come there, and at the earliest.

At Dunbar he found a state of urgency prevailing, and a large company sharing it. Not only the state of the Chancellor was responsible; there was much else. Down in his Borders valley, John had heard little or nothing of it all. Albany, whose position had seemed fairly secure now, was no longer sure of it, either as to his status or indeed his person – for there was a circumstantial report from a servant at Stirling that the King had been overheard discussing the poisoning of his brother with one Anselm Adournes, one of his strange familiars. With proof so evident that this threat was not to be taken lightly, and knowing what had happened to his brother Mar, the duke was in a state of apprehension as to what he ate and drank.

But this was only one aspect of the situation. A so-called

parliament had been held some six days previously, in his absence, in the absence of all there indeed, and dire pronouncements made therefrom; so-called, in that it could indeed be declared to be no parliament, even though the King presided, like John, none of the Albany supporters had been informed or summoned, no forty days' notice given. It had been, rather, just a secret council of the James and Sheves faction, at Stirling, and given the name and authority of a parliament by the device of saying that it was but a continuation of the December one, which the then Chancellor, Laing, had allegedly said was to be continued at an unspecified date in the future, prorogued not stood down; so this was merely a renewal of a suspended sitting. Whether Laing had indeed made any such statement was in doubt, but being safely dead, it could not be pronounced an invention. That was the excuse. And having the King's and the Primate's presence gave it some air of legality. Unfortunately, from Albany's point of view, certain prominent individuals had evidently elected to throw in their lot with the James and Sheves party, including Argyll – who, in the absence of the ailing Bishop Livingstone, was appointed acting Chancellor – the Earls of Huntly, Crawford and Menteith, the Lords Home, Kennedy, Fleming, Glamis, Montgomery and old Avondale, and only one named prelate, the Bishop of Aberdeen. No doubt there had been sundry lesser adherents present, to make it look sufficiently like a parliament.

At any rate, its decisions, however valid, were positive enough. Albany was deprived again of all offices, including governor, and forbidden to come within six miles of his royal brother; also to make written promise of manrent, homage and lifelong loyalty to James. The King's three uncles were dismissed from all official positions which they occupied, Buchan, here present, deprived of his valuable office of Lord High Chamberlain, this given to Crawford. The other Albany supporters ordered to surrender their appointments as justiciars, sheriffs, wardens and other offices of state. So Archie was no longer Warden of the March, this going to Home, which left John mercifully free of his deputy's duties there, the only advantage that man could see in the situation.

William Sheves seemed to have won the day.

There was, to be sure, great talk and discussion as to what was to be done about it all, as well as vows of vengeance upon backsliders and defectors. Lord Gray and others, Archie included, were for an armed solution of the situation. After all, between those present here at Dunbar, apart from other major supporters throughout the land, they could muster at least forty or fifty thousand men; whereas it was very doubtful whether James and Shreve could match that, even with Argyll's Campbells and Huntly's Gordons. But Albany himself was hesitant, indeed uncharacteristically uncertain of himself. He was, it appeared, preoccupied with this threat of poison, which seemed to affect him direly; after all, any servant could be bribed to do the deed.

Also, Albany had to consider the English question, and Gloucester, as a result of Archie's embassage and its findings. If, as seemed likely, King Edward died, there would be a totally changed situation, and one which demanded positive action, knowing Richard Crookback. Civil war in Scotland, between the royal brothers, was not the answer to Gloucester's implied threats. It would make an English assault all but inevitable, to gain not only paramouncy but complete domination of the northern kingdom. Albany, it became evident, was for temporising in this present pass, waiting to see how events materialised – and taking stringent precautions against poison. It might even be advisable for him to pay a personal visit to England, in the interim, indeed it might.

This reaction was less than popular at Dunbar. But, apart from the civil war option, no very effective proposals were forthcoming. So much would depend on how the majority of the earls, lords and magnates of Scotland behaved now. Albany's popularity was unlikely just to evaporate, nor James's enhance; and Sheves undoubtedly would still have most of the land against him. So waiting, not idly here but dispersing about the country to test and organise opinion, might indeed be the best course meantime, however uncharacteristic of most present.

For John's part, with no large personal manpower to muster, and considerable doubts in his own mind as to what line should be pursued, it seemed to him that a visit to Arran, to consult with the clever and resourceful Princess Mary, would be his best contribution. Archie, at something of a loss himself, did not this time demur.

Before John, with a lifting heart, prepared to depart, his brother revealed, in confidence, an item of news. Albany's possible visit to the south might have more than the one intention. The fact was that his beloved Anne de la Tour, the duchess, had in France given birth to a boy, and the proud father was eager to see his son and heir. A brief trip across the Channel might well be in the offing.

27

Spring had come to Arran with John Douglas, more obviously
than it had done on the colder Norse Sea coast, even though
the mountain-tops still held traces of snow. But the trees were
budding, the grass greener, the wild crocus blooming purple
and the wild hyacinth sky-blue, while the larks carolled and the
eiders crooned. This was a different world, and the new arrival
revelled in it, as in his affectionate reception by all, and Mary's
glowing warmth in especial. This was what that man wanted
from life. He was no schemer and plotter, power-seeker or
manipulator of men, any more than a warrior or a judge, which
seemed to have been largely his fate. He never should have
been born brother to Archibald Bell-the-Cat. A sheep-rearer
in the Lammermuirs would have better suited him – although
in that event he would never have met Mary Stewart.

John was received into the life at Brodick Castle as though
he had never been away, the youngsters looking on him almost
as a favourite uncle, Anna and her Patrick his friends, and
Mary accepting him almost as though he was indeed her
husband, and making no bones about it. Strangely, this now
felt almost more of a home to him than did Tantallon.

Mary was, of course, much concerned over all that he had
to tell her about events on the mainland – not that she
was wholly ignorant of much of it, her visiting Kilwinning
Abbey friars keeping her fairly well informed as to the general
situation. She knew of the so-called parliament and some of
its enactments, however questionable, and Argyll's change of
allegiance. Also of Sheves's unfortunate return to influence.
She expressed her fears as to what he might seek to do now.
She was even able to inform John to the effect that the Queen
had already returned to Linlithgow, from Stirling Castle, with

her children, James apparently showing little interest in their presence. There was no word of any visit to Denmark.

As to the Albany situation she was surprised and distressed, in particular about his fears of poison. On the results of Archie's embassage to Edward, and Gloucester's proposals regarding Tynedale, she was unhappy, declaring that on no account should her brother be persuaded to offer fealty to the King of England for it, a grievous move towards admission of paramouncy, however much of a mere gesture Alexander might rate it. Indeed, she was against her brother's suggested visit to England again, deeming it a mistake and dangerous. But she was interested to hear of Albany's acquisition of a son; although there could be a complication here also, for if Alexander did gain James's crown, he might well become anxious for this child to become heir to the throne, displacing young Rothesay, which would be wrong, and productive of much trouble. She would write him a letter to that effect.

However, although concern over events across the water was never entirely banished from their minds, events on the island itself were sufficiently positive, pleasing and varied to keep them preoccupied and cheerful. The children were demanding and vigorous, finding new challenges daily; and Arran was a great place for challenges, with its mountains to climb, its cliffs to scale, its rivers and waterfalls and bays to fish, its salmon to spear – or to try to – its sandy beaches to swim from and its Pictish remains to trace and explore. Spring was not the deer-stalking season, but they did go stalking in the corries and on the high slopes, nevertheless, to watch and admire, not to kill. Mary took her responsibilities as Countess of Arran seriously, and made a point of frequently visiting all the island's communities, farms, churches and properties, no light task, with the earldom twenty miles by ten, two hundred square miles. With her, John came to know a great many of the island's population, from lairds and friars to humble crofters, herdsmen and fisherfolk.

The days were seldom long enough for all that they found to do, and the weather on the whole was kind. What John rather dreaded, a demand from Archie for his return, did not materialise. Presumably his brother was lying fairly low, as was advisable, however unlike that man.

News, when it did reach them, came as so often by one of the Kilwinning monks. King Edward of England was dead, his young son nominated Edward the Fifth, and the Duke of Gloucester appointed Regent and governor of the kingdom. The Duke of Albany had departed for England. Pope Sixtus was sinking fast, and Cardinal Giovanni Cibo acting pontiff in his name. And the Chancellor, Bishop Livingstone, was in a coma, still alive but barely so. The Archbishop of St Andrews and the Earl of Argyll ruled the land in King James's name.

These tidings, although none really unexpected, did concern Mary and John – especially, as it happened, the situation at the Vatican. Sixtus all along had been Sheves's ally and supporter. When he was gone, things might change drastically. This new Giovanni, said to be no friend of Sixtus, as Pope might well elect to unseat Sheves and appoint her uncle, Andrew, Bishop of Moray, as archbishop and Primate, especially with rumours of poison circulating. That would greatly reduce Sheves's power in the realm and deprive him of his patronage and the use of the vast wealth of Holy Church, even though James still clung to him. So that was hopeful. Whether Gloucester ruling England would be any better than his brother remained to be seen. If Albany was now with him, it was to be hoped that he was agreeing to nothing foolish. Poor Bishop Livingstone. Could poison have this effect? To turn a man into a living corpse? Perhaps it was not poison at all, just coincidence that the three bishops, all officers of state and enemies of Sheves, should go down in such quick succession? If it was indeed poison, or witchcraft as was being increasingly declared, it represented a terrible stain on James's name and reputation, since he would have to bear some of the responsibility, as he had done over his brother John's death.

Mary was much distressed about James. And not altogether happy about Alexander either. The royal credit was at a low ebb.

If Scots royal credit was low, the next important news to

reach Arran intimated that the English one was no better. Unexpectedly, it was George, Lord Seton, who brought it. He informed that Gloucester had confined the twelve-year-old King Edward, and his brother the Duke of York, to the Tower of London, got parliament to declare them illegitimate, and there they had been smothered to death, almost certainly by his orders. He was now on the throne of England as Richard the Third.

Appalled, his hearers digested this, eyeing each other.

Seton's visit, of course, was not primarily as news-bearer. He had come as envoy to his friend, royal envoy no less, from the heir to the throne, James, Duke of Rothesay. Because his secondary seat, Niddry Castle, or Niddry Seton, was near to Linlithgow, he was quite frequently at that palace. And because he had married, wisely or otherwise, his love the Lady Margaret Campbell, daughter of the Earl of Argyll, acting Chancellor, he had been appointed lord-in-waiting to the Queen, to ensure her well-being and the safety of the royal children. And he had grown fond of young James, a very likeable boy.

His errand was this. The lad was Duke of Rothesay, but he had never been to Rothesay and desired to see it. He understood that Rothesay was on Bute, another island near to Arran; and he wanted his friend the Lord Johnnie to take him there and show him it all. There was a fine castle, he was told, *his* castle. And, of course, he wanted to go soon.

John was nowise averse. How was it to be arranged?

Mary said that she had been to Rothesay as a girl. It was a notable place, Bute a pleasant and sizeable island although smaller than Arran. Why not make a summer-time expedition of it, a family affair? Bring her nephew here, and all embark on one of the ferry-boats, to sail up the Kyles of Bute, round the island, and land at Rothesay. They would all enjoy it, and her children be interested to meet their cousin.

This was agreed. Seton said that he would return to Linlithgow, and, if the Queen allowed it, bring young James back here. That might take some time, but a little delay should ensure suitable sailing weather, even if the duke complained. John said that he thought that he ought to go back with his friend. He tended to feel a little guilty about prolonged stays on Arran, even though now he held no actual office in the state, apart from his baronial duties in Douglasdale. He felt somewhat concerned as to his impetuous brother, and that he ought at least to go enquire about him, and see his sisters likewise. This would be an opportunity to show himself briefly, and then return for another stay.

So it was arranged. John and George Seton sailed over to the mainland, and then crossed Lowland Scotland to Lothian, where the latter stopped at Seton Palace and John went on to Tantallon, to meet again in two days' time.

At home, John did not find Archie, as he had hoped; but he was surprised to find Mary's sister Margaret lodging there meantime as a guest. It seemed that her husband, William, Lord Crichton, was away with Archie seeking to organise the pro-Albany supporters south of Forth and Clyde to be ready for action at any time now, making their headquarters at Lochmaben in Annandale, leaving Dunbar Castle strongly held. Atholl and Buchan were doing the same in the northern half of the country. In the circumstances it had been felt that the Princess Margaret, left alone at Crichton Castle, could be in danger of being snatched by the King's faction, and that she would be safe at the all but impregnable Tantallon.

Archie's wife and sisters, glad to see him, poured out news – although how much of it all was fact and how much speculation and rumour, was hard to ascertain. It was feared that Albany, in England, was perhaps co-operating too closely with Richard Crookback. A group of English expert cannoneers had arrived by sea at Dunbar, sent by Albany to strengthen the defences of that castle, now his Scottish base; and it was doubtful whether Richard would have lent him these without promises of some real advantage to himself. Indeed the leader of the cannoneers had declared that the duke was again agreeing to English paramouncy. That might well be mere wishful thinking, but the word of it had worried Archie, as it now worried his brother.

There was news from even further afield – France. King

Louis had died, to be succeeded by the thirteen-year-old Charles the Eighth; and to try to ensure better relations therewith, especially with English threats in the offing, a most notable embassage had been sent to renew the Auld Alliance. James, apparently, had wanted to go himself, his previous Amiens pilgrimage notion revived, but Sheves had persuaded him otherwise. Indeed, Sheves himself, with Argyll and old Avondale, had gone instead, and were presently in France. Clearly they were much concerned over King Richard's intentions towards Scotland, and France was the obvious counter-influence in that. Sheves was thought to intend to go on to Rome, while he was thus far, to seek to establish good relations with the Pope-to-be, Giovanni.

Meanwhile at Stirling, of all men, the insufferable survivor of Lauder Brig, John Ramsay, was in high favour, elevated to be Lord Bothwell and given that great castle and its surroundings in Lanarkshire. Indeed there was talk of him being sent to England as ambassador, to win Richard away from Albany's cause by offering various inducements, including the betrothal of young Rothesay to one of the late Edward's daughters or other bride selected by Richard, much to the offence of most of James's proud supporters like Crawford, Glamis, Fleming and the Bishop of Aberdeen.

So matters had scarcely stood still whilst John had sojourned on Arran. Unhappy over nearly all that he had heard, he wondered whether young Rothesay would be allowed to make the proposed trip with him to the islands.

Two days later he expressed his fear to Seton. That man admitted that the news was disturbing in many respects – he had not known that his father-in-law, Argyll, was off to France – but thought that the King was so uninterested in his wife and children, personally, as distinct from letting them be used as pawns on Sheves's board, that he cared not what they did meantime. He was apt to be much more interested in the kindnesses of such as Ramsay.

They rode on to Linlithgow, skirting Edinburgh, unsure now in whose camp that city and citadel were.

They had a joyful, all but riotous reception at the Queen's

palace by the loch, at any rate, if scarcely from the mother, who was not made that way, but from her elder son, who was. John was moved by the boy's so evident affection for himself, and the complete trust in his ability to achieve all that was demanded of him.

The Queen made no objection to the Rothesay expedition, indeed she was probably quite relieved to have her so lively and urgent son off her hands for a spell. She was seldom in the best of health, and the reverse of spirited, an unlikely sea-king's daughter. Although the visitors did not question her, she clearly had no orders from Stirling limiting her son's activities.

George Seton would have liked to have joined the little expedition, but it was obvious that the Queen expected him to remain with her now, after this absence – as indeed did his wife, who was also at Linlithgow, acting as lady-in-waiting. So next day John, with the boy, set off for Irvine and the Firth of Clyde, with a mere four Douglas horsemen as escort, promising to deliver the prince to his mother again, safe and sound, in two or three weeks.

They made an all but hectic journey of it. Extraordinary it was how many matters this young James Stewart found to challenge him, an improbable son of his parents as could ever have been imagined. Almost any hill that they passed had to be climbed, every castle inspected, rivers forded in unusual places, any deer seen chased, woodland rides explored – and this delay attempted to be made up for by horse-racing. Rothesay was already an excellent horseman, and eager to prove it. He also proved to John to have a good memory as well as a keen eye, for he pointed out sundry birds that they roused, and gave them the local names John had told him of on their trip to the Bass Rock – which clearly had been a high spot in the prince's experience – gowks for cuckoos, pyots for magpies, marlezones for merlins and gleds for kites. No doubt when they reached salt water he would demonstrate his expertise on the seabirds.

Inevitably, owing to all this excitement *en route*, they got only as far as Strathaven by nightfall, not a few miles less than intended, where they had to put up at a lesser monkish hospice than Kilwinning Abbey. Not that the boy cared; he found plenty to interest him in the vicinity, after the meal, but was soon yawning, and went to sleep thereafter like any snuffed candle.

Even calling in at Kilwinning, to ensure the availability of a boat and crew, they reached Irvine in the early afternoon, and embarked, to further excitement, especially over the dramatic mountain silhouette of Arran, across the firth. Also comparisons between this scow, necessary for the transport of horses, and the boat they had used to visit the Craig of Bass.

Sure enough, they were not far out from land before John was having black doukers or shags pointed out to him, tarrocks or kittiwakes, sea-coulters or puffins. Where had these last come from? Only one, gormaws or cormorants, the boy forgot the name of, and that was because he mixed them up with shags. He was explaining this when suddenly he was smitten by something still more riveting – another Bass Rock, no less. Perhaps fifteen miles away, down-firth, a great rock-stack rose out of the waters, remarkably like the Bass. A flood of questions burst forth.

This was Ailsa Craig, it was explained. Strange that the two firths which so nearly cut Scotland in two, Forth and Clyde, should each display such extraordinary and similar features. John was not sufficiently well informed to explain why and how these enormous cliff-girt isles came to be formed, much disappointing his questioner, who however advanced his own theories. And, of course, had this Ailsa a saint like Baldred? John had never heard of any such, but the monk-sailors informed that the craig, belonging to Crossraguel Abbey, had the ruins of an ancient chapel on it, so there must have been some Columban saint using it for a refuge. And the name Ailsa meant the Fairy Rock. This matter kept them going for most of the sixteen-mile voyage. Then with Arran itself beginning to produce a further flood of question and comment, and especially Holy Isle in Lamlash Bay demanding attention, John at least was able to expand on

411

St Molaise, one of Columba's assistants who made a refuge there. He was beginning to realise that being sole companion to the heir to the Scots throne was an exhausting business.

Their arrival up at Brodick Castle diluted the inquisition, or at least transferred it to others. The prince's aunts and cousins, with Anna and Patrick, now shared the load, and gladly. For however demanding, young Rothesay was friendliness itself, with no notions of grandeur, the way he had been reared perhaps ensuring that.

Almost at once the problem of names came up, and hilariously – for of course Mary's two sons by her different husbands were also both called James, in the royal tradition. So there were three of them, and none to be *referred* to as James, this being reserved for the monarch. So there was already a Jamie and a Seumas there; now what were they to call their cousin? Clearly they were not going to address him as duke or prince or highness. John suggested Jacques, the Latin form, such as one day the boy would have to sign on charters; but this was too formal, and Jay was accepted by all.

Mary presently took charge. Although her nephew was already talking about climbing those mountains, especially the mighty Goat Fell and the splendid pointed one, Cir Mhor, she pointed out that he had come principally to visit his own Isle of Bute, and Rothesay. So they ought to go there first and then, depending on how much time they had left, come back and explore Arran later. This was accepted, if doubtfully, immediacy being obviously part of this youngster's make-up. A ferry-boat was arranged, for they would need horses. They would all sail north on the morrow.

Getting the young people to bed that night was a delayed process.

At least there was no problem about delays at getting the five of them down to the scow in the morning; they were agitating to make a start considerably before their elders were so inclined, especially John and Mary whose night's slumber had been intermittent. Anna and Patrick came too, so they made a party of nine, leaving the escorting Douglases to their own devices meantime – thirteen horses would have been just too much for their craft to transport, sizeable as it was.

Actually Bute was only six miles from the nearest point of Arran, but the sail from Invercloy Bay would take them most of the day, for Mary planned to show young Jay something of his island's size and perimeter before ever they landed at Rothesay, which was midway down the eastern shore. This entailed going north-abouts up the western side, firstly by the Sound of Bute and then into the Kyles – a word which had to be explained to the prince as coming from the Gaelic *caol* meaning narrows – and these Kyles of Bute were lengthy, for the island, although varying between three and five miles' width, was some sixteen miles long; and the objective was not to hurry but to see as much as they could of the place without actually landing, at this stage, in and out of the innumerable bays, round the headlands and offshore isles, so that its boy duke would have some notion of his domain without having to traverse it all on horseback.

Nevertheless it was the highly dramatic features and outlines of Arran itself, so much more spectacular than Bute's, which tended to preoccupy the lad as they sailed north, the jagged mountains and deep corries and tall cliffs of this top end challenging indeed. All were to be climbed, he asserted, the other two Jameses declaring that they would show him how – which, indicating competition, further stimulated ambitions. The Cock of Arran, the final northerly headland, of course, drew its own comments. Garroch Head, the corresponding southern tip of Bute, fell to be pointed out as equally worthy of consideration, even though the name was less evocative – although Garroch, after all, came from the Gaelic *garbh* meaning rough; and on closer inspection, rough it was.

Derogatory comparisons with the splendid mountains of Arran were not long in forthcoming, and pointings to a miserable pimple of a hill near Garroch Point, which Mary named St Blane's Hill. John was quick to point out that Blane was another Celtic Church saint, nephew of St Catan or Chattan – Kilchattan Bay was just across the island from here. Actually, or at least reputedly, Uncle Chattan,

413

one of Columba's lieutenants, seems to have been a stern disciplinarian, for when his sister, Ertha or Bertha, got herself pregnant, allegedly to King Aidan of Dalriada, he had her, with her nephew Blane, cast off in a coracle, without oars, as punishment. They drifted across the Irish Sea to Ulster, safely fortunately, where Ertha redeemed herself in a nunnery, and Blane was educated by the famous St Comgall, eventually to return to Bute to aid stern Uncle Chattan in Christianising this island. Mary added that he seemed to have had a lot of help other than Blane's, for Bute was full of saints' names – Marnoch, Michael, Davanan, Ninian, Calmac and Bridget. Her daughter, Grizel, observed that Jay's island must have been a very wicked place to require all this attention; perhaps her cousin matched his island?

However, this concern with the distinctly vigorous and venturesome Celtic clerics, so different from their present-day variety, kept the young duke interested in the less exciting landscape of his Bute, all the way up the coast, searching for Kil-this and Kil-that, So-and-So's Point or chapel or cairn, the two-mile-long isle of Inchmarnock especially intriguing him, as they sailed right round it. His demands as to who St Marnock was had Mary explaining that this was not rightly known, for there were over twenty-five Celtic saints of the name, or variations of it, including an uncle and nephew of Columba himself.

The top end of Bute was quite different from the rest, rough and hilly and unpopulated, without being particularly challenging to view, although stone circles and cairns and one chapel ruin, Kilmichael, were to be seen. The dramatic narrowing of the Kyles, to less than half a mile across from mainland Cowal, made up for this, however, the communities on the other shore to be identified, Lamont and Campbell country. What did arouse mirth from the youngsters, to be sure, was that while Arran had its Cock, Bute's northern headland was called Buttock Point, the inevitable connection duly emphasised to the girls, especially with standing-stones called Maids of Bute.

And now the Kyles, which had been north-going, became

suddenly the opposite, to lead down the eastern side of the island, their scow having to thread the cluster of islets at the mouth of Loch Riddon to make their turn southwards. These were called the Burnt Islands, and references made to the similar name over in Fife. And, of course, why burnt, and by whom? This was not known. Coping with the future monarch's thirst for information was a taxing task.

It was ten miles down this shore until they came to Rothesay, and the first six or so provided little of especial feature, uninhabited upland – although opposite Colintraive, on the mainland, it was demanded to know who this Colin was? It was Patrick who could reveal that the name was really Caol-an-t'-Snamh, meaning the Swimming Narrows, for here it was that the Bute cattle were swum across salt water on their long drove to the Falkirk markets.

At the mouth of Loch Striven they came to the great bays of Kames and Rothesay itself, populous and fertile land now, worthy of being duke of. They could see two castles at Kames, and a quite large community called Bannatyne, the prince assuming this to be Rothesay. But wait, he was told. Round the next headland.

Rothesay and its bay were indeed worth waiting for, a great bight into the centre of the island, with pleasant shores with gently rising slopes behind, tilled land now almost ready for harvest, and woodland higher. And at the head of the bay a town climbing to a great fortress-type castle, the former main seat of the High Stewards of Scotland, not on a rock-top site as at Stirling and Edinburgh but in the middle of the town itself. It was unique in that it was round, its high curtain walls forming a circle, such as John had never seen before, these amplified by a gatehouse keep and four round angle-towers, only there were no angles.

There was a great scramble to get up to this dominant feature, the youngsters not prepared to wait for the disembarkation of the horses but, whenever the scow was moored at the quayside, jumping ashore and running off up through the narrow streets, the Duke of Rothesay, the Earl of Arran and the Lord Boyd leading the way, but the girls not to be left behind. Their elders were not concerned for their safety here, and followed on, mounted, in more dignified fashion.

They found the five grouped in the street under the mighty frowning walls, gazing up in a mixture of admiration and frustration. It was magnificent, but they could not get in. There was a deep water-filled moat all round, and the drawbridge was up. They had shouted and shouted but nobody appeared, only these gaping townsfolk. It had to be pointed out that none here could know that the lord of it all was arriving; and the keeper of the castle would be unlikely to spend his time watching for unexpected visitors.

John added his voice to the hallooing, but with no effect. He should have brought a hunting horn with him. At Mary's suggestion they made a circuit of moat and unwelcoming walls, and at the second round tower they came to, at the other side from the keep gatehouse, they saw smoke rising from a chimney. At least the place was inhabited. There was no other drawbridge, however.

How to attract attention? They tried the shouting again, but without result. The master of it all declared that bombardment was the answer. Stones. So the youngsters set about gathering small stones and pebbles from the side of the moat, and a competition started as to who would aim best. The girls proved useless at it, tossing rather than throwing, their missiles apt to go anywhere, scorn expressed. The boys had to be warned, in their enthusiasm. There were only small and infrequent windows as targets, and it had to be the lower parts of these to aim for, the wooden shutters, not the upper parts where they could break the glass. It was a strange besiegement.

There were only the two windows to choose from in that tower, at second- and third-floor levels, and both received a battering of small missiles, although many of the stones missed or fell short, the boys cheering each other on. Quite a crowd of locals had now assembled, wonderingly, to watch and question, children to shout and dogs to bark. When some of the town's youth decided to join in the throwing, John concluded that it was time to call a halt. Which was not so

416

easy. Just as he attempted it, a bearded face appeared at the lower window-glass, glaring out. Then a fist was shaken at them and the face disappeared.

Distinctly at a loss at what to do now, although the youngsters had no such doubts, continuing with the bombardment the more enthusiastically, their elders were debating the issue when a burly character wearing a leather apron came up, frowning, to demand what was going on, and declaring that he was provost of the royal burgh of Rothesay. John, feeling rather foolish, sought to explain the situation, whilst maintaining some degree of dignity, although by this time the Lady Anna was laughing happily, Sir Patrick Fullarton grinning, and even the Princess Mary looking less than sombre.

The provost, all but unbelieving at first when told of the identity of the visitors, and taking in their attire and the quality of their horses, evidently decided that it must all be true. Shaking his greying head and pointing a finger at that window, he sought for words.

"Och . . . aye, weel . . . i'ph'mm . . . he's a right crabbit, thrawn auld chiel, yon Alicky Shand," he admitted. "You'll no' get inbye, wi' him, lord. His auld wife's nae better. They'll no' open the yett nor let doon the brig to ye, yon yins."

"But . . . this is ridiculous! Here's the Duke of Rothesay himself! And the King's sister. Come to this royal castle, and denied entry by some wretched keeper . . ."

"Och, yon's no' the keeper, lord. Yon's Alicky Shand, who bides in yon bit tower. The keeper's the constable. Constable o' Bute. Sir Hugh Spens, just. Leastwise, he's *deputy* keeper, mind."

"Spens? Where is he, then?"

"Doonbye, lord. Doon at Wester Kames. He's the keeper's deputy. No' far. Three mile, just . . ."

John glanced at Mary, and she nodded. "We will go see this Spens, then." They could not remain there, shouting and hurling stones.

So a halt was called to the assault, and orders given to mount, the boys rather reluctant to end their aiming contest.

417

The provost gave them approximate instructions as to where to find the House of Spens, as the castle at Wester Kames seemed to be called.

As they rode off down to the shore again, and then north-wards towards the smaller township of Bannatyne-Kames, Patrick told them that he had heard of this Sir Hugh Spens, Constable of Bute, an amiable man apparently, who really governed the island for the crown. Actually, the keeper of the castle was Bannatyne of Kames, but he, owning larger lands on the mainland, was seldom here and Spens deputised in the keepership. For the children's sake, Patrick recounted how the Spens name and constableship came about – at least as he had been told it by his own father, the coroner of Arran. In King Robert the Bruce's time, Wester Kames belonged to a family of MacKinlays. There was an archery contest at Rothesay to celebrate something, at which the three MacKinlay sons won. But the bad losers thereafter made a descent on the winners' house at Wester Kames. The archers there demonstrated their expertise with bow and arrow, and slew no fewer than fifteen of their assailants. This was a bit much for even Bute, and King Robert decided to remove the MacKinlays to lands in Perthshire, and put in their place here his own butler or dispenser at his table, one MacDonald. In time his descendants anglicised their name to Dispenser, Spencer or Spens, and they became Constables of Bute, Sir Hugh the present incumbent.

This story satisfactorily mollified the interrupted stone-throwers, and whiled away the ride round Kames Bay to the small castle of Wester Kames, passing the larger one of Kames itself on the way. It was explained that Kames was just the Gaelic word for bay – *camus*.

They found a cheerfully sweating gentleman assisting his farm-workers to harvest the oats, who, after initial surprise, most heartily welcomed the newcomers, said that he was glad to have excuse to halt his back-breaking labours at building stooks, and announced that he would conduct them back to Rothesay Castle, apologising for the ill-manners of the caretaking Shands, who were admittedly boors but useful in keeping intruders out of the unused castle. Spens pointed out, however, that the said castle *was* unused, and in consequence cold, damp and less than hospitable. He suggested that, if the royal party intended to stay a day or two on Bute, they should quarter themselves here at the House of Spens, where they would be entirely welcome.

From what they had seen of Rothesay Castle, handsome as it was, the callers, the women in especial, were entirely agreeable and grateful. Was there a Lady Spens? And if so, would not this invasion be rather too much for her? It was not a large house . . .

There was indeed a Lady Spens, a large, motherly and capable personage, who took charge of all without the least hesitation. Four rooms she could manage, two for the children and one each for the men and women. Food was no problem – they had great stocks prepared for the harvesters anyway, simple but adequate. But she suggested that, since the travellers had been at it all day, this was no time to go back to that chilly and draughty fortress. Let them bide here for the night and go to see Rothesay Castle, and whatever else they wanted, in the morning. That was in the nature of a command, and was gladly adhered to by the adults at least.

So whilst the ladies assisted at the settling-in process and preparing the rooms, the men and boys went out to make a token assistance with the oats whilst waiting for the promised adequate meal.

After a doubtful start, they seemed to have fallen on their feet.

Access to Rothesay Castle next day, in company with Sir Hugh, presented no problems, his horn-blowing producing a fairly prompt lowering of the drawbridge across the moat, the caretaking Shands thereafter keeping themselves discreetly out of sight.

It was a notable structure, but as warned, draughty and cold, even in this August weather, scantily furnished however commodious. There was a magnificent great hall, with a huge fireplace and a withdrawing-room at the far end, passages in the ten-foot-thick walling leading to little mural chambers and stairways to the upper floors, and on to the circular curtain-walling parapet-walk, up and down which the children scampered. The courtyard was very spacious and contained a deep well, a chapel and subsidiary lean-to buildings, also access to the angle-towers.

Sir Hugh explained that it was a thirteenth-century fortalice, made so strong to resist the encroachments of the Norsemen who then so grievously terrorised this Hebridean seaboard. It had been attacked in Alexander the Third's time by no fewer than eighty Norse longships, and taken, but won back after the Battle of Largs in 1263. Given to the High Stewards, who in time became the Stewart kings, it was a favourite residence of Roberts the Second and Third, the latter of whom created his elder son first Duke of Rothesay.

The youngsters fairly quickly had enough of listening to all the history, and instead resumed their racing round the parapet-walk, hiding from each other amongst the mural passages, dropping stones down the well, and the like. When, however, the boys began to scare the caretaking Shands in their single occupied tower, their elders decided that it was time to move on to alternative attractions.

Sir Hugh seemed entirely happy to act as guide to all that they might want to see – after all, he *was* Constable of Bute, by royal appointment, and this might be construed as part of his duties. So he took them to see the Cathedral of the Sudreys, no very large fane but important as the seat of the bishopric of Sodor and Man. It had to be explained that Sudreys or Sodor referred to the southern parts of the Hebrides, below the Point of Ardnamurchan. Oddly enough, its jurisdiction had been transferred to Nidaros in Norway, in 1154, during the Norse domination of this seaboard. This interested Mary in especial, who had been partly responsible for winning Orkney and Shetland from Norse rule to Scots, only a few years before. The girls were pleased to discover in the cathedral, amongst other recumbent effigies of bishops and Stewarts, one of a woman with a baby, something unknown elsewhere.

After exploring the rest of the town, Spens took them to see Barone Hill nearby to the west, where he proudly described a victory of two centuries before, in which his Spens ancestor had taken a prominent part, after the Bruce's death when Edward Baliol invaded Scotland with English help, and the Bute islanders had managed to surprise and defeat the English garrison, slaying the English governor, Sir Adam Lisle.

Return was made to the House of Spens, a section of the party now clamouring for food. And there was still the harvesting to assist.

Thus commenced four days of quartering the island and discovering much more of interest, even to children, than had appeared from shipboard. From the northern tip at Buttock Point – which the boys insisted on examining in detail, along with the Maids of Bute standing-stones nearby, comparisons being made with the girls – right down to Garroch Head, sixteen miles away, they rode. They visited everything worth seeing, stone circles, burial cairns, sculptured stones, ruined chapels, lairds' houses, sandy beaches, the Uamh Capuill, or Chapel Cave of St Blane, being a special attraction. Patrick was somewhat jealous of the Jamiesons' crowners' castle at Kilmory, no mighty fortalice but better than his own father, the crowner or coroner of Arran, was allotted. They even found a Viking grave, to one Gutlief, on the isle of Inchmarnock.

Throughout, the Lady Spens acted the most generous and attentive hostess, to the gratitude of all.

When they sailed back to Arran eventually, the Duke of Rothesay was much more enamoured of his titular isle and style than heretofore.

There followed almost two weeks on the larger island, for here there was so much more to see and savour, so much demanding assault, all those mountains in particular – needless to say, the Cioch-na-h-Oighe peak, the Maiden's Breast, not the highest but the most shapely, requesting special attention. But John at least became very much aware of the swift passage of time, and the Queen's possible anxiety for her son, and reluctantly had to call a halt.

But they would be back; that was promised to all concerned.

The visitors' eventual send-off from the bay below Brodick Castle was an event in itself, with the heir to the throne all but tearful. As well as fulfilling himself, he had made real friends – something new for young James Stewart.

On their return to Linlithgow Palace, John learned extraordinary news from George Seton. Albany, with the Earl of Douglas and an English force of only some five hundred horsemen, had made a sudden and entirely unlooked-for raid from the Carlisle area into the Scots West March, aimed at Lochmaben Castle apparently. Perhaps they had been expecting Archie Douglas to be there, although he was in fact at besieged Dunbar. Strange to say, this had taken place on St Magdalene's Day, 22nd July, when there had also been taking place the great annual fair and gathering, which presumably Albany had not known about. At any rate, the invaders, whatever their purpose, were vastly outnumbered by the tough West March Borderers, Armstrongs, Maxwells, Kirkpatricks, Johnstones and the like, all assembled for trials of strength, tournaments, joustings, archery contests and so on, and roundly beaten back and put to flight. But the old Earl of Douglas had been captured, to be duly brought to Stirling to King James. No doubt, had Sheves been back from the Continent, he would have been executed there and then, earl or none; but James, on less drastic advice, merely banished him to perpetual imprisonment in the Abbey of Lindores, in Fife, the earl remarking reputedly to the monarch, "He who may be no better, must needs turn monk!"

Albany had turned and hastily ridden back to English soil.

This scarcely believable story set John wondering indeed. Had that duke taken leave of his senses?

It was not until considerably later, when back at Tantallon, that John was able to visit the defended castle of Dunbar, by boat, and saw his brother there, that Archie told him that it all might in fact have been a device on Albany's part, with two objectives: one, to satisfy Richard Crookback's requirement of

422

making some armed gesture against James, to indicate that that King's replacement was still very much a live issue; and two, to show some gratitude towards himself, Archie by getting rid of the Black Douglas conveniently, who was no asset to the cause, and much of whose lands were now of course in *Red* Douglas hands. They were now in no danger of having to hand them back.

Ruminating on all this, less than satisfied or joyful, John returned to Tantallon.

28

That winter was one full of rumours, for John Douglas at least. Many came via George Seton – for John was frequently at Linlithgow for short visits at the behest of young Rothesay – and some from William Crichton, who, being very unpopular with the ruling faction over his marriage with Princess Margaret, spent much of his time at Dunbar Castle, still besieged but readily accessible by sea for identified friendly visitors however defensive against others, that is when he was not up at his Aberdeenshire seat of Frendraught with his wife. Also, of course, reports emanated from Archie, who came and went all over the land, largely secretly, keeping the Albany supporters in touch, although not always informed.

For instance, Archie did not always tell everyone that Albany had in fact gone over to France, feeling that this might tend to lessen enthusiasm and a sense of urgency. The duke went to see his wife and son, admittedly; but Archie felt that he could have instead brought *them* over to England.

From Seton he learned that Pope Sixtus had at last died, and Cardinal Giovanni had ascended to the papal throne as Innocent the Eighth, however suitable or otherwise that style. This had caused Sheves to remain at Rome, seeking to ingratiate himself with the new pontiff, which at least pleased those who considered that Scotland was better without him. The rumour was that, amongst other things, he was trying to get a new low-born familiar of James, one Alexander Inglis, whom he had appointed Dean of Dunkeld, promoted to be bishop thereof in place of the late Chancellor, Bishop Livingstone having died, however lacking in qualifications for the position, the Vatican being understandably doubtful. Also, allegedly, Sheves was trying to win the Holy See's support for the betrothal of James, Duke of Rothesay, to the King of England's niece, little Anne de la Pole, presumably to help counter Albany's ambitions.

There was another advantage, in the opinion of many, in Sheves's extended absence. In the interim, one William Elphinstone, Bishop of Ross and a former colleague of the late Laing of Glasgow, had been appointed to the vacant and more important see of Aberdeen, and was taking an ever more prominent part in national affairs. This was good, for it seemed that he was a man of ability and integrity, and appeared to know how to handle the King. Already he had effected some distinct improvements in the management of affairs, although whether Sheves would countenance Elphinstone and his doings when he got home remained to be seen – by which time, of course, Albany might have regained the upper hand. What Sheves thought of Elphinstone's petition to Rome for a papal bull to allow the establishment of a new university at Aberdeen, possible rival to St Andrews, was not disclosed.

Another of the new Bishop of Aberdeen's achievements, it seemed, was getting the insufferable John Ramsay, Lord Bothwell, away from the King's presence by having him sent as ambassador to Richard Crookback's court, however odd an envoy he might make. He was to try to arrange a three-year truce, and to discuss this of the proposed Rothesay betrothal. If Elphinstone could get rid of a few more such, it would be all to the good. This hoped-for truce was apparently to try to reassure King Richard over the arrival in Scotland of Bernard Stewart d'Aubigny, actually Lieutenant-General of the French army, as ambassador from the new King of France to make firm and detailed renewal of the traditional Auld Alliance. King James, or at least his advisers, were certainly seeking to walk a tightrope in international affairs.

Lord Crichton, who in John's absence in Arran had more or less become Archie's peripatetic lieutenant, had different stories to tell. He reported that the lords of Scotland, at least those who supported Albany, were getting impatient. They could not keep their men permanently on call for armed service, to the neglect of their normal duties on the land; and the duke's present dilatoriness, with the extraordinary Lochmaben fiasco, was upsetting them, in especial the Earls of Buchan and Huntly, of whom Crichton saw much, his Frendraught estates being in their area of Aberdeenshire. They were supporting their new bishop meantime, but were demanding that Albany made a positive move soon. Archie was apparently thinking of sending him, Crichton, to France to urge the duke to come back to Scotland quickly and make an all-out grasp for the throne.

And so on – reports, stories, suppositions, hearsay, but little of definite advancement in the nation's best interests.

Then in late February, Crichton brought further and dire news, no rumour. He was a true fugitive now. Ramsay – few ever called him Bothwell – had returned from England, and whether or not his mission there had been successful in gaining a three-year truce, he had concocted a plot to enhance his own fortunes and to damage Crichton. It so happened that Ramsay's mother, formerly Janet Napier and now married to an Edinburgh merchant, had inherited a small property in the barony of Crichton, in Lothian. Ramsay now held this, and wished to enlarge it, possibly to gain the entire barony; and to this end accused Lord Crichton before King and council of theft and spoliation, to the tune of eight hundred pounds and a golden chain from his mother, a quite ridiculous charge, but one which Crichton had not risked challenging in person before the hostile monarch in case he was arrested. As a consequence he had been found guilty and declared forfeit, his title and estates; and not only himself but his two brothers, who might have claimed the lordship and who were also known to favour Albany. So now all three were outlaws, and Ramsay, in name at least, the owner of Crichton Castle and lands. Frendraught too, no doubt, but that northern property he would never be able to grasp, not while the Earls of Huntly, Buchan and Atholl ruled up there. The Crichtons, therefore, were meantime going to leave Dunbar Castle and Archie's service in and for the Albany cause, and hide themselves up in Aberdeenshire until better days dawned and Albany was King.

John was sympathetic. He learned more of Ramsay's doings from another source, Mary Stewart. She kept in touch with him by sending letters, usually by travelling friars. In one of these she informed, a month or so later, that her uncle, Hearty James, Earl of Buchan, was in a fury. Ramsay, while at King Richard's court, had managed to extract quite a large sum of money from that monarch to help ensure the issue of paramouncy over Scotland, and had named Buchan as one of the key figures in the shameful business. Whether this was done actually to help that cause, so important to the English crown, by implicating one of King James's kin; or whether it was merely Ramsay seeking to get his own back over his fright at Lauder Brig, while adding to his personal wealth, was not known – perhaps both. But at least the moneys seemed to have stuck to Ramsay's fingers. He was clearly of an acquisitive nature, that one.

With the new campaigning season well started, yet no sign of Albany returning from France, and Sheves still apparently in Rome, that summer continued the unaccustomed lull in dramatic developments in Scotland, with Ramsay and Inglis continuing to dominate the King, but Bishop Elphinstone proving a good influence and the strongest figure in the Church, talk now of him succeeding Argyll as Chancellor, this being normally accepted as a position best suited for churchmen. John, in the circumstances, contrived another visit to Arran, although Archie stipulated that it must be brief, for any day they might hear that Albany had returned and was coming to take the crown, presumably with French support; this time there must be no foolish mistakes and delays, and every supporter must play his part. John claimed, as a species of excuse for this trip, that it was at young Rothesay's command – which was certainly true enough, this being the boy's constant litany; and his mother's continuing ill-health making her grateful to be relieved of her so energetic son's demanding presence for a space. This time George Seton did come with them.

It proved the usual delight for all concerned. Even the year's interval had made a noticeable effect on the development of all the young people, with their ambitions nowise reduced. So physical, intellectual and certainly vocal and argumentative activity was the order of the days – which had the effect perhaps of making the nights the more blissful for some at least.

The promised brevity of the visit, unfortunately, had to be observed, despite loud pleas to the contrary, and reluctantly the mainland trio departed, at the end of August. They came back to extraordinary news indeed. There was a new King of England. Richard Crookback was dead, slain at a battle at Bosworth Field. The Lancastrians, long lying low, had arisen, under the half-Welsh Henry Tudor, Earl of Richmond, and the Yorkist house had at last fallen. Now, of course, an entirely new situation could develop between England and Scotland.

The stir and excitement occasioned by this unlooked-for event was, inevitably, great, since it could, indeed must, mean a very different approach towards the new English power. Few doubted that this Henry the Seventh would not relinquish the age-old claims to suzerainty over Scotland; but undoubtedly he would be busy for some period consolidating his hold on his kingdom, and in the meantime Scotland's relations might be improved. The first hint of this was word that the ever astute William Sheves had abruptly cut short his prolonged stay at Rome and crossed to London to establish contact with the new monarch there. To what end was uncertain, but undoubtedly it would seek to be to his own advantage, whether or not it was to Scotland's.

Henry Tudor was the grandson of John of Gaunt, Duke of Lancaster, and had married a daughter of Edward the Fourth. He was something of an unknown quantity as far as Scotland was concerned; but no doubt they would discover his potentialities before long.

Yet, whatever the stir *this* death occasioned in the northern kingdom, it was as nothing compared with the tidings which reached them only a few weeks later. Alexander, Duke of

428

Albany was also dead, killed by nothing more than a splinter of a lance broken in a tournament contest with the Duke of Orleans.

The realm of Scotland reeled.

29

It would be hard to overestimate the impact on Scotland of the death of Albany. Suddenly and utterly all was changed. The hopes of most of the nation were dashed, obliterated, and James's throne no longer endangered. Unpopular, weak, ineffective as he was, the King was now secure, for there was no alternative lawful contender for the crown, other than his own young son and heir, Rothesay – since the baby child of Albany in France could hardly be considered. A kind of depression settled on the land, or the larger proportion of it. Albany *had* been popular with the common folk as his brother never was, despite his fondness for low-born associates. So it was not only the lords and magnates who knew almost despair.

Sheves duly returned, his power strengthened and, reputedly, with a valuable agreement with King Henry. It was said that he had not done quite so well at the Vatican. Inglis, for instance, was not made a bishop. And he had not been able to prevent the new Pope's favourable consideration of a bull to permit the establishment of a third Scots university at Aberdeen. The archbishop's attitude towards Elphinstone could be imagined.

Nevertheless, Sheves and Ramsay now all but ruled Scotland almost unchallenged. The former declared that he had papal authority to interdict and excommunicate all nobles and others who showed disobedience to the royal will; and not only that, but to refuse pardon to those who had done so in the past, a dire threat indeed – although even Sheves could hardly excommunicate half the realm. And Elphinstone's moderating influence with some of the bishops and most of the abbots was a factor which had to be reckoned with.

It all made for a winter of discontent, fears and uncertainty – and a wet and cold one into the bargain.

Then, in the spring of 1486 there was a development which was to have momentous consequences, on the face of it no earth-shattering happening, and sparked off by a seemingly unlikely event, the arrival in Scotland of a new papal legate, the Bishop of Imola. This dignitary came, as it were, as first representative of the new Pope, to declare Innocent's support for the lawful King James and his officers, to consider appointments to the two vacant bishoprics, to enquire further into the Aberdeen university project, to hear the new Bishop Blackadder's plea for Glasgow's see to be raised to the status of archdiocese – which Sheves of course was wholly against – and lastly to indicate the Vatican's goodwill towards the King of Scots by changing and raising the status of the Priory of Coldinghame, in the Merse, to be a crown appendage collegiate church and to attach it to the Chapel Royal at Stirling. This last it was, so minor apparently compared with the rest, which nevertheless touched off the gunpowder-train which led to explosion.

The reason was that Coldinghame was one of the richest Church properties in the kingdom, owning vast lands in the Merse and elsewhere, indeed having its own major territory of Coldinghamshire, which no doubt was why Sheves had promoted the project. But it had been held by the Homes, the greatest of the Merse clans, for centuries, and had always been their private benefice – or, at least, only once had a non-Home prior been appointed, and the Homes had promptly ejected him and his assistants with cold steel. So now there was uproar in the borderland.

The Homes had played a peculiar role of recent years, not only as to Albany but in the realm's affairs generally: Laodicean, Archie called them, neither hot nor cold, tending to keep a foot in both camps. It was said that the Lord Home could put the holders of thirty baronies in the field, with their mosstroopers, a major force indeed. But he had seldom done so, for his own reasons, and in consequence had been made Warden of the East March in succession to

Archie, earl's task as it normally was. However, he had kept in touch with the Albany camp, largely through the Lord Hepburn of Hailes, whose mother was Home's sister. They were neighbours and had long been linked by marriages and by similar interests. Sheves and James, if not the Vatican, should have remembered this.

Fury erupted in the Merse of Berwickshire. The papal and royal emissaries were not only denied admittance to Coldinghame Priory and its grounds but warned to keep away from the Merse itself. Even the rest of the Borders expressed solidarity in this grievous interference in their affairs, despite many of the clans being at feud with the Homes.

A parliament was called for May, properly summoned this time but mighty poorly attended – Archie and John being amongst the absentees – to which the Homes were commanded personally to appear to answer for their intransigence. Neither the Lords Home nor Hepburn came which, in the circumstances, amounted to treason. The proceedings were reportedly brief in the extreme, and culminated in the forfeiture of Home, which of course could nowise be effected without major civil war. But sundry penalties were imposed, at least nominally, and his wardenship taken from him; but discreetly no replacement was nominated there and then, since nobody with any sense, in the circumstances, would have taken on the position. However, to the astonishment of the absent Archie, and no doubt others, *he* was appointed to be Warden of the Middle March, commissioned to keep the peace in the borderland – no doubt on the assumption that now that Albany was gone, Archie was no longer any threat. That man's first reaction was to refuse the appointment with scorn; but on second thoughts, and John's counselling, he perceived that there could be advantages in this, and without actually assailing the Homes, help to keep the Borders from any cooperation with the Sheves faction.

So John found himself busy acting deputy again, an odd situation admittedly.

Then, a month or so after the 1486 parliament, Queen Margaret, sickly as she had been for long, died, a sad end to a sad life, for she was only in her thirtieth year. Again this in turn created something of a crisis, for more than her immediate young family but especially for the heir to the throne. For Rothesay and his brother and sister could not be left alone at Linlithgow; and however lacking in fatherly love the King might be, he took them to Stirling Castle. And there they were all but prisoners – a dire fate for young Jay. John's heart bled for him, but there was little that he could do about it. Nothing was less likely than that James, or his associates, would permit such as the Lord of Douglasdale to come and take the boy on excursions. The crisis, on the wider scale, developed later.

It took some time for any amelioration of Rothesay's plight to eventuate. When it did, to some small extent, it was his Aunt Mary who contrived it. A messenger reached John, in the autumn, to say that she was at Stirling temporarily, and if he could spare the time could he pay a visit there, for young Jay was vehemently demanding his presence. It did not take long for John, who was holding wardency courts at Jedburgh, to transfer himself to Stirling, justiciary or none.

With Princess Mary's presence and authority he had no difficulty in gaining access to the castle. There he found the boy-duke in a state of clamorous revolt – not that this had any effect on his father. Even Mary was not permitted to take him outside the citadel, allegedly for fear of kidnapping attempts by wicked traitors.

Strangely, in their entertainment of the young people, Mary and John obtained unexpected co-operation from none other than Sir James Schaw of Sauchie, the present keeper of the castle, who they found sympathetic to the boys' needs, and who, it seemed, had a Home mother.

Clearly no more than a few days of this was practicable for those with responsibilities elsewhere; but before they left the sorrowing Jay they learned of trouble involving the Home–Hepburn alliance. Oddly, this emanated from Ayrshire. Coldinghame Priory owned lands and subordinate chapelries in more than the Borders, and had no fewer than six such in Ayrshire. Apparently the King's emissaries had arrived

433

there, at Crenoch and Roberton, to try to collect revenues and establish control. They were repulsed, and when reinforced by the royal guard, a force of Homes and Hepburns arrived from the east to assail them. Fighting developed on quite a major scale, and the royal party had to retire. It looked like rebellion, even the commencement of civil war, as sides lined up.

That winter was a tense one, as men assessed chances and duties and their best interests. It became evident that the lords and magnates, the wielders of manpower, might well have to choose whom to support, the wretched monarch or the forces coalescing against him – for it was now not just Home and Hepburn. More and more saw it as necessary to get rid of James and his associates, even though Albany was no longer available to replace him. The Lords Gray, Lyle and Drummond led the way in this, announcing that if the crown could at will seek to take over properties like Coldinghamshire for no reason other than greed, then none of them was safe. This sentiment was echoed all over the land, even by some of the bishops, in especial the powerful Blackadder of Glasgow, since it had been Church property involved, in name at least.

It was a particularly tense time for Archie and John, of course, since they were supposed to be representing the King in the Middle March, where the Borderers' attitude was almost wholly against the crown in this, as indeed were the Douglases' own. And the strife was brought very near to home when a royal force was sent, under Ramsay, to Fast Castle, not so very far south of Tantallon and Dunbar.

This was fairly obviously a pointless exercise, but then, James's present familiars were scarcely capable militarily, however effective at plotting and scheming. Fast Castle was one of the most inaccessible holds in all Scotland, a Home possession, built halfway down a lofty Berwickshire cliff above the waves, a sea-eagle's eyrie if ever there was one. Certainly the least vulnerable to assault of all the Home castles, approachable, save by sea and a cave beneath, only by a narrow ladder-like track down the cliff, impassable for horses. Fast had been chosen by the Lord Home as a sure and safe base from which to defy the throne, however inconvenient as a residence meantime. So when Ramsay's force arrived, and gazed down in disbelief and frustration from the dizzy cliff-top, all that they could do was to shout threats and royal fulminations against the rebels, and then turn inland to ravage one or two of the lesser Home properties on their way back to Edinburgh.

This episode did not advance the King's cause.

Another of the pseudo-parliaments was held in Edinburgh in May, attended almost solely by James's adherents, a farce really, since few of its enactments could be implemented. But it did produce two notable developments. The first, that Argyll, who apparently had fallen out with Sheves, was replaced as Chancellor by Bishop Elphinstone – which was good, as that man ever sought to be a mediator and moderating influence, so desperately required. And second, that Sir James Schaw, keeper of Stirling Castle, took the opportunity to depart therefrom, while the King was in Edinburgh, and carried off the young Duke of Rothesay with him, to Fast Castle, an astonishing gesture indeed. He was half a Home, of course. So now Scotland's heir was a hostage of the Home–Hepburn faction.

When John and Archie heard of this they were not long in repairing to Fast, although they were each far apart at the time. John arrived first and was met by Home guards at the Dowlaw farmery, a mile short of the castle, the nearest point for horses nevertheless. Satisfied that he represented no threat to their lord, they let him past, but on foot and under escort.

It was an extraordinary approach to make to any fortalice, indeed to any haunt of man other than some sort of agile hermit, firstly a walk along a sheep-track through heather at the lips of the enormous cliffs, with the roar of the breakers coming from far below – this not so different as within Tantallon's walls admittedly, but not in an approach. Then, after half a mile, the descent began, with the castle itself only just becoming visible part-way down, perched seemingly precariously on a slender rock-stack column of the cliff, a drawbridge crossing the gap. But that was relatively far ahead, and considerable goat-like picking of way to be achieved first.

Much shouting, when eventually down at the gap between cliff and stack, produced, in no hurry, a lowering of the half-raised drawbridge. John was led across, to peerings from the small gatehouse-parapet. Before he was over, there were yells therefrom of "Lord Johnnie! Lord Johnnie!" so that, whatever the attitude of the owners, a warm welcome for the visitor was assured, the young duke evidently on the watch.

Greetings were ecstatic, not to say tumultuous, the boy actually pummelling his friend in his excitement, amidst a flood of exclamation.

The Lord Home proved to be considerably less demonstrative when John was brought before him, a reserved, cool individual who scarcely gave the impression of being a leader of revolt. Perhaps he was doubtful as to the reliability of one who was still, in theory at least, the King's Warden-Depute of the Middle March. The various Home lairds present took their cue from him; but at least there was a warmer welcome from Sir James Schaw, who had remained at Fast.

The boy was urgency personified, eager to drag John off to see the extraordinary sights of this place, dramatic even for one used to the spectacles of Tantallon and the Bass. Towers here actually overhung the frightening drop to the sea – how many men had died in the building of such masonry was a thought to ponder on. For anyone lacking a head for heights the wall-walks would be a nightmare. Seabirds were everywhere, clustering on ledges, clinging to knobs of rock close enough to peck at the boy's hands outstretched to pat them, and filling the air with their skimmings, divings, circlings and screamings, the smell strong. But the prime fascination was the shaft. This was a hole, a great chimney or funnel cut down through the solid rock, from one of the little courtyards at differing levels which the stack-top dictated, this with a trap-door which opened to reveal a black abyss with an iron ladder leading down into it, with the curious, gurgling whisper of the surging waters below. Jay would have led the way down into it there and then, but indignantly informed that he had been sternly forbidden by the Home man to do anything of the sort. Perhaps Lord Johnnie could get permission? It went down to the roof of a great cave, apparently, into which the seas washed at all states of the tide, and by which the castle could be supplied by sea, while representing no risk of attack therefrom. This was how the wreckers' booty was brought up from the cruel reefs of the shoreline. Jay thought that wrecking ships was not very fair.

All this clearly enthralled the boy. But equally evident was that he grievously resented restrictions imposed by this cliff-side roost, for he was confined within its precipitous walls and was not allowed to go outside. So he could not walk nor run, save up and down twisting narrow stairs. Because Fast was so much smaller, it was worse than Stirling Castle in this. And there was no hurly-hackit, no hawking even. Complaints poured out. John pointed out that it *was* a highly dangerous place, outside as well as in, and these cliffs less than apt for walking, much less running and climbing. Young Rothesay thought that a defeatist attitude, obviously.

When the boy was in bed, with John promising to come and sleep in the same room, the latter consulted with Home and his friends as to what now? The situation could not remain thus.

There was no doubt about the Home–Hepburn view of what must follow, and quickly. With the heir to the throne in their hands, they must strike, get rid of James and his familiars, and establish his son as King – and this before the father had time to try to muster forces to his aid. Outright war was inevitable now, and the sooner the better, the rallying of their utmost strength the priority. The Douglas full strength would be important.

Archie arrived next day from Hermitage Castle in Liddesdale, much exercised over it all. He argued that, with Rothesay in their hands, the only course was armed rising to put him on the throne, otherwise all would be forfeited for treason. So it was all forces to be summoned to the fight. This agreed with the Home decision. Only he was in still more of a hurry. Where would they muster?

437

John pointed out that it all would take some time, whatever the need for haste. Although the same would apply to King James, to be sure. The hay-harvest would be upon them soon, and lords reluctant to summon their fullest strength in men until that was over. If this drastic effort was to be successful, they would require every man who could be raised.

Home agreed with this assessment. Six weeks, perhaps two months, and they should be ready, Archie claiming that half of this time should serve. The King, or Sheves and Ramsay, should not be allowed time to assemble *their* supporters. James might even appeal to the new Henry of England for aid. Sheves had allegedly struck some sort of bargain with him. The King was apparently remaining at Edinburgh Castle meantime. Once he realised that they were mustering against him in arms, he would no doubt seek to assemble an army on the Burgh Muir there. Haste was of the essence, therefore. All lords, lairds and chiefs must be approached immediately for fullest numbers to assail him. That was Archie Douglas.

John, while accepting some of all this, asserted that, in the circumstances, they could not keep young Rothesay cooped up in this cramped and confined hold, however secure. Already he was complaining of it. They were going to need the boy's goodwill and co-operation, as King, and this was not the way to gain it. He suggested that his security would be adequately ensured at Arran, in care of his aunt the Princess Mary of whom the boy was very fond. And to counter any objections from Archie, he added that he himself, in so escorting and guarding Rothesay, would be playing his part in mobilising the insurgent forces by visiting the magnates of Ayrshire and Renfrewshire, this easily enough done from his base on Arran – much more so indeed than from the Borders.

His persuasions prevailed, and it was agreed that he should be entrusted with the care of the prince. When needed, they would be sent for. Sir James Schaw should accompany them to Arran, for added safeguard. On the way there, they should call in at Douglasdale and its lands, to ready the Douglas manpower there.

So the matter was settled. Young Jay's restraints and confinements were over meantime. They would be off next day.

30

In 1488 considering the circumstances, with major civil war and uprising against the crown imminent, John spent a remarkably congenial summery six weeks on Arran. He did his duty by his brother and their allies in visiting the lords and lairds of Ayrshire, Renfrewshire and western Lanarkshire, the Montgomeries, Cunninghams, Kennedys, Cathcarts, Dalrymples, Dunlops and the like, and finding most prepared to support the cause, although a few, Lord Kilmaurs the Cunningham chief in especial, contrary-minded and some doubtful about actually taking to arms against the monarch however unpopular he might be. John understood their reluctance, knowing something of it himself, but claimed that the nation's well-being was more important than their liege-lord's, with the latter wholly controlled by evil men. His arguments usually prevailed.

The coming and going from Arran was no problem, the passage across the firth taking only a couple of hours at most, so that he could spend the larger part of his time, and nights, on the island. Sometimes Sir James Schaw or Sir Patrick Fullarton came with him in supporting role; but they told none that the heir to the throne was on Arran, just in case word got round, and efforts be made to retake him.

The said heir, like the other youngsters of Brodick Castle, was well pleased with life, and undoubtedly would have been quite content to remain so indefinitely. But John, and Mary also, tried to warn and guide him as to the future, pointing out that he would assuredly be required to take some fairly active part, or at least make some prominent appearance, in the forthcoming campaign to unseat his father and put him on the throne, with something of what that would mean.

High-spirited as he was, the boy, almost a youth now, took all this more or less in his stride, and having little or no affection for his sire, suffered no qualms. Not that he showed much ambition actually to be King, save in that it would enable him suitably to reward his friends.

Meantime, however, there were all the delights of Arran to enjoy. It is safe to say that never had that island's possibilities been so thoroughly exploited.

John savoured his own delights, needless to say.

On his visits to the mainland he did learn something of how affairs went – even though Archie did not communicate. The hay generally and fairly satisfactorily harvested, men everywhere were beginning to gird themselves for action. The response from the anti-James faction was good, heartening; indeed few, even of those who refused to join the rising, seemed prepared to take up arms on the other side. There was a rather notable silence, however, as to the attitude of the earls; but by the nature of things these, being the descendants or representatives of the ancient mormaors of Alba, the *ri*, were mainly domiciled north of the Forth and Clyde, and so news of them was hard to come by hereabouts. But John, for one, was a little concerned.

Then, at the beginning of June, more detailed and dramatic tidings did reach them. The King, most of this time at Edinburgh Castle, and finding that city turning hostile as stories of the coming rising proliferated, made a move. He announced, presumably on advice, that he was, of all things, going to Flanders – just why was not stipulated – and called upon the famous captain of shipping, Sir Andrew Wood of Largo, to have vessels ready at Leith to transport him and his. Whatever Wood thought of this odd development for a threatened monarch, he did produce two sea-going vessels at Leith, the port of Edinburgh. James duly left the castle with his friends and considerable baggage – and, as it transpired, considerable treasure also, in gold and silver, presumably provided by Holy Church in the person of William Sheves. Whether or not word of this latter was leaked from the castle garrison, an Edinburgh mob hastily assembled and attacked the baggage-train on its way to Leith haven, and captured the booty. The King's party escaped, to reach the ships, and duly sailed – but not to Flanders. That seemed to have been but a ruse. The two vessels had merely taken the royal party across the Forth to Fife, from where James and his company had headed northwards, to raise his army, not on the Burgh Muir of Edinburgh but in what was presumably considered to be the more loyal lands of Perth, Strathearn, Angus, the Mearns and even Aberdeenshire.

This extraordinary news set tongues wagging indeed. James must have had some information to make him believe that major support would be forthcoming from up there. The earls? Strathearn, Erroll, Lennox, Mar, Huntly, even Argyll? Were they, the *ri*, in the end rallying to the *Ard Righ*? And what of Atholl and Buchan? Did their recent silence imply a change of attitude? If so, it was distinctly worrying for the insurgents.

That this concern was not confined to Arran and Ayrshire was proved a couple of days later, when at last Archie sent an urgent courier. John was to come, with young Rothesay, at once. Their army was to assemble, not at Edinburgh but at Linlithgow, with the enemy mustered at Perth. He was, of course, to bring Rothesay with him, and also the Douglasdale contingent, which Archie had sent orders to be ready.

So it was a hurried farewell, hurried but emotional, especially on the part of those left behind, Mary in particular. For those leaving were off to war. Many and great were the urgings and warnings as to care to be taken, military flourishes left to others less precious, follies avoided, and the like. John at least recognised how blest he was in all this concern, and found the parting sore indeed. Young Jay was disappointed to be taken away from the delights of Arran, with so much still to be savoured there, but was rather looking forward also to what was to come, seeing it all as an exciting adventure. Sir James Schaw came with them. Patrick Fullarton would have done the same, but John insisted that *his* duty was on Arran, looking after those at Brodick Castle.

They sailed off, to wavings from the shore which persisted until such were no longer visible.

At Douglasdale, in due course, they picked up over two hundred mounted men-at-arms, enthusiasts now that the hay was in, but hoping that hostilities would not persist to interfere with the grain harvest.

They reached Linlithgow two days later, to find the place changed out of all recognition, in the hands of a vast armed host, the little town all but submerged under the tide of men with nothing to do meantime but make nuisances of themselves, the palace full to overflowing with the leadership, the loch surrounded by the encampments of the various contingents, Allegedly there were some seventeen thousand men assembled, and more to come. John was surprised to see the Earl of Argyll among the lords, after his having seemed to veer towards the other side. Presumably the wily and careful Campbell had summed up the situation and considered the chances to be in favour of the insurgents, and made his choice accordingly. Which might be taken as a good omen. It was good to meet up with George Seton again.

The Duke of Rothesay's arrival was made much of, and the boy was paraded round the town and encampments as evidence of authority and assured success – indeed some were already calling him His Grace James the Fourth. He both showed and aroused enthusiasm, and clearly made a much more effective figurehead than ever would his father.

Archie gave his brother news of events which had taken place while John had been hiding away on Arran, the most important of which was that there had been a preliminary skirmish, two weeks before, and not far from here, at Blackness, the port of Linlithgow. It had developed into more of a parley than a battle, for the King had sent a modest force under the Earl of Crawford and the Cunningham Lord Kilmaurs – who had evidently made contrary choice from John's urgings – with Bishop Elphinstone as councillor. These had been met by Home, Hailes and Bishop Blackadder of Glasgow, the nucleus of the insurgent leadership, and after only token display of fight, a mere tournament according to Archie who had been elsewhere raising men, had come together to confer, the two prelates acting as mediators. James's people had offered free pardon if the insurgents laid down their arms and dispersed, with no persecutions to follow. And the opposition had demanded the dismissal of the King's present advisers – save Elphinstone – and consultation in any future important appointments, neither side expecting results from the other. There *had* been results from Perth, however – odd ones, but significant. James and his familiars were claiming the incident as a victory, the Earl of Crawford was created Duke of Montrose for his leadership – extraordinary style for a non-royal noble – the Lord Kilmaurs made Earl of Glencairn and, most notable of all, James's second son raised to the dignity of Duke of Ross, this indicating an alternative heir to the throne to the errant Rothesay.

None of this greatly troubled the insurgent faction.

Another account was arousing hilarity. It seemed that the King, on his way north, had actually called at Lindores Abbey to offer the incarcerated Earl of Douglas freedom and pardon and return of his honours and lands if he would order all Douglas insurgents either to change their allegiance or to return home without fighting – an offer which that earl had rejected with scorn.

Linlithgow's was a large palace, hitherto apt to be more than half empty; but that night its former royal denizen had difficulty in finding a room for himself and his Lord Johnnie to sleep in.

In the morning, spies from the Perth area arrived to say that the King's army had started on its march southwards, very large in numbers. This produced immediate claims for the insurgent force not to wait any longer for reinforcements but to strike northwards to engage the enemy before *they* could receive any additional support such as was rumoured they were expecting from the Earls of Caithness and Sutherland, Archie being foremost in this demand. But cooler heads, notably those of Home and Argyll, counselled delay. Let the enemy come across Forth first, before they themselves moved. Remember the strategies and successes of Wallace and Bruce, at Stirling Bridge and Bannockburn, to make the land and water fight for them there. They could, quite possibly, prevent the King's army from crossing the Forth; but what would that serve if it remained undefeated? Especially with Andrew Wood and his ships available to ferry forces across further down the firth and get behind them. Much better to contrive a battle, once the foe was over Stirling Bridge, in the soft lands known as the Pows of Forth, the pools that is, where Bruce had won his mighty victory. It would take a couple of days probably for the enemy to march from Perth to Stirling, some thirty miles, whereas they were only eighteen miles away. Give them another day, and then move north.

This was accepted. And in the interval they gained fully another thousand men, come up from Galloway, Agnews, MacCullochs and the like.

Two mornings later then, at dawn, eighteen thousand strong, they marched, the Duke of Rothesay, all excitement, at their head. Scouts informed that the King's army was indeed at Stirling now. It was St Barnabas's Day.

With only fifteen miles to cover to their chosen battleground, even so large a force was able to reach the Pows of Forth area before midday, their forward scouts saying that the King's host was also on the move south from Stirling. There was some talk of halting at the very marshy bank of the River Carron, which would offer a serious hazard for the enemy to seek to cross; but those who knew the area best pointed out that the foe would not have to go far upstream to be able to send an outflanking force to get behind them here, endangering them. Admittedly *they* could do the same but, if as was now reported, the King's army was much larger than their own, the situation could be difficult. Better to try to use the much larger boggy area of the Pows, near Bannockburn.

Unfortunately, they learned presently that the enemy were evidently thinking along the same lines, Crawford – or Montrose as he now was to be thought of – being no fool and presumably commanding in the King's name. They would be at Bannockburn first, and if they waited for the assault there, they could have the distinct advantage. It was at this point that Sir James Schaw of Sauchie again proved his usefulness – after

445

all, this was his calf-country. There was alternative territory which they could make use of, he informed. The Bannock Burn entered the Pows of Forth, yes, but inland some little way it was joined by a tributary, the Sauchie Burn – actually nothing to do with his own lands of Sauchie, just across Forth from here, saughs merely being willows. And this Sauchie Burn, rising in the hilly ground which was part of the great Tor Wood, meandered its way down from Loch Coulter to join Bannock. If indeed the King's array was holding the famous Bannockburn positions of strength, then it would be folly to attempt to assail them there. Instead they should turn inland for a couple of miles or so and make for an area he knew of where this Sauchie Burn wound through a fairly wide little vale, always flooded in winter and boggy at other times, at a spot known as Little Conglar. On the east side of this they would be in a good position, first to resist enemy attack and then to go over to the offensive, with the enemy cavalry bogged down, as at Bannockburn itself – that is, if the foe could be lured away from their own strong position.

There was much debate about this, but with none of the leaders really knowing the terrain and all concerned over the numbers of the royal force, now estimated at thirty thousand, and the Bannockburn strategic situation so firmly implanted in all their minds, it was decided that they ought to follow Schaw's directive. A move westwards was made, by Plean and Durieshill, crossing the ancient Roman road. But would the King's army move away from its chosen position to challenge them? If it did not, the situation would have to be reconsidered; and with the enemy almost double their numbers, reconsidered carefully.

All were relieved, presently, when their forward scouts sent back word that the enemy was indeed on the move westwards. Evidently *their* scouts were equally active and informative.

Soon they were into low hilly country, away from the coastal plain, and not seeming to be in the least like the required marshland for bogging down cavalry. There were murmurs amongst the lords, John and Seton explaining to young Rothesay what they were seeking, and why, the boy clearly thinking that these tactics of foundering the enemy in mud and mire were not at all admirable when a good hearty charge and swordery were what was called for.

Moreover, not far beyond a laird's house, called apparently Auchenbowie, there opened a wider vale between the hillocks, through which the Sauchie Burn coiled lazily, the stunted willows on its wet verges much in evidence. Leaving the small farmeries of Meikle and Nether Conglar, the army moved down towards the water-meadows. So far as they could see, the ground across the burn was equally wet, and wider, before it began to rise towards more foothills.

It was early afternoon when a halt was called, and tentative positions marked out. The insurgent army would form three divisions, the left under Hailes and the Master of Home, the right under Archie and Lyle, the centre and main strength under Home himself, Argyll and Gray. The royal standard of the red rampant lion on gold was raised, and Bishop Blackadder said a prayer before the leadership, however inattentive and unheeding the rank and file. Jay, too, doubted whether this was necessary.

The question arose: where was the said young doubter to station himself? All his wise elders declared that this must be well to the rear, in a place of safety, which was not their figurehead's notion at all. He was going to be King, was he not? Therefore he must be at the front, taking the lead. That was the King's place. He took a deal of persuading otherwise, but presently a compromise was reached. There was a small mound to the left, not far back from the stream, where he could take up position and survey all the scene, in John's and George Seton's care, Hailes's left wing stretching away westwards. He wanted the larger royal standard flown above him there, but John pointed out that this would be better with the main body – and it would only draw attention to the prince's position – so a smaller one had to be found.

Now it was a matter of waiting to see if the enemy co-operated. Meanwhile various alternative stratagems were debated. Schaw, knowing the terrain, was in much demand for guidance.

447

Their scouts were not long in reporting that the King's army was indeed moving in this direction also, through Howiestoun and the Cauldbarns area. So it looked hopeful.

They waited.

Oddly, they heard the enemy approach before ever they saw movement in the hillocky country eastwards – bagpipes. This, of course, implied the presence of Highlandmen, a sobering thought, for such were usually doughty fighters and, not being apt to be mounted, would be able to negotiate the boggy ground better. How many of these might there be? Presumably Huntly's Gordons and Sutherland's and Caithness's Rosses and Sinclairs, rather than Islesmen. If they represented any large proportion of the King's host. then the outlook was the less hopeful.

Argyll might be reconsidering his choice.

At length they saw the other army coming into view – and all fell silent as the size of it became apparent, emerging from the slopes into this vale. On and on they came, pipes playing, banners flying, steel armour gleaming, the column elongated by the terrain. Fortunately it looked as though most were mounted, but that might just be that horsemen were the more kenspeckle at a distance. Thirty thousand seemed a most moderate estimate.

It took a considerable time for the opposing force to form itself up on the other side of the Sauchie Burn, perhaps five hundred yards away, close enough to distinguish the flags and banners, and the fact that there were indeed a great many kilted Highlanders. Their line stretched for almost a mile, also in three divisions, and from the heraldic ensigns it appeared that the right was under Crawford and Erroll and the Earl Marischal, mainly cavalry, this opposite Hailes's left wing. At the other end, under the banners of Huntly, Caithness and Menteith were the Highlanders, or most of them, numbers hard to gauge, but many, with some mounted men also. And in the centre, with the royal standard prominent, were the flags of the Lords Glamis, Semple, Ruthven, Erskine, Lindsay of the Byres and Bothwell. It seemed to have become largely a confrontation between north and south of Forth and Clyde.

King James could be seen sitting a magnificent grey charger, under the largest of the flags, an unlikely warrior at his first battle, fine armour reflecting the sunlight.

For some time the two armies facing each other waited to see which would make the first move – to John Douglas at least an unreal situation, such calm before the storm and bloodshed. Rothesay seemed to think the same, for he demanded to know what the delay was for? Should they not be at them, with swords and spears? Indeed, he shouted this out loud, in ringing tones.

Undoubtedly Archie Douglas could not have heard him, for he was almost as far away as were the enemy, on the right wing. Moreover the pipes were still playing. But presumably he was of the same mind, and a man of urgency anyway. His force was all mounted mosstroopers. With typical flourish he waved them all forward, shouting "A Douglas! A Douglas!" and led the way down to the stream, the battle started.

They were soon in trouble in the soft marshy ground amongst the willows, even though Borderers' horses were used to this sort of thing. But such had been expected, and the same conditions would apply to the enemy. It was not all display and bravado, of course. Directly opposite was Huntly and the Highland contingent. The objective was to get these foot-fighters involved right at the beginning, and if possible on firmish terrain where the horsemen would be at an advantage, rather than let them attack on the soft ground where the horses would be sinking hock-deep and therefore disadvantaged. Archie's aim in starting first was to get across the burn and as far beyond as possible before the Highland host was given orders to move.

It did not work out quite like that, with the Gordons and their allies responding too swiftly at sight of the attack, whether ordered to or not, and coming charging down yelling, claymores waving, targes held high. So, after splashing across the stream, the horsemen did not get far on the other side before the Highlandmen were amongst them, and still on fairly soggy ground. It was spears and broadswords against claymores and dirks, the Borderers having

449

the benefit of height but the enemy of mobility and numbers.

Nearer at hand, Hailes now used his left wing to make a gesture. They moved forward, but not nearly so far as the Douglases had done, only to the beginning of the boggy ground, where their beasts were still not sinking in too deeply. From there only a few plunged on for the stream, seeming as though to prospect the best crossing. The strategy worked, for Crawford, opposite, accepted the challenge, and led the King's right wing down, in fine style and great numbers.

Soon these also were slowed up, floundering and the rear ranks riding into the front. Hailes and the Master of Home ordered the next stage. Their men of the Merse and Lothian leapt down from their horses and advanced racing on foot, stabbing spears pointing and held short, daggers drawn. Leaping the tussocks and puddles and dodging the dwarf willows of the burnside so much more nimbly than could the horses, they splashed across the shallow burn and charged in amongst the bemired cavalry, thrusting and slashing, the horses themselves rather than their armour-clad riders their targets – the exact reverse of the situation on the right wing.

Home ordered the main division to a slow and careful advance, hoping to use the same tactics. The King's centre moved down to meet them.

After that, so far as John and his royal charge were concerned, it was progressive chaos, details all but impossible to distinguish in the storm and fury of battle, and the ebb and flow of attack and defence. No doubt some pattern of events and advantage might have been evident for a military expert stationed above it all, but the little group on the mound were not so privileged. All was just a pandemonium of smiting, thrusting, shouting, screaming men, neighing, rearing horses and the clash of steel against steel. Young Rothesay fell silent, biting his lip, wide-eyed.

There was no clear line of either side now, no distinction between the divisions, as much fighting going on at one side of the Sauchie Burn as at the other. The only definite and evident feature of it all was that a rearguard of the enemy had come forward only so far, and halted, remaining detached meantime from the turmoil, no doubt to move in to best effect where and when required, this quite a large grouping. And in the centre of it flew the large royal standard, under which sat the King on his great grey charger.

For how long it all went on there was no knowing. At some stage, John perceived that a column of the enemy right wing cavalry had detached itself and was streaming off westwards, up the valley. That, he recognised, could spell danger, if these found a firm fording-place further up, crossed and came down on their flank. But no doubt Hailes and Home would see that also, and take the necessary precautions. He was gazing in the other direction altogether, to try to see how Archie and his right wing were faring, when George Seton grabbed his arm, and pointed. Across there, behind the battle, there was another detaching process – a single horseman this time, and him riding off eastwards, not westwards. The mount was the splendid grey charger. The King was leaving the field, and alone.

Astonished, the watchers stared, until the single, lonely figure disappeared from view amongst the green slopes. Then they eyed each other, and the boy, whose father could so act, wordless. Rothesay had seen where they gazed, and recognised the significance, the shame of it. He was swallowing.

Preoccupied by the monarch's desertion, John, himself all but conscience-stricken at sitting his horse idle when others were fighting and dying around him, yet knowing well that his own duty was to watch over and protect the boy at his side, suddenly became aware that it was not all to be watching and sitting. The party of Crawford's wing which had ridden off westwards was now coming fast down *this* side of the burn – and in larger numbers than he had realised. They were not far away. Hailes saw them also, of course, and ordered part of his force to detach itself from the present fighting to swing round to face this new threat. And at this precise stage, part of the enemy reserve, from which the King had fled, moved into action, and came pounding down to reinforce Crawford's frontal attack. Suddenly this insurgent left wing

451

was grievously endangered, clearly the chosen main target of the foe's command. And why? John had little doubt that it was because of Rothesay's presence with it. The enemy wanted the heir to the throne either captured or disposed of.

What was the best course? To remain on top of this mound and trust that the defence would prevail? Or to hurry off to join Home's main central division while still there was time? John was urgently putting this choice to George Seton when he perceived a new dimension, a third enemy enterprise. This was a smaller, hard-riding group which, after crossing the burn higher up, must have left the others to head for higher ground southwards, to swing round in an encircling move, and so to descend upon the beleaguered left wing from directly behind. They were coming down fast, and only some three hundred yards away.

If it was indeed the young duke who was the target, then now the threat was three-sided – and this new assault was bearing down on their all but unprotected rear. John made up his mind. They had only moments to escape eastwards, to the main body. Reaching over to grab the preoccupied boy's arm, and point, he shouted to Seton, and reined round, spurred heels kicking.

Down that mound the trio plunged, Seton behind, to the wetter ground. They had not far to ride to safety, perhaps four hundred yards, although the enemy was closer. There was a line of leaning, stunted willows below. Jay, looking over his right shoulder, failed to rein his beast over to follow through the same gap between the straggling trees which John was using, good horseman although the boy was. His mount, left to choose its own course, made for a lesser space to the left, wide enough to pass through but partly blocked near the ground by a fallen trunk amongst reeds. The horse leapt this easily enough but Rothesay, looking elsewhere and unsteady in his saddle, was unready for that jump. Thrown askew as the animal brushed through the branches, a larger bough struck the youth's shoulder and, unbalanced as he already was, toppled him out of his seat. Yelling, he fell to the ground.

Hearing the cry, and Seton's shout from behind, John looked back. He reined round. Rothesay's horse had plunged on. The boy was sprawled amongst the reeds. John shouted to him to rise, to reach up. He would take him behind him on his horse. Seton sought to rein up beside them.

The boy duke was on his knees now, but seemed to be having difficulty in rising, perhaps part-stunned, or merely winded, by his fall. John yelled to Seton, pointing, to head the approaching enemy off, head them off. That man, nodding, pulled his mount round to ride courageously towards the descending assault. John jumped down, to assist his young charge, but still gripping his own horse's reins.

The boy was gasping, bent double, trying to speak, clearly winded. Grasping him, all but shaking him in his urgency, the man told him to climb to the saddle. Jay tried but the horse, agitated by all this, was sidling, head-tossing amongst the willow branches, and the boy, seeking to gain control of his breathing, just could not get up into the saddle.

John was about to mount himself, and to hoist up Rothesay after him, when, round the other side of the mound from where Seton had spurred off, two horsemen rode down on them, one with sword drawn, the other wielding a battle-axe. Shouting, they came at them.

John tugged out his own sword, yelling to the boy to run, run amongst the willows. But Jay did not leave him, or would not. In some measure those straggling, spreading trees helped then, for the riders could not descend directly upon them without entanglement. Backing himself, and the duke, against a twisted trunk, John, sword out-thrust, crouched on the defensive.

The two attackers were young troopers, no doubt on their first battlefield. Since in that confined space both horsemen could not attack at once, one spurred round, the axeman, while the sworder came on. John, although dismounted, was not wholly at a disadvantage, for the other had to bend low in his saddle to attack, well enough for slashing but in poor position for pointing and thrusting downwards. John, no very expert swordsman as he might be, was better placed. As the other reared close, he jerked aside to avoid the first furious slash, and then lunged forward with his own point, up to the trooper's thigh, unprotected by the quilted leather jerkin he wore as armour. The steel drove in, and with a scream the young attacker, spouting blood, toppled and fell from his horse.

Rothesay, recovering, was crying out, and pointing. There, up on the top of their mound, more horsemen had appeared. But even as he cursed, John perceived that one of them was the Master of Home, come to the rescue. He raised sword to wave. Then Jay yelled again, this time pointing in the other direction, behind. The axeman had come to his colleague's assistance, and recognising the difficulty of attacking successfully amongst those intervening willow branches on a horse, had dismounted and was coming at them, axe in one hand, dirk in the other.

John had to turn right round. But he was hindered by the boy, the reeds, two now riderless horses stamping and tossing, and by those same branches. Before he could get his blooded sword into a thrusting position and himself steady, the axe struck down. Down it smashed on his neck and shoulder with pulverising force.

John knew no pain then, only sudden and complete collapse of all strength, feeling, balance. Reeling, knees buckling under him, knowing that he was finished, he yet retained sufficient of his wits to direct his pitching-forward person directly against his attacker, to ensure that the next blow did not strike young Jay. The trooper did indeed strike again, but with his dirk, as he was bowled over by the weight of the man falling against him. Deep the steel blade plunged.

Darkness mercifully engulfed John Douglas.

But only temporarily. Presently he knew awareness. He was seeing, through a strange dark haze, shot with deep red, which seethed and swayed and eddied. He was seeing. It was young Jay's eyes that he was seeing, gazing down into his own, tear-filled. There were others there too, now, he was aware. The boy was saying something, pleading, but the roar in his ears was too insistent to hear it.

There was no need for pleading, none at all. John managed a smile, or thought that he did. Then the kindly darkness descended again, this time for good, for very good.

454

Historical Note

Only one James Stewart survived the Battle of Sauchieburn, young Rothesay, to become James the Fourth; for the other, who had fled the field, did not get far, only to the edge of the Bannock Burn itself, at the mill thereof, where his spirited grey charger, the gift of Lord Lindsay of the Byres, took fright at the miller's wife dropping a pitcher in alarm, and threw its royal rider. Injured inside his splendid armour, the King was found and carried into a stable by the miller, and there, in panic, believing that God and His strange spirits were against him, called for a priest to shrive him. It was no priest who was eventually brought to him but a very different attendant, some records say the Lord Gray himself, a sworn and harsh enemy, some say Gray's servant. And the shriving took the form of a dagger's stabbing. James the Third, sad and ineffective monarch, born probably centuries out of his time, died there in the stable of Bannockburn Mill.

Disheartened by the desertion of their liege-lord, the royal army fairly soon recognised a lost cause, and began haphazard withdrawal.

James the Fourth, all that his father was not, proved to be one of the best monarchs Scotland ever had, sure of hand, courageous, just, popular, reigning for twenty-six years. Yet he too may have been born out of his time, for his notions of chivalry led to perhaps the greatest disaster in his realm's fairly disastrous history, Flodden Field, when the floors o' the forest were a' wede awa', himself with them, in a romantic and unnecessary gesture towards the Queen of France. It was at Flodden that his hitherto loyal supporter the Earl of Angus, Archibald Bell-the-Cat, now a man of sixty, who had been Chancellor of Scotland, so strongly countered the

King's will in this gesture as to turn back before the battle in ever-impetuous heat, although his sons went on to die with their sovereign-lord. Archibald died a monk, broken-hearted, a year later.

Mary Stewart, Countess of Arran and Lady Hamilton, lived to a notable age, a notable woman to the end, one of Scotland's great women and a power behind her young great-nephew James the Fifth when he succeeded, aged one year, in 1513.

As for William Sheves, his power largely gone with the death of James the Third, he lived for another ten years, nominally Archbishop of St Andrews but able to exercise little of his former domination, Bishop Elphinstone of Aberdeen becoming a power for good in Church and state, and founding the University of Aberdeen. Sheves, oddly, was succeeded as Primate by none other than the twenty-year-old James, Duke of Ross, the King's younger brother, who also died at Flodden.

Other players on this stage went on to act their due parts, some worthily, dramatically, some less so. But that is another story.

NIGEL TRANTER

THE JAMES V TRILOGY

In 1513 – two hundred years after Robert the Bruce routed the English and restored his nation's pride – King James IV of Scotland lies slaughtered on Flodden's field. With Scotland in a state of turmoil, his seventeen-month-old heir lies at the mercy of ruthless rival factions.

Two men have been entrusted with the new king's welfare: loyal and steadfast David Lindsay and David Beaton. Sons of lowland lairds, they struggle in their role as royal protectors. For there are many who would seek to supplant or control the boy-king James V – his stepfather, the power-hungry Earl of Angus, is one; Henry VIII of England, his greedy eyes never far from the tempting realm of Scotland, is another. Even the boy's mother, Margaret Tudor, plots against her son.

And as he grows up, the young and handsome James V proves to be impetuous, hot-blooded, interested more in wine and women than matters of state. The two Davids have preserved him so far but the threats to James and his country seem to grow by the year . . .

In this fascinating trilogy, Nigel Tranter paints a vivid picture of a turbulent period, an unruly, perplexed and endangered nation, and an attractive but weak-willed king.

'Colourful, fast-moving and well written' – *The Times Literary Supplement*

HODDER AND STOUGHTON PAPERBACKS

NIGEL TRANTER

THE BRUCE TRILOGY

In 1296 Edward Plantagenet, King of England, was determined to bludgeon the freedom-loving Scots into submission. Despite internal clashes and his fierce love for his antagonist's goddaughter, Robert the Bruce, both Norman lord and Celtic earl, took up the challenge of leading his people against the invaders from the South.

After a desperate struggle, Bruce rose finally to face the English at the memorable battle of Bannockburn. But far from bringing peace, his mighty victory was to herald fourteen years of infighting, savagery, heroism and treachery before the English could be brought to sit at a peace-table and to acknowledge Bruce as a sovereign king.

In this bestselling trilogy, Nigel Tranter charts these turbulent years, revealing the flowering of Bruce's character; how, tutored and encouraged by the heroic William Wallace, he determined to continue the fight for an independent Scotland, sustained by a passionate love for his land and devotion to his people.

'Absorbing . . . a notable achievement' – *The Scotsman*

HODDER AND STOUGHTON PAPERBACKS